D1188924

Peter James was educated at Charterhouse then at film school. He lived in North America for a number of years, working as a screenwriter and film producer before returning to England. His novels, including the number one bestseller *Possession*, have been translated into thirty languages and three have been filmed. All his novels reflect his deep interest in the world of the police, with whom he does in-depth research, as well as science, medicine and the paranormal. He has produced numerous films, including *The Merchant Of Venice*, starring Al Pacino, Jeremy Irons and Joseph Fiennes. He also co-created the hit Channel 4 series, *Bedsitcom*, which was nominated for a Rose d'Or. He is currently, as co-producer, developing his Roy Grace novels for television with ITV Productions. Peter James won the Krimi-Blitz 2005 Crime Writer of the Year award in Germany, and *Dead Simple* won both the 2006 Prix Polar International award and the 2007 Prix Coeur Noir award in France. *Looking Good Dead* was shortlisted for the 2007 Richard and Judy Crime Thriller of the Year award, France's SNCF and Le Grand Prix de Littérature award. *Not Dead Enough* was shortlisted for the Theakstons Old Peculier Crime Thriller of the Year award and the ITV3 Crime Thriller Of The Year award. He divides his time between his homes in Notting Hill, London and near Brighton in Sussex. Visit his website at www.peterjames.com.

By Peter James

Dead Letter Drop
Atom Bomb Angel
Billionaire
Possession
Dreamer
Sweet Heart
Twilight
Prophecy
Alchemist
Host
The Truth
Denial
Faith
Dead Simple
Looking Good Dead
Not Dead Enough
Dead Man's Footsteps
Dead Tomorrow
Dead Like You

CHILDREN'S NOVEL
Getting Wired!

PETER JAMES

POSSESSION

PROPHECY

Possession
First published in Great Britain by Victor Gollancz Ltd in 1988

Prophecy
First published in Great Britain by Victor Gollancz Ltd in 1992

This omnibus edition published in 2011
by Orion Books Ltd
Orion House, 5 Upper St Martin's Lane, London WC2H 9EA

A CIP catalogue record for this book is available
from the British Library.

ISBN 9781407230962

Printed in Great Britain by Clays Ltd, St Ives plc

www.orionbooks.co.uk

POSSESSION

ACKNOWLEDGEMENTS

A very special thank you is owed to my Agent, Jon Thurley, whose faith, encouragement and advice has been a constant source of strength. And to Joanna Goldsworthy and the team at Victor Gollancz for immensely constructive input, and for having the belief and the courage to take the ball. . . .

A mention is long overdue to David Summerscale, who taught me English at Charterhouse, who, probably unknowingly, gave me the confidence to start writing.

Many people have helped me with my research, both directly and indirectly, and it is to them that much of the authenticity of this book is due. The list is long, and so many have given much more than I ever asked for: especially Canon Dominic Walker, O.G.S.; the Reverend David Gutsell; the Reverend Jim Mynors; the staff of the College of Psychic Studies; the Reverend Gerald Shaw, Hospital Chaplain, Broadmoor; Dr Duncan Stewart; Tim Parker of St Cuthmans Wines; Peter Hall of Breaky Bottom; Renée-Jean Wilkin; Peter Lee; Jim Sitford; my secretary, Peggy Fletcher; and my wife Georgina who gave me tireless patience and encouragement.

To Georgina

'For life is but a dream, whose shapes return, some frequently some seldom, some by night and some by day'

James Thomson

CHAPTER ONE

Fabian lay cocooned in the rich warm softness of the bedding, and stared out through the open curtains. Shafts of red speared the dawn sky, pink, bloody.

He rolled over and studied the sleeping girl beside him. Then he slipped out of bed and walked naked through the tangle of clothes on the floor to the window. He stared out at the morning mist, and at the thick coils of smoke from the last of the winter prunings in the vineyards. Like the aftermath of a battle, he thought, and shuddered suddenly, his thin sinewy body covered in goose-pimples.

The air was good, filled with dew and the strange animal smells of the girl that were all over him; he scratched himself, then stared once more out of the window, uneasily.

'Fabian?' There was a gentle rap on the door, followed by a clumsy thump.

'Two minutes.' He felt the strain on his throat as he tried to shout and whisper at the same time. The girl stirred slightly, rustling like a leaf in a breeze, and was silent again.

He pulled on his jeans, collarless shirt and pullover, stuffed the rest of his clothes into his bag, and sloshed some cold water on his face. He dried it off, took half a step towards the girl, then stopped, picked up his bag and went out of the room, closing the heavy door silently behind him.

Otto, Charles and Henry were already outside, waiting. Otto, tall, with his hooked nose that overhung his mouth, his black hair raked sharply back from his pockmarked face, his herringbone coat hanging from his gangly frame, looked like a huge bird of prey. Charles stood beside him, rubbing his hands, bleary eyed, with his usual baffled expression, as if the morning had crept up and caught him unawares.

I

'God, I feel bozoed,' he said, yawning. Henry leaned against the car, hands sunk deep in his coat pockets, his eyes closed.

'I'm sorry, I overslept,' said Fabian, unlocking the rear hatch of the Volkswagen and pulling out the scraper.

'Any chance of a coffee before we go?' said Charles.

'Let's get some en route,' said Fabian, dragging the rubber scraper through the heavy dew on the windows. It was still almost dark out here. He stared at the black, threatening silhouettes of the tall pines, and at the cold grey walls of the château. He glanced up at the windows, and tried to spot the one with the open curtains; he thought he saw a face there and looked away. 'I'll drive the first leg.'

Charles and Henry squeezed through into the rear seat, and Otto sank down in the passenger seat. Fabian switched on the ignition. The engine turned over noisily, clattering, popping, caught for an instance, then died.

'Ace,' said Charles. 'Going to be an absolutely ace morning.'

'Yurr, really nice,' said Henry in his slow, deep voice. He closed his eyes again. 'Wake me up in Calais.'

'I would prefer to be heading south rather than north,' said Otto, toying with his seat-belt. 'Bloody thing; I can never remember how this goes.'

The engine clattered, then fired again, rasping furiously.

'Sorry that we're dragging you away, Fabian,' said Charles.

Fabian shrugged, leaned forward and switched on the lights.

'Is she a good screw?' said Otto.

Fabian smiled, and said nothing. He never discussed women.

The girl stood by the window, a flat, drained expression on her face as she watched the red Golf drive off into the mist. She touched her left arm gently; it hurt like hell. She walked over and sat in front of the dressing table and stared in the mirror. She flinched, then stared again closely at the purple bruises on her breasts, at the gouge down her left cheek, at the swelling around her right eye, and at her puffy lip, cracked and stained with dried blood. She stared for a long time, straight into her own eyes, unable to avert her gaze, then gently lowered her fingers between her legs and winced in pain at the touch. '*Salaud*,' she said.

'What ferry do you think we'll make?' said Charles.

'If the road's this empty, we should be at Calais around four.'

'You're a jammy bastard, Fabian, aren't you.'

'Jammy?'

'Yes, jammy.'

DIJON ... MACON ... LYONS ... PARIS ... The jumble of autoroute signs flashed past as Fabian accelerated hard around the flyover, feeling the tyres bite into the tarmac, the tightness of the steering wheel, the crisp roar of the warmed-up engine, the pure thrill of an open, empty road. As the curve straightened out on to the autoroute approach, he flattened the accelerator and the Volkswagen leapt forwards. Sometimes it seemed to him the car would take off, be free of the road and fly, fly straight up into the stars. He watched the curve of the rev counter needle, flicked up through the gears each time the needle touched the red sector, until he was in fifth, staring at the speedometer, his foot still hard on the floor. One hundred and twenty-five. One hundred and thirty.

'What are your plans this term?' said Fabian, above the roar of the engine and the wind.

Otto and Charles looked at each other, not sure to whom the remark was addressed. Otto pushed in the lighter and shook a crumpled Marlboro out of a dented pack.

'I don't make plans,' said Otto. 'I never make plans.'

'How are your parents?' said Charles.

'Mine?' said Fabian.

'Yes.'

'O.K.' He hesitated, uncomfortably. 'Still apart. How's

your mother?' He raised his arm and wound the roof back, letting in a blast of fridge-cold air and a roar which drowned Charles's reply. He stared at the sun to the right, a low red ball rising above the hills of Burgundy, the sun that would warm the grapes that would be made into wines, great whites, great reds, blood red. In twenty years' time he might open a bottle of Clos de Vougeot and lean over to someone and say, 'I saw the sun that went into that bottle; I was there.'

The sense of doom enveloped him again; the ball of sun seemed too close, suddenly. He wanted to open his window and push it further away. A shaft of light played for an instant down the dashboard, ran down it, vibrant, lively, like fresh blood, he thought.

'I'm going to try and play cricket this term,' said Charles.

'Cricket,' said Otto, staring at him oddly.

'Cambridge might be my last chance to play.'

'Did you say cricket?' shouted Fabian.

'Yes,' Charles shouted back.

Fabian saw a cluster of red lights in the distance; there was still not enough daylight to make things out clearly. Several vehicles, bunched together: an amber indicator flashed; something was moving out into the middle lane. He pulled the Golf over into the fast lane, eased his foot slightly on the accelerator, and flashed his lights. 'I didn't know you played.'

'I was in the First Eleven at Winchester.'

'First Eleven Wankers,' grinned Fabian, turning round for an instant.

'What?'

'Wankers!'

'Fabian!'

Fabian heard Otto's voice, strange, garbled, cut short, and sensed him flinch, tighten up. He stared back at the road.

There were headlights coming straight at them. Big, blinding lights, towering above them, coming the wrong way in the fast lane.

'Lorry!' he shouted. 'Christ!'

His foot dived for the brake pedal, but he knew there was no point, knew he was too late. Through the glare of the yellow lights he saw the last two digits of the registration plate: 75. Paris, he thought to himself.

Then suddenly he was above the Golf, looking down: through the open roof he could see Otto, Charles and Henry, jerking around like puppets. He watched, fascinated, everything in slow motion now, as the Golf began to crumple against the front of the lorry, then he realized it wasn't a lorry at all, but another car, a Citroën, one of the large old models, upright, high off the ground.

First the nose buckled, then the roof twisted, then the windscreen seemed to turn to feathers, hundreds of thousands of feathers all floating around; things were flying through the air now, shapes, large and small. The rear doors of the Citroën opened, one inwards, one outwards, and the Citroën seemed to turn sideways. The back seat was filled with parcels which began to rise up, slowly, and break open as they hit the roof; little men, white, brown, black, all furry, with their arms opened, gyrated through the air together in a strange ritualized dance. Teddy bears, he realized, as they fell and bounced, then fell.

There was a smell of petrol; a tremendous powerful smell. Everything was obscured for a moment in a shimmer, as though a layer of frosted glass had been slipped beneath him, then there was a strange dull boom, like a tyre bursting, followed by an intense searing heat. The bears burnt first, then the paint on the cars started to blister.

Fabian began to vibrate in the heat, shaking uncontrollably. He tried to move, but could not; all around was shimmering now, and it moved in closer, tighter. 'No,' he said, suddenly. 'No!' He looked wildly around, struggled again. 'Carrie!' he shouted. 'Carrie!'

Then, suddenly, he was free of the heat, racing again down the autoroute. The light was brilliant white – the sun must have come up fast, he thought – as he gripped the wheel, felt the car accelerating. There was no need to change gear, it was accelerating by itself, free of the road now, gliding just above the surface. The road markings had gone, the road signs, everything. He was flying now, he could fly to the stars! He pulled the wheel back, but the car would not climb, and instead flew on silently through the light, towards a vanishing point in the white mist of the horizon. He passed a wrecked car smouldering by the side of the road, then a coach on its side, a lorry, its cab torn in half, two cars interlocked like fighting beetles, rusted, abandoned, another car, burning figures dimly visible through the flames, the light ahead getting more brilliant each second. He looked around. Otto's seat was empty. 'Where's Otto?'

'Must have fallen out,' said Charles.

'He's just lit a cigarette. Where's the cigarette?'

'Probably taken it with him.'

Charles's voice sounded strange, a long way off. Fabian looked over his shoulder. He thought Charles and Henry were there, but was not sure.

'Did we hit that car, Charles?'

'I don't know. I think so.'

The brilliant light was hurting his eyes. Fabian leaned forward and fumbled for his sunglasses. Ahead he saw shadows in the white mist, shapes moving. '*Péage*,' he said. 'I need some money.'

'No,' said Charles. 'No, I don't think we need any money.'

Fabian felt the car lifting up, then drop away from him, found himself suspended in the white light; it was warm, and he sank back in it, and saw figures coming towards him.

Then he remembered again, and began to shake. 'Carrie!' He tried to shout at the figures, but nothing came out. 'Carrie! You must let me. You must!'

The figures were standing around him now, smiling, kind, pleased to see him.

6

CHAPTER TWO

Alex watched the waiter pour an inch of Chambertin into her husband's glass, retreat and stand stiffly beside him. David held the glass up to the dim light, swirled it around in his hand, hurtling the wine around the wall of the glass, and then examined the tears of glycerol after the wine had dropped down. He sniffed deeply, frowned, drained the glass into his mouth, sluiced it noisily around, then began to chew it as if it were a tough piece of steak. Don't send it back, please God don't send it back, she said to herself; I can't bear it when you send it back.

To her relief he gave a single nod to the waiter and the ordeal was over.

'Chambertin '71,' said David, proudly, as if he had made it himself.

'Ah,' she said, trying to look enthusiastic, trying to pretend for his sake that she really could appreciate a good burgundy, that she could tell a burgundy from a claret, which she never could and doubted she ever would. 'Thank you, that's a treat.'

'You sound very formal tonight,' he said. 'It's like taking a maiden aunt out to tea.'

'I'm sorry, I'll try and be less formal.' She stared at his hands which had become so coarse, his stubby fingers red, almost raw, with the black grime under the nails, and at the battered tweed suit and the frayed woollen shirt; was it part of his new image, or did he genuinely not care any more? She stared at his face, tanned, relaxed, even turned a little leathery from the outdoor life, his hair ragged, almost bushy now, like the thick tangle of his beard. He raised his glass and pointed it at her.

7

'Cheers.'

She raised hers and the glasses clinked.

'Know why people touch glasses?' he said.

'No.'

'You can see wine, smell it, touch it, taste it. But you can't hear it! So we touch glasses; it completes the five senses.'

'Ever the advertising man. It's still in your blood.' She smiled, and pulled out a cigarette. 'What about telepathy? Can you communicate with wine?'

'I communicate with it all the time. I even talk to my vines.'

'Do they talk back?'

'They're not great conversationalists. I thought you'd given up smoking.'

'I have.'

'That's what London does for you. Eats you up; screws you up. You do things you've given up, and you don't do the things you've promised yourself.'

'I do.'

He nodded, with a reluctant grin. 'Yes. Perhaps you do.'

Alex smiled and raised her eyebrows.

'You're looking very pretty.'

She blushed. She had never been very good at taking compliments. 'Thank you,' she said, stiffly.

'There you go. The maiden aunt again.'

'What do you want me to say?'

He shrugged and sniffed his wine. 'Have you heard from Fabian?'

'Not for a few days. He'll be back tomorrow evening.'

'When does he go back to Cambridge?'

'At the weekend.' Alex saw her husband's face drop. 'What's the matter?'

'I was hoping he might come down this weekend. We're doing some planting.'

Alex brushed some long strands of blonde hair off her face. David noticed the petulance in the motion. Fabian was a touchy subject. 'You know, darling,' he said, 'it's silly, this separation – surely we could . . .?'

He felt the wall, even before she replied.

Alex fumbled with her cigarette, rolled it around, then tapped it several times in the ashtray.

'I've been thinking a lot about things, David.' The cigarette fell on to the pink tablecloth and she picked it up again, quickly, and rubbed the mark on the cloth with her finger. 'I want a divorce.'

David swirled the wine in his glass, carelessly this time, so that some spilled over and ran down his hand. 'Do you have somebody?'

'No.'

She swept away a few more hairs, too quickly, he thought, trying to read the truth in the blush of her face and the blue eyes that were staring down at the tablecloth. God, she looked lovely. The confidence of her success and the toughness that had come with it had changed her, but nicely; changed her into a fine midway stage between prettiness and handsomeness.

'Would it bother you if I stayed up here tonight?'

She shook her head. 'No, David, I don't want you to stay up here.'

'It is my house.'

'Our house.'

He drank some wine, then sniffed it again, testily, disappointed. 'I'll go down to Sussex.'

He dropped her off in the King's Road, at the top of the cul-de-sac. 'I'll call you,' he said.

She nodded, and bit her lip, fighting back the sadness. 'That would be nice.'

She slammed the door of the grimy Land Rover and turned away, hurrying down the terrace, past the smart doors of the Regency town-houses, squeezing her eyes against the rain and her tears. She threw her coat on to the stand, then walked into the drawing room and paced

9

around, restlessly. She looked at her watch. Eleven-thirty. She felt too churned up to sleep.

She opened the door under the stairs, and walked down the steep narrow staircase into the basement, through the light trap and into the familiar smells of developer and fixer of her darkroom. She closed the door behind her with a click that sounded like a pistol shot. She felt acutely aware, suddenly, of the silence in the room and wondered, for a moment, was noise carried in light? Did you cut out noise when you cut out light? She listened to her own sounds, her breathing, the rustle of her blouse, and for an instant she felt like an intruder in her own room.

She snapped on the light-box, unpegged a roll of negatives from the drying line and laid it on the box. She looked closely at one of the frames; a fat black tubular object with two heads stared back.

Alex cut the roll into four strips, and laid them in the contact printer. She switched on the red safety light, took a sheet of bromide paper out of the box and fed it into the printer. 'One thousand and one, one thousand and two, one thousand and three.' She counted to fifteen, then snapped the light off and dropped the sheet into the shallow plastic developer tray. She up-ended the tray and rocked it sharply, sending the sheet down to the far end with a loud clack.

She watched the image on one frame, white on white, then a smudge of silvery grey appeared. Next came the perforated holes, then the outlines of the two ovals, one lower than the other. What was it? Something long, suspended between the ovals began to take shape, and then she realized. 'Bastard!' she said, grinning. Some of the hairs began to appear, then the phallus itself, fat, limp, the skin at the head saggy, the small slit in the front, like an ugly grinning reptile. What did it belong to, she wondered. An elephant? It wasn't human. Couldn't have been.

She shook her head, smiling, pulled the sheet out of the developer and dropped it into the fixing bath. She rocked the bath gently for a few seconds, then looked at her watch and waited another forty seconds. She pulled the sheet out and dropped it in the wash, checking her watch again. She tidied up, then looked at her watch again, impatiently. When the five minutes were up, she lifted the sheet out and pegged it on the drying line. Thirty-six phalluses stared at her, all the same, taken each time from a slightly different angle.

She grinned again as she went upstairs, feeling better, as if she had scored a secret personal triumph over David.

She woke with a start in the large bed and wondered if she'd overslept. She reached over and picked up her watch. Six-fifteen. Relieved, she sank back on to the pillow and closed her eyes. In the distance she heard a lorry thunder down the King's Road. Then she heard the click of a door; it sounded like her front door. She listened intently, but realized she must have imagined it, and closed her eyes. Another hour of sleep. She needed it. Her lungs felt sore and there was a sharp throbbing pain in her head. She always smoked too much and drank too much when she saw David. Separating wasn't easy; sometimes it seemed harder than staying together.

A shadow passed in front of her eyes in the dark room and she felt cold suddenly. She opened her eyes and saw Fabian standing over her bed, could see him clearly in spite of the dark.

'Darling!' she said.

'Hi, Mum.'

She stared up at him; he looked worried, agitated.

'I wasn't expecting you back until tonight, darling.'

'I'll get some rest now, I'm very tired.'

'You must have driven through the night.'

Fabian smiled. 'Go back to sleep, Mum.'

'I'll see you later,' she said, and closed her eyes, waiting for the click of her door closing. But she heard no click. 'Fabian, darling, close the door,' she called out. Then she opened her eyes and looked at the door and saw it was closed. She smiled, confused, and lapsed back into a doze.

It seemed only seconds later she heard the shrill cry of an insect in trouble, urgent, insistent, growing louder. She fumbled for her clock, wanting to stop it before it woke Fabian. Her hand groped about on the bedside table, found keys, a book, a glass of water, the hard scaly cover of her Filofax. The shrill insistent beep continued; she lay back for a moment and waited for it to stop, then remembered it would not; the wonderful solar clock that would never switch off by itself, programmed to beep, if necessary, until the end of time. It became, instantly, yet another reason to dislike David. What a damned stupid Christmas present to give; cruel, masochistic. He had bought it because it amused him; wines and gadgets. For a man who had turned his back on urban civilization, he was too damned fond of gadgets.

She pulled on her track suit and padded out into the corridor, quietly, not wanting to wake Fabian, pleased he was back, making a mental note to cancel a meeting that evening so they could do something together, maybe go out and see a film and have a Chinese afterwards. He was at a nice age now, in his second year at Cambridge, beginning to see clearly how the world worked, yet still filled with the enthusiasm of youth; he was a good companion, a mate.

She pounded her two mile route up to the Fulham Road and round the Brompton Cemetery, then scooped the papers and the milk from the doorstep and went back indoors. It struck her as mildly odd that Fabian had not left his usual trail of clobber all over the hallway. She hadn't noticed his car outside either, but maybe he'd had to park in another street. She went back upstairs, quietly, to shower and dress.

She wondered whether to wake him up before she left, but went to the kitchen instead and scribbled a note. 'Back at seven, darling. If you're free we could go to the cinema. Love, Mum.' Then she looked at her watch and flew.

By the time she reached the Poland Street car park her

mood had changed to a sense of gloom. She nodded mechanically at the attendant as she drove up the ramp. Something wasn't right, and she couldn't place it; she felt depressed, flat, and blamed David. Something in Fabian's expression had unsettled her, as if he had a secret he was keeping from her, as if there was a conspiracy and she was the only one not to know.

CHAPTER THREE

Alex stared in disbelief as her secretary laid a third stack of Jiffy bags on her desk.

'All this is today's, Julie?' She picked up one of the packages and looked dubiously at the label. 'Ms Alex Hightower, Hightower Literary Agency' was spelt out in huge jittery letters. 'Hope he hasn't handwritten the manuscript.'

'Philip Main called a few minutes ago. Asked whether you had deciphered the message. He may have been joking, but I wasn't quite sure.'

Alex thought of the negatives she had developed and grinned. 'I'll call him back after I've opened the post.'

'In about two weeks.'

Alex picked up her paper-knife and searched, bewildered, for a gap in the Sellotape.

'A Walter Fletcher rang – wanted to know if you've read his manuscript yet.'

'Doesn't ring a bell.'

'He was complaining bitterly that you'd had it for almost a week.'

Alex stared at the shelves beside her desk, piled high with manuscripts of novels, plays, film scripts. 'Walter Fletcher? What was the title?'

'*The Development of Tribal Dances in the Middle Ages.*'

'You're joking!' Alex sipped her coffee. 'Did you tell him we don't handle that sort of thing?'

'I tried to. He seems fairly convinced it's going to be big.'

Alex ripped open the bag and pulled out a shapeless wodge of dog-eared papers, several inches thick, and loosely bound with elastic bands. 'This one's yours,' she said, passing it straight to her secretary, who flinched under the weight.

Julie put it down on the desk and stared at the first page, a barely decipherable code of misspellings, crossings out and red underlining. 'He appears to have typed this without a ribbon.'

'Look on the bright side,' said Alex. 'At least it's typed.'

The intercom buzzed and she picked up her phone.

'Philip Main for you.'

Alex hesitated for a moment. 'O.K.' She pushed the button. 'You're mad,' she said. 'Completely mad.'

She listened to the usual sniff, followed by the clearing of the throat that always sounded like a grunt, followed by the long hiss as he drew deeply on the inevitable Capstan Full Strength that he poked in and out of his moustache with his nicotine-stained forefinger and thumb. 'Did you understand it?' His deep, quiet voice was tinged with a boyish excitement.

'Understand it? What was I meant to understand?'

Sniff; grunt; hiss. 'It's a whole new form of communication; a new language. We're evolving from dialogue; it's a random communication mutated into celluloid. Nobody bothers talking any more, that's too trite; we make films, shoot pictures, pass them round. Dialogue is too dominating – you don't get a chance to develop your thoughts if you're listening to dialogue – but you develop someone's pictures and they talk to you – part of your soul goes into them.'

Alex looked up at her secretary and tapped her head.

'So, thirty-six photographs of an animal's genitals were meant to communicate something to me.'

Grunt. Hiss. 'Yes.'

'All it communicated to me was that it was far too small.' She heard a giggle from Julie.

'*Organs of the Species*.'

'*Organs of the Species?*'

'It's the title; I've got the title.'

'Of what?'

'A new book; we're going to write it together.' Grunt.

Hiss. 'Your passion for photography. My obsession with the sex organs.'

'Philip, I have a lot of work to do. Friday's my worst day.'

'Let me buy you lunch next week.'

'I have a very busy week.'

'How about dinner?'

'I think lunch would be better.'

'You don't trust me.' He sounded offended.

'Tuesday. I could do a short lunch on Tuesday.'

'I'll pick you up at one. All right?'

'Fine. Bye.'

Alex shook her head and put the phone down.

'Philip Main?' said Julie.

Alex nodded, and smiled. 'Mad. Completely mad, but the book he's writing could be brilliant – the bizz – if he ever finishes it.'

'Will anyone be able to understand it?'

'No, so it should win a few awards.'

The intercom buzzed again.

'Yes?' said Alex.

'There's a policeman down here, Mrs Hightower.'

'A policeman?' Her instinctive reaction was guilt, and she raked through her mind, trying to remember if she had any parking tickets outstanding? Or had she been reported for reckless driving? Surely not? 'What does he want?'

'He'd like to have a word with you.' There seemed to be an insistency in her receptionist's voice; perhaps she too was intimidated by policemen?

'Maybe he's written a book?' said Julie.

Alex shrugged. 'Ask him to come up.'

He came through the door with his cap in his hand, looked down at the ground, at his immaculately polished shoes, then up, aiming his eyes at a level just below the top of Alex's desk. He was young, she realized with a shock; she had expected someone old, but he was as young as her son.

He had a flat boxer's nose, but soft, kindly blue eyes, shy eyes. 'Mrs Hightower?' he said, expectantly, to both women.

'Yes,' said Alex.

He looked nervously at Julie, then at Alex, put his hands behind his back and swayed slightly from side to side. 'Do you think I could have a word with you alone?'

'It's all right, officer – my secretary works with me all the time.'

He looked at Julie then at Alex. 'I think it would be better if I could speak to you on your own.'

Alex nodded at Julie. She went out of the room and closed the door behind her.

'Mrs Hightower – I'm Constable Harper, from the Metropolitan Police.' He blinked furiously.

Alex watched him quizzically; he was making her feel uncomfortable.

'You have a son, I believe – Fabian?'

'Yes?' She felt cold, stared past him, out through the horizontal venetian slats at the grey rooftops beyond, saw the rain sliding down the window leaving trails like snails. Her mind started racing.

The policeman unbuttoned the top button of his tunic, then did it up again; he dropped his hat on the floor, and knelt down to pick it up, then composed himself. 'He owns a red Volkswagen Golf G Ti?'

Alex nodded. What the hell has he done this time? The police had been before, eighteen months ago, when someone had reported him for reckless driving. She nodded blankly as the policeman read out the registration number.

'He's been travelling in France?'

'Yes. Been skiing with some friends – and then he went to Burgundy to a party – a twenty-first – the daughter of a friend of my husband's.'

The policeman's eyes were wide, staring, and his mouth was twitching as if an electric current were running through it. Alex looked away from him again, and stared at her face in the word-processor screen at the side of her desk. She looked old, suddenly, she thought, incongruously, old.

'We've had a phone call from the police – gendarmerie – er – police, in Mâcon. I'm afraid there's been an accident.' The words began to float around her, as if each was contained in a watery bubble; she saw them, heard them, again, repeatedly, in different sequences. Taken. Hospital. Arrival. To. On. Found. Was. But. Be. To. Arrival. Dead. She felt one of her knees hit something hard, then again. She stared at the policeman's face, saw two faces, then four.

'Would you like a cup of tea?'

Who had said that, she wondered, suddenly. Him? Her? She spoke mechanically, positively, tried to be courteous; tried not to make the man feel like an idiot, in spite of her mounting anger. 'I'm very sorry,' she said. 'There has been a mistake; a very terrible mistake. My son is at home, asleep in bed; he arrived back safely this morning.'

CHAPTER FOUR

Constable Harper departed in a flurry of staccato apologies and twitches. Alex sat down, staring at the spats of rain on the window, and dialled her home phone number.

She heard the click as it answered, and a dull roar. Over the roar, she heard the voice of her cleaning lady. 'Hold on, you don't go no away please.' There was a clunk, the roar stopped and her voice came on again, clearer. 'Very sorry; go turn off 'oover. Missy Eyetoya 'ouse.'

'Mimsa, it's Mrs Hightower speaking.'

'Missy Eyetoya no here; you telephone please at office.'

Alex waited patiently, and then repeated herself, slowly, louder.

'Allo Missy Eyetoya.' There was a pause as if Mimsa was looking something up in a phrase book. 'How you you?' she said positively, slowly, triumphantly.

'Fine, may I speak to Fabian please.'

'Misser Fibbian? He no here.'

'He's asleep in bed.'

'No, he no sleeping. I just clean his room. You say he come back tonight; I just clean room for him.'

Alex hung up, grabbed her coat and went out into the corridor. She put her head through Julie's office door. 'I'll be back in an hour.'

Julie looked at her anxiously. 'Is everything all right?'

'Yes, it's fine,' she snapped.

She double parked in the street, ran to the house and up the steps. There was a drowning roar from the vacuum cleaner and a strong smell of polish. She walked through and saw Mimsa, arched like a chicken, hoovering the drawing room. She ran up the stairs and along the corridor to Fabian's bedroom, paused outside and knocked gently. She opened the door. The bed was neatly made and there were no suitcases, nor any clobber lying on the floor. It smelt clean, freshly aired, unused.

She looked around the room, up at the strange gaunt portrait of her son. He stared back down, sternly, arrogantly, hand slipped inside his jacket like Napoleon. The eyes were all wrong; they looked cold, cruel, not those warm eyes that were full of life that was the real him. Fabian had given it to her last year as a birthday present, but it had unsettled her; she had tried it on a few different walls, and eventually hung it in his own room. She felt a shiver as she looked at it now.

She went up and looked in the spare room, then the bathroom; but there was no sign of Fabian having returned. She went to her bedroom, picked up the phone and dialled her husband.

'Can I call you back?' he said. 'I'm right in the middle of something urgent.'

'So am I,' she said, conscious of sounding more hysterical than she had intended. 'Is Fabian with you?'

'No,' he said, impatiently. 'He was going to that twenty-first at the Arboisses' last night. He wouldn't be back in England yet.'

'David, something very strange is happening.'

'Look – I'll call you back in half an hour. Are you at the office?'

'No. I'm at home.'

Alex was conscious of the sound of hooting outside. It was getting increasingly impatient. She hung up and ran down the stairs. Mimsa jumped in shock as she saw her. 'Missy Eyetoya, oh you give me fright!' Alex dashed outside. 'Sorry,' she shouted at a small, thin-lipped man in a large BMW who glared and shook his head. She jumped into her Mercedes, moved down the road, then reversed into the space the BMW had left. She went back into the house.

'You did not see Fabian, Mimsa?'

Mimsa shook her head; the whole top half of her stooped body shook as though it were attached to her legs by a fulcrum. 'Don't see no Misser Fibbian. Don't been back yet.'

Alex went through into the drawing room and sat down on a sofa, looking around at the apricot walls, thinking, suddenly, how pretty the room looked, and then, suddenly, how strange it felt being at home on a weekday morning. She stared at the bowl of red roses on the table by the door, and smiled. They had arrived by Interflora on her birthday, three days ago. The card from Fabian was still tucked in with them. Red roses; his favourite flowers. He always gave her red roses. She closed her eyes and heard the vacuum rev up again to a crescendo and then undulate, as Mimsa pushed the machine backwards and forwards over the carpet, relentlessly.

He had come into her room this morning; she had seen him; surely to God she had seen him?

She heard the front door and ignored it; probably the milkman; Mimsa could deal with it.

'Missy Eyetoya.' She opened her eyes and saw Mimsa looking agitated. 'Policeman here.' Mimsa's eyes were wide open, bulging; she jerked over her shoulder with her thumb.

'That's all right, Mimsa, show him in.'

Mimsa stared at her, and Alex smiled reassuringly, nodding.

A moment later, Constable Harper was standing awkwardly in the doorway, cap in hand, and mouth twitching like a rabbit. 'Sorry to bother you again,' he said.

Alex swept some hair from her face and pointed to a chair. He sat down and placed his cap on his knees. 'Nice house.'

Alex nodded and smiled. 'Thank you.'

'We seem to have a problem.' He turned the cap over a couple of times. 'I don't know quite how to say this. There is a young man in hospital in Mâcon, who was in the – er – the accident, Mr Otto –' he pulled out his notebook and

21

looked at it. 'Mr Otto von Essenberg. He says that the other three in the car were a Mr Charles Heathfield, a Mr Henry Heathfield and Mr Fabian Hightower. Obviously he's still in a state of shock.'

'Charles and Henry Heathfield?'

'Yes.'

She nodded.

'Do you know them?'

'Yes, their parents live in Hong Kong. Charles is at Cambridge with Fabian. Henry's his younger brother. Are they all right?'

Harper paled, looked at the ground, and shook his head. 'I understand that –' he shook his head '– that they were killed.' He looked back at Alex, and turned the hat over again. 'You said you saw your son this morning.'

Alex nodded bleakly.

'I'm sorry, this is very difficult.' He looked away from her again. 'Where exactly did you see him?'

'He came into my bedroom.'

'What time would that have been?'

'About six. I think I looked at the clock, I'm not sure.'

He wrote carefully in his notebook, his hand shaking. 'About six?'

'Yes.'

'Here?'

'Yes.'

'But he's not here now?'

'No.' She sensed an inevitability dawning on her and she bit her lip.

'Do you know where he's gone?'

She shook her head. It was getting harder to speak.

'Did he say anything?'

Alex nodded. 'He said "Hi, Mum". I told him I was surprised to see him back so soon; he said he was tired and was going to get some sleep. He was in his room this morning when I left.'

'You saw him again?'

22

Alex stared directly into the policeman's eyes. 'No, I didn't see him; the door was shut, and I didn't want to wake him.'

'Then you went to the office?'

She nodded.

He made another note. 'What time did you leave?'

'About quarter to nine.'

'And what time does your cleaning lady come?'

'About nine-fifteen.'

'Was she on time this morning?'

'I'll ask her.' Alex went out of the room. 'Mimsa!' she called. Mimsa, intent on her hoovering, did not hear. Alex tapped her on the shoulder. 'Mimsa!'

The cleaning woman jumped. 'The second fright you give me today. We don't got no Vim. You forgot?'

Alex nodded. 'Sorry, I'll try to remember.'

'The winnow cleaner no come. He lazy bassard.'

'Mimsa – what time did you get here this morning? It's very important.'

'This morning, I early. Five to nine. I catch earlier bus – I don' normally catch it, 'cos have to make husban' breakfast; he no have breakfast this morning – got to go to the doctor for the tests, so I catch early; I go early too if O.K.?'

'Fine.' Alex nodded and went back into the drawing room. 'She was here at five to nine.'

'Only ten minutes after you left?'

Alex nodded.

'Forgive me, this may sound a little rude – do you think you might have imagined your son coming home – dreamt it perhaps?'

The phone rang; she listened for a second to the shrill echoing of the bell, the very normality of it calming her down. She picked up the receiver. 'Hallo?'

'Hi, darling, sorry about that.'

She wished her husband would stop calling her darling; she wasn't his darling any more; why did he keep having to pretend that everything was all right between them?

'I was right in the middle of a crucial experiment – I've got a catalyst that I think is going to enable me to produce a Chardonnay to rival Chablis; and it'll be cheaper. Can you imagine a really good British Chablis?'

'Sounds very exciting,' she said, flatly.

'I'm talking about Premier Cru Chablis, at least! Did you sleep O.K. last night?'

'Yes,' she said, surprised. 'Fine. Did you get down all right?'

'Yes, no problems – can you hold on a second?'

Alex heard voices shouting in the background.

'Listen, darling, I've got to get back to the lab – there's a slight problem – it's turning brown. Actually I had a weird dream – well I didn't think it was a dream but it must have been. I was woken up by it, about six this morning; I could have sworn that Fabian came into my bedroom. He said "Hi, Dad", then disappeared. I looked all over the house for him when I woke up, I was so convinced I'd seen him. This country life can't be doing me much good after all – I must be cracking up!'

CHAPTER FIVE

She stared at the light oak coffin, with its brass handles, and the red roses that lay on top of it; at the shafts of sunlight playing through the stained glass window; at the kindly face of the clergyman at the lectern. 'Now we see through a glass darkly,' he read, calmly, serenely.

They were picking up the coffin now, they picked it up easily. Her son was in that; she wondered what he looked like. They hadn't let David see him when he'd gone to France. Too badly burned to identify, they had said. She felt David's hand tugging now. Do I have to stand, she thought, panicking suddenly. Do I have to walk down that aisle, in front of those staring faces? Then she remembered they were friends, all friends, and she followed her husband, lamely, through the haze of tears she was trying to hold back, outside and into the black Daimler.

The cortège stopped in front of the neat red-brick crematorium; they got out into the sunlight and stood silently watching the pall-bearers unload the coffin. Two men took the roses off around the corner, and the others carried the coffin into the building and set it down in front of the dark blue curtains. Alex walked up to the coffin and laid a single red rose on the lid. She spoke quietly, with her head bowed. 'Goodbye, darling.'

She walked back and sat in the front pew beside David. She knelt and closed her eyes, trying to find some prayers, but could think of nothing; she heard the building filling with people and the soft organ music. She tried to listen to the words of the committal service, but could hear nothing, nothing but the sudden click and hum of the blue curtains sliding apart and the coffin starting to move slowly through them.

She felt uncomfortable at the wake, standing in the crush of people in her house, and drained a glass of champagne straight down. A bottle popped loudly, near her ear, frothing and spraying, and she was swept backwards helplessly in the retreating surge of people, like being carried on a huge wave, she thought.

'I'm sorry, Alex,' said a woman in a black veil whom she did not recognize.

'He was a nice chap,' said Alex. 'They never take the shits, do they?' She fumbled for her cigarettes. Through the crowd she saw Sandy making towards her, her hair a mad cauldron of tangled jet-black strands held vaguely together with what looked like knitting needles. Instinctively she turned away; Sandy's theatrical emotions were more than she could cope with right now. She saw Otto's sharp bird-of-prey face staring down at her, hideously lacerated, a mass of weals and sticking plasters. 'Thank you for coming, Otto,' she said.

He nodded, gave a half-smile that turned into a cruel grin. 'Fabian asked me to,' he said.

Alex stared at him, but he turned away from her, back to his conversation.

She closed the door on the last of the guests, took another drag on her cigarette and another long pull on the glass. She was feeling better, from the buzz of the drink, from the cheer of the friends and family who had been around. Only David still lingered, lurking in the entrance to the kitchen, leaning against the wall, glass in his hand. 'Would you like me to stay?' he said.

'No, David.'

'I don't think you should be alone tonight.'

'I really would prefer to be on my own. Please; I have to get over this my way.'

'Why don't you come down to Lewes?'

'I'll be O.K. here.'

David shrugged. 'I suppose you blame me.'

'Blame you?'

'For buying him the car.'

'No. Accidents happen; I don't think it would have made any difference, whatever the car.'

'If he had been going a bit slower?'

Alex smiled and shook her head.

David picked up a bottle and poured into his glass; only a dribble came out. He looked at the label. 'Veuve Clicquot.'

'Fabian's favourite; he always thought it was a smart champagne.'

'The widow Clicquot.' He paused, looked awkwardly at Alex, and blushed. He sniffed the wine. 'Could have done with a bit more bottle age.'

'I'm sorry,' said Alex. 'Perhaps if you'd asked him he might have waited a couple of years before he died.' She walked past him into the kitchen and switched on the kettle. David followed her and put his arm gently around her.

'You know,' he said, 'it's incredible we should have both had the same dream about him, at the same time. I've been thinking about that.'

'It must have been about the time he died,' said Alex.

'Most extraordinary coincidence.'

Alex opened the jar of Nescafé and spooned some into two cups. 'Still taking sugar?'

'One spoon.'

'You think it was coincidence?' she said, testily.

David held the glass up to the light and examined the colour carefully. 'You know I'm sure this used to be a deeper yellow. I wonder if they've cut the ageing time down – or perhaps I'm mistaken. The bouquet's fine.'

Alex glared at him. 'You think it was coincidence?'

'Coincidence?' he said blankly. 'Ah, yes, well of course.' He caught the look in her eyes. 'Oh, come on now, Alex, you think it was something else?'

She shrugged. 'It was very strange; it was just so real.'

'We'll have to let Cambridge know,' he said, changing the subject.

'I hadn't thought of that.'

'I'll call them tomorrow.'

'I'd better write to Charles and Henry's parents too.'

'Yes.'

They sat opposite each other and drank their coffee. 'How's your Chardonnay?' said Alex.

David smiled. 'One step forward, two steps back; can't get it to stabilize. How's the agency?'

'Busy.'

'Got any blockbusters on the stocks?'

'An anthology of Urdu war chants.'

'Is that what the world's been waiting for?'

'I doubt it.'

He raised his eyebrows. 'I'm thinking of writing a book on wine.'

'Good subject,' she said. 'I've only had sixty-four manuscripts on wine land on my desk this year.'

David stood up. 'You know what they say, sixty-fifth time lucky.'

Alex smiled. 'Give me a call when you get home.'

'You want me to?'

'I want to know you've arrived safely.' She kissed him and closed the door, and suddenly felt very alone.

The hallway was dark, with its sombre black and white tiles and high ceiling, and she switched on the light. She walked into the drawing room, with its thick pallor of smoke and perfume and the vinous acidity of the champagne, parted the net curtains and looked through the bay window at the street; the colour had drained out of the clear sky and it was now a darkening wash. She thought again of Otto's strange words, 'Fabian asked me to'. Something moved behind her, suddenly. She sensed it, and felt fear, stronger than any fear she had ever felt before; she was cold and her skin was prickling, bristling with cold needles. She felt the room closing in on her and she wanted to tap on the window, shout for help, but she was paralysed. She saw a shadow moving out of the corner of her eye, rising from a chair behind her.

'Oh darling, excuse me, I must have dozed off,' said the shadow.

She stared, transfixed, as she suddenly realized it was Sandy.

'Quite overcome by the emotion of it all – I'm on these tranquillizers, you see, and they just don't go with booze.' She yawned, and stretched. 'Has everyone gone?'

'Yes.' Alex said, weakly. She switched on a table lamp, and felt comforted by the warm glow as the colour came back to the room. 'You gave me a fright.'

'I'm sorry, darling.' Sandy blinked, then prodded her haystack of black hair with her fingers, and adjusted a couple of the knitting needles.

'Like some coffee?' said Alex, relieved, and grateful now for the company, even, she thought, Sandy's.

'I'd love some. What are you doing tonight?'

'Nothing.'

'What – you're going to be here on your own?'

Alex nodded. 'I want to be alone.'

'You can't, darling, not tonight.'

'I have been every other night; I don't mind it.'

They walked through to the kitchen. Alex suddenly found herself acutely aware of the objects that were in the house, as if she had entered a museum. She saw the stern portrait of David's great-grandfather in his cavalry uniform. 'Fabian has his eyes,' David used to boast proudly, and she had always demurred, there was no point in disillusioning him, no point in spoiling the pretence. Only she knew that Fabian had inherited nothing of David's, not one single gene; it was her secret, and she had kept it for twenty-two years.

'Dreadful,' said Sandy. 'The whole thing. There were two other boys also who . . .?'

Alex nodded. 'Brothers. Charles and Henry Heathfield.'

'Shocking. So shocking. What a terrible thing. A lorry on the wrong side of the motorway, wasn't it?'

'A car,' said Alex.

29

Sandy frowned. 'I was certain it said lorry in the paper.'

'It did. They got it wrong.'

'A drunk Frenchman?'

Alex nodded.

'How can anyone drive down the wrong side of an Autoroute? However drunk they are?'

The kettle clicked.

'Do you know anything about him, darling?'

'No, not really,' said Alex. 'Apparently he'd had a row with his wife and stormed out. Been drinking all night; his business was going bust. Soft toys, or something.' She shrugged. 'David knows more about it.'

'Dreadful.'

Alex carried the cups through into the drawing room, and they sat down. Her head was beginning to ache, and she closed her eyes.

'I think you should see a medium, darling,' said Sandy, staring down at the swirling coffee, trying to dissolve the last of the grains.

'A medium?'

'Yes.'

'No, Sandy, that's not for me; I'm afraid I don't believe in that sort of stuff.'

'I think you do.'

'You think I do?' she said, incredulous.

'You're a Christian; so you believe in life everlasting.'

'I'm not sure that I do.' Alex stared at the nervy mess of a woman sitting opposite, who was now trying to push a cigarette into the end of a long thin holder and was having a harder time than if she were trying to thread a needle. The girl she had known since schooldays, mad, cranky, but kind; a girl who had been through three divorces, who had been a drug addict, an alcoholic, a Christian Scientist, a vegan, who had meditated under the Maharishi Yogi and tried virtually every other religion under the sun, who had made just about every kind of a mess of her life it was possible to make; this girl was trying to give her some advice.

'David told me that Fabian came to see him the morning he died, and he came to see you too.'

'We both had the same dream.'

'Dream?' She shook her head. 'That wasn't a dream, darling, he came to see you; very common occurrence.'

'What do you mean?'

Sandy stared at her, her thin tortured face that had once been so pretty, but was now looking so jaded and her huge blue eyes, like forgotten ponds, she thought. 'We all have spirit guides, darling, keeping a watch on us, but they're not around all the time. If someone dies suddenly, when the guides aren't expecting it, they can lose contact and the person's spirit can wander around, lost. That may have happened to Fabian; that's why you both saw him; he was trying to get his bearings.'

Alex sipped her coffee and stared at her friend with a mixture of contempt and pity.

'You think I'm an old crank, darling, don't you, someone who's made a mess of their life? Well, maybe I have in your terms, but I've had lots of other lives, some extremely happy ones, and I've been sent back this time in order to learn to cope better with rough times. I'm an old spirit, darling, I'm toughened to it all; you're not, I can tell, you're a young spirit, and you must accept my help, that's one of the things I'm here for, to help others.'

Alex shook her head. She felt tired, suddenly, hemmed in, as if the room was full of people; she wanted to get away, go out of the front door, walk about outside. 'Maybe the dream was telepathy,' she said. 'That's possible, isn't it?'

'It's possible, darling – plenty of that in the spirit world, but why should it be? We don't know much more about telepathy than we do about spirits. I think he came to you because he needed help.'

'What sort of help?'

'He may be all right now, darling; he may have been reunited with his guides, they may have taken him off. But if they haven't, then he could just be wandering around, lost.'

'How long would he do that?'

'Time has a different perspective on the other side, darling; it could be forever. You owe it to him to make sure he is all right, and try to help him if he isn't.'

'How?'

'By seeing a medium; a medium will know. If you do that, darling, then at least you will know you have done everything you can. I can put you in touch with an excellent one.' She paused and dragged hard on her cigarette holder; she blew the smoke out then flapped it away with her hand. 'You don't believe what I'm saying, do you, darling?'

'No,' said Alex, shaking her head. 'No, I'm sorry, I don't.'

CHAPTER SIX

Alex woke suddenly, afraid. There was a light pulsating in the room; she felt her hair prickling, did not dare open her eyes, but instead, squeezed them even tighter shut, so she could not open them accidentally; she waited. Something was in the room, she could feel it.

She saw the stark wood coffin, the red rose; her face suddenly began to feel hot; she smelt petrol fumes, then heat; her face was burning. Her breathing began to get out of control, she was panting, her knees were crashing together under the bedclothes. Her eyes sprang wide open. She sensed a green pulsating light. The light turned from a blur into sharp focus. Four noughts. On, off, on, off. The burning subsided and she felt only cold, and the fear began to subside too.

She watched the dial on the alarm clock, the four noughts blinking on, off. Midnight, she thought. She looked around the room, saw the shapes, the familiar shapes. She'd been afraid of the dark when she was a child, always slept with the light on; but that fear had gone a long time ago, long before she'd married. The noughts blinked.

She snapped on the bedside light; the room seemed normal, everything seemed normal, sounded normal. She heard a lorry in the distance, sloshing down the King's Road; it sounded as though it had been raining. She picked up her watch. Five o'clock, but the four noughts continued to blink. Then she remembered that had happened once before to her previous clock in a power cut; it had automatically reset itself to zero. She fumbled with it, trying to remember how to reset it, staring with tired, strained eyes at the blinking lights, and shivering in the cold. It was almost unbearably cold.

She got out of bed and walked to the window, parted the heavy curtains and put a hand outside. The air there was warm and mild; she held her hand out, puzzled. She saw steam from her breath and let out a small shriek of surprise, felt the hair prickling again down her neck. She stared out through the curtains once more, at the parked cars, at the glow of the street lamp; it was calm out there, normal. She pulled the curtains apart slightly and let the orange light into the room. A floorboard creaked under her foot and she jumped. Then she climbed back into bed, pulled the clothes up and closed her eyes, but still she felt cold, bitterly cold, and the cold made her feel afraid. She picked up the telephone, listened to the hum as it pierced the silence, then she punched out the numbers that she knew by heart, and waited.

It rang, once, twice, please be there, three times, four times. 'Oh please be there,' she whispered.

'Yurlo?' She listened to the grunt, filled with relief and felt warm again.

'David?' She was whispering still.

There was another bewildered grunt.

'I'm sorry to wake you, David.'

'Alex?'

'Are you awake?'

'Yrr.'

'You didn't call me.'

'Didn't call you?' He still sounded half asleep.

'You were going to call me when you got home. I was worried.'

'Wassertime?'

'Half five.'

There was a pause, and she heard the rustling of sheets.

'I didn't think you really wanted me to.'

She felt his voice, warm, smiling, comforting; it was like talking to a teddy bear. 'I was worried about you,' she said.

'I'm O.K. How are you feeling?'

'Not great. How about you?'

'I feel bloody awful. It's so lousy. I keep thinking about that other driver, that bastard.'

'Don't.'

'If he'd survived, I would have killed him.'

'Don't.'

'I'm sorry.'

'I feel so bad about Otto and those Heathfield boys.'

'At least Otto's alive,' he said.

'It must be pretty difficult for him, you know, to accept that he's survived.'

'I should never have bought Fabian that car.'

'That's not your fault, darling; you were always so kind to him.'

'I should have got him something slower.'

'I don't think it would have made any difference. Listen, go back to sleep, I'm sorry I woke you.'

'It's O.K.; I'm wide awake now.'

'Go back to sleep. I'll call you later.'

'I love you,' he said.

She stared at the receiver and smiled sadly, then hung up, slowly, gently, and lay back on the pillows. She loved him too, she knew, missed his big warm body, missed his tenderness; why the hell had they parted? She felt tired, suddenly, tired and warm, and cheered up, and fell into a heavy sleep, and dreamed dreams of Fabian, light and airy, then suddenly menacing and confused; he held her hand and laughed and then taunted her like a child, except he wasn't a child any more, but a grown man, older suddenly, so old she could see wrinkles in his face. She awoke shivering, afraid to open her eyes in the dark room. Then she slept again and did not dream.

When the alarm went at seven, she ignored it, and when she looked at the clock again, it was ten to eight. Back to normality today, she knew; it was over. There was the scattering of the ashes, but she needed time to think about that, to think where Fabian would have liked them. The last ten days had been a haze, a blur, waiting for the French bureaucracy, trying to get the body released, brought back to England. David had been over to France, taken care of all the arrangements, and had made no demands on her. He had been marvellous. Now she had to get on with her life again, try to concentrate on her work. At least she had that; staff, partners, clients. She couldn't fall apart on them, had to prove to them that she could do it, had to prove it to David; most of all had to prove it to herself.

She toyed around with her wardrobe, trying to decide what to wear. Fabian had always been particular about what she wore, far more so than David. The right colours, the right shape, the right names – God, he had been an unbearable clothes snob at times. She smiled, half-cheered, a damp, tearful smile, and rummaged through a drawer full of silk scarves, all of them Cornelia James, and most of them bought by Fabian. Which ones? She tried to remember, pulling various scarves out and letting them gently drop back in, like cascading waterfalls, she thought. She draped a turquoise and grey one carefully around her neck, and tied it so the Cornelia James signature was clearly showing. Are you pleased, darling, she thought? Do I look O.K.?

She gulped down half the cup of coffee, left the rest which was too hot, grabbed her coat and hurried to the front door. The bell rang just as she reached it, and she opened it almost before the bell had stopped ringing. The woman looked up at her in surprise and stepped back, a buxom, peroxided blonde, neatly but dramatically dressed in black and white, who looked like she had come from a casting agency for film extras and spoke through tiny rosebud lips that were too small for the expanse of her face. 'Mrs Hightower?' She spoke in a definite, precise voice as if she had been having elocution lessons to shed her East London accent.

'Yes?' Alex hesitated, on the defensive, wondering what she was trying to sell. She looked too dolled up to be a Jehovah's Witness, and anyway they normally came in pairs.

36

'I'm Iris Tremayne. Sandy suggested I pop round – she said you went out early and this was the best time to catch you.'

The woman stared straight into Alex's eyes, and she found it unsettling, found it hard to disconnect from her gaze. She wondered for a moment whether she was selling Tupperware, or Avon cosmetics; yes, cosmetics looked likely, except that she didn't have a sample case. 'Actually, I'm rather late for the office.' Alex spoke pleasantly, trying to be polite.

'No, of course, if this isn't convenient I fully understand, but I thought I'd better come round right away. In case you wanted news about your son.'

Alex realized suddenly who she was. 'No,' she said. 'Thank you, but I don't want any news about my son.'

'I'm very sorry to hear about what happened.'

'Thank you.'

'Sandy's very worried about him.'

'Is she?' said Alex, conscious that her tone was becoming belligerent.

'If you'd like to have a sitting, I'd be very pleased. There'd be no charge; Sandy is a good friend.'

'Mrs Tremayne,' said Alex, coldly, 'my son is dead. Nothing you or anyone else can do can change that; I'm afraid I'm just not a believer in –' she paused '– in whatever you call it – the spirit world.'

'I think he wants to talk to you.'

There was a sincerity in the woman's expression, a sincerity ingrained deep beneath the make-up, beneath the dramatic hair, a sincerity and a naïvety, Alex thought. You poor deluded fool, she wanted to say, but did not. 'Thank you,' she said. 'But I have to go now.'

Alex nodded to her receptionist, avoided catching her eye, and went upstairs to her office.

Julie looked up from her typewriter as she walked past her office, and smiled gently. 'Good morning. I'll let you catch up with your post,' she said. 'Do you want me to cancel any of your appointments this week?'

'No, Julie, we cancelled enough last week. The show goes on.' Alex closed her door and stared at the bewildering stack of mail on her desk. She looked at the wooden calendar which Julie adjusted every day. April 21st. The last ten days had disappeared as if she had been in a hole in time.

She slit open a Jiffy bag and pulled out a neatly typed and bound manuscript. '*Lives Foreseen – My Powers and Others*'.' She flipped open the cover and turned to the first chapter; the first page always determined whether she would read it herself, or pass it to Julie.

'I always used to see a hand in the dark, beckoning. When I saw that hand, I knew someone would die. The first time was when I was seven, and the next day, my sister was run over by a tractor. That was the first time I became aware of my powers of clairvoyance.'

She turned back to the cover, then buzzed Julie. 'Does an author called Stanley Hill ring a bell?'

'No.'

'I think we may have had something from him before.'

'Do you want me to look it up for you?'

'No, I'll do it.' Alex switched on her VDU screen and saw three words, clearly, in the centre, in bright green letters: HELP ME MOTHER.

She felt as if cold water was being flushed through her tubes. The words faded and the screen became blank. The cold turned to hot, her forehead was burning and she felt sweat running down her face. She switched the unit off, then on again, but this time there was nothing but the words MENU and the list of functions.

Fearfully, she tapped a couple of keys, the menu disappeared and was replaced by the words CLIENT FILE. She moved her shaking hands across the keyboard, tried to tap the search key, but pressed the wrong key, and the machine bleeped angrily at her.

'Are you O.K., Alex?'

She watched Julie put down the cup of coffee almost as if in slow motion, and she was conscious of the sound of her own words when she spoke.

'Yes, I'm fine.'

'You look as white as a sheet.'

'I'm very tired. I haven't been sleeping too well.'

'Maybe you should take some pills – you know, just until you get over the worst –'

Alex smiled. 'I am over the worst.'

'I think you've been very brave.'

Alex felt her eyes watering, and squeezed them tightly shut; but the emotion welled up inside her until she could not contain it, and she felt the tears flooding out through her eyelids. She felt a hand squeeze hers and squeezed back hard, opened her eyes and saw Julie's pretty face staring kindly; she noticed that Julie had changed her hairstyle; it had been cropped short and she realized she had not commented. 'I'm sorry,' she said. 'I like your hair.'

'Thanks.'

'You needn't worry, I'm not going to crack up on you all.'

'We know that.' Julie handed Alex a handkerchief.

'It's O.K., I've got one.' She blew her nose. 'When people call, tell them not to ask me how I am, all right?'

Julie nodded.

'Tell them also not to mention Fabian; it would be much easier for me.'

'Yes, of course.'

Alex looked fearfully at the word-processor. She saw the imprint of the words in her mind. Clear. Unmistakable. 'I can't remember how this thing works – I want to find the name of an author – this chap.'

Julie tapped the keyboard, and a moment later the words STANLEY HILL appeared.

'Submitted a manuscript to us in 1982, called *Star-Gazer to the Stars*.'

'A modest title,' said Alex. 'Why did we reject it?'

Julie leaned closer to the screen. 'Not enough meat.'

'There are dozens of other agents – why did he send us his next one?'

'You must have written him a very nice letter.'

'I doubt it,' said Alex.

'Do you want me to read this one?'

'No, send it straight back; tell him we're not interested in this sort of stuff.'

'It sells well,' said Julie. 'Look at Doris Stokes.'

'I don't care if it sells a million; I don't want to handle it.'

She watched Julie take the manuscript and walk out of the room, then stared again at the screen. She switched it off. Help Me Mother. The words went round in her mind. She switched on the machine again and the words stared back at her, calmly, unflickering:

HELP ME MOTHER.

CHAPTER SEVEN

'You look very preoccupied.'

Alex waved away the smoke with her hand. 'You keep disappearing.'

Philip Main pushed the Capstan cigarette through the hairs of his walrus moustache, emitted a long slow grunt which had a rasp to it like a moped racing down a distant lane, and released another explosion of smoke. 'In the cosmic sense?'

'No,' Alex smiled. 'In the physical sense.'

'Hrrr,' he said, thoughtfully.

She waved her hand again. 'The smoke, you're getting worse.'

'Ah,' he said in his soft low voice, shrugging his shoulders apologetically. 'A chap's few pleasures; still, this is only a transient inconvenience, for a few more thousand years, five, six maybe at the most – an insignificant time.'

'Before?'

'Before we have evolved enough to stay on our own all of the time; no need to meet; all communication will be by telepathy and unexposed film; the thrill of exposure, that will replace all of today's social contact – the pleasures and –' he held up his cigarette '– and the inconveniences.'

She stared, smiling, at his elongated frame, shoulders hunched in his battered tweed jacket and up at his gaunt fiery face, with the moustache that hung down like a statement. In his forties, he still looked more like an overgrown student revolutionary than a scientist with three respected, if controversial, books to his name. 'How's the book coming?'

He lowered his head and stared at her as if she was a

goldfish in a bowl. 'Proof; there is proof.' He raised his wine glass, drank and lowered it again, leaving his moustache looking like a damp rug.

'What proof?'

'You'll see. You'll be stunned, girl, stunned.' His face changed as he spoke, becoming animated.

'Good,' she said, feeling rather lost.

'Irrefutable proof that Darwin was right.'

'You've been able to recreate the origins of the universe in a repeatable laboratory experiment?'

'There's a little bit of fine tuning, but yes, good Lord yes, I've seen it done. DNA, girl, out of two bits of dust.'

'And where did the dust come from?'

'Thin air, girl' he said, triumphantly. 'Thin air!'

A waiter presented her Dover sole for inspection and then began to fillet it.

The tone of Main's voice suddenly became gentle. 'Has your husband been around the past couple of weeks?'

'What do you mean?' She felt herself blushing, saw the almost imperceptible motion of the waiter's head as he tuned his ears in.

'Has he been of help?'

'Yes, he's been a brick.'

'Good,' he said, without enthusiasm.

She blushed again and looked at the waiter, who was having problems with the sole.

'Does he still want you back?'

'I, er –' she said, and faltered. She looked at her watch and pressed the date button. 5.4 it read. She stared at it, puzzled. May 4th? 'What's the date today? It's April still, isn't it?'

She stared at her watch again, confused.

'Alex? Alex?' She heard the words echoing around her head, tried to work out where they were coming from; she saw the face across the table, his mouth opening, closing. 'Alex? Are you all right?'

The face went out of focus then came back in again. 'Yes,' she said. 'Yes, I'm fine.'

'You've gone very white.'

'I'm sorry.' She looked down at her watch again and frowned. 'What's the time?'

'Twenty to two.'

Her watch was correct. 'Was there a thunderstorm last night?' she said.

Main frowned, then eyed the sole that was placed in front of him suspiciously. 'Was this in a fight?' he said to the waiter, his voice suddenly stern and loud.

'A fight, sir?'

'Looks like it's been in a massacre.'

'I'm sorry, sir.' The waiter hesitated, then retreated.

'Thunderstorm?'

'Or an electrical storm?'

'There may have been; it was very humid last night.'

Alex felt liberated suddenly. 'And could that affect electrics – clocks, things like that?'

He frowned. 'Possibly. Can cause interruptions in the power supply.'

She was silent for a moment, thinking. 'Could it affect solar powered things too?'

He nodded slowly. 'Possibly. Why?'

'Oh, nothing.'

He looked down and glared at the fish malevolently, then drank some more wine and dabbed his moustache with his napkin.

'What's your opinion of mediums, Philip?'

'Mediums?'

'A friend of mine said I ought to go and see one.'

He spooned carrots out of a partitioned dish of vegetables and looked uncomfortable. 'Have some carrots,' he said. 'They do them well here.'

She took the bowl. 'You haven't answered.'

'There are some people who find mediums helpful.'

'Who? People who can't accept that someone's dead?'

He shrugged. 'Are you a Christian?'

'I suppose so.'

43

'Therefore you believe in eternal life.'

'I'm not sure what I believe in any longer.'

'Excellent piece of evolution, the Dover sole.' He speared a bit with his fork and lifted it. 'Used to swim upright.' He put his fork down and held up his hand, vertically. 'Didn't start swimming flat until they moved to the bottom of the sea – realized they would be less visible.'

'Smart.'

'They had a – problem with their eyes. One either side of their head. Fine upright, but swimming flat, one eye always looking at the sea bed, one up at the sky; one day, pop, both eyes appeared on top.'

'What's that got to do with mediums?'

'Can't you see? Evolution is about making nature work. We can prove God did not make man. But what about the other way round?'

'That's an old argument.'

'No, it's new; brand new.'

'That man may have invented God?'

He speared his fish and held it up in front of his mouth, examining it carefully. 'No, girl, not invented. Made! Made! If the whole animal world has evolved from two specks of dust and a bolt of electricity, why not a spiritual world too?'

'You're bonkers.'

'I'm smarter than this fish.'

'How do you know?'

'Because otherwise it would be eating me.'

She grinned. 'At least you're cheering me up.'

'Yes, well, we all need a bit of cheering up from time to time.'

She ate a mouthful of fish. 'It's good, even if it does look like something that survived Glencoe.'

He put his knife and fork down, and blushed slightly. 'I – er – I was wondering – would you let me buy you dinner one evening? You know – not just yet awhile – but perhaps in a bit?'

She shook her head. 'I like my relationships with my clients to be strictly professional.'

He dabbed his moustache with his napkin and spoke at the same time, so that his words were muffled. 'We – er – could have a strictly professional dinner.'

She shook her head. 'Don't, Philip. I'm not in any state to start trying to cope with a relationship.'

'I'm just offering the hand of friendship; nothing more.'

'O.K., thanks, I understand. Let's just keep it a lunch-time friendship.'

'Are you free for lunch tomorrow?'

She laughed. 'Tomorrow's Saturday.'

'Saturday's a good day for lunch.'

'I'm going to Cambridge tomorrow – I have to sort out Fabian's things.'

'Maybe next week?'

'Maybe.'

Lunch with Philip Main had lifted her, and she was feeling considerably cheered when she got home. She thought again of the three words on the screen. The strain, she thought. It must be.

The house was quiet, peaceful, and smelt strongly of polish. It was growing dark. The clocks had gone forward. Summer Time had started, but it didn't feel much like summer.

She stood in the hall and felt suddenly in a vacuum. The last ten days had passed in a haze and now there was a return to normality that seemed flattening. She wished she had taken up Philip's offer of dinner, or her husband's. She did not want to be alone this evening, to dwell on her thoughts. She looked up the television programmes in the *Standard*, but there was nothing she fancied. She dropped the paper on to a sofa and went down the narrow staircase into her darkroom.

Photography; there was something intensely personal about photography, and it was instant, told the story without having to wade through the manuscript. Perhaps Philip was right. But there was so much to learn about it.

45

She'd missed the last classes; time, there was never enough time. When David had built her the darkroom she had loved locking herself away down here; she had felt peaceful and safe with the silence and the strange smells of the chemicals. But tonight she felt uncomfortable here; the silence was oppressive.

Philip Main's disgusting contact sheet was still on the drying rack. She unpegged it, hoping Mimsa hadn't noticed it, and was about to tear it up when something caught her eye, a mark, very small, on one of the frames. She picked up her magnifying glass, switched on the light box, and looked at the print.

Fabian's face stared back, clearly, from the bottom right-hand corner. And then she noticed it was on every frame, in the same position.

She dropped the magnifying glass; it hit the white perspex of the light box, cracking it badly, and she stood, shuddering, her skin prickling.

Fabian's face had appeared on the print since she had developed it.

The walls seemed to be closing in. She spun around; the door had moved, she was certain. She grabbed the handle, pulled it open. There was nothing there. 'Hallo,' she said. 'Hallo?' She stared through the door, but everything was quiet.

There was a shrill rasping which seemed to shake the whole foundations of the house. She let out a small yelp of fear and clutched the door frame, fearful. The rasping ended in a series of metallic pings. Doorbell! She felt the relief surge through her. Don't go away, oh please, don't go away! She ran out of the room and up the stairs, desperate to catch whoever it was before they went away, desperate for some company, some human contact, any.

She opened the door and stood, gasping for breath, as she stared at a young man with an earnest, scrubbed face and short curly hair. He was wearing a shabby grey suit, too old for him, probably a cast-off from someone, she thought, and a polo neck sweater. She looked down at his shoes, scuffed, shapeless black shoes that badly needed a polish. Perhaps they were cast-offs too?

He spoke slowly in a gentle voice, carefully articulated. 'Mrs Hightower?'

Alex nodded. He had a familiar look about him, like an old newspaper she had already read. He didn't look like a salesman, and she wondered for a moment if he was another medium sent by Sandy; she did not mind, at this moment anyone was welcome.

'I'm John Allsop, the curate – I cover your area – er – the vicar told me of your bereavement, so I thought I would pop in and introduce myself – if it's convenient.' His right eye twitched sharply, twice.

'Please – yes, of course.' She closed the door behind him. 'I'm afraid we didn't use the vicar for the funeral service – it was done by an old schoolfriend of my husband's – John Lambourne – he's down near Hastings. I hope the vicar didn't feel his nose put out?'

'No, not at all; this is quite usual.'

They went into the drawing room. 'I'm afraid we've been a little remiss about church.'

'I wouldn't worry,' he said kindly. 'But you'd be very welcome if you'd like to come and worship at any of our churches.'

'Thank you.'

'And how are you coping? You look as if you are still in a great deal of shock.'

'You don't expect to go to the funeral of your child,' she said.

'No,' he said. 'No; to have a child taken is a terrible thing. Do you have any other – er – children?'

She shook her head.

'That makes it even worse, if that is possible.' He twitched again. 'I suffered a bereavement myself recently – my wife. I found it very helpful to look at photographs.'

She stared at him wide-eyed, and thought of the face

47

staring out from the photographs of the genitals. How? How? How had it got there? Was it some kind of macabre joke? 'I'm sorry,' she said.

He smiled sadly and nodded. 'Thank you.'

'Was it –?' she fumbled for words.

'Cancer,' he said.

Alex nodded, unsure what to say. 'Terrible.' Fabian's face stared at her again. 'Terrible.' She stood up abruptly, then wondered why she was standing up. 'I'll – er – can I get you some coffee?'

'Oh, no, really, thank you.'

'Do you like coffee, or would you prefer tea – or whisky or something?'

'Nothing, really.'

But she was already on her way to the kitchen, desperate for a moment on her own to pull herself together. She made the coffee, opened a pack of chocolate digestives and was about to take them back out, when she noticed a business card on the kitchen table. 'Iris Tremayne' it read, with an address in Earls Court. She dropped it in the bin, then pulled it out and put it on the dresser. She picked up the tray and went back into the drawing room. 'Please help yourself to milk and sugar.'

'Thank you.'

She was conscious of him looking at her oddly; how bad do I look, she wondered. How shocked?

'Yes,' he twitched again. 'Photographs; bringing back the memories. It can be very therapeutic. The pain does go, in time, believe me.' He smiled and bit into a biscuit nervously, as if worried it might bite him back.

She saw him staring at the bowl of wilting red roses.

'Fabian gave them to me for my birthday – he always gave me red roses; he loved them.'

'Do you – er – garden?'

'I'm hopeless, I'm afraid. My husband's the gardener.'

'Ah. You're separated, I understand?'

'Yes. My husband used to be in advertising – but wine

48

was always his big love; he decided to jack it all in and start a vineyard. Unfortunately, country life did not agree with me.'

'Very difficult, the country; sometimes it can be too peaceful.'

'Yes.'

'You're a literary agent, I believe.'

She nodded.

'I'm writing a book myself. Just a little one.'

Alex felt a sense of disappointment; was this the reason why he had come round? 'Do you have a publisher?'

'Oh, I'm a long way from finishing it – I don't know that it would be good enough.'

'If you'd like me to look at it . . .'

'Oh no, I wouldn't want to put you to any trouble. Perhaps, if I finish it, thank you.'

'Have some more coffee.'

'I'll have another biscuit if I may.' He leaned forward and took one from the plate. 'You might find it comforting, you know, to talk to some of your son's friends. We often know so little about those that are close to us when they are alive, and yet we can learn nice things after they have departed; it can be of great comfort.'

'Thank you. That's good advice. But he was a bit of a loner really. He had only two close friends that I knew, and one of them was killed in the accident.'

He shook his head. 'Some things are very difficult to understand, Mrs Hightower.'

She nodded. 'Yes.'

'But you look as if you are the sort who can cope.'

'Yes,' she sighed. 'I can cope.' She smiled. 'Somehow.'

He smiled back and stirred his coffee.

'Do you have any –' she paused, and blushed '– any views on spiritualism?'

She saw the frown come across his face, like a cloud.

'I would not advise that, Mrs Hightower, I would not advise that at all. Have you –?' He hesitated.

49

'No, absolutely not. But people have been suggesting it to me.'

'I have only come across misery caused by that, never any good.' He looked uncomfortable, suddenly, as if he wanted to go.

'I don't believe in it at all.'

'Very sensible. If any friend suggests it to you, they are not truly a friend. Prayer, love, happy memories and time will heal; nothing can be gained by trying to summon up the departed, nothing but disappointment and –' he hesitated.

'And?' she said.

'There are many evil forces, Mrs Hightower. There is much evil in the world; those that dabble in the occult expose both themselves and others to it.'

She nodded. 'I'm not about to start dabbling.'

'Good.' He smiled. 'Would you like to say a prayer together?'

'A prayer?' She blinked, and felt herself blushing. 'Yes – er – thank you,' she said, awkwardly.

The curate closed his eyes and they said the Lord's Prayer. He then continued into more prayers and she sat, with her eyes tightly shut; it seemed strange, just the two of them in her drawing room, but when she opened her eyes again, she felt stronger, comforted.

'Would you like me to visit you again?'

'Please, whenever you are passing.'

He left, almost as if he was in a hurry to get away, she thought; something had changed in him the moment she had mentioned spiritualism, some concern that she had been unable to allay.

She closed the front door and walked back down the hallway. The light was still on down the stairs to the darkroom, and she wondered whether to go and look again at the photographs. No, she decided, she would look in the morning, in the daylight, when she was rested and her eyes were not playing tricks. She sighed; some time she would have to tackle Fabian's room, do something with his clothes, his belongings. She wondered, suddenly, if he had made a will.

She went upstairs into his bedroom and turned on the light. The room seemed very peaceful, almost welcoming. His slippers by the bed, laid out by Mimsa; silly Mimsa, she thought with a smile. Mimsa had taken it badly; violent floods of emotion, the best way to get grief out, she knew, envious for a moment of Mimsa's simplicity, of her Latin temperament. She wished that sometimes she too could let her emotion go.

She looked up at the stern portrait on the wall, and Fabian's cold eyes stared down; she shuddered. 'Don't look like that, darling,' she said. She closed her eyes. 'Oh, God, look after my darling Fabian; protect him wherever he is.' She opened them again and her eyes were wet. She sat down on the bed and sobbed, gently.

Then she stood up, looked at the framed photograph of a Jaguar sports car on the wall and the huge stylized coloured posters of old cars, racing. She looked at his books, rows and rows of science fiction, astronomy. She looked at the telescope set up at the window, that David had given him for his sixteenth birthday. She walked over, removed the lens cap and looked through it. She could remember Fabian patiently pointing out the stars to her, the Bear, the Plough, Uranus, Jupiter, he knew them all. She could never really be sure which was which; she even had difficulty in recognizing the Plough. She stared at the stars now. They looked huge. She wondered if Fabian was up there, somewhere, among them.

She opened a drawer and rummaged through his socks, lurid greens, yellows, pinks; he always wore bright socks. Something caught her eye at the bottom of the drawer, and she moved the socks aside. It was a postcard depicting a long red-brick building with shops and an outdoor café. The Quincy Markets, Boston, Mass. There were more cards underneath, all of different scenes of Boston: the river,

M.I.T., Harvard University, the harbour, 'Scene of the historic Boston Tea Party', she read. Strange, she thought, he'd never been to the States, never even talked about it; why the postcards at the bottom of the drawer, almost as if he had been hiding them?

She slept with the light on that night, as she had done when she was a child. It would go in time; as the curate had said, the wounds would heal. She slept for a while then woke up, stared at the green glow of her clock, and lay with a sense of dread, covered in pins and needles listening to the silence of the night. She looked up at the ceiling, then across at the wall, at Fabian's room.

She saw the words on the VDU. Fabian's face staring from the photograph.

She closed her eyes tightly, tried to shut them out, tried to shut out everything.

CHAPTER EIGHT

It was drizzling as Alex drove over the Cam, the same as it had been when she had driven Fabian up for the start of his first term. It was strange, she thought, the odd details she could remember. The car crammed full of his luggage. Their conversation. 'Had any more thoughts about what you want to do after Cambridge, darling?'

He had stared ahead as if brooding. 'No,' he had replied, flatly, but a little too quickly.

She realized the curate had been right; one knew very little about one's children, however much they hugged you, gave you roses and could sense your own moods. She remembered the day she had told Fabian she and David were separating. 'I've known you would for years, Mother,' he had said, walking over and kissing her, this strange tall thin son, stronger now than when he had been a child with his weak chest and his fearful rages and his strange dark brooding moods and the hours he would spend in his room with the door locked.

She walked around the quadrangle, listening to the echo of her footsteps, up the stone staircase, along the corridor and found room 35. She was nervous, she realized suddenly, nervous of knocking on the door.

It opened almost instantly, and she jumped.

'Hallo, Mrs Hightower,' said Otto.

Why did he always have to sound as if he was mocking, she wondered? She stared up at his brooding, menacing face, made all the more satanic by the cuts and bruising and his strange eyes, smiling, like a pair of conspirators, two hideous cold mocking objects. Had this really been her son's best friend?

'Hallo, Otto, how are you?' she said, gently.

'Oh, I'm fine, Mrs Hightower. Would you like some coffee?' She noticed the lilt of German that just took the knife-edge off his Eton accent; she could not work out whether he was trying to accentuate or obscure it.

'Thank you.'

He poured some coffee beans into an electric grinder, laid out the pot, the cups, the milk, as if performing a ritual.

'This is very nice, Otto, I thought most students only knew how to make instant.' She looked around the room.

'Most students probably do.'

There were few clues about his personality in the battered undergraduate furniture, the bare walls, the rows of books, mostly scientific. There were piles of papers and clothes strewn untidily around. A couple of empty bottles of champagne lay by the wastepaper basket. 'How are you feeling now, Otto?'

'Feeling?'

She nodded. 'Emotionally.'

He shrugged, put a cigarette in his mouth and lit it. 'Would you like one?'

She shook her head. 'I hope you don't feel guilty.'

'Guilty?'

'Yes. That you – you know – survived.'

'I don't feel guilty.'

The coffee pot hissed and spat.

'Maybe I will have one,' she said. He handed her the pack. 'I don't think it's fair that three young boys were killed by a drunk.' She leaned forward and took the light Otto held out. 'A sad drunk.'

'Perhaps it was meant, Mrs Hightower.'

'Meant?' She drew on the cigarette. 'Meant that they should be taken or that you should have survived?'

He raised his eyebrows.

'Tell me,' she said, and paused, feeling silly. 'At the funeral, when I thanked you for coming, you said that Fabian had asked you to come. What did you mean?'

Otto leaned against the window-sill and looked down at the quadrangle.

She stared at him, realizing what he must be going through, and said nothing; she sipped her coffee and tapped the ash off her cigarette. 'Was Fabian happy here at Cambridge, Otto?'

'Happy? I don't know how you tell if anyone is happy?' He turned and gave a strange, leering smile.

'I got the feeling he enjoyed it here; he liked you and Charles very much.'

Otto shrugged.

'I think he was very fond of Carrie too. He brought her home a couple of times; I didn't really think she was right for him. All the same, I was sorry when he ditched her. In a funny way, she was quite good for him.'

'Ditched her?' Otto marched across the room and stubbed his cigarette out in the ashtray. 'He didn't ditch Carrie, she ditched him. She went off to find herself in America.'

Alex smiled wryly. 'Children never tell their parents much, do they?'

'That depends on the parents,' said Otto.

The tone of his voice made Alex feel uncomfortable. 'I thought Fabian and I had a close relationship.' She shrugged and stared out through the grimy window at the grey sky; the springs in the armchair were tilting her slightly over to one side, and as she moved there was a loud twang beneath her. 'He told me that he'd given her up – I suppose he was embarrassed – felt it might be bad for his ego to admit he'd been ditched; one thing he never had any problems with was girls.'

'Why do you say that Mrs Hightower?'

'What do you mean?'

'He was always having problems with girls.'

'What sort of problems?'

'I'd rather not say.' He smiled, a curious private smile to himself. She looked at his eyes, puzzled, but they gave nothing away. 'I'll take you to his room.'

'It's next door isn't it?'

Otto nodded.

'I'll go on my own first, if you don't mind. If there's anything of his that you'd like – books, whatever, please take them.'

'Thank you.'

She felt nothing as she walked into Fabian's room; it could have been the room of a total stranger. It was chilly, damp, and smelt of old furniture. She stared at the thin carpet with the floorboards showing through in patches, the single bar electric heater and the grill for toasting sandwiches which she had given him. She looked at the rows of decanters on the mantelpiece. One was half full; she removed the top and sniffed. There was a musty sweetness that reminded her of liquorice; port, she thought. Wine racks were piled against the wall, with dusty necks of bottles poking out here and there. Near the floor were several bottles grouped together, their necks wrapped smartly in gold foil, with orange bands around their necks. She leaned down to read the writing, Veuve Clicquot Ponsardin.

There were some papers on the desk, held down by a biro, and she looked at them. 'Were Goneril and Regan evil? Or just practical businesswomen? Was Shakespeare trying to tell us all something, centuries before his time? Had the Business Woman of the Year Award existed in Elizabethan times, could they have won it?' Alex smiled. She remembered Fabian discussing this with her only a few weeks ago; she could picture him clearly, walking around the kitchen, hand in his jeans pocket, firing questions at her.

She looked around; it seemed almost as if he had just popped out for a few minutes. She pulled up a chair, stood on it, and lifted his trunk from the top of the wardrobe. The clips opened with dull metallic thuds and she raised the lid, staring at the torn yellowing lining inside, at the broken plastic coat hanger and the single black sock that lay in there, and remembered the first day she had ever packed this, fourteen years before. She could see the clothes lying neatly pressed and folded, the regulation string vests and Airtex shirts and the grey prep-school pullovers with the name tags neatly stitched in, and she felt herself crying and did not want to cry in case Otto came in and saw her.

She opened the top drawer in his desk and saw his diary. She flipped through a couple of pages from March, but could see nothing of interest: dates and times of lectures; the start of the holiday marked with a thick line and the word SKIING written after. She turned back a few pages, to January 15th. '8pm. Dinner. Carrie.' The previous day read: '7.30. Cinema. Carrie.' There were no more entries mentioning Carrie after the fifteenth. A couple of days were blank, but with large asterisks marked on them. She turned forward to April 7th and smiled through her wet eyes at the black circle around the date, neat handwriting underneath. 'MOTHER'S B'DAY.'

She turned the pages forward and noticed a few other asterisks; they seemed to be about two weeks apart. She noticed an asterisk against May 4th and the date rang a bell. She felt suddenly as if an unseen hand had picked her up and dunked her in cold water; she felt the cold seep through her, as if she were litmus paper. May 4th; that was the date her watch had shown in the middle of her lunch with Philip Main.

'How are you getting on?'

She turned around. Otto was standing in the doorway, smiling that hideous knowing smile, the grotesque slashed and bruised mask that contained, she knew, so many secrets about her son. 'O.K.,' she said. 'Fine. There's some port in that decanter – you may as well have it.'

'Port doesn't last,' said Otto, disdainfully. 'That won't be any good now.'

'Oh,' she said flatly. 'There's quite a lot of wine – you're welcome to that.' She wanted Otto to take something, desperately wanted him to take something, but she did not fully understand why, whether it was to have him in her debt, or simply to atone.

He nodded uninterestedly. 'I don't think Fabian had that good taste in wine.'

'His father was –' she began, indignantly, then stopped, realizing she was rising to the bait. 'What did you mean just now, Otto, that Fabian was always having problems with girls?'

Otto walked over to the bookshelves and plucked a book out; he flipped through the pages. 'I don't think you knew very much about your son, Mrs Hightower,' he said, absently.

'Do your parents know much about you, Otto?'

'My mother has been in a home since I was four. My father –' he shrugged '– yes, I see him often.'

'What sort of home?'

'A home.'

'A mental home?' she said, gently.

He looked away from her. 'What are you going to do with everything?'

'I don't know. Take it back and –' She realized she did not know. She closed the diary and looked at the rest of the papers. Puzzled, she noticed a wodge of postcards and a letter addressed to Fabian at Cambridge in a girl's handwriting, all held together by a rubber band. She pushed them into the diary and put it into the bottom of the trunk. She could sense Otto watching her, but each time she turned around he was still leafing backwards and forwards through the pages. She folded a pair of trousers and laid them in the trunk, feeling embarrassed, as if she was looting.

'I'll take this book, if I may.'

'Of course. Take anything you want – it's no use – I mean – I'm just going to give this all away, so take anything.'

Otto shrugged. 'Just this.'

'What is it?'

He held up the cover. It was a slim paperback, F. R. Leavis on T. S. Eliot.

She smiled. 'I thought you were studying chemistry?'

'I study lots of things.'

He walked out of the room without saying anything further.

As she drove back towards London, with the trunk wedged in the passenger seat, the drizzle turned to pelting rain. She watched the wipers clouting away the water, like angry hands, she thought.

The rain turned to hail; the stones rattled on the car's bodywork, drumming on the soft hood above her, and then turned back to rain again. She thought about Otto's strange behaviour. He had always struck her as being weird, now he was even more so; anything was understandable, she supposed, after what he had been through; but there was a malevolence about him which seemed to have intensified, as if it was a joke that he had survived, some sort of bizarre personal joke. And his strange comments about Fabian; maybe it was true, maybe Carrie had ditched him, but his remark about Fabian always having problems with girls mystified her; what had he meant? Was he gay? Had he and Otto been lovers? She thought about Carrie again. A pretty little thing, with her spiky punk blonde hair and her chirpy South London accent and the awe in which she had walked round the house. 'Like bloomin' Bucknam Palace,' she had said. Alex smiled. Hardly.

'Actually, I like scrubbers, Mother,' Fabian had said. God, he could be a ghastly snob at times, and then do something totally out of character, like bringing this girl home for Christmas and fawning all over her, as if it were a game. Carrie had been no fool, that was for sure. She tried to remember what she had been doing at Cambridge; reporting for some strange left wing magazine, something to do with ecology. She remembered driving down through Streatham with Fabian and his pointing out a dismal council high-rise complex, telling her proudly that was where Carrie's mother lived.

Suddenly there was a sharp scratching noise on the

windscreen in front of her and she flinched; a car passed her in the fast lane, chucking up a heavy spray which blinded her for a moment; there was another sharp crunch and then another.

Then the spray cleared, and she stared, transfixed with horror, at the single red rose entangled in the wiper arm, sweeping backwards and forwards across the windscreen.

CHAPTER NINE

She stopped on the hard shoulder, got out of the car and stood in the lashing wind and driving rain. A lorry thundered past, inches from her, the blast of its slipstream catching her, throwing her against the side of the Mercedes. She walked forward, put her hand out, and the wipers swept again, the rose scratching, shrieking against the howl of the wind and the whine of the traffic. She grabbed the wiper arm and lifted out the rose. It pricked her finger badly, and she swore; she released the arm and the wipers swept again, angrily. Another lorry passed, close, sucking her in its slipstream, then throwing spray like a breaking wave over her. She jumped back into the car, slammed the door against the elements, and switched on the interior light.

The rose was red, blood red, like the stain trickling down from her finger which she put to her mouth and sucked. She stared out through her window at the rain, at the demoniac lights which hurtled past, at the roars and whines which faded away into the black.

Then she looked down at the rose. Who had flung it from their car, or left it loose on the back of a lorry, or . . .? But no, that was impossible, a coincidence, that was all, she told herself half-heartedly. She sat, shaking, wanting to throw it back out there where it had come from, but she could not, instead she laid it down in front of the gear stick and drove off slowly, frightened.

She carried the rose into the house and stood in the gloomy hallway, leaving the front door open behind her, not wanting to close it yet. She did not know why, but she did not want to cut off contact with the outside world.

She sucked her finger again, which was still painful, and

felt the wet damp stem; some of the petals had fallen off. She went through into the drawing room and placed it in the bowl among the roses Fabian had given her for her birthday. It stood out, fresh and vibrant among the others which had now wilted and were dying or dead; but she couldn't throw them out, not yet.

There was a loud bang as the wind blew the front door against the wall; there was another bang and then it slammed shut, as if an unseen hand had hurled it in a rage.

The trunk would have to stay in the car until Monday when she could get Mimsa to help her lift it out, she thought, walking through into the kitchen to turn the heating on, and was surprised to see that it was on, had been on all day, according to the time switch. She suddenly noticed that she could see the vapour of her breath and breathed out again, puzzled, then rubbed her hands together against the cold.

Something moved upstairs, a creak of a spring or a floorboard. She stood and listened. The cold permeated through her, made her tingle; she curled her toes, silently, listening. There was another clunk, and then the sound of water in pipes; the boiler made two loud clanks and switched itself off. She breathed out; stupid, she knew, the house always made strange noises when the heating was on.

She filled the kettle, then walked into the drawing room, glanced nervously at the rose again and switched on the television. There was a roar of applause from a studio audience and the camera panned along a row of beaming antiseptic faces: second division showbiz celebrities playing a panel game, trying a little too hard to be jolly; there was a cut to a slick quiz-master holding his microphone up close to a brunette who rolled her tongue round the inside of her mouth. Alex continued to watch for a few moments, cringing. The series had been devised by one of her clients; the critics had called it tasteless, banal and degrading, and they were right. But it had paid the rent for the past four years.

It was too cold to relax. She jumped to her feet, walked across to the roses, sniffed the new one and gave it a light caress with her finger.

She thought of Fabian's trunk lying out there on the front seat of the Mercedes, wondering why she had bothered to bring the clothes back and worried for a moment that someone might steal it. Then she shrugged; perhaps that would be the best thing.

If David had been around, he could have got the trunk; she wished she had been able to swallow her pride and ask him to. She rubbed her hands together again and shivered and felt sad, wanted to be with Fabian, wanted to hold him, hug him, wanted him to walk in the door and unpack the trunk himself.

She went up to his bedroom; the temperature seemed even lower in here; had Mimsa turned off the radiator? She put her hand on it, then lifted it away smartly, feeling the heat burning her skin. She looked at the brass telescope, the posters on the wall, and then up at the painting, almost expecting a reaction, a slight movement, but there was nothing, just the cold arrogant stare. She knelt down under it and buried her head in her hands. 'I love you, darling; I hope you're all right wherever you are; I hope you're happy; happier than you were here. I miss you; I wonder if you miss me; take care, darling, wherever you are. Please God, take care of Fabian.' She stayed kneeling, then slowly rose to her feet, and felt more peaceful.

She slipped out, gently shutting the door behind her, stood in the corridor and closed her eyes tightly. 'Goodnight, darling,' she said, and opened her eyes again; they were brimming with tears. She stopped at the top of the stairs, sat down and sobbed.

She thought of Otto's lacerated face; thought of him being catapulted from the car; what had happened, she wondered, at that moment of impact? How had Fabian reacted? What had he thought? Who was the driver of the other car? How could he have done this? The questions seemed to appear in her mind in bright green letters printed on a black void. How did Otto feel about surviving? Why was he so damned weird? He'd given her the creeps; what did he know? Some secret about Fabian? Was the whole thing a hoax, some sick joke; were he and Fabian about to come waltzing in through the door, laughing, brushing past her and going straight to his room and locking the door, and do what? Watch the stars? Make love?

She heard a roar of laughter from downstairs, and then applause and a voice saying something she could not make out; she felt peaceful, sad and a sudden overwhelming desire to be kind. She thought of David alone in the farmhouse with the dog and the sheep, tired, lonely, baffled and she went into her bedroom and dialled his number.

'David?' she said, when he answered.

'How are you?' He sounded pleased; she knew, sadly, that he always sounded pleased when she rang, and she wished sometimes that he would sound angry, or disturbed from something, or distracted, anything to stop her feeling guilty about what she had done to him.

'I just thought I'd say hi.'

'What have you been up to?'

'I went to Cambridge today – to clear out Fabian's room.'

'Thanks for doing that; must have been a bit of an ordeal.'

'It was O.K.; except I have a bit of a problem.'

'What's that?'

'I can't get his trunk out of my car.'

She heard him laugh.

'Want me to come up and help you?'

'Don't be silly.'

'I don't mind – I'll come now – or –' his voice became quieter, testing. 'Do you have a date?'

'No, I haven't got a date.'

'Well I'll come now; take you to dinner.'

'I don't want to drag you all the way up.'

'I'll be there in an hour – hour and a half. Better than talking to the sheep.'

Alex hung up feeling angry with herself, angry at her weakness; giving David hope, allowing the wound to continue festering. She was startled by the vapour of her breath, and stared at it, thinking for a moment it must be cigarette smoke that she had exhaled. But she wasn't smoking. She watched the cloud, thick and heavy, so heavy she could almost see ice crystals form as it drifted up in front of her; she was cold again, suddenly, almost unbearably cold. She felt as if something had come into the room, something unpleasant, malevolent; something very angry.

She got up, went out into the corridor and into the kitchen, but it stayed with her. Her hands were shaking with the cold, shaking so hard she dropped the tea bag on the floor; she heard the clunk upstairs again, a different clunk this time, not like the boiler. She walked out of the kitchen in long positive strides, down the corridor and out of the front door, into the orange glow of the streetlighting.

The rain had stopped and the wind was still strong, but felt warm and enveloped her like an eiderdown. She walked down the street, slowly, hugging it around her shoulders.

She heard the toot of a horn and the rattle of an engine and was engulfed by the stench of pigs, a strange, unfamiliar smell in the middle of Chelsea. She looked around and saw David's mud-caked Land Rover. He was leaning over, sliding open the window. 'Alex!'

She waved, surprised. 'You were quick! I didn't think you'd be here till well after eight.'

'It's half past eight.'

'Half past eight?' She frowned, and looked at her watch. No, it wasn't possible. Surely it had only been a few minutes? She shivered. What was happening?

'What are you doing out without a coat?'

'Just came out to get some air.'

'Jump in.'

'There's a space just there – you'd better take it, you won't get any closer.'

He nodded. 'Saturday night, I was forgetting.'

She watched him reverse into the space, then jump out. 'Aren't you going to lock it?'

'I'm out of the habit of locking cars.' He gave her a kiss, and they walked down the road to the house.

How long had she spent walking around outside? An hour and a half could not have gone by. Surely not?

'You look frozen,' he said.

'I – er – was a bit hot in the house – had the heating up too much. Let's get the trunk – I'm parked just there.'

She staggered backwards into the house, sagging under the weight, and heard a crunch as the trunk swung into the wall. 'Careful,' she said, testily.

'Sorry.'

They laid the trunk down and David closed the front door; she saw a flat piece of dried mud on the carpet. 'For Chrissake, David, you're bringing bloody mud in!' she shouted, livid suddenly.

He blushed apologetically, as if in the house of a complete stranger, bent down and untied his brogues. 'Sorry,' he muttered, sheepishly. 'Bit muddy down there at the moment.'

She instantly regretted her outburst, and guiltily watched him stooping over, removing his shoes. She stared at his faded roll-neck sweater, battered tweed jacket with its haphazard patches and his shapeless brown corduroy trousers. His beard was tinged with white strands and his face had a ruddy weatherbeaten complexion. It was hard to imagine, she thought, watching him standing there in his grey woollen socks, with his big toes poking through, that he had once been so fastidious about his appearance; that he had once worn nothing but sharp designer suits, silk shirts, Gucci loafers; that he used to gad about in a Ferrari, that he had loved to strut into Tramp in the early hours of the morning, greeting Johnny Gold and every waiter by name.

'You're right,' he said, 'it is hot in here. Incredibly hot. How are you?' He leaned forward to kiss her, staggered and nearly fell. 'Ooops.'

66

She felt the bristles of his moustache, smelled the alcohol, felt his tongue poke through and push in between her lips. She recoiled. 'David,' she said, reproachfully.

'Just giving my wife a kiss.'

'Do you have to get drunk before you can come and see me?'

He shifted his weight, uncomfortably.

'If you got breathalysed, you'd be really stuck. Want some coffee?'

'I'd prefer some whisky.'

'I think you've had enough.'

God, why had she asked him up, she thought, riddled with guilt; she just wanted him to go away; she did not need him, did not need anyone. It had all been a mistake, tricks of her imagination; or was it? Somehow, she had to be sure. At least it was comforting, having another human here; at least she felt safe.

She made him a coffee and took it through to the drawing room. Angrily, she snatched the glass of whisky out of his hand. 'Drink this; I want you sober; I need to talk to you.'

'I can stay the night here,' he said.

'No you can't.'

'It is my house.'

'David; we have an agreement.'

He stared at the coffee and wrinkled his nose. God, he really looked like one of those ruddy bucolic picture-book farmers, she thought. How could anyone change so much, so quickly? Just a couple of years; or had he been changing for much longer without her noticing? He was an alien here, hopelessly uncomfortable in the surroundings; she had to concentrate hard to remember that it was he who had decorated this house, his taste, his furniture, his colours. And yet, she felt strangely safe with him here; it was like being in the presence of a great cuddly bear. She sat down on the arm of the chair beside him, trying to sort out the confusion of her thoughts, the violent swings of her emotions, and listened to the noisy slurp as he tested the coffee. She twisted the whisky glass guiltily around in her hands, then put it down gently beside him.

'This may sound strange, David, but I think Fabian's still around.'

He looked up at her, frowning. 'Still around?'

'Yes.'

'You mean you don't think he's dead?'

Alex took out a cigarette and offered him the pack. He shook his head and pulled a tin of tobacco out of his pocket. 'I went to the morgue. I spent six bloody days in France with the body of my son – our son.'

'But you didn't see him?'

'No, thank God, I didn't have to; anyway, they wouldn't let me – they said he was too badly –'

Alex shuddered. 'I know he's dead, David. But I can – I don't know – sort of feel his presence still around.'

'You're always going to remember him – we both will, that's natural.'

'Don't you think that dream you had when you saw him, the morning he was killed – that we both had – don't you think that was strange?'

He prised open the lid of the tin and pulled out a cigarette paper; she looked at his grubby hands, the yellow-stained fingers, his filthy nails.

'Coincidence. Maybe telepathy; my mother had a similar experience during the war, the day my father was killed; she swore she saw him sitting under a hedge at the end of their lane. She went to mediums, had séances in the house and claimed she spoke to him regularly.'

'What did he say?'

'Nothing; used to tell her it was very blue out there. That's the problem, the dead never seem to have anything very interesting to say.' He licked the gum on the paper and closed up his cigarette.

The door suddenly moved, several inches; Alex jumped, her heart racing, and it moved again; she felt a cold chill down her neck and spun round; the curtain was billowing out. 'Did you open the window?'

'Yes,' he said.

She felt the relief seep through her, like warmth from a bath.

'You're very edgy,' he said. 'You should have a holiday — go away somewhere.'

'I can't spare the time at the moment; I've got two very important deals I have to close.'

'Come down to Château Hightower — you can have your own room, come and go as you like. It's peaceful — you can do your deals over the phone.'

'I'll be all right.'

'If you want to come down at any time just turn up, you'll be very welcome.'

'Thanks.' She smiled. 'Maybe.' She hesitated, leaned over, and stroked the side of the whisky glass. 'I want to show you something.'

She led him down into her darkroom and picked the contact sheet off the table, then stared at it in disbelief; it had completely fogged into a haze of white and grey tones. She shook her head, picked up the negatives and dropped them on to the cracked light box. There was nothing there; nothing on them. Nothing at all. It was as if they had never been exposed.

'You didn't fix them properly,' he said.

'Don't be ridiculous. Of course I did.'

'You must have had the solution too long — got too weak — these have all carried on developing. What were they of?'

'That's the whole point; they were pictures a client sent me — a roll of film — he's a bit eccentric — they were pictures of some animal's genitals.'

She saw David's probing stare and blushed.

'He knew of my interest in photography. Anyhow, I developed them, made a contact sheet and they were fine; I put it on the drying rack, and when I came down to check it, I could see Fabian's face on every frame – it had just appeared there.'

David looked at her, and shrugged. 'Double exposure.'

She shook her head. 'No. No way.'

'Did he know Fabian, this client of yours?'

'No; he had no reason to take pictures of Fabian. Anyhow, it wasn't on the neg.'

'You mean you hadn't noticed it on the neg.'

'No. It wasn't on the neg.'

'You sure you didn't imagine it?'

She shook her head.

'Alex, you know you are very tense at the moment –'

'It's nothing to do with that,' she snapped. 'Jesus, what do you want to do? Commit me to a loony bin?'

'Perhaps you should see the doctor.'

'David, I am perfectly O.K.; I'm coping with everything; it's just there is something very strange going on. I feel that Fabian is still around, that's why his face appeared.'

'And Fabian fogged the film?'

She shrugged. 'Maybe.'

'What else?'

'Silly things.' She shook her head. 'Probably nothing. I just wonder – maybe I should go and see a medium. If I did, would you come?'

He shook his head. 'Forget it, darling; you'll make it worse for yourself. If you went to a medium and you got in touch with Fabian – what would you say to him?'

She stared at her husband, and then had to look away, red in the face; I know what I'd say, she thought.

'And what would you expect him to say to you?'

She shrugged. 'I've always been as cynical as you about that sort of thing, David, it's just –' she paused. 'Maybe you're right, maybe I should have a break. Help me get the trunk upstairs.'

'And afterwards I'll buy you dinner; we'll go out somewhere nice, O.K.?'

She looked at him and nodded.

'Christ it's cold in here,' he said, as they carried the trunk into Fabian's room. 'Where do you want it?'

'On the floor.'

'Let's put it on the bed,' he said. 'Be easier for you. You ought to have the heating on in here, otherwise you'll get damp in.'

'It is on. I think the floor would be –' But David had propelled them over to the bed, and they laid the trunk down on to it, with a loud clank from the springs.

Alex watched David look around the room, lost, like a visitor trying to find his bearings in a museum. 'There's his telescope; God, I remember giving him that.'

'He loved it.'

David stared up at the portrait, and Alex noticed the look of discomfort on his face. He looked away. 'Still got that Brooklands poster – worth a few bob now.'

Alex looked at the old racing car, hurtling around the banking. David walked over to it. 'I remember hanging this for him – he can't have been more than seven or eight. I made a real botch up of it – couldn't get it to the right height – had to take the bloody nail out half a dozen times.' He lifted the picture off the wall. 'Look, there they all are!' He pointed to the chipped plaster and the haphazard holes.

'It's funny what one remembers,' said Alex, watching him carefully re-hanging it. For whom?

She walked out into the corridor, suddenly wanting to be away from the room, wanting David away from it as well; his presence there was annoying her, poking about, moving things. Let him rest, she wanted to say, let him rest you fool!

He came out of the room, with his head bowed and the colour gone from his cheeks, and she immediately felt angry with herself now for her feelings, angry at being so blind to his own grief. The child had meant so much to both of them, after the endless visits to the specialists, the ectopic pregnancy that had to be terminated and then finally, the last hope; and her secret.

They walked slowly down the stairs and stopped on the

71

landing. She felt David's arm around her, squeezing her, and she leaned into him. It was cold once more suddenly and she wanted to go down and close the window. Grief crept up around her, the cold empty room, the trunk on the bed that Fabian would never again unpack. She felt the warmth of her husband, felt his strong powerful frame, the squeeze of his large hand. She nestled into the soft brush of his face and kissed his cheek. She felt his face stir and his moist lips on her own cheek and she found herself being manoeuvred, slowly, step by step in through her bedroom door; she felt his kisses becoming passionate, moving down her neck.

'No, David.'

He kissed her chin, then pushed his lips on to hers. She broke her face away. 'No, David.'

'Yes,' he said. 'Yes, we must.'

It was Fabian's voice; she opened her eyes and saw Fabian's face. 'No,' she said, pushing him away. 'No, get out!' He came back towards her. 'Get out!' she screamed. 'Get out!'

Fabian stared at her, frozen for an instant in shock, then became David again, and then Fabian, until she could not tell who it was.

'Get out, get out!'

'Alex, darling, calm down!'

She kicked him hard, straight up between the legs, saw the wince of pain, the shock in his face, then pummelled him in the chest. She felt hands grasping her. 'Calm down,' she heard. 'Alex, calm down!'

'I'm calm!' she yelled back. 'For Chrissake, I'm completely calm. Just get out!'

'I'm sorry, darling, I didn't mean to –'

She stared at him, wide-eyed, filled with an inexplicable sudden hatred for him. 'Go,' she shouted, in a voice she scarcely recognized as hers. 'Go, go, I can't stand you being here.' She saw the shock in his face, saw his hands crossed between his legs. 'Please, David,' she said. 'Please go.'

'What about dinner?' he said, bewildered.

'I want to be on my own. I can't explain it; I just need to be on my own. I'm sorry, it was a mistake asking you to come.' She stared at him, fearful that at any moment he would turn back again into Fabian. 'I'm just not ready at the moment, not ready for anything; I've got to come to terms with this myself.'

She followed him down the stairs. 'Will you be all right – to drive home?'

David looked at her and shrugged. 'I drove up here.'

'I'm sorry,' she said. 'I'm sorry.'

'Do you want me to call you when I get home?'

'Call?' she said, weakly. 'Sure, if you like.'

She closed the door, went into the drawing room and sank down in a chair. Outside, a short way off, she heard the Land Rover's engine rattle into life and the crunch of the gears.

And then the guilt hit her.

'David!' She ran to the front door. 'David. Wait!' She fumbled with the catch, pulled the door open, tripped out, down the steps, on to the pavement. The tail lights were disappearing down the road. She ran after them. 'David! Darling! Stop, please stop! I didn't mean to. Please stop, oh please stop.'

She saw the amber flashing indicator getting closer as she sprinted down the road. Then it pulled away from her and vanished around the corner.

'David!'

She ran on after it down the King's Road. Don't get those lights; please don't get those lights!

But they turned green and he was gone.

She collapsed, sobbing, against a lamp post. 'David, darling. I'm sorry. I'm so terribly sorry.'

Slowly, she turned, and walked back to the house. The front door was still open. She closed it behind her, then went through into the drawing room, completely drained, weeping. She lay down on the sofa and lapsed into a doze.

She wasn't sure what woke her, whether it was the chill air

in the room again, or the smell of cooking, the tantalizing smell of a fry-up.

In spite of the cold she felt better, more peaceful. Had David really come, she wondered, or had it all been part of a terrible dream? She sniffed the rich heady smell of the frying and thought of Fabian's passion for fried eggs; sunny side up, always; there were times, as a child, when he had his moods, he would refuse to eat anything except fried eggs for days.

It was an unusual smell for a Saturday night in Chelsea, in the heart of foodie land; she looked at her watch. Ten o'clock; the smell was growing stronger and she realized she was feeling hungry; she'd eaten nothing since the apple and a piece of toast for breakfast. She wondered which of her neighbours it was, and walked to the window. To her surprise, it was shut. She stood still, trying to work out how the smell could be so strong, and then she heard a hissing and crackling, close, so close it sounded like her own kitchen.

She walked out into the hallway and saw the kitchen light on.

The hissing and the crackling were coming from there.

She sprinted the twenty feet and stood, staring at the empty hob. The smell of fried eggs was overpowering. She opened the window and leaned out, but there was nothing: the familiar night odours of the neighbourhood, of dustbins, wet grass, diesel fumes and a faint hint of curry. She closed the window.

The smell was in here.

She saw the vapour of her breath again, smelt the smell even more intensely, felt terror surging through her. She walked out of the kitchen, closed the door, went through into the drawing room and picked up the telephone directory.

Mankletow. Manly. Main. Her finger was shaking uncontrollably. There were seventeen P Mains listed. She knew the road he lived in, Chalcot Road, but there was none

74

there. She dialled Directory Enquiries, conscious of her strained, high-pitched voice. The operator was kindly, as helpful as she could be. 'Sorry, dear,' she said, 'he's ex-directory.'

'Could you phone him and ask him to call me?'

'Can't do that, I'm sorry. He's down as "no connection". I don't even have his number myself.'

Alex walked back into the hallway, stared fearfully at the kitchen door, felt the ice-cold air. She pulled her coat down from the rack, grabbed her keys off the table, went outside and locked the front door behind her.

CHAPTER TEN

A drunken gaggle of businessmen wandered past Alex; in town for a conference, she judged, by the name tags some of them had forgotten to remove from their lapels.

'Here's a bit of crumpet, Jimmy,' said a Scottish accent.

She let herself into the office, and as she locked the door behind her, there was a roar of laughter in the street, probably at her expense, she thought.

It was quiet inside, unnaturally quiet; the room was dark, the random streaks of harsh white light from the massage parlour across the road flickered on the walls and furniture, giving a strange chiaroscuro effect.

She stared at the intense blackness of the staircase, pressed the light switch, and instantly it was banished and she was in her own familiar surroundings, with the soft greys of the walls and carpets, the crimson lamps and banister rail and the framed dust jackets lining the walls.

She walked past the receptionist's dark silent switchboard and began to climb the stairs. She saw the shadow on the floor above, and for a moment was reluctant to climb further; it seemed the shadow was moving. She hesitated, but knew she had to get to the landing, to the next switch. She watched the shadow; when she moved, it moved; when she stopped, it stopped.

Stupid, she thought, suddenly realizing it was her own shadow.

She walked up into the dark, found the switch, pressed it with a quick nervous stab of her finger and jumped as the light came on, then walked up the next flight and on to the landing. Julie's office door was open and the room was pitch dark. She stared at it nervously, reached in and switched on the light, and again felt relieved by the normality. She stared, irritated for a moment, at the black Olivetti sitting there without its cover. Julie was always leaving it off. Why did she do that? The grey plastic cover was screwed up behind the filing tray. She straightened it out, put it on carefully, then the manuscript on the desk caught her eye. 'Lives Foreseen – My Power and Others'', with a bookmark halfway through it. She had told Julie to send it back, she thought, annoyed, picking it up and carrying it through into her office. She'd speak to her about it on Monday.

Down in the street below, the drunks were bunched up around the doorway of the massage parlour, peering at the blanked-off windows. She let go of the blinds, walked away from the window, shivering from the cold, switched on the heater, then pulled out her address file. She dialled his number and waited, knowing that he always took a long time to answer. Relieved, she heard the click of the receiver being picked up, and was about to speak, when she realized that the phone was still ringing.

Someone in her own building had picked up an extension.

She stood, frozen for a moment, paralysed with fear.

Who, she thought, who? The cleaner? No, impossible. One of her partners? No. She listened for a sound, for breathing, a cough; the phone rang on. She could feel the presence, feel the person waiting, listening. Who? Who? Who? She was shaking now, heard her own heart thumping, louder than the ringing. She felt a pain below her ear; she was banging her cheekbone with the receiver. It rang on, unanswered. Fearfully, she turned around, looked through her open doorway at the passage. The ringing echoed around her office. Something moved, at the end of the passage, or had she imagined it? Lock the door, she said to herself. Lock the door! The key was on the outside.

Carefully, gently, she laid the receiver down on her blotter, and tiptoed over to the door. The ringing continued. She tried to pull the key out silently, but she was shaking

77

too much, it scraped, clanked, then fell to the floor, bounced and clattered against the skirting board, with a noise like two trains colliding. 'No,' she said aloud, 'no, no.' She dived on to her knees and scrabbled her hands across the carpet after it. She closed her fingers around it, turned and stared fearfully again down the passage at the stairwell, heard the ringing continue, then flung herself back into her office, slammed the door and leaned against it. She tried to get the key in, fumbled, dropped it again. 'No,' she said. She picked it up, pushed it in, and tried to turn it. It would not move.

She turned it so hard she could feel it bending. 'Please lock, please lock.' She pushed it in further, and suddenly it turned easily, without pressure, and the lock clicked home almost silently.

Alex rested her head against the door, relief swimming through her, her heart beating so hard it was like a fist punching her chest. She was sweating, gulping for air.

'Hallo? Hallo?' The voice sounded tinny, as if a radio had been left on. 'Hallo? Hallo?'

She fell on to the receiver, as if it was the first piece of food she had seen for a week. 'Hallo?'

She heard the familiar hiss of air and tobacco smoke.

'Alex?' said Philip Main's voice, whispering, almost incredulous.

Suddenly, she was conscious again of the presence and did not want to speak, did not want to give herself away. 'Yes,' she found herself whispering back, softly, almost hissing.

'Hallo?'

'Help me,' she hissed, louder, suddenly beginning to feel vulnerable again; the door was strong, but it would not hold someone determined.

'Is that you, Alex?'

'Yes.' The sound came out, a strange, high-pitched squawk from deep inside her that she scarcely recognized.

'Are you all right?' He sounded gentle, concerned.

She didn't want to say it, did not want the other person listening to know she was afraid. Normal. Sound normal.

78

For God's sake sound normal. 'I want to see a medium. I wondered if you knew anyone?' She was conscious that her voice had changed again, into a flat monotone automaton; it sounded like the voice of a complete stranger.

'Are you sure about this?'

Christ, don't start querying things; for God's sake don't. Not now.

'Alex?'

'Yes I am sure,' said the automaton.

'You sound a little strange.'

'I'm fine,' said the automaton.

'I don't know about mediums. You ought to think about it very carefully.'

'Please, Philip. I have to.'

'I don't know. I think we should talk about it.'

'Please, Philip, do you know any?'

She listened, agitated, to the silence.

'Not personally, no; good Lord, no.' He paused. 'You told me that a friend of yours had suggested this – doesn't she know any?'

'She sent one round. She was horrible.'

Silence again.

'You must know someone, Philip.'

'You could try the Yellow Pages.'

'Please, Philip, be serious.'

There was another silence; Alex listened hard, trying to hear something, anything. She looked around at the door, stared at the handle. It was moving, turning.

She screamed; a dreadful, piercing scream, then stopped, as abruptly as she had started; it wasn't moving at all; it was the blinds that were moving in the air of the heater, sending shadows across the handle.

'Alex? What's the matter?'

'There's someone here, in the office, listening to this phone call. Please call the police; I think I'm about to be attacked.'

She put down the phone, saw the light on the panel go

out. Light. She breathed gulps of air; light; there was only one light, wasn't there? If there had been someone else listening, then another light would have come on on the panel; wouldn't it? She stared around at the door, then at the window, at the restless blinds, then something caught her eye on her desk: the calendar; she stared at it and was filled instantly with a sensation that felt like ice cold water flushing through her, filling every blood vessel in her body.

The date on the calendar read **Thu May 4th.**

'Oh, God,' she said. 'Don't let me be mad; please don't let me be mad.' She stared again at the letters, the digits, checked the date on her Rolex. April 22nd. She looked around the room, expecting to see something, a phantom, a spectre – a – she hesitated, thinking about the smell of eggs, the rose in the windscreen. Fearfully she looked to her right, at the VDU screen that was under its cover; she wanted to lift the cover, stare at the blank screen. Then, suddenly, she felt angry. She wanted to get up, throw open the door and shout out: 'Here I am. Take me. Do what you want.' Instead she found herself pulling out the Yellow Pages.

She heaved a wadge of pages over. Mediums. Mediums. Nothing under Mediums. What else? Psychics? She turned more pages. Again nothing. Then she tried Clairvoyants. Something, there was something. 'See Palmists and Clairvoyants.'

The list was short. There was an Indian-sounding name, repeated twice, and only one other. She hesitated; the names didn't feel right. She stared at Stanley Hill's manuscript, '*Lives Foreseen – My Power and Others*''. Reluctantly she opened it and flipped through the pages. The manuscript seemed comfortable suddenly. She was on familiar territory.

Then she realized the words were blurred; she couldn't read them. She saw her hands shaking wildly, and put the manuscript down on the desk.

A name caught her eye. Morgan Ford. She saw it again, a couple of pages later, and then again, her eyes drawn to it as if by a magnet. 'Modest trance medium Morgan Ford would strenuously deny that he frequently arranges sittings for royalty in his Cornwall Gardens flat.'

'Modest.' She liked that word. She pulled out the directory from the shelf behind her, and leafed through the pages.

She picked up the receiver and listened to the harsh crackle, then the rasping hum; she waited for the click of the extension again, watching the panel for the tell-tale light, but nothing happened; the line was private now. She punched the number and waited.

The tone of the man's voice surprised her. For some reason she had expected it to be kindly, warm, welcoming; instead it was cold, irritated, the Welsh accent further alienating him. She had expected him to say, 'Yes, Alex, I've been expecting you. I knew you would call, the spirits told me.' Instead he said, 'Morgan Ford, who is speaking?'

Name. Don't give him your name. Think of a false name. 'I hope you don't mind my calling you at this hour,' she said nervously, unsure how to react, and listening, all the time listening, for the sound of the receiver being picked up below her. 'It's just – so terribly urgent.'

'Who are you, please?'

'I need help. I need to see a medium. I'm sorry, are you a medium?'

'Yes,' he said, as if she was mad.

'Is it possible to come and see you?'

'You'd like a sitting?'

'Yes.'

'I have a cancellation on Monday, 10 am, if that's any good?'

'I don't suppose there's any chance tomorrow?'

'Tomorrow?' he sounded indignant. 'Absolutely not, I'm afraid. Monday – or – otherwise it won't be until May, I'm afraid. Let me see. May 4th, I could do.'

May 4th. She stared at the calendar again. What was it? What the hell was it?

'No, Monday, please.' She was conscious of the sound of

a car approaching fast and pulling up outside. She heard a door slam, the bark of a dog.

'May I have your name, please?'

'It's –' she hesitated. What name? What name? 'Shoona Johnson,' she said, wildly. She thought she could detect cynicism in his voice as he repeated it, as though he could tell somehow that she was lying, and she felt embarrassed.

'And may I have a phone number?'

'I'm er – staying –' Don't give a number where he could check up and find your name, give him no clues. She stared around for inspiration, read the wording 'South East Business Systems' on the base of her VDU, and gave him the number printed beneath it. 'See you Monday,' she said.

'Goodbye.'

She did not like the way he had sounded, as if she had been a nuisance to him, as if he had not cared whether she'd rung him or not. It was now a quarter past ten on a Saturday night, she reminded herself; she wouldn't have been too impressed if someone had rung her at this hour, asking if she'd look at a manuscript. She heard a harsh rattle. Oh, Christ, someone was trying to get in the door.

She spun around, but there was nothing. She heard the sound again, distant, below her, and the bark of a dog again. She ran to the window and looked down. She saw a car with its wheels on the kerb, then Philip Main looking up, anxious.

Already? How could he be here already? She fumbled with the window lock, pushed it open, and stared down. No, he couldn't be here yet, too soon. Much too soon.

'Alex, are you O.K.?'

Chunks of time were disappearing. What was happening? What the hell was happening?

'Alex? Shall I break the door down?'

'No,' she said, weakly. 'I'll give you the keys.' She threw them down, saw him jump out of the way, heard the faint clank as they hit the pavement.

Sighing with relief, she walked across her office. There was a growl outside her door. She opened it and saw a small

82

black bull-terrier standing belligerently, baring its teeth, with a stream of slobber dribbling from its black gums. It gave a low rumbling growl.

Footsteps raced up the stairs and Main appeared on the landing, puffing, dishevelled. 'Black!' he shouted. 'Leave!'

The dog glared at Alex, hungry for action.

'Black!'

Reluctantly, it backed off.

Main put his hands out and rested them on her shoulders. 'Are you all right?'

'Yes, I'm O.K.'

'I decided to come myself. What's the matter? What's happened?'

Alex stared at him, then burst into tears. 'I don't know, Philip. I don't know what's happening.'

'Oh, Lord,' he fumbled in his pockets and pulled out a handkerchief. 'You are in a bad state.'

'It was the phone; I heard someone on the phone.'

'In here?'

She nodded and took the handkerchief.

'Sorry, it's a bit grubby.'

She squeezed it tightly, then dabbed her eyes with it. He led her over to the sofa and they sat down. He fumbled in his pocket and pulled out his cigarette. She watched the dog look around, uninterestedly, then trot out of the room.

'Someone lifted up the receiver when I was calling you.'

'There's no one here now, I looked as I came up; the windows are all locked, as far as I could see. Are you sure?'

She nodded.

'It wasn't a crossed line, outside somewhere?'

She stared at him. 'It felt so close.'

'What did?'

'The person, whoever it was.'

Main offered her a cigarette. 'What are you doing here, at this hour, on a Saturday night?'

'I – I needed your number – I didn't have it at home. I'm sorry – did I disturb you?'

'No more than the chap from Porlock disturbed Coleridge; you may have deprived mankind of the greatest poem of all time – I was about to write it –' He smiled.

'I'm sorry; I don't know what is happening.'

'I'll drive you home.'

'No,' she shook her head. 'I don't want to go home.'

'You're not staying here, I won't let you. I think you need some rest.' He held out his lighter. 'You can come and stay at my place,' he caught her eye and stared straight back. 'In the spare room. O.K.?'

She smiled, and nodded, then winced at the strength of the cigarette. She stood up, and took Stanley Hill's manuscript back into her secretary's office, replacing it where she had found it. 'I didn't know scientists wrote poetry,' she said, walking back into her office. 'Are you ever going to let me see any?'

'We'll see.' He smiled, mysteriously.

She felt better after the first whisky, curled up on the floor on the thick rugs in front of the log fire. The walls of the room were lined with books, shelves of battered, loved books that went up to the high stuccoed ceiling. There was wood and leather everywhere; fine wood panelling, solid wooden furniture, antique but simple, well restored, and leather chairs, big, thick leather chairs and a massive leather sofa.

'I don't understand. Why are you so against it?'

'Mumbo jumbo, it's a load of nonsense; we die and we're gone.' He clapped his hands together, suddenly, violently; it made her jump, and the dog rushed over to him, barking excitedly.

'How can you say that?'

'I know it; it's proven. Down, boy, down! Good Lord, you're an intelligent woman, you can't still believe in God! Darwin's proven; the game's up for the Holy Joes.' He exhaled a lungful of smoke and the sharp gaunt features of his face became hazy and soft for a moment as the smoke wafted up around him; he looked demoniac, she thought, satanic, and for an instant she felt a tiny shudder of doubt about him.

'If we were part-spirit, part-man, we'd have free will, girl. We don't, we're all prisoners of our genes; it's all laid out, the DNA, the computer program in your genes, from your mother and your father; the colour of your eyes, the size of your fanny.'

She grinned, relaxing again.

'Even the way you're going to think.'

'We have free will, Philip.'

'Rubbish. You and I have no more free will than a dog, than Black.'

'I thought dogs had free will?'

Main pointed a finger at his dog. 'Black kills cats; if he sees a cat when he's not on the lead, he'll kill it; it's in his genes, he can't help it, and he can't be stopped.'

'What do you mean?'

'You saw how obedient he was in your office. I told him to stop and he did. He'll obey me on everything, except a cat; if he sees a cat, that's it; he'll tear its throat out.'

'That's bad training.'

'No, there's nothing I could do about it; there's nothing any trainer in the world could do about it; it's in his genes and it can never be removed.'

'You said that spirits could have genes too.'

'We've evolved God in our minds; it's our survival mechanism, dates back thousands of years, when man first tried to explain why he was here. You've met spiritualists, mediums; they're all loopy or else they're very smooth. The loopy ones think they're genuine, the smooth ones are hoods; they're good at telepathy, they pluck Uncle Harry out of your memory banks, tell you things you already knew, throw in a few others for good measure, you go "Gosh, Wow, Triff!" Then you think a bit, and you say "How is Uncle Harry?" And he says, "Fine," and you go away, and you start thinking about it, and the doubt sets in.

85

Look, you think, I buried Uncle Harry last week. He's in his grave, or his ashes are in this urn, and now we're talking to each other again and you want to talk more and more and you'll find you can't, because Uncle Harry can't think of anything else to say.'

He drew deeply on his cigarette, and smiled. 'He was a boring old fart when he was alive and you suddenly expect him to become interesting because he's dead.' He stopped, seeing the tears in her eyes. 'I'm sorry, girl, but you'll only do yourself harm up there.' He tapped his head. 'Your son was a nice lad; but you've just got to accept that he's dead.'

She stared at him for a long time. 'I can accept it, Philip. But I'm not sure he can.'

CHAPTER ELEVEN

The bright London Sunday morning unfurled through the grimy windscreen of Philip Main's Volvo; it was like trying to watch television through a frosted glass window, Alex thought. London looked different on Sundays, the sense of urgency had gone from it. There was time on Sundays, time to walk, time to think; London was a good place on Sundays.

She felt rested, having slept well for the first time, she realized, since the news about Fabian.

She looked down at the car's ashtray, jammed open and thick with butts, at the piles of papers, magazines, documents, cassettes lying in the floorwell around her feet. 'Thank you,' she said, 'for last night. It did me a lot of good.'

'We managed,' he said gently.

'Managed what?'

'Managed.'

'You talk in riddles sometimes.'

'Managed to restrain ourselves.'

She smiled and looked at him, cigarette protruding from his moustache, head hunched slightly forward, as if he was too tall for the car. 'You have quite an ego, don't you?'

'No – just sometimes –' he trailed off.

'Sometimes what?'

'Sometimes –' the words trailed away and evaporated. He leaned forward, pushed a cassette into the player, and a second later Elkie Brooks sang, loud and clear, all around her. He grunted, leaned forward again and turned the volume down. 'So, the vicar told you to try to find out more about Fabian?'

'The curate. Yes.'

'And what have you found out so far?'

'That he didn't ditch his girlfriend, Carrie – she ditched him.'

'What does that tell you? That he was proud?'

Alex laughed. 'I feel so stupid, you know, about last night.'

'The mind plays tricks when you get tired.'

'Have you ever heard of a medium called Morgan Ford?'

He shook his head and inhaled deeply on his cigarette.

'How can you tell a genuine one from a fake?'

'There are no genuine ones.'

Alex stared at him. 'You scientists can be so damned smug, you're infuriating.'

He pressed the horn irritably at a small rented car, all four of its occupants gawping at Liberty's façade. 'No, we just state truths people don't like to hear.'

'That's equally smug.'

She was mildly surprised to see her Mercedes standing where she had left it, not towed away, ticketed or vandalized. She leaned over and gave him a kiss on the cheek.

'You're going to be all right now?'

'Yes.'

'I think I'll take you out to dinner tonight, just to make sure.'

She shook her head. 'I don't really like going back to an empty house in the evening. Come round to me and I'll make some supper.'

'About eight?'

Alex drove off feeling cheerful, relaxed; but the pain would come back, she knew. It was all piled up in her head, waiting to avalanche; it would be worst in the late afternoon when the sunlight began to fade; the depression would come, the way it always had, late afternoon on Sundays, all her life, since she was a small child.

She drove south over Vauxhall Bridge and down towards

Streatham, not relishing the task she faced of trying to find Carrie and breaking the news to her. She didn't even have an address. All she could remember was that they had been passing an antique shop with a row of chairs out on the pavement, when Fabian had said, 'That's where Carrie lives, Mother,' and she had looked over to the right and seen the tower blocks. It was at the start of a hill, very similar to the hill she was on now; she saw an antique shop, closed, boarded up and two grey towers in the distance to the right. She turned and headed towards them, down a narrow street lined with beat-up cars and grimy vans: a tight hemmed-in street. Two black kids were playing a game on the pavement; they stopped and looked at her and she felt herself blushing, felt somehow that she had no right to be here, that she was out of her allotted territory.

The road wound round and up through a seemingly endless row of two-storey council dwellings, stark metal staircases leading to the upper floors. Towels, sheets and underwear hung from the balconies and windows; it felt like a ghetto.

The two tower blocks now loomed straight up in front of her, crumbling, pre-cast concrete; they stretched into the sky like a pair of giant dismal tombstones.

Alex got out of the Mercedes, locked it carefully and walked into the lobby of the nearest building. Most of the glass from one door panel was lying on the floor and the other door was wedged permanently open. The word FUCK had been aerosolled across a wall in large crimson letters, and there was an unpleasant smell she could not identify.

She looked down the name panel. It was there: E. Needham. She felt a confusion of emotions suddenly. It would have been easier if there had been no name; the decision would have been made, and she could let it rest.

She pushed the button and the huge lift door slid open; it was more like a goods lift than a passenger lift. SUCK YOUR BALLS. The crimson aerosol artist had been at work in here too. She pushed the button for the third floor and the door shut, slowly, jerkily. She wondered if she would have been more sensible to have walked. There was an almost imperceptible jolt and the doors in front of her began to slide downwards, slowly, almost agonizingly slowly. The lift smelt foul, like a public lavatory, and suddenly she noticed, to her horror, a puddle of urine on the floor beside her. She moved away. There was a clunk and a judder and the lift passed a marker for the first floor.

Finally, it jerked to a halt and she stepped out into a grimy stone-floored corridor. There was a faded ban-the-bomb roundel sprayed on the wall, and further along someone had carved PIGS into the wall with a chisel. She stopped outside number 33, a blue door with a spyhole, and looked for the bell. She pushed it, heard a rasp like an angry insect, and waited. A moment later a woman's voice called out, 'Yeah?'

Alex stared at the door. 'Mrs Needham?' She waited, but nothing happened. Somewhere down the corridor she could hear a baby crying, and above her the faint blare of pop music. She rang the bell again.

There was another long pause. 'Yeah, who is it?'

Alex stared at the door. 'Mrs Needham?'

'Who is it?' The voice was closer now and she heard the shuffle of footsteps, saw the glint of movement in the spyhole. 'What yer want?' said the voice, hostile.

'I want to speak to Mrs Needham, please.'

'You from the Council?'

'No. My name's Alex Hightower. My son used to go out with your daughter.'

There was a long silence. Alex heard a hacking cough, then silence again. 'Hallo?' she said, nervously.

'So what yer want? I've paid me TV licence.'

Alex frowned, baffled. 'I just want to have a word with you about your daughter, Carrie. Do you have a daughter, Carrie?'

A pause. 'Yeah.' Another pause. 'What she done?'

'Nothing, Mrs Needham. I have some news to give her. Please open the door.'

There was another hacking cough and she heard the sound of bolts sliding; the door opened a few inches. She saw a much younger woman than she had expected, someone her own age, but a pinched, hardened face, aged by neglect, sourness and a sallow complexion that was desperately in need of some fresh air. She must once have been very pretty, and she could be attractive now if she made the effort. She stood there, her hair a nest of curlers, cigarette hanging from her lips, in a dirty blue dressing gown, looking her up and down. 'You're not from the Council?'

'No.'

'Yeah, well, they got some funny ideas.' Alex saw the eyes stare at her shiftily, then dart nervously around. The woman jerked her head and stepped back; Alex took this to be an invitation and stepped into a short hallway which stank of sour milk and cigarette smoke. Through the door to the right she could see the kitchen, the table stacked with a pile of empty beer bottles. The woman led her into an L-shaped bedsitting room. 'Carrie, you said?'

Alex nodded and stared around at the unmade bed, the bare walls, the clothes, trash, magazines and unwashed dishes strewn around at random, at the filthy windows and the magnificent views out over London beyond.

'My son, Fabian, used to go out with your daughter – until quite recently; I think they split up just after Christmas.'

The woman stared blankly, drew heavily on her cigarette, even though it was down to the filter, screwed up her nose, took another drag and stubbed it out. 'Ain't seen her; she don't come here much.' She turned her face away from Alex and coughed again, a long, hacking cough. She turned back. 'Sit down, throw those papers on the floor. I'm afraid it's not much here; they don't give you much now, the Council, if you're on your own.'

Alex removed a pile of newspapers and a half-completed pools coupon from the sofa, and sat down.

'Gone her own way, if you know what I mean.'

Alex sensed the woman eyeing her up and down. 'All children are difficult, one way or another.'

'I don't know about no Fibbin – wozzisname, Fibbin?'

'Fabian.'

'Don't know about 'im. She din't say nothing about him.'

'He was killed in a car crash two and a half weeks ago. I know he was very fond of Carrie; I thought she ought to know.'

'Oh yes?' the woman said, matter-of-fact, and Alex wondered if perhaps the woman had misheard her.

'I thought Carrie might have come to the funeral, you see.' Alex bit her lip; she wanted to get out of here, away from the stench, this wretched woman, the filthy flat.

'I'll tell her when I see her, dear – dunno when that'll be. I'm sorry, haven't offered you nothing – don't get many visitors, see, except from the Council.'

'I'm fine, thanks.'

'Cup of tea or something.'

'No thank you, really.'

'She's in America.' She nodded at the mantelpiece and Alex saw a postcard with a picture of a skyscraper.

'How long has she been there?'

The woman shrugged. 'Dunno how long she been anywhere; just get postcards, nothing else; get 'em regular, I suppose,' she shrugged. 'Know some mums don't even get that.'

Alex smiled. 'I thought Carrie was very nice; pretty girl.'

The woman shrugged. 'I wouldn't know, wouldn't know what she looks like these days; had some photographs of her once, dunno what I done with 'em.'

There was a rasp from the doorbell and an urgent pounding on the front door.

'Who is it?' she shouted sharply.

It rang again twice and there was more urgent knocking.

'All right, all right!' She stood up, coughing, and shuffled out.

Alex went over to the mantelpiece and looked at the postcard. In small white print at the bottom were the words: 'John Hancock Tower'. There were several more cards stacked up beside it. Massachusetts Institute of Technology, Cambridge, Mass. Newport, Rhode Island. Vermont, New Hampshire. She heard the click of the door opening, heard laughter and footsteps, looked around nervously and slipped the card from the Massachusetts Institute of Technology into her handbag.

'Bugger off! You fuckers!' she heard Mrs Needham yell; there was a crash as the door slammed shut, and Mrs Needham shuffled back into her room, holding a beer bottle, her face flushed with rage. 'Buggers, the kids round here. Buggers.' She prised the top off the bottle, took a swig, and offered it to Alex.

She shook her head. 'No, thank you.'

The woman wiped her mouth with the back of her hand. 'Get 'em all the time. The Council say they can't do nothing.' She took another swig from her bottle. 'How did you say your son was?'

Alex looked at her, horrified, as she realized that the woman was drunk and had been all along.

'He's dead, Mrs Needham,' she said, as calmly as she could, feeling pity and anger fighting their way up her throat. 'Dead.'

'Yeah, well, gets us all,' said Mrs Needham.

CHAPTER TWELVE

Alex drove down the King's Road, glad to be out of Mrs Needham's flat and away from the claustrophobic desolation of the estate.

She felt anger rising in her, anger at the woman for living like that, for not caring that Fabian was dead; anger at her being so pathetic, anger that anywhere as ghastly as that place could even exist. Then she thought of the view, that stunning view from the window, and it seemed absurd that the only thing of beauty about the whole place should be the view of somewhere else.

The house was peaceful; she picked the Sunday papers off the doormat and took them through to the kitchen. She heard the whirr of the kitchen clock, the soft breathing of the boiler. Everything felt normal, smelt normal, sounded normal. The house hummed, sighed, creaked, like the old friend it had always been. She felt comfortable, safe. Home.

The phone rang; it was David. 'Alex, are you O.K.?'

His voice sounded clumsy, intruded on her peace, and she felt instantly annoyed with him; then she remembered how she had treated him and felt sorry. 'Hallo, David,' she said, making an effort to sound pleased to hear him. 'I'm fine – look – I'm sorry about last night – I don't know what happened –'

'It must have been the strain, darling. We've both been under terrible strain; the shock of the whole thing.'

Swear at me, for Christ's sake, be firm with me, don't be so bloody nice to me all the time; call me a bitch, shout at me; make me afraid of you, she thought, but could not say it. 'Yes, you're right,' she said, flatly. 'I ran after you last night, shouting at you, waving – everyone must have thought I was bonkers.'

He laughed. 'Why?'

'I wanted to apologize.'

'I rang you when I got back; there was no answer; I was worried sick.'

'I went to the office.'

'The office?'

'I thought I'd try and do some work; I ended up sleeping there.'

'I think it's good to work hard at the moment, take your mind off – you know – but don't overdo it – you must try and rest.'

She watched her reflection in the toaster, saw her eyes and looked away, unable to face them. It was a lousy feeling, lying when you knew you were being believed, she thought; it was like cheating against yourself. 'I went to see Carrie's mother today.

'Carrie? Did she know?'

'No. Nothing. She hardly ever sees Carrie, apparently. She's in the States somewhere at the moment.'

'She was a sweet little thing.' His voice tailed off. 'How about some dinner one night this week?'

'That would be nice.'

'How's your diary?'

'I've left it in the office. Let's talk tomorrow.'

She sighed as she hung up, thinking for a moment of the times they had been together, when they had been happy; or had it all been a pretence then? All just a larger lie? She made a sandwich, then went through into the drawing room, lit the fire, put on a cassette of *Don Giovanni* and curled up on the sofa.

It was late afternoon when she woke up with a start out of a heavy dream. She felt confused and hot; she had been driving somewhere with Fabian; he had made a joke about something and they had been laughing; he seemed so real in the dream, so incredibly real, it took her several seconds to remember . . . that they would never drive anywhere, never laugh together again. She felt sad and cheated, cheated by the dream and cheated by life, and stood up with a heavy heart, walked to the window and drew the curtains against the darkening light.

She wished her mother was still alive, that there was someone older and wiser in whom she could confide; someone who had been through it all before. There were things about being an adult she had never got used to; sometimes it seemed she had become a parent without ever having ceased to be a child.

She opened her handbag and took out the postcard she had taken from Carrie's mother: it was a wide riverside panorama, showing an avenue of grand university buildings. She turned it over. 'Massachusetts Institute of Technology, Boston, Mass.' was printed on the bottom. Boston, she thought; Boston, Boston, Boston. She looked at the handwriting, large neat upright letters:

'Hi Mum, This is a really friendly place, lots of things happening, met some great people. Will write again soon. Love C.'

There was one half-hearted 'X' after the initial. She carried the card upstairs and went into Fabian's room.

His trunk sat on the bed, like a coffin, she thought, shuddering. F.M.R. Hightower was stencilled in faded white letters amid the scratches and dents on the lid. She opened the first catch, which sprang back sharply and caught her finger a painful blow, and opened the second more cautiously. She raised the lid, rummaged through the clothing, and pulled out Fabian's diary. She opened it up and pulled out the blank postcards she had found in his desk at Cambridge, and compared them with the one she had in her hand from Carrie; although the pictures were different, the printed layout on all of them was exactly the same. She frowned, puzzled, looked around the room, caught Fabian's eye staring down from the portrait and looked away, guiltily, embarrassed about what she was doing.

There was a zipped pocket at the back of the diary, which she opened; inside was some pink notepaper, with handwriting that looked like Carrie's, and it was dated January 5th. The address, in Cambridge, was also handwritten:

'Dear Fabian,
Please stop these persistent phone calls which are annoying and distressing for everyone. I have told you I do not want to see you again, and there is nothing that is going to change my mind. There is no one else, as you seem to insist, I just cannot cope with your weird habits any more. So please leave me alone. With love. C.'

The same curly 'C' and the same style of handwriting as on the postcard, but something struck Alex as being different about it, and she could not work out what. She read the letter again. Weird habits. Weird habits, she thought, puzzled, conscious that she was beginning to feel cold again in the room, cold and uncomfortable. The doorbell rang. She looked at her watch: it was six-fifteen. She slipped everything back inside the diary, laid it on top of the trunk, and went downstairs.

She opened the front door and felt immediately unsettled by the large woman with the peroxided hair who stood there.

'Hallo, Mrs Hightower.'

Alex stared at her neat black pill-box hat, her leather gloves and her immaculately pressed white blouse.

'Iris Tremayne; I popped round last week.'

Alex watched her tiny rosebud lips parting as she spoke, like a secret door in the soft folds of her face. There was a determination in the woman's eyes, a determination that this time she would not be sent away. 'Come in,' she said, unable for a moment to think of anything else to say.

'You need me, dear, I can tell,' the woman said, stepping possessively into the house.

Alex still had the words of the letter going round in her mind. Weird; weird; the glare of the portrait, the sudden chill in the room. Surely it was Morgan Ford she was seeing, and that was tomorrow? 'I think there's a mistake –' she began.

97

Iris Tremayne stared imperiously around the hallway, then followed Alex into the drawing room. 'You're being troubled dear, aren't you?' There was a gentleness that just stopped her voice short of being bossy.

'I've been a bit jumpy, that's all.'

'I should think you would be, with what's been happening.'

Alex stared at her warily. 'What do you mean – with what's been happening?'

'You're being troubled dear, aren't you? I could sense it when I came round before, you were going to be troubled; tell me, I'm right, aren't I dear?'

Alex glared at her, annoyed suddenly for the intrusion into her privacy. She had the appointment for tomorrow; she did not need to speak to anyone now. She wondered if Morgan Ford and Iris Tremayne were connected, whether he had tracked her down through the Olivetti service number she had given him and sent Iris Tremayne round? Ridiculous. 'Would you like a cup of tea?'

'Oh no dear, thank you.'

She looked around her again. 'This is a very nice house dear.' A painting on the wall caught her attention and she walked over towards it, then pointed her finger. 'Is that a Stubbs?'

'No.'

'He's the only painter of horses that I know.'

'It's one of my husband's.'

'He's a painter is he?'

Alex looked at her coldly. 'No, the horse; he used to own it. One of his hobbies.'

'Not a betting person myself; suppose I should be . . . with my sensitivity . . . but it never seems to work for us sensitives, dear, I never knew anyone who could predict winners for themselves. Restful, aren't they, pictures of horses.'

'I've never really thought about it.' Alex stared at her impatiently. 'What did you mean just now, when you said I was being troubled?'

'His spirit is restless, isn't it dear? He wants some help.' She lowered herself carefully into an armchair, like a crate being lowered into a hold, thought Alex. The woman closed her eyes tightly, inclined her body forward and, keeping her gloves on, held her right wrist in her left hand. She opened her eyes and looked up and Alex detected, for the first time, a flicker of doubt in the woman's positive manner.

'Don't worry, dear.' The lips parted, stretched into a nervous smile, then shrank back, as if they had a life of their own. 'There's no charge, no charge at all. Of course, you can give a donation to charity if you wish, but that's optional, quite optional.' She raised her large false eyelashes up to the ceiling, frowned, as if detecting a flaw in the paintwork, then smiled again uncertainly. 'Coping are you, dear?'

'Yes,' said Alex coldly. 'I'm coping.'

'He's around, isn't he dear?'

'What do you mean?'

Iris Tremayne shook her head and breathed in sharply; her shoulders suddenly contracted, then relaxed again. She closed her eyes and sat very still. Alex watched her curiously, and felt a sudden deep sense of dread.

The woman began to twitch, almost imperceptibly. Then suddenly she stopped and stood up straight, opening her eyes. 'I'm sorry dear,' she said, 'I've made a terrible mistake. I shouldn't have come.' Her voice had changed, it was icy cold now; the calm had gone from her face and she looked almost as if she was frightened. 'No, I shouldn't have come at all. A terrible mistake.'

'What do you mean?'

She shook her head. 'I'd better go now dear,' she said abruptly, picking up her handbag.

Alex felt afraid suddenly. 'What do you mean?'

'It'll be much better if I go, dear; it's not what I thought at all.'

Alex stared at the round whiteness of her eyeballs, the

dark pupils scanning the room, darting about, the furrows of the frown lines in her fleshy forehead. 'Can't you at least tell me what you mean?'

Iris Tremayne sat down for a moment, rummaged in her handbag and took out her powder compact. She opened it with a loud click and stared at the mirror. 'I look a sight,' she said, dabbing her nose with some powder.

Alex felt her anger rising. 'Please tell me what this is all about.'

The woman looked at her, then snapped shut the compact. She hesitated, then shook her head. 'You must believe me dear, it's better if I go, best not to talk about it, forget it dear, forget I came. You were right, you were quite right last time.' She stood up again and edged towards the door. She stopped, tried to give Alex a kindly smile, but she was trembling too much. 'I really think I'd better go; leave it all alone, I think that would be best. Don't worry about my payment.'

'Look, I want an explanation. Please?'

There was a dull crash from upstairs; Alex wondered for a moment if she had imagined it, but she saw the woman's nervous glance.

'He's troubled dear.'

'I'll just go and see what that was.'

'No dear, I wouldn't; I've disturbed him, you see,' she said, hesitantly. 'He's not pleased about my coming, not pleased at all.' The woman shook her head. 'Leave it dear, take my advice – I've never had – never known – not like this, you must leave it alone, leave him alone; ignore him.' She suddenly took a step towards Alex and gripped her hand firmly. Alex felt the cold leather of the glove. 'You must dear.' She turned and marched out into the hallway. There was a click of the door and she was gone.

Alex stared around the room, her head spinning, and walked to the window; she parted the curtains and stared out. She could see Iris Tremayne walking down the street, in short duck-like steps, each one growing faster, more determined, almost as if she was trying to run but wasn't quite able to.

CHAPTER THIRTEEN

Alex released the curtains and stared around the room. What had Iris Tremayne seen, she wondered? Was she a loony, or –? She lit a cigarette and took a deep drag; it had a foul, unfamiliar taste, like burned rubber. Fabian hated her smoking and she had always tried not to when she was with him; she felt suddenly as if she was cheating on him now, took another drag, almost surreptitiously, and stubbed it out, screwing her nose up at the stench.

She went through to the kitchen, trying to ignore the crash from upstairs. Just another trick of her mind, she told herself, but she could still see Iris Tremayne's face, the fearful glance upwards. Probably just the boiler again. She opened the freezer door, and rummaged through the frozen packs, wondering what to cook for Philip, then closed the door again, restlessly. She looked at her watch, seven o'clock; he would be here soon. He could decide and she'd bung it in the microwave.

She looked up at the ceiling and listened. Everything was quiet. What the hell had she meant, that damned woman? She walked down the passageway, climbed the stairs, stood on the landing and listened again. She felt nervous suddenly, uncomfortable, wished for a moment she was not alone. In the distance she heard the siren of an ambulance. She opened her bedroom door and turned on the light; everything was normal. She checked the bathroom; nothing wrong there either. She went down the corridor, stood outside Fabian's room, and listened again. She pushed open his door, turned on the light, and felt the blood drain out of her.

The trunk was lying upside down on the floor, the contents spewed out all around it.

She felt herself reeling and clutched the wall for support; it seemed to slide away from her and she stumbled, grabbed the side of his armchair. She closed her eyes, breathed deeply, opened them again, looked around, bewildered for a moment, then went out of the room, down the corridor and into his bathroom. Had there been someone in here? No, impossible; the windows were all closed, secure. Could it have fallen by itself – had she left it balanced on the edge of the bed? No, that was not possible. So how? How?

She went back into the room, stared at the jumble of belongings on the floor, clothes, books, his diary, his battered straw boater, then up at his portrait. How?

The doorbell rang. She turned off the light, closed the door and went downstairs.

'Sit!' she heard, followed by an angry snarl. 'Sit!'

Shaking, she opened the door and saw Philip Main standing there in a battered cord jacket, holding a crumpled paper bag under one arm and Black's lead, with some difficulty, in the other.

'Black, sit!' Main looked at her. 'Sorry if I'm a bit early, couldn't remember what time.' He turned back to the dog. 'Sit!'

'I don't think I said a time.'

He thrust the paper bag at her. 'Didn't know what we were eating, so I bought red and white.'

'Thanks.' She took the bag.

Main was physically jerked backwards. 'Black, sit!'

The dog let out a slow rumbling growl, like a powerful motorbike idling. 'Come in.'

Main jerked the dog's lead hard and Black gave a surprised choking cough. 'He's – er – not best pleased – hasn't had much of a walk today.' The dog dug its toes into the concrete step and slid, reluctantly, a few inches under Main's determined pull. 'Black!' The dog looked up, sensing defeat, and reluctantly followed its master into the house, then stopped inside the hallway and sat down.

'Hallo, boy,' said Alex, patting him but the dog ignored

her completely and stared, suspiciously, at the ground. Main unclipped the lead. 'Gets these moods.'

'Must be difficult, keeping a dog in London.'

'Sometimes.' He rolled the lead up and pushed it into his pocket. 'We seem to manage.'

They went through into the drawing room. 'What would you like?'

'You look terrible.'

'Thanks a lot,' she smiled.

'White; you look white as a sheet.'

'Scotch?'

'I don't suppose you've any Paddy?'

'Paddy?'

'Irish whisky.'

She shook her head. 'Sorry.' She was conscious of his stare and felt uncomfortable. 'I'm probably a bit tired.'

He sat down and slowly eased his cigarette pack out of his jacket pocket.

She handed him his drink. 'Actually, I've had a bit of a bummer of a day. How was yours?'

'All right.' He leaned forward and sniffed his whisky.

'Make any progress? Am I any nearer getting a book?'

'A little bit.' He sniffed the whisky again. 'A little bit.'

'I wouldn't make much of a living if all my clients were like you; three years and I still don't know what it's about.'

'Did all right with the last one, girl.'

She smiled; his last one had been published in fifteen countries; it had been translated into twelve languages, and it was incomprehensible in all of them. 'Will I be able to understand this one?'

'The whole world will be able to understand it, girl. But they won't want to.' He struck a Swan Vesta match and held it to the end of his cigarette.

'You're very determined, aren't you?'

'Determined?'

'To prove that God does not exist.'

He shook out the match. 'Hokum, girl; there's too much hokum in the world.'

'Are you sure it's not a vendetta?'

'Vendetta?'

'Against your father. He was a clergyman, wasn't he?'

He shook his head in a cloud of smoke, then stared sadly at the carpet. 'Lost his faith; decided he had it all wrong, that he wasn't a vicar at all.'

'So what was he?'

'He became a medium.'

Alex stared at him. 'You never told me that.'

'No, well, there are certain things one doesn't tell.'

She shrugged. 'Why not, it doesn't matter. Did he get you involved in anything?'

'Good Lord yes; all the time.'

She watched him sitting there, his tall frame crumpled awkwardly in the chair, gripping his glass clumsily with both hands, like an old man. She felt comfortable with him, safe with his mysteries and his answers and his knowledge; he always gave her the impression that somewhere, deep inside him, was the truth about life, that only he knew it and one day, if she pried hard enough and deeply enough, he would reveal it to her. 'In what sort of things?'

He went red and stared hard at his glass, as if trying to read something that was written in the whisky. 'Spirit rescues, he used to call them.'

'Spirit rescues?'

'Hmmm!' He shuffled awkwardly about in the chair.

'Tell me about them.'

He looked around, embarrassed, as if to check no one else was listening, then gave her an apologetic smile. 'Used to take me along, as a sort of earth.' He shrugged. 'Exorcisms, spirit rescues, that sort of thing.'

'I don't understand.'

'There was a stretch of road, near Guildford, that people seemed to think was haunted; some chap wandering around in the middle of the road. Several police patrols saw him too. My father went along, took me with him, took me because I wasn't psychic, couldn't be affected by spirits; I was like an earth wire on a plug.' He pushed his cigarette into his mouth and drew deeply on it. 'It turned out to be a lorry driver who had been killed in a crash a few years before; he didn't realize he was dead, was wandering around trying to find his wife and kids. My father told him what had happened, explained he was dead and put him in contact with some spirit guides; they took him off and he was quite happy.' Main looked up at Alex, sheepishly, then looked down at his whisky and turned the glass around in his hand.

'Did you see this man?'

'Lord, no. Just heard my father speak to him.'

'And what did you think about it?'

He drank some whisky and looked up at her. 'I thought my father was round the twist.'

Alex stared at him, and they sat in silence for a long time. 'I don't think you did,' she said, finally.

He shifted again, uncomfortably. 'It was all a long time ago.' He paused. 'Gosh yes, a very long time.'

'And you've spent the rest of your life trying to prove him wrong?'

Main sat and stared silently at her. 'My father ended up in a funny farm.'

'I'm sorry,' she said.

He shrugged.

'Perhaps he couldn't cope with his powers.'

'Hmmm.'

She shuddered. 'Creepy.'

'There's a link between the old brain, mental illness and psychic powers. Weird lot, mediums.'

'I've never heard of a vicar becoming a medium.'

'Have you ever heard of a vicar who ended up in a funny farm?'

She looked at him, uncertain whether to smile. 'Was there ever a time when you did believe in it?'

'It destroyed my father.' He looked down at his drink.

'Don't you think sometimes good comes of it? People with healing powers?'

'The National Health has healing powers; and statistically a better record.'

'And when they fail?'

He stared into his whisky. 'Nothing's proven.'

'People have been healed when doctors have given up hope.'

'They've done that for centuries, girl; long before mediums.'

'And before Christ?'

He shifted again. 'You need rest, girl, a holiday; get away from it all; you don't need mediums stirring it all up again for you.'

'One came round this afternoon.'

'That explains it.'

'What?'

'Why you looked white as a sheet when I arrived.'

'She was odd. She really spooked me.' She looked at him, but he said nothing. 'I hadn't asked her to come; she said she sensed I was being troubled, that – Fabian – was still around.' Alex smiled nervously and pulled out a cigarette. 'She sat down, in here, closed her eyes and started shaking like a leaf; then she stood up, looking very frightened and said she had made a mistake, a terrible mistake, that I should leave him alone.'

'Very sensible.'

'Then there was a crash upstairs.'

Main looked at her, his eyes probing. 'Some stupid woman trying to con you into something.'

'No,' said Alex, 'that's the point – she wasn't. She just left; wouldn't say anything, wouldn't answer me. Just rushed out, looking terrified.'

'Loonies; they're all loonies.'

'Even Morgan Ford?'

'Yes, girl. Bound to be.'

'Thanks a lot; I should have a great time with him tomorrow then.'

'I've already told you.'

She shrugged. 'I want to go; I can make up my own mind. I especially want to go now, after what's happened – I –'

He was looking at her, his eyes penetrating. 'Something else has happened, hasn't it?'

She twiddled with her cigarette. 'I brought Fabian's old school trunk down from Cambridge yesterday; it was on his bed, full of stuff, very heavy. The crash I heard – I went upstairs; it had fallen off his bed, on to the floor. There's no way it could have fallen on its own, Philip.'

'So how do you think it got there?'

She smiled, nervously, and felt herself blushing. 'This may sound crazy – maybe you should put me in a funny farm too – Fabian always used to have a violent temper; most of the time he was sweet and gentle, but when he didn't get his way, particularly as a child, he used to have the most terrible tantrums. Sometimes he was so strong, I couldn't hold him. Maybe he got angry just now, with that woman.' She smiled again and stared at Main, hopefully.

He grinned. 'There are a hundred reasons why something can fall on to the floor.'

She shook her head adamantly. 'No. There's no way; that trunk did not fall.' She looked at him. 'Why are you grinning?'

He shook his head, slowly. 'Yesterday you were being attacked in your office; today someone's throwing trunks around your bedrooms; think about it.'

'It's different, Philip; last night I was all wound up, I admit that; but not tonight, tonight I was feeling O.K.' She paused. 'Come and see for yourself.'

He shrugged and stood up.

For a dreadful moment Alex thought they were going to

walk into the room and see the trunk lying on the bed again, still neatly packed. She pushed open the door and turned on the light; the trunk lay there, everything spilled out on the floor, as she had left it.

'See?'

He looked down at the trunk, studied the clothes and the books strewn around. 'It was on the bed?'

'Yes.'

Main looked around the room, stared up at the portrait of Fabian, and lingered on it, thoughtfully; he walked over and fondled the telescope. 'Fine instrument.'

'You can have it, if it's useful.'

Main knelt down and stared through it; he focused the eyepiece. 'Bad place, London, for astronomy; too much pollution in the air.'

'Take it, if you like.'

He shook his head. 'Not my field. Queen Victoria used to loathe microscopes. Said they enabled you to see things so closely, you could not tell what they were. I feel that way about telescopes; they enable you to see things so far away you still cannot tell what they are.'

She smiled.

'Give me a microscope any day. It's all there, girl, under the microscope; all of it.' He stood up, stretched, looked down at the trunk. 'Want a hand?'

'No. I've got to sort it out, anyway; might as well leave it there.' She saw Main stare at the portrait, then look away, uncomfortably. 'Has that effect, doesn't it?'

'The portrait?'

She nodded.

'Looks like one of those van Eyck characters.' He looked up, then turned away again, sharply.

'Are you hungry?'

'Well,' he sighed, 'I suppose a chap could eat something.'

'Perhaps a chap would like to choose it? And the chappess will cook it.'

'Bona,' he said, turning and staring at the picture again. A perturbed look came across his face and he walked out of the room, a little too hurriedly, thought Alex, surprised at the sudden change that had come over him.

CHAPTER FOURTEEN

Black made a noise like a child gargling, and Alex jumped. The pitch deepened again into a low rumble.

Main prised some lasagne out of his moustache, dabbed his lips with his napkin, then turned his head towards the passageway. 'Quiet, boy!'

The rumble continued. He picked up his wine glass and drained it. 'Bona,' he said.

'You've been very quiet.'

He leaned back in his chair and pulled his cigarettes out of his jacket. He lifted the bottle and poured some wine into Alex's glass, then refilled his own.

'Nice wine.'

'Montepulciano d'Abruzzo.'

'Pardon?'

There was another rumble from Black. Philip turned and looked at the passageway again. 'Quiet!' he shouted. 'Some remarkably good wines, from Italy. Stunning.'

'You should get together with David; write a book.'

He paused, then looked up at her. 'Jesus knew a bit about wine.'

'Jesus?'

'He didn't turn the water into ordinary plonk. Someone asked the host why he'd saved the best wine to the end.'

She smiled. 'Italian?'

'No, good God no. Probably Lebanese.'

Black rumbled again. Philip frowned but said nothing.

'So what do you think about the trunk?'

He did not speak until he had lit his cigarette, as if it was a drug he needed to give him the power of speech. 'I think you had it too near the edge of the bed.'

She looked down. 'No, Philip, I didn't, and you know I didn't.'

Main stood up and ambled towards the doorway. 'Black!' He walked down the passage and saw the dog standing staring up the stairs. It started its low growl once more. 'What's the matter, boy?'

The dog ignored him.

'There's nothing up there, boy.' Main stared at the dog, puzzled, beginning to feel uncomfortable himself. He turned back, walked a short way down the passage and went into the lavatory under the stairs. He closed the door, turned on the light and lifted the seat. He found himself shivering. It was like an icebox in here. He looked at the sharp black and white pattern on the wallpaper and noticed a sheen on it; he ran his finger along a strip and it felt wet. He looked at the moisture on his finger; the temperature seemed to be dropping as he stood. There was a crack like a pistol beside his right ear, he saw a shadow and flinched reflexively. An entire panel of paper fell away from the wall and on to him. He fielded it off with his arm and it dropped down beside him; he saw another panel in front of him begin to slide slowly down. He opened the door, snapped off the light and backed out, closing the door firmly. He stood in the passageway for a moment, wondering if he had imagined it. He put his hand on the handle again, then turned away and walked back into the kitchen.

Alex was looking at him, anxiously. 'Everything all right?'

He said nothing.

'You look worried about something.'

'Have you had that damp in the loo long?'

'Damp? What damp?'

'The wallpaper's dripping; it's coming away from the walls.' He saw the frown on her face.

'Can't be. The house is bone dry.'

'Perhaps you've got a leaking pipe.'

'I'll call the plumber in the morning.'

'I'll have a dekko; may be something simple.' He took off his jacket and hung it on his chair.

'I'll make some coffee,' she said, as he walked out of the room.

She heard Main scrabbling about upstairs as she carried the coffee through into the drawing room. Black was sitting by the front door. 'Hallo, boy!' she said. 'Want to go out?' The dog ignored her.

She put the tray down, pulled *Don Giovanni* out of the tape player, and pushed in a Mozart compilation tape. She saw the stack of unopened letters on her bureau, walked over and sifted through them. She recognized the handwriting on one or two of them, but could not bring herself to open them; not yet, she thought. Later, one day when she was strong again; for a moment, she wondered if she ever would be strong again. She filled her cup and sat down on the sofa.

Main came into the room, wiping his hands on his corduroy trousers.

'Black or white?'

'Black, please.'

'Did you find the problem?'

'No.'

'Thanks, anyway.'

He sat down beside her and began to stir his coffee thoughtfully. 'I'll bring some tools round tomorrow. Lift up some floorboards; probably a leak in a join somewhere.'

'I didn't realize you were such a handyman.'

'No, well, we all have hidden talents.'

'You could write a book on do-it-yourself.'

'Going to be busy, with do-it-yourself and the origins of life.'

'Not to mention poetry.'

Alex sensed him tense up. Suddenly, he looked over his shoulder.

'Everything O.K.?' She found herself turning around too, and felt a prickle of anxiety. Philip was looking uneasy, frowning. She listened to the music and said nothing. Slowly she felt him relax again; she watched him put down his cup and felt his arm gently touch her shoulders. She leaned back slightly, affectionately, but still she didn't feel comfortable. She shivered.

'Figaro?'

'Yes. An excerpt; various different Mozart –'

She wanted to speak, converse, to hear his voice, put this strange fear that was engulfing her out of her mind. Her Sunday afternoon fear had come late today, she thought. 'You're very quiet.'

He raised his eyebrows.

'Penny for your thoughts.'

'You won't get rich on that; you're meant to be my agent.'

She laughed, then was silent again, and listened to the music. A french horn was blowing a gallop; it was Mozart at his most rousing, most cheering. She found her feet tapping to the tune, felt the rhythmic thump of Main's arm on her shoulder. She sighed. 'Oh God,' she said, 'why did this have to happen, why?'

'Hrrr.'

'Is that your explanation for the origin of life?'

'What?'

'Hrrrr!' she imitated.

She felt him lean forward, heard the clink of the cup, the faint slurp, the clink of the cup again. 'You'll get over it, old girl; it'll take time, a long time. I wish I'd met him.'

She suddenly had an impulsive wish to say 'You will!'; she felt a sudden strange tingling of excitement, of optimism. She drank some more coffee. 'You know, it's funny – my mood swings so much at the moment – I go up and down, often several times in an hour.'

He nodded. 'That'll keep happening, for a while.'

She looked at him. 'Are you an expert on everything?'

'No, gosh, my word no. A little knowledge is a dangerous thing.'

'So you have a lot?' She felt his arm squeezing her shoulder.

'No, good Lord no.' He sat in silence for a moment. 'There was a master at school, a pompous little man, who used to tell us with great satisfaction that he had never driven a motor car and did not know how to. But he was, however, fully qualified to drive a steam locomotive.'

Alex smiled.

'He'd driven one in the 1926 General Strike: from King's Cross to Edinburgh non-stop. He claimed still to hold the unofficial record for the fastest time.'

'Life's full of odd little people doing odd little things.' She saw Main's face close to hers, saw the pock marks in the white bony flesh, the gingery bristles of the moustache; she jerked back, surprised, then felt the soft bristles brushing her nose, brushing around the top of her mouth, saw his blue staring eyes going out of focus, like the view of a dentist's eyes, she thought for a moment.

Then suddenly the face changed and it was Fabian.

'No!' she screamed, pulling sharply back. 'No!' Fabian's face dissolved, and she saw the shock on Main's face; it remained there, frozen for a moment, and then turned to an embarrassed sheepish expression.

'Sorry,' he said, lamely. 'I – cr –'

She continued to stare at him, shaking, wide-eyed. She had seen him so clearly, so vividly. There was something touching and at the same time hideously obscene; Christ, what weird tricks her mind was playing. 'I'm sorry, Philip,' she said. 'I'm really not – I don't know – ready.' She felt his arm slip away from her shoulders, saw him lean forward, rest his elbows on his thighs.

'No, my fault, my fault entirely,' he said. 'I just find you – so immensely attractive, I – I –' He sat upright, gave her a benign, lost smile.

'I think maybe I'd better go to bed now,' she said.

He looked at his watch. 'Yes, good Lord, it's getting late.' He stood up, slowly, looked around again and she saw the sudden expression of fear on his face. 'You'll be all right?'

She nodded, and grimaced. 'I'll have to be, won't I?'

Main wandered out into the hallway. It felt cold out here now; he rubbed his arms and walked into the kitchen. It was freezing. He looked around; were the walls damp in here too, or was it his imagination? He suddenly felt very uncomfortable, an intruder; the house didn't want him, was telling him to go. He removed his jacket deliberately slowly from the chair and pulled it on, then stood still and looked around. He felt the cold seeping through his skin. He walked over and touched a wall, ran his finger down and lifted it away; it was dry. He looked up at the ceiling, feeling so cold he could barely stop himself from shaking, then marched to the door, turned and stared back at the kitchen. 'Fuck off,' he said, loudly, firmly; then he turned and walked through into the hallway.

'Did you say something?' said Alex, carrying the tray out of the drawing room.

'Me? No.'

'I was sure I heard you speak.'

'Just to Black, that was all.'

'Ah.'

He pulled the dog's lead out of his pocket and Black suddenly became animated, jumping up, barking cheerfully.

'Home, boy!'

'Goodnight, Philip.'

'Thanks for supper.'

'Thanks for the wine.' She leaned forward and gave him a light kiss on the cheek. 'Drive carefully.'

'You can come and stay with me if you – er – if you want. You can have your own room, come and go – if you don't feel like –'

She shook her head. 'Thanks, but this is my home. I've just got to get used to it again, that's all. Fabian was never here much, you know, anyway.' She closed the door, heard the dog bark cheerfully at the night, and turned the key. She felt peaceful suddenly. Immensely peaceful and relaxed, as if an evil presence had suddenly been exorcised from the house.

CHAPTER FIFTEEN

She parked in the gloomy terrace off the Gloucester Road and crossed her fingers that she would not get clamped. The numbers on the buildings were illogical, and she paced the length of the terrace, crossing the road, getting increasingly anxious that she was going to be late and might miss the appointment altogether.

Then she saw it. 49. On the building directly in front of her car, staring her in the face, almost taunting her, she thought, angrily. She walked up the steps and scanned the names on the entryphone panel. Goldsworthy, Maguire, Thomas, Kay, Blackstock, Pocock, Azziz. Several of the names had been written in a scrawling pen; one, Azziz, had a line through it. Amongst them she found a fading yellow label with neat typing which simply said 'Ford'.

For an instant she felt relieved; then she began to feel nervous. She looked around uncertainly, wondering whether the neighbours all knew, whether the people walking past on the pavement were nudging each other and pointing at her. She wondered whether mediums made a lot of money; Morgan Ford certainly did not spend any on the outside of the building. The porch tiles were cracked and the plaster was peeling off the columns.

A cold unwelcoming voice crackled through the entryphone. 'Yes?'

'It's –' Oh, Christ, what the hell was the name she had given? She couldn't remember; stall, she thought, stall for time. 'Johnson!' she said, suddenly, feeling the relief. 'Mrs Johnson.' She'd given a Christian name too, what was that? She racked her brains again, feverishly.

The grimy, dimly lit hallway gave nothing away about

the identity of the tenants. There were several piles of mail on a shelf and a battered bicycle leaned against the wall.

Ford's flat was on the third floor and the door opened as she reached it. His appearance surprised her and she wondered what she had been expecting – some ageing bearded weirdo left over from the sixties, dressed in a kaftan and sandals and holding a joss stick. Instead she was staring at a short man with neat grey hair and a neat grey suit; in his early fifties, she guessed.

'Shoona Johnson?'

For a moment Alex nearly said, 'No, no, Alex Hightower,' but just managed to stop. She stared through a doorway behind him, into a tiny office where a pile of letters and newspapers were laid out neatly on a small desk. 'Yes.' That was it, Shoona. Why the hell had she chosen Shoona, she wondered? She'd never met anyone called Shoona in her life.

He held out a small pink hand dominated by a vulgar rhinestone ring, a hand so small she wondered if it was a deformity. It was like shaking hands with a child.

'Come in. Thank you for being so punctual.' There was a warm sing-song lilt to his Welsh accent that seemed totally different from how he had sounded over the phone. 'I'm afraid I'm a bit disorganized today, my secretary hasn't turned up.'

Alex felt a sense of disappointment as she stepped into the plain dim hallway. It all seemed so ordinary; there was no feeling of magic, of occasion, of great ceremony. Business suits, secretaries, an office. She hadn't somehow expected him to be doing this for a living.

The drawing room changed her opinion. A huge burgundy-coloured room with a view out across the gardens. It was over-furnished with fine antiques in an almost vulgar display of money. A gas log fire burned with a low hissing sound. Two cats sat either side of the grate, motionless, like sentinels, a ginger tom and a smoke-grey Burmese; the tom jumped forward on to the carpet and circled curiously around her.

And then she saw the bowl of roses on the table in the centre of the room.

She began to tremble, and started to back away. The phone rang.

'Please, take a seat.' Ford brushed past her and picked up the receiver. 'Hallo.' She watched him stiffen, saw him speak in the same cold, aloof way. 'I have a cancellation on Thursday at half past eleven. I could fit you in then. Very good, and what is your name please?'

Did he tell everyone that he had a cancellation, she wondered? She sat down in an uncomfortable Victorian armchair and stared at the roses again.

'Just one second, I'll fetch my diary and confirm that.' She looked up and caught his eye. 'Like roses do you? They're nice those, aren't they?'

She wondered, as he left the room, whether it had been an innocent remark, or whether she had detected a mischievous wink in his eye. She looked again at the roses; no, maybe it was just coincidence; they went with the cats and the fire and the ornate furniture. A strange room for a middle-aged man, she thought; it seemed more like the room of an elderly titled widow.

She stared at a painting on the wall. Three phantom-like faces with slits for their eyes, huddled together, white on a white background. On a shelf just below them was a menacing buddhaesque statue. She noticed more paintings as she looked around, all sinister; the room was beginning to frighten her. She stared at the roses, so like the ones Fabian had given her. She went over to the bowl and counted them. The same number. The same colour. Was it a message, she wondered. A sign? Ridiculous. As she watched them, they seemed to be glowing; she closed her eyes, shook her head and turned away. She heard Ford's footsteps, a loud snort as he blew his nose. Instantly she sensed the atmosphere change as he entered the room. Everything became calm, peaceful again; she felt at ease. She glanced again at the roses; they were pretty, cheerful, made her suddenly, inexplicably, feel good.

The tom looked up at her, then jumped on to her lap. She smiled down at it, nervously, wondering whether it was about to attack her, and tentatively stroked its neck. It settled down, resting its head on her thigh and looked up at her unblinkingly. She felt comforted by the contact, rested her hand on its belly, felt the warm skin beneath the fur, its assured relaxed breathing.

'Put him on the floor if he's a nuisance.'

'No, he's fine.'

'Some people are funny about cats.'

'He's a nice chap.'

Ford stood in front of her, hands clasped behind his back, and gave her a gentle smile. He looked up at the mantelpiece. 'We've started a little late, so I'll give you some extra time.'

Again Alex felt unsettled by his businesslike attitude. Surely you couldn't be a medium in units of quarter of an hour, like a lawyer or an accountant?

'Do you have anything I can hold?'

'I'm sorry?'

'Something you wear a lot. Your watch, a bracelet?'

She took off her Rolex and handed it to him.

'Now, is there anything in particular you want, or shall we just start and see how we go?'

She shrugged, wondering what to say.

Without waiting, he sat down in a chair beside her, held her watch outstretched in his hand for a moment, then curled his fingers over it. 'Upheaval,' he said gently. 'I sense upheaval. Something's upset the rhythm, something tragic, I feel, recently, very recently, within the last few weeks perhaps?' He looked at her.

'Do you want me to answer you?'

'As you like.' He smiled. 'There's no need if you don't want to, but it would be helpful, guiding me, if I'm on the right track.'

'You're on the right track.'

He sat still and frowned, then tilted his head back, keeping his eyes wide open. 'Yes,' he said. 'Yes, I'm feeling something very distinctive, something very close, young, energy, a lot of energy. It's a child – no, not a child, but not an adult, definitely. Someone in their teens perhaps, or early twenties?' He stared questioningly at her. She said nothing. 'Male.' He frowned, and Alex saw the strange, nervous expression she had seen on Iris Tremayne's face the previous day. He sat very still for a moment and said nothing.

Alex stroked the cat, looked again at the roses, at the three phantoms, at the leaping flames with their unaltering pattern, then again at Morgan Ford. His whole body seemed clenched like a fist, shaking, grim determination on his face, as if fighting a tremendous battle of will.

'This is extraordinary,' he said, continuing to stare straight ahead. 'He's trying to tell me his name. But it's too soon, much too soon, it takes several months for the spirits to settle down, they're too frisky in the first few weeks, it's difficult.' His voice tailed away. 'Clarity, clarity is difficult. Something violent, not here, not in England, somewhere overseas, I sense flames, an explosion. A lorry is involved? Yes, a lorry, someone's shouting about a lorry!'

Alex watched him, his eyes shut now, trembling like a child.

'Something else now, someone's shouting, Harry? No, not Harry, sounds like Harry. I can sense terrible anger, terrible violence, someone is screaming "Lorry! Lorry!" There's an explosion, someone's shouting out "Harry" again; this Harry seems very important.'

Alex watched him, transfixed, as sweat poured from his sheet-white face.

'Now it's clearing a little, there's this young person again, a young man, he's trying to tell me his name. It's not clear, not clear at all, David could it be? No, Adrian? Maybe Adrian.' He shook suddenly, violently, as if an electric current had been passed through him. 'Something's not right, not right at all; there's a terrible conflict going on, something very disturbed; there's a lot of anger, so much anger. Fabian, could it be Fabian?' He continued without opening his eyes. 'Yes, he's telling me something, he's clear now, incredibly clear.'

Alex felt the cat breathing softly under her hand. She looked at the roses, at the medium, felt herself trembling strangely, almost as if she wasn't actually sitting in the chair but was suspended a few inches above it.

The medium suddenly shouted out at the top of his voice, and startled her. 'MY GOD HE'S CLEAR!' His hands were shaking, as if the watch was a mad wild thing. 'There's someone else now, trying to come through; a girl, she's trying to tell me something, but it doesn't make much sense, she's saying her name's Harry. There's so much disturbance, Fabian's making this disturbance; it's a game, he's larking around, that's the trouble, it's too soon, he's too frisky, it's all a game at the moment. Now, she's coming through again, more clearly now, no there's Fabian again, it's almost as if he's trying to – yes – trying to stop – jealousy, of course, oh it's become all so unclear again.' Alex saw Ford relax, lean back, turn to her. 'It's as bad as the telephone system up there sometimes.'

She stared, puzzled for a moment by the remark, then realized he had cracked a joke.

'Extraordinary, quite extraordinary; I've never known anything like this, never.' He leaned towards her. 'This is something really quite incredible.'

Alex stroked the nape of the cat's neck mechanically and listened to it purring. 'In what way?'

'Extraordinary; did it make sense?'

'I'm very confused.'

'I'm very confused too,' smiled Ford.

'What do you mean?'

'Have you had much experience in this field, Mrs – er – I'm sorry – I can't remember your name?'

'High – Johnson.'

'Ah, yes.'

'What do you mean, experience?'

'In the spiritual world?'

'No.'

'Your son came through very clearly; I am correct, yes? It was your son you wanted to contact? His name is Fabian, or Adrian?'

He knew who she really was; somehow he had found out.

'You've done your research well,' she said, coldly. 'You've been very thorough; but you've made just one mistake.'

He raised a single eyebrow.

'My son wasn't killed by a lorry, but by another motor car.'

'Mrs Johnson, I wasn't there; I can only go by what I'm told.'

'Or by what you've read.'

He pulled out his handkerchief and blew his nose. 'Read?'

'The crash was reported in the newspapers, Mr Ford,' she said. 'I don't know how many papers, but it was in the *Daily Mail*. They reported that it was a lorry. I noticed, as I came in, the *Daily Mail* on your desk.' She waited for the explosion of anger, but none came. Instead, he looked hurt, puzzled, and shook his head thoughtfully.

'I'm sorry,' he said, quietly, 'you obviously have a poor opinion of the integrity of mediums.'

The sincerity of his voice made her hesitate, and she felt herself begin to blush. She looked at his neatly groomed hair, his immaculate white shirt and snappy grey tie and the matching handkerchief bouffed out of the breast pocket of his suit. She looked at his tiny pink hands with their manicured nails and the huge vulgar ring, and then back at his face. Smooth. He could have been an insurance salesman.

'I don't do research, Mrs Johnson. I don't read obituary notices. I don't scan the papers for reports on road accidents and try to link them up with my clients; I don't delve back into the old school records of my clients, trying to dig up facts they've long forgotten that I can hit them with.' He smiled. 'In any event, with the amount of people who come here giving me fictitious names, how could I get anywhere with any consistency?'

Alex looked away guiltily from his searching eyes, and heard his gentle voice continue.

'Nor do I dole out only good news to the bereaved; I relate what I hear. That's my gift, that's all I can do.' He raised his eyebrows apologetically. 'We have a misconception about the departed. We think that because they have moved on, they have gained integrity.' He shook his head. 'It takes more than one life and one passing to gain integrity – and integrity is just one of many things we have to learn in our journeys through this life and the next. Spirits can tell lies, frequently they do; they can get things wrong too. You see, things don't get improved, suddenly, by passing into the next plane. If you have a lousy memory in this life, it isn't going to alter suddenly in the next.'

She saw his meek, apologetic smile and did not want to hurt him. 'My son had a very good memory.'

'Accidents happen very fast. They can be very confusing; the whole business of going over is very confusing, that's why I don't like to try to communicate with the very recently departed, not really before at least three months; this was only in the last few weeks, wasn't it?'

She nodded.

'Normally, I am not aware of much of what I am saying during a sitting, and at the end I can scarcely remember it at all; this is quite different; never in all my life have I known anything so vivid. Please don't be cynical, we should continue.'

'You got something else wrong too,' she said.

He smiled. 'What was that?'

'You were talking about someone called Harry – you said that something was odd, that it seemed to be a girl called Harry.'

'Yes?'

'Could she have been called Carrie?'

'Carrie?'

Alex nodded.

'Sometimes,' he said, 'with all the interference – things aren't distinct. Carrie? Yes, Carrie.' He closed his eyes for a moment and then opened them again. 'Yes, it could have been.'

'Tell me, at these sessions, do you talk to the living or the departed?'

He stared at her, unruffled. 'I'm what is called a medium, Mrs Johnson; I'm a link between the earth plane and the departed.'

'Then I don't understand how you could have spoken to Carrie.'

'Why not?'

'Because she's not dead. She's very much alive, and well, in America.'

She saw doubt flit across his face, like the shadow of a bird, saw a strange look appear in his eyes, as if something had profoundly disturbed him. He shook his head. 'She was trying to come through, Mrs Johnson, that's all I can tell you. You're sure that she's still on this plane? That she hasn't been in an accident?'

'Isn't it possible you might have picked her up telepathically?'

'That's how a lot of people try to explain mediums, Mrs Johnson. That we pick up the information telepathically from our client's brain. You couldn't use that old chestnut today, could you? Because I've stated two things that aren't in your brain: that your son was in collision with a lorry; and that Carrie, whoever she is, has passed across to the other side.'

She stared at him, trying to think clearly.

'I'm sorry that you're sceptical, Mrs Johnson. I don't know how I can change that, but I've got to, somehow.'

'What do you mean?'

He sat in silence for a long time. Alex listened to the hiss of the gas, the purring of the cat; outside she heard the rattle of a taxi and the slam of its door, and wondered it it was his next client arriving.

Suddenly he leaned towards her, until his face was close to hers, so close she could feel the warmth of his breath.

'Mrs Johnson,' he said. 'Fabian wants to come back.'

CHAPTER SIXTEEN

She felt confused and disillusioned as she drove away. Main had been right in his advice; it was exactly how he had told her she would feel. The curate had been right too. Nothing could be gained by summoning up the departed, he had said, nothing but, what was it – disappointment and evil? Strong words from the fire-and-brimstone brigade. Pastoral care, he had recommended; that had a nice gentle ring to it.

She thought about the evil; mischief, perhaps, but not evil. Games, perhaps; tricks. She thought about his room, how it had seemed so menacing without the presence of Ford; did evil take place there? Did he hold strange séances where they drew the curtains, turned up the wick, and sat in circles with the cats hissing? She shuddered. There seemed to be so much about life, so much that went on in the world that she could never know, that most human beings could never know: secret societies, strange practices, communions with gods, devils, departed ones. Did any of them know the secret? The truth? Was Morgan Ford, in his smooth suit and his grand drawing room, one of the few people on earth privy to the meaning of life? Had he alone been entrusted with the secret? And if so, what had he done with it? What was he doing with it? Sitting in his strange room telling lies to grieving women?

She heard angry hooting behind her and looked up; the light was green. She glanced in the mirror, saw the nose of the taxi, raised a hand and drove into Hyde Park. She pulled over to the left, driving slowly, and put her indicator on. Where was she going? It was eleven o'clock on Monday morning and she had important work to do in the office, but she couldn't face it, not yet; it seemed unimportant compared to her disappointment. What had she been expecting, she wondered, and shrugged, privately, to herself.

It had really seemed, she thought sadly, that Fabian had been trying to tell her something; that there had been a meaning to all the strange goings on, to the weird tricks her mind had been playing. She had been convinced, she knew, that Fabian had been telling her to go to a medium. She smiled, and felt her eyes watering. She had hoped, she supposed, that she was going to discover some point to his death, that he would explain it to her; but now all that had been shattered; it had been a delusion, another of life's dirty tricks.

Yes, Main was right. He and his kind were closer to the truth, sitting there in their laboratories with their pipettes and their glass tubes and their Bunsen burners, and their computers, searching all the time for their equations, searching for that one big ultimate equation.

Was it there, a palimpsest, lying quietly somewhere under the DNA code, waiting for that one scientist more patient, or just luckier than the rest, who would forever render the entire paraphernalia of religion redundant?

She parked and walked along beside the Serpentine, feeling the enormity of the world all around her. She looked at the London skyline beyond the trees, the buildings bunched together, rubbing shoulders, like passengers in a crowded tube. An old man sat staring out across the water, raising his arms up and down as if making a strange gesture to the futility of it all. She shivered, wrapped her arms around herself, afraid suddenly of being old, old and staring at the water and making futile gestures.

The roses in the room; the rose on the car windscreen. What were the odds of that happening? The odds of there being the same number of roses in the bowl? The same colour?

What were the odds for Morgan Ford? Had he known who she really was? Was linking her with the car crash he'd read about in the papers a good guess, or had she given him some clue when they'd begun to talk? Had he picked it up telepathically? That was the only other rational explanation – but then how had he made the mistake about the lorry? And the mistake about Carrie?

Too many things were contradicting each other. Where was the truth? Was there a personal palimpsest put there by Fabian? Was she looking at the face value of everything, and not beneath? She shook her head, stared at the boathouse, watched a horse canter by on Rotten Row, a young smart girl in one of those new-style crash helmets; change, she thought, change, progress. Everything seemed to be converging to a vanishing point somewhere in the distance. There was a growing sameness about everything; even horse riders now all looked like mounted police. God, she had never been any good at puzzles, riddles; was there a vanishing point for this riddle now? Would the puzzle stay unresolved for ever, parallel lines that would never change, or was there a junction, somewhere in the distance out there, where the answer lay?

Otto came into her mind, quietly, unobtrusively at first, as if he had slipped in through an open door and was waiting quietly in the shadows for her to notice him. She watched a young girl with her nanny throwing crumbs to the ducks, and felt Otto, lurking, smirking. Why? What was he doing, she thought, irritated. She tried to ignore him, to put him out of her mind, but that only made him clearer still. She could see his room, the empty champagne bottles, the hum of his coffee grinder, the careless, arrogant stirring of the cups, and the contempt in his eyes, with their secrets about her son, and the look which said 'I could have you any time I wanted, but I wouldn't bother.'

What did he know?

She found herself walking back to the car, working out in her mind the best route to the motorway, wondering if he would be there, or would she have to wait out in the corridor? It was no good resisting, there was nothing she could do to stop herself. She could think of nothing, nothing except the dark oak door of his room.

She arrived in Cambridge shortly before two, parked outside Magdalene and ran through the archway. She hurried up the steps and down the corridor which now seemed familiar, then stopped outside his door, breathless, and hesitated, listening, for floorboards creaking, for a clink of a cup, for music, voices, a rustle of paper. There was nothing. She knocked, timidly, knowing it was futile, heard the dull echo of the knock, sensed the flat emptiness of the room beyond.

The door opened, and she jumped back. Otto stood there, one hand in the pocket of his heavy cardigan, and nodded at her, the knowing smirk on his lacerated face, the leer in his eyes. 'You're earlier than I expected.'

She frowned, thrown by the remark, stared back into his eyes, trying to understand what he meant, then looked away, uncomfortably, and gazed for a moment at the flaking lintel above the door. 'I'm sorry, I don't understand – I didn't leave any message.'

He turned and walked inside. 'I've put coffee on. Would you like some?'

She saw the percolator bubbling, the two cups laid out beside it.

'Thank you.'

'I knew you were coming,' he said, matter-of-factly.

'How?'

He shrugged. 'I know a lot of things.'

'What sort of things?'

He gave a short contemptuous laugh, and for an instant she would have loved to hit him.

'You didn't know enough to save my son from being killed,' she said suddenly, vitriolically, unable to prevent the words from coming out.

He knelt down beside the percolator and lifted it up. 'Black, no sugar.'

'Thank you.'

She waited for his retort, but none came; he stayed kneeling by the coffee pot, and she watched him, feeling strangely sickened.

When he finally turned around, his eyes were livid.

'I'm sorry, Otto,' she said, nervous suddenly. 'That wasn't very nice of me.' She felt the rage burning silently inside him; he seemed much older than a student, suddenly, older than her. 'Sometimes I say things,' she said, 'things I don't mean.'

He sat down on the floor and leaned against the wall, his anger subsiding, the youth returning.

She smiled tentatively. 'How did you know I was coming?'

He sounded distant, as though he was dictating into a microphone. 'I get feelings about things sometimes, something that's going to happen, sometimes big things, sometimes little things, sometimes nothing.'

'And what happens?'

He took a sip of his coffee. 'They come true.' He stared, probing. 'But I can't do anything about them; it's all useless, this information.'

'Why?' she said uncomfortably.

'It's as though it has already happened; so I can do nothing.'

'You got the coffee ready for me.'

He shrugged. 'Got the coffee ready, sure; but that's really no big deal.'

'Did you know about the accident? That it was going to happen?'

'No. Nothing.' He paused. 'Even if I had –' He shrugged.

'Do you know why I've come?'

He said nothing.

She looked into his eyes, tried to read them. She tried to ignore the faint mocking smile that was in them, and looked beyond; but there was nothing. It was like staring through panes of glass at a dark night.

'Otto, I want you to try to remember something; it's not going to be very nice for you, but it's really very important to me; will you help me?'

'If I can.'

'It was a car you hit, wasn't it?'

'Yes, for sure.'

'What happened just before?'

'I don't remember; one moment I was in the car, the next I was outside.'

'Please try.'

'I had a hangover; the party was a good party; I don't know about Fabian.' He smirked.

'Why are you smiling?'

'He scored with the host's daughter; spent the night with her.' He shook his head. 'Incredible, you know, he was always scoring with girls.'

'But never keeping them?'

He looked at her, then looked away. 'It wasn't important.'

'Not to you; what about to him?'

Otto shrugged. 'Your son was a bastard to women, Mrs Hightower; better to leave it at that.'

'What do you mean?'

He shook his head.

'Does it really matter, now that he's –' she paused. 'Can't you tell me?'

He smiled strangely. 'It's not important, really it's not important.' He stirred his coffee. 'We drove, we were just talking; I was in the front passenger seat, Charles and Henry were in the back; for some reason I hadn't put my seat-belt on, the catch in the Golf is awkward, you know. It was dawn, we had our lights on; Fabian was talking to Charles, looking around; suddenly I saw these lights in front of us, coming straight at us, high up; I thought it was a lorry.'

'What?' Alex heard herself shout the word out, involuntarily; she felt herself shaking, trembling in disbelief, confusion; she felt giddy, saw the floor slope suddenly away

132

from her, as if she was in a boat hit by wash, and had to hold on to both arms to prevent herself falling sideways from the chair. 'A lorry?'

'It was an old Citroën, apparently, big, upright; we were sitting in the Golf, low down. It looked like a lorry. Fabian must have thought so too. He shouted out "Lorry!" After that, I was lying on grass, or mud – I don't really remember.'

The chair felt like a seesaw; it swayed from side to side as if it had a life of its own; she fought it, leaned against it, and watched his eyes all the time, those eyes that were like the night.

'I'm afraid it does not tell you much.'

'Sometimes,' she said, distantly, vaguely conscious of the curious flutter in her stomach, 'one doesn't need to be told much.'

CHAPTER SEVENTEEN

The house looked fresh and clean and smelt of polish. Mimsa had left one of her usual indecipherable notes: 'Dere Misy Higtow, dun al jobbs. Don got no more clenning for winnow stuff. Got problims in dounstair toilee, paper no stick wall. See yoo tummorro.'

She frowned, and made a note on the shopping pad. She hesitated outside the downstairs lavatory, then went up to Fabian's room. Mimsa had left everything as it was, as she had told her. She picked up his diary, sat down on the bed and took out the postcard she had taken from Carrie's mother, and the letter Carrie had written to Fabian, which she opened out and pressed flat. Then she laid the postcard beside it, and began to compare the handwriting, going through each letter of the alphabet in turn.

She began to feel chilly as she worked, and sensed the temperature dropping. She stood up and left the room, without looking up at the portrait, went downstairs into the drawing room and sat beside the phone. She picked up the receiver, hesitated, and dropped it back on the rest. She stared again at the letter and the postcard, then picked up the receiver again and dialled Philip Main.

'I'm sorry,' she said, 'if I was a bit abrupt last night.'

'No, gosh, quite understand – I behaved –'

'No, you didn't, you were nice and kind.'

'Did you go to – today?'

'Yes.'

'I see.' He sounded disapproving.

'That's why I'm calling you. I want to talk to you about it. I wondered if you were doing anything this evening?'

'Oh, nothing important; only about to prove conclusively the origins of man.'

'I'm sorry.'

'It's waited two billion years, I don't suppose one more night's really here nor there.'

'Want to try another of my frozen dinners?'

There was a silence. He coughed and sounded uncomfortable. 'I – er – I'd rather take you out somewhere. Nothing to do with the cooking, you understand. Think it's good for you to get out.'

'Want me to meet you somewhere?'

'No, gosh, no; I'll pick you up – I'll wait outside and hoot.'

'You are allowed in,' she said, smiling.

'It's – er – jolly difficult to park outside sometimes.'

He sounded evasive, and it puzzled her; she shrugged. 'Fine. What time?'

'About an hour?'

'I'll be ready.' She replaced the receiver, then slipped the postcard and letter underneath the phone, and carefully placed it on top to weigh them down.

The restaurant was small and simple, with an empty Monday evening air about it. Candles burned optimistically on each of the bare wooden tables and the staff hovered earnestly, as if to assure them that they hadn't made a mistake in coming here, that they were not normally empty like this.

'If you stand at the bottom of a mine shaft in the middle of the day and look up at the sky, you can see Venus. It's up there, all the time. In the fifteenth century sailors used to navigate by it.'

'Did they have mine shafts on their ships?'

Main smiled wistfully. 'Didn't need to, girl.' He tapped his eyes. 'They could see it, just by looking.'

'So why can't we?'

'Evolution; we've moved on; our senses are getting dulled; we have computers to navigate for us now.'

'So we can't see Venus because of pollution in the sky?'

'No, good Lord, no; we can't see it because we don't know how to see it any more; perhaps primitive man in the jungle in other countries can still see it, but if we had the sensitivity to see it, we'd be blinded by the dazzle of electric lights.'

'So evolution isn't always too smart.'

He swirled his wine glass and stared down at the table. 'It gets the job done,' he said, defensively.

'With every generation our senses get dulled?'

'Old senses get dulled; new senses develop.' He paused. 'There's a certain irrational streak.'

'What do you think is irrational?'

'Man's ability to run fast; getting faster every generation. No one had run a four-minute mile until 1954; now people do it in three minutes fifty. And yet, we don't even need to run at all these days.' He shrugged.

'I thought that was because the athletes take drugs?'

'In part; only in part; evolution has something to do with it.'

'So our legs should be getting shorter?'

'And our arms; don't need them. All we're going to need is fingers to push buttons.'

'So, in thirty-two million years' time we'll just be bodies with fingers and feet, all looking like potato men?'

He scrabbled in his pocket and pulled out his cigarettes. 'So, you went to your medium.'

She nodded, and took the cigarette he offered. 'Mr Ford has given me rather a lot to think about. He claimed to have got through to Fabian; he was describing the accident.' She lit the cigarette from the candle, looked around to see if any waiter was listening, and leaned across the table. 'He said that someone in the car was shouting out that a lorry was coming straight at them.'

'Could have picked that up from the papers — or telepathically from you.'

She shook her head. 'He was killed by a car, not by a lorry; there was no lorry.'

Main looked puzzled. 'It said in the paper –'

'That's the point,' she interrupted. 'That's the whole point! It said in the papers that it was a lorry, so I was convinced he had read the papers, and put two and two together. I went to Cambridge this afternoon and had a chat with Otto, the boy who survived. I asked him to tell me what happened just before the accident. He said that they'd seen what they thought was a lorry coming, and that Fabian had shouted out that there was a lorry.' She drank some wine and drew heavily on her cigarette, then stared hard back at him.

He shrugged. 'Could be telepathy: you picked the message up from Fabian, just before the accident, in your subconscious, but it did not register, then Ford picked it up from you.' He shrugged again. 'That's rather a complex way of looking at things. Or –'

'Or Ford is genuine?'

'I don't know about that. Remarkable.'

A waiter appeared. 'Was it the pigeon for you, madam?'

'No, me.'

Alex waited in silence until the food had been served, then leaned forward again. Do you know where I could find a handwriting expert?'

'Handwriting?'

'Yes, I don't know what they're called – the sort of person the police would use to see if something was forged.'

'There's a chap I've used from time to time in my research; thought I'd have a go at disproving the Dead Sea Scrolls.' He smiled, wryly.

'To annoy your father?'

He looked pensive. 'No, a long time after –' he paused, and stared sternly at his pigeon, as if it had committed a misdemeanour.

'Looks very nice,' she said.

'Dead rat,' he said.

'What?'

'Dead rat,' he repeated.

'Dead rat?'

'Yes. Had a name like Dead Rat. Derat, Durat, Dendret. Dendret he was called.'

'Is there anything that you don't know?' she smiled.

'I don't know why I ordered pigeon; I just remembered I can't stand the stuff.'

'I'll swap with you.'

'No, no, good Lord, no. A chap's got to accept the consequences of his actions.' He gave her a strange look, which for an instant disturbed her.

'You don't have to be a martyr any more these days, we've evolved past that.'

'Touché,' he said, prodding the pigeon dubiously with his fork.

She felt comfortable with all the junk in the Volvo around her, her feet nestling in an undergrowth of papers, parking tickets, cassettes. The car had a homely, lived-in feeling, like an old boat. 'Do you ever clean your car out?'

'No, gosh, no. Usually change it when the ashtray gets full.'

She smiled, and stared at the ashtray, jammed open, crammed with dried out butts. 'What do you call full?'

The wipers smeared the rainwater across the screen, splaying out the lights of London in front of her like a kaleidoscope.

'Does it bother you, going back to the house on your own?'

She shrugged. 'No. I've got used to it; Fabian only came down in the holidays.'

'Would you ever like to have any more children?'

She shook her head. 'I'm too old, too set in my ways.'

'How old are you?'

'Ancient,' she smiled. 'Sometimes I feel very ancient.'

She watched the white, oranges, reds, exploding and sliding away in front of her eyes, heard the roar of the engine, felt the force of braking, heard the sluicing of the tyres cease suddenly. The wipers clacked in front of her, clack, clack, clack, almost in tune with the rattle of a taxi engine and the beat of the music from a disco nearby; clack, clack, two tiny instruments in the orchestra of the London night.

'I can't have any more children,' she said. 'We had –' she paused; the knowledge was still painful, perhaps now more so than it ever used to be; she ran her tongue along her lower lip and watched the show.

He double-parked outside her house and kept the engine running. 'Thanks for the meal,' she said. 'Would you like to come in?'

She noticed a strange expression flicker across his face for an instant, almost of fear, she thought.

'I'd better get back to work.'

'Tonight?'

'A chap can't keep the world waiting for ever.'

'Nor his agent.'

'No. Gosh, no.'

'Look – would you mind just coming in for a second, so I can show you the postcard, see what you think?'

Again she saw that same flicker across his face and this time there was no doubting the fear that was there. She stared at him, feeling uncomfortable herself now, wondering what was disturbing him, what had been able to break through the seemingly impenetrable defences that he carried around with him, like a shell.

He stared through the windscreen for a moment, saying nothing, then pushed the gear lever into reverse, with a strange, resigned motion, as if conceding defeat, and turned to look over his shoulder.

He seemed to be having difficulty climbing the steps, as if pushing against some unseen force. She watched him, hesitantly; it was as if he was wading through deep water.

He stopped as they reached the front door, and swayed, putting his hand on to the door frame for support. His face went sheet white, and he began to sweat. He closed his eyes tightly, and she looked at him, afraid.

'Philip? What's the matter?'

He looked up, rivers of sweat torrenting down his face. 'Fine,' he said. 'Fine. I'm fine. It's going; I'll be all right.'

'What, Philip?'

'It's all right.' He looked at her nervously. 'It's all right. Fine.' He smiled.

The smell hit them as they walked in through the front door. A vile, hideous stench. Alex gagged, turned around, and gulped in lungfuls of air from the street. Main put his hand over his nose, and looked around, silently.

'What is it?' She turned on the hall light; everything looked normal. 'It's like a dog –'

He shook his head. 'No, not a dog.'

She went into the kitchen, with her handkerchief over her nose. 'Not in here,' she said, lifting it away. 'Hardly smells at all in here.'

Main came down the stairs. 'No smell upstairs either.'

She went back into the hallway, where the stench was far worse, then outside and stood on the doorstep and sniffed the wet night air. 'It's inside, Philip,' she said. 'Maybe it's a dead mouse or something?' She looked at him, and saw him staring around wide-eyed, his face sheet white. 'Philip? Why don't you sit down? I'll open the windows.' She went into the drawing room and turned on the light; she felt her eyes pulled sharply down to the floor.

Lying there, as if they had been flung, were the postcard and the letter from Carrie.

The wall sloped sharply away from her. For an instant she had to bend her legs under the pressure, and then there was nothing beneath her at all, and she found herself running across the floor and crashing into the wall; she put her arms up for support and the wall seemed to push her away; she tottered back a few steps and fell over.

'Alex? Are you all right?'

She stared up giddily and saw Main staring down; it was almost as if she was watching everything from a distance, that she could see herself lying on the floor, looking up at

Main. She heard a voice, and it took a moment to recognize it as her own. 'I – I must have tripped.'

She saw a hand floating in the air; it gripped hers, pulled her up; she watched herself put her arms around Main, then suddenly, quite vividly, felt the crumpled softness of his jacket and the warmth of his chest. She hugged hard and felt his strong back muscles. 'On the floor,' she said. 'They were under the telephone when I went out, weighed down; someone's moved them.'

She felt his firm hands on her back, trembling; or was it she who was trembling, she wondered.

'Calm down, girl, calm down.'

She could tell from his tone that he was struggling to suppress the anxiety in his voice. What's the matter with you, she wanted to say. What the hell's the matter with you? She stared at him. 'Just another of those tricks of my mind?'

He looked down at his battered brown brogues, and coughed. His voice went into a quiet whisper, as if he was talking to himself. 'No, good Lord, no, it's not a trick.' He looked up at the ceiling and around the walls, pensively, still ruffled by anxiety. 'Drains, most likely.'

'I'm sorry,' she said, bending down and picking up the card and letter. 'Do you want some coffee?'

'Could I have a drop of whisky?'

'Help yourself; I'll put some coffee on.' She went out of the room.

Main walked to the cabinet, and poured himself a large whisky. Then he picked up the card and letter and walked over to an armchair. He sniffed again, and winced, looking up at the ceiling, then sat down, slowly. He held the whisky under his nose, and sniffed it gradually, then closed his eyes tight.

'Our Father,' he said, 'which art in Heaven, hallowed be Thy Name. Thy Kingdom come –'

'Philip? Are you asleep?'

He opened his eyes with a start, and felt his cheeks

reddening. 'Hmmm,' he replied, fumbling for his cig-arettes.

'What do you think?'

'Think?'

'About the letter?'

He looked down at the letter and read it carefully. He shrugged. 'Seems pretty definite. What does she mean, "weird"?'

'Not the content,' she said. 'The handwriting. Look at the postcard.'

'It's a little different,' he said. 'Might have been written balanced on her knees, or when she was stoned; looks basically the same.'

'But your friend Dead Rat would be able to tell?'

'Dendret?'

Alex saw his head suddenly whiplash around, as if trying to catch sight of something behind his shoulder, staring wildly. 'Are you O.K.?'

'What?'

She sat down on the arm of the chair and shivered. 'I don't think I can keep the windows open for ever; they don't seem to be making much difference.'

'Much difference?'

She put her hand on his forehead. It was damp and cold. 'Do you want to lie down?'

He stared blankly ahead, across the top of his whisky, and said nothing. Alex went out to pour her coffee; when she came back in, he was still sitting there. The smell in the room was venomous.

She sat down beside him again, on the arm of his chair, and saw the sweat again on his face. 'We'd be better in the kitchen – it's fine in there.' She looked at him, unsure that he had heard, and put her hand on his forehead again; she wondered for a terrible moment if he had had a stroke.

'I don't belong here,' he said, suddenly. 'I'm not wanted here.'

'Do you want me to call a doctor?' she said, becoming

alarmed at his incoherence. She waved her fingers in front of his eyes, looking for a flicker of movement, but there was none. 'Philip, do you want me to call a doctor?' She waited. 'Can you hear me?'

'Hallo, Mother.'

The words were gentle, crystal clear, as if Fabian was standing right beside her.

She whirled around, stared out at the hallway, then at the open windows. She ran over to them and looked out. The street was empty, nothing out there except the dark and the parked cars and the rain.

She had not imagined it.

She stared at Main, who was now trembling violently.

'Mother.'

The words had come from Main.

She watched him shaking, breathing heavily, and sensed the room getting colder. She saw the sweat running down his face, and watched him clenching his knuckles, so tight she thought his hands would break.

She stayed watching him.

Mother.

The word rang around inside her.

Suddenly he sprang to his feet, pushed his arms away from his body, and shouted in his own voice, 'No, I say, no!' He stared around the room, as if lost, confused, breathing deeply, then stared at Alex with eyes filled with terror, eyes that scarcely recognized her. 'I – must – go,' he said, slowly, hesitating after each word. 'I – must – go – now. I should not have come.'

'What's happening, Philip, please tell me.'

He stared fearfully around the room with the same expression on his face that she had seen on Iris Tremayne's, then he walked determinedly out into the hallway.

'Stay and talk to me.'

'Come with me.'

She shook her head.

'I'll wait for you in the car.'

'Dendret,' she said. 'Where do I find Dendret?'

He opened the front door and went outside, a complete stranger suddenly.

'Philip!' She heard her own voice, shrill, afraid, like the call of a lost chick. She turned and looked around the hall. She grabbed her bag, her coat and her keys, closed the door and ran down to the pavement.

Main was sitting in the Volvo in a thick cloud of cigarette smoke; as she slammed the door, he started the engine and drove off

'Philip, I want to stay here.'

He ignored her, and turned left into the King's Road. She looked at his face, which was expressionless. He was driving fast and she was being thrown around in her seat. The seat-belt warning light was flashing and clicking like a furious insect and she tried to ignore it. He said nothing until they were inside his flat.

He gave Alex a brandy and sat down with his whisky, stared at the floor then let out a low whistle. Alex sniffed the brandy and drank some; she felt it burning deep inside her stomach, clutched the huge balloon tightly with both hands and drank again, gratefully.

'What happened?'

He whistled again and pulled out his cigarettes.

'Was that Fabian speaking, or you?'

He offered her the pack, still without saying anything, and she shook her head, pulling one of her own out.

'You don't want to admit it, do you?' She watched his face redden, as the torment built up inside him, and wished for a moment that she too had said nothing. 'I'm sorry.'

She heard the click of his lighter and watched him stare at the tiny flame that was dancing in the draught; he stared at it intensely as if it was a genie he had summoned up to help him.

'Very unusual,' he said, suddenly.

Alex noticed for the first time how tired he was looking; his skin seemed to be hanging limply from his face, like a flannel on a washing line, everything wrung out of it.

'What do you mean?'

He shrugged and said nothing.

'Do you remember, in your last book, something you wrote?'

He drew hard on his cigarette and stared out into space; Alex shuddered; for an instant as the smoke drifted around him, he reminded her of a picture she had once seen of sallow ghouls in an opium den.

'You said that we are all prisoners of our genes.'

There was no flicker of response.

'You said that we cannot fight the programmes we are born with, and we cannot change them; the only liberty we have is to disagree with them.'

Slowly he nodded his head.

'That they were chosen for us at the moment of conception, random pickings from the selection of genes in the father's sperm and the mother's egg. In that split second is determined everything that is to be inherited or left out from each parent. Right?'

He turned and looked vaguely in her direction.

'You've inherited your father's powers, and you don't want to admit it.'

He looked away from her again and into space.

'Please explain it to me Philip; please explain what happened.'

'Just a theory, that's all,' he said, without looking at her. 'Just a theory, girl. There's no proof.'

'Not in genetic engineering?'

'That's a different sphere.'

'But I'm right, aren't I?'

He stared down at the floor. 'Maybe,' he said quietly. 'But it is considered unlikely. The colour of your hair is transmitted in genes, the shape of your nose. Psychic power is something different –' He shrugged. 'It's meant to be a gift.'

'Intelligence isn't passed on in genes?'

'Yes, of course it is.'

'I always thought intelligence was considered a gift.'

'Not at all.'

'What about behaviour? Is that passed on in genes?'

'To an extent.'

'So why not psychic powers?'

He stared at her for a moment, then looked away.

'Why didn't you want to come into the house? What happened?'

'It's all hokum, girl; I don't know where these spirits, voices, manifestations, whatever come from. We can only see a very narrow band of light waves, hear a narrow band of sound waves. Perhaps when we die we leave behind us imprints in other waves outside these, and some people are able to tune into them and pick them up. It doesn't mean they are still alive, somewhere else, doesn't mean that at all.'

'What does it mean?'

'That they've left an imprint, like a photograph. The trick is being able to see it.' He tapped his head. 'We probably all have the power, but most of us don't know how to use it; some do and keep quiet all their lives; some become mediums; it's a good con.' He looked at her, colour beginning to return to his face. 'I didn't want to con you.'

'Con me?'

He thought carefully before speaking. 'I had a feeling I might pick Fabian up; what good would it do you? Raking it all up, giving you some false hope that he's out there somewhere.'

She stared at him, leaned forward and crushed out her cigarette, startled at how fast she had smoked it. 'You're lying, Philip,' she said.

'I'm not lying, girl. I'm just trying to put it into plain English.'

'If that's all it was, you wouldn't have been so frightened. You were terrified about something. About what?'

He shook his head. 'You're imagining it; that's what happens when people dabble in this.'

'Philip.' She looked at him. 'Please look at me. You're my

146

friend. Do you seriously expect me to believe that if there is such a thing as an imprint that can be left behind, that after twenty-one years, all that is left of Fabian are two words? Hallo, Mother? Stop being evasive and tell me the truth.'

He picked up his whisky glass and studied it; he swirled the whisky around, sniffed it testily, then studied the glass again, carefully, as if searching for a hidden hallmark. He spoke without looking at her. 'It's possible there's a presence in your house; a malevolent one.'

Something wet and slimy trickled down her spine. She shivered, and drank some more brandy; it tasted like dry ice. She pulled the glass away sharply, her mouth burning, stared around the room, closed her eyes and tried to clear her mind. 'Surely, if there's a presence, it's Fabian?'

'Those who – believe in this are of the opinion that evil can be a very mischievous thing: that it can prey on the victims of grief, take advantage of their weakness, and their blindness to the truth.'

'What are you saying?'

'Rogue spirits, girl. One of them might be conning you now; trying to pretend he's your son.'

She stared at him for a long time in silence, trembling, despair soaking through her; she stared at him as if he was an outcrop of land to which she was moored; the last piece of land on earth.

'Why?' she said, finally, helplessly.

'Spirits sometimes try to come back.'

'Do they succeed?'

'There is evidence that they can possess people; and influence them. For good and – for bad.' He smiled, wryly.

Alex shook her head. 'You amaze me; you're so cynical, and yet – I don't know – you know so much more, don't you; you're like a stage, sometimes, with a hundred back-drops.'

He smiled. 'No, good Lord, no.' He shook his head. 'Don't overestimate me, girl.'

'Why do they try to come back?'

He twisted his glass round in his hand, then looked at Alex. He looked away, around the room, then back at his glass, twisting it again. Finally he looked up at her, his face heavy with doubt. The words came out slowly, as if dragged against some tremendous inner reluctance. 'Because they have unfinished business.'

CHAPTER EIGHTEEN

Arthur Dendret had a sharp pointed beard and a sharp pointed head; he moved around his office in short clockwork-like stages, as if governed by a program inside him.

Every inch of the available floor and shelving space of the cramped office was covered with untidy bundles of documents, and equally untidy stacks of reference books, and the walls were hung with cold, lifeless prints of Regency Terraces which revealed nothing about him. In contrast to his own size, his desk was vast and almost completely empty. The only relief on the acreage of flat green leather was a neat blotter, a magnifying glass and a framed photograph of a stern woman.

'Please, sit down.' He pulled off his gold half-rimmed glasses, peered accusingly at them and then replaced them. He laid both hands on the blotter, squinted at Alex and gave a wide, almost imbecilic grin.

She stared at his brightly checked suit, and his drab woollen tie, the colour of slime. 'Philip Main gave me your name.'

'Ah, yes.' His face screwed up like a sponge, he blinked furiously, and raised an arm in the air as if hailing a taxi. 'Dead Sea Scrolls. Very interesting. Thought he might have been on to something, for a time, but of course it ended up a blind alley; always does with the Scrolls, don't you think?'

Alex smiled politely. 'I'm afraid I wouldn't know.'

'No, well, he's a determined chap. Still –' He leaned back and looked expectantly at her.

Alex opened her handbag and laid the postcard and the letter on the wilderness. He stared at them for a moment, opened his drawer and pulled out a pair of tweezers. In turn he picked each one up and placed it down in front of him. 'Not Dead Sea Scrolls, these,' he said, 'not Dead Sea Scrolls at all.' He grinned, then chuckled, his shoulders moving up and down several times as if pulled by strings. He turned the postcard over with the tweezers. 'Ah, Boston, Cambridge, MIT, know this view well. Had a puncture on this bridge once; not a good place to have a puncture; not a good country to have a puncture in, America; not in a Peugeot, anyway.'

Alex stared at him curiously.

He pointed his index finger upwards. 'They have these spikes they put through the wheel, to get the tyre off; you can't do it on a Peugeot.' He turned the postcard back over. 'What can I do for you?'

'I want to know if the person who wrote the letter is the same person who wrote the postcard?'

Dendret picked up the magnifying glass and studied several lines of the letter carefully, then leaned over slightly and studied the postcard. As he read, his lips pursed and the action elongated his nose. He reminded Alex of a rather aggressive rodent.

Quite decisively, he put down the glass and leaned back in his chair; he looked up at the ceiling, closed his eyes for a second, then opened them again and stared directly at Alex. 'No, not at all. The writing on the postcard's a very poor imitation of the writing on the letter; there are eight points of difference clearly visible, just through the glass. The t bars for instance.' He shook his head. 'No, quite different. The spacing; pressure, slant, the loops – look at the loops! There really is no comparison to be had.'

He looked irritated, thought Alex, as if he had been expecting a glass of fine claret and only been given plonk. He picked the tweezers up and placed the items in front of her, without attempting to hide his disdain.

'I – er – I'm sorry,' she said. 'As a layman, I –'

'No, of course, you wouldn't.' His tone had become

almost belligerent. He took a deep breath and stared for a moment at the photograph of the stern woman; it seemed to calm him down, very slightly. He no longer stared at Alex, but through her. 'Frankly, I would have thought a child of six could have told those weren't the same.'

'Unfortunately,' said Alex, equally acidly, 'I don't have a child of six.'

Dendret produced an invoice pad from his drawer, pulled out a gold pen from his pocket. He wrote on the pad, then turned it upside down on to his clean blotter. 'That will be thirty pounds.'

Alex looked down at the imprint of the writing on the blotter, then at the crisp white piece of paper that he put down in front of her, using his fingers this time, not the tweezers.

She paid him in cash, and he slipped the notes possessively into his wallet, like a rat storing away food, she thought.

'Do give my regards to Mr Main.'

She sat in her car and stared at the postcard with a heavy heart. She read it for the hundredth time: 'Hi Mum, This is a really friendly place, lots of things happening, met some great people. Will write again soon. Love C.'

She looked at the franking. The word 'Boston' was just discernible. She tried to concentrate; who did she know in Boston? Or had been to Boston? Or anywhere in the States? Who had posted it? And the others? Who? Fabian? He'd never been to America, so far as she knew.

She drove straight to Cornwall Gardens, and rang Morgan Ford's bell. A woman's voice crackled through the entry-phone, and the latch released with a loud buzz.

She walked nervously up the stairs, and Ford's door was opened by a cluttered-looking girl with thickly lensed glasses and a thatch of floppy hair that covered most of the rest of her face; she reminded Alex of an Old English Sheepdog.

'Ah-ah,' said the girl, 'Mrs Willingham? Mr Ford won't keep you a moment.'

Alex shook her head. 'No, I don't have an appointment. I wondered if it was possible to see Mr Ford just for a quick moment?'

The girl smiled nervously. 'I think it would be best to – ah – make an appointment.' She shifted her weight from one foot to the other, then back again, whilst her head nodded up and down.

'I saw him yesterday, you see. It's just something I want to ask him – it's very important.'

The shifting of the girl's weight increased in tempo. 'I'll speak to him for you,' she said, earnestly but dubiously. 'Ah – ah – what did you say your name was?'

'Mrs Hightower.'

The girl nodded her head again and marched off in great long ungainly strides, her body stooped forward. Alex looked around the corridor; it was narrow and drab, with a gaudy red carpet and rough white rendering on the walls; it gave no clue at all as to the almost baroque magnificence of the drawing room it led to.

The girl clumped back towards her clutching a large diary. 'I'm afraid Mr Ford doesn't remember you at all.'

'But it was only yesterday!'

The girl shook her head. 'That's what he said.'

'It must be in your book, surely?'

The girl opened the diary. 'What time was it?'

'Half past ten.'

'No,' she shook her head. 'We had a Mrs Johnson then.'

Alex felt herself blushing. She stared at the thick lenses: it was like looking at the girl's eyes through the wrong end of a telescope. 'Ah, yes, of course; I gave my maiden name.'

'Mrs Shoona Johnson?' said the girl, dubiously.

'Yes.'

'One moment.' She trotted off again. This time Morgan Ford himself followed her out. He looked up at Alex, and smiled politely. 'Ah yes, you came – wasn't it yesterday?'

Alex nodded, and looked at his tiny pink hands and the enormous rhinestone ring. He was in a different grey suit today, a snappier one, with a louder tie and grey shoes with large gold buckles; yesterday he had looked like an insurance salesman, today he looked more like a games show host. 'I'm sorry to barge in on you,' she said, 'but I need to talk to you very urgently.'

He looked at his watch, and she saw the faint flicker of irritation on his face, which he managed to keep from his voice. 'I can give you just a couple of minutes, until my appointment arrives; I mustn't keep people waiting, you see,' he said, kindly.

The cats were still on sentry duty by the gas log fire, and watched her suspiciously.

'Perhaps you could remind me,' he said.

'My son was killed in a road accident in France; when a driver drove on the wrong side of the autoroute.'

'It does ring a bell.' He nodded to himself. 'You must forgive me – I see so many people.'

'You got very excited yesterday.'

He frowned. 'I did?'

For a moment she wanted to shout at him, clout him on the ear. Then despair took over and the anger slipped away. 'It's no good,' she said, 'if you can't remember what happened; I wanted to ask you about something my son said.'

'Please – sit down.'

Alex sat in the same chair and saw the tom approaching her, slowly, walking in a wide arc.

Ford smiled at her, with a slightly distant look in his eyes. 'Perhaps if you gave me something close to you, a bracelet or a watch?'

'I gave you my watch yesterday.'

'That would be the best, then.'

She nodded and unclipped the clasp.

He sat down beside her, and held the watch out. 'Ah yes,' he said, 'ah yes. Very strong feelings.' He shook his head. 'Incredible; remarkable. What is it you want to know?'

'I was rude to you yesterday, because I didn't believe

what you told me. Certain things have happened since then.'
She looked at him carefully, searching for something shifty
in his face, for a flicker, a blush, for the hint of something
uncomfortable. But all she saw was a polite smile. 'You told
me that my son, Fabian, wanted to come back; what did
you mean?'

Ford looked at her. 'There are feelings coming through
that are immensely strong. There is a spirit here who is
earthbound, presumably your son, but there are so many
other things going on, much conflict, I sense a girl, I'm
sorry, there isn't time now, but we must do something. He
is earthbound, confused; we must do something for him.'

'What do you mean, earthbound?' She heard the buzzer
ring in the hallway.

'That he hasn't gone over. It's a common occurrence, I'm
afraid, in a sudden death, like an accident or a murder; the
spirit needs to be helped over. He may not be aware that he
has died, you see.' He smiled.

'There's nothing –' she paused '– nothing malevolent?'

He smiled and handed her back the watch. 'There's evil
everywhere; but we protect ourselves against it. Simple
procedures – there is no need to worry – providing we
conduct everything properly.' He looked at her and she
tried to read his expression.

Without warning, the cat jumped into her lap, and she
felt her heart miss a beat.

'The environment is very important. You see, an earthbound spirit gets lost very easily; nothing is familiar; he tries to
talk to people and wonders why they don't answer back.' Ford
smiled. 'He has no energy, because he has no body to give him
energy. We have a circle, and the circle creates energy, like a
beacon. He can find his way to the circle, then we can bring in
spirit guides who can take him off, over to the other side.'

'Do you mean a séance?'

Ford winced. 'Circle is better; I think séance has a rather
vulgar tone to it; seaside gypsy ladies and all that.' He smiled
again.

'I know you're in a hurry – I'll be quick. You said yesterday that a girl was coming through, someone called Carrie. Can you remember anything about that?'

He shrugged. 'There were so many channels yesterday, all trying to come through, so much confusion.'

'It's very important.'

'I'm sure it will all become clear when we start the circle. Now, we need somewhere suitable, somewhere familiar to your son; in your home would be best, if you have no objections?'

Alex shook her head.

'What about your husband?'

'We're separated.'

He nodded. 'Was your son fond of your husband?'

'Yes.'

'Then I would like your husband to be there. We need people to give the power; it's very important to have some people close to him. Are there any brothers or sisters?'

Alex shook her head.

'Do you have any other relatives?'

'No.' She paused. 'My husband's very sceptical, I'm afraid.'

'So are you.' He smiled, a warm kind smile. 'It is important. A father can give you so much energy in a situation like this.'

Alex stared at him hesitantly, but said nothing.

'Also, if you have any other friends, people that knew him, who would be prepared to come, it would be helpful. I can bring people, you see, but it is much better if there are others that knew him.'

'How many others?'

'At least two others. We must have a minimum of five, preferably more. Now, let's make a date. The evening would be best; do you have a room without windows?'

'I have a photographic darkroom.'

'Perfect.'

'No, I'm sorry, it wouldn't be big enough.'

'Any room would do, perhaps his own bedroom would be best; but it's a room you should not use for anything else as long as the circle continues. You must make sure the windows are well sealed, so that no light can come in, no light at all, do you understand?'

'Yes.'

'And you must eat nothing for six hours before. No one must.'

'Six hours?'

'And everyone must have a bath before and wear clean clothes. These are my rules and they must be obeyed.'

Alex listened to the gentle lilt of his voice and frowned at the detail; why did these people have to be so obsessed with ritual, she wondered? Why couldn't they just get on with it?

'You must clean the room thoroughly, hoover very carefully. Evil attaches to dirt, you see, the dirt in the room, on our bodies, the waste products in our systems; we must give evil the least possible chance.' He stood up and she followed him down the corridor; the new arrival was nowhere to be seen. Who was it, Alex wondered? What did they look like? Why had they come?

'Margaret!' said Ford, loudly. 'Could I have the diary?'

The secretary trotted obediently out of a door and handed the book to him. 'A Tuesday or a Thursday would be best,' he said, 'and you must keep the same day each week clear for several weeks ahead. It may be immediate, it may take a while; continuity is essential. Now, today is Tuesday; no, there wouldn't be enough time. How about this Thursday? Could you manage that?'

She nodded. 'Somehow.'

He showed her out himself. 'You must persuade your husband,' he said. 'It really is most important.'

'Yes.'

She tried once more to read his face. It seemed that there was something beyond that gentle smile; something that he knew and did not want to tell.

CHAPTER NINETEEN

'I believe everyone is wonderful and has something special to offer the world.' The woman whispered the words in an awestruck Californian accent, as if her personal discovery was a secret she wished to keep from the three million radio listeners. Alex wondered if she was holding the interviewer's hands and staring into her eyes. 'Tibetans will tell people if they're troubled to go and walk under pines, they've been doing it for fifteen hundred years.'

'Gosh!' said the interviewer.

'Crap,' said Alex, leaning forward and snapping off the radio. The world was full of people who'd discovered the secret of life, who saw it lying in undigested lumps of sweetcorn in their stools; Christ, did you have to stare down lavatories or walk under pines to cope with life? Lucky for them that they had the time. Lucky for them that they had nothing better to do.

She swung the Mercedes off the road and onto the rough cart track, through the gateposts with the small hand painted sign that read 'Château Hightower', and smiled. At least David had never lost his sense of humour; nor, she thought fondly, his patience. He should have divorced her and got another woman by now, someone who would love him, make him happy. He deserved that; but right now she was glad he hadn't.

After a few hundred yards the track, as usual, turned into a quagmire, and the car lurched and bumped through the gates of the pig farm with its appalling stench; muddy water splashed on to the windscreen and she put the wipers on. A filthy dog ran out of an outhouse and barked at her. She passed the pens and the farmhouse, and drove through another gate, past another sign marked 'Château Hightower', with an arrow underneath it. She could see the small cluster of buildings a mile or so down to her right, nestling in the valley of the South Downs, the fields of vines staked out, and sheep scattered incongruously on the slopes around, like white bushes.

As she drove down the steep hill the lake came into view on the left, a weird lifeless expanse of water with a strange man-made island in the centre. The estate agent's blurb had described it as a unique medieval pond believed to contain rare carp; it had excited David at the time more than the buildings. Carp, she thought, there were people who believed eating carp was the secret to eternal youth.

She passed the huge open-sided barn that contained a rusting tractor and a pyramid of manure, and pulled up in the muddy courtyard in front of the ramshackle flint cottage that was David's home and, for a brief time, until the isolation and the cold had finally become too much, had been hers also.

It had been a long time since she had been down here and little had changed. The stable block on the far side of the courtyard still looked as if it was about to collapse, in spite of the freshly painted sign of the wall which read: 'Château Hightower Reception'. She smiled again; the absurd grandeur of the name always made her smile. A mud-spattered Collie sloped out of a doorway and looked at her dozily.

'Hallo, Vendange,' she said.

The dog managed a single flick of its tail, then dipped its nose and sniffed something on the ground. She walked past David's Land Rover over to the stables, opened the reception door, and looked in. It was a cold, musty room, with a stone floor and an old kitchen table with an even older cash register perched on top. Two half-empty bottles with Château Hightower labels stood there, their corks sticking out of their necks like ill-fitting top hats. The rest of the room was piled high with white boxes, all with Château Hightower stencilled in green. She went out and the door swung shut behind her with a loud bang.

She walked the length of the courtyard to a tall flint barn at the end, which looked as if it might once have been a chapel, and went in. It was dank and cold, with a stale vinous smell like an empty pub.

Her husband was standing down at the far end between two massive plastic vats, deep in thought. She walked past a shiny red grape-crushing machine, past a row of smaller plastic vats, and a large glass jar filled with an opaque liquid. He raised a wine glass to his nose, sniffed thoughtfully, then tipped the contents into a drain cut into the centre of the floor.

'Hallo, David,' she said.

He looked up with a start. 'Good God!' He smiled and scratched his beard. 'You gave me a fright!'

'I'm sorry.'

He walked towards her, his arms open; he was wearing a grimy denim jacket and tattered cotton trousers. She felt the prickle of his beard against her face and the cold wetness of his lips.

'Aren't you frozen in that?'

'Is it cold? I hadn't noticed.'

She looked down at his feet. 'I thought farmers wore wellies – not bedroom slippers.'

'I'm not a farmer,' he said, with a hurt expression. 'I'm a chatelain.'

She smiled. 'I'm sorry, I forgot.'

'Anyway, they keep my feet warm. Here, I want you to taste this.' He walked over to one of the giant vats and half-filled the glass from a tap on the side. 'Forget the colour, it's very young; it'll clarify.'

She looked dubiously at the murky grey liquid, then sniffed it; there was a soft, flowery smell.

'Good nose, eh?'

She nodded.

'It'll get stronger. But not bad, eh?'

She tasted the wine and winced at the coldness. Dutifully, she swilled it around in her mouth, looking at him for instructions as to whether to swallow it or spit it out. She saw the desperate eagerness in his eyes, like a child waiting for praise. In contrast to its nose, the wine had a dull steely taste; something almost buttery. She swallowed, wondering if it was the right thing to do. 'Hmmm,' she said, pensively. She saw the enthusiasm waver on his face and doubt appear. 'It's very nice. Very nice.'

Happiness flooded across him, and he rubbed his hands together gleefully. 'I think I've cracked it, don't you?'

'All your wines are very nice, David.'

He shook his head. 'Everything I've done to date has been rubbish, a con, a copy of something else; second rate Alsace. I've tried to copy Breaky Bottom, St Cuthmans, and everything else that I thought was good.' He shook his head and clapped his hands. 'Originality. I want to create a great English wine, something distinctive, unique.' He formed a circle between his forefinger and his thumb. 'And limit the production; that's the secret. They'll be queueing all the way to the road for it.'

'If they can stand the smell of pigs.'

He looked hurt and she was sorry she had made the remark.

'Did you – did you really like it?' he said.

She nodded.

'It's got a long way to go yet; you realize what it is don't you?'

'Yes,' she lied, giving him a reassuring smile.

He looked relieved. 'I knew you would; at least if you picked up nothing else from being married to me, you learned your wines.'

She smiled again, reassuringly.

'I think Fabian would have been proud of this. He came down for the vendange last year; he helped pick these grapes. It's going to be very special, isn't it?'

She nodded.

'Chardonnay!' he exclaimed, looking up at the ceiling; he repeated the word, loudly, clearly, like a Bible thumper in the pulpit. 'Chardonnay!' The word echoed around the cold damp barn, and his teeth shone maniacally through his beard.

Alex shuddered; he seemed such a stranger, suddenly.

'Montrachet, Corton Charlemagne!' He kissed the tips of his fingers.

'I need to talk to you,' she said.

'I could make twenty-five thousand bottles this year; that's not bad is it?'

'I need to talk to you, David.'

He held out his hands. 'Look, look at these.'

She stared at the grime in his nails and in the pores of the skin.

'I used to have them manicured in London, didn't I? Do you remember?'

She nodded.

'My hands were beautiful – it's just everything I did with them was crap. Now they're filthy, ugly, but with them I create great beauty. Isn't that wine wonderful?'

'Yes; I hope it does very well for you. Can we go in the house and talk?'

'Sure.' He took the glass from her and walked towards the door; he stopped and patted a huge stainless steel trough. 'For fermentation,' he said proudly. 'No other winery in England has one like this.' He looked up at Alex, and she stared into his sad brown eyes. This was the world he'd rejected London for, the life he'd rejected his big salary and fast cars and smart suits and expensive manicures to live; to do his own thing: this cold dingy building with its sour smell and strange machines, the rows of vines and the sheep and the solitude.

'Are you happy?' she said.

'I'm doing what I want.'

'But are you happy?'

He shrugged and walked in. She followed him out of the building into the bright daylight, across the yard with the smell of mud and dog and manure, and ducked after him through the low doorway into the cottage.

He filled the kettle from the tap in the stone sink and put it on the Aga. Alex sat down at the pine table and instinctively brushed some breadcrumbs into the palm of her hand.

'Do you want anything to eat?'

She shook her head, and emptied the crumbs into the large brown paper bag that was the waste bin.

'It's nice seeing you. You haven't been down for a long time.'

She looked at the heap of plates and dishes piled around the drying rack, and smiled. 'You ought to get a dish-washer.'

He shook his head. 'No good for wine glasses; leaves a deposit.'

'You make it hard.'

He shrugged. 'Not much else to do when it's dark; might as well wash the dishes.'

The kettle made a faint-hearted hiss, like a sigh, she thought. 'I went to a medium.'

He wiped a mug carefully with a dishcloth and looked at her. 'And?'

'He got in touch with Fabian.'

David put the mug down and pulled a tobacco tin out of his pocket.

'I know what your feelings are on the subject, but there are some things that have been happening – some very strange things.'

'What sort of things?'

Alex stared at an old wooden clock on a shelf. Four-fifteen. 'Is that the time?' she said weakly, looking at her own watch for confirmation.

'It's usually a few minutes fast.'

'I was meant to be at Penguin at four.' She shook her head.

David looked at her. 'Important?'

She nodded. 'It's taken a month to set it up.'

'Can't someone else go for you?'

'No.'

'I thought you had some good assistants.'

'I do, but I have to be there myself for this one.' She looked at her watch. 'I'd be lucky to get there by six.' She found herself blaming David; it was his fault that she had forgotten, that she was stuck down here, in this filthy kitchen, in the middle of bloody nowhere. His fault that she might have blown one of her best-ever deals. 'Can I use your phone?' she said, lamely.

'You don't need to ask; you own half of it.'

'I don't want a lecture,' she snapped, 'I just want to use the bloody –' She paused, bit her lip; there was no point in getting mad; no point in trying to blame David, or anyone else.

'You were pretty convincing.'

'I think I've salvaged it.' She dug her hands into her coat pocket. The wellingtons were slightly too big and her feet slipped about inside them; she wondered whose they were.

The track squelched and moved beneath the weight of their feet as they walked along below the fields of vines; endless rows of thin gnarled branches, unrelieved by any greenery or flowers, they stood like a regiment of skeletons at the gates to Hades. Alex shuddered, worried by the horrific thoughts that had been coming into her mind recently. She slipped, and grabbed on to David's arm; it was rigid, powerful, and his strength surprised her; she had forgotten how strong he was.

'O.K.?'

'Fine.'

'Finished pruning on Sunday,' he said, proudly. 'Three months, almost to the day.'

'Good,' she said, enthusiastically, assuming that it was. The afternoon light was fading, and the air was turning sharp. She heard the bleat of a sheep, and a light aircraft droned high above them.

'You think I'm cracking up, don't you?' she said.

'No, I don't think that,' he said, looking annoyed suddenly. 'How the hell did the sheep get up there, look.' He pointed, and Alex followed the line of his finger up the hillside beyond the vineyard.

'Doesn't Vendange keep them under control?'

'Bloody dog's not interested in sheep; all he wants to do is sleep and chase rabbits.'

'There must be something wrong with his genes.'

David looked at her oddly, then up at his vineyard again. 'Bloody things. Must be another hole in the fence.' He shook his head. 'I think you're under a lot of strain and it's showing, isn't it? You've always been super-efficient, that's how you've succeeded; you'd never have forgotten an appointment in the past. Roses in windscreens, in bowls. There are a lot of red roses in the world, Alex. Nice to think they're a message from Fabian, but it's a little improbable; you're clutching at coincidences, putting a meaning to them, and screwing yourself up in the process.'

'I am not screwing myself up,' she said angrily.

At the end of the vineyard the track forked. 'Shall we walk around the lake?'

'Sure,' she said.

They walked through a short wood and came out on to the bank of the lake. Alex stared at it and felt unsettled; she had never felt comfortable with it, and now it had a sinister, almost menacing feel. Medieval pond: the estate agent's description had never left her mind since she had first read the blurb. She wondered if it had ever been drained. and what secrets were buried at the bottom of it. She smelt the flat stagnant smell, saw the thick reeds, like dead men's fingers, and the strange octagonal concrete island a hundred yards out in the middle. There was a ballroom underneath, at the bottom of the lake. The agent had taken them there once, hastily. It had been built at the end of the last century by an eccentric engineer who had had something to do with designing the London Underground, according to the agent. Now it wasn't considered safe any more.

She shuddered at the memory of the place; they had gone in through a door in the bushes somewhere nearby and down into a tunnel under the lake, opening and closing various watertight doors as they went – a precaution against flooding, the agent had said. And then they had come into a vast room, with a domed glass roof covered in slime and tendrils of weed, the occasional dark shape of a fish just distinguishable from the murky water. There had been an ominous puddle of water on the floor, and the agent had looked up nervously and declared that the roof could cave in at any time. That was four years ago.

'Remember going into that ballroom?' she said to David.

He nodded.

'Is it still standing?'

'I've been meaning to have a look; I'll go out in the boat with a snorkel one day and see if it's still there.'

'You could go down the tunnel.'

He shook his head. 'Too dangerous; if there's a leak and one of the sections has filled up, you'd be drowned if you opened the door. Fabian used to be obsessed by the place; I gave him quite a bollocking last year when I caught him going down there.' He shrugged. 'It's a pity; it would have been a good place for a party.'

'I thought you didn't like parties any more.'

'It would go with my chatelain image, don't you think? Launching the new vintage with a party under the lake?'

She smiled.

He pulled his tobacco tin out and prised off the lid. 'Look, Alex, I didn't mean what I said as a criticism. I'm very fond of you still; I always will be – that's my problem and I have to cope with it. Fabian's dead. Mediums are charlatans. They'll take your money for as long as you'll pay them.' He rubbed the cigarette tightly between his fingers, then put it between his lips; they stopped and he clacked his lighter; Alex smelt the sweet smoke for an instant.

'How did the medium know the truth about the lorry?'

'He didn't. He read in the papers that it was a lorry,

which you knew was wrong; by a sheer fluke the boys in the car thought it was a lorry, and that makes you think the medium is a genius. Anyway, you gave a false name – there probably was someone called Johnson whose son was killed by a lorry; there are hundreds killed on the roads every week. Think about it.'

'He didn't say that it was a lorry. He said that Fabian was saying it was a lorry.'

'Look, see what we're doing; raking it all up again.' He shook his head. 'Your medium chap, Ford, or whatever his name is, told you that he was in touch with Fabian?'

Alex nodded.

'So what you're implying is that Fabian's lived on – is still living on, since the accident, albeit in another world – the spirit world, or whatever?'

She nodded again.

'So surely he would have realized after the accident that he was mistaken, that it was a car not a lorry? Why didn't he tell the medium?'

She stared ahead across the water and tried to block out his words. A ripple appeared suddenly and she wondered if it was a fish. She felt tired and drained, as if all the energy had been vacuumed out of her body, and she was left weighed down by a coat of heavy lifeless flesh. 'How do you explain Philip Main?' she said, but there was no fight left in her words.

'Your hearing Fabian's voice coming from him?'

'Yes.'

'He's probably acting; maybe he's a good actor.'

'Why should he do that? Anyway, it happened with you, too, David. It was as if you'd – you changed into him. I heard his voice coming from you.'

He shrugged. 'The mind can play strange tricks.'

They stood in silence for a moment.

'I'm cold,' she said. 'I'd like to go back now.'

They turned around and walked in silence. There was a loud plop near them.

'A fish!' said David.

'It sounded big.'

He nodded, and smiled sadly. 'Fabian would have made a much better fisherman than me; he had more patience.'

'It's funny how you can see different sides of your own child; I never thought he was patient; he used to fly into the most frightful tantrums when he was younger, if he didn't get what he wanted immediately. Dreadful, it used to frighten me.'

'He had a good nose for wine. I think he could have gone a long way in wine, if he'd wanted.' He noticed the scorn on Alex's face. 'A growth industry,' he said, defensively. 'When he was last down here, only a few weeks ago, he tasted the Chardonnay; got it right away. That's pretty good.'

'A few weeks ago?'

'Yes.'

'He told me he hadn't been down since before Christmas.'

David smiled apologetically. 'Perhaps he didn't want to offend you, make you – I don't know – jealous or something.' He shrugged. 'He'd been coming down a lot just lately, particularly since Christmas.'

Alex felt uncomfortable and wasn't sure why. 'What was he doing?'

'Helping me a bit with the pruning. He really seemed to be getting quite interested in the place. I got the feeling he was thinking of joining me here after Cambridge. Of course it wouldn't have been practical, not at the moment anyway, because of the money. A couple of years, though, and we could be in profit.'

'Did he come alone?'

'Yes. I'm sorry – you're not upset are you?'

'No, no of course not; I'm pleased that you were such good friends; it's nice.'

'I wish I'd got to know him better, really; he was very deep. I used to watch him sitting out there on the island, fishing for hours on end, and wonder what he was thinking.'

'What do you think about when you're fishing?'

He shrugged. 'You, I suppose.'

'Me?' she smiled.

He relit his cigarette. 'The happy times we had together. When we first met. How I can win you back.' He turned and looked at her, and for a moment then they stopped walking and stared at each other; then Alex looked down at the ground.

'It's really turning cold,' she said, starting to walk on again.

'Do you have to go back to London tonight?'

'Why?'

'I'd like you to stay and have dinner. Or we could go out. We were going to have a date this week.'

'Haven't you got some bird turning up?'

'Bird? No, crikey, no.'

'The one that owns these boots?' She saw him go red.

'I don't know whose those are,' he muttered, awkwardly. 'I think we inherited them with the house.'

She smiled. 'I don't mind, if you – you know –'

He shook his head. 'Are you going to stay?'

'I'll have supper, then I must get back.'

'Stay down tonight, unwind; you look so tensed up – I'll sleep in the spare room – you can have my room – it's nice and warm.'

'I'll see,' she said.

They went into the tiny drawing room, and Alex kept her coat on whilst David lit the fire. 'Only use this room when I have visitors, otherwise I live in the kitchen.'

'I'm happy in the kitchen.'

'No, it's cosy here once it warms up. You used to like this room.'

She nodded and stared around at the photographs, at the old battered furniture, and the elderly Bang and Olufsen music centre. She remembered the day they bought it; she had been knocked out by the design of the thing. How large and clumsy it looked now. There was a picture of Fabian on

168

a tricycle, and a very recent black and white close up, face on to the camera, with a penetrating stare that unsettled her, made her turn away. She watched the flames dancing in the grate, and savoured the smell of the smoke.

'Give it a few minutes and it'll be nice and snug. Put some music on if you like.' David started to walk out of the room.

'What sort of music do you listen to these days?'

He shrugged. 'Mostly Beethoven.' He looked at her. 'Why are you smiling?'

'Nothing.'

He went through into the kitchen and Alex followed him, smiling again, to herself.

'I just find that amusing, I suppose. I tried to teach you to appreciate classical music and you wouldn't have it, you said it made you feel too old; you'd never listen to anything but pop.'

'I quite liked jazz,' he said, defensively.

'It's funny, isn't it, how we all change.'

'Have you changed?' he said, running the tap and washing his hands.

'Yes.'

'I don't think you have.'

'I used to be frivolous, like you; now I'm serious and so are you.'

'At least we've changed together.'

I wish we had, she thought, sadly.

They sat at the kitchen table, facing each other across a candle flickering in a saucer, and David ladled out the stew.

'It doesn't bother you, that it's your own sheep?'

'No. Probably would have done when I lived in London. The country changes your attitudes.'

She dipped her fork into her plate, blew on the end then tasted it. 'Good; very good.'

He shrugged and looked proud.

'There's another reason why I want to see the medium again, David.'

'Potatoes?'

She nodded. 'I think Fabian may have —'

'Carrots?'

'Thanks.'

'May have what?'

'You know the girl, Carrie, he was going out with?'

'Yes.'

'She ditched him after Christmas.'

'Did she? He never mentioned it.'

'He did to me. He told me he'd ditched her — probably just his pride.'

'No one likes admitting they've been ditched.'

'No. But I thought she should be told, you know —'

'Of course.'

'I went to see her mother; the mother hasn't seen her for a long time; she said she was in the States and showed me some postcards, recent ones, that Carrie had written.'

David poured some wine.

'When I was going through Fabian's things, I found some identical postcards, and a letter from Carrie in which she told him she didn't want to see him again. I thought it rather odd that he should have the same postcards — what did he want with blank postcards — all from Boston?'

He shrugged.

'I'd pinched one of the postcards from Carrie's mother, and I compared the handwriting with her letter; it didn't look quite the same, so I took them along to a handwriting expert.'

'A graphologist?'

'Yes. I was trying to remember the word.' She stared at him. 'David, the postcard Carrie sent to her mother from Boston, postmarked seven days ago, wasn't written by Carrie. It was written by Fabian.'

He sat down and stared at her through the steam of the stew and the flickering light. 'Are you absolutely sure?'

'Yes.'

He shook his head. 'What are you saying?'

Alex shrugged.

'Are you trying to say that he is still alive?'

'You went to France.'

He swallowed and went white, nodding slowly. 'So what's it all about?'

'That's why I want to see the medium.'

He was silent for a long time, while the food cooled in front of him. 'I'm sure there's an explanation,' he said, finally. 'Probably a very simple one.'

'We have a choice, don't we. Either a medium, or the police.'

'Or we could do nothing.'

Alex shook her head. 'No, we can't.'

CHAPTER TWENTY

She hoovered Fabian's room herself, drew the curtains and taped them all the way around against the wall. Then she turned out the light and stood in the pitch dark. She felt a chill like a cold draught down her neck and began to tremble. She fumbled for the light switch and couldn't find it. She heard the scraping of her hand against the flat wall. The switch had gone. No. She felt the crack of the door, heard the clunk as she rubbed against the handle, saw the faintest glow of light through the curtains, heard her own heavy breathing.

She found the switch and snapped on the light, sighing with relief, too scared to look at Fabian's portrait on the wall.

The room had a strange emptiness without the bed, which Mimsa had helped her to move out in the morning, and she stared at the six empty chairs, wondering how Ford would want them arranged. There was so much she should have asked him, she realized, as she unplugged the hoover and carried it downstairs.

It was six o'clock. She wondered whether to put peanuts out; were they allowed to drink? To smoke? The house had a cheerless, expectant feel. Could she put music on, she wondered?

The doorbell rang and she went down. David stood there in a sombre suit and dark tie and for a moment she hardly recognized him.

'Hi,' he said.

She blinked. 'You came!'

'I said I would.'

'Thank you.' She leaned forward and kissed him lightly. 'I – I thought you might not. You're looking very smart.'

'I wasn't sure what to wear.'

They went through to the drawing room. 'Would you like a drink?'

'Am I allowed one?'

She smiled, nervously. 'I don't know. I think I need one.'

He pulled out his tin of tobacco. 'Is it all right if –?'

She shrugged.

'I don't think Fabian would mind.'

'Oh sod it, let's have a drink.' She poured out two generous whiskys. They clinked glasses.

'Cheers,' he said.

She smiled, nervously.

'Who's coming?'

'Sandy.'

'Sandy? That loony.'

'She's the only person – friend – I could think of who wouldn't think we were bonkers.'

They sat down and she watched David roll a cigarette.

'Thanks for Tuesday night.'

'It was nice having you down.'

'It can't have been very comfy for you; that room was never warm.'

'I was fine. Having you in the house warmed it up. It gets lonely down there at nights.'

'I thought you enjoyed that.'

He shrugged. 'We make our beds, we have to lie in them.'

She smiled again, trying to think of something else to say; it was like making small talk with a stranger. She drank some whisky and felt more confident. She looked up at the wall. 'You never took that picture of the horse.'

'It looks good where it is, I don't mind; anyhow, the damned thing never brought me much luck.' He lit his cigarette and took a long pull on his whisky. 'Seven o'clock?'

She nodded.

He checked his watch. 'Been doing any more photography?'

She shook her head. 'Not since —'

He smiled and shook his head. 'What did you do last night?'

'Stayed at the office till about eleven, then brought a pile of work home. I didn't sleep much — I couldn't — I was thinking about this evening all the time.'

'Don't expect too much.'

She smiled, wearily, then looked up at the ceiling; she heard the beating of her own heart, as loud as war drums, she thought, and wondered if David could hear it too. The doorbell rang, a long positive ring, so long it became almost aggressive. She saw David start to get up. 'I'll go,' she said.

A tall meek-looking man in his early sixties stood there; he had grey hair cropped to a close stubble and his ears, which were too large, looked as if they had been stuck on as an afterthought. He was far too thin, she thought.

'Oh, er, is Mr Ford here?' He stooped, as if embarrassed about his height, and spoke in a timid voice that was scarcely louder than a whisper.

'He should be here any minute.'

'Ah. I'll wait outside then.'

'You're very welcome to come in.'

The man smiled. 'Thank you. I'm here for the circle, you see, tonight.'

Alex nodded, closed the door behind him, and ushered him into the drawing room. 'This is my husband, David.' She looked at the man's creased brown polyester suit and noticed he had huge feet.

'How do you do,' said David, standing up. 'David Hightower.'

'Pleased to meet you.' He raised a hand nervously forward then withdrew it again, before David had had time to shake it. 'Milsom.'

'Come for the er —?'

Milsom nodded.

'Would you like a drink?' said Alex.

The man looked around, hesitantly. 'A squash, if you have one, please.'

Alex went out of the room. 'What do you – do?' she heard David say. She paused in the hallway.

'I'm with the Post Office.'

'Ah. What do you do for them?'

'I deliver letters.'

'Ah. A postman?'

'Yes, yes.'

'Ah,' she heard David pause. 'Interesting.'

'Yes.'

There was a silence. She went into the kitchen and poured out an orange juice. When she returned to the drawing room, they were still standing facing each other, both staring at the ground in silence.

'Mr Milsom's a postman,' said David, brightly.

'Really?' She handed Milsom his drink. 'You're a friend of Morgan Ford?'

Milsom went red. 'Well, colleague, really; I help out sometimes.' He went even redder, and tapped his throat. 'Sometimes the spirits speak through me, you see.' He gave a nervous embarrassed laugh.

Alex caught David's eye and saw him fight the smirk off his face.

'Ah,' said David.

The doorbell rang again and Alex escaped, relieved, to answer it. Morgan Ford, Sandy, and a young man she had never seen before were standing there.

'Darling!' said Sandy, her jet black haystack of hair wilder than ever, a purple cloak billowing around her. 'You never told me it was Morgan Ford – we just met here on the doorstep! This is the finest medium in the country. Why didn't you tell me? How did you persuade him to come?'

Ford stood quietly like a man standing in his own shadow, holding an enormous tape recorder. He looked even smaller out of his own environment, Alex thought.

'Hallo, Mrs Hightower,' he smiled politely, and she shook his tiny hand, feeling the sharp edges of the rhinestone ring. 'May I introduce Steven Orme.'

'How do you do.' She held out her hand, and shook his; it felt cold and bony and had no energy in it, as if it was completely detached from him. Orme was in his early twenties, with slicked back hair and a large gold earring in one ear. He had an elongated deadpan face and cold half-closed eyes. A creep, she thought, and wondered if he was Ford's boyfriend.

'Please, come in.'

'There's one other who should be arriving.'

'I think he's already here.'

Ford nodded.

They went through into the drawing room. 'I wasn't sure,' she said to Ford, 'whether we are allowed to drink or smoke?'

'It's best to avoid anything, if you can.' He stared at David. 'Good,' he said. 'This must be your husband?'

'Yes,' said Alex.

'Excellent; perfect.'

'Why?' said Alex, curiously.

'He's exactly what I imagined; not psychic. It's important to have an earth, you see, like the earth wire in an electric plug, there should be one person in the circle who is not receptive; it helps a great deal in protecting the circle.'

'So clever of you, darling, you couldn't have a better person,' said Sandy, shedding her cloak and allowing a gossamer purple gown to unfurl around her.

Ford smiled modestly, or at least made a good pretence of modesty, thought Alex.

'Perhaps I could see the room, Mrs Hightower?'

She led Ford upstairs. He was immaculately dressed in grey, as before. Everything about him looked freshly pressed; even his grey socks.

'Perfect,' he said, laying down the cassette player. He looked up at the portrait. 'Yes, exactly as I imagined him. It's good, to have that. Yes, this is a good room, I can feel him here, he's comfortable here, he knows this room.'

He walked around the room, looking at the posters on the

wall, the telescope and examined the curtains. 'Is there a socket?'

She showed him.

'Saves the batteries,' he smiled, uncoiling a wire from the player. 'He's here already, you know, just waiting for us.' He turned and smiled again, and Alex had a sudden urge to throw him and the rest of them out, now. He was annoying her, kneeling on the floor, fiddling with his cassette, too mean to use his own batteries.

She looked at the portrait on the wall and Fabian stared back, coldly, arrogantly; she thought of his charred corpse, and shuddered, and wondered.

'Are we doing the right thing?' she said, suddenly.

'It's entirely up to you, Mrs Hightower. If you don't want to go ahead, just say so, please. There's no point in proceeding unless you want to communicate with your son, no point at all.' He pushed a switch on the player and she saw a green light come on. 'I'm ready,' he said.

'Would you like me to fetch them?'

'Thank you.'

She went down the stairs slowly, heard the stilted murmur of uncertain conversation, and stopped, feeling a sense of dread. It wasn't right. Nothing was right. Iris Tremayne might have been loopy; Philip Main was eccentric, yes, but not loopy. Something had frightened him, frightened a man she had thought was beyond fear; something in this house. Was she going to be destroyed tonight? Made mad? She felt a cold draught again, down her neck. It wasn't too late, she thought, she could stop it now.

Sandy came out into the hall. 'Must just nip to the loo, darling.'

'Under the stairs,' said Alex.

'Won't be a sec.'

'Sandy,' she said, walking down the rest of the stairs. 'Have you seen Iris Tremayne recently?'

Sandy looked at her oddly. 'No darling.'

She was lying.

Alex walked into the drawing room trembling. Why had Sandy lied? She picked up a pack of cigarettes and shook one out; her hands were shaking so much, she couldn't open her lighter. David suddenly stood in front of her holding a match. She inhaled the smoke and then took another deep drag. 'I think we're ready,' she said. 'Would you all like to come upstairs?'

She stubbed out the cigarette, reluctantly, and led them into the hallway. There was a dreadful scream, the sound of the lavatory flushing, and Sandy burst out of the door, her face white. Everyone stared at her. She looked around, wildly, and patted her chest. 'I'm sorry,' she said, 'the wallpaper – some of it fell on to me.'

'We've got a problem, with damp,' said Alex, falteringly.

'It gave me such a fright!'

Alex went to the lavatory and opened the door. There was a crack as she did so and the last remaining sheet of paper curled away from the wall and fell down on to the seat. She slammed the door shut and turned to face the others who were standing, silently, watching. 'Damp,' she said, trying to smile, and pointed a finger up the stairs.

Ford had arranged the chairs in a tight circle. He placed Alex on his right and asked the others to sit down as they liked. He closed the door firmly, with finality, and stood in front of it. 'I think I'm right that there are some of you here who have never sat in a circle before?' He looked at David, then at Alex. They both nodded.

'We never know if anything will happen, so we have to be patient. It's a good night tonight, clear, there should not be too much interference. Does anyone have any objections to my leading tonight's circle?' He looked around. 'Good.' He spoke gently, but authoritatively. 'You must all do exactly what I say; if I feel things are getting out of hand in any way, I will stop it.' He looked around and everyone nodded.

Alex felt slightly absurd, sitting in the bedroom, surrounded by these strange, earnest people. She was glad

David was with her and she wished she had more friends around; she felt vulnerable and very scared. She looked up at Fabian's portrait. 'Don't harm me, darling,' she said, silently.

'We conduct our circles in three stages. We begin with prayers, to protect the circle against evil spirits and simply mischievous spirits. Then we go into meditation. After that we will try to communicate directly with the spirits. We would like to communicate with Fabian, and we believe he would like to communicate with us; we will try to give him energy.' He looked at Alex and then at David. 'You see, spirits have no energy of their own – but it is possible for them to use the energy we create in our circles to speak, and sometimes even to appear.' He smiled and clasped his hands gently together, like a master giving a lesson to school children, thought Alex. 'If you want to speak, or ask questions at any stage, please do so.'

'What do you mean, evil?' said David.

'What we are doing is trying to open up channels for the spirits to come through. We want to communicate with good spirits, but in opening channels, in giving our energy for spirit use, we are exposing ourselves to misuse. There are evil spirits around, evil forces that try to come in through these channels, make use of the energy. That is why we protect our circle by prayer, and why I must stop it instantly if I sense the forces of evil.'

'What happens if evil comes through?' said David.

Ford smiled. 'Usually it is mischievous spirits more than evil ones, they play pranks, try to confuse, try to get their own messages through – strangers to us who would like to communicate with the earth plane – get messages through to other carnates. But we will be protected; the power of prayer is strong. This is why it is so dangerous for amateurs to tamper with the spirit world, for people to play dangerous games with Ouija boards.' He smiled again. 'Are we ready?' He looked pointedly at Alex and she nodded.

Ford switched off the light and the room was plunged into darkness. Alex felt calm. Suddenly the room seemed warm and friendly; it was going to be all right. She cupped her hands together and leaned forward.

'Dear God,' said Ford's gentle assured Welsh lilt. 'We pray to you that you will look after our circle and that we shall come to no harm.'

She closed her eyes out of respect and felt faintly silly.

'Guide us safely throughout this evening.'

The prayers continued for an eternity, it seemed. Ford asked for healing for people whose names she had never heard of, for peace in the world, for someone called Mrs Ebron's leg to get better quickly.

Finally they stopped and the room was very still. She heard a siren a long way off in the distance, and then it was gone; even the traffic seemed still. She thought again of the terror in Sandy's scream. What was going on in that lavatory, she wondered, opening her eyes and looking nervously around. She could see shadows, silhouettes. She looked towards the window and saw a faint streak of light down one side. She hoped the room was dark enough. The silence continued; she wondered if Fabian was watching them and tried to imagine him, but could feel nothing.

There was a click, and she suddenly heard Spring from Vivaldi's *Four Seasons*, light, sad, airy. 'We'll begin our meditation now,' said Ford gently. 'I want you to close your eyes and imagine you are walking on soft grass, in a field. It's a warm spring day, a clear sky, you feel the sun warming the air, feel the grass soft and springy beneath your feet. It's good to walk on, you're enjoying walking, breathing in the air, cool and fresh, the start of a fine day. The field is gently sloping up a hillside; you walk across it, imagine the grass beneath your feet, the sky above you. Now you see a path in front of you.'

Alex thought of a field at David's vineyard, tried to imagine it, as the medium said, tried to feel the grass beneath her feet, tried to stop feeling self-conscious and go with his words, relax with his soothing voice.

'Go along the path, it's nice to be walking along a firm

path again, enjoy it. You can see a white gate ahead of you now; open the gate and go through and you can see a river, a wide gently flowing river, with trees and rushes and lilies. It is peaceful, so peaceful. There's a bridge across the river, you can see it clearly.'

Alex thought of a river she had once known, with an old stone bridge, arched across it, crumbling.

'You can see people on the far side, standing there. Your friends, waiting to greet you. Cross over the bridge now, go to them, greet them, hug them, spend time with them. Don't be afraid, go, enjoy, be happy with them.'

Alex saw white ghosts on the far bank, swaying and opening their arms; she saw the slits which were their eyes, like the painting of the three phantoms she had seen on Ford's wall, and she hesitated. She saw Philip Main standing amongst them in a shabby corduroy suit, shrugging, then she saw Ford standing there. What friends does he mean, she wondered? Living or dead? She stepped on to the bridge and the ghosts swayed towards her, stretched out their arms, like faceless monks with cowls over their heads. Main and Ford disappeared. Then she saw Fabian standing among them, looking away from her, his head bowed, as if he were ashamed.

She felt herself hurrying anxiously; she stumbled on a loose brick, and when she looked up, the ghosts had closed ranks and he had disappeared. She stood among them, staring into their cowled hoods, into voids. 'Fabian?' she said, trembling. She pushed her way among them and saw one, taller than the rest, Fabian's height, facing away from her. 'Fabian?' She tapped him on the shoulder. 'Darling?'

Slowly he turned around. Inside the cowled hood was a charred skull that stared at her helplessly, with an almost apologetic look.

She felt herself about to scream and sat upright with a start, opened her eyes and looked around. Where was she? Where the hell was she? She heard her own breathing; it was the middle of the night, surely? Had she imagined it all?

Weren't they having a séance? Where was everyone? She felt sweat pouring down her, looked around, trying to see in the dark. She saw a faint streak of light; was that the curtain? The streak of light she had seen before? She wanted to call out, say something, but she was afraid of speaking to an empty room. Weren't there people here? Surely they hadn't left her alone? But why couldn't she hear them?

There was a tinkle of music and the strains of Vivaldi's Summer filled the room; the speakers were slightly tinny and she could hear the hiss of the tape. She breathed out slowly, relief flooding through her. Baloney. It was a con; hypnotism; a cheap trick dressed up in an elaborate production. She closed her eyes, thought again of the charred skull and shuddered. She opened her eyes and looked around, restless, her backside was stiff in the chair and she wanted to move, but was afraid to break the silence. She could sense David now, restless too; what must he be thinking?

She heard the shuffle of a foot on the carpet, the creak of a spring, the rustle of fabric and smelled Sandy's pungent perfume. What was she meant to do now? Would Fabian suddenly appear? She looked around again at the dark shapes; what were they all doing? Were they in hypnotic trances? Asleep? Or sitting there in the dark, thinking, like her?

She closed her eyes again, and tried to concentrate on the river. But it had gone and, instead, she saw David's lake, the medieval pond, the expanse of flat black water with its fringe of reeds like dead men's fingers, and the crumbling octagonal island in the middle.

She tried to imagine a bridge across to it, but no bridge would come, only the tunnel underneath. She thought of the entrance, like the steps down to an air raid shelter, overgrown with grass and weeds. She saw the rotting oak door, turned the key, stiff in the rusting lock, and pushed the door open. She felt it scrape across the concrete, warped and sagging on its hinges, heard it clacking like the laughter of crows as it vibrated. She could smell the must and the damp and could hear, a long way off, the echo of dripping water. It was cold in here, so cold. Gingerly she walked forward, listening to the echo of her own footsteps, and the splashes of dripping water like pistol shots.

She came to the inner door, unlocked that, and walked into the dark passageway, her feet squelching on the unseen floor, wondering whether she was treading on frogs or toads or just water and slime. Deep under the lake now, she came to the next door, which led into the domed ballroom, a heavy steel watertight door, the door David said she must never open. If there was a leak in the ballroom, and it had flooded, then opening this door . . . She unwound the huge handle, like a steering wheel, four, five, six turns, and the door swung open, outwards, as if she had been expected.

She stood back blinking in surprise, and stared around the huge domed room. It was snug, warm, cosy. Up in the ceiling, through the glass roof, carp and trout swam round, lazing, playing in warm pools of light. There was soft carpeting on the floor and a fireplace burning cheerfully. A woman stood there in a nursemaid's outfit; she stooped down, lifted a thin charred branch out of the fire with her bare hands, and held it high above her, a tiny gnarled object with burned twigs coming from it. The twigs began to move, at first as if in a breeze, but then they took on a life of their own and became little pink arms; tiny fingers curled and opened and she heard a baby cry.

'Don't cry; you're going to see Mummy now.' The nursemaid carried the baby across towards her with a smile, and Alex shuddered as she realized how like Iris Tremayne the woman looked.

Then she felt the weight of the baby in her arms, saw the pinkness of his hands and his legs, and looked down at his face.

A charred skull stared back.

A dim red light came on, and she blinked, startled. The music had stopped, she realized. She saw Ford standing by the door, and she looked at Steven Orme, Milsom, then at Sandy, who smiled reassuringly. She avoided David.

'How did everyone get on?' asked Ford. 'That was a long meditation – I felt it was going well, so I didn't interrupt.'

Alex looked at her watch. Ten to eight; it had been over half an hour. Impossible. She steeled up the courage and looked at David; his head was bent over, his ear pressed to his jacket and he had a strange preoccupied expression on his face.

'Sandy,' said Ford in his gentle voice. 'How did it go for you?'

'Incredible, Morgan. I saw Jesus.'

Ford inclined his head slightly and smiled.

'He was standing in front of me with a basket; he told me I must try to develop my healing and he showed me how to do several things that have been confusing me.'

Ford looked at Sandy, puzzled.

'I sensed Jesus was in here too,' said Steven Orme, in an enthusiastic, nasally voice. 'I felt him come in.'

They're all bloody bonkers, thought Alex.

'I think,' said Orme, 'that he may come in to protect the circle. What do you think, Morgan?'

'Sandy's healing is very important; he may have felt it was necessary to come and see her.' He looked at Milsom. 'Arthur?'

'My wife,' said Milsom, his gruff voice tinged with a boyish excitement. 'Always pop over and see her when I can.'

'How was she?'

'Fine; she was showing me what she's doing. She's working on a project with some others, building this huge column of light, you see.'

'Ah, yes,' said Ford, nodding. Alex watched him, wondering what she should say.

'And Mr Hightower?' asked Ford.

'Think I fell asleep,' said David.

'Very easy,' said Ford, dismissively. Alex felt Ford's eyes

on her. 'Would you like to tell us what you saw, Mrs High-tower?'

Alex looked at David and regretted it. Don't be conned, he was saying; don't be a clot.

'I saw Fabian,' she said, and was reassured by the approving look in Ford's eyes.

'Yes, I thought you would; I thought he would be there. I could sense him very strongly; he's around now; I think we're going to be in touch tonight, it's very strong.'

'His face was all burned and charred, like a skull.'

Ford nodded. 'It is natural in meditation for the subliminal to play a part. You are projecting to him from the earth plane. The image you have is his carnate one, and it is inevitable that is how you will see him. Later, when he comes through to you, he will project his incarnate body, and that will be as you would like to remember him.'

'He was running away from me,' she felt herself blush, feeling ridiculous; she glanced at David, saw him trying to say something with his eyes, some warning, but she looked away before the message could get through.

'Probably your subliminal again, your fear of losing him forever. This will pass after your first communication; after that, you will be able to join him in your meditation whenever you like, and I think you'll find he'll be very helpful to you.' Ford smiled again and walked over to the tape recorder. He knelt down, ejected the tape and turned it over.

Alex looked around the room and felt herself trembling again. Fabian's portrait looked sterner than ever in the red lighting and Orme's cruel cold face unsettled her. She looked at Milsom, and he smiled cheerfully back.

'You may hear a strange voice, Mrs Hightower,' said Ford. 'I have a guide, called Herbert Lengeur – he was a doctor in Vienna in the 1880s; a nice chap; he moved to Paris in the '90s. He looked after Oscar Wilde for a time.'

She stared at him; he said it casually, as if it were normal. She was too nervous to ask him what he meant.

'Is everyone ready to go on? I sense strong influences tonight; you must all remember to do what I say, it's very important. All right?' He stared at Alex, and Alex stared back.

She shivered and felt a deep sense of dread. She did not want to go any further, did not want him to turn out the light.

There was a loud click and a weird drumbeat came out of the player, at a quick tempo that seemed to be increasing all the time.

Then the light went out.

She sensed him almost immediately, as clearly as if he had opened the door and slammed it shut behind him. He was in the room, standing behind her, watching.

She felt the shivers racing down her arms. She saw a shadow cross the room, she was certain, something darker than the dark, and she wanted the light on, wanted to touch someone. But she dared not move, dared not give way to her son, to his strange penetrating gaze, that she could feel, that she was frightened. This is what you want, darling, isn't it? That was the reason for all the signs you gave me; we're here now, for you. Be kind, please be kind.

God, she thought suddenly, it all seemed so long ago now. So long ago that he had been alive and everything had been normal.

There was a mournful hideous wail, like the cry of a vixen in the night, separate from the beat of the drums and way above it; it came from someone in the circle around her. She heard it again. Lower, slower, it dissolved into a ghastly choking sound, as if someone was trying to breathe through a broken throat. Who had made it, she wondered? Ford? Milsom? Orme? Sandy? It was impossible to tell.

'Mother.'

Fabian's voice, weak and frightened. There was a click and the music stopped.

'Mother.' Not one shadow of a doubt; it was her son speaking. She felt cold, the room was turning to ice, felt herself shaking so much she could hardly bear to sit still.

'Darling?' she said, nervously, out loud. 'Hallo, darling.'

She heard the hideous choking sound again, then suddenly a single dreadful piercing scream, a young woman's scream, the most pitiful frightened scream she had ever heard; she thought it would echo around the room for ever.

Oh, Christ, please stop this, she thought, please stop it now.

'Who is there?' she heard Ford's voice, calm, assured.

A voice replied with a heavy Germanic accent; the voice was cultured and had completely different intonations from anyone in the room. 'This is Herbert. There is a young man here who would like to speak with his mother.'

'Please tell him we are waiting for him. He has already started to come through.'

Alex stared at Ford through the dark. He had heard Fabian too. It wasn't a trick of her imagination. There was no way that his voice had been faked. She tried to feel excited, to put away the fear, but the dread and the cold encircled her; it was impossible, surely, she thought, for anyone to feel so alone in a room full of people? And yet, she knew, as she felt the force of the cold and the fear, like hands on her shoulders, that she might have been the only person left in the world.

'He is needing some energy,' the Germanic accent was almost chiding.

'I want everyone to hold hands,' said Ford. 'We will allow our energy to surge through us, to give power to the spirit.'

Alex felt her hand seized; Ford's tiny hand was so warm it felt as if it was burning her. The rhinestone cut into her skin, but she did not dare change the position. She pushed out her right hand and felt a limp, bony hand; who was that on her right, she tried to remember. Milsom. The hand responded, tentatively.

'Feel the power,' said Ford, 'let it surge, let it surge!'

She sensed Ford and Milsom rocking backwards and forwards, and rocked with them. Then suddenly they

187

stopped; Ford's hand closed tight over hers, a clamp, and he had become immovable, like stone.

'Mother!'

Fabian's voice hung in the air.

She heard the strange choking again and realized it was coming from Milsom. She looked at him, tried to see something of him, then suddenly she heard Carrie's voice from directly opposite her, where Orme was sitting.

'Don't let him, Mrs Hightower.'

Pitiful, frightened, the words unmistakably Carrie's, pierced the air like a knife scraped against marble.

'There seems to be a young woman coming through our channel,' said Ford, patiently.

'There is no young woman,' said the German voice.

'Who is there?' said Ford, calmly. 'Please tell us your name?'

There was a ferocious snarl, which made Ford and Milsom both jump, almost jerking Alex's arms out of their sockets.

She felt a cold draught of air blowing down the back of her neck, spreading out over her shoulders and down her body.

'Please help me, Mother.' Fabian's voice came through again.

He sounded so close, she felt she could reach out and touch him. She stared around the darkness. 'Where are you, darling?'

A strange deep nasal voice suddenly snarled back. 'Don't listen to the little bastard.'

She jumped again, shaking, staring wildly around at the dark.

'Who are you, please?' she heard Ford say, still calm. 'Kindly tell us your name, or else leave the medium at once, in the name of God.'

'Mother!' shouted Fabian, desperately.

The deep voice snarled again in the dark: 'I'm his father.'

Alex's head was swimming; she swayed, felt the grips of Ford and Milsom's hands.

'No,' said Ford. 'His father is here in the room with us.'

'Mother,' Fabian's voice whimpered again.

'Please stop this,' said Alex. 'I want to stop.'

'The spirit's father is here with us; please leave us, whoever you are,' said Ford, his voice growing sterner.

'My name is John Bosley. I am the boy's father,' snarled the voice again.

Alex tried to free her hands from Milsom and Ford, but could not. 'Oh God, please stop this.' She was shaking uncontrollably and felt as if she was going to vomit at any moment. 'Morgan, please stop this!' she shouted.

'Darling?' She heard David's voice, anxious, soft. 'Are you all right, darling.'

'I want to stop. Please ask them to stop.'

'Mother!' Fabian screamed again. 'Carrie!'

She curled up in the chair, tried to free her arms, tried to tuck her head under her arms. 'Help me,' she said. 'Help me.'

Then she heard Carrie's voice again, quietly imploring. 'Please don't let him, Mrs Hightower.'

'Don't let him what?' she said, weakly. 'Tell me. Don't let him what?'

'May 4th, Mother.' She heard Fabian's voice, different now, gently, confiding, just like he had always sounded. 'They're going to let me out on May 4th.'

'Out of where, darling?' she said, weakly. 'Out of where?'

There was a long silence and she found herself becoming conscious of the room again, of the creaking of chairs, of breathing and the rustle of clothes. Ford's grip relaxed on her hand, then let go completely.

She sensed that Fabian had gone, as definitely as he had arrived. There was nothing in the room any more, except the darkness and the silence. She freed her right hand from Milsom and gingerly touched her face with her fingers; it was soaking wet.

'Mr Ford,' she heard David say. 'I think you should stop; my wife is frightened.'

There was no response; she looked round, tried to see the silhouettes, but could see nothing; she felt her heart thumping so hard it was making her chest ache. 'David?' she whispered.

'Are you all right, darling?'

'I'm –' she paused. 'I'm O.K.'

There was a long pause, then she heard Ford's voice, gentle again. 'The spirits have gone.'

She heard the creak of a chair, the sound of feet on the carpet, and then the light came on and she closed her eyes against the brightness. When she opened them again Ford was standing by the door, his head bowed slightly, deep in thought.

She looked around the room; nothing had changed, nothing had moved. Still trembling, she wondered what she had expected to see, then sank back in her chair, totally drained. Opposite her, Orme was slumped at a hideously contorted angle across the arm of his chair. His mouth was open and his chin pushed forward like a beached fish; his eyes, wide open, stared up at the ceiling. For a moment she thought he was dead. Then he moaned softly and rolled back into the chair.

Milsom was leaning forward with his hands clasped and resting on his knees. Sandy was lying back in her chair, dabbing her forehead with a handkerchief.

Alex glanced nervously at David, who had his hand inside his jacket and was looking suspiciously at everyone.

She stared at Ford. 'What happened?' she said.

Ford looked strangely back at her and said nothing.

'Please tell me,' she said, trembling. 'Please tell me what happened?' She looked across at Orme again, then at Milsom, then Sandy. Everyone was strange, so strange. She stared at Fabian's portrait on the wall and at the cold brass telescope underneath the window. She thought how stark the room felt without the bed, how cold and flat the lighting seemed, how normal the room suddenly seemed again. Had she been in a trance, she wondered. Yes, perhaps that was it, all a weird dream. She relaxed very slightly, and looked at the people again. Why won't anyone look at me? She stared at Milsom, at Sandy, at David. Look at me someone, please. Smile at me, tell me it was all a bad dream; tell me that you've all been sitting here and no one saw anything. Please, please tell me.

The fear slowly subsided and was replaced with a flatness. Was that it, she thought. Just voices? Where was the ectoplasm? The spectres? Green slime hurtling from people's mouths? Levitations?

David was fiddling around inside his jacket again. Am I still alive, she wondered, suddenly. Is that why they're not looking at me? Panic gripped her. Can't they see me? I've died, that's what's happened, I've died. Look at me, please David. What are you doing? Suddenly her hands touched something in her lap, something hard and prickly which made a crackling sound like parchment, and she recoiled in shock. It felt like a huge dead insect. She tried to move her hands away, but they were entangled in it, and she felt the skin on her fingers tearing. She stared around wide-eyed, shaking wildly, too afraid to look down. What was it, what the hell was it?

She looked again at David for help, but he was still concentrating on his jacket. She felt a sharp pain in her finger, like a bite, that made her cry out in pain, and she had to look down. For a moment she stared in disbelief. Then she let out a scream which filled the room.

It was not an insect but a small shrivelled rose, black and charred.

CHAPTER TWENTY-ONE

Alex opened her eyes and focused hazily on the portrait of the horse on the wall. Somewhere in the distance she heard the murmur of voices. She looked around, puzzled, trying to get her bearings. Surely she had been in Fabian's room? Now she was downstairs in the drawing room. There had been people all around, now she could see only two, David and Morgan Ford, and they seemed a long way away, so far they might have been in another room, or even in another house.

'I never said goodbye to anyone.'

They didn't notice her.

'Your conjuring tricks might be fine for little old ladies,' she heard David say.

'Apports are common occurrences, Mr Hightower.'

What time was it, she wondered. How long had she been here on the sofa? What had happened to everyone else?

'You really mean that roses can dematerialize, travel across time and space and rematerialize?' said David.

'Many things happen in the spirit world that cannot be explained in ordinary terms. Apports are messages from the departed to their loved ones; their only way of offering tangible proof.'

'What sort of proof is a burnt rose?'

'I never said goodbye to anyone,' she said again. Still they did not notice her.

'We know only very little about the spirit world; we are learning all the time.'

'By experimenting on people when they are at their weakest?'

'I would never allow anyone into a circle who I felt was not strong enough.'

'My wife wasn't. Look what happened to her.'

'She'll be fine; she's just very tired. Giving power is very draining. It's very soon, you see, very soon after the bereavement. It's best normally to leave these things for a few months, at least.'

'So why didn't you?' said David.

'It was important.'

There was a long silence. 'What do you mean?'

'There is a mischievous spirit around.'

'No,' said Alex, suddenly, loudly. 'No there isn't.'

She saw them turn and look down in her direction, as if they were trying to confirm a distant landmark.

'How are you feeling, darling?' said David, tenderly.

She saw him lean over her, saw the tangle of his beard and his eyes peering down at her in turn, first one then the other.

'Would you like me to call the doctor?'

'She's calming down now,' said Ford. 'In another half an hour she'll be fine. Apports do cause great emotional stress.'

'Apports,' said David. Alex heard the crackle, like parchment, and saw David turn a blackened object around in his hand. 'Just a rose, an old dead rose plucked off someone's bonfire, that you or one of your accomplices dropped in her lap whilst we were holding hands in the dark. Someone with a very sick sense of humour.'

'David,' said Alex. 'Please, darling, don't be angry.'

'I'm not angry, darling. I'm sure Mr Ford meant well. Perhaps people are comforted by these things; you obviously weren't. Try and sleep some more.'

'I'd like a cigarette,' she said, sitting up on the sofa. The room seemed to slip sideways, and for a moment she was looking down at the wall; then it righted itself with a heave that churned her stomach.

'Don't sit up just yet, darling. Wait a few minutes.'

'It wasn't how I thought it would be,' she said, and looked up at Ford.

'It never is,' said Ford, smiling, gently.

'Fabian was so clear.'

'What do you mean?' said David.

'Fabian.'

'Fabian?' he echoed, blankly.

'Fabian, darling; surely you heard him?'

She watched the puzzlement on David's face, saw him turn to Ford, and then look back at her again. 'Heard him?'

'Yes. And Carrie. And –' she paused and went red.

'Nothing happened, darling, you must have imagined it.' Again he looked at Ford, and she saw Ford turn dismissively away from him to look back at her.

'Fabian spoke to me,' she said.

'Well he didn't speak to me. The only person who spoke was Mr Ford. And those two odd chaps; one sounded as if he was being sick, and the other as if he was being strangled.'

Alex felt frightened again, suddenly, frightened and isolated. 'You mean you heard nothing?'

'He wouldn't, Mrs Hightower,' said Ford reassuringly. 'He is not a sensitive.' Ford coughed, and turned to David. 'But your role was essential, there was mischief around tonight; you kept us earthed; without you we would have achieved far less.'

'Achieved?' said David, incredulously. 'What on earth did you achieve?'

'I think you should ask your wife that,' said Ford.

Alex saw David staring at her.

'Darling,' she said, feeling herself blushing, 'would you mind terribly if I had a word in private with Mr Ford?'

David looked at her, then at Ford.

'Perhaps you could make us a cup of tea?'

He stood up awkwardly and rubbed his beard. 'Yes – I'll –' he looked around, put his hand in his jacket pocket and took it out again. 'I'll go and put the kettle on.' He walked out of the room and Alex heard the click of the door closing. She stood up and the floor tilted away from her. She swayed, then felt steadier, and walked across to the drinks cabinet.

'Are you feeling better now, Alex?'

She took a cigarette out of the box, noticing that it was the first time Ford had called her by her Christian name.

'Thank you. I think so. There's been rather a lot to take in.' Her eye caught the rose David had left on a side table; she wandered over and touched it gently. 'Did Fabian really send this?'

'Something happened to it. Someone burned it on the way.'

'A spirit?'

'Yes,' he said, quietly.

'He often brought me roses; perhaps he was bringing me one back from France and it got burned in the accident. Could that be it?'

Ford nodded. 'It's a possibility.' He frowned.

'But you don't think so.'

'There were other spirits around tonight, making mischief. Herbert, my guide, warned us.'

'What do you mean?'

'When we hold circles, we are opening channels for communications from the spirit world. I can never know who is going to come through. We hoped tonight it was going to be Fabian, but often others come through; sometimes total strangers. And sometimes evil spirits will try to influence the circle, and try to manifest.'

'Evil spirits?'

Ford nodded. 'Evil spirits can be very cunning. Good mimics. Take on a departed person's characteristics: voice; mannerisms; appearance. They try to use the energy we create in the circles.'

'Why?'

'For their own purposes.'

'Do you believe in evil?'

Ford was silent for a moment. 'Of course. The positive and the negative, Mrs Hightower. All existence, both here and in the spirit world, is a balance between the two.'

'And one of these – evil – spirits might have burned the rose?'

'It's possible. There was much that happened tonight that I do not understand.'

'So it wasn't successful?'

'I don't know. Our intention was to rescue Fabian, free him from the earth plane. But there was too much interference, too much confusion. I cannot be sure that he has gone over.' She saw him shake his head.

'Interference from the girl, you mean?'

Ford nodded. 'Partly.'

Alex lit her cigarette and sat down again on the sofa. 'She came through before, in the sitting room in your house. A girl called Carrie whom Fabian used to go out with.'

Ford nodded. 'But this man claiming to be Fabian's father?' He stared at Alex. 'John Bosley, or something like that? I don't understand why he came through; but sometimes these mischief-makers do.'

Alex felt her face burning again. 'Have you ever had any experiences,' she said, 'of spirits who want to come back?'

'To human form?'

She nodded.

'You mean possession?'

'I'm not sure what it's called. Someone who wants to come back because they have unfinished business.'

Ford glanced at his watch. 'Many spirits are confused after death – the earthbound ones; often they do not realize they are dead; it is only when they try to talk to their loved ones and their friends and they discover no one can see them, no one can hear them, that they start to realize what has happened. Until that point many of them try to carry on as before, turning up to work, imagining they are doing everything they used to do before they departed.'

'Has anyone ever succeeded?' she said.

'In carrying on with their work?'

She nodded.

'Yes.'

'How do they do it?'

'They use the physical mind and body of someone living.

They take them over – so that person becomes a host body That's what we know as the state of possession.' He smiled. 'There are well-documented instances of spirits continuing their work through influencing living persons. There have been cases of surgeons, painters – and composers. Mozart was composing at four years old; it is very likely that he was under the influence of a spirit.'

'What about evil?'

'Hitler,' said Ford. 'There is no proof, but much evidence that Hitler – and several other members of the Third Reich – were possessed by evil spirits, which would account for their actions.'

'When I came to see you and we had our sitting, you told me at the end that Fabian wanted to come back. Is that what you meant? That he had unfinished business?'

Ford looked nervous, suddenly. He wasn't comfortable with this subject. She wondered if it was out of his depth. 'Unfinished business?'

'Yes.'

Ford smiled. 'What sort of business do you think?'

Alex looked down at the carpet. 'It seems so strange, talking about him as if he's –' She paused then stood up abruptly, walked across the room, and tapped the ash from her cigarette into the wastepaper basket.

'As if he's still alive?'

She nodded.

Ford smiled mysteriously. 'You're a very sensible lady; perhaps too sensible.'

'What on earth do you mean?'

Ford shook his head and smiled again.

'I don't understand.'

'I think one day you will.'

His face darkened and she felt uncomfortable again.

'I think we should have another circle, next Thursday.'

'No.'

'It's important; for your son.'

'I found it too frightening.'

'The first time is. But things are not resolved.' He looked anxiously round the room. 'You will feel better when they are.'

'I can't imagine ever feeling better.'

'No,' he said. 'You won't as long as the spirit is around. When we have helped the spirit across, then you will have peace and the healing will start.'

'Don't you think perhaps I've just been raking things up; that it would be better to leave them as they are?'

'You must think of your son.'

She stared at him, again trying to figure him out. Was it all a con, as David had insinuated? Had she been hypnotized, imagined everything? No, the voices had been too clear, too real, surely? And yet a small piece of doubt nagged at her. It was, after all, in Ford's interest to go on for as long as he could spin it out, for as long as he could give work to his strange colleagues with their gold earrings and their big feet. 'I also have to think of my husband.'

'Because he is sceptical?'

'There's another reason.' She paced around the room then sat down again. 'This man who came through, claiming to be Fabian's father –'

'The mischievous spirit?'

Alex shook her head. 'No, not necessarily a mischievous spirit.' She paused. 'David is not Fabian's father.'

Ford stared at her, searching, and looked down at his fingernails, checking his immaculate manicure. Something was disturbing him, she thought. The revelation should have clarified things for him, but it seemed to have made them worse. 'Bosley wasn't it – a name like that?' he said.

'I wouldn't know who he was.'

She saw Ford look at her oddly, and she smiled awkwardly. 'I don't mean it like that,' she said. 'We couldn't have children, you see.' She felt herself blushing. 'My husband's sperm count was too low.'

'You had a donor?'

'Not exactly – well, sort of.' She sighed and inhaled

deeply. 'I didn't want to have artificial insemination – some stranger's sperm – I wanted to have David's child. We were put in touch with a specialist who was experimenting at the time, mixing one's husband's sperm with a donor sperm, a high-mobility sperm, they called it.'

She smiled sadly. 'That way you were supposed never to know whether it was your husband or –' She tailed off.

'And now you think that –?'

She blushed. 'David's always been convinced Fabian was his, which is good. But I've always known he wasn't.'

'How?'

She felt herself going even redder. 'It wasn't working. The specialist told me he felt David's sperm was too hostile – I never quite understood – something in the chemistry wasn't right. I asked the specialist to let me have it neat – without David knowing.'

Ford nodded. 'Genes are important to the spirit world, you see,' he said. 'The blueprint for character. We know that they are essential to the carnate mind and body, that they shape and control everything, but I believe they are just as important to the discarnate state.'

'That we take our genes with us?'

'The part that relates to our character.'

'So Fabian has found his real father now?'

'It's a possibility.'

She shook her head. 'I don't want David to know. He was so proud of Fabian. I don't want his pride to be taken too.'

Ford nodded. 'I understand. But your husband is not what we call a "sensitive". He won't pick it up from the spirit; he won't know unless you tell him.'

She sank her face in her hands. 'Oh God, I feel so confused, so confused and frightened.'

'Alex,' said Ford gently. 'There is a terrible conflict going on between your son and his real father. It is something we must try to resolve, because it could harm your son – and it could harm you.'

'How do you mean?'

'There is a very strong dark force present; I have been trying to play it down, not to frighten you, but I have never in my life experienced anything stronger. Your husband reckons I am a charlatan; you, I think, believe me, although you have doubts. To prove my sincerity, I am prepared to waive all my fees, but you in turn must do exactly what I say. Do you understand?'

She shook her head. 'No,' she said. 'I don't want to go on.'

'Alex,' he said gently, 'you cannot turn the spirit world on and off at the touch of a button or at the twist of a tap. These things have to be seen through, or else they will see it through themselves.'

Alex felt an ice-cold shiver again, felt a draught blowing down inside her blouse, a hideous damp cold wind that made her blouse stick to her skin, as if she had just put it on sopping wet.

'Is there any way you can find out the real identity of your son's father?'

'I went to a man in Wimpole Street. A specialist in infertility. Saffier. Dr Saffier. He used sperm from donors – he told me they were very careful in matching up the donors – features –' she paused. 'Hair colour, eyes, that sort of thing.'

'And he helped you.'

'Yes.'

'I think you should go and see him. Try and find out more about this John Bosley.'

'I don't even know if he's still alive.'

'It's very important,' said Ford.

'Why?'

'You'll understand.'

The door opened and David came in. 'Do you take milk, Mr Ford?'

Ford stood up. 'I'm sorry, I'm very late. I must be on my way.'

'Do you want a broomstick, or did you bring your own?' said David, smiling.

Ford stood up and smiled politely back. 'Oh, I don't need things like that; I'll just dematerialize in front of your eyes, if I may?'

CHAPTER TWENTY-TWO

The Land Rover lurched, jolted and slithered on the muddy track. Alex smelt the stench of the pigs, saw several rabbits staring into the headlights, twitching; they turned and fled away through the fencing and into the fields.

It was a clear night; she could see the stars, the half-moon and the dark contours of the land like a never-ending shadow.

'Thanks for letting me come down.'

'Don't be silly.'

'I didn't want to stay in the house tonight.'

'I'm not surprised. That chap, what's-his-name, Ford, has scared you silly with his tricks.'

She stared through the windscreen, across the spare wheel. The nose of the Land Rover dipped and she could see the sheen of the lake, almost as if it was glowing from some light inside it. Medieval pond. She shuddered; why could she never get those words out of her mind, why did they always sound so sinister? She thought of ancient carp, hundreds of years old, menacingly guarding the deeps. She tried to look away from the lake, but her eyes were drawn there as if it were a magnet.

'He wasn't what I'd imagined,' he said.

'What do you mean?'

'Well – he had a bit of a sense of humour really; I never thought of people like that having a sense of humour – always thought they were deadly serious. He looked more like an insurance salesman than a medium.'

She smiled. 'That's what I thought when I saw him. Apparently he has a very fine reputation.'

David stopped the Land Rover sharply, yanked on the handbrake, and peered out of his side window.

Alex looked at him anxiously. 'What's the matter?'

He raised a finger and continued staring. She listened to the beat of the engine, like a heart racing, looked around, and felt vulnerable, afraid, wanted to get to the farmhouse, not be stopped out here in the dark, beside the lake and the fields.

'Buggers,' he said.

'What is it?'

'Some sheep have got through into the vineyard – I've got my Chardonnay in that one; I don't want them in there.'

She felt the relief surging through her.

'I'll have to sort that fence out in the morning.'

'You don't mind if I borrow the Land Rover tomorrow?'

'It's not much fun grinding it up to London – you'd be better to take the train from Lewes.'

She nodded.

'But you just do whatever you like; I want you to rest, relax, get strong again.'

She smiled and rested her arm along the back of his seat. She wanted to hug him, squeeze him, but no, she knew, deep down, it was bad enough what she was doing to him already; she didn't want to open all the old wounds again; it wasn't fair to him, or to herself, she realized as an afterthought.

She sat down at the kitchen table and watched David opening a bottle of his own wine. Vendange padded into the room, looked around, and padded out again.

'You really did what he said and didn't eat for six hours before?'

She nodded. 'Not since breakfast. And you?'

'I usually only eat twice these days, breakfast and dinner.' He opened the fridge. 'Like an omelette?'

'I'm surprised you don't have your own hens; you always wanted to in London.'

'That was for the novelty of keeping them in London; they wouldn't be such a novelty out here.'

She smiled.

'Anyway, wine and eggs don't go that brilliantly together.'

'Even if you were to bring the hens up on Chardonnay vines?'

He put a handful of eggs down on the draining board.

'What were you doing during the séance – the circle, David?'

He looked at her and went red. 'Doing?'

'You seemed to be fiddling around a lot.'

He grinned and patted his chest. Carefully, he removed his jacket, to reveal a tape recorder strapped to his chest. 'It's all there. We'll see which one of us is right.' He unbuckled the straps, pressed the rewind button and put the machine down on the table in front of Alex. She heard the shuffling whirr and looked up at him.

'Do you think that was wise?'

'What do you mean?'

'It might have put the spirits off.'

'No one said that tape recorders were banned.'

'I think you might have told me.'

'If I had, you wouldn't have allowed it.' He filled her glass, then frowned as the wine settled and clarified. He raised the glass by the stem and turned it around under the light bulb. 'Colour's good,' he said.

'Very clear.'

'Not too watery, you don't think?'

'No.'

'Just a hint of yellow, isn't there?' he said, excitedly. 'The last lot came out a bit greeny.'

'What do you do? Put colouring in?'

He frowned at her disapprovingly. 'Never; not me. It's the skins of the grapes that give the colour: depends how long you leave them in the must.'

Alex sniffed the wine. It had a tart, slightly oily smell at first, and she puckered her nose; on the second sniff, she detected a faint sweet scent of grapes.

'Still very young,' he said, defensively.

'You must be careful not to make them too sophisticated, David. The majority of people aren't connoisseurs – they just want something that tastes pleasant.'

'Bugger the majority; they can have their Blue Nun and Hirondelle. God, you don't understand, do you? It's greatness I want; the great English wine.'

She sipped and closed her eyes and swilled the wine noisily around in her mouth, hoping that was what he wanted. It was sharp and stung her palate, making her wince; then she swallowed and felt it slide down her throat; as it hit her empty churned-up stomach, she flinched. 'Good,' she said, opening her eyes again. 'Good, but a little sharp.'

There was a loud click from the tape recorder. David leaned down and pushed the play button. There was a cacophony of sound and he turned down the volume. 'I didn't bother with all the prayers and stuff,' he said.

She heard Vivaldi's Spring, tinkling, pretty, sadness tinged with optimism. '. . . feel the grass soft and springy beneath your feet,' said Ford's voice. '. . . you can see a white gate ahead of you . . .'

'I'll run through this bit,' said David, pushing the fast-forward. Alex sat watching the machine, afraid. She heard the weird drum-beat, then the mournful hideous wail, like the cry of a vixen; slowly it dissolved into a ghastly choking sound. She felt a cold prickle seeping down her spine as she waited for the words to come.

But the choking faded into a quiet crackle of static.

Frowning, David twiddled with the knobs, turning the volume up and down, but there was nothing but crackle. He ran it forward a few seconds and tried again; still the static. He stared dubiously at Alex.

'What's the matter?' she said.

'I think he's jammed it.'

'Jammed?'

'Your friend; I think he must have brought a jamming device with him.'

'Why should he have done that?'

'For precisely this reason.'

He played it on at fast-forward and the crackle continued, snapping, popping, hissing. Then, suddenly, they heard high-pitched voices, like chipmunks. David slammed his thumb down on the stop button and wound the tape back a short way. Then he pushed the start button again:

'Are you all right, darling?' It was his own voice. He stared, knowingly, at Alex.

'I'm – O.K.,' said Alex's voice.

There was a pause and then she heard Ford. 'The spirits have gone.'

David switched off the machine.

'Don't spirits and electricity have something to do with each other?' said Alex, trembling, conscious of sounding slightly ridiculous.

'A con, darling.'

She shook her head.

'All a con.'

She shook her head again. 'I wish you were right.'

Alex slept with the light on in the lumpy double bed. Throughout the night her waking thoughts and her sleeping thoughts were peppered with wails and screams and Fabian's voice. Every time she lapsed into a doze she woke again, hearing him, close, right beside her. She felt the sweat pouring from her and sipped the water from the glass, afraid in case she should finish it before dawn, too afraid to go out of the room for more.

The night outside was full of sounds; an owl's hoot echoed across the water. The medieval pond. She dozed and heard the sound of carp swimming, strange echoing bleeps, ripples of water, saw one larger than the rest racing to the surface, crashing upwards between the weeds and its face came out into the daylight, a hideous burnt human face, and she screamed, wildly.

There was a gentle knock on her door. 'Darling, are you all right?'

She closed her eyes and tried to go back to sleep. 'Yes, I'm fine, thank you.'

She heard him wander around and felt safer. She heard him go downstairs, heard a tap in the kitchen, the clank of a door opening and closing. The noises outside were different now. Birds were singing; it was peaceful and she opened her eyes and saw that the morning had come.

David was already at work in his winery. She pushed open the heavy door and walked into the huge flint barn. How could he put up with the smell all day, the stale dull acidy smell of yesterday's party?

There was a massive block and tackle hanging from a central beam, above a huge plastic vat in the middle of the floor. David was standing on top of the vat, adjusting the rope.

'I'm ready,' she shouted up to him.

'I'll come down!'

She watched him shin down the precarious ladder. 'What are you doing?'

'A new vat – only had it delivered yesterday. I want to move it over slightly. You're welcome to stay tonight, too; stay for the weekend, at least.'

'Thanks. Do you mind if I see how I feel?'

'If you're definitely coming back, you might as well take the Land Rover and leave it at the station.'

'You'll be stranded if I don't.'

He turned and gave his winery a loving glance, as if he could hardly bring himself to leave it, even for a few minutes. 'I'll be O.K.'

'You're lucky,' she said, 'having something you're so passionate about.'

'You have too.'

She shook her head. 'I've hardly been in the office since –' She shrugged. 'I suppose there are times in life when certain things become unimportant.'

'Do you think your clients would agree with you?'

She looked away and blushed guiltily.

CHAPTER TWENTY-THREE

It felt comfortable to be in the bustle of London, to travel on the underground amid the surge of the commuters. London had a good feeling on Fridays. You could see it in their faces, in their slightly brighter clothes and in the holdalls and suitcases some of them carried, stuffed with green wellies and baggy pullovers.

She walked down Wimpole Street. It had been a long time since she had last been here, she thought, and nothing in the street seemed to have changed.

She could not remember Saffier's number, but she knew the house by heart; over a dozen visits before he hit the jackpot. Over a dozen visits, clutching David's hand, trying to ignore his sheepish expression and feeling the little plastic pot wedged inside her blouse between her breasts to keep it warm.

She could still remember which button to push, the second from the top. 'R. Beard F R C S , M R C O G' it said. She scanned the rest of the names. D. B. Stewart, B. Kirkland, M. J. Sword-Daniels. No Saffier. She stood back, and double checked, then rang the bell marked Beard, and waited.

There was a sharp buzz and the latch clicked open. She pushed the door and went in. The hallway was painted a brighter colour, but otherwise was exactly as she remembered it. She climbed the stairs and pushed open the door. A smart beanpole of a girl looked up from her desk and stared at her from under her neat straw fringe. 'I wonder if you can help me,' said Alex. 'I'm looking for Dr Saffier?'

The girl opened her lips and spoke in an unintelligible

voice that sounded like a distant racing car; she tossed her fringe, which promptly fell back into place.

'Pardon?' said Alex, leaning forward, trying to tune in her hearing.

'Years,' she picked up. 'Gosh,' she also managed to decipher.

'Do you have any idea where he might have gone to?'

The door behind the girl opened and a gentle-looking man in a dark suit that was too large for him came out. 'Have you forgotten my coffee, Lucy?' The girl turned round and made a sound like a bunch of racing cars negotiating a chicane.

The man ran a huge hairy hand over the back of his head and stared at Alex with wide blue eyes. 'Julian Saffier,' he said, in a soft, husky voice, and shook his head. 'He left here a long time ago – I've been here fourteen years.'

'Would you know if he's still alive?'

He raised his eyebrows. 'Used to be in the press a lot – haven't seen anything about him for a long time. Infertility?' The man looked at her quizzically.

Alex nodded.

'I have a feeling he bought a place somewhere in Surrey, set up a clinic down there. I may be wrong.'

'It's very important that I get in touch with him.'

The man smiled. 'I'll look him up in the register for you.' He went into his office and came out holding a heavy red book and leafed through it. 'No, not in here.' He looked thoughtful, then turned to his secretary. 'See if you can get me Douglas Kerr.'

'Yah, O.K.,' Alex deciphered, and watched her tap some numbers out on the phone as elegantly as if she was playing a piano. She looked around. There was a framed picture of a yacht under full sail on the wall; a large expensive yacht, with *Houdini* emblazoned on its side.

'Are you an old friend of, er?'

She shook her head. 'I was a patient.'

'Ah. Clever man, I believe.'

'Are you in the same line?'

'Well – not really – I'm a conventional gynaecologist.'

Alex nodded. Several racing cars accelerated down a long straight and the beanpole thrust the receiver at him.

'Hallo,' he said, 'Douglas? Bob Beard here. Yes, fine, and you? Yes, Felicity's fine too; had a hole-in-one last week, would you believe? Yes ... at the Dyke. Listen, must be brief. Tell me, does the name Saffier ring any bells?'

Alex watched him, nervously.

'Julian Saffier?' He turned to Alex.

Alex nodded. 'Yes.'

'Yes, that's the one.' He paused. 'Yes, infertility ... about eighty? Maybe; yes, I suppose he would. I just wondered, on the off-chance, whether you knew him? Similar line of work ... yes, I thought you did.' He paused. 'No, no, nothing like that – just someone wants his address.' Again he paused. 'Guildford? Yes, I thought it was somewhere around there. Any idea who might have his address? I've tried the register.' He frowned. 'Good Lord; was he? How long ago? I see, that would explain it. Listen, thanks very much, talk to you soon.'

He turned to Alex, clasping his two huge hands together. 'He was struck off, I'm afraid,' he said, almost apologetically.

'Struck off?'

He nodded and smiled awkwardly.

What for? she wondered, feeling very uncomfortable. What for? 'I don't suppose you know why?'

He shook his head. 'I'm sorry, no, I don't.' He looked at his watch.

'I've taken enough of your time, thank you.'

He smiled. 'You might find him in the phone book, or directory enquiries. But I don't know if he's still alive, even.'

She could hear the hoovering from the street as she climbed out of the taxi. Mimsa's hoovering always had a particularly frenetic quality to it, as if she was trying to catch the dust before it hid.

The house felt light, airy, safe. The smell of polish, the grinding of the hoover and the grunting of Mimsa reassured her. Normality. Perhaps David was right. Perhaps.

'Ah, Missy Eyetoya. Much messing in toilet. Is a no paper on wall.'

'I know, Mimsa,' she nodded. 'There's a problem with damp.'

'I getty fixed for you. My humsbund, he good fixing toilet paper.'

'Thanks, Mimsa, but don't worry.' She recoiled at the memory of the last time Mimsa's husband had come to fix something. She took the small pile of mail on the hall table, went through to the drawing room, picked up the phone and dialled directory enquiries. 'Mimsa!' she shouted. 'What did you do with that rose that was on the side table?'

'I putty in dustbin.'

'Could you get it out.'

'Eh?'

'Enquiries. Which town please?'

'Guildford,' she said, sifting through the envelopes; one, a fat buff envelope, was postmarked Cambridge. Then she heard the operator's voice and her heart leapt. Saffier was listed. She scrawled the address on the back of the buff envelope, her hand shaking so much that she could hardly read her writing. 'Thank you,' she said, weakly, and glanced at her watch. Eleven o'clock.

She tore open the envelope; there was a compliments slip from the Bursar's Office and several letters addressed to Fabian at Cambridge. She glanced through them: an American Express bill, a bank statement, a large envelope marked PRIZE DRAW PRIORITY and an airmail letter from the United States, postmarked Boston, Mass; Fabian's name and address was typed on the front by a dot matrix printer. Inside was a letter, similarly typed, and two sheets of computer printout.

The paper was headed in block capitals NEW ENGLAND BUREAU. In smaller letters underneath were

211

the words: Office rentals – weekly, daily, hourly. Secretarial services. Accommodation addresses. Confidentiality assured.

The letter read simply:

'Dear Customer, We have now despatched the last postcard, and await your further instructions. Please find enclosed your statement for the quarter ending March 31st, and your invoice for the next quarter should you wish to continue with our services. Faithfully yours, Melanie Hart, Executive Administrator.'

Alex felt herself going white. She read the letter through again and began to shiver; the room was turning cold and something seemed to be turning her inside out. The asterisks in Fabian's diary. Two weeks apart. The postcards. Two weeks apart. She took out her cigarette lighter, walked over to the fireplace, lit the letter, the printouts and the envelope and dropped them into the grate.

'You want light fire? Now? I light for you.'

She turned and saw Mimsa standing in the doorway. 'No, it's fine, thanks, Mimsa.'

'Cold in 'ere. Sheesh, it cold.' Mimsa rubbed her hands and frowned. Then she held her hands up to Alex. 'Been in dustbins, both dustbins. Ees not there.'

'Who's not there?'

'Rose.'

'Rose?' Then she remembered and began trembling. 'Not there? What do you mean? You said you put it there?' She watched the last corner of the paper go brown, blacken and then erupt into flame.

Mimsa shrugged.

She felt her muscles tensing, saw Mimsa only dimly, as if she was staring at her from a long way away. 'When did you put it there?'

Mimsa shrugged again. 'I don know. Hour ago?'

'Have the dustbins been emptied today?'

'No, dey don come today.'

'I'll have a look.'

Mimsa followed her out, protesting. 'What you want get dirty for? It no good rose, finish.'

Alex turned the dustbins on their sides, and tipped the contents out on to the pavement. A wine bottle rolled past her and into the gutter. She knelt in the stench and the gunge, peering into the empty tins, shaking them, checking the cartons, poking her fingers through the fluff and the rotten fruit and the plastic bags and the dust.

Mimsa watched her for a moment, as if she was mad, and then dutifully joined her. 'Ees better get fresh roses.'

Alex stared at the rubbish on the pavement and inside the dark empty bins.

'Maybe someone took,' said Mimsa.

'Maybe,' said Alex, as she began to put everything back in. She looked around nervously at the quiet street. 'Maybe.'

CHAPTER TWENTY-FOUR

Alex floored the accelerator, felt the clunk of the kick-down and heard the aggressive bellow of the engine as the Mercedes surged forward past the line of traffic. She cut sharply in front of a Sierra, which hooted angrily at her. New England Bureau. The charred rose. She wondered if the world had finally gone completely mad. Perhaps we have moved nearer to the moon, she thought, or Jupiter, or perhaps they have moved nearer to us? What was going on? What the hell was going on?

She turned the Mercedes off the Guildford bypass on to the narrow country lane. The road became dark, shrouded with overhanging trees which blotted out the afternoon sun. It wound up a steep hill, under a stone bridge, then dropped down sharply into a small village, which seemed to consist of a couple of houses, a pub and a garage.

A youth on the forecourt gave her the directions and she found the entrance half a mile further on, marked by a large white sign almost hidden by shrubbery, which read 'Witley Grove'. She drove through two tall stone pillars, each topped with a black cast-iron falcon, over a cattle grid and down a long pot-holed tarmac drive between two fenced-in fields.

Rounding a bend, she saw a sprawling Victorian Gothic mansion, wildly asymmetrical, with stark red-brick walls and steeply pitched half-timbered roofs, like witches' hats, she thought.

Several cars were parked in front of the house, and she was relieved by the sign of life. She climbed out of the Mercedes, feeling butterflies in her stomach, and glanced uncomfortably at the house. It was stark, bare, an institution, not a home. She had the distinct feeling someone in the house was watching her but, glancing around at the dark leaded windows, she could see no sign of movement.

There was a black Daimler limousine outside the front door, the chauffeur sitting inside with his hat off, reading a newspaper. As she walked past it and up the steps to an imposing porch, she wondered who it belonged to. Some Arab client? She stared nervously at the small brass plaque beside the huge oak door: 'Witley Grove Clinic'. Was he still practising – in spite of having been –? Would she be able to see him now, today, right away – or was some starchy secretary going to make her wait three months for an appointment? God, he used to have a real gorgon in London. She tried to remember Saffier himself, but his face was fuzzy. She remembered how much she had depended on him; hope when there had been no hope, when the doctors had told her to forget it, they could never have children, adopt. His memory was coming clearer now: the voice, the faint hint of an accent; permanent suntan, the stiff handsome face, a good looking mid-European; a smoothie, with a sparkle in his eyes and short neat hair that had been dyed to match his face-lift; the smart suits and the ties that were too loud with the white shoes; he always wore white shoes. In a showroom she wouldn't have bought a used car from him; in Wimpole Street he was her god.

They'd sent him a present when Fabian was born: a case of champagne. She wondered whether Saffier would remember, whether that would stand her in good stead twenty-one years on. Would he allow her to see the records? Did he still have them? She leaned forward to press the bell, but at that moment the front door swung open. She looked up and to her amazement saw Otto staring down at her.

She stood back, blinking, confused, and tried to focus. She saw the raked back hair, the lacerations, the weals, the pockmarks, the hooked nose, the mocking eyes.

'Hallo, Mrs Hightower,' he said. 'Won't you come in?'

I'm going mad, she thought. I'm going mad. Somehow I

have driven to Cambridge by mistake, come to Otto's room. She glanced over her shoulder. The driveway was still there, the chauffeur in the Daimler turning the page of his paper. Am I in the middle of Cambridge? Are there fields in the middle of Cambridge?

She followed him into the huge dark hallway and gazed in amazement at the ornate carved oak staircase with hideous gargoyles on the newel posts. No, this is not his room, surely his room didn't look like this? A suit of armour stood stiffly on guard at the bottom of the stairs and she looked away from the dark eye slits of the visor, shuddering; suits of armour had always frightened her.

'You didn't make the service,' he said.

In a room nearby she could hear the hubbub of voices. She could smell sherry, cigar smoke. Was it a dining hall? Had she come to a Cambridge dining hall?

'The service?' she echoed blankly. Otto was looking smart, oddly smart, in a dark grey suit and black knitted tie. 'Have you been to church, Otto?'

The eyes. Oh, God, stop smiling, stop looking like that.

A woman appeared in front of her, small, in a black and white outfit, carrying something. 'Dry or medium, madam?'

'Dry, please, thank you.'

Alex took the glass, felt its weight, felt it gone, suddenly. There was a noise, a long way away, a distant tinkle.

'Don't worry, madam, I'll get a cloth; please take another one.'

She took the glass, clutched it in both hands, holding it to her body as if it was a new-born infant.

Otto smiled, his knowing smile. 'Of course. I thought you would be there.'

Riddles. Riddles were everywhere; the world was becoming a riddle. She sipped the sherry, dry, nutty, it warmed her stomach; she sipped again and realized she had drained the glass. 'I don't understand.'

Stop smiling, for Christ's sake stop smiling. Think; be

216

rational; calm down. 'I – I thought this was Dr Saffier's house.'

'It was.' The answer came back straight at her, like a hard-hit ball.

'I –' She stared at her empty glass and smiled, nervously. 'I'm just a bit surprised to see you.'

The two eyes stared knowingly, smiling, mocking.

She stumbled, trying to find the words, trying to put them together. 'Do you know where – where? –' she looked at the black tie again. Black tie; dark suit. Black tie. 'Where Dr Saffier has moved to?'

The eyes smiled back, laughing at her, and his mouth joined them, silently. 'Yes, sure, of course.'

'I – er – didn't know you knew him.'

'I know lots of people, Mrs Hightower.'

'Another sherry, madam?'

She took the glass from the tray, holding it tightly, and put her empty one down.

'Would you like to meet some of them?'

'Some of whom?'

'Dr Saffier's relatives. Dr Saffier's friends.'

'Well –' she shrugged, puzzled, 'yes – I suppose –'

But he had already turned and was walking down the corridor towards the room full of people.

It was a huge panelled room, the walls hung with massive oil canvases, ancestral portraits, hunting scenes, naked cherubs, all larger than life, and she hesitated in the doorway, staring at the pall of smoke, the men in their sober, formal suits, the women in dark dresses, wearing hats, veils, the waitress with her tray of drinks weaving her way through them like a native in a jungle.

'This is Dr Saffier's brother,' said Otto, leading her to a group of three people.

A frail, elderly man, white haired, with a skinny, almost skeletal face, held out a hand heavily marked with liver spots. His grip was much firmer than she had expected. 'How do you do?' he said in a cultured voice with the tiniest trace of a mid-European accent.

217

'Alex Hightower,' she said, thinking how different from his brother he looked, yet how similar he sounded.

He nodded, pensively, with a sad expression. 'You were a friend of my brother's?'

Were? Were? She saw that he too was wearing a black tie; and the man next to him. 'Er – no – I was a patient of his – a long time ago – he helped me a lot.'

'He helped many people.' He shook his head. 'And then they did that to him.'

She was conscious of the other man and the elderly woman, standing beside them, whose conversation Otto had interrupted, and glanced at them; they both nodded and smiled.

'My sister,' said Saffier's brother. 'And my brother-in-law, Mr and Mrs Templeman.'

'How do you do?' said Alex.

They both smiled again, but said nothing.

It was beginning to sink in. It was a wake. There had been a funeral. Whose? Whose? Panic was beginning to grip her. Not Saffier, please not.

'It was all a set-up,' said the woman, indignantly, in an accent far more guttural than her brother's. 'The Establishment wanted to get him, and that was their way of doing it.'

'Absolutely,' nodded Saffier's brother. He looked at Alex again. 'Never recovered from that you know; that's what did it. I saw him last week – the day before he died. Destroyed, you know; he was destroyed. A brilliant man, brilliant. He helped so many people. So many letters, you know, so many.'

The three of them stood silently, nodding their heads sadly, like puppets. She felt trapped suddenly, cornered, and wanted to get away, outside, wanted air.

'He carried on working of course,' said his brother. 'Wasn't allowed to call himself Doctor, any more – but they couldn't stop his clinic. Do you know what he did? He bought a doctorate by mail order from America. By mail order! So he could call himself Doctor again; they couldn't stop him!' He chuckled, looked at his sister and brother-in-law who smiled, and began nodding again.

Mail order, thought Alex. The New England Bureau. There was a heavy silence; Alex stared at them awkwardly, feeling like an imposter. 'Would you excuse me, just a moment?' she said, backing away from them; she turned and walked back into the hallway, feeling the tears streaming down her cheeks. She stopped and wiped her eyes, dabbing them gently.

'Leaving already?' She heard Otto's voice, and turned round.

'I have to get back to London.'

He smiled, the knowing smile again, she thought. 'With your business unfinished?'

She blushed. What did Otto know? How much did he know? What the hell was he doing here? 'Are you related to Dr Saffier, Otto?'

He shook his head. 'Just a pupil.'

'A pupil?' She felt his eyes raking her, boring into her.

'I wrote a thesis on him – on his work.'

'I – I thought you were studying chemistry?'

'Yes. His work was chemistry; chemistry and biology.' He smiled and stared, mockingly. 'Biology and chemistry are very intertwined, Mrs Hightower – I think you understand that more than most people.'

She felt herself reddening even more. How much do you know, she wanted to say, feeling her embarrassment beginning to turn to anger; how much do you know, you bastard?

He turned away from her, looked around the hall, and studied the suit of armour at the bottom of the stairs. Then suddenly he spun around and stared hard at her. 'I know why you have come here.'

She was startled by his words and by his movement; she tried to compose herself, tried to stare him back and show nothing. 'Do you?' she said acidly. 'Do you really?'

'Oh yes.' He smiled. 'I can help you. I know where the files are. I know where all of them are.' He turned away again, and began to walk across the hall towards a corridor.

She felt the anger draining away and helplessness replacing it. Limply, she followed him.

The drawer slid open silently and stopped with a sharp metallic clang.

'Tell me, Otto,' she said, 'why was Dr Saffier struck off?'

He stared inside the drawer at the files. 'He interfered with young boys in a public lavatory.'

She reeled as the words sank in, then watched his face, to see if it was a joke, something from his odd sense of humour. But there was nothing; a fact, that was all.

Did he interfere with you too, you bastard, she wondered.

'No,' he said, turning to face her.

'Pardon?' she said, feeling a flush sweeping through her that was both cold and hot at the same time.

'No, he did not interfere with me.'

She stared at him, feeling her head hot, so hot it was sweating. How? Had it shown in her face? Or had he picked it out of her mind?

She looked around the dank cellar, lit by one naked bulb, at the shadows that danced menacingly against the walls each time she or Otto moved, at the old green filing cabinets that stood in a row in the middle of the room like sentinels. What did they contain, she wondered, what secrets were there that should have been in Somerset House? What secrets were there that Saffier had not taken with him to the grave? This strange, brilliant man who interfered with boys. Public lavatories? Surely he had style? Surely he could have at least –? Frightened, she stared up at the stairs they had come down, up at the door at the top which Otto had closed and locked from the inside.

Otto ran his fingers through the files with a sharp clacking that echoed around, then stopped. He pulled out a slim green file and held it up to the light, studied it for a moment, then walked across the cellar floor to a metal table directly beneath the light bulb. He laid it down, nodded at her, then stood back.

Holding her breath, Alex walked over to the table and looked down; she saw the name typed on the index tab: **Hightower. Mrs A.** Nervously she lifted the flap. There was a wodge of graph paper and several index cards held together with a paper clip.

She felt her face go red as she looked at the graphs and remembered. Temperature charts, with the most likely days of each month circled in black. God, what they'd gone through. She looked at the top index card. Her date of birth. David's date of birth. His sperm count. Then a list of dates, with tiny illegible handwriting in faded ink beside each one. Her heart began to sink. Nothing. There was nothing here. Nothing that was going to help.

And then she saw it.

She began to tremble as she read, and then re-read, the tiny slanting handwriting beneath the date on the last card: 'J. T. Bosley'.

She heard again the echo of the sharp nasal voice. *My name is John Bosley. I'm the boy's father.*

She tried to hold the card, but her hand was shaking wildly. She looked around and saw strange shapes flickering in the shadows, flickering among the filing cabinets and along the walls that seemed to stretch away into the dark for ever.

She saw Otto's face; the smile. The smile. Otto walked to another filing cabinet, opened the drawer, pulled out another file, carried it to the table as if it were a priceless jewel, and laid it down. Again he stood back and folded his arms behind him.

The tab was marked, simply: **Donors.**

Inside was a thick wodge of computer printout. Names in alphabetical order, pages and pages. On the fourth page she found it: 'Bosley. John Terence. Guy's Hospital, Lon. Date of Birth: 27.4.46.' He would have been twenty-one then, she thought. It was followed by several lines of minute detail; the colour and texture of his hair, size of forehead, colour of eyes, exact length and shape of his nose, mouth, chin, teeth, neck, his build. She shivered. It could have been a description of Fabian.

At the end of his section were the words: 'Donations used: 1 time. Ref. Hightower, Mrs A.'

She turned and looked at Otto.

'Have you seen enough?' he said.

'Is there any more?' she said, weakly, trembling.

He smiled again; that hideous knowing smile; the mocking eyes. 'Not down here.'

'So where?'

'That depends on what you want to know.'

'Don't play games with me, please, Otto.'

'I don't play games.'

'Who was John Bosley? What was he like? How did he die?'

'He's a doctor. But I don't think he died.'

Alex shuddered as the snarling in the séance came back. Bosley's words. *Don't let the little bastard* . . . 'Yes; he's dead; I know that.'

Otto looked at her scornfully and shook his head. 'He didn't die.'

'How do you know?' she demanded, feeling her temper flaring.

'I already told you. I know a lot of things.'

'Well this is one that you don't.'

He smiled. 'Would you like his address?'

She looked, hesitantly. Something; there was something in the way he spoke. 'What is it?'

'It's easy to remember. Dover Ward, Kent House, Broadmoor.'

'He's a staff doctor there?'

'Oh no, Mrs Hightower.' Otto smiled. 'He's an inmate.'

The words sank in slowly. Inmate. Inmate. She wanted to

escape from here, be somewhere, anywhere, alone. She wanted to be away from the eyes, from the smile, from the pleasure that was in that smile. Inmate. Public lavatories. What had Saffier been up to? How much damage had he done, to her, to others? Christ, what the hell had he been playing at? Impregnating her with the sperm from a criminal lunatic. 'What – why – was – is he there, Otto?'

Otto shrugged. 'Murder; I don't remember how many.'

'Who – how –?' She wanted to sit down, wanted desperately to sit; she leaned against the table, let it take her weight, tried to think clearly. 'Who did he murder?'

Otto shrugged, and smiled. 'Women.'

'Did Fabian know?' She stared at the floor.

'Yes.'

'You told him?'

'A son has a right to know who his parents are.'

She felt a flash of rage, but bit her lip, somehow contained it.

'I showed him the file.'

Alex glared at Otto. 'And you thought you were being frightfully clever?'

'Your son was kind to his father, Mrs Hightower. Kinder than you will ever know.'

What did he mean? A knife. It was as if he had a knife inside her and kept on twisting it. 'He was a very kind boy,' she said, helplessly.

Otto glanced up at the door and smiled again. 'Shall we go back and join the party?'

CHAPTER TWENTY-FIVE

She drove up the hill through the messy High Street of the village; an uneasy blend of neat Victorian red brick houses and modern urban sprawl. Plenty of money. How did they feel, she wondered, living here, so close?

The sign was like any other road sign, small, unobtrusive: Broadmoor. 1/2 mile.

She felt her pulse racing as she turned off into a much steeper road. It did not feel right, it was too quiet, too residential. She wondered whether she had misread the direction: she saw an elderly man weeding the front garden of his bungalow and she stopped the Mercedes. Then she hesitated for a moment, embarrassed, suddenly, embarrassed to ask the way, embarrassed to admit to a stranger that she was going there.

'Is this the right road for Broadmoor.'

'Straight up; you'll see the sign.'

She felt herself blushing under his gaze; what did he think her business was? Was there something wrong in going there? In merely being even associated with the place?

The sign rose up from behind a tall hedgerow. 'Broadmoor Hospital. Private.' Grey with black and red lettering. She turned into a road with neatly trimmed grass verges. 'Private Road Patrolled by Wardens.'

A few hundred yards further up the hill, she rounded a corner, and gasped. Christ. The massive buttressed red-brick wall and the huge Victorian red-brick institution rising up behind it, with the barred windows and the steep slate roof. More unfolded; it seemed to go on for ever. A huge red-brick tower with guard rails, a weather vane and a massive radio aerial at the top and the wall, stretching away out of sight. The wall. She shivered. Bosley was in there, somewhere. The father of her child.

There was a maze of roads and signs and triangles of neatly mown grass in front of her. 'Staff Club, Access to Main Gate For Collections, Deliveries & Emergencies Only, Cricket Ground.' Signs. Everywhere. Everything labelled. Was John Bosley labelled too? 'Upper Broadmoor Road, Terrace, Chaplain's Hill, Drive Carefully, Speed Controlled Ramps.' She looked around, bewildered, for the road name she had been given. Then she saw it, right beside her. Kentigern Road.

She followed along and it dipped down away from the wall, past a sloping lawn with two fir trees and a small statue of a winged angel. Salvation, she thought, staring at it puzzled. Then she saw the house, Redwoods. A sizeable modern brick house, standing back from the road behind another grass triangle, with a parking area in front of it.

The door opened before she had got out of her car and the chaplain stepped out, a sturdy middle-aged man with greying hair and a kindly face; he was dressed in conventional black, with a white dog-collar, and wore sandals, she noticed. His glasses were turning dark in the sunlight, blotting out his eyes.

'Mrs Hightower?'

She nodded and his hand enveloped hers, warm, firm, comforting.

'You found it all right?'

'Thank you.'

He looked at his watch. 'I'm afraid we will have to be brief – unfortunately one of our patients has had a sudden family bereavement and I must . . .'

'Of course,' she said. 'It's kind of you to see me at such short notice.'

He led her through into a large drawing room with a pink carpet and pointed her to a sofa. He sat down in an armchair and put his feet up on a pink pouffe. She looked around the room. Everything was in soft pinks and browns;

the colours were unobtrusive, like the furniture, but did not quite blend. The room felt oddly bare to Alex, lacking bits and pieces, ornaments, as if it had recently been burgled. There was a solitary Coalport statuette on the mantelpiece, a young courting couple, a framed photograph of a schoolboy on the wall and a television; but little else, nothing to dominate, nothing to distract from the presence of the man in the armchair opposite her. She wrung her hands together. 'It's very kind of you to see me,' she repeated.

He smiled benignly. 'Not at all.' He paused. 'John Bosley?'

She nodded.

'Know him well.'

'He really is still alive, is he?'

There was a strange flicker across his face. 'He was yesterday, yes. Very much so.'

'I wasn't sure – that was all.'

'Oh yes, very much alive.' He stood up. 'I've just remembered – one moment.' He went out of the room and she stared around again, at the television, the video, then back at the statuette on the mantelpiece. Two young things from another century, elegant, in love, carefree. Carefree. Was there such a place, she wondered?

'I brought this – just to make sure.' He walked back into the room and handed her a small black and white photograph.

She stared down. The photograph was shaking in her hands, shaking so much it was almost a blur. She saw a double portrait, one face-on, the other in profile, with a row of numbers printed beneath, a pale gaunt face; a shock of fair hair. And the eyes. The eyes. 'Oh my God,' she mouthed. 'Fabian. It's just so incredibly like him.' The photograph fell out of her hands into her lap. She tried to pick it up, but it danced in her trembling fingers then flipped on to the floor. She leaned over, feeling sick suddenly, violently sick, and put her hand in front of her mouth.

She breathed deeply and it passed. Then she looked at the chaplain again. He was back in his chair, smiling gently.

'Very difficult,' he said, gently. 'Very difficult.'

'The likeness,' she said. 'It's incredible.'

He nodded; there was something about his expression that she thought was odd.

'You've never seen him before?'

She shook her head.

'Forgive me – I don't quite understand. You say he's the father of your – er – son?'

She nodded.

'But you've never seen him?'

She felt herself going red. 'My husband was – er – is – infertile. I was inseminated by semen from a donor – John Bosley was the donor. It was all done through a specialist in London.'

He nodded, frowning. 'So you're not, strictly speaking, related?' He paused. 'Well, I suppose you must be; an interesting one, that.' He smiled, happier.

'Would it be possible to see him?'

'I'd have to get the Governor's consent.'

'I'd like to see him.'

He smiled. 'I don't know.' He shook his head. 'It may be opening a whole can of worms that's not good for his treatment. I can put your request forward – but I'm not optimistic. He's making progress you see, but the treatment of schizophrenia is a very slow and difficult business, and he has of course already had a major set-back.'

'Am I allowed to know why he's here?'

He stood up again. 'I brought the file – I think it's probably quite irregular – but under the circumstances – I'm sure we can make an exception.'

She pushed the sheaf of stiff typewritten sheets back into the yellow envelope and wound the cotton back around the fastener.

'Oh – before you do that, we'd better put the photograph back.'

'Photograph,' she said, mechanically. The blood was drained out of her and she felt exhausted. She unwound the cotton again, grateful to have something to do for a moment, to occupy her mind, anything. 'Photograph,' she said, again.

'Mrs Hightower, there's nowhere in the Bible,' he said gently, 'nowhere where it says that a person has to be a good person to be of value.'

She stared at him blankly, seeing only the stark paper and the clinical black typing, and nodded, trying to fight back the tears. 'If someone is mad,' she said, falteringly, feeling a tear running down her cheek, 'if someone is mad, can they be absolved of blame?'

'God laid down the Ten Commandments. We cannot break them without responsibility. There is sin and there is responsibility, even in the mentally ill. Psychiatrists cannot wipe a slate clean. I cannot either.' He smiled again and crossed his legs. 'A person who has committed a crime when ill can only become better when he becomes aware of what he has done, when he can say "I was ill then, but now I feel I need to be forgiven".'

'Has John Bosley said that?'

He shook his head. 'I'm afraid he's confused, terribly confused.'

'It seems very cruel,' she said.

'Cruel?'

'Cruel of God to make that condition.'

'We take the view, in the Church of England, that evil will not enter a person who will not receive it.' He smiled. 'Evil must be invited in – Satan must be invited by that person into his life. Satan will not come on his own.'

She looked at him, chilled. 'You're saying that John Bosley, in spite of his madness, is fundamentally evil?'

He lifted his arms, slowly, with a sad bemused expression on his face. 'Perhaps not in spite of his madness – we must consider the possibility that the mental problems of someone who has committed a terrible crime are a symptom of their evil.'

She shuddered. There was a long silence and she sensed him looking at his watch.

'Can schizophrenia be passed on – inherited?'

'There is a lot of evidence, yes. The Schizophrenics Society could give you information – they have been making some very interesting discoveries.'

'So my son –?'

'It's a possibility to be aware of.' He looked at his watch again. 'Perhaps you could come back and we can have a longer chat?'

'Thank you. I'd like that.'

He stood up and straightened his shirt.

'You said that there had been a set-back in his treatment – what was that?'

His face reddened and he touched his hands together, awkwardly. 'Just a foolish incident,' he said. 'Very foolish.'

'What happened?'

He looked again at his watch. 'Nothing. It was nothing.' He paused. 'Perhaps you should know. Next time – I'll tell you next time – I'll have to think about it.'

She stared. What was it? What the hell was it?

'You'll be able to find your way out all right? Back to the main road? Just turn right.'

'Thank you, Father – er – Reverend – er –' she said.

He smiled. 'Call me. I'm very busy for the next few weeks – perhaps in June sometime?'

'Thank you,' she said. 'You've been very kind.' But his mind was somewhere else, somewhere a long way away.

CHAPTER TWENTY-SIX

'He wouldn't let me keep the photo.'

Philip Main lay back with his feet on his desk. He crossed his legs, uncrossed them, and ground his heels into the pile of papers, then raised himself up on his elbows and shifted his weight in the armchair. He stared, pensively, at the phone. 'Extraordinary, this man Bosley. Just left her?'

'Apparently.'

'Chained her up in a cellar?'

Alex nodded, white-faced.

'And left her?'

'Yes.'

'Without telling anyone.'

She said nothing.

'Did he have a grudge – against women?'

Alex turned her cigarette over in her fingers. 'She'd jilted him.'

'Extraordinary. Quite extraordinary. A doctor; must be an intelligent chap – you expect this sort of – in –' He opened his hands out. 'People do extraordinary things.'

'Why, Philip?'

The room darkened suddenly and she heard a spatter of rain outside. She thought of a cold cellar, a woman, chained, sitting, whimpering, shivering and heard the drip of water. She shuddered.

Main pushed a cigarette through the fronds of his moustache and let it hang there, unlit. 'What gave you the idea?'

'The idea?'

'To see the chaplain?'

She shrugged. 'I don't know. I rang up Broadmoor to see

if I could see Bosley.' She smiled, suddenly, weakly. 'When they answered they sounded just like a hotel.'

'And they wouldn't let you see him?'

'You have to write to the Board of Governors. I asked if there was anyone I could speak to.' She shrugged. 'They put me through to the chaplain.'

Alex stared around the chaotic study, at Black, asleep on the sofa. His desk, work table, filing cabinets, military chest and almost every inch of floor space were covered in piles of paper. An ancient electric typewriter was buried under it, so were the printer, screen and keyboard of his computer. It was everywhere, like snow. 'It reminds me of your car,' she said.

'My car?'

'Your study. How do you work in here?'

'I manage.'

She smiled. 'I don't think I've ever been in one of my author's studies before. It's quite an insight.'

He looked around, nodding. 'You haven't been in the office much.'

'Are you keeping tabs on me?'

'No, good Lord, no. I think it's good that you are staying down with David.'

'He's trying to keep me sane.'

He fumbled with a box of matches. 'Will you –' He sounded embarrassed. 'Will you get back together?'

She shook her head.

He struck a match and lit his cigarette, looking at her quizzically. She blushed.

'He's being very kind to me; he has a lot of strength. I suppose I need him at the moment, and I wish I didn't; I don't want to hurt him again.' She paused. 'He deserves someone nicer than me.'

'Gosh, don't underestimate yourself, girl.'

She felt weepy and closed her eyes tightly for a moment, nodding her head. 'I'm so frightened, Philip.'

'What's David's view?'

She stared out through the window at the grimy rear wall of the house behind. 'He wants me to see a psychiatrist.'

Main shook his head. 'No,' he said. 'Gosh, no.'

'What do you think I should do? You're so full of contradictions, aren't you. I need help, Philip. I must have help.' She looked at him again. 'You said, last time we spoke, that sometimes spirits try to come back because they have unfinished business.'

'It's a theory. Just a theory.'

'Everything's just a bloody theory to you.'

He looked hurt and stared around the room, helplessly.

'I'm sorry,' she said. 'I didn't mean to get angry. But all you ever do is give me theories; all everyone does is give me damned theories. Last night I had three hours of David's theory, how I'm emotionally disturbed, in need of psychiatric help. I had the curate's theory, a few days ago, that I'm in need of pastoral help. I have Morgan Ford's theory, about dark forces of evil. And I have you, going on about genes, what is it? That we are prisoners of our genes?' She leaned forward in the hard chair. 'The chaplain talked about genes, too; that schizophrenia could be passed on. Ford talked about genes as well. He said they were important to the spirit world; something about them being the blue-print for character.'

Main nodded, slowly. 'They are.'

The phone rang. Main leaned over and picked up the receiver. 'Hallo?' he said, thoughtfully.

Alex watched him. She felt safe here, safe with his clouds of smoke and his crumpled jacket and his solid furniture. Knowledge; he knew things, knew so much, had the answers to so many mysteries. He was comfortable with life.

Except. She thought with a shudder of the last time he had sat in her drawing room.

He picked up a pen and scribbled on the back of the nearest sheet of paper. 'Good Lord.' He paused, then continued scribbling for a long time. 'Right,' he said, finally. 'Terrific. See you.' He hung up and looked at Alex.

There was something in his eyes, a heavy weight, hanging there awkwardly. 'That was my – er – chum, the prison psychiatrist.'

'Yes?'

He smoothed out his moustache with his fingers. 'The one who used to work in Broadmoor.'

'He came back quickly.'

Main picked up the sheet of paper and looked at it, then peered at her with a worried expression.

'Did the chaplain say anything to you about –' he hesitated, '– about Fabian visiting?'

She went white. 'When?'

'About a year ago.'

She shook her head. 'Nothing, except –' she paused. 'He was going to tell me about something, but didn't. He seemed to change his mind; it might have been because we were short of time – but I don't think so. Fabian went there? To see Bosley?'

'There was quite a to-do, apparently.' He crushed out his cigarette and shook another one out of the pack. 'Quite a to-do.' He glanced down at his notes, then struck a match and lit his cigarette.

She stared at his two black boots on the desk, and noticed the heels were scuffed down at the back.

'While the chaplain was away on holiday, apparently. They have a locum – the vicar of Sandhurst – he is cleared for security – and his curates –' He turned his cigarette over in his hand. 'Fabian got hold of some theology student, managed to pass him and some other chap off as curates from Sandhurst, and got inside.' He looked across at her.

She stared back at him puzzled. 'Why?'

'They carried out an exorcism.'

The room darkened suddenly and she felt afraid. 'And what happened?'

'It wasn't discovered until too late.'

'Too late?'

He shrugged.

'Don't you think,' she said, slowly, 'that Fabian probably

233

meant it kindly? That he thought he was doing the right thing. Wouldn't you try to help your father?'

The room was becoming cold, bitterly cold, and she could feel draughts all around her.

Black sat up on the sofa and gave a low rumbling growl.

Main drew hard on his cigarette.

She stared at him, afraid, terribly afraid. 'He was a kind boy; I'm sure he would have tried to help him.' She thought of a cold dark cellar, a woman, chained, sitting, whimpering, shivering and heard the drip of water. 'Who was there?'

'Fabian, the theology student chap called Andrew Castle and another chap from Cambridge, not a priest at all –' Philip leaned across to study his notes '– someone called Otto von Essenberg.'

The room seemed to slip sideways. 'Of course,' she said, bitterly, 'Otto. Fabian followed him around like a lamb.' She shook her head. 'What happens at exorcisms?'

'They try to drive the demons – the evil spirits – out of the person.'

'It sounds slightly barbaric.'

'It is barbaric,' he said, then raised his eyebrows mysteriously. 'But sometimes the old remedies are best.'

'Are you serious?'

'There is evidence, girl, it does seem to have worked, sometimes.'

'Did it work on Bosley?'

He glanced at his scrawled notes. 'His personality changed – and remained changed. He was aggressive and cruel before – then he became very docile, confused.'

'Isn't that his schizophrenia?'

He drew deeply again on his cigarette and said nothing.

'Don't you think, Philip?' she insisted. 'Surely that could have been part of his condition?'

'Perhaps,' he said, distantly.

She shivered, and saw Philip watching her with a worried frown, saw him toy with his moustache. 'I'm frightened, Philip.' She closed her eyes. 'Oh, God, Philip, help me.'

'I did suggest that you left it alone.'

'No.' She shook her head violently. 'No!'

'It would have been better.'

She looked up at him. 'It's easy to say that. He's not your son.'

Main stood up and laid his hand gently on her shoulder. 'You'll be all right, girl, don't worry. Would you like some coffee?'

She nodded and closed her eyes; she heard him walk out into the hall and listened to the steady drip of the rain, echoing around the room, around her head, around a dark empty chamber.

'It's hot.'

She looked up and took the mug carefully. A car hooted outside. Normality; there was a real world somewhere out there, with ordinary people doing ordinary things. She wanted to be out there among them. 'What am I going to do?' she said.

'Go away, have a holiday.'

'You're not even trying to understand.'

He smiled, kindly. 'I am, believe me.'

'Nothing will change if I go away; it'll all be the same when I come back.' She felt the fear and her helplessness overwhelm her.

He sank back down into the armchair. 'Oh dear, girl,' he said. 'Oh dear.'

She fumbled for her handkerchief as the tears streamed down her cheek, then sniffed and blew her nose. 'Otto said that Saffier didn't know.'

'Didn't know?' said Philip, puzzled. 'Didn't know what?'

'About Bosley. About his condition. Thought he was just a normal healthy student. None of this – it didn't happen until years after.'

'How did he find out?'

'It was Otto that –' she paused, suddenly, as if a curtain had come down inside her mind. 'It was Otto,' she repeated, the words sounding like an echo. 'I – er –' but she had forgotten what she was going to say.

It seemed that the temperature in the room dropped even further. She sipped her coffee and sniffed again. Philip lit another cigarette and snorted the smoke through his nostrils. She watched the steam rise from her coffee.

'If an exorcism is successful, Philip, what happens to the spirit – the demon – whatever it is that's driven out?' She shuddered as a cold chill eddied through her.

He tested his coffee with his finger and stared thoughtfully at it. 'It has to find a new host.'

'Someone with the same genetic make-up?'

'It's a possibility.' He tested his coffee again. 'There's a scene in the Bible – Jesus casting out devils – sent them into swine.'

'I didn't see any pigs at Broadmoor.'

He stared at her and she felt her face reddening; she felt his gaze penetrating through, inside, deep into the innermost sanctum of her mind. He understood.

'Perhaps, girl,' he said.

'It might explain a lot of things, Philip.'

'Perhaps,' he said. 'It's a job to know.'

'Everything's a bloody job to know.'

He nodded, looking worried again. 'You should be careful of your medium,' he said, suddenly.

She looked at him. 'Why?'

'Sometimes they can be dangerous.'

She tried to read his face, but it was impossible. 'What do you mean, dangerous?'

'Having a go at –' he paused '– at things even they are not sure about.'

She blew her nose and sniffed again. 'You know, don't you, Philip? You know it all.'

He paused for a long time before answering. 'No, I don't know.' He shook his head slowly from side to side, then he stood up and walked over to his bookshelves, and stared at the titles. 'No, good Lord no, far from it.'

There was a long silence. 'Philip,' she said, finally, 'last time we spoke, you said that sometimes spirits try to come back –' she felt acutely self-conscious saying the words '– because they have unfinished business. How would they do that?'

He spoke softly, almost apologetically. 'The spiritualist view is that – that they would have to come back through someone.'

'Through someone?'

'Someone carnate. Living.'

'Possess them?'

Main nodded. 'Discarnate spirits have no energy.'

'So they would use a human's energy?'

'That is the spiritualist view.'

'A host?'

He nodded.

'The same as a spirit that has been exorcised?'

He nodded again, warily.

'How would they find someone?' she said, sensing a sudden dryness in her throat.

He shrugged. 'The spirit would look for someone with a weakness.'

'What do you mean, weakness?'

'Unguarded.' He pushed his cigarette into his mouth and puffed furiously on it, then inhaled the smoke sharply, with a hiss. She looked at him and saw that he was shaking, deeply distressed.

'Evil spirits are cunning. They can con people.'

'Con?'

'It's been known.'

'What sort of con?'

'Often they pretend to be someone else.'

She felt the single shiver roller-coaster through her, like a tidal wave; it nearly swept her out of her chair.

'They pick on someone who is down; bereaved people make the easiest targets of all.'

Stop looking at me, she thought; please stop looking at me like that. 'No,' she said, shaking her head. 'No.'

'They can be very clever. Far more clever than it is possible to imagine.'

237

She shook her head. 'How can you stop them?' she said, her voice barely even a whisper.

'As a scientist?' he said.

She shook her head. 'No,' she said, and her voice became bolder. 'As a person honest with himself.'

He looked at her, then away, down at the ground, and shifted his weight, embarrassed. He crushed out his cigarette and pulled out a fresh pack from under a deep layer of paper.

'There has only been one effective way through the ages.' He looked at her, then turned his attentions to opening the cigarette pack. 'The power of prayer.'

He looked relieved suddenly, she thought, as if he had overcome some deep inner conflict to get the words out.

'Prayer?'

'Hrrr.'

'What sort of prayer?'

His face went red and he stared at the ground as if reading from a prompter's script. 'Exorcism.'

She began to shiver violently; the temperature in the room seemed to have dropped even further, 'Is it cold in here?'

There was no answer.

'Philip?' She felt her voice quavering. 'Philip?' She looked wildly from side to side then spun around; he was standing behind her, a gentle worried look in his eyes. 'Is it cold in here?'

'I'll shut the window.'

'No.' She did not want it to be shut, did not want the outside world excluded. 'Perhaps I've just got a chill.'

She felt his strong hands squeeze her shoulders and she tried to stop shaking, but she couldn't. 'I would do anything in the world to stop this nightmare.'

'Then see a priest,' he said, quietly, squeezing her shoulders again. 'It would be best for both of us.'

CHAPTER TWENTY-SEVEN

She drove up the narrow road behind Chelsea football ground, into a sprawling modern housing estate, and leaned over towards the passenger window trying to read the numbers. She hoped he wouldn't mind being disturbed at lunch-time.

Number 38, like all the rest, was a small semi with a prim front garden, and she was slightly embarrassed about parking the Mercedes outside. She walked down the short path and rang the doorbell. Please be in, she thought, please be in.

The curate came to the door in clean and neatly pressed jeans and an old pullover, holding a piece of Lego in his hand. He looked younger than she remembered.

'Hallo,' she said, tentatively, then fumbled, wondering what to call him. Reverend? Mr?

'John Allsop,' he said helpfully, sensing her difficulty, and stared at her, trying to place her. There was a slight twitch of his right eye. 'Mrs Hightower, isn't it?'

She nodded.

'How nice to see you. How are you?'

The enthusiasm of his greeting stumped her and she was lost for words for a moment. 'I'm fine,' she said, nodding, then wondered why she had said that.

'Good.' He rocked from foot to foot and stared at the piece of Lego in his hand; she wondered if he was about to throw it in the air, like a juggler. 'Good,' he said again.

'I wondered if it would be possible to have a word?'

'Of course, come in.'

She followed him into the narrow hallway. The sitting room floor was covered in Lego bricks, with what looked like a half-built crane in their midst.

He smiled apologetically. 'Dreadful stuff this, far too complicated for me. Gave it to my son for his birthday. Ever tried it?'

She shook her head. 'Looks very good.'

'I'm afraid that was my son, not me.'

They went into a tiny study at the rear of the house and he pointed her to the one armchair. She sat down, looking around. The room was blandly furnished and, in contrast to Philip's study, immaculately tidy. There was a small home-made bookshelf, filled with religious reference books which looked as if they were dusted every day, and several fossils and fragments of pottery on a mantelpiece above an electric fire.

'Is that your hobby, archaeology?' she said.

'Yes.' His face became animated. 'Those are all from digs I've been on.'

'Interesting,' she said, hoping her voice reciprocated some measure of enthusiasm.

'How are you getting on? It was about ten days ago that I came to see you, wasn't it?'

She nodded. 'Not very well, I'm afraid.'

'It's a difficult time this. He was your only child, wasn't he?'

'Yes.'

'And you have marriage difficulties too, I believe?'

'Yes.'

'Sometimes,' he said, gently, 'this sort of thing can bring people closer together.'

She shook her head and smiled sadly. 'We have a good relationship, but I'm afraid we won't ever get back together.' She remembered, suddenly, Allsop had told her that his own wife had died recently, and blushed, not wanting to make him feel ill at ease. 'How are you coping, bringing up your son?'

'All right,' he said, and a sad look came across his face. 'People think it must be easier for people like me, in the clergy, to cope with things; but we go through the same feelings too.'

'You have your faith, though.'

He smiled again. 'That gets sorely tested at times. Especially when your son eats your sermon.'

She grinned. 'How is your book going?'

'Ah, you remembered. Slowly, I'm afraid.'

'That's what my clients always say.'

'It's difficult, applying oneself. I'm – ah – digressing.' He looked at her questioningly.

'I don't know quite where to begin.' She clasped her hands together and interlocked her fingers. 'There are some very strange things that have been happening, and I'm frightened.'

His eye twitched again. 'What sort of things?'

'I'm not quite sure how to describe them. Weird things, things that there's not really any explanation for.'

'Do you mean perhaps that your mind is playing tricks?'

'No, not tricks.'

'Bereavement causes all sorts of tricks to be played on the mind.'

She shook her head. 'These aren't tricks. Really they aren't. I'm not a nervy person; I don't have a wild imagination.' She looked at him and knotted her fingers even tighter. 'There are some very strange things happening in my house, and I'm not the only one who thinks that.' She looked at him and wished he was older; he looked so young, so green, she thought. 'I've been advised –' she paused again, feeling slightly foolish under his concerned gaze '– that I ought to bring in an exorcist.'

His eyes widened and she felt him staring at her for a long time.

'An exorcist?'

'You probably think I'm mad.'

'No, I don't think that at all. But I think we should talk about these things that are frightening you, see if we can find a reason for them –' he paused '– and perhaps look at some alternative solutions.'

'Would it be possible, do you think, for us to talk at my house?'

He looked hesitant. 'Of course, if that would be easier for you? I'll have a look in my diary.'

'Is there any chance that you could come now?'

He frowned at his watch. 'I have to pick up my son from school at four.' He looked at her again and his face mirrored her seriousness. 'Yes, that would be all right.'

She saw a parking spot a short way down from her house and slowed down.

'Very nice motor car,' he said.

'It's only an old one,' she said, and instantly regretted the patronising tone of her voice. 'Over twenty years old.'

'I'm afraid the Church doesn't run to Mercedes cars.'

She detected the note of envy. 'They're a bit silly really. Very expensive to service.'

'We all need our compensations,' he said.

She looked at him; what were his compensations, she wondered. God? The fossils?

Mimsa had gone, leaving behind one of her usual barely decipherable notes. She switched the kettle on then went out into the hallway. The curate was pacing around the drawing room, looking up at the ceiling, frowning.

'White or black?'

'White, without, please.'

She took the coffee in. 'Must just pop to the loo. There's one just under the stairs, if you —?'

'Ah.' He nodded politely.

As she climbed the stairs she realized that the house felt curiously hot, muggy, as if the heating had been left on all day. It felt even hotter upstairs. She tested the radiator on the landing; it was stone cold. She looked around uncomfortably, then went into her bedroom and walked into her bathroom. It felt like an airing cupboard.

She stood at the basin washing her hands and examined her face in the mirror. It was wet with perspiration. She pressed her hand against her forehead, but it was cold, almost icily cold, she thought, and wondered if she was going down with flu. She dabbed her face gently with a towel, careful not to smudge her make-up, closed her eyes and patted the lids.

There was a sudden cold blast of air, as if a freezer door had opened, and she felt the presence of someone watching her. She opened her eyes slowly and looked in the mirror.

Fabian was standing, motionless, right behind her.

She was conscious of a terrible jerk inside her chest, as if she had pushed a finger into an electrical socket, and then her body was wracked with pins and needles, hurting her so much she wanted to cry out in pain.

As she turned around to face him she realized there was no air in the room. She could not breathe.

He stood there, wearing a white shirt and his favourite floppy jumper, solid, so solid it seemed she could reach out and touch him.

But there was no air.

He was smiling a strange unfamiliar wry smile, and there was something in the dark of his eyes that was mocking her, something she had never seen before in her son, something that was ringing a terrible bell.

She felt herself beginning to panic. The pain of the pins and needles was unbearable; she was shaking, her lungs ached, and she felt violently sick.

Tricks of your mind, she heard the curate's voice echo. Tricks of your mind.

She swayed, beginning to black out, pushed her trembling hands out behind her and clutched the basin.

And then he was gone.

She staggered into her bedroom, gasping, looking wildly around. She ran, tripping down the stairs, and stood in the hallway gulping air, shivering and itching all over. She went through into the drawing room. Allsop was staring at his coffee with intense concentration. He looked up uneasily as she came in. 'I didn't realize — you have another son?'

'Eh?' She blinked at him, unable to speak.

'The young man who just went up the stairs.'

Why was he smiling? What did he think was so funny? Then she realized it wasn't a smile at all but his nervous twitch.

'Fair-haired?' she gulped.

'Yes,' he said, quietly.

'In a floppy sort of pullover?'

Again he nodded.

She clutched the arm of a chair for support, unable to stand any more, sat down and closed her eyes. Then she opened them and stared at him again. 'I don't have another son. That was Fabian.'

She heard a sharp clack, followed by another, as his cup rattled in the saucer. She saw the spoon vibrating in his hand, rattling against the side of the cup as if he were playing a tiny musical instrument, and she saw the coffee slopping over the side.

'I see,' he said finally, his right eye opening and closing. With great difficulty he put the cup and saucer down and looked around the room, clearly badly shaken, trying to compose himself. 'Is that what you meant?'

Alex felt something soft and realized she was still holding the towel. She began to fold it, pressing carefully along the creases. 'Yes.'

'There is no possibility of there being someone else in the house?'

'What do you mean?'

'Like a window cleaner or a plumber, someone like that?'

She shook her head.

'No,' he said, opening and closing his mouth several times, like a goldfish, she thought.

'Do you understand now what I mean?'

He looked around the room again and then at her. 'About an exorcism?'

'Can you help me?'

He cupped his hands together and gently rocked backwards and forwards in his chair. He looked into his hands, frowning in deep concentration. 'There are alternatives to –

er – exorcism, which have the same effect. Exorcism is seldom advisable, I'm afraid there is rather a lot of bureaucracy surrounding it these days. One has to present a case to the bishop and it's up to him to decide; it can take several weeks at the very least.' He looked up at her, fearful. 'You see, it's rather frowned upon these days; ordinary clergy like me are not allowed to perform the exorcism service.'

'I can't wait several weeks,' said Alex. 'Please, you must do something.'

'It could be very much longer in your case, under our current guidelines.'

'What do you mean?'

'Permission would not normally be given after a bereavement for at least two years.'

She thought again of the terror in the bathroom and felt overwhelmed with helplessness. 'Two years?' she echoed, weakly.

'I'm afraid the Church considers the balance of people's minds can be in a troubled state for a long time after bereavement. It is only if things continue after this period that the service of Deliverance can be considered.'

'Deliverance?'

'The modern terminology.' He smiled and she saw the twitch again. 'The Church prefers the word Deliverance – it sounds perhaps a little less dramatic.'

'But surely,' said Alex, 'if it can be proven – you've just seen yourself.'

'The Church has been aware for centuries that the state of possession is normally caused by mental illness and not by spirits. The Church of England leaders have become increasingly involved in psychology these days; there is a strong awareness that not all problems can be resolved by pastoral care alone. I suppose it is an effort by the Church to move with the times, to become more responsible. Frequently, the circumstances in which clergymen have diagnosed the need for exorcism and carried it out have turned out to be mental illness, and they have sometimes made matters worse.'

'And you think I'm mentally ill?'

He looked at her, then around the room again. 'No. I think that you may be right. There is a presence in this house. Something troubled. But I don't think an exorcism is necessary. We need to try to establish why the spirit is troubled, then perhaps we can lay it to rest.' He rocked backwards and forwards again.

'I know why he is troubled.'

Allsop looked at her, continuing to rock backwards and forwards. 'Would you like to tell me?' he said gently.

She looked at him, then shook her head. 'No. I can't.'

'It would be helpful to know the reason.'

She looked out of the window, then suddenly at the hallway, convinced she saw something move. She listened hard, watching, but there was nothing more. She stared at the curate. 'I think that he had unfinished business.'

He stopped rocking, then started again. 'I'm afraid most of us depart unprepared, with much that we have planned to do in life still undone.'

She nodded.

'Is that what you mean?'

'No.' She looked down at the towel, then at Allsop. 'I think he wants to come back to kill someone.'

She looked down again, unable to face his stare, unable to face the knowledge that he thought she was mad.

'I think a Requiem Mass would be the answer,' she heard him say, gently, quietly.

She looked up at him. 'What do you mean?'

'We could hold a simple Requiem Mass service here in the house. I think you'd find that would lay everything to rest.'

She felt uncomfortable, frightened by the words. 'How – would – what – I'm not sure exactly what you mean.'

'We could have it today, if you like, after I've collected my son. I'd just have a few things to bring.'

She stared at him. 'What things?'

He looked at his watch. 'About six o'clock, would that suit you?'

246

Could he help her, this solemn young man with his nervous twitch and his pristine jeans? Could he confound all that was going on with a few prayers? Or would the spirits laugh him out of the house?

'Fine,' she heard herself say. 'Thank you.'

'What will you do until then?'

'Do?' her voice said.

'I think it would be best if you did not remain in the house this afternoon. Is there somewhere you could go? Some friend you could visit?'

'The office. I'll go to the office.'

'Yes,' he said. 'A good idea. Try to concentrate on something different.'

He stood up, looked around nervously, and made his way to the front door. He stared at the staircase and his eyes widened, filled with uncertainty.

She followed him out of the house without looking back.

CHAPTER TWENTY-EIGHT

'There's an Andrew Mallins on the line; he says he has an idea for a play he would like to discuss.'

She shook her head. 'No, Julie,' she said into the intercom. 'Not today.'

'Do you want to speak to him at all?'

'Ask him to call me next week.'

She stared hopelessly at her desk; Christ, how it had piled up. She looked at the wooden calendar. Wed. May 3rd. The intercom buzzed again.

'There's a Mr Prior on the line,' said Julie.

'Mr Prior? I don't know him.'

Julie's voice dropped. 'From the crematorium,' she said sympathetically.

'O.K.'

Mr Prior's tone was deferential but to the point. 'I was wondering,' he said, 'if you have had time to consider what you would like to do with the ashes?'

She looked at the calendar again. May 3rd. The chill went through her. May 3rd. Tomorrow, she thought. Tomorrow. May 4th. 'The ashes?'

'Of course, we could scatter them for you, if you'd prefer.'

'No,' she said.

'We do offer several very nice options. Perhaps a rose bush? We could scatter them over it, or bury the ashes under. Not in the urn of course, there's not really the room.'

'No,' she said, absently, 'Of course not.'

'There's no need to make a decision now – we will hold them for you for three months.'

Urn, she thought. A small black polystyrene pot. God, if only it was that simple. May 4th. May 4th. Tomorrow.

'A carved plaque on the wall is very popular; of course, you do have to renew it every fifteen years.'

'Of course.'

'An entry in the Book of Remembrance is permanent; that's a once-only payment.'

A small black pot filled with fine white powder. Her child.

'There are some spaces still available in the rockery – but they are a little inaccessible. I'm afraid there's a waiting list for the more popular sites.'

May 4th.

'Or, of course, you could have the urn; a lot of people do that now; scatter them in his favourite place. Very popular these days; no cost involved, you see.'

Favourite place. Scatter them over the lake. She thought of holding the pot, unscrewing the lid, the ashes blowing in her face, and shuddered.

'Perhaps I could think it over,' she said.

'Yes, there's no hurry, we hold them for three months before – er – disposing of them. Of course, we would notify you first.'

'Of course.'

May 4th.

Philip Main was on the line. Did she want to speak to him? Where was the man from the crematorium, she thought, suddenly. Had she finished speaking with him? How had she left it with him?

'How are you?' he said softly.

'O.K.'

'Did you . . .?'

'Yes. This evening.' She felt tears flooding into her eyes. 'They're doing a Requiem Mass. He said an exorcism would take a long time to arrange – that they wouldn't do one so soon after – Oh God, Philip, I'm so frightened.'

'It'll be all right.'

'I wish you could come too.'

'You'll be all right, girl.'

She blew her nose. 'Shall I call you afterwards?'

'Yes, we'll have a drink.'

She sniffed and felt good suddenly, felt good having him on the end of the phone, felt a great flood of warmth come down and through her. 'I'd like that.'

She managed to park right outside her house. It was quarter to six. She switched off the engine and closed her eyes. She heard footsteps and looked up with a start; a man was walking past with a Labrador on a lead; he glanced admiringly through the windscreen at her. She looked away blushing, and felt strangely cheered for a moment. Normality, there was still normality; normality was possible. She clenched the steering wheel tightly with both hands and peered out at her house, like a rabbit, she thought, a frightened rabbit in its hutch.

May 4th.

What the hell did it mean? Why did it keep coming back into her head?

How could she be sitting in her car like this, a few feet from her front door, and not dare to go inside? Her house? Her home? She stared at the blue front door, and the white paintwork of the walls; looking a little tatty perhaps, could do with a repaint soon. She tried to remember when it had last been painted. Five years ago at least. God, it looked so solid, so normal, would it ever be normal again? Could she ever live there again?

She trembled. In the wing mirror she could see the curate and another man, both in black cassocks, walking down the street, lugging something between them; a brown vinyl holdall, she realized, as they came closer.

The other man was older than Allsop, in his early forties, she guessed.

She got out of the car.

'Ah, good,' said Allsop, 'you've just arrived. We were worrying that we were late. You know each other of course, don't you?'

Alex smiled politely at the older man; he had a suave dry

face, the face of a career clergyman, not a pastoral one. In a suit, instead of his cassock, he could have been a high-flying lawyer. 'No,' she said.

'Derek Matthews,' said the man in a clipped voice, holding out his hand, unsmiling. 'The Vicar of St Mary's.'

'Ah,' she said feeling the firm shake of his hand. 'I'm afraid I've been a bit remiss in my church-going.'

'Most people are, Mrs Hightower,' he said humourlessly.

'I hope you didn't mind – that we didn't ask you to take the funeral service – it was a friend of my husband's – who knew my son – our son –' she shrugged. 'We thought it would be appropriate.'

'Naturally.'

'Shall we – ah?' said Allsop.

'Yes.' She was unsettled by Matthews. 'Of course, please come in.' She looked down at the holdall. It looked as if it might have contained sandwiches for a picnic. 'It's a – very pretty church, St Mary's.'

'Not to the purist,' said Matthews, tersely. 'It's an architectural disaster.'

She closed the front door behind her. Matthews looked around, dismissively.

'Would anyone like any – er – tea?'

'I think we'll proceed straight away,' said Matthews, looking at his watch. 'I have a meeting I must get to.'

She looked at Allsop and he tried too late to avoid her eyes. He blushed. 'I – er – I thought it might be helpful if Derek were present; he has had much more experience in these things than me.' His right eye twitched furiously.

'Yes, of course.' She looked nervously at Matthews. 'Which room should we use?' she said.

'The room in which the manifestation occurred,' said Matthews, curtly, as if he were addressing a hotel clerk.

'The manifestation has occurred in every room,' she replied, acidly.

'May I ask if you've been dabbling in the occult in here at all, Mrs Hightower?'

'I don't dabble in anything.' She was conscious of the anger rising in her voice.

'You've held no séance in here, nothing like that?'

Look, she wanted to say, I'm not at school. But she restrained herself, and nodded. 'We held a circle here, last week.' She felt her face redden, and stared apologetically at Allsop, feeling she had let him down.

'Then I think we should go to the room where you held it,' said Matthews, becoming increasingly impatient.

'I'm sorry,' she said, feeling foolish and helpless.

She led the way up the stairs; nothing was going to happen, she knew, nothing at all, and Matthews was going to think she was an even bigger fool.

Oh, God, she thought as she opened the door, feeling her face go red hot with embarrassment at the sight of the chairs, still arranged in a circle.

She sensed Matthews' glare and was unable to face him. She looked up at the portrait of Fabian, then at the curtains, the sticky tape still holding them tightly to the wall.

'These practices are very dangerous, Mrs Hightower,' said Matthews.

'I know,' she said lamely, like a schoolgirl, looking at the mortified expression on Allsop's face.

Allsop put the holdall on the floor, and something inside made a loud clank. Matthews knelt down and unzipped it. 'We'll need a table; and we'll need some salt.'

'Salt?' she said.

'Just ordinary salt. Have you a salt-cellar?'

'I'll get one.' Alex fetched a salt-cellar from the kitchen, then went up into her bedroom. The room felt chillingly cold, and she was frightened to be separated from the others even for a moment. She grabbed the small table from the end of the bed and hurried back to Fabian's room.

'Thank you.' Matthews took the table and the salt-cellar from her as if they were toys he was confiscating from a child.

They set about their preparations as if they had rehearsed

them beforehand. Allsop pushed three of the chairs away, while Matthews began to pull objects out of the holdall and lay them out on the table.

He carefully arranged two small candles like night-lights in the centre, then a chalice, a bottle of wine, and a silver tray. They worked silently, ignoring her, as if oblivious of her, as if, she thought uncomfortably, she did not count.

Matthews pulled out a silver stoup, and poured a small amount of water into it from a container, mouthing a silent prayer as he did so. Then he poured some salt in. He picked up the stoup and turned, staring past Alex. 'Protect us, Oh Lord, we beseech you.' He pulled a silver aspergillum out of the bag, dipped the head into the water, then stepped past Alex, and flicked it hard at the wall. He turned and solemnly repeated the procedure at each of the other walls. Then he put the stoup and the aspergillum down, pulled a gold Dunhill from his pocket, and lit the candles.

Allsop carefully poured the remaining water back into the container, and replaced the stoup in the holdall.

'Shall we begin?' said Matthews.

Alex sat facing the two clergymen.

'You are confirmed, I take it?' said Matthews.

Alex nodded.

'Let us pray,' he said loudly, sternly, as if addressing a courtroom.

The curate pressed his hands neatly together and brought them up to his face.

It felt more like a school class than a religious service. Silently, she copied him, trembling with anger and humiliation.

'Listen to our prayers, Lord, as we humbly beg your mercy.'

Did they know any more these two? With their plastic bag and their ornate silverware? Did they know any more than Morgan Ford? Than Philip? Were they just a couple of well-meaning charlatans under a massive flag of convenience? Or did they carry the authority and the clout of the divine power, the power above all else? What power?

She leaned forward and closed her eyes, trying to concentrate, trying to feel the bond with the God she used to talk to when she was a little girl, the God who used to listen to her and protect her, and make everything all right.

'Listen to our prayers, Lord, as we humbly beg your mercy, that the soul of your servant Fabian, whom you have called from this life, may be brought by you to a place of peace and light, and so be enabled to share the life of all your saints. Through Christ our Lord.'

'Amen,' said Allsop.

'Amen,' she echoed, quietly, self-conscious about the sound of her voice.

'We pray you, Lord our God, to receive the soul of this your servant Fabian, for whom your blood was shed. Remember, Lord, that we are but dust and that man is like grass and the flower of the field.'

Put some feeling into it man, she wanted to shout out, put some bloody feeling into it. She opened her eyes, and watched him through her cupped hands, angrily.

'Lord grant him everlasting rest.' Matthews paused to look at his watch. 'And let perpetual light shine upon him. Grant to your servant Fabian, Lord, a place of rest and pardon.'

She looked up at Fabian's portrait, then closed her eyes and covered them again with her hands. What do you think of all this darling? Do you mind? Do you understand?

'Oh God, it is your nature to have mercy and to spare. You have called to yourself your servant Fabian who believed in you and placed in you his hope.'

Nothing. She could feel nothing except disbelief that this was all happening. She watched Allsop, hands piously together, eyes tightly closed. The room was feeling stuffy; she could smell the melting candlewax, and felt herself perspiring.

'Oh God, you measure the life and times of all men. While we grieve that your servant Fabian was with us for so short a time, we humbly pray you that he may enjoy eternal youth in the joy of your presence for ever.'

The candles flickered, throwing their shadows over Matthews' face, as if they were throwing back the holy water in disgust.

'Our brother was nourished by Christ's body, the bread of eternal life. May he rise again on the last day. Through Christ our Lord.'

'Amen,' said Allsop.

She couldn't bring herself to say anything.

There was a long silence.

The room was getting even hotter.

'Holy, holy, holy Lord, God of power and might, heaven and earth are full of your glory. Hosanna in the highest.'

Matthews fixed his eyes on hers.

'Our Father, who art in heaven, Hallowed be thy name, Thy kingdom come. Thy will be done on earth as it is in Heaven. Give us this day our daily bread, And forgive our trespasses, As we forgive those who trespass against us, And lead us not into temptation, But deliver us from evil.'

Matthews paused, then stared up, over her head, as if the words were too important to be addressed solely to her.

'For thine is the kingdom, the power and the glory, for ever and ever. Amen.'

He stood up silently and turned to the table. He picked up the host, and broke a piece into the chalice.

'Lamb of God, you take away the sins of the world; have mercy on us.' He turned, and stared directly at her. 'May this mingling of the body and blood of our Lord Jesus Christ bring eternal life to us who receive it.' He beckoned her.

Slowly she stood up and stepped falteringly forward.

He signalled her to kneel, then held out a wafer.

'Take, eat,' he said, staring past her again, as he placed the wafer in her cupped hand.

She tasted the dry sweetness, then felt the sharp cold rim of the chalice, and the sudden heady wetness of the wine.

'This is the blood of Christ.'

She walked silently back to her chair, a dull metallic taste in her mouth.

'Lord God, your Son gave us the sacrament of his Body to support us in our last journey. Grant that our brother Fabian may take his seat with Christ at his eternal banquet: who lives and reigns for ever and ever.'

'Amen,' she whispered.

Allsop said nothing, and Matthews glared contemptuously at her, a little girl, not concentrating, speaking out of turn. She closed her eyes.

'Almighty God, you have destroyed death for us, through the dying of your son Jesus Christ.'

The words began to echo in her head, like hammering.

'Through his lying in the tomb, and his glorious resurrection from the dead, you have sanctified the grave.'

She heard the dripping of water, sharp, fierce drips, like shots. One hit her forehead, like a punch from a fist, then another. They ran down into her eyes, salty and stinging. She put her hand up to her forehead. But there was nothing there, nothing but the slight damp of her perspiration.

'Receive our prayers for those who have died with Christ, and been buried with him, as with heaven-sent hope they await their resurrection. Grant, we pray you, God of the living and the dead, eternal rest for Fabian. Through Christ our Lord. Amen.' He looked at his watch again.

'Amen,' said Allsop.

Matthews knelt down and blew out the candles, then began to pack the items away in the bag.

Allsop opened his eyes, smiled gently at Alex, then stood up and helped him.

She sat watching them. Is that it, she wanted to say, is that it? But she doubted whether Matthews would have even bothered to reply.

They went down into the hallway, and she opened the front door for them. Matthews went outside, then turned to her. 'I hope you'll consider very carefully before dabbling in the occult again, Mrs Hightower.'

She nodded, sheepishly.

He turned away, and walked down the steps. Allsop

picked up the bag and smiled at her. 'I'll call you in a couple of days, to see how you are getting on.'

'Thank you.'

She closed the door gently and turned around.

Fabian was standing at the bottom of the staircase.

She smelt petrol suddenly; the whole hallway seemed to be filled with fumes. Then Fabian began to move towards her, gliding silently, without moving his legs, until all she could see were his eyes, someone else's eyes, not her son's, cold malevolent eyes glaring hatred.

'No!' she screamed, closing her eyes, turning to the door, scrabbling blindly with the catch. She wrenched it open and stumbled out into the street. 'Help me!'

But no words were coming out.

'Help me!'

Nothing.

'Oh God, stop, come back, please come back!'

She stared after them, helplessly. 'Please help me,' she whimpered. But the two clergymen were almost at the end of the street, bobbing along in their cassocks with the bag strung out between them, like a pair of Humpty-Dumptys off to a picnic.

CHAPTER TWENTY-NINE

She drove too fast through the gates, and hit the water-logged cart track with a thump that bottomed the suspension and jarred through the whole car. Muddy blobs of water spattered the windscreen, and she switched on the wipers, swerving to avoid a deep rut; the nose of the Mercedes dipped sharply, rose in the air, then crashed down again with a bang that deflected it sideways, almost pushing the car into the fencing.

The wipers clawed at the windscreen, screeching like angry birds. She smelt the stench of pigs and saw a small dark object scurrying out of the dull beam of the headlights. The Mercedes bounced again and crashed down. Still she kept the accelerator hard on the floor.

Ahead, down to the left, through the muddy streaks and the rubber talons of the wipers, she could see the lake covered in a thin canopy of mist, like a shroud, she thought, and shuddered. It always looked its most sinister at twilight.

She saw David's Land Rover parked outside the house and pulled up beside it. She switched off the engine, closed her eyes and almost wept with relief. The engine made several loud ticking sounds, then pinged, registering its protest, the smell of hot oil overlaying the stench of pigs. It ticked again, pinged again. Somewhere in the falling dark beyond her a sheep bleated.

She climbed out of the car and stood still, her legs trembling. There was another bleat, then the distant splash of a fish rising carried across the still air. She took a few faltering steps towards the house, then stopped, swaying, and nearly fell. She felt the crunch of mud beneath her feet, moved forward again, heard a plop and a squelching sound and felt her right shoe suddenly become very cold.

'Blast,' she said, pulling her foot out carefully, trying not to leave her shoe behind in the puddle. The house was in darkness, but she saw a light shining behind the barn door and walked across the courtyard towards it.

David was standing with his back to her, staring up at the gantry he had rigged from the beam. The block and tackle hung down, swinging gently just above the large new vat, which was still in the middle of the floor.

'Hi,' he said, without turning round. 'Have a good day?'

'No,' she said, quietly.

'This is a bugger this; a real bugger.'

'How did you know it was me?'

He still didn't turn around. 'The car. Can always recognize your car – although you were driving a bit faster than usual. It's a real bugger – what do you think?'

'About what?'

'I'm wondering if I might leave it where it is – do you think it looks odd?'

Alex stared at the rope. 'It looks like gallows.'

'Gallows?' He turned around, then leaned forward, to look closer at her. 'Christ, you look terrible.'

She lowered her head and felt the tears welling; she sniffed.

'Come on,' he said, gently putting an arm around her. 'Let's get you a drink.'

They sat down in the kitchen.

'I think that's nice,' he said. 'Your own personal service.' He smiled. 'Shows the Church is having to get competitive. If the congregation won't come to the Church, send the Church out to the congregation. Go do battle with the pizzas and curries and the visiting masseuses. Dial-A-Service, eh? Communion delivered to your own home – and there's no collection box to worry about. I assume there wasn't a collection?'

'No, there wasn't a collection.'

'Wouldn't put it past the buggers.'

'David,' she said sharply.

'I'm sorry.'

He picked his glass up by the stem and swirled the wine around. 'Getting better by the day this, you know.'

Alex smiled and sipped her whisky. 'Good.'

'So does this mean you'll be going back now?'

She detected the note of sadness in his voice and held her glass tightly in her hands.

'I thought – you know . . .' he said, blushing, 'we seem to be getting on pretty well. I thought – maybe – perhaps . . .'

She closed her eyes tightly, felt the tears welling again, and sat, clenched up, shaking, rocking the chair backwards and forwards. She sipped her whisky again and could taste the salt from her tears. She opened her eyes and looked at him. 'It's not over yet, David.' A single violent convulsion rippled through her body, jerking her so hard it hurt. 'It's only just beginning.'

She felt his firm strong arm around her shoulder, his rough fingers caressing her face.

'You're safe here, darling,' he said. 'I'll look after you, don't worry. Don't go back to London for a while – not until you – everything – has settled down.'

She nodded; a huge single tear rolled down her cheek, just as far as his finger which stopped it, like a dam.

She was woken by the sound of water dripping, sharp, fierce drips, like shots from an airgun. One hit her forehead, like a punch from a fist, then another. Plop. Plang. The sound echoed around the room, as if she were in a cave.

Her feet felt like ice. There was a bitter cold draught blowing on her face. Plang, she heard. She put her hand up to wipe away the water.

But her face was completely dry.

She frowned, felt her heart thumping, and thought again of Fabian's pitiful cry in the circle. 'Help me, Mother.'

And then the snarling voice: 'Don't listen to the little bastard.'

What's happening to you, darling? Please tell me. Please.

Plang. It stung, as hard as if she had been hit by a tennis ball; she felt the water roll down the side of her head, and again touched it with her fingers. Nothing.

And then suddenly she understood.

She closed her eyes, shivering. She knew what she had to do; but she did not know if she had the courage to do it.

There were two sharp pings from the drawing room clock. She heard a slithering sound, the rustle of fabric, then a sharp intake of air. The window creaked, there was a sharp exhalation, then the sound of the curtains flapping and billowing.

Her heart slowed down; the wind; just the wind and the curtains. That was all. She smiled in relief, and sank back into the soft pillow, felt her feet warming, her skin relaxing, the pain subsiding.

There was a sharp, stabbing pain in her finger and her whole body convulsed. Agonising pins and needles wracked her and she convulsed again. Equally suddenly, the pain subsided and she was left tingling all over, as if she had fallen into a bed of nettles.

Then a violent shock-wave passed through her, flinging her up in the bed, sitting her upright against the headboard. She whimpered. Something was standing in front of her, by the foot of the bed. A shadow, darker than the dark.

'Today, Mother.'

The voice was clear; so incredibly clear.

'What do you mean, darling?'

The tingling was going.

'Darling?'

She put her hand out towards the bedside table, scrabbling for the light switch. The light came on and she blinked, her eyes sore and stinging, blinked at the dark wardrobe at the end of the bed.

The curtain billowed wildly out into the room, as if someone was shaking it in anger, and she heard the hissing of the wind as it gusted. She cupped her hands together and closed her eyes. 'Oh God, please help me. Please give me the strength to cope. Please protect Fabian's spirit, and bless him, and let him rest peacefully. Please, dear God, don't let him . . .' she paused.

Someone was looking at her.

She opened her eyes, but there was nothing, nothing but the furniture and the restless curtains and the sounds of the wind in the night.

She was surprised to see David sitting in the kitchen when she came down in the morning.

'How did you sleep?'

'O.K.,' she said. 'I was kept awake a bit by the wind.'

He looked out of the window. 'Seems to have blown itself out; going to be a fine day. Are you going to stay down today?'

She nodded.

'Good. Like some coffee?'

'Thanks.'

He put the kettle on the hob.

'I thought you were usually at work by now?'

'I'm expecting a phone call. Think I may have tied up something really good. This is the only phone that's working – I dropped the one in the office the other day and the bell doesn't ring.'

'I'll stay in here, and call you.' She smiled. 'I can play at being your secretary.'

'It's O.K. I have some paperwork to catch up on – I'll do it in here.'

Damn, she thought.

'Anyway, it's not often I'm lucky enough to have your company on a weekday.'

Don't you understand, she thought, oh, Christ, don't you understand?

He frowned at her, and she smiled back reassuringly; then she glanced past him to the rusty key on the hook on the wall behind him.

'I think I'll go for a walk.'

'It's gorgeous at this hour.' He smiled. 'One of the compensations. I'll have the coffee waiting for you. Oh – er could you keep an eye out for any sheep in the vines?'

She nodded and looked at her watch. 'I'd better call the office when I get back.'

'I'll do it for you. I'll tell them you're not well, won't be in for a couple of days.'

'You always make things sound so simple,' she said, conscious of the irritated tone of her voice. She smiled at him, trying to compensate. 'Can you just walk away from your work here, for as long as you like?'

He shook his head.

'Nor can I.'

'There are times when you just have to.'

She sighed and went out into the morning air, into the stale stench of the pigs and the fresh sweet scent of wet grass. There was a chill tang in the air and a translucence in the early morning sunlight, something watery, almost ethereal.

She walked up the track, away from the house, and forked off right towards the lake. The concrete island was visible only as a shadow through the shroud of mist which lay just above the water. Medieval pond. She shuddered, her nostrils filled with the stagnant smell. Not even the birds sang near this lake. She stopped and looked at the tiny track overgrown with brambles. She picked one stem up, carefully avoiding prickles, and it came away in her hand.

Someone had snapped it off and replaced it.

She stood still, frozen, and stared at it. She looked, carefully, either side of her, then stared into the under-growth; she sensed someone behind her, and spun around, her heart racing. No one. Warily, she tested another stem; that too came away.

Whoever it was had done a good job. The path and the dry, rotting oak door, with its concrete surround, had been very carefully camouflaged.

She turned the handle and pushed, but it was locked. Again, she sensed someone behind her, and turned around, trembling. But there was nothing. She stood still for a long time, and listened. The only sounds were the throb of a tractor and the distant bleating of sheep.

She carefully replaced the brambles in front of the door, and across the path, then looked at her watch. 9.15. Too early, much too early. She turned and stared at the lake again, then walked slowly, reluctantly, back to the house.

David was sitting at the kitchen table, a crumpled cigarette in his mouth, surrounded by his paperwork; he appeared entrenched for the morning.

'Did you get your call?'

He shook his head. 'Don't expect I'll hear till later.'

Alex nodded, walked into the drawing room and sat down. It was dark in here, quiet.

Leave it alone, her instincts told her; leave it alone, forget it, walk away from it, go back to the curate. Tell him.

'*If there was a leak and one of the sections has filled up, you'd be drowned if you opened the door.*'

'*Don't let him, Mrs Hightower.*'

'*Mother.*'

'*Don't listen to the little bastard.*'

'*May 4th.*'

May 4th.

Today.

She stood up, restlessly, and walked over to the unlit fireplace. She held up the photograph of Fabian on his tricycle. Tiny little eyes stared innocently from his plump giggling face. You could only see it if you looked closely, so closely. She put it back, slowly, heavily.

May 4th.

Today.

'*Today, Mother.*'

'*Don't let him, Mrs Hightower.*'

Carrie.

'*They let me out today, Mother.*'

She got up and walked through into the kitchen. David smiled up at her.

For Christ's sake, go out to your barn, go out somewhere, anywhere. Why do you have to pick this morning? Let me have that key. I must have it.

'We could go to a pub somewhere and have a nice lunch.'

'A nice lunch?' she echoed, blankly.

'A pub lunch? A real pub lunch? We haven't done that for years.'

'We haven't?'

She was conscious of him staring at her.

'Alex? Are you O.K.?'

She stared blankly. His words echoed round in her head.

'O.K.? O.K.? O.K.?' She felt herself falling and grabbed the wall, but it slipped away from her. She heard the scrape of a chair, then felt the hard grip of his hand.

'Sit down . . . down . . . down . . .'

She felt the wooden chair creak slightly, saw the walls slip sideways and the ceiling dip suddenly, sharply. Then the whole room tilted on its side and the floor rushed up to her, punched her hard in the shoulder.

David was kneeling over her. She heard his voice, somewhere, a long way away. 'I'll call a doctor . . . doctor . . . doctor . . . doctor . . .'

She shook her head, and the ceiling seemed to spin round, as if it was attached to her head by a piece of string. She felt the hard wooden floorboard against the back of her head. 'No,' she said. 'I'm fine. Really, I'll be fine.'

She looked up at his face, straight into the curled barbs of his beard. 'I'm fine.' She stood up, unsteadily, and looked around. The walls stayed where they were. She sat back in the chair. 'Must be the strain,' she said.

'You should have a holiday. We could go together somewhere – separate rooms –'

She smiled sadly. 'I wish it were that simple.'

The phone pinged, then rang. David watched it, let it ring several times. 'Don't want to seem too keen,' he smiled at her.

Answer it, for God's sake, answer it; I can't bear this. Please answer it.

He spoke briefly, curtly, then hung up and looked at her. 'Not the one I was expecting.' He looked at his watch.

Please ring soon. You must ring soon. You must.

By lunchtime he was bored with his paperwork. 'I'd better get over to the winery,' he said, 'just check everything's O.K.'

The barn, with its vats and strange machines and vinous smell. That was his happy hunting ground, she realized. He could not bear to be away from it, even for a few hours.

'I'll shout,' she said.

'Butler. His name. Geoffrey Butler.'

'Fine,' she said. She watched him walk across the courtyard, then went into the hallway and opened the boot cupboard. She reached up to the top shelf and pulled down the large rubber torch. She switched it on, pointed it at her face, and blinked at the brightness of its beam. She switched it off and put it back.

It was two more hours before Geoffrey Butler rang. A quarter past four. Two more hours of staring at the key, at the torch on the shelf beside it, two more hours of waiting, fidgeting the day away. May 4th.

'Geoffrey Butler's on the line,' she shouted, finally, through the winery door, then hurried back across the courtyard, terrified in case Geoffrey Butler might have changed his mind, might have hung up. 'He'll be with you in a moment, Mr Butler,' she said, staring at the key, the key that was so nearly hers.

Oh God, please be quick. But no, he scrabbled among his sheets of paper, made notes, more notes. She could take the key now and go whilst he was concentrating on his call. But if he saw it was missing? Too much of a risk.

'Calcium carbonate,' said David. 'Chalk. Yes,' he chuckled, 'yes, common chalk; reduces the acidity. No, that's right, just ordinary chalk. Anyhow everyone's into calcium these days – meant to be good for you. Yes, of course, well within the EEC prescribed measures.'

Come on, come on.

266

Finally, he hung up; then he walked over to her, flung his arms around her neck and kissed both her cheeks with gusto. 'I've got it,' he said. 'I've got it! It's going to be mega-huge!'

'Good.'

'Geoffrey Butler. He's going to stock it permanently, put it on his lists.'

'I'm very pleased.'

'I tell you something, for him to like it, it must be good. We're going to go out tonight; celebrate. Fancy that?'

'Sure.'

'Would you mind if I just went back to the winery for a bit – just got to try a few things out for him – would you mind terribly?'

'No,' she said. 'No, I wouldn't mind at all.'

She watched through the window as he walked across the courtyard and into the winery, and was about to lean forward and take the key, when she heard the sound of a car. A customer, or a tourist, she thought. Free tasting any time. Visitors welcome. Go away, she said to herself, go away, whoever the hell you are.

She left the key where it was; he would come running in here in a moment, for a corkscrew, or a couple of glasses, or some damn thing.

Angrily, she went through into the drawing room, sat down on the sofa and stared at the little boy on the tricycle, the plump little chap, with the dark brooding eyes.

There was a commotion outside and then she heard David shouting, furious. 'Alex? Alex? Where are you? What the hell's all this? Did you arrange this? These bloody loonies again?'

She looked up at the mantelpiece and Fabian grinned back at her from his tricycle.

'David,' she called, her voice scarcely louder than a whisper, and heard his voice, heated, in the distance.

'Can't you see – she's come here to get away from it. All you're going to do is bring it down here – whatever the hell it is. Why can't you just leave her alone? She'll be all right, she'll get over it; a few days of country air is what she needs.'

'It's not that simple, Mr Hightower. I wish it was.' She recognized the sing song voice of Morgan Ford instantly.

'David.'

There was a long silence.

May 4th.

She shuddered.

'David.'

She heard Ford's voice, gentle, but firm. 'I think we should start now.'

'No,' said David. 'She doesn't want to.'

'For both your sakes,' said Ford.

No, she tried to say. No. But nothing came out.

'Your son's spirit is disturbed, Mr Hightower. You cannot leave him like this. Until we have helped his spirit over, your wife will have no peace.'

Don't let him, David, please don't let him.

'Couldn't you do this some other time? When she is stronger?'

'She won't get stronger whilst he is around. He's using her power all the time, draining her energy.'

No. You've got it wrong. Can't you see? Oh God, can't you see?

'She's acting like a battery to him; he's taking, all the time. We must put something back in – or free them from each other.'

'What do you mean, a battery?'

'Spirits have no energy of their own, Mr Hightower. They draw their energy from carnate beings.'

'And you say he's drawing his energy from Alex?'

'Earthbound spirits live in a world of darkness, Mr Hightower. Just as humans in darkness head towards any light they can see, spirits make for sources of energy. Grief is a strong source of energy. Your wife's grief is acting like a beacon to him.'

There was a silence. 'And that's your theory?'

'No, Mr Hightower; it is not my theory. It is what I know.'

'And if we do nothing, what will happen?'

'There is a danger that he could end up possessing her completely.'

'I'd like to have a word with my wife in private.'

'Yes, of course. There is an important consideration. You see, she must understand that she may be responsible.'

She heard David's voice rise. 'Responsible?'

'We believe your son's spirit is still on the earth plane,' said Ford, very matter of fact. 'But we do not know whether that is because he did not depart from it, or whether he has been brought back. You see, Mrs Hightower may have disturbed his spirit by coming to see me in the first place. Often spirits do not want to return – they are summoned unwillingly, like Samuel when Saul consulted a medium. And sometimes it is the power of the grief of a bereaved one that pulls the spirit back.'

There was another silence.

'I just wanted to make that point, Mr Hightower. It is important.'

'So it's all my wife's fault is it?'

'Not necessarily, Mr Hightower. Not necessarily at all. But it is a possibility.'

There was a long silence. Then she heard David shouting. 'Alex? Alex!'

She looked around.

'Where the hell is she?'

She heard footsteps, then his voice again.

'Here you are! Have you gone deaf – I've been looking all over the place for you?'

She said nothing.

She heard the door close.

'Your damned medium friend is here – and that bloody loony Sandy – and the rest of them. Why the hell did you ask them down?'

'I didn't.'

'What?'

'I didn't.'

'So who the hell did then?'

'Fabian,' she said simply.

She heard the click of his tobacco tin, the rustling of paper, and then silence again.

'What do you mean?'

She stared at the child on the tricycle; her child, that she had brought into the world. Her infant crying in the night. Her infant crying for the light. She shuddered. The smiling child on the tricycle was out there in the darkness, confused and frightened.

'*Help me, Mother.*'

How?

'I don't know. I don't know what I mean.'

'What do you want to do?'

'*Help me, Mother.*'

She heard a click, saw a brief flash of light, then smelt the sweet smoke of his cigarette.

'Morgan Ford upset you last time.'

'*Help me, Mother.*'

'It's my fault,' she said, trembling. 'It's all my fault.'

'Of course it's not.'

May 4th.

The door opened.

'Shall we begin?' said Ford.

Alex turned around. A young man with a gold earring carried a wooden chair into the room, bashing the doorway with it in the process. He looked down at her and nodded. The slicked back hair; the creepy face. Orme, she remembered. Orme.

A tall meek man in a brown suit followed him in, also carrying a chair. He held it off the ground, and looked around apologetically, as if waiting for someone to tell him he could put it down. The postman.

David stood, silently, frowning, uncertain, his anger abated.

Morgan Ford was standing over her. Grey suit, grey shirt, grey tie, grey hair, all perfectly colour-coordinated. He gave her a firm, assured smile. She saw the glint of the rhinestone ring and looked up at his face, at the black haystack of Sandy's hair, at Orme's gold ring, at Milsom's brown polyester suit; at the reluctant nod of David's head and the strange look of anxiety in his eyes.

No. Don't let them David. Oh God, don't let them.

'There is so much power here,' said Ford. 'So much power.'

Don't let them David.

'Let her stay there,' said Ford. 'She's fine like that. Let her be comfortable.'

No. Please. No.

'The process of releasing the spirit can sometimes be a little distressing,' said Ford, gently, looking at David, then Alex. 'Sometimes the spirit will relive those last few moments of his carnate existence.'

The light went out.

'Dear God, we pray to you that you will look after our circle and that we shall come to no harm.'

Don't you realize what's going to happen?

There was a click and she heard Vivaldi, light, airy, sad.

'Feel the grass, soft and springy; it's good to walk on. You see a white gate ahead of you. Go through the gate and you can see a river.'

Stop them. Please David. Stop them.

'You can see people on the far side, standing there. Your friends, waiting to greet you. Cross over the bridge now, go to them, greet them, hug them, spend time with them. Don't be afraid, go, enjoy, be happy with them.'

She stared across the river, to the far side of the old stone bridge, and saw Ford, standing in his immaculate grey suit, waving at her, beckoning. Behind him were more people, grouped around, chatting as if they were at a cocktail party. Sandy, Orme, Milsom and David.

I'm here. Over here.

She put a foot on the bridge, but they all turned away, ignoring her.

I'm here.

She tried to step on to the bridge, but a pair of hands gripped her arms, held her back.

Let me go.

You'll drown; it's a trap; the bridge isn't safe.

Who are you?

There was a click, then silence; complete silence. She opened her eyes and stared, terrified, around the dark room.

'It's started,' said Ford. 'He is impatient. He is not willing to wait for us to finish our meditation.'

She felt icy air swirling around her.

A car roared past outside the window, followed by a heavy lorry. The room shook with the vibration. She stared wildly around. Impossible. There was no road. No road, she thought, again. Had David heard it? Had they all heard it?

'Mother!' A gruff, rasping whisper, scarcely louder than the silence. It was coming from the postman.

'What is your name?' said Ford, in a plain businesslike tone, as if he was answering a telephone call.

There was another long silence.

It's a con. That's not his voice. Don't you realize it's a con?

'Will you please tell us your name? If not, kindly leave the medium at once.'

Alex heard breathing, right beside her, halting erratic breathing, deep gulps, then long pauses.

'Are you Fabian Hightower?'

There was a sharp smell of petrol. She heard others sniffing; they could smell it too.

'Are you Fabian Hightower?'

The smell increased suddenly and the fumes stung her eyes.

'We're going to help you, Fabian.'

She couldn't breathe.

'To help you go over to the other side.'

It was as if a mask had been pressed over her face. The harder she tried to breathe, the closer she sucked the mask into her face. The breathing beside her was becoming calmer, more rhythmic, like the breathing of a diver.

No.

She was beginning to shake. Give me some, don't take it all; oh God, don't take it all. Air. Oh God, give me some air.

She fought with the vacuum around her face, tried to push it away, to duck under it, to turn away from it. Her chest was aching.

The fumes; the fumes had taken the air.

Then she noticed. The breathing beside her. Rhythmic, contented.

No.

She rocked violently backwards and forwards, shaking, more and more.

The fumes. Petrol. It was going to explode.

Let me breathe, darling. Give me air. Please give me air.

Something was moving inside her; something cold, bitterly cold. A cold hand brushed her forehead, gently pushed her hair back from her forehead, squeezed her shoulders. She heard the sofa shaking, rattling, clattering in the silence, as she shuddered, fighting for breath. There was something cold inside her ear now, seeping into her head like liquid.

And then, suddenly, she felt strong. Stronger than she had ever felt before. So strong, she no longer even needed to breathe. No. Please no. Please no.

Another car hurtled past outside and into the distance. Suddenly there was a slithering sound, a desperate, frightening sound, which seemed to go on for ever. No. She tried to stand up, but an immense force pushed her back on to the sofa. She tried again, and a hand tugged her back, insistent; whose? David's? Ford's? She tore it free, and stood up again. Something tried to push her back, some huge force like a falling wall. She pushed against it, with all her new strength, and felt the floor rise up sharply in front of her. She went on to her hands and knees, and slowly inched her way across, tugging at the strands of carpet with her fingers; she reached the door and clung to the handle, which took all her weight, clung to it to prevent herself falling backwards into the dark room.

Still the slithering sound continued, eerily, a car with locked wheels sliding across a damp road.

She forced the door open, then tumbled through it, suddenly, rolled over and over across to the kitchen wall and hit the sink with a thump that jarred her.

Her lungs were bursting. She gulped down air ravenously, long deep breaths, then lay there for a moment, exhausted, staring fearfully at the door to the drawing room, the door she had just come through that had closed behind her. She felt a cold prickling down the back of her neck, climbed unsteadily to her feet and listened. But she could hear nothing. She stared at the key hanging on the nail, and at the cupboard with the torch. Time. Was there time? The key felt cold, rough, heavy. Was there time?

The key turned easily, too easily. The lock had been oiled. The door was harder to open; warped, and sagging on its hinges, she had to push hard to make a gap big enough to go in, then she closed it behind her.

She turned to face the darkness, breathing in the dank, lifeless smell, and heard the scrape of her foot echo around her.

'I'm here, darling,' she said, and heard her voice fall flatly away into the dark. She switched on the torch, and saw the stone steps, a few feet in front of her. Exactly as she remembered.

She went down them and felt the air getting damper, and colder. At the bottom was a massive watertight steel door, with a huge round wheel on the front of it, like a submarine.

'If there is a leak and one of the sections has filled up, you'd be drowned if you opened the door.'

She tested the handle and it rotated easily. She gave it six full turns before it stopped. She swallowed, then pushed the door. It swung open with no effort at all and just the merest groan from one of its hinges which echoed along the dark tunnel ahead like the cry of a wounded animal.

She shone her torch at the concrete floor then up around the curved walls. To her right was a series of valves, dominated by another huge wheel on the wall. 'Never touch these,' the estate agent had warned; 'no one is sure what they do.' Dimly, at the end of the beam, she could see another door, like the one she had just opened. She shone the torch down at the floor again and a puddle glinted at her. Nervously she pointed the beam up at the ceiling. The plasterwork was mottled with fat brown blotches and flaking away.

A tiny blob of water launched itself from the centre of the blotches with a faint plop. It smacked into the concrete floor. Plang. The sound echoed around her, and she shuddered, spun around, beamed her torch back where she had come from. She heard breathing, heavy breathing, and stiffened. She held her breath and the sound stopped. She breathed out again with relief, then stepped forward into the tunnel, deep under the silent black water of the lake, under the mist and the fish that jumped and the reeds like dead men's fingers.

There was slime on the floor and patches of mould on the walls. The beam of the torch threw streaks of light and long shadows all around her and the dull echo of her footsteps followed her at first and then overtook her. The door was coming closer, the door to the ballroom. If the ballroom was flooded . . . If.

She stopped when she reached it and looked behind her, fearfully.

Plop. Plang. The noise echoed around like the slamming of a door. Oh Christ, no. She shone the beam back where she had come from, saw the prick of light dance on the roof, then on the floor. The door was still open.

Plop. Plang.

She rotated the wheel, and it turned silently, well oiled, six turns, exactly as the previous one.

Then her torch went out.

No. She shook it. No. She shook it again. No. She switched it on, off. Nothing; she shook it. Nothing. Please, she whimpered. Please. She shook it again, and she heard the faint tinkling of glass inside the lens. She closed her eyes, then opened them again. There was no difference. She held her breath and listened to the silence. She had never before heard such silence.

Plop. Plang.

And then silence again.

She pushed open the door. Light. There was light; so bright it startled her. She stared in wonder up at the domed roof, its thick panels of glass, coated in slime and limp strands of weed, exactly as she had remembered. The panels were so bright, almost as if they had lights behind them; it felt as if you could reach through them and touch the sky.

For a moment she was dazzled by the brightness, too dazzled to see anything in the green light that filtered down and around the room.

Then the stench hit her. A horrendous pungent stench, that flooded through her nostrils, down her throat, deep into her stomach, unlike anything she had ever smelt before.

She pinched her nostrils together tightly with her fingers, felt her stomach heave, and then gagged. Something banged into her shoulder, and she shrieked, then felt stupid. It was the wall, which she had backed into.

The stench hit her again; she cupped her hands over her nose and took a deep breath through her mouth.

And then she saw the person on the floor on the far side of the room, watching her.

She froze.

Slowly, she felt her legs buckling. She tried to back out of the room, felt the jarring thump of the hard slimy wall. She pressed her hands against it, feeling her way, inching along. Where was the passage? Where was it? Where was it?

Someone had closed the door.

'No. No.' She spun around and saw the wall right behind her. The door was still open, through to the blackness of the passageway, just a couple of feet to her right.

She looked over her shoulder. The person was laughing at her, laughing silently, motionless. The stench filled her nostrils again and she gagged.

'*They let me out today.*'

'*Don't let him, Mrs Hightower.*'

'*Don't listen to the little bastard.*'

I want to get out. Please, God, I want to get out. She turned and looked down the tunnel, then back over her shoulder. Who are you? What do you want?

Plop. Plang.

Are you going to come for me here? Or in the dark of the tunnel? She gripped the torch, tightly. But she knew who it was. And she knew that she wouldn't be after her; not after her, nor anyone.

She heard a cry; a single tiny whimper. Her own. It echoed around the room, came back at her.

'I'm sorry,' she said. 'I'm so sorry.'

She left the safety of the wall and began to walk across the room. A shadow flitted past her and she spun around. Nothing. The shadow flitted again; she looked up, and saw the dark silhouette of a fish nibbling at the weed on the outside of the glass.

She took another step forward, then another.

Move. Please move. Please say something.

The stench was getting worse.

There was a sharp crack, right underneath her. She screamed, wildly, then again, and again. Then her scream subsided into a whimper, as she looked down and saw a plate, split in half by her foot.

She took another step forward and then she was close enough. She stared, shivering in horror, at the girl's face, shrivelled, like dried leather, at the eyes, staring hopelessly ahead at the door she had opened far too late and the twist of her mouth, like a hideous laugh.

'No,' Alex whimpered. 'No,' as she stared at the chain around the girl's neck that trailed off to an anchorage somewhere beyond in the gloom. 'No.'

'He'd been coming down a lot, just lately.' David's voice echoed through her head. 'Since around about Christmas. Really seemed to be taking an interest in the place. I used to watch him, sitting out there on the island, fishing, for hours on end. I used to wonder what he was thinking.'

'No.'

She backed away, slowly, desperately slowly, inching her way as if she was pushing against a huge force. She tried to look away, at the walls, at the ceiling, but she was drawn back, like a magnet, to the face: 'Hi Mum. This is a really friendly place, lots of things happening, met some great people. Will write again soon.'

I'm sorry. She mouthed the words, but nothing came out. I'm sorry; I'm so desperately . . .

There was a noise right behind her.

She froze, felt the terror surging. She looked down at the ground, unable to turn around, then back again at the face like leather.

A shadow moved, the shadow of the person who was standing behind her.

She shook her head. Please no.

The scrape of a foot.

Please no.

The rustle of a coat.

No.

She spun round.

Nothing.

Nothing, but the black entrance of the tunnel.

Then she heard a noise behind her, from the girl.

Oh no. Oh Christ, no.

She turned around, slowly, fearfully.

The girl was grinning. Grinning at her, grinning at her fear.

No. Please don't do that. Please don't.

'Admiring your son's handiwork, Mrs Hightower?'

The voice ripped through her like an electric shock; she lost her balance, and nearly fell on to the girl. She blinked, felt a surge of nausea, lost focus for a moment. Otto. She mouthed the word but nothing came out. Otto.

He was standing in the doorway, coat slung over his shoulders.

She began to shiver violently. Something in his expression; something terrible. She tried to scream, but nothing came out. She put her hand in front of her mouth, staring at the eyes, the two different mocking eyes. And then she realized. The eyes; the same expression in the eyes. Fabian on his tricycle. The portrait on the wall. Bosley. Otto.

She stepped back, trod on something which crunched under her foot, and jumped in fear. She spun around, saw the girl staring at her, stepped back, stared up at the ceiling, around at the walls and then back at Otto in the only doorway.

She tried to speak but still nothing would come out. She spun around again, stared at the girl, the girl seemed to move. She tried to scream. Nothing. Oh God help me. She turned back. Move, oh Christ, move! Say something. She was shivering wildly; it was freezing in here now; as she breathed, her lungs hurt, and her breath hung in front of her, like a cloud.

'What do you want?' she mouthed the words, her voice tight, cracking, faint, as if it were a long way away.

He smiled.

Say something; for God's sake, say something.

Otto continued to smile.

The air was going, it was getting harder to breathe; she started gulping, looking around wildly; panic seized her.

'I – want – to – go – now ...' she said, and began walking towards Otto, walking against a huge force that was pushing her back.

'He'll be here in a minute, Mrs Hightower, aren't you going to wait for him?'

'Will you let me by, please Otto.' Her voice was calm, suddenly, firm, normal.

Still smiling, Otto stepped out of the way. It took her what seemed like an eternity to reach the doorway. She stood there, staring fearfully at him, waiting for his move, waiting for him to grab her, but he just smiled, his expression unchanging.

'He'll be so disappointed to have missed you.'

She turned away and ran, stumbling, down the tunnel.

Plang. The droplet of water hit her like a fist, knocked her sideways.

'No!'

She stumbled forward.

Another drop hit her on the forehead, like a hammer. She reeled, crashed into the wall, fell on her face into the slime. Another drop hit her on the back of her neck, like a kick. She picked herself up, stumbled forward. Which way was she going? The wrong way. No. She could see the light. The ballroom. 'Oh God help me.'

Another droplet smashed on to the bridge of her nose; her eyes watered. The ballroom disappeared, she stumbled forward into the wall. A droplet smacked her scalp and stung like acid. She turned and staggered towards the dark; the dark that seemed to go on for ever. 'Help me, God, please help me.'

A beam of light shone in her face, dazzling her.

Her scream echoed down the tunnel and came back at her from every direction at once.

Then she stood for a moment, frozen like an animal.

Two arms closed around her.

She felt the rough denim of David's jacket, hugged it tight.

'Oh God.' The emotion welled up inside her and burst over and she began to sob. She ran her hands up and down the jacket, up into the soft curly hair at the back of his neck.

'Thank God, thank God.' She felt his neck and the thick tangle of beard and sobbed uncontrollably. Then she heard his voice.

'It's all right, Mother, it's all right.'

The shiver ran through her.

'It's going to be all right.'

'No.'

She felt the grip on her arm like a pincer of iron.

Chained her up in a cellar.

'David?'

And left her?

'David, please let me go.'

The voice was gentle, soothing. 'Don't worry, Mother.'

She screamed, pulled herself away, tripped, fell over into the slime, rolled hysterically.

She stood up, saw the light at the end of the tunnel, saw a dark shape block it out suddenly. She turned again, ran, slipped and fell. She flailed around with her arms, slithering, scrambled back on to her feet and ran as fast as she could. Then she tripped and fell again hard, winded. Door. Close door. She climbed back on to her knees, trying not to pant, and cracked her head. She cried out in pain and put her hands up. Something round, cold. The door handle.

She stood up, seized the huge wheel with both hands. But it would not move. Come on; come on. She turned the wheel, sharply, rotated it completely and pulled again. Oh, come on, please; she rotated it again; stiff, creaking, grating. They'll hear; they'll hear. Christ, it wasn't stiff before.

A fine spray of water hit her in the face.

She rotated it again and pulled. A jet of water hit her in the chest and flung her against something. The wall. She heard the hissing of the water, venomous, getting louder.

'Mother!' She heard Fabian's piercing scream.

Never touch these; no one is sure what they do.

The wrong wheel; that's why it would not move. No, oh Christ, no.

The water stung her eyes, like acid. She opened them,

blinking against the pain. Where was the light? Which way? Water was spraying at her from every direction.

There was a creaking sound; faint at first, then a louder cracking, like the splintering of wood. It sounded as if someone was opening a gigantic packing case. The noise spread, surrounding her, deafening her. Then suddenly it stopped and for a moment there was no sound at all.

She stared wildly around in the dark, trying to orientate herself, trying to find the way. But there was nothing but the black.

She heard a rumble, faint at first, like distant thunder. It turned into a raging bellow, right behind her. She spun around, and for an instant she saw it; the light; the ballroom. Then the wall of water.

No.

The wall of water that was hurtling at her.

The light went first. Then the sound. It was silent as the water scooped her up, enveloped her, swept her down.

Completely silent.

CHAPTER THIRTY

Everything was very white, soft, diffused, milky. White fingers glided noiselessly around her leaving silent ripples in their wake. Consciousness was still only dimly registering. Pills, she thought; pills that made her feel good, dream good dreams; they were hard to wake up from.

The stern gaze; fronds of moustache; steely blue eyes. How long had he been there?

'All right, girl?'

She smiled weakly.

'It's jolly stuffy – shall I open a window?'

She nodded. There was a sharp clack as the blind shot up and the room suddenly filled with bright light. The illusion was gone and reality had intruded again. Another day. Another day that would not matter.

'What's the date, Philip?'

'May 18th.'

Christ. She tried to sit up suddenly, but the pain in her shoulder prevented her.

'No change?'

'I think it's a little better.'

They sat in silence for a few minutes. She watched Philip smoking, saw the flickering of his eyelashes, then tried to think again, fighting against the drugs that were meant to stop her from thinking.

'I killed them,' she said, suddenly.

'It was unsafe. Could have gone at any time. Should have been sealed off.'

'I thought that David had become Fabian, that he – that they were going to chain me – I opened the valve. I thought it was the door.'

She stared at the blue of his eyes. Light danced on them, like ponds. Medieval ponds. The shudder ran through her. 'I killed them.'

'No, gosh, good Lord no.'

'I did.'

'An accident, girl. An accident.'

'I didn't even go to his funeral. I didn't go to my own husband's funeral.' She watched as Philip stood up and walked over to the window. He leaned on the sill and looked out. 'I should have gone to Otto's too. He came to Fabian's.'

'Germany,' Philip said gently. 'I gather they took him back to Germany.'

'So many funerals,' she said.

There was another long silence. She shivered. 'I didn't even send any flowers to Otto – or to the girl.'

'The girl?'

'Carrie.'

'Carrie?'

'The girl who,' she paused, and stared at him. 'You know. Who was there.'

'Who was where?'

'Under the lake.'

'What girl under the lake?'

'The one that Fabian –' She paused. Why wouldn't he talk about it? Why did he keep denying it?

He walked back over and sat down beside the bed. 'The lake was drained.' He pulled out another cigarette. 'There was just Otto and David. No one else.'

'But – I – I saw – Philip?'

He shook his head, firmly.

'In the ballroom,' she said, lowering her voice.

'Rubble,' he said. 'All rubble. Whole thing imploded. Extraordinary piece of engineering.' He stood up again and walked back towards the window.

'She's under there,' Alex said, softly.

He stared out of the window again. 'It's what saved you,' he said.

'What do you mean?'

'The engineering. Stressed in sections. You must have been pushed out like toothpaste.'

'Why didn't it save them?'

He stared out of the window in silence.

'Philip – she was there.'

He continued to stare out of the window again, for a long time. 'There's a balance,' he said softly, without turning around. 'Always a balance. Two bits of dust; positive and negative; meeting in a void; bang. One without the other would have been useless – no life; nothing.' He turned and stared at her. 'The sun's out there.' He nodded towards the window. 'Can you imagine going there? Hell. The inferno. Hell, girl. But we need it; we need it to exist. Do you understand?'

The door opened and a nurse walked in dressed in white. She lifted her arm and looked at her watch. 'I'm afraid it's time for your –' She looked at Philip.

He stood up awkwardly and blushed. 'Righty-ho – I'll er – tomorrow?'

Alex listened for the click of the door closing. The new routine of life. Easy; so easy; sometimes she wished she could stay here for ever.

CHAPTER THIRTY-ONE

The removal van arrived at nine. She could see it without looking up; a great blue shadow across the window. She heard the rattle of the engine, the slamming of doors, voices.

'They 'ere, Missy Eyetoya, they 'ere.'

'Let them in Mimsa.'

Mimsa stared at her, wide-eyed, uncertain.

'Go on,' she nodded, smiling.

They carried the packing cases out first, then the furniture. She watched the house, now already bare, being gutted. Cleansed, she thought to herself, walking around the rooms, checking. God, they looked small, suddenly. Tiny.

She stood on the pavement and watched the van reverse away. Eighteen years. Eighteen years and she wasn't sure what her next door neighbours looked like. They wouldn't miss her; the street wouldn't miss her; there was no sentiment here. Only inside her own heart.

As she climbed into her Mercedes, she saw the young couple arrive in their blue BMW and park opposite her. He was smart, trendy, in a Paul Smith suit; she was a willowy blonde. He lifted a small boy out of a car seat and plonked him on the pavement. Then the three stood, looking at the house.

'I think red for the front door,' she heard her say.

'Or black,' he said. 'Black would be smart. Look, there, 46, that's black.'

The same conversation they had had, she thought, a tear rolling slowly down her cheek; eighteen years ago; they had stood on that pavement, the three of them; David in his Tom Gilbey suit, herself and their son. Fabian. The thrill. The hope, the dreams, the plans. Plans. She sighed, and started the engine.

286

A new beginning. It was a bright day for it, a fine August morning. She felt a twinge of pain in her shoulder as she turned the wheel. They told her it would still hurt for a while to come. But it was healing, all the wounds were healing, both the physical and the mental. It was the memories that would last the longest. She wished it was as easy to empty her mind as it had been her house.

The removal van was already at Cheyne Walk and they were piling her furniture on to the pavement.

She climbed the stairs to the top floor and walked around the huge empty apartment. She felt free, suddenly, free of so many things. She hardly noticed the removal men bringing everything in; there seemed to be no effort, no effort at all. Even the huge bouquet of flowers that arrived from Philip scarcely registered more than a gentle smile.

She slept well that night, without pills, without anything; slept well for the first time, she realized, since it had begun.

There was so much that had passed. People had attempted explanations. The chaplain of Broadmoor. The psychiatrist at the hospital. But they could only ever know part of the story. Without the body, Fabian had done nothing wrong. Without the body that was buried under the rubble at the bottom of the lake, buried under the rubble of her mind. Without the body, it could all be a product of her mind. And they believed it was. All of them, except Philip. Who knew.

It was Philip who had got her through the past months. Philip, with his theories and explanations, who helped her peel away the layers. It was Philip who dismissed the idea each time she thought of telling.

'If they did look . . . and found nothing? What then girl?'

That, she knew, would be the worst horror of all.

She stared out across the Thames streaked with the morning sunlight at the trees of the park on the far side, at the rooftops of Battersea, Clapham, Wandsworth and beyond.

She smelt David, suddenly, the musty vinous smell of his denim jacket, felt the warmth of his body, the bristles of his moustache and heard Fabian's voice calling out from inside him and shivered. Conductors; conduits; receptors; the technical jargon; the explanations; Philip; the chaplain; Morgan Ford; it sounded like something to do with electricity, not with the . . . She stumbled on her thoughts.

'In a violent death, usually an accident or a murder, the spirit needs to be helped over. He may not be aware that he has died.'

'If a possessed person dies, what happens to the evil spirit?'

'It goes with him to Hell.'

'Could someone bring it back?'

'Perhaps.'

'If an exorcism is successful, where does the spirit – the demon – whatever it is that's driven out, go?'

'It has to find a new host.'

'It was horrible, Philip. It was David, but he spoke with Fabian's voice.'

'That happened before.'

'This time it was different.'

'Because the tunnel made you scared.'

'No. It was Fabian. He had made David his host. Ford was wrong. He said David wasn't receptive. I knew he was.'

'How?'

'I knew.'

'No, girl. If David had been receptive, you wouldn't have got out of there.'

'Evil will not enter a person who will not receive it.'

'Do you think David had come down to find me? To help me?'

'Perhaps.'

'The spirit wanted me. I wouldn't receive it so it tried to enter David?'

'Perhaps.'

'And he was fighting it too?'

'Evil spirits can be very cunning. Good mimics. Take on a

288

departed person's characteristics. Voices. Mannerisms. Appearance.'

'The circle creates energy, like a beacon. He can find his way to the circle.'

'Does evil have beacons too? Could Otto have been a beacon?'

'Mrs Hightower, no clergyman who is a true believer can rule out the diabolical.'

A lone jogger, in a singlet and shorts, was running across the Albert Bridge. Jogging, she thought. It had been a long time. Tomorrow she would jog again.

She felt a strange stillness and calm. David's dying had released her from something. She was sad, deeply sad, and sometimes she missed his phone calls and the glee in his voice when he talked about his wine, but in a strange way, in her grieving she was free.

It was as if the past had begun to exorcise itself.

She walked up the stairs to her office. She was looking forward, once more, to work. To the deals; to the piles of manuscripts. To concentrating on something different.

'How did it go?' said Julie.

'Fine; I thought it would be much worse. The flat is gorgeous – the view this morning was quite fantastic.'

'I'd like a view,' she said.

Alex smiled. 'Anything happen yesterday?'

'Nothing urgent. Philip left a message – something about the theatre on Thursday; he said your phone wasn't working yesterday.'

Alex walked through into her office. It felt chilly after the warm sunlight and she pulled up the blinds, opened the window and let the warm summer air soak in.

Her desk was stacked with letters, manuscripts, message slips. Challenges. God, she was so far behind, from her weeks in hospital and from the preoccupation with moving. She stared around the room for a moment, collecting her thoughts, making a mental schedule for the day. Then she smiled to herself again. It was over. She stared out at the blue sky. The long climb had begun, back to where she had been once, back to somewhere that could never be the same. Sighing, she stretched out her arm and switched on her VDU.

Two green words stared back at her, bright, unflickering.
HALLO, MOTHER.

PROPHECY

To Jesse

ACKNOWLEDGEMENTS

As ever, I am indebted to many people and organizations whose help, knowledge and input has been invaluable. In particular, a very special thank you to the following:

The Viscount Hampden for allowing me to use Glynde Place as the model for Meston Hall (although I should add that Glynde Place is in very considerably better condition than Meston and I have made changes both to the house and grounds). I should also add that the Halkin/Sherfield family are entirely fictitious and bear no relationship to any of the Viscount Hampden's family nor previous occupants of Glynde Place.

Brian Inglis. Roderick Main of Scarab Research for his invaluable help also on coincidence (and for the coincidences!). Robert Knox, Deputy Keeper of Oriental Antiquities at the British Museum. Frances Wollen. Canon Dominic Walker OGS. Dr Robert Morris of Edinburgh University. Miss Eleanor O'Keefe of the Society for Psychical Research. Jane Henry. Ruth West. Brian Dickinson. Tim Mair. Pippa Hooley, Bovine Consultant. Councillor Pam Stiles. Kathryn Bailey. Sophie Allen, Game Boy Consultant. Dr Nigel Kirkham. Dr Tim Carter. Dr Duncan Stewart. Dr Brian Kirkland. Mick Harris. David Garbutt. Nina Mackay (for lightning calculations on the backs of envelopes!). Ray Hazan and Peter Marshall of St Dunstan's. Adrian Elliott. Mark Towse. Peter Orpen of AVT. Dr Robert Wilkins. Roy Gambier of the Shuttleworth Collection.

I am indebted also to the hard work of Sue Ansell;

to my agent, Jon Thurley; to my editors, Joanna Golds-worthy and Richard Evans and my copy-editor Eliza-beth Reeves. And to Bertie, for not eating all of the manuscript. And to my wife, Georgina, who through all the bludgeonings of chance kept me bloody but unbowed . . .

PROLOGUE

The man and boy walked along the London street trying to keep clear of the gutter, the man hurrying, clutching the boy with sharp, bony fingers, turning down one dark alley then another, like a rat that has learned its way through a maze.

The boy was confused and uncertain; he did not know who the man was and did not like him. His mother and the man had talked in low voices and his mother had not kissed him or looked him in the eye when the man had taken him away. They had walked for a long time through the failing light and the rain, and he was tired and hungry. And becoming afraid.

After a while they stopped in the rear yard of a large house and the man knocked loudly. The door opened a few inches and dark, suspicious eyes peered out. 'Come in,' a woman said and the door opened wider. The man pushed the boy ahead of him into the kitchen.

The woman frightened the boy. She was tall, dressed in a black gown, and had a skeletal face with eyes that seemed to scold him.

'How many years has he?'

'Eight,' the man said.

'He stinks.'

'He needs a wash, that's all.'

The woman studied the boy carefully. He had fair curls that were unkempt and matted, large blue eyes and a snub nose; his lips were drawn sullenly down, and his clothes were little more than grimy rags; his feet were bare. 'Wait here,' she said.

The boy stood gazing at the stone floor, aware of the flames in the hearth and the pot above it from which came an acrid, unpleasant smell.

After a few moments the door opened and the woman came back in, followed by a tall man with a limp. He was wearing a gold, full-length robe, and had a cruel, vain face framed with a carefully trimmed beard. He stood in the doorway and smiled approvingly at the boy. 'Yes,' he said. 'You have done well.'

He came closer to the boy, dragging his club-foot across the floor with a scrape, and stood still again, admiring him. 'Very good.'

The boy was impressed by the man's robe and by his noble appearance. The man moved closer, then in one fast movement tore the clothes off the boy, letting them drop around his ankles.

The boy looked at him in shock. The nobleman took a step towards him and laid a hand on his shoulder. The boy whipped his head around, bit the man's wrist hard and bolted for the door on the far side of the kitchen.

The man who had brought him grabbed him by his hair and held him tightly. The nobleman roared with laughter.

'He is fine and spirited. You have done *very* well, for a change.'

'Thank you, my Lord.'

'Yes,' he said. He eyed the boy's body with mounting satisfaction. 'I will reward –' He broke off as a commotion beyond the kitchen disturbed him. He frowned; they were early. Much too early. They were not due for at least two hours yet, surely? He turned, staring through the open door and down the passageway.

A man in a tall black hat, a high white collar and a

black coat over tight, ribboned breeches strode through the doorway. He was followed by a group of soldiers wearing the red coats, grey breeches and waist sashes of the Parliamentarian Army.

His grey eyes scanned the room then fixed on the nobleman. He spoke with a humourless smile. 'Good evening, Francis,' he said. 'Have I interrupted some sport?'

'What do you mean by this intrusion, Thomas?' The nobleman stared with a vexed expression at the soldiers who were clustered inside the door; their faces beneath their buff leather hats carried an air of intent that disturbed him.

The man in the black hat looked at the woman and the rat-faced man beside her. 'Who brought this child?' When they remained silent, his voice became hard and stern. 'Who brought him?'

''Twas I,' the rat-faced man said.

'Clothe him and take him back.' And then, to the woman, 'How many servants are here in the house now?'

The woman glanced at her master as if for approval to speak.

The nobleman's vexation was tempered by uncertainty. 'Thomas, I'll not have this. Take your men and leave forthwith.'

The man in the black hat ignored him and continued to stare at the woman. 'I want all the servants to be gone immediately and not return until curfew time. Understand?' He turned and nodded at the soldiers.

They moved forwards and seized the nobleman's arms. His expression turned to fury. 'Thomas – my brother, man! For God's sake! What do you think you are doing?'

'For God? For *God's* sake?' his brother echoed

mockingly. 'What dost thou know of God whom thou hast abandoned these five and twenty years?' He led the way out of the door and down a passageway into a fine hall with a black-and-white tiled floor, candles in ornate sconces on the walls and gilt furniture. The soldiers, headed by their sergeant, frogmarched the robed nobleman, ignoring, as his brother did, his protestations.

They went downstairs into a dark, evil-smelling cellar and halted at a door outside which a candle burned. Thomas jangled a key tauntingly at his brother, unlocked the door and led the way into a huge cellar chamber.

A massive fire blazed in a hearth beneath a brick flue on the far wall, the echoes of its cracking and spitting resounding like gunshots around the brick walls and flagstone floor. There were stone tablets fixed to the walls, some containing five-pointed stars, others squares of numbers. Skulls and bones, human and animal, were laid out on shelves between lit black candles.

On a raised dais like an altar at the far end was a bed covered with tasselled cloth. There were massive black candles at each corner and, beyond, a leather-bound book lay on a lectern.

The man in the black hat nodded at his brother, whilst the soldiers stared round in awe and horror. 'The fires of Hell already lit, my Lord?'

'I'll have no more of these games, Thomas. What do you want?'

''Tis no game, Francis, I assure you. None but that of your own making. I must depart, for I've a long way to go before dark. I'll take my leave of you, if you'll forgive me. Sergeant Proudlove will attend your needs; a good man by all accounts and a father of three young boys.'

He nodded to the sergeant who had a blunt face with a broad, flat nose and dull eyes, and walked out. Ignoring the shouts of his brother, he closed the door of the chamber behind him.

'Like to sport with young boys, your Lordship?' the sergeant said.

As the nobleman looked at him, and at each of the deadpan faces of the other six soldiers, the heat of his anger began to turn into the cold uncertainty of fear. 'Your intrusion is intolerable,' he said stiffly.

'We has but only one more intrusion to make and we'lst be gone, my Lord.' The sergeant grinned and several of the other soldiers let out coarse sniggers. Then he nodded and they gripped their prey tighter.

'Unhand me at once, I say! What do you mean by all this?'

The sergeant pointed to the bed. The soldiers pulled the nobleman over and thrust him face down on to it. The sergeant removed his waist sash and tied it across Francis' mouth as a gag, yanking it so tightly that there was a grunt of pain. Then he carefully eased up the gold robe, exposing the nobleman's naked, bony backside. Francis began to struggle harder, grunting louder. The soldiers moved as if they had done this before, four of them each using his own body weight to pin down an arm or a leg, the other two sitting on the small of his back. 'Careful not to bruise him,' the sergeant said.

He walked slowly across to the fire, knelt and picked up the poker then ambled back to the front of the bed and held the poker up so that Francis could see it. 'Thou enjoyest sporting with backsides, let's see how thou enjoyest this, my Lord.'

The nobleman's eyes widened; the cruelness of them was gone now, replaced with a look of pleading. He mumbled desperately and incoherently through the gag.

The sergeant removed from inside his jacket a slim hollow ox-horn and checked that the poker would slide freely through it. Then he placed his hands on his captive's buttocks, which were slippery with the perspiration of fear, and pushed them apart, locating with his eyes the circular orifice of the anus. Using some of his own spittle he lubricated the end of the ox-horn, then again located the orifice and slowly but firmly inserted the horn, easing it in further and further.

'Gently does it, my Lord,' he said. 'Wouldn't want to hurt you.'

There was a guffaw from the soldiers. The nobleman struggled, his buttocks twitching fiercely, but the sergeant continued pushing the tube in for several inches until only the tip was still showing.

A low whine of fear escaped through the gag. Rivulets of sweat ran down the small of the victim's back. Sergeant Proudlove carried the poker across to the fire and prodded the tip deep into the burning coals. The nobleman grunted, trying to speak, to call out to him, but the sergeant stood in steadfast silence, watching the poker, carefully pulling on a thick gauntlet.

After a few minutes he removed the poker. The last twelve inches of the tip were glowing red and white hot. He walked around and held it up in front of the nobleman's face. 'Ready, my Lord?'

The nobleman's eyes skittered as if they had broken loose in their mountings. Another, longer, whine of fear came through the gag, then another. He tried to speak, choked on his own saliva and coughed, then tried frantically to speak again. He writhed and thrashed, throwing one soldier off his back on to the

6

floor, and pulling an arm free. A soldier grabbed it again, pinned it down and the other climbed back on to him, holding him down grimly. The sergeant thrust the poker back into the coals, holding it for some seconds with his gloved hand. The nobleman whined again, then again.

The sergeant removed the poker, walked up to him, gripped the hollow horn, which had slid out a couple of inches, carefully inserted the red-hot poker into the end of it as if he was locating his sword into his scabbard, then slid it in, pushing firmly and grimly.

There was a sharp hiss and bubbling sound as it burned through the soft rectal flesh, and the sudden sweet smell of roasting meat.

A convulsion of agony bulged every muscle of the nobleman's body and a scream tore free of the gag and bounced around the room like an unleashed demon; it came back at the soldiers from the ceiling, from the walls, from the floor: a screeching banshee that became louder every second as the sergeant pushed the poker relentlessly, holding it with both hands, twisting it, working it further and further in, forcing it up through the rectum, the colon, tearing through the peritoneum, melting and cauterizing a passage through the liver, gall-bladder and pancreas; through muscles, tendons, gristle, piercing the stomach wall, stirring the nobleman's bowels and organs like a giant pudding until the poker was in up to the handle.

The victim arched backwards, scattering all six of the soldiers. His neck twisted like a serpent, his head almost turning completely backwards as if his neck was broken. He stared the sergeant full in the eye and for a moment the sergeant thought he was going to clamber off the bed. Then the nobleman's mouth contorted as if it were melting, and let out a low, barely audible moan of agony; slowly this began to rise into a howl, becoming louder and louder until, in its crescendo, it seemed to detach itself from the writhing, almost inhuman, object on the bed and explode in an independent ball of energy.

The soldiers stood back, covering their ears now, unable to bear the sound that threatened to shatter the insides of their own heads. Even the sergeant released his grip and covered his ears.

Long after the poker had cooled and the nobleman lay motionless in his own slime and vomit, his finger-nails embedded into the palms of his hands, the scream remained, echoing back at them as if it would never fade.

CHAPTER ONE

26th March, 1988

The father and son walked along the London pavement
in the warmth of the spring mid-morning sunshine.
The father ambled at a leisurely stride; a tall man in
his late thirties, in an unbuttoned Harris Tweed coat,
whose thoughts seemed to be elsewhere, as if he was
pondering the cosmos above him rather than concentrating on his immediate environs.

He had a strong, open face, with handsome features
and an amiable, if rather absent-minded, expression.
His brown hair was parted high and was a little long,
covering the tips of his ears and the top of his collar.
His bearing was distinctly aristocratic, but in spite of
his City suit he looked more like an academic than
someone who fitted into a business community.

The five-year-old boy had his mother's looks: short
ginger curls, a serious, freckled face, wide, innocent
green eyes. He was wearing a tiny corduroy jacket,
grey flannel shorts, grey knee-length socks and polished black shoes. He wished his father would walk
faster; this part of London did not interest him –
except for the Dungeon and the Tower, and the Docklands train, and they had already done those. The
thought of the shop in Regent Street filled him with
an excitement he could barely contain, and the prospect of the tube train they were going to take to it was
something he looked forward to also, but now that
they had left the boring office where he had had to
wait for an hour with nothing much to read, his father
seemed in no hurry and he panicked for a moment.

'Daddy, we are going to Hamleys, aren't we? You promised.'

'Hamleys?' The father stared at his son as if he had momentarily forgotten him.

'You promised!'

'Righty ho, suppose we'd better head there, then.'

The boy looked at his father, never sure when he was joking and when he was serious. 'Is this the right way?'

'We've got to wait for Mummy.'

The boy's face fell. 'Where is she?'

'At the hairdresser's. She's coming to my office at half past twelve. That's in twenty minutes.'

'That's not for ages! Where are we going now?'

'I have to pick up Mummy's wedding bracelet from the mender.'

The boy's face fell further. 'You said we were going to Hamleys.'

'We're going to have lunch with Mummy, *then* we're going to Hamleys.'

'I want to go now! You promised!' The boy was sobbing.

They were blocking a busy pavement, being jostled by passers-by. There was an alley-way beside them, with a café a short distance down on the right. The father pulled his fractious son past an employment bureau, a travel agent, a heel bar and a few other shops, then stopped outside a dingy, unprepossessing sandwich bar with words above it, in twelve-inch-high dayglo letters, two of which were missing: SANDW CH S LUIGI CAFE. Four small suction cups held a white plastic menu against the inside of the window. EAT IN OR TAKE AWAY was printed along the bottom.

'Look, they have milkshakes,' the father said. 'Let's have one.'

A small queue stood at the counter and all but one of the tiny handful of tables were taken. There was a strong smell of coffee and of frying food; a dying fly fizzed and crackled in the mesh of an ultraviolet trap. Two posters, discoloured with age, one of Amalfi and one of Naples, were stuck to the back wall.

His father propelled his charge to the empty table and sat him down. The boy placed his fists on the table. 'You promised! You promised – you –' The boy was silent suddenly and a strange look came into his eyes, a mixture of both fear and recognition as he stared past his father at the counter.

His father turned his head, surprised, failing to see what he was looking at. Behind the counter a thin, unshaven man in his fifties greeted a customer with a cheery: 'Hi, how y'doin? What y'gonna 'ave today?' Next to him, a short, plump woman with lifeless black hair and a haggard, drained face, was buttering bread. There was a sharp ping and a girl in a white apron removed a dish from the microwave.

'Chocolate milkshake?' the father suggested, pulling out a handkerchief and wiping the tears from his son's face. He went to the counter and bought a milkshake and an espresso.

The boy concentrated on his drink, his tantrum forgotten. Soon he was spooning the dregs from the bottom of the glass, and then he became absorbed in scooping up the last of the froth with a straw.

When they left the café and were walking back down the alley into the street, he asked, 'Are we meeting Mummy, now?'

'Yes, for lunch. Then we're going to Hamleys, and then the Planetarium. You want to see the stars, don't you?'

The boy nodded dubiously.

In the distance, they both heard a siren; it sounded like a bag of stones being swirled through the air.

'Daddy, why does Mummy always go to the hairdresser every time we come to London?'

'Because she likes to look nice,' he was told.

They walked on for a moment in silence. The shops here contained nothing to distract the boy. Stationery. Men's clothes. Masonic regalia. A bank. A silversmith.

The swishing of the siren was coming closer and the boy heard the roar of an engine. They stopped, waiting for the lights to change to cross the road. A cyclist pedalled across, wearing a crash-helmet, his face covered in a smog mask which the boy thought made him look frightening. Then he saw a woman with short red hair on the other side of the road, and for a moment he thought it was his mother and tugged excitedly on his father's hand, wanting to pull him across the road to greet her. Until he realized she was a stranger. His mother had long hair.

The siren was still coming closer. The boy looked up at his father and tugged his sleeve. 'Daddy, do you think I should have my hair done in London?'

The father tousled his son's curls fondly. 'Like to come to Trumper's with me next time I go?'

The boy nodded, waited until his father was looking away, slid a hand up and flattened his hair down again. Then he looked across the road at the woman with red hair. She looked like his mother again now. It was his mother! It was. His heart leapt, then her hair blew in a gust, and it wasn't; it was someone quite different.

The lights changed to green, and the boy ran forward. Something jerked him back, holding his collar, a sharp yank. There was the roar of an engine, a shadow bearing down, the siren deafening now. The red-haired woman was halfway out in the road. His mother? Not his mother? She was staring at him, her mouth open. She was trying to run backwards now.

Tyres screamed. A shadow crossed, blocked his view for an instant. A van with two young men in it braking furiously, slewing across the road. Going to hit the woman.

'Mummy!' he screamed.

The woman was splayed out on the van's bonnet. It was careering across the road, mounting the pavement. A man in a business suit dived out of its path. A traffic-light post snapped and the coloured lights shattered on to the road. Then came an explosion like a bomb as the van, with the woman still on the bonnet, smashed through the plate-glass window of a bookshop.

The woman seemed to elongate then disappear. For an instant the entire surroundings seemed paralysed. In the silence there was nothing but the sound of breaking glass. The boy saw a chunk of window fall. He heard a scream, followed by another. Doors slamming. A siren winding down. Policemen leaping out of a car. Doors of the van opening: one easily, one with difficulty, the man inside forcing it. The van's engine was still running.

'*Mummy!*'

The boy broke free of his father's grip and ran in terror across the road, through the crowd that was forming, pushing his way, sidestepping the opening door of the van. Another pane of glass crashed down. Blood. Books scattered everywhere. A poster lay on the ground, covered in blood. An assistant was standing in the shop, hand over her mouth, screaming. The boy stared in the direction she was looking. His mouth opened but no sound came out. The woman's body lay on the floor, blood jetting intermittently from her neck. Red bubbles lay on the grey carpet tiles. A rubber mask with hair attached lay nearby, leaking blood into a fallen dumpbin of paperbacks.

Then he realized it wasn't a rubber mask. It was his mother's head.

CHAPTER TWO

August 1991

Summer had finally come to London a week ago after two months of almost continuous rain, and already the grass in the parks was parched. Seven days of heat seemed to have drawn every last drop of moisture from the soil – from the pavements, from the cement in the eternal building works – and dust that was loose and weightless hung like a permanent haze in the air. Frannie Monsanto had breathed it in, washed it out of her hair at night. She felt it now, clinging like pollen to her skin, which was already sticky with perspiration.

Normally Frannie's Mediterranean genes reacted automatically to sunshine, flooding her with a deep sense of well-being. But at work today she had been glad of the coolness of the basement vault of the Museum, and she was thankful to be heading away from the claustrophobic oven of the city and *en route* to catch a train up to the Yorkshire countryside.

The rush-hour tube was crowded and she felt faintly ridiculous holding the double bass, her overnight suitcase wedged between her legs. Air blasted her face through the open windows: hot, rank draughts that smelled of soot and something more unpleasant, reminiscent of unwashed feet, as the carriage rocked and screamed through a long stretch of darkness.

Frannie was twenty-five, with attractive Latin looks and a slender figure that she kept well toned by twice-weekly aerobics, and by swimming fifty lengths on Sunday mornings at her local pool. Like many Latins, her family had a tendency towards fatness in middle age, and Frannie was determined never to let that happen to her, the way she was determined about many things in life.

Capriciousness sometimes broke through her barrier of reserve and, on rarer occasions, a fiery temper; but mostly Frannie applied herself with single-minded quietness and dedication to her work. She did not consider herself academic, or intellectual, and had to compensate by sheer slog. That was how she had got into university in the first place, and how she had got her degree in Archaeology and Anthropology. Frannie would have been pleased just to have scraped a third and had surprised herself by getting an upper second. She had scarcely been able to believe her good fortune when she had been offered a post as a research assistant at the British Museum within weeks of leaving university, where she had remained since.

She had wispy chestnut-brown hair that was clipped to each side of her head and rested on her shoulders, a straight nose, intelligent olive eyes and an expressive, sensual mouth prone to smiling, although at heart she was a serious girl. At five feet four inches, she wished she was a little taller, but by and large she was happy about her appearance.

She was wearing Nike trainers, blue jeans, an orange T-shirt and a black cotton jacket. Slung over her arm was a large untreated leather handbag she had bought in Naples four years previously on a family visit, and which was now comfortably hammered from its daily use. Frannie was not particularly interested in clothes and loathed shopping for them. In any event, archaeology did not pay well and she was saving as hard as she could to buy a small flat of her own and get out of the crummy place she rented. Jeans were fine for her work and she lived in them most of the time, except when she had a smart date.

She had had no such date for a while. It had been over six months since her relationship with her last boyfriend had ended and, to her surprise, she was really enjoying her freedom. She was reading a lot, catching up on movies, going to exhibitions.

It would not last, she knew. Something intrinsically excited her about men, and sex was something she enjoyed deeply.

'Dreaming of nothing in particular?' said an advertisement on a panel in front of her.

A lanky youth with goofy front teeth stood opposite her. He looked at her face, down at the double bass, then back at her again. She caught his eye, stared back, and he looked away hastily. The train swayed and she nearly lost her balance, bumped into a large man in a singlet, with tattoos on his arms, and the double bass rocked precariously. She was already regretting having so readily agreed to bring it.

It belonged to Meredith Minns, a fellow Archaeology student at the University of London, with whom she had shared a room for their last year there. Meredith had wavered all that year between becoming a professional archaeologist or musician, then had fallen in love with a farmer and was now living in North Yorkshire, had produced two children, one of whom Frannie was a godmother to, and seemed content being a farmer's wife.

When she had invited Frannie up to stay, she had asked if she would mind collecting the instrument from a man who was repairing it in Covent Garden. Meredith had told her to take a taxi and she would pay, but Frannie did not like squandering money, neither her own nor anyone else's, and she had decided when she collected it that although it was bulky it was not heavy, and she could manage it on the tube. Now she was beginning to realize she had been a bit optimistic.

The train was slowing and she gripped the grab-handle harder, lurching towards the goofy-toothed youth. Bright lights slid past the window as they came into a station. She saw the sign KING'S CROSS, and the train halted. She lugged her case and the double bass out, along the platform and on to the escalator.

On the station concourse, long lines stretched back from the ticket offices and the platform gates. Commuters hurried, some trying impossibly to sprint through the crowds.

People clambered over suitcases; a toothless old lady halted her luggage trolley, lips chomping impatiently, waiting for Frannie to move out of her path. But Frannie had not noticed her; she was standing, trying to fathom out the departures board. YORK, she saw, 17.34. PLATFORM 3. She looked around for a luggage trolley but could not see one, and hefted her double bass and suitcase over to a queue at the ticket offices. An announcement rang out. Beads of perspiration trickled down her neck. She bought her ticket, then queued again at the platform gate. The train was coming in now, and the Tannoy announced: 'Arrival of the 14.52 from York. British Rail apologizes for the late arrival of this train.'

She saw carriage doors opening in line before the train had stopped moving, and the empty platform erupted in seconds into a surging wall of people. Frannie heard a shout and a small boy ran past the ticket inspector and headlong into the mêlée, followed by a harassed-looking man. Frannie gripped her ticket in her teeth, picked up her case and slid the double bass forward, stopped, repeated the procedure until she had reached the gate, then handed the ticket to the inspector.

He clipped it without looking at it, distracted by a colleague, and handed it back. She struggled forwards, the double bass getting heavier by the moment, got a few yards down the platform then stopped for a rest. Somewhere in front of her she heard a child shouting.

'No! I don't want to! I don't want to!'

The sound rang out above the clattering of feet. Several people glanced around.

'I hate you!'

The crowd was thinning and she could now see a boy of about eight – the boy who had run through the barrier a few minutes before – fighting to free himself from the grip of the man who had been chasing him and who was pulling him down the platform towards the gate.

'Let me go, let me –' As they reached Frannie, the boy suddenly stopped shouting and stared at her intently. Frannie felt a strange sense of recognition, as if she had seen him before somewhere. The man looked familiar also. In his mid-thirties, she estimated. Tall, a handsome, distinctive face; brown hair parted high up; he reminded her a little of the movie actor Harrison Ford and she wondered fleetingly where she had seen him before; perhaps he was an actor, or maybe a politician.

He stopped, sensing the boy's change of mood and interest, and smiled apologetically at Frannie; he seemed a little embarrassed by the child's behaviour. The boy was looking curiously at her double bass.

'Can I – er – give you a hand?' the man said in a quiet, assertive voice that carried both a hint of humour and the plummy confidence of the English upper classes. He was wearing an old-fashioned but rather stylish linen suit, a faded denim shirt and a pink-and-green tie, and he had an endearing air that made Frannie instantly attracted to him.

'It's OK,' she said. 'Thanks – I can –'

'It's – er – no problem. Which carriage do you want? Have you got a reservation?'

'Any carriage – I didn't reserve.'

'Where are you going?'

'To York.'

'Oh right – we'll – umm – take you down to the front – it'll be easier for you the other end.' He picked up the double bass and the suitcase.

'Really, it's –'

'What's in there?' the boy asked, touching the case. He was serious-looking, with an open, freckled face and curly ginger hair.

'It's a double bass,' she said as she walked behind the man, the boy walking beside her.

'Why's it in the box?'

'Because it's easier to carry.' She smiled, feeling a curious affinity for him.

'We've just been to an air museum and the zoo,' the boy said.

'Have you?' Frannie said politely.

'Whipsnade Zoo, in Bedfordshire. I had a ride on an elephant and on a camel. The camel sat down first so I could get on. They always do that. Did you know?'

'I didn't realize they were so polite. Which did you like best – the camel or the elephant?'

The boy thought for a moment. 'I think the camel – because if you have one you don't have to remember to give it water every day. But they can kill you.'

'Can they?' she said, amused by the boy's reasoning.

'Oh yes,' he said solemnly.

'How about here?' said the man.

'Perfect. That's very kind – just leave them here.'

The man lugged the double bass on to the train and wedged it into the luggage space at the end of the compartment. Frannie picked up her bag, but he took it insistently from her, carried that on to the train too and put it beside the double bass. 'Beautiful city, York,' he said.

'Eboracum,' Frannie replied, then immediately wondered why she had said that.

He gave her an intense look, as if he was examining an exhibit in a glass case. His eyes were a brilliant, cornflower blue, beneath thick eyebrows that were well apart. 'Ah,' he said with a warm grin. 'A Latin scholar.'

Frannie smiled back. 'No, I'm not a scholar, I'm afraid.'

'I'm having piano lessons,' the boy said.

'Are you?'

'Yes. My teacher's not very nice, though. I'd like to learn the guitar when I'm older.'

Frannie caught his father's eye. Caught the *frisson* of interest that flickered in it. He hesitated, as if about to say something, then he blushed and glanced at the boy.

'Well – er –' the man patted his pockets. His jacket was crumpled and his shoes were old brown brogues, well polished but battered. The boy was by far the neater of the two, in a white open-necked, button-down shirt, grey shorts with turn-ups, white socks and laced rubber-soled shoes. 'Better not – er – get stranded on the train,' he smiled at Frannie, hesitating again, as if trying to summon the courage to say something else.

'Thank you,' Frannie said as they parted. 'Thank

you very much.' She wished she could have kept the conversation going, but found herself watching him walk towards the exit, the boy at his side.

She went into the compartment, which was beginning to fill, and managed to claim a seat by the window. The image of the man's face stayed in her mind. Excitement burned inside her. The fleeting look of recognition of something in his eyes; of the mutual attraction. She wanted suddenly to get up and run down the platform after him. To prevent the parting that had just taken place.

Except, she might just have been imagining his interest. And at least she hadn't made a fool of herself. She smiled, feeling good suddenly. Good to have found herself attracted again to a man after so many months. She sat back, opened her bag and took out two magazines, *Antiquity* and the *Antiquaries Journal*. And she also took out the novel she was reading, *Take No Farewell* by Robert Goddard, which seemed oddly appropriate, she thought.

As the train jolted, then jolted again and began, silently, to roll forward, she flipped open one of the magazines at the last page, where she always started. But it was an hour before she was able to settle down and concentrate on her reading.

CHAPTER THREE

The traffic was snarled. Engines blattered and rattled and horns blared. The air above the bonnets of cars was corrugated by the heat and the gold spikes of the railings across the road bent and shimmered like reflections in a disturbed pond. Beyond them the British Museum sat, serious and graceful in the block it occupied in Bloomsbury, bounded by four roads like an island to which time was anchored.

In the rooms and galleries beyond the graceful portals, fragments of the past were laid out and neatly labelled, tens of thousands of years of chaos put into semblances of order: *Ancient Iran*; *Coptic Art*; Italy *Before the Roman Empire*. Visitors could stare through polished glass at the corpse of a man preserved in a peatbog; at jewelled crowns from the heads of dead emperors; at clay tablets and carved gods and Ming vases and fragments of neolithic artisan soup mugs; at pages of manuscripts left open as though waiting for their long-dead authors to return for final amendments.

Few people left the building unimpressed, untouched by something, by a memory or a thought, by a sense both of man's insignificance and of his resources, by an awe of being in a place the sum of whose parts was greater than any single human being could ever be.

Behind the quiet order of the galleries lay a labyrinth of corridors, book-lined offices and basements where many of the thousand-strong staff worked, and where some of the priceless exhibits had been stored during the war. Frannie's office was cramped and one of the few without a window, but she did not mind. She loved this museum and still, some mornings, after nearly three years, got a kick just out of walking in through its majestic front, unable to believe that this was really where she worked. And sometimes, when the monotony of her current assignment got her down, she reminded herself that it was early days in her career and there were more exciting landmarks ahead.

She had been working for twelve months on checking and recataloguing the countless basement treasures not on view to the public because of lack of space. It was tedious work, but she was learning all the time, broadening her knowledge both in her own subject, oriental antiquities, and beyond. After Christmas she was going for the first time to the Himalayas, for six weeks, on a dig. She was looking forward to that, and her mercurial boss, Declan O'Hare, the head of her department, had been hinting about a new and more exciting project at the Museum to follow.

In truth, the hope and excitement she had felt after leaving university had been dulled just a little by the tantalizing enormity of reality. By the knowledge that one human being with a trowel could unearth at the most a few square feet a day. Maybe a dozen square yards in a fortnight. That he or she could dig on the same small site for a lifetime and still examine only one tiny part of it, and find only fragments within that. There was far more still buried than had ever been discovered. Earth did not yield its secrets easily. It seemed at times as if there was some superior force at work, toying with them all, letting them build up theories then fragmenting those theories. As if the rules did not permit that you could ever piece together the whole.

Part of the excitement of archaeology for Frannie was to look at artefacts, to hold them and try to let the past come back to life in her imagination. It was something she had found herself doing ever since she had first read a book on Roman history at school. Caesar's world had come vividly alive through those pages, and the hundreds of historical books she had devoured since then. It had come alive through tiny fragments – the spoon handles, brooches, beads, rims of pots, pieces of tessera – that she had unearthed on the digs she had done.

On fine days Frannie spent her lunch-breaks outside, usually taking a sandwich to a bench in a nearby square. Sometimes one of her friends working in the West End managed to bus over and join her, or else she might be accompanied by some of the younger crowd from the Museum, but today was an exception. She felt a sense of dread as she left the massive front hall, negotiating the stream of visitors, and went out through the gateway between the black-and-gold railings into the solid, fumy jam of Great Russell Street.

She had been scared of dentists all her life. Her stomach felt like a hollow metal bowl as she walked down Charing Cross Road and turned into the narrow alley where she stopped beneath the small plastic DENTIST sign that needed a wipe. Once inside and upstairs, she announced herself to the blonde receptionist.

'Francesca Monsanto. I have an appointment with Mr Gebbie,' she said.

The girl checked her name off a list. 'Go through – first door on the right.'

Frannie went into a tiny waiting-room with half a dozen plastic chairs. A messy-looking woman with a bag of groceries spilling on to the floor beside her chair eyed Frannie hopefully, as if willing her to jump the queue.

She sat down, opened her handbag and took out her diary, determined to distract herself while she waited. Ignoring the National Health booklets scattered on a small coffee-table, she opened the diary by pulling the ribbon marker and checked the weekend and the week ahead. Clive Bracewell's party on Saturday night. It would be a crush in his tiny flat just behind the Portobello Road, but he knew a lot of people and there was always a chance of a decent spare man being there.

Clive was a research assistant at the Museum like herself. Life at the Museum wasn't that different from college, she reflected. Similar social functions, similar cliques. The same air of studiousness. It was more serious, and there was an underlying good feeling of purpose and shared aims. She had a good circle of friends there, but tried not to make it the whole focus of her life, and she particularly treasured get-away-from-it-all occasions, like the recent weekend in York with Meredith Minns, that were completely away from this community.

A breezy voice broke her train of thought, 'Mrs Lowe?'

The grocery bag rustled as its owner walked heavily through the door. Frannie put the diary back into her handbag and noticed that there were some magazines among the booklets on the coffee-table. She spotted *New Woman* lying beneath a copy of *Private Eye*, and tugged it out. As she did so, *Private Eye* fell on to the floor and lay up-ended, its covers spread open. Frannie leaned over and picked it up. It was open at the personal ads page. 'Eye Love' was the headline of one column. She glanced at it out of curiosity.

'BALDING 50-SOMETHING not fat if stomach held

in. Own London house plus inadequate income. Separated. Chain-smoker not interested in star signs. Any
offers?'

'NICE BOTTOM washes quite regularly, clever 28 and
tailormade for the beautiful young London career
woman. One only remaining. A giveaway at 24p . . .'

'FEMALE SEEKS eccentric to delight in. Midlands.
Box . . .'

She wondered what sort of people put these ads in.
Whether they were like herself. Or whether they were
desperate. Maybe it was all in code. She glanced across
the page and read down the 'Eye Need' column.

'DESPAIRING STUDENT urgently needs funds to continue education. Genuine. Thanks. Box . . .'

Then a headline in another column caught her attention: 'GIRL WITH DOUBLE BASS! Are you the girl who
was struggling down the platform of King's Cross
Station carrying a double bass, on Friday, 10th August,
catching a train to Eboracum? I am the man who
helped you. I'd like to see you again.'

Frannie looked at the advertisement in disbelief,
thinking for a moment she must have imagined it.
Eboracum. The Roman name for York. She had mentioned it to the man and he had understood it.

She read through the ad again, feeling strangely
disconcerted. Yet a tiny pulse of excitement beat deep
inside her. There might have been other girls struggling with other double basses down that platform.
But not going to *Eboracum*.

'Jesus!' she blurted out in excitement, and then felt
slightly foolish. A brake of caution suddenly applied
itself in her mind and she wondered for a moment if
she was the butt of some elaborate joke. She bit her lip
and looked up at the ceiling, and then around her.

Then she read the ad once more. It had to be her!

Had to be. A grin spread across her face as if she was sharing the joke with the man she had met. Of all the tens of thousands of people reading this ad, it was for her, her alone. And she had seen it.

She tried to recall the man's face, but it was hazy. The intense stare of his blue eyes, the resemblance to Harrison Ford. The warmth in his face, in his voice. The strange way the boy had looked at her. The ginger curls, the freckles; the serious, tear-stained face.

She remembered the humour in the man's face as he had spoken to her. The pulse of excitement beat again, more strongly. Crazy; she could remember that sudden thrill of attraction, could feel it now. It was like that sometimes; you met a total stranger and you immediately clicked, as if you were soul mates.

Frannie dug her pen out of her bag, took her diary out again and wrote down the box number of the advertisement, then the address of the magazine.

It was only as she closed her diary that the doubts began. As if there was something not quite right, that she had not yet spotted. The big snag. She shrugged them off, read the ad again, and grinned again. She was still smiling ten minutes later as she walked through into the dentist's surgery.

When she got back to the Museum, complete with two new fillings, Penrose Spode was seated at his desk with the quiet demeanour of a statue of Buddha. And the same aura of benign domination. He was her colleague and they shared an office.

Like most of the offices in the building, it was taller than it was wide, the walls on all four sides lined floor to ceiling with books and catalogues. The word-processor terminals and digital telephones on each of their ancient wooden desks looked incongruous, as if they were stage props that had been put on the wrong set.

Their desks faced each other: Spode's, like himself, immaculate; the stacks of paper laid out in careful geometric asymmetry in contrast to the post-nuclear-holocaust appearance of her own desk. Spode sat very erect, his chest indented, the knot of his lichen-coloured tie protruding the same distance as his Adam's apple; his black hair drawn smooth and flat like sealskin; his eyes small and myopic behind lenses like magnifying glasses and frames the size of protective goggles; his closed mouth, small and tight, formed a perfect circle like a rubber bung.

He was a man of twenty-eight with a dry, anarchic humour and an obsession with routine, punctuality and consistency, which he maintained were essential for a harmonious life. He did everything at the same steady pace, as if aware that energy was a commodity not to be squandered, and went about his work and his life with an air of constipated inertness. Archaeology was his world; he had no outside interests and he exercised by cycling to work on an old-fashioned upright bicycle. His clips hung on a hook on the back of the door, along with his crash-helmet, smog mask and fluorescent sash.

Frannie's hurried late arrival from lunch seemed to throw the rhythm of his concentration and, between entering the room and settling at her desk, she noticed him type and erase the same line three times on his word processor.

He stopped, clearly irritated. 'I didn't know you would be up here this afternoon,' he said. 'Thought you were down in the basement.'

'Dentist,' she mumbled through her frozen mouth.

He sighed as Frannie noisily opened and shut a drawer in her desk, looking for plain paper.

'Oh – there was a call I took for you,' he said. 'A Mr Jupp from the Bodleian. He says he's found the reference you wanted.'

'Thanks,' she said, distractedly.

'He said he thought you'd be extremely pleased.' There was a slightly pained note in Spode's voice as she continued to rummage, cleared a space on her desk, laid down a sheet of paper and started to write.

'He asked if you could call back before three,' Spode said, looking at his watch pointedly.

Frannie did not notice. She was concentrating on her handwriting, trying to make it legible for once. She wondered whether it was sensible to give her home address and phone number just in case, then realized how embarrassed she might be if he rang her at the office. Penrose Spode always listened to her calls with one ear. She decided to include her home number but not her address. Even so, her surname was not common and he could get the address by matching her name and number but she felt it at least afforded her some protection if he turned out to be a nutter.

She tore up five attempts before she was satisfied that she had got the tone right:

'I am the girl who was carrying a double bass down the platform of King's Cross Station on Friday, 10th August. Were you the very kind man with the young boy who had just been to the zoo? I would be delighted to see you again. Francesca Monsanto.'

She called at a post office on the way home, stuck a first-class stamp carefully on the envelope, then held the letter for a long time before letting it drop, with a strange feeling of finality, through the slit of the post box into the darkness.

As she walked on towards the tube station, there was a light spring in her step.

CHAPTER FOUR

Frannie's misgivings began a couple of hours after she had posted the letter. It was nothing she could put her finger on, more the feeling that what she had done was rash and she needed to be careful. There was something about the chance of having seen the advertisement that nagged her.

She wondered where else he had advertised, and whether he had done it of his own volition, or had been goaded into it for a bet by friends. And she wondered, more darkly, whether he did this as a regular way of picking up women.

She had posted the letter on Friday and it would have reached *Private Eye* on Monday. Depending how quickly they forwarded it, she knew that the earliest he could receive it would be Tuesday. Even so, every time the phone had rung over the weekend she had stiffened and answered it with a mixture of trepidation and excitement.

At the party on Saturday night she had confided in Carol Bolton, who was her closest friend at the Museum. Carol had surprised and worried her by being alarmist. She told Frannie that if he contacted her she should make sure they met in a public place, and offered to go along and lurk in the background as her minder. Frannie promised she would meet him in a public place, but said she would not be able to relax if she knew Carol was lurking, watching her.

On Monday she had lunch in a café round the corner from the Museum with Debbie Johnson, an old friend, with whom she had been at school from the age of thirteen. Debbie had a rough-and-tumble impishness about her; she was short, but prettier than she normally allowed herself to look, with large doe-like eyes and fair hair that sprouted like wild grass around a badly tied bandanna.

'Hm,' said Debbie, 'he sounds *very* dishy. Nothing like that ever happens to me.'

Debbie worked as public relations officer for a chain of fashion shops and was always enthusiastic about everything, which was one of the many things Frannie liked about her. She told Frannie she thought it sounded incredibly romantic but, like Carol Bolton, warned her to meet in a public place. Even if he was a maniac, she said, he could hardly murder her in a crowded bar.

They discussed whether the fact that he had been on his own with his son meant that he was divorced or a widower, or even that he was happily married and seeking an affair. Debbie ruled out the happily married option; she did not think he would have dared risk an advert. Frannie agreed with that.

There was no call on Tuesday. Frannie did not go to her aerobics on Wednesday in order to be at home in case he rang. But the phone remained obstinately silent.

He called the following night when she was in the bath. It was half past nine. She had for the moment forgotten about the ad and the letter, and was thinking about the argument she had had with her parents when she had gone to their Bethnal Green flat for Sunday lunch, as she usually did. Her mother had loosed off one of her regular salvoes at her for being nearly twenty-six and not married, not even going out with anyone; for not having started to make babies.

Her father had been in one of his despairing moods

in which he shook his head at her and questioned her wisdom in choosing archaeology. He could not understand how his daughter could get into university then not go into industry or law, how she could be content to make do on a meagre salary and spend her time looking at what he called old stones and bones. Frannie had heard the same argument with weary monotony two or three times a year ever since she had first made the decision to study archaeology. During her university years her father had not been so forceful, wondering perhaps at the back of his mind whether she had a smart commercial motive he had not spotted. Now, when he was in a bad mood, he vented his anger at his own failure to prosper at Frannie's betrayal, as he saw it, of all he had worked for. She had no ambition to be rich. He could not understand her. He and her mother had sacrificed everything to come to England to try to make money.

She had replied angrily that she could not understand how they had run a café for thirty years in London's Square Mile and made no money. Lunch had ended in a shouting match, with her kid sister Maria-Angela taking her side and her brother Paolo taking her parents' side. The row had eventually petered out, but the acrimony had not, and she had returned to Clapham on Sunday evening angry at herself for having erupted, angry at her parents, and with a sense of desolation about her life.

Her parents had worked hard, they had tried, they had given her the opportunities. Maybe they were right and she was letting them down. It was much easier for animals who left their families for ever the moment they could feed themselves, she thought. Then she remembered the numerous times she had gone back to her parents after she'd split up with boyfriends or was just down in the dumps, and they'd sat with their arms around her and talked wisely, made jokes, made her feel strong again, and she felt lousy for having shouted at them.

She lay back in the bath in her rented flat, her knees drawn up. The bathroom was crummy: a tiny, cramped, windowless room with a mean, narrow bath-tub that was too short to stretch out in and taps that had been loose ever since she had moved in three years ago. Despite her frequent calls to her landlord's office, the wash-basin was still coming away from the wall and was so small it was almost impossible to get both hands in together.

The hallway by contrast was vast, larger than both her bedroom and the small sitting/dining-room. It was dark and dingy, with massive pipes that gurgled and vibrated alarmingly in winter when the central heating was on, serving as an echo chamber for the boiler that switched noisily on and off at irregular intervals. One day, she was convinced, it would explode and blow the entire terraced house above her down.

She sat up and began to soap her breasts. The first ring of the telephone startled her, and water slopped over the end of the bath as she stood up, the soap submarining down between her legs.

She knew instinctively that it was him, and as she scrambled out she tried to recall his face, tried to picture him, but all she could see was a little boy with ginger hair and freckles pointing at the double bass. She managed to conjure up a crumpled linen suit but the face above it eluded her.

Water streamed down her face and her neck. Her fingers slid without purchase on the door-handle and she wrapped an end of the towel around it to open it, then hurried out, straggles of wet hair draped down the side of her face and the back of her neck, across the hall and the pea-green carpet of the sitting-room to the brown telephone which sat on a cheap, spindly table of its own.

'Hello?' she said, trying to sound nonchalant, but it came out as a strangled squawk.

'Is that – er – Francesca Monsanto?'

She recognized the voice immediately. The hesitation, then the quiet authority.

'Yes, speaking,' she said. His voice clarified his image and a clear picture of him flashed in her mind.

'It's your railway porter here.'

The remark threw her for a moment, then she laughed. 'Oh – right – hi – you got my letter?' she said, aware too late of the dumbness of her reply.

'This morning.'

Water ran down her cheek. There was an awkward silence. 'I – er – posted it on Friday.'

'How – ah – how was the concert?' he said.

'Concert?' she said blankly.

'In York?'

'Concert? Oh –' She gave a nervous laugh that sounded like she had swallowed a fish bone. 'It wasn't my double bass. I was taking it to York for a friend; it was being repaired in London.'

'Ah – I see – I – I thought you were a musician.'

'No – I'm – not terribly musical at all.'

There was another awkward silence. 'I'm sorry – I didn't introduce myself – I'm Oliver Halkin.'

'Hello,' she said, the formality of her tone striking her as absurd.

'Are you any connection with the company?'

'Company?'

'Monsanto – it's rather famous in textiles.'

'No – I don't think so.' Without meaning to, she

found herself noting the people who were walking down the street. Above the parapet she saw trousers, then a woman's legs. Water trickled down the small of her back into the towel.

'I'm really pleased you saw the ad,' he said.

'It was pretty amazing seeing it!' She relaxed a little. 'I never thought – I – I don't read *Private Eye*. I saw it by accident.'

'You were awfully decent to write.'

'I – I didn't really believe it was for me, you know? I thought it must be for someone else. Except for the Eboracum bit, that was clever.'

'Could we – er – meet up? Perhaps I could – er – could buy you some lunch?'

Lunch. She liked the idea of lunch. Daytime. There was an almost disappointing innocence about it. Lunch wasn't easy for her, it was meant to be an hour; not that anyone kept a stopwatch on it, but she felt guilty about abusing it. She remembered Carol Bolton's caution, and Debbie's. Lunch would be safer, although she did not believe he could be a threat to her. And she could compensate by working late. 'Great! Thank you.'

'Do you work in London?'

'Yes.'

'Are you anywhere near the City?'

'In Bloomsbury.'

'Right. Is next Tuesday any good for you?'

'Next Tuesday? I'll just check.' She clamped the receiver against her towelled thigh, her brain racing. Tuesday. Nothing. Her diary was through in her bedroom, but she knew she was free. 'Tuesday would be fine.'

'I'm trying to think of somewhere that's easy for you. Do you know Greville Street?'

'Off Gray's Inn Road?'

'Yes. There's a wine bar in a little alley called Bleeding Heart Yard. We can sit outside if it's nice.'

'Great. I'll find it.'

'One o'clock OK for you?'

'Yes, fine,' she said. 'See you then.'

Frannie found the Bleeding Heart wine bar more quickly than she had expected and was ten minutes early. She had dressed in the only really smart summer outfit she had, a navy two-piece, a white open-neck blouse and her one pair of decent navy shoes, and she had felt good when she had left the Museum twenty minutes ago. Now she was a bag of nerves.

She walked on past the courtyard and crossed over to the cool of the shaded side of the street, out of the cloying lunch-time heat, wondering if there was some subtle humour in his choice of venue that was eluding her.

She checked her reflection in a shop window, making sure her face and nose had not gone shiny, then ambled on edgily, unable to stand still, glancing at other windows but barely registering what was in them. Instead she was thinking about him. Oliver Halkin. All worked up, she thought, for someone I met at a railway station and will probably never see again after today. Someone whose face I can't even remember clearly without his voice to prompt me. She even wondered whether she would recognize him instantly or not.

At five to one she made her way back up the street and into the pretty, cobbled courtyard with tables outside laid for lunch, several of which were already occupied. A waitress asked if she had a reservation and she told her there might be one in the name of Oliver Halkin.

The girl disappeared inside, then came back out a moment later. 'He's not here yet.' She led Frannie to a table in the sun, saying 'Would you like a drink?'

'I'll wait for a few minutes,' Frannie said.

She sat, glancing around. There were three women at the next table, smartly dressed and chattering. Two men sat at the table in front of her, one having soup, the other pulling an artichoke apart. A blond man in a brightly checked jacket walked arm in arm with a smartly dressed woman across the cobbles, and into the interior. She heard the faint clatter of cutlery, the clink of glasses around her, and smelled the aroma of grilled fish.

A tall brown-haired man hurried in from the street; he was the right age and build and she wondered, just for an instant, whether it could possibly be Oliver Halkin. He caught her glance and hesitated, looking at her expectantly but equally without recognition, then walked past her and inside.

A striking-looking woman in her early thirties, in a white trouser suit and jangling gold chains, strutted past, heels clicking on the cobbles. Her wake of perfume drifted over Frannie. A siren wailed a few blocks away. Then Oliver Halkin came in.

She stood up as he ambled towards her with a shy smile on his face, everything else in the courtyard dissolving into the background. He stopped in front of her, seemed to pluck up courage and held out his arm, stiffly, giving her hand a firm, curiously formal shake. 'Francesca. Sorry I'm late – the traffic –' He raised his arms then let them drop to his side by way of apology. 'You haven't been waiting long?'

'Just a couple of minutes. I was a little early.'

He was taller and more powerfully built than she remembered, and in the bright sunlight she could see he was closer to forty than thirty-five. He was dressed similarly to before, although he looked smarter and fresher in a well-pressed linen suit, a blue-and-white striped shirt and a tie which had what looked like hippopotamuses on it. He was as good-looking as she had remembered. Even more so.

They studied each other for a moment, as if each was uncertain of their memory and was seeking reassurance, then he leaned forward and lowered his voice conspiratorially. 'You know, you look much better without your double bass.'

'You don't get to meet such nice strangers without it.' She smiled, surprised by the flirtatiousness of her reply. Now that he was here, her nervousness had gone almost completely, and she was feeling the same immediate attraction to him that she had before.

He sat down opposite her and the waitress came over with two menus. 'Can I get you something to drink?' she said.

Frannie opted for a spritzer and Oliver joined her. He glanced down towards his lap, then up, touched the edge of the table as if he was going to adjust it, then seemed to have difficulty in deciding what to do with his arms. He folded them, unfolded them, then rested his hands on the edge of the table. They were large, strong-looking hands with slender, elegant fingers and rather bluntly clipped nails, which he examined for a moment before looking directly back at her. She noticed the signet ring on his wedding finger.

'So, tell me about Francesca Monsanto.'

She interlocked her fingers in her lap, amazed how relaxed she still felt. 'You tell me about Oliver Halkin first.'

'There's nothing very exciting to tell.' Oliver tapped his menu as she grinned at him disbelievingly. 'I'm a

39

widower with a son of eight, Edward, whom you've met. I have a farm which my brother runs – I help him out at weekends. And I'm a mathematician at a bank in the week.'

'Oh?' She tilted her head inquiringly.

'Yes; mathematics and flying have always been my two big loves. But I can't afford to fly much these days.'

'Do you have a plane?'

'I have an ancient Tiger Moth I've been restoring. But she's not airworthy yet.' When her eyes widened, he said, 'Your turn! Tell me about Francesca now.'

'Right, well . . .' She pursed her lips and smiled, infected by his own expectant air. 'She's an archaeologist.' She paused to take in his reaction, which seemed to be of approval. 'She has graduated in Archaeology and Anthropology at the University of London. She's a Libra.' She thought for a moment, swinging her tongue inside her mouth. 'Her lucky number is four and her favourite colour is blue. She's quite superstitious. She has two brothers and one sister.'

The waitress arrived with their drinks and as Oliver leaned back a little Frannie noticed his broad shoulders. She brought to mind an expression about the boy being father of the man. In Oliver Halkin she could see both. There was a boyishness about his features, his hair, about the faint trace of sadness in his eyes, and yet a manliness in his physique, in the lines of his face, the crow's-feet, in the confidence with which he carried himself, the assurance with which he sat here like a lion in its own habitat.

'What do they do?' he asked. 'Your brothers and sister?'

'My little sister Maria-Angela's at catering college.

My eldest brother, Vittorio, is a doctor – he's a house-man in Durham, and my younger brother, Paolo, is a lorry driver.'

'Quite a mixture, your family.' He held his glass forward. 'Cheers.'

'Cheers,' Frannie said.

He clinked his glass against hers and there was a rich chime. Their eyes met and Frannie felt a beat of excitement as she drank. He lifted his menu. 'Shall we order? Get these out the way.'

They studied the menus in silence for a few moments. Frannie ordered melon followed by turbot, and Oliver Halkin ordered pâté and the turbot.

She wondered how his wife had died but did not like to ask. 'Which bank are you with?' she said.

'It's a small merchant bank, called the Halkin-Northrop.' He raised his eyebrows. 'I shouldn't think you've heard of it.'

'Halkin? Is that a family connection?'

'More by name than much else, these days. We don't own many shares any more. They give me something to do out of kindness.'

'I don't believe that! What do you actually do there? Chairman?'

'No, gosh, I'm just a sort of consultant. I dabble away with my mathematics and every now and then if I get something right they give me a pat on the head and a biscuit.'

'You do their accounts?'

'No. I'm a statistics analyst. I study trends, patterns, assess the odds of risks. We do quite a bit of reinsurance financing – I have to try to work out things like how many people are going to be killed in road accidents over the next decade, how many in plane crashes and how many are going to get bitten by dogs.' He smiled wryly. 'Or how many cavalry officers are going to get kicked to death by horses.'

'Do many?'

'It's a very consistent figure.'

'I've never been much good at maths.'

'Have you ever been interested in it?'

'No, I've never really thought about it very much – probably because I'm so hopeless at it.'

He looked reprovingly. 'That's a shame.'

'Why?'

He patted the table with the palm of his hand, lightly but with a sudden look of zeal on his face, and leaned forward. 'Because so many bright people do ignore it. So few teachers make it exciting at school – they teach it as just another boring thing you have to learn.' His eyes brightened, coming alive like a dormant fire blasted by bellows. 'Archaeology – beauty – symmetry. Think about the proportions of buildings, of vases, furniture. Mathematics and design are inseparable. The design of objects,' he raised his side plate then put it down; 'the design of the world.'

'Of the world?' she said.

He picked up his glass and swirled the liquid inside it. His eyes were alight and Frannie was captivated by his enthusiasm. 'Mathematics is the most exciting thing of all. It holds the key to the universe.'

She looked at him and asked dubiously. 'In what way?'

'You said you're a Libra. Do you read your horoscope?'

'Sometimes.'

'Do you believe in fortune-tellers?'

'I'm not sure. I suppose I do, a little.'

'I'm a fortune-teller.'

Her eyes widened. 'Do you have a crystal ball?'

'No. Just a calculator.' He smiled. 'At a simple level, mathematics can predict the most extraordinary things.'

'Like what?' She leaned towards him.

'I can tell you how many people are going to die next year, in every country of the world, in any kind of accident you can name. And from any kind of disease. What's more, I'll be more accurate than any seaside clairvoyant.'

Frannie savoured her spritzer then cupped her glass in both hands. 'Except you can't predict who the victims will be, can you?'

He smiled. 'No, that's right. Not yet.'

'Not *yet*? You think you'll be able to one day?'

'There are patterns to everything. By understanding patterns you can make order out of chaos.' He raised his glass. 'I'm getting far too serious.'

'No, I'm interested.'

He drank and then set the glass down with exaggerated care. 'Tell me about your parents. What do they do?'

The time slipped by easily, almost unnoticed, as they chatted. Their table had become a private island where they sat alone, absorbed in each other and undisturbed except for the arrival of food and more drinks and the removal of plates, and at some point, even when Frannie already thought she was feeling far too drunk, a bottle of Sancerre was presented and poured. She became increasingly surprised at the things they had in common. Attitudes and interests. She told him how she had first become interested in archaeology as a child, from a book on the Romans at school, and had persuaded her parents to take her to stately homes and museums at weekends.

43

Oliver elaborated on his love of mathematics and how he believed that it was both an art and a science, one which could ultimately solve all the mysteries of the universe. She talked about her love of archaeology and how she believed that it was through uncovering the secrets of the past that the mysteries of the universe would be solved.

Finally, Frannie noticed there was no one left in the courtyard except themselves. She looked at her watch, and saw with shock that it was four o'clock.

Oliver took her back to the Museum in a taxi, and asked her if she would have a meal with him on Friday. She told him she would like that very much.

She hurried back up the steps into the shadow of the colonnaded portals, stepping on air, her guilt at being so late back cushioned by the haze of alcohol.

An hour later, as she began to sober up, she had a slight sense of unease about Oliver and she was not sure why. He seemed almost too good to be true. It was as if there was something about him that did not totally fit together; a piece missing from the equation. Something about himself that he wasn't telling her, perhaps; that he was either hiding or holding back. And she was still bothered, also, by the feeling that she had seen him before.

Normally Frannie was confident and looked on the bright side and she found it unsettling to feel this way. All the more so as she realized quite how deeply she fancied him.

CHAPTER FIVE

Debbie Johnson rang her late on Wednesday evening, curious to know how her date had turned out. Just back from her aerobics, Frannie tried not to say too much, afraid it might be bad luck to talk about it too soon. She promised to call her friend back on Saturday and report on Friday's date.

As she hung up, the phone rang again. It was Oliver. He apologized for having made her so late in getting back to work on Tuesday afternoon and she told him it had not mattered, although actually she'd been carpeted by the unpredictable Declan O'Hare. They chatted easily. He asked her what she had been doing at work and she told him she had spent the day cataloguing Indian daggers and had then been to her aerobics class; and he said he had just got back from playing tennis. There had been a pause in which she had been tempted to say, 'Why don't you come over?' but she did not want to seem pushy or too keen. It was enough that he had called. And she was secretly pleased that at nine o'clock he was at home and not out on a date.

On Thursday evening she washed her hair but could not settle down and relax. She was unable to concentrate on reading, or on the television and instead spring-cleaned the flat. She knew she was behaving like a besotted teenager and was angry with herself. But she could not help it.

On Friday she left work punctually at half past five and hurried home, having a sudden, uncustomary panic about what to wear. She unhooked the black dress, a high-street version of Chanel, which she had decided on. She liked it because it was short and neat, but she was worried in case it didn't make her look attractive enough for Oliver Halkin. She tugged several more outfits out, but nothing else looked right, so it was going to have to do.

A narrow rectangle of sunlight lay across the bedroom floor, touching the edge of the white rug she had bought in Petticoat Lane a few months ago to try to brighten up the room. Sometimes it could feel dark and oppressive even though the walls were white and the ceiling was high, and at times it had an atmosphere that made her feel distinctly uncomfortable. A window opened on to a basement well which only accentuated the subterranean feel of the room.

Frannie had hung a couple of Egyptian prints on the walls, and on the mantelpiece were her family photographs, as well as two small fragments of tessera that she had pocketed from one of the first digs she had ever been on, and which still gave her a thrill. In spite of all the objects she handled daily at the Museum, nothing quite measured the feelings she got from the few treasures of her own.

She had finished getting ready by twenty past seven and had forty minutes to kill. She looked around the sitting-room. Her efforts of last night had improved it a little. It was the first flat she had ever had of her own and she did not mind the cheap furniture and the drabness because it had given her freedom and independence. She always enjoyed playing hostess when her friends came round. But most of them were as used to the flat's less-than-impressive air as she was. It was only now, with Oliver coming, that Frannie suddenly found herself gazing uncomfortably at the ugly vinyl sofa and armchairs, the dining-table with its peeling mahogany laminate, and the shabby net curtains.

The only stamp of her own personality on the room lay in the framed posters of past exhibitions at the Museum, her books and her pride and joy – a small, plain earthenware Roman vase that sat on the coffee table. It was pear-shaped and rather dumpy, with the handle and part of the rim missing, and had been carefully glued back together by the amateur archaeologist who had dug up the pieces in 1925.

Often Frannie wondered about the life of the Roman artisan who had made it, imagined what he or she had looked like. The clay indicated it had been made in Italy and brought over maybe by an immigrant like her own parents. She had paid five hundred pounds for the vase three years ago in the Portobello Road, on the day she had received the letter from the Museum telling her she had got the job. It had been a spur-of-the-moment bit of madness that had blown her savings, but she had never regretted it.

She switched off the overhead light, leaving just a table light and the wonky lamp standard and that made a further improvement, made the room seem almost cosy. Another year and she would buy somewhere of her own. It would be tiny but it would be tasteful, she resolved.

She picked the Jilly Cooper novel she had just started off the sofa, made a mental note of the page number and closed it, tucking it into her bookshelves, and pulled out instead a paperback of Guy de Maupassant short stories, which she opened and placed casually, face down, in the same position on the sofa.

As eight o'clock approached, Frannie began to feel nervous. She went into the bedroom, and felt a bit reassured by the girl who stared back at her from the mirror. The short dress showed off her legs and her figure well. She had frown lines from anxiety so she deliberately relaxed and smiled. A sultry girl with dark, shiny hair that framed her face and touched her shoulders smiled back. The girl looked OK.

She looked great.

She went back into the sitting-room, sat down and picked up the Maupassant, glancing through, unable to concentrate. She could hear muffled gunshots ringing out from the television in the flat above. Her watch said eight-fifteen. Then eight-thirty. He wasn't coming. Chickened out. Stood her up. Going to end up spending the evening watching the box.

Then she heard footsteps. A shadow crossed the curtains. The doorbell rang.

She jumped up, went into the hall and opened the front door. Oliver Halkin peered over the huge bunch of flowers in his hands, looking relieved that he had found the right place. 'Sorry I'm so late,' he said. He pushed the flowers forward as if he was slightly embarrassed by them. 'I hope you – sort of like these –'

'Wow!' she said. Their scents blotted out for a brief moment the rank, humid smells of London at night, of unemptied dustbins, exhaust fumes and dust, reminding her that there was another world of parkland and countryside. 'They're gorgeous!' She took the flowers, brought the heads close to her nose and inhaled deeply. 'Thank you.' She kissed him spontaneously on his cheek, but he made no response and the gesture left a moment of awkward silence between them.

He was wearing a navy double-breasted suit that looked good on him, a soft-collared blue shirt and a yellow tie. His hair seemed more carefully groomed than before and he was wearing black Oxfords that looked fairly new. The neatness of his appearance belied her original image of him. When she offered him a drink, he looked at his watch, then back at her, expressionlessly.

'I think perhaps we ought to make tracks – I booked for eight-thirty.'

'I'll just put these in some water.' The flat suddenly seemed dingier than ever. She ushered him through into the living-room, then walked with a heavy heart into the kitchen, and ran the cold tap into the sink; a feeling of unease was establishing itself inside her. He seemed a bit distant.

As she went into the sitting-room she was pleased to see him staring with interest at the Roman vase.

'Is this one of your finds?' he said.

'Yes – well – sort of – I found it in a shop.' Her confidence had gone and she realized she was sounding stiff and nervous.

'How old is it?'

'About 50 BC.'

'Good Lord.' He squatted and stared at it more closely. 'I've got one very similar at home. I'd no idea it was as old as that. What would it have been used for?'

'Probably for water or wine. I could have a look at it for you if you like.'

'Yes, I would.'

'I sometimes feel guilty about owning it.'

'Why?' He stood up again.

She shrugged. 'I suppose it's the same as I feel about the treasures locked away in the vaults in the Museum. That things from the past like this ought to be accessible to everyone – that maybe it shouldn't be tucked away down here – a secret little treasure hoard.'

'You could always open your flat to the public.' He grinned, fleetingly.

'Great idea. England's first stately basement!'

He laughed, and although it was a little forced, the atmosphere seemed to improve between them.

It was now dark outside. She followed him to a small Renault that was either grey or blue beneath a London patina of grime and dust; it was badly dented down the passenger side, and there was a row of holes where a chromium or plastic strip had been torn away.

He held the door for her, scooped a clutch of papers off the passenger seat, and she climbed in. The interior of the car was full of clutter. She carefully placed her feet between several library books that lay on the floor. A residents' parking sticker, Borough of Chelsea, was stuck on the windscreen beside the licence roundel, plus another permit that she could not read. Several parking-tickets in cellophane bags lay in the indent above the glove compartment, along with a packet of Fisherman's Friends, a couple of ball-point pens, several loose pieces of paper and a tennis ball.

She pulled the seat-belt over her chest and found the buckle. He climbed in and sat slightly hunched, his head touching the roof lining, as if the car were a suit that was a size too small. He twisted the ignition key and the engine clattered into life, then he turned towards her. 'I apologize if I'm not quite with it at the moment. I had a bit of grim news just before I came to pick you up.'

'I'm sorry,' she said.

'No – it's –' he shrugged. 'My son's on holiday in the South of France, staying with some friends who've a boy his age – they have a villa down there.' His voice tailed and he pulled the car out, accelerating harshly. 'I just had a phone call this evening – they had a ghastly accident on a speedboat yesterday.' He braked at the junction and peered sternly out into the main road, as if he expected the traffic to stop under his withering gaze. 'Apparently they all went out in the boat to find a bay for a picnic and water-skiing. On the way back they ran over a swimmer – a girl.'

'God!' Frannie said. 'Awful. Is she –' she hesitated. 'Badly hurt?'

'She was killed.'

'That's terrible.'

He accelerated decisively out into a gap, alarmingly close to an oncoming car.

'Is your son all right?'

He drove on without replying for some moments. 'Fine. Edward's fine.' He said it rather oddly, she thought; quite defensively.

'Shock sometimes hits people later,' she said, remembering the time she had been a passenger in a motorway pile-up four years ago, and one of the cars behind had caught fire. Just a few flames under the bonnet at first. Everyone had tried to get the trapped driver out, but the flames had soon engulfed the car and beaten them back. She'd watched him banging the windscreen and yelling until she could bear it no longer and had had to turn away. It had been a week later that she'd had the first nightmare about it. She still dreamed of it now, occasionally.

'Yes,' he said.

'Who was driving the boat?'

'I'm not sure. It wasn't Edward.' He was about to say something else, then was silent.

'What a horrible thing for a child to see,' Frannie said.

'I had a word with him over the phone. He seemed fine – far more concerned about whether I'd got his Scalextric working again – there was a problem with the transformer.'

She smiled. But there was no humour in Oliver's

expression and he lapsed into silence. She watched him, the glare of each passing street light flaring on his face then fading. Something about his taut profile reminded her of a rabbit when it is caught in the glare of the headlights and doesn't know which way to turn. Just for a moment. Then the impression was gone.

The restaurant was a cheap and cheery trattoria, with red-and-white tablecloths, strips of fish netting and wickered Chianti bottles strung from the walls. The air was heavy with cigarette smoke, and stronger, sumptuous smells of hot olive oil and garlic, of searing meats and grilling fish. All the tables were occupied and the place had a crammed, lively atmosphere which made Frannie immediately feel comfortable.

A waiter with an accent Frannie recognized as Neapolitan led them down a staircase into an equally packed basement. There was a burst of raucous laughter from a large party of people in their twenties at the far end. Only two tables were unoccupied and he led them to one tucked in a corner alcove near the party. 'You like an aperitif, perhaps?' he said as he pushed Frannie's chair in.

'Yes, I – er –' Oliver raised his eyes quizzically at Frannie.

'Love one.' She felt in need of a drink.

'A couple of your cocktails.'

'*Due Vito Fizzo*,' he proclaimed, presented each of them with a large, handwritten menu and wheeled away. A packet of *pannini* lay beside each of their places. Oliver picked his up and tore open the top.

There was a deafening eruption of laughter from the party behind them, and Frannie instinctively turned her head. As she did so, a chuckling face looked familiar. The luxuriant hair was shorter than when she had last seen it, but there was no mistaking the thick lips, the burly frame, the booming voice. She watched as Seb Holland banged the table and called out: 'Hey, Luigi, bring me an alligator sandwich and make it snappy!' He turned, roaring with laughter at his joke, to his companions.

She hadn't seen Seb since university, over three years ago. He was going into his family business, she remembered. They were in insurance, something large in the City, and he looked like a prosperous City businessman now, in his chalk-striped suit and loud tie. Their eyes met and he beamed in recognition, stood up, stumbled slightly drunkenly out of his chair, came over, and leaned across the table. 'Frannie! Hi! How are you? You look gorgeous.' He gave Oliver Halkin a cursory glance. 'Sorry, 'scuse me,' he said. 'I've always been in love with this girl – might try and pinch her from you later on if I get pissed enough.' Seb Holland's voice was slurred with booze and he spoke too loudly.

Frannie blushed and introduced the two men.

'Hello,' Oliver said. There was a brief silence as Oliver and Seb frowned at each other in vague recognition.

'Met you before,' Seb said. He was having difficulty in standing upright without swaying, and held on to Frannie's chair-back.

'Yes,' Oliver said good-humouredly, 'I – seem to think we – have –' He frowned which made him look rather fierce, Frannie thought.

'Halkin? Halkin-Northrop bank?'

'Yes,' Oliver said. 'Seb Holland? Any connection with Holland Delarue?'

'Yah.'

'Ah!' Oliver's face relaxed into a beam as recognition dawned. 'I know Victor Holland.'

''S'my brother.'

'Good Lord! Your brother! I play tennis with him occasionally at Queen's.'

'Didn't you come to our Christmas party last year? That's where we met.'

'At your rather super building?' Oliver's eyes narrowed as if he was trying to remember its name. 'That's right. We talked about cricket! How is Vic? Haven't seen him for a while.'

'He's fine.'

'Good – well –' Oliver looked awkward suddenly, as if unsure how to end the conversation. 'Give him my regards.'

'Yes, I will.' Seb turned to Frannie. 'So, how are you? What are you up to?'

'Fine. Working at the British Museum. How about you?'

'Great.' He sniffed. 'Getting married next month. That's my fiancée.' He pointed at the table, but Frannie could not work out which of the girls he meant. 'Lucy – d'yever meet her?' He screwed up his eyes as if finding it hard to focus. 'No – that was after university. Getting married next month,' he repeated. 'Hey, you must come! Send you an invite. I've still got your family address. We must have a drink sometime before that, anyway.'

'Love to. Congratulations.'

'Yah, thanks.'

Frannie was secretly pleased at being recognized; it helped her stand on her own two feet with Oliver. Seb showed no signs of moving away and she felt a bit embarrassed about prolonging the conversation. 'Still in your family business?'

'Yah, it's OK. Spend half the time in the States.' He sniffed. 'Still see any of the people I'd remember?'

'Meredith. I stayed with her a couple of weekends ago up in York.'

'Meredith! Great girl! Really liked her. How is she?'

'Fine. Very married.'

He grinned, then looked solemn. 'Hey – remember Jonathan Mountjoy?'

'Yes.' She remembered him clearly, a tall, quiet boy, always intensely serious, who never said very much.

'Poor bugger got shot dead in Washington a few weeks ago.'

Frannie stared at him in shocked silence. Her stomach felt as if a drum of cold water had been emptied into it. 'What – what happened?'

'Mugger. Gave him his wallet apparently and the bastard still shot him.'

'God, poor Jonathan!' she said. 'That's awful. Horrible.' She shivered, feeling oddly disoriented suddenly.

Seb dug his finger into his breast pocket and pulled out a card. 'Give me a buzz – come and have lunch or something sometime.' He gave Oliver a smile. 'I'll tell Vic I met you,' he said, then moved away from the table, hesitated for a moment and turned towards Frannie. 'Great seeing you.'

'You too.'

Jonathan Mountjoy. Shot. Dead. Gone.

'Were you at school together?'

Oliver's voice startled her. She collected her thoughts and smiled at him apologetically. 'University.'

A waiter presented them with their cocktails.

Oliver raised his glass. 'Cheers,' he said, quietly. 'It's good to see you again.'

'You too,' Frannie said and sipped the pink-tinged fizzing concoction. It had a pleasant taste of apricots but she barely registered it.

'I'm sorry about the news – about your friend being killed.'

'Thanks,' she said heavily. 'I didn't really know him that well – hadn't seen him since university. But he was nice.' She hunched her shoulders and smiled more brightly. 'Doesn't seem as if either of us are having much good news tonight.'

'No,' he said. 'Well – except that you're here, and that's pretty good news.'

Their eyes met. 'Thank you,' she said.

Someone at Seb's table was telling a story and a girl was squealing in protest. Frannie felt a chilly draught from the air-conditioning against her neck, then a sudden rash of goose-pimples down between her shoulder-blades. She drank some more of the cocktail, but could not feel any effects from it yet. Oliver Halkin and Jonathan Mountjoy's death were now intertwined in her mind, as if somehow connected. She tried to control the crazy notion that the news was an omen about her and Oliver. That she should pull out now, while she still could.

A waiter hovered; they looked at their menus and ordered, then there was an awkward silence. Oliver shook a stick out of his packet of *pannini*, then laid both the stick and the packet down, aligning them carefully so they lay parallel to his cutlery. 'Penny for your thoughts,' he said.

'I was thinking about the coincidence – of bumping into Seb – and that we should both know him.'

Oliver broke a piece off the end of his *pannini* stick and ate it in silence. 'Coincidences make me uneasy,' he said.

'Why's that?'

He shrugged, then lowered his eyes to the tablecloth, as if embarrassed by what he was about to say. 'I've had rather too many in the past few years; not very happy ones. I find them bad news. They bother me. Probably sounds daft.'

Frannie smiled back at him, surprised that he was superstitious. 'They happen to everybody, surely? Don't you ever have harmless coincidences – like when you're thinking about someone and they phone you?'

'I'm not sure there is such a thing as a meaningless coincidence.'

As she watched his serious face, she began to feel excluded, and her sceptical grin faded. 'What's happened to make you feel that way?'

He fiddled around for some moments with the *pan-nini* packet, then responded in a way that did nothing to make her feel better. 'I suppose the worst was my wife's death.' He moved his hands in a gesture of helplessness.

'I'm sorry,' Frannie said. 'What happened?' She felt that she needed to know.

He leaned forward, pressed his fingernail hard into the tablecloth, and with intense concentration began to make a straight line across. 'Almost any sort of coincidence,' he said distantly, as if he had not heard her question. 'Bumping into someone like Seb Holland. The same number coming up a couple of times. Anything.'

His expression suddenly changed into a distant smile that seemed to be directed at the universe in general rather than at her. 'The French mathematician Laplace said that chance is the expression of man's ignorance.'

'Is that what you believe?'

He picked his glass up by the stem, cupped the base in the palm of his hand and twisted it round slowly, studying the contents with an air of suspicion. 'Chaos. All these bubbles firing off in here at random. But the effect works; it tastes good and it's intoxicating. Order from chaos! See?' He continued to hold the glass in the air as if in a mood of childish contentment.

'Perhaps the next coincidence is going to change your luck,' she said and drank some more.

'Maybe,' he said, unconvinced.

An image slipped silently through her mind. Jonathan Mountjoy wearing a battered old greatcoat, standing with his hands in his pockets, staring into space. That was how she remembered him, always slightly out of it, in his own world. Dozy, silent Jonathan, handing over his wallet, then the gun coming up, firing.

Over.

She swallowed, placed her hands on the tablecloth, reached out awkwardly for her glass, then stopped as she realized there was nothing left in it.

I'm not sure there is such a thing as a meaningless coincidence.

'Mozzarella for the signorina!' A waiter placed their plates in front of them, then brandished a pepper grinder above Oliver's minestrone. He gave the handle several sharp, crunching twists.

Another waiter appeared with a bottle of wine, which he ceremoniously opened. Frannie looked at her plate, but her appetite had gone. She wanted someone to tell her that it was quite safe to fall in love with Oliver Halkin. She looked across the table at him. He was tasting the wine, holding the glass with one hand, the other lying on the table, large and solid, the winder of his watch nestling in the hairs of his wrist. The sadness had returned to his eyes and she felt an urge to put her own hand out and touch his, to reassure him, to reassure herself.

Her attraction towards him was growing, but her

unease grew with it. Almost as if he were reading her thoughts, he smiled at her.

They talked deeply throughout the meal, which Frannie managed to pick at, mostly discussing their views on the meaning of life, and carrying on their arguments from where they had left off at lunch on Tuesday. She found him challenging to talk to, and he opened her mind further to the world of mathematics and physics. Starting to relax, she told him she had tried to read *A Brief History of Time* but had abandoned it halfway through, and he laughed and told her he'd abandoned it a quarter of the way through, and talked her through the theories in a way that made more, if not total, sense to her.

Frannie had two Sambucas with her coffee, and was pleasantly drunk as they left the restaurant shortly after one; she felt on safer ground with him now. As she fumbled with the seat-belt she was vaguely aware that it was she who had done most of the drinking tonight. She had not even noticed whether Seb Holland was still there or had left.

Oliver dropped her home and escorted her down the steps to her front door. She hoped he would not make an advance because she would find it hard to resist him if he did, and she wanted it to be special when they made love, and she was too drunk for it to be like that now. 'Would you like to come in for a coffee?' she said.

'I – ought to get back – it's pretty late.' He looked awkward suddenly. 'I was wondering – Edward's coming back tomorrow – this is his last weekend at home before he goes back to school.' In the haze of the street-lighting Frannie could see that he was blushing, and wasn't sure what was coming next. 'If – if you're not doing anything, would you – like to come down to the country for the weekend? He took a bit of a shine to you at King's Cross.'

She tried to think of the implications, but her heart overruled everything. There was a party tomorrow that she was not particularly looking forward to, and she was meant to be going to her parents for Sunday lunch, but had already been thinking of ducking out of that. After the fracas of last Sunday, she could do without seeing her parents for a few weeks. 'I'd love to,' she said.

He looked really pleased. 'How about if I pick you up at about ten?'

'Do I need to bring anything?'

'Some wellies. I don't know what the forecast is. We're very informal. And swimming gear.'

'I'll be ready at ten.'

He held her gaze for a moment, gave her a light peck on the cheek, walked back up the steps, and stood waiting until she was safely inside.

As she closed the front door and pressed the latch, she felt as if she had been scooped up and put on a pedestal. Her emotions came to the surface so that her earlier fears were buried by a glow of pleasure and a sense of anticipation. The very word *country* conjured an image in her mind of a ramshackle farmhouse, with a flagstone floor and log fire, acres of fields and woods. She could see them taking long walks, maybe having lunch in a pub garden. Lazing around a swimming-pool, with sheep on the far side of the fence. The boy had taken 'a shine' to her. Edward. She was pleased about that, rather flattered.

She went through into the kitchen, switched on the light and stared at Oliver's flowers in the sink, then hunted for something suitable to put them in. She remembered a plain white vase with a green ceramic bow which she had been given a couple of birthdays ago by Meredith Minns, and retrieved it from behind a stack of bowls.

She carefully arranged the flowers in the vase, feeling wide awake and almost deliriously happy, then carried it through into her bedroom and placed it in the centre of the mantelpiece, spreading out the white and peach carnations, the yellow and orange lilies, smelling their scents in turn, then standing back to admire them.

It was after two when Frannie went to bed, and she set her alarm for eight. After she switched the light out she lay awake for a long time, her brain buzzing.

When she eventually slept, she sank into a sinister dream in which she was running through dark empty streets in a city. Ahead of her she could see Jonathan Mountjoy, silhouetted against a high-rise building. But although he was not moving and she was sprinting, she was not getting any nearer. Footsteps were clacking down an alley. Someone was running towards him holding a gun. She tried to scream at him, to warn him, but her voice would not work. She could see the gun pointing at him, the wild, shaky hand holding it. 'Jonathannnnnnnnnn!'

The shot woke her with a start.

People were screaming. The sirens of the police and the ambulance were wailing. Then she realized it was a real siren, somewhere in the distance. But the shot had been here, in this room. A bang, or a slap.

Someone in here.

A deep chill of fear spread through her. For a moment she was too scared to move. Then slowly she put out her hand, groping for the light switch. Snapped it on.

The darkness leapt back into the walls. She stared around with frightened eyes. Only an eerie silence filled the room. Nothing moved, nothing breathed, but something was wrong. Shadows from the lamp lay across the ceiling; a fly sat directly above her. She stared at her prints on the walls; at the wardrobe. Her throat was parched, her mouth dry. She stared at the mantelpiece. The mantelpiece where she had carefully put the vase with the flowers.

The vase was still there but there were no flowers in it.

She sat bolt upright. The flowers lay strewn across the floor, as if they had been hurled there by someone or something in a rage.

CHAPTER SIX

Oliver turned up shortly after ten, wearing a rugger shirt, baggy red trousers and ancient laced yachting shoes; he carried Frannie's bag to an elderly mud-caked Range Rover.

'What happened? Did you put the Renault in a grow-bag?' she asked.

He laughed. 'I just use the Renault for hacking around London; it's so clapped out I don't think it would survive a long journey.'

The interior of the Range Rover was as cluttered and untidy as his Renault, with the addition of crum-pled rugs and an assortment of chewed rings and rubber bones on the rear seat. 'Captain Kirk's,' he said by the way of explanation.

'Captain Kirk?'

'Edward's dog; he treats this bus as his kennel.'

They drove south out of London, through traffic that was heavy and slow at first, but which thinned out on the motorway. The sun beat down ahead of them out of a cloudless sky. Frannie had on a checked shirt, with a thin jumper slung around her shoulders, white cotton trousers and trainers, and she felt cool and comfortable in her clothes. Her thoughts were less comfortable and she felt tired, her eyes sandpapery from the fitful sleep she had had.

The flowers churned in her mind. She had checked the flat, but the windows were shut, the front door was locked and no one could have been in. She had put them back in the vase and in the morning they were still there, and she had begun to wonder seriously whether it had simply been a dream. Or just a household accident to which she'd overreacted.

She asked Oliver more about his farm, trying to build up a picture of it. He told her his manager and younger brother, Charles, was a very committed Green, and the farm was now almost completely organic. They were building up large herds of organically reared cattle and sheep, although both were fraught with problems, and he explained some of them. She learned also that Charles was divorced and had custody at the weekends of his son, Tristram, who was the same age as Edward.

Oliver was not a driver she would have liked to have been following, she thought. He drove well if a bit fast most of the time, but occasionally, when he talked about something that particularly excited him, he would go for several miles oblivious of an indicator he'd left flashing, or forgetting to change up into top gear so that the engine raced, maddeningly. Several times she had been quite convinced he was not going to stop for a red light, and had found herself jabbing her foot down.

Now, cruising on the motorway, everything had settled down. The windows were open and air billowed through the car, batting strands of Frannie's hair across her face, and she lounged back in her seat, beginning to relax, surveying the scenery through her sunglasses.

As London receded, the disconcerting memory of her sleepless night receded with it. The weekend ahead was full of promise and she was determined to enjoy herself. Her return journey seemed a hundred years away, and she wondered whether she and Oliver would have become lovers by then.

The friends with whom Edward had been staying in France were catching a ferry to Dover this morning and would be dropping him home around midday. The accident on the powerboat had clearly distressed Oliver; he had not talked about the boy very much, yet she had the feeling that Edward had a strong influence on him. She realized how very little she really knew about Oliver. Their conversations had all been about their subjects, their views on life, and they had talked only very sketchily about their families. She had not been able to draw him back on to the topic of his wife's death and she was curious to know both how she had died, and what the coincidences were that had distressed him so much. But she did not want to be morbid.

The silhouette of the South Downs, like a huge barrier wedged across the horizon, drew closer, and a few miles on they turned eastwards off the motorway, on to a busy country road. They drove into a heavy stench of manure, but even that she found refreshing after the cloying, greasy air of London.

'Where does Edward go to school?' she asked.

'A place called Stowell Park. A prep school about ten miles away. It's easy for picking him up at weekends.'

'Does he board?'

'Yes.'

'He doesn't mind?'

'No. That's what he wants to do.'

Through an opening in a hedgerow she glimpsed a flurry of activity at a car-boot sale. 'Did you board?' she asked.

'Yes, from the time I was seven.'

'How did you find it?'

'I hated it. I loathed school altogether.'

'Why?'

He shrugged. 'I couldn't do what I wanted, I

suppose. And I didn't care about team games.' He smiled and scratched his ear. 'I was only interested in mathematics and aeroplanes as a child. We could only do one afternoon a week of gliding, and that was in summer, and I used to think the maths teachers were a load of bozos.' He smiled again. 'I don't think I was very well adjusted to school. Did you like it?'

'Yes, most of the time, I loved it. Particularly history, and the classics. I used to long in the holidays for term to start. People probably thought I was an awful swot.'

'And they all thought I was a lazy bugger who didn't like being prodded. They were probably right.'

'And Edward really enjoys it?'

'Yes,' he said, then he went silent for a while.

They drove along a bypass, past an old town built over a hill; at the top she could see the ramparts of a castle.

'Lewes,' he said. 'County town of Sussex.'

'Where Simon de Montfort defeated and captured Henry the Third in 1264.'

He glanced at her quizzically.

'Once the home town of Gideon Mantell, who discovered the dinosaur,' she added. 'Originally a Saxon stronghold then a Cluniac priory.'

'Smart alec!'

She grinned.

They drove through a deep cut in the Downs and along a wide, flat valley for a couple of miles, then slowed and turned into a lane that wound up a steady gradient, bounded on both sides by overgrown verges. As they drove down a dip, she saw a tarpaulin of mist suspended over a boggy field. They passed a 30mph speed-limit sign, then another sign that was partly obscured by a cluster of tall nettles: MESTON. PLEASE DRIVE SLOWLY.

The lane levelled out. There was an elegant Sussex flint farmhouse ahead on the left, and she wondered if he was going to turn in there, but he drove on, without glancing at it, into a small, unspoilt-looking village of flint houses. They passed an old-fashioned village store, a pub called the Sherfield Arms and a Norman church that Frannie thought looked interesting.

The lane climbed steeply out of the village, bounded on the right by a continuous brick wall, beyond which she could see thick, mature trees in a rather grand, sweeping park, and on the left by a railed field. Oliver changed down a gear, and as they rounded a bend, Frannie noticed something odd rising above the brow of the hill ahead. It looked like a giant bird suspended in mid flight. As they got closer she could see that it was one of a pair of massive carved stone wyverns on top of brick gate pillars.

Oliver slowed and indicated. A white sign with black lettering, on a weighted pedestal, said: MESTON HALL. OPEN TODAY. 10a.m. – 5p.m.

Frannie looked at Oliver but his expression told her nothing. The wyverns towered above them, menacing creatures with snarling faces and scaly tails. He turned in through the gates and drove down a formal drive, walled on either side by tall yew hedges, towards a handsome flint stable-block. There was an archway through the centre of it, above which a gold clock face was housed in a domed Venetian cupola. The hands said 11.40.

They drove through the arch, and came out into a junction flanked by more yew hedges and with signs pointing in various directions: CHAPEL. TEA ROOM. CAR PARK. HOUSE. GARDENS. FARM. Another, on a free-standing plinth, said: THE MARQUESS OF SHERFIELD REGRETS ANY INCONVENIENCE TO VISITORS DURING NECESSARY BUILDING REPAIRS.

Uncertainty welled inside her; she wondered if Oliver was playing a game on her. He followed the drive in the direction labelled HOUSE and CAR PARK, and as they rounded the end of a hedge, the house suddenly appeared in front of them.

It was a red brick Elizabethan stately home, as large as many of the great houses she had visited with her parents when she was a child, built in a fold on the hilltop and dominating the entire valley.

The architecture was romantic and imperious: brick chimneys that rose majestically into the sky, banks of tall, mullioned windows with Gothic drip-stones, the baronial front door in its own crenellated tower. A gravel drive ran in front of the façade, separating it from a formal, stone-balustraded lawn below which the park swept away down into the valley.

'Is that it?'

He nodded with a guilty schoolboy smile.

The road ahead was marked NO VEHICLES BEYOND THIS POINT. To the right was a ticket hut, with a wooden bridge beyond that spanned a ditch into a sloping field containing a massive gnarled oak and half a dozen cars parked haphazardly. In spite of its grandeur, the house had a forlorn air of neglect about it. The grounds also, as if it was a struggle to keep them up, and probably a losing battle.

Oliver braked to a halt as a solidly built woman in her sixties hurried towards them, her hand raised in a greeting. A springer spaniel raced past her and stood outside Oliver's door, barking furiously. He opened the door and the dog scrambled in and on to his lap, licking his face.

'Captain Kirk! Hello, chap! Hello! Hello! Say hello to Frannie!'

The dog jumped on to Frannie's lap, its tail thumping as she stroked it, then scrambled frantically over Oliver's lap, jumped back down and barked expectantly at them.

The woman reached the car and paused for breath, wheezing heavily, and gave Frannie a quick but absorbing glance. She had a kind, rather handsome face, and was wearing an ill-fitting cobalt-blue T-shirt printed with the words MESTON HALL, EAST SUSSEX in gold letters. Her voice was doughty, with a faint rural burr. 'Good morning, Lord Sherfield.'

'Morning, Mrs B. How are we doing?'

Frannie looked at him, her surprise increasing. She began to feel slightly out of her depth. The woman ran her eyes over her again, making Frannie feel like an object in a display case, and she felt a flash of irritation that Oliver made no immediate effort to introduce her.

'Not a bad week,' the woman said. 'And a good start so far today. About a dozen already.'

Oliver nodded approvingly. The dog was still barking. 'Quiet!' he yelled.

The woman wheezed again, and dabbed her brow with the back of her hand by way of signalling her dislike of the heat. 'Good day yesterday in the tearooms. Party of ramblers. Twenty-four of them. All had high teas.'

'Excellent. Jolly good. Well done.'

The engine rumbled busily and Frannie sat with a polite smile on her face, aware of the woman's scrutiny. There was obviously a lot that she had not been told and she hoped she could get through the next twenty-four hours without showing herself up in any way. She listened carefully as the woman addressed Oliver again. Despite a feeling of nervous excitement verging on panic, she was determined not to miss a trick.

'We can do a lot more with that catering side. We

ought to consider keeping it open during the winter. I think we could do a good trade with the ramblers.'

'Yes – ah – yes, I'm sure you're right – I'll – er –' he nodded thoughtfully, glancing at Frannie. 'This is – ah – Miss Monsanto,' Oliver said. 'Mrs Beakbane.'

Mrs Beakbane arched her back and tilted her head sideways in order to present herself with a better view of Frannie. 'How do you do?' she said in a pleasant but rather servile tone that Frannie found slightly embarrassing.

'Hello,' she replied, feeling her way.

Oliver pushed the gear lever forwards. 'Right, I'll – ah – see you a bit later on.'

'Oh, one more thing – young Cliff Webber in the village is anxious to have a word.'

He disengaged the gear. 'Cliff Webber?' He looked distant.

'Charley Webber's boy.'

'Ah.' Oliver still looked a little blank.

Mrs Beakbane glanced around as if to make sure no one was in earshot. 'Getting married. Wants to talk to you about a house.'

'I was planning to go down to the estate office this afternoon.'

'I'll let him know to pop in, shall I?'

'Yes, right, about three o'clock.'

He drove on slowly, with Captain Kirk chasing along beside, down on to the gravel and along the front of the house. 'Mrs B,' he said, 'can be a bit of a dragon but she runs the place with an iron rod.' He stopped and waited patiently for a Japanese youth to take a photograph of his girl by the front door.

Frannie turned to Oliver with a quizzical air. 'Lord Sherfield?'

He had the grace to look slightly embarrassed. 'I – I

don't use it very much. My wife used to –' He fell silent.

'So you're a peer?'

'Not a very active one, I'm afraid. When I'm not at the bank I spend most of my time trying to keep this place going.'

Frannie stared out of the window. Close up, the neglected condition of the house was much worse. The stone casements had been painted at some stage, and now the paint was flaking off. Chunks of the masonry had fallen away. The brickwork badly needed repointing, and the bricks themselves had been rubbed raw by centuries of wind and rain. Green slime coated the walls behind the downpipes of the guttering. Shrubbery climbed unchecked, blocking the light from some of the windows, and had even found a way inside some of them.

She focused on the coat of arms carved in a stone tablet above the front door, noticing a wyvern among the symbols, and a Latin inscription that was too worn to read. The Japanese smiled cheerily and Oliver drove on again. Frannie felt an air of unreality as she attempted to take it all in, trying to accept that this was not a dream, that this really was Oliver's home and she was going to be staying here. She pictured her father's approval.

The drive ended at a low wall, beyond which was an ornamental circular pond, with a stone fountain that was not working. A large sign said: PRIVATE. NO VISITORS BEYOND THIS POINT.

Oliver pulled on the brake and switched off the engine. Outside the car, Captain Kirk's barking penetrated the silence. Frannie jumped down, and the dog suddenly went mad, chasing its tail around in several wide loops, skidding on the gravel, then it jumped the wall, skirted the pond and hurtled off towards some beech trees beyond. She shut her door; the clang hung in the air for a moment, then there was complete silence again. It was broken after a few seconds by the distant bleat of a sheep.

Oliver opened the tailgate and hauled their bags out. She walked across the lawn to the balustrading and surveyed the acres of parkland into the valley, savouring the smell of the grass. Rolling meadows, one of which contained a couple of horses, and another a large flock of sheep, dropped down towards the dense, mature woodland that covered the floor of the valley, and through which she could see pearly glimmers of a lake. The woods rose up the far side and gave way near the top to downland pasture sprinkled with sheep. The entire vista was peppered with stone obelisks, classical columns, statues and follies, adding further to the unreality for Frannie.

She turned to Oliver, who was standing quietly beside her, holding their bags. 'It's really stunning,' she said, her excitement tempered by unease, then a sudden feeling of anger. 'I could kill you,' she added.

'Why? What's the matter?'

'Why didn't you tell me about all this? Did you think it would frighten me off?'

'How was I supposed to tell you?'

She walked on a few steps, pushing her feet through the swaying fronds of grass. 'I don't know.'

'Why are you upset?'

'You've made it embarrassing for me. I haven't even brought a decent dress.'

'God! We're not formal – it's only you and me.'

'And all your staff?'

He put an arm around her and squeezed gently. 'You look wonderful as you are, you don't need a ball gown. We live in jeans down here.' He gave her a light kiss on her cheek. 'Come on, let's go and dump our bags.'

She gave him a glare that was part anger, part smile. 'How long have you lived here?'

'Since 1580.'

'I didn't realize you were that old.'

The corners of his eyes creased in a smile and the breeze lifted his hair and rearranged it across his forehead. 'Halkins have lived here ever since it was built. It hasn't always passed from father to son – the lineage has become a bit diluted over the centuries.' He turned and carried the bags through the gap in the walls, and as she followed she saw to her surprise that the house continued with another wing. It was in the same style as the façade, but set well back behind a group of rectangular parterres that badly needed tidying. Beyond it she could see a row of greenhouses and the wall of a kitchen garden. A plume of thick blue bonfire smoke reminded her that summer was nearly over.

'This is the bit I – ah – we – inhabit,' Oliver said.

She followed him along a narrow gravel path bounded by a rampant herbaceous border, down the side of the house, past a bumble bee clinging like a circus acrobat on to the swaying stem of a climbing rose, and a hydrangea that was out of control, then stopped at the front door. It was oak, in the same style as the main front door of the house, but not extended forwards. Above it, Frannie noticed there was again a carved heraldic crest with a wyvern on one of the lozenges.

As Oliver slid the key into the lock and turned it with a sharp clunk, her brain registered something familiar about the Latin motto that was written in the scroll beneath the crest. In the distance she heard the single, mournful toll of a bell, and glanced at her watch. It was 11.45.

She looked up at the crest and read the motto again. *Non Omnis Moriar*. Automatically, she translated it to herself. *I shall not altogether die.*

Oliver held the door for her and she frowned as she stepped into the large, dark hall. Although she had come across that motto in her Latin studies at school, she had come across it somewhere else, also, and the thought disturbed her. She was not sure why.

CHAPTER SEVEN

Oliver waited for Captain Kirk, then closed the front door. It was pleasantly cool inside and very dim. Frannie realized she still had her sunglasses on, and removed them, but even when her eyes had adjusted it was not much brighter. Sunlight shone through the narrow windows, creating a dramatic chiaroscuro effect and trapping motes of dust in its rays.

They were in a large panelled hall with a flagstone floor partially covered with fine rugs. In the centre was a round inlaid table with a vase of fresh flowers. A wide oak staircase rose up to a half-landing on which stood a suit of armour.

Frannie's gaze fell on a squat bronze container in the shape of two back-to-back rams, standing on the floor. She went over to it, examining it more closely. It was cold and felt smooth in spite of the intricate carving representing the coat. She turned to Oliver, feelings of inadequacy forgotten, excitement brimming inside her. 'How long have you had this?'

Oliver looked at it with a faintly bemused air. 'Never quite worked out what it is,' he said.

'It's Chinese,' she said. 'Called a *zun*.'

'*Zun*?' He mocked her with his eyes.

'They would have put wine in it. Know how old it is?'

'About two hundred years, I should think. It was brought back from the Orient by one of my ancestors – the family used to have business interests out there.'

Frannie studied the carving of the horns and squinted carefully at the pattern in the poor light. She raised one end up with some difficulty, and looked beneath one of the legs. 'I think it's Shang dynasty; somewhere between 1700–1050 BC.'

Oliver appeared startled. 'My father used it as an umbrella stand,' he said.

She wondered if he was joking, then realized from his expression that he wasn't. 'It's priceless.'

'We've got all sorts of bits and pieces here. Nothing's ever been properly catalogued. Maybe I should hire you to do that.'

'So long as everything's Oriental or Roman I'll be OK; I'm not much good on anything else.'

'There was a Roman villa here originally, before the house.'

'Has anyone ever done any excavations?'

'In about 1820. They found a tessellated pavement and baths, then they filled it all in and planted beech trees on top.'

'God, why?'

'I think they got fed up with people coming and poking around.' He picked the bags up. 'Right – let's dump these.'

They climbed the stairs, which were lined with painted panels of hunting scenes, went through a pedimented door, past a fire bucket and extinguisher which added a rather institutional feel, she thought, and down a wide, dark landing. Their shoes squeaked on the polished wooden floorboards.

Oliver stopped by a door and pointed to the end of the corridor. 'That takes you through into the main part of the house – the section that's open to the public – if you want to have a wander any time. You'd have to buy a ticket, of course.'

'A ticket?' Then she saw his expression and realized he was teasing.

He opened the door for her. Frannie went into a large, sparsely furnished bedroom that smelled of musty fabric. In spite of the sunlight streaming in, the room had a cold, damp feel, as if it were rarely used, and it had not been redecorated for decades.

Oliver pressed the light switch by the door and seemed surprised that the bulb came on, regarding it for some moments with an expression of almost primitive wonder, then he switched it off and carried Frannie's bag over to a *chaise-longue* at the end of a funereal-looking two-poster bed. 'There's a loo just down the corridor, second door on the left, and a bathroom next to it. I'm afraid the Elizabethans didn't go in for *en-suite* bathrooms.'

Frannie gazed out of the window across the valley. 'Incredible view. How much of it's your land?'

'To the north as far as the main road we turned off, and to the south down to the river, which you can't see from here.'

'Your land goes as far as the village we came through?'

'I – um – own the village.'

'Own it?'

'Yes.' He scratched the top of his nose, and had the grace to smile. 'There are about seventy houses – all peppercorn rents. A lot of the farmland's tenanted out, so most of the houses are let to the farmworkers.'

'How feudal!'

'Very. Look, you'll want to freshen up or something. I'll go and make some coffee and meet you downstairs.'

In the bathroom there was a chipped and stained cast-iron bathtub and wash-basin. When she turned the brass tap it rattled with a sharp knocking sound for some moments, then rust-coloured water hurtled out with the ferocity of a fire hose.

She checked her face in the large mirror and tidied her hair. An air of unreality surrounded her, almost as if she had entered a new dimension where she didn't really know the rules.

A strong smell of coffee filled the hall as she went downstairs and along a short passageway into a large kitchen that had a homely, lived-in feel. Copper pots sat on a rack above the Aga oven; strings of onions and another of garlic cloves hung from hooks; toy cars were strewn across a Welsh dresser; a chewed plimsole lay on a decrepit sofa. An open door led through to a scullery.

Oliver was seated at an old pine table, phone to his ear, tilting back precariously in a chair and tapping his knee with a pencil. Behind him, a red light glowed on a gurgling percolator.

'Yup, well, I'll be in the estate office for an hour or so this afternoon but that's all. I'm not going to have too much time free this weekend.' He winked at Frannie as she came in.

In a corner, Captain Kirk was busily digging toys out of his basket and rearranging the blanket inside it, snorting and panting, his tail wagging furiously. The windows looked out on to an internal courtyard that was in the shade. She could see a rusty barbecue and some garden furniture.

'OK, three o'clock. See you then,' Oliver said with some reluctance and hung up. 'No peace for the wicked.'

Frannie looked at him.

'Tenants. Always problems. I'm like a marriage-guidance counsellor half the time.' He sifted uninterestedly through a stack of post. 'The really frightening thing is that they actually take my advice.'

'Perhaps you give good advice,' she said.

'No, I just sound convincing.' He went over to the dresser and unhooked two mugs.

'How many staff live here?' she said.

He shook his head. 'None.'

'None?' she said, surprised. 'Doesn't the woman who met us – Mrs Deakdene?'

He put the mugs on the table. 'Beakbane. No, she lives with her husband in the village. She stays here and looks after Edward if I have to be away, and there are four ladies who come in every day to clean.' He frowned at an envelope and ripped it open with his finger, glanced at the letter then dropped it in the waste-bin.

'What about cooking?'

'Either Mrs B or me.' He tapped his chest with his thumb, then switched the percolator off and filled the mugs. 'I'm afraid it's a bit frugal and rather primitive here. All the money gets gobbled up on maintenance. The house went through a long spell when almost nothing was done and it's now in a pretty desperate condition. Sugar or milk?'

'Black, thanks. Do you get any grants?'

'A bit – English Heritage and the local council – but you only get a portion of the total cost or a small contribution.' He took a bottle of milk out of the fridge and eased off the top. 'There's subsidence on the north wing, where the scaffolding is. It's costing three quarters of a million to underpin and make good the damage.' He smiled grimly.

'Is that why you're open to the public?'

'We don't make much from the public. There are about six thousand visitors a year at three quid a head, and we pick up a bit from brochures and teas and things, but it all goes on wages for the staff. We have to employ a sitter for each room, for instance. But we have to be open to the public to qualify for grants for the repairs – we're getting about £400,000 towards the costs.'

'And you have to find the rest?'

'Yes.' He brought her mug over to her and put it on the table. He stood beside her and gave her a long, fond look. 'Thanks for coming.'

She smiled, touched. 'Thanks for inviting me.'

There was an easy, warm silence and Frannie wished suddenly that Edward was not about to turn up, and that they could be on their own together. 'Did you inherit this from your parents?'

He sat on the edge of the table and blew into his mug. 'My father made it over to me to avoid death duties. They moved into a smaller house on the farm.' He stared into the rising steam. 'To avoid inheritance tax you have to survive for seven years after handing the property over. He died twenty-four hours before the seven years was up.'

'God! So you had to pay?'

'Yes.' He shrugged. 'They were pretty crippling. I'm still paying them off.'

'Did you have to sell anything?'

'Our two finest paintings – a Canaletto and a Vermeer.' He hunched his shoulders and pulled the mug closer to his chest, as if he were drawing warmth from it. 'I don't believe in flogging things off. I feel that each person who lives here has an obligation to pass on what he inherits intact, and in better condition. I have to do what I can, and one day, I hope, Edward will do what he can.'

'The *zun* would be worth a lot, if –'

The doorbell rang and there was a sharp rapping of the knocker at the same time. Captain Kirk raced across the kitchen and down the passageway, barking furiously. Oliver put his mug on the table and jumped down. 'Might be them!' he said and hurried out.

Frannie hesitated, uncertain whether to follow. She heard the sound of the door opening and then a commotion of voices.

'Edward! Hey, hey, hey! How are you?'

'Captain Kirk! Hello, Captain Kirk! Good boy! Daddy, guess what? We nearly had an accident! We nearly had a crash!' Although Frannie had only heard Edward's voice once before, she recognized it instantly.

'No we didn't, stupid!' said another boy's voice, very insistent.

'We did, Daddy! This car pulled out right in front of us. We had to brake really hard.'

'The car was miles away, stupid. We hardly had to brake at all!'

'Clive, hi!' Oliver said. 'Caroline! You all look wonderful!'

A collage of photographs on the wall caught Frannie's eye, and she walked across to it. There were several of a pretty red-haired woman of about her own age, one of Oliver, a boy she recognized as Edward, and the woman – whom she presumed must be Oliver's late wife – standing by the wing of a small aeroplane. The resemblance between the woman and the boy was striking. Unable to restrain her curiosity, Frannie looked more closely at Lady Sherfield and noted the classical English rose features. The designer country-wear. She felt she could imagine the voice: cut glass, precious, confident. And hard?

There was a happy innocence in the photograph. A family together, going off somewhere or just posing. She looked at the woman again, wondering, absurdly, whether it was possible to tell from a photograph that someone was going to die. Then she stepped back, disturbed by the darkness of her own thought. She felt awkward doing nothing, she wanted to look interesting in case Oliver brought his visitors in to meet her.

'We're bloody tired,' said a woman's voice in the hall. 'The hotel we stayed in last night had lorries thundering past non-stop.'

'Hey, Daddy, I had snails for dinner,' she heard Edward say. She was beginning to feel like an eaves-dropper.

'No you didn't,' said the other boy. 'They weren't real snails, anyhow.'

'Yes they were. You can't have pretend snails.'

'They weren't, were they, Mummy?'

'Like some coffee, or a drink?'

'We ought to get going,' a man's voice said. 'Caroline's mother's expecting us for lunch.'

'I've got a surprise for you, Edward!' Oliver said.

'What? Tell me!'

There was a sudden silence as if Oliver was whisper-ing. And Frannie felt her remaining confidence evaporate. She heard footsteps and turned round, prepared to be intimidated. Edward was standing in the doorway, in a white T-shirt, jeans and espadrilles. His face was tanned, bringing out more freckles than when she had seen him before, and the tip of his nose was peeling.

His intelligent, brown eyes widened and his mouth broke into a grin that was an exact replica of Oliver's. 'Hey! You're the lady from the railway station!'

She relaxed and grinned back, warming to him in-stantly as she had before. 'That's right.'

He looked more serious suddenly. 'We nearly had an accident.'

'Did you?'

'A woman pulled right out in front of our car. Uncle

Clive had to brake very hard indeed.' He paused. 'He's not my real uncle, but I call him that.'

'How was your holiday?'

He stood, studying her without replying, as if he had not heard her.

'Ghastly business,' said the woman out in the hall.

'Who was driving the boat?' Oliver's voice asked.

'Jean-Luc's boy, Albert. He's normally quite a careful lad. You know what it's like. The kids love driving boats – Edward drove it quite a bit too, and Dominic. Problem was that the adults were a bit pissed – had a boozy day – left the kids to it really.'

'And no one saw the swimmer?'

'She was quite a long way out but it was fairly calm. He should have been able to see her, and he wasn't fooling around or anything. He can't explain it. Poor Jean-Luc's in a terrible state.'

'Can you water-ski?' Edward asked Frannie.

'No.'

'I can mono-ski now. It's really great. I can get out of the water with one ski. Dominic couldn't do that; he could only start on both skis then kick one off.'

Another boy came into the room. He had a fat, aggressive face, untidy tufts of fair hair, and was wearing a gaudy shirt and Bermuda shorts. He stopped a safe distance from Edward, his face screwed up into a knot of anger and shouted at him. 'You know something? You're weird! Really weird! And you're really stupid and I never want to see you again. You're a stupid, stupid bumhole!' He ran straight at Edward and pummelled him on his right arm and chest, then ran out of the room.

Edward stood his ground without flinching, barely even acknowledging the assault, and Frannie admired his restraint. 'Dominic got scared to go into the water because he saw a jellyfish,' he said as if nothing had happened.

A tall, fine-boned woman appeared in the doorway, looking tired and hot from travelling; her dry blond hair was scraped back beneath a floral printed headband and she was wearing a creased, lightweight shift-dress. Her face had a haughty, rather disdainful expression, and she had a matching accent, elongating each of her words as she spoke, with virtually no movement of her lips.

'Oh, hello,' she said.

'Hello,' Frannie replied, feeling slightly undermined by her.

The woman gave her a thin, patronizing smile and went back down the corridor.

In the hallway, Frannie heard her say: 'Is she the new nanny, Oliver?'

Bitch, Frannie thought.

Oliver sounded embarrassed. 'No – that's Frannie – let me introduce you, I'm not thinking –'

'No, we really must be on our way,' the woman insisted. She and the man called their goodbyes to Edward in turn.

'Box jellyfish can kill you within seconds,' Edward said, ignoring the farewells.

Oliver called out: 'Edward, they're off, come and say goodbye and thank you.'

Edward screwed up his face, then marched reluctantly out of the door.

'I'm going to give you a ring, Oliver,' the woman's voice said. 'There's someone I absolutely want you to meet. Great friend of mine, stunning looking. Just been through a horrendous divorce. I think you'd like her. And this is the best bit: she has a degree from Cambridge in mathematics! I'll fix something up in the next couple of weeks.'

Frannie strained hard, unsuccessfully, to hear Oliver's reply, feeling a strong twinge of jealousy, and a desire to go out into the hall and throttle the woman. She seemed to be the odd one out. She suddenly wondered if she should have stayed in London and gone partying after all.

The voices faded. With relief, Frannie glanced back at the photographs, thinking about the boy's attack on Edward and his oddly mature response. There was a shot of Edward fishing in a small rowing-boat on a lake. Behind him was a boat-house and overhanging trees. The water was flat and he was holding his rod with deadly serious intent.

'Can you ride?'

Edward's voice startled her. 'No,' she said, turning round.

'I could teach you, if you like. My horse Sheba's very docile.'

She smiled. 'I'll have a go.'

His face lit up. 'Would you? She's quite old – she's fourteen; she's a hunter.'

'Do you hunt?'

Outside there was the slam of a car door. Then another. Then a scream that started low and slowly and built up to a high-pitched howl like a siren. It took her a moment to realize that it was a human scream.

'I think I'd quite like to hunt, really, but I'm worried because it's cruel,' Edward said as if he could not hear the scream at all.

'I think we'd better see what's happening,' Frannie said as the scream worsened. She went to the door. Edward stayed where he was. She ran across the hall, out of the front door and down the gravel path.

There was a commotion around a silver Volvo estate car parked beside the Range Rover. The blond woman was shouting hysterically. A balding, rather plump man was trying desperately to open the rear door of the Volvo. He had one foot pressed against the wheel fairing for leverage while he heaved with both hands on the door handle.

The scream was coming from inside the car.

The boy's face was visible through the open rear window. It was he who was screaming, his face stretched and twisted in agony.

Frannie saw to her horror that his hand had been shut in the hinged end of the door; his fingers were trapped between the edge of the window frame and the door pillar.

A man was running towards the car. So were Mrs Beakbane and another woman in their Meston Hall T-shirts. The woman in the bandanna, the boy's mother Frannie presumed, clambered frantically in through the opposite door, leaned across, and pushed the door from the inside.

The boy's screaming continued, getting even louder, whooping with pain and shock. Droplets of blood slid down the paintwork, deep crimson against dusty metallic silver. Oliver ran across, found a grip on the door's top edge and pulled too. Both the balding man's legs left the ground for a moment as he used every ounce of leverage he could. The door finally came open with a splitting sound like a safe that had been jemmied.

For a brief instant the screaming stopped. And the footsteps.

Three fingers detached themselves from the door pillar, one after the other. At first Frannie thought the boy was relaxing his grip. Then his fingers fell limply on to the gravel. In the silence she could hear each one land.

*

Oliver took charge. He sent Mrs Beakbane to phone for an ambulance, and told Frannie to come with him. They sprinted into the house and through to the kitchen. Edward had disappeared but in her panic she hardly noticed. Captain Kirk bounded in after them, barking.

'Towels, that drawer!' Oliver said, turning on a tap, hunting around the room with his eyes. 'Soak them!' He yanked open a drawer, then another, rummaged through it and pulled out a long knife steel. Frannie bundled tea towels into her arms and dunked them in the sink. He helped her wring them out, then they raced back to the car.

The boy's stunned mother held a bloodstained handkerchief over his hand. Oliver took his arm and removed the handkerchief. The forefinger was hanging from a thread of skin. Blood spurted unevenly from the stumps of the other fingers; some pattered like rain onto Frannie's trousers as she knelt with wet towels at the ready, and she swallowed the bile that rose in her throat. The boy screamed relentlessly, emptying one lungful of air after another and pausing only for choking gulps. A slick of warm blood struck Frannie's cheek, then another her forehead and she felt it sliding down towards her eye. She turned away, swallowing hard again, fighting not to be sick, unable to look at the hand or the boy's twisted, boiling face.

Oliver swathed the hand in a tea towel, and she helped him wind it around the wrist, then repeated the process with a second one. He put a third over the top, and with Frannie and the boy's mother's help, using the knife steel as the lever, wound the towel tightly into a tourniquet. The boy's father leaned over, agitatedly crowding them, a feeble twitch animating his expression of utter helplessness.

Oliver scooped up the fingers and parcelled them in another towel, which he gave to Frannie. 'Pack these in ice.'

The commotion had attracted the attention of several visitors, who watched in a group a short distance off. They were talking amongst themselves, trying to work out what had happened. One woman said she thought the dog must have bitten the boy.

'Dom? You OK, Dom?'

Edward was rushing towards them, his face horrified. 'Dom?' He looked at his friend, then at Frannie. 'What's happened?' His eyes shot to the tourniquet. 'Hey, Dom –' He blanched.

As Frannie ran into the house she wondered where he had been during the past few minutes, and why he had not come with her. She unfolded the towel on the draining-board, and stared at the three fingers, each of which was leaking blood. Like joke fingers, she thought. Then a wave of giddiness struck her; her stomach up-ended; she swayed, gripped the edge of the sink and threw up into it. Her eyes streamed and she wiped them with her shirtsleeve, then rinsed the sink out, washed her hands and forced herself into sensible action.

There were several trays of ice cubes in the fridge, and she searched for a suitable receptacle. The screaming was coming closer and Oliver carried the boy in, followed by the parents and Edward. Mrs Beakbane was trying to comfort the boy by assuring him the ambulance would be there any moment. Oliver laid him on the sofa, and Mrs Beakbane went to the sink and peered at the fingers with a surprising nonchalance that made Frannie feel displaced.

'I was a Red Cross nurse in the war,' she said, as if by way of explanation, and helped free the ice cubes,

88

again making Frannie feel inexperienced and in the way.

The screaming abated into an undulating, sobbing moan of pain. Edward hovered, looking very distressed. He put his arm around his friend but the boy shook him away and began screaming again, even more vehemently than before. His mother sat beside him, white-faced.

'Look,' the father said, 'this bloody ambulance could take hours. I'll drive him myself.'

'No,' Oliver said. 'He's got to go somewhere they can do microsurgery – they might be able to sew the fingers back. If you go to the wrong place you could waste valuable time; I think you only have a few hours before the nerve endings die.'

'Six,' Mrs Beakbane said, authoritatively. 'My Harry lost his little finger in a lawnmower but we never found it until the following day.'

The father paced over to the sink, then turned away rapidly at the sight of the fingers. Frannie stood back and let Mrs Beakbane pack them carefully, using all the cubes, then they were placed with a couple of freeze packs inside a picnic cool-box.

Oliver phoned a doctor friend who gave him some names and suggested a hospital less than half an hour away, which seemed to relieve the father.

The ambulance arrived a few minutes later. The boy and his mother went in it, and his father followed in the Volvo. Frannie, Oliver and Edward watched numbly as they left. A couple of short pulses of the siren pricked the air and then there was silence.

They walked back towards the house, Oliver with his head sunk in thought, Frannie uncertain what to say. Edward stopped by the pond. Frannie waited a moment for him, then went inside. Mrs Beakbane excused herself, saying she had to go to a problem she had been dealing with in the tearoom.

Oliver poured the remnants of coffee in the percolator down the sink and turned the tap on. Frannie gathered the two mugs from the table and carried them across.

'It's OK – they can go in the machine.' His words made Frannie feel even more useless. As if she hadn't yet found her role. His eyes skimmed her face and he lowered his voice. 'You have a bit of – er – warpaint on you.'

She touched her cheek with her fingers and saw blood on them. 'Oh, God!'

She hurried upstairs to the bathroom. Her reflection in the mirror startled her. Streaks of blood ran down her forehead and cheeks. Her eye make-up had smudged and run. Her stomach rolled again. Sour bile rose in her throat and she puked it out. Then she stripped off and washed herself, put her trousers and top into the sink to soak, wrapped herself in a towel and went to her bedroom to change.

When she returned, Edward was sitting in the kitchen, glancing in a rather adult way through a newspaper. He looked up at his father.

'Do you think they will be able to sew Dom's fingers back on, Daddy?'

'They can do pretty clever things with microsurgery these days.'

'It's a pity it wasn't his left hand,' Edward said. 'Then at least he could still do sport.'

The comment hung over them and there was a long silence broken only by the sound of Captain Kirk grinding on a bone. Edward closed the *Daily Mail* and began turning the pages of *The Times*. 'You didn't remember to fix my Scalextric, Daddy.'

'I did. The brushes had gone on one of the cars.'

'It's not working.'

Frannie frowned, wondered when Edward would have had time to play with any toys. And what he was searching for in the newspaper.

'It is. Did you switch the transformer on?'

'You're useless, Daddy. You should have taken it to the man in Lewes to fix.'

'Well, it was working last Sunday. I spent an hour on it.'

Edward seemed unconvinced. Oliver looked at his watch. 'Right, let's make some plans for this afternoon.' He shrugged apologetically at Frannie. 'I have to do a few things. Would you like to lounge around the pool? Have a swim? The water's very warm.'

'Can I show Frannie round the grounds?'

Oliver signalled Frannie with his eyes that she did not have to.

She winked, then smiled at Edward. 'Thank you, I'd love that.'

'Can I show Frannie the aeroplane, Daddy?'

'I have to go down and turn the engine over; I might catch up with you.'

'Is your name really Frannie?' Edward said.

'Yes.'

He held out his hand for hers and for a moment she thought he was going to shake it. Instead he held it firmly, pulling her very slightly towards him, as if there was an urgent message he needed to communicate. Then slowly, without slackening his grip, he led her towards the door.

She glanced at Oliver and noticed a strange look of apprehension on his face as he watched his son. The shadow that crossed his eyes was one of fear. She turned to Edward but all she could see was the trusting face of a small boy who has found a new friend.

CHAPTER EIGHT

Frannie and Edward, closely followed by Captain Kirk, ambled past the Range Rover and along the front of the house. A bird chirruped with a ping that sounded like a spoon against china and as Frannie breathed in the scents of the air and felt the afternoon sun on her face, the horror of an hour ago receded a little in her mind; but not the unease. She still wondered why Oliver had kept quiet about his title; quiet about Meston Hall; wondered if it had anything to do with his wife's death, for instance. And was there anything else he was keeping quiet about?

She avoided looking at the gravel in case she saw the stain of blood and stared up at the façade, picking out details of its decaying state: a chunk missing from the coping-stone of the parapet; a cracked window; a bird's nest under the eaves; wasps going in and out of a hole in the roof.

An elderly man with a shiny camera case and a woman in a straw hat were going in through the front door and Frannie caught a glimpse of a marble floor and white columns. Edward pointed across the valley. 'The English Channel's the other side of those hills. Brighton's over there to the right – you can see the glow of the lights on a clear night.'

'Do you like living here?' Frannie asked.

'Yes, quite.'

'Only *quite*?'

'I like some things,' he said, more brightly.

'Have you got many friends here?'

'Yes, I suppose so.' He seemed about to say something else, then changed his mind.

They walked past the end of the house and up the private road towards the junction bounded by hedges.

'Is Frannie short for something?'

'My full name's Francesca.'

'Is that Italian?'

'Yes.'

'Does that mean you're a Catholic?'

'I am a Catholic, yes.' She was surprised by the question. 'What are you?'

Edward was silent for some moments, then he pushed his hands into his pockets and stared down. 'We have our own chapel.'

'Can I see it?'

'There's not much to see.'

'I'd be interested.'

He pointed in front of them. 'It's through there, but it's not worth going in.'

'Couldn't I have a quick peep inside?'

'Why?'

There was something oddly strained about his voice and she almost wished she hadn't pursued the idea. 'I'm very interested in churches,' she said.

'All right.'

They waited for a car full of visitors to pass, then crossed, went through an opening in the hedge and the chapel was in front of them. It was small and narrow, rising out of a riot of weeds and in the same poor state of repair as everything else. A well-trodden cinder path went up to the door, through a tiny graveyard peppered with old tombstones.

The interior felt more cared for. Marble and alabaster tombs were spaced along the sides and there were plaques on the floor. Frannie read one of them. *Lord Thomas Bouverie Henry Halkin. 15th Marquess of Sherfield. 1787–1821.*

While Edward walked on slowly down the centre of the aisle, running his hand nonchalantly from the top of each pew to the next, Frannie scanned the structure of the building, trying to date it. Deep, solid buttresses and well-dressed stones; classic Perpendicular tracery in an elaborate geometric pattern. Geometry, she thought suddenly. Mathematics. Oliver's words at lunch on Tuesday echoed suddenly in her head. *Mathematics and design are inseparable.*

'Every Marquess of Sherfield for four hundred and fifty years is buried in here,' Edward said. 'Except one.' He stood gazing at the floor in front of him. Frannie joined him. He was looking at an onyx rectangle, with a brass plaque in the centre which read: *Lady Sarah Henrietta Louise Halkin, Marchioness of Sherfield. 1963–1988.*

Edward's face reddened, and Frannie sensed a tension in the air between them as if she had intruded into something private. She wondered if that was the reason he had been reluctant to show her in here. She kicked herself for not having realized that his mother would be buried here.

He began to hum softly, and after a few bars she recognized the tune as 'Swing Low Sweet Chariot'. Then he turned and began to saunter as if he was in no hurry – as if he had all the time in the world – towards the exit, humming more loudly now, the way someone might who is alone in the dark and wants to demonstrate that he is not afraid.

Captain Kirk was lying obediently outside. Edward stopped humming and knelt beside him, telling him he had been good. Then they left the graveyard and walked along a cart track that sloped downwards towards a cluster of farm buildings. An invisible barrier separated them. Frannie wondered what to say to repair the situation, realizing how very little she knew about children. She was not used to dealing with the problems of motherless young boys and she simply didn't know what to do. She almost wished that Mrs Beakbane would appear. She had no idea of how Edward felt about seeing his father with another woman.

A vapour trail was unravelling across the sky. Grit crunched beneath their feet. 'You said there was one Marquess who was not buried in your chapel – who was that?'

'Lord Francis Halkin,' he said. 'The second Marquess.'

'Where is he buried?'

'I don't know.' He lowered his voice as if he were letting her in on a secret. 'There were quite a lot of people who didn't like him very much.'

'Why was that?'

'I'd like to be buried somewhere that's completely secret. Where no one knows where I am,' he said, not answering her.

'So you don't have to spend eternity with your ancient relatives? You'd like to meet some new people when you die?'

Edward broke into a fit of giggles. 'I think they'd be *dead* boring, don't you?' He giggled again.

'*Dead* right.'

'*Dead* on!' he said. 'Hold out your hand.'

She held it out and he turned it palm up, then slapped it with his own palm. '*Dead* on!' he said again as he did so. 'You have to do that when you say "dead on"!'

'I'll remember. *Dead* – cert!' She stopped as a stone on the ground caught her eye, knelt, and picked it up. She pulled her handkerchief out of her pocket, spat on it and rubbed one side that was almost flat. She examined it carefully, whilst Edward watched her in silence, then she held it in front of him. 'Look!'

He stared blankly. 'What at?'

Frannie pointed carefully with her finger. 'Can you see? The shape of the shell?'

He peered closer, still uncertain.

'It's a fossil – of a seashell – an oyster or something.'

His eyes brightened. 'Gosh, yes! Is that really old?'

She nodded. 'Ten thousand years; perhaps more.'

'Do you think it's worth a lot of money?'

She shook her head. 'The countryside's covered in them.'

'I've never seen one before.'

'You've probably never looked.' She handed it to him. 'You keep it.'

'You should keep it really, because you found it.'

'It's a present.'

'Hey! That's great, wow! Thank you.'

She walked on, feeling she was getting somewhere with Oliver's son after all. But she was taken aback by his next remark.

'Do you think the dead stay dead, Frannie?'

Mindful of his mother, she deliberately played down her response. 'I don't think that oyster's going to come back to life.'

'Its spirit might.'

A combine harvester chomped through a cornfield on their right. The stubble stretched out into the distance, short and spiky, and Frannie breathed in its dry, prickly smell. Edward was a strange boy, she thought. Old for his years, he slouched as he walked, as if burdened by a thousand worries.

As they approached the rear of a massive corrugated-iron barn, a bang like a muffled gunshot rang out, making Frannie jump. Captain Kirk barked. There was the clatter of what sounded like an enormous ratchet, and another bang. Edward sprinted on ahead.

Oliver's Range Rover was parked on the concrete hard in front of the barn. The barn's doors were open and there was an old-looking single-engined biplane inside, its wingspan taking up almost the entire width.

Oliver had both hands close together in the centre of one blade of the propeller and slowly rotated it anti-clockwise, while Edward stood several feet away, watching him. There was a deep sucking noise from the engine. He rotated the propeller completely a couple of times, then tensed up, gave the blade a sharp downward pull, and stepped quickly back and to the side. There was another much louder bang as the engine fired and died, a splutter as the propeller made a half-turn, then the ratchet sound again as it swung to a halt. A small puff of oily blue smoke drifted over Frannie. Oliver looked engrossed and Frannie began to wonder if he'd simply wanted to be on his own for a bit.

He turned and smiled cheerily at her, pushing his hair back from his forehead with a grimy hand, sweat pouring down his face. 'Got her started last weekend; have to try to run her again for a few minutes to get the oil circulating, but she doesn't seem to want to know.' He gazed at the aeroplane admiringly. 'What do you think of her?'

The plane reminded Frannie of First World War movies. A primitive, open two-seater, with struts and wire rigging between the wings, it sat on a flimsy-looking undercarriage, its nose in the air. Parts of the skin of the fuselage and wings were missing, exposing the skeletal frame beneath and the cylinder block of the engine protruding from the nose. In contrast, the propeller appeared immaculate; it was made of dark, varnished wood and held in place with a polished aluminium spinner.

'It's beautiful,' Frannie said. 'Have you actually flown her?'

'Not this old girl. She hasn't been airborne for about thirty years. I bought her as a complete wreck five years ago. A few more months and she'll be up there.'

'Yeah!' Edward said excitedly. 'Daddy said we can fly to France!'

Oliver looked at his watch. 'I'd better get to the estate office. My three o'clock appointment will be waiting.'

'No peace for the wicked,' Frannie said.

'None. See you in an hour or so.' He began closing the barn doors. Frannie and Edward helped him, then Oliver drove off in the Range Rover.

'Would you like to see the lake now?' Edward said.

'Yes, sure,' she said, feeling slightly out on a limb at being abandoned again by Oliver, and wondering suddenly if Dom's snobby mother hadn't been too far off the mark when she had asked Oliver if she was the nanny. She felt a sudden flash of anger as she wondered whether Oliver had conned her into coming down here in order to look after Edward. Once again, she pictured the party taking place that night in London. Had she made a mistake?

They skirted around the side of a ploughed field, jumped a ditch and came out at the bottom of the visitors' car park. Captain Kirk ran on ahead then bounded back and walked beside them. They climbed over a fence and walked across a broad, sloping meadow. 'Do you like it here, Frannie?' Edward asked.

'It's very beautiful.'

'I had to really twist Daddy's arm to make him see you again.'

She stopped and stared at him. 'Pardon?'

'Daddy wasn't brave enough. He said he'd be too embarrassed and that anyway you might not like him.'

'It was you? You made him put the advertisement in?'

He shook his head. 'I told him that he had to try to find you. He thought you were nice, but he's very shy, really.'

'So how did you persuade him?' Frannie asked.

He looked rather pleased with himself. 'I did keep nagging him a bit. But I don't think he needed that much pushing.'

They walked on through some trees, and Frannie smiled to herself, her anger fading. She was amused by the boy's precociousness. A clock chimed three times in the distance. They passed a collapsed stone folly, and came into a walk of lavender bushes past a cluster of small headstones, most of them overgrown with moss and lichen. On one she could just make out the words: *Sam (Nimo San). Labrador. 1912–1925.*

Edward stopped by a lavender bush, and pointed at it, announcing '*Nana atropurpurea.*'

'What?' she said, unsure if she had heard correctly. She was startled by a growl from Captain Kirk and turned, wondering what was wrong with the spaniel. Then she realized it was growling at Edward.

Edward walked on down some timber steps and stopped by a rhododendron. '*Rhododendron campanulatum,*' he said.

The spaniel growled again more deeply, baring sharp white teeth that rose from gums brimming with saliva; its soft hair seemed to rise and harden like spines and its dark brown eyes boiled inside their whites with a sudden rage that frightened Frannie. The dog was crouching on its rear haunches, as if its rear paws were embedded in the earth, its head craning forward, the growl deepening into a ferocious snarl. It pulled itself forward in sharp jerks as if trying to free its rear legs from the ground and launch itself at the boy, and she dived in panic, grabbing it by the collar to restrain it.

Captain Kirk's head spun round, the jaws showering her with saliva and she just managed to withdraw her hand and jump back before the teeth snapped on air. The dog turned to Edward again, simmering, the snarl deepening. Edward stood his ground in silence, staring back hypnotically. Frannie felt the hairs rising on her own body, the onlooker in a private duel. The dog made a lunge forward towards the boy, then stopped as if restrained by an unseen force. It tried to lunge again, and stopped once more, seemingly made powerless by Edward's concentrated stare.

Frannie watched in horror as the spaniel's hair slackened, then it let out a whine and began to shake, backing away, whimpering, and finally retreating like a banished demon.

There was a strange hush. The sun went behind a cloud and Edward stood in silence, as if nothing had happened. Frannie turned to watch the dog but it was almost out of sight, heading back towards the house. She was shaking, not knowing exactly what she had just witnessed.

'What's the matter with Captain Kirk, Edward?'

He said nothing at first. Then he suddenly pointed to another rhododendron across the track that had white, trumpet-shaped flowers. '*Auriculatum*,' he said.

'Have you been learning Latin at school?' she asked, her voice quavering.

He studied the bush for some moments again, as if he had not heard her, then continued along the track through increasingly dense shrubbery until they came down on to level ground, and Frannie could see water beyond a screen of reeds. The lake was a good quarter of a mile across and longer in length.

She followed him along the bank towards a sorry-looking boat-house, its white paint stained green with moss and peeling away in chunks. Edward pulled open the rotting door with some difficulty and they went into the dank, shadowy interior. A cobweb brushed Frannie's face and she jerked her head to one side, instinctively putting up her hands and feeling the sticky strands on her fingers. Her nostrils were filled with the unpleasant mushroomy stench of rot.

'You get in first and sit down,' Edward commanded, pointing to a narrow wooden pontoon.

Dazed into compliance, she placed a foot carefully in the bottom of the boat, avoiding the oars. It rocked precariously and she grabbed the side with her hand, steadied herself, then brought the other foot in and sat down quickly.

Edward untied the boat, pushed it forward and stepped in, sat down and fitted each of the oars into the rowlocks. They drifted out of the boat-house into the sunlight, now bright again.

As the boy rowed, Frannie felt the pull of the little boat through the water and listened to the splash of the oars. Then Edward let the boat drift forwards on its own momentum, and she let her own thoughts do the same: Jonathan Mountjoy; 'Is she the new nanny?'; Sarah Henrietta Louise Halkin. The onyx slab on the floor. 1963–1988.

'I hope you're not planning to sleep with my daddy.'

Her mouth dropped open in amazement. Edward was leaning over to one side, staring idly at the water the way she had been, with a distant expression on his face. She watched him for a moment, wondering if she had misunderstood. 'Pardon?'

He did not look up or acknowledge her. His face remained blank and unreadable. Was it his mind that was disconnected or hers? she wondered.

A fish rose near them and left behind an eddy of disturbed water that slowly broadened out until the surface was smooth again, as if the water had forgotten it had ever happened. Oliver had told her last night at dinner, when he had been talking about mathematics and gambling, that a coin could not remember which way up it had landed the previous time it was flipped. It was always an even chance whether it would be heads or tails the next time, regardless of how many times one or the other had come up before. Water had no memory either. Humans remembered everything – too much sometimes – Oliver said, so that at times it was difficult to look back clearly to both before and after an event had happened. The brain played tricks constantly, he said.

She watched the small boy with the intelligent brown eyes and sad, freckled face, and tried to work out what trick her own brain might have just played on herself.

Frannie was hot and sticky and her top was damp with perspiration after the climb back up from the lake. They emerged through a ride of giant beech trees at the rear of the walled kitchen garden. The intensity of light had gone from the sun and the caw-caw-kercaw of a pigeon carried through the air like the last post from a lone bugler.

She felt uncomfortable, as if Edward was playing a

game with her for which she had not been given the rules, and she wondered if he was deliberately trying to undermine her confidence. Yet he was only eight; surely he was too young to be that devious? His mood changes left her not knowing whether left was right or right was left. She couldn't find her feet with the boy and she wondered if it was her fault or if there was another reason. She thought about the dog, wondering where it was now and whether its fury had been deliberately provoked by Edward for her benefit. She found that hard to believe because it had seemed so spontaneous.

Edward had become chatty again in the last ten minutes. He asked her more about fossils and she explained to him how you could date the past from them, enjoying seeing the deep interest he took.

As they reached the front door, he said to her: 'Can you play ping-pong?'

'I haven't for ages.'

'Would you like to have a game?'

She smiled, feeling a bit weary. 'All right, but a quick one. I'm tired.'

He gave her such a mischievous look that she felt like putting her hand out and tousling his hair as a gesture of affection, but remembered the faint look of irritation on his face when his father had done that. Something else stopped her too: she daren't.

Before their game, they both went into the kitchen to make themselves a quick sandwich. Frannie finished hers first and she wandered off to look in the library as she waited for Edward. It was a surprisingly small and narrow room that seemed to double as a study. Several large hand-drawn charts were pinned to the walls either side of the desk. One looked like a family tree. Another was a mass of mathematical calculations. All the rest of the walls were lined floor to ceiling with bookshelves, which she would have liked to look at instead of playing ping-pong but she felt that duty called.

Her reverie was broken with the arrival of Edward who, worried in case she changed her mind, led her upstairs and along the dark corridor past her room. As they drew up to the next door, Edward said: 'That's my room. I'll show it to you later if you like.'

'Thank you.'

They passed a couple more doors, then the passage dog-legged left. Edward climbed up a narrow staircase into a huge, gloomy attic-playroom that seemed to span the entire wing of the house and which housed the ping-pong table.

She acquitted herself well at the ping-pong table despite losing. After promising to go with Edward to see the orchard the next day, she made her excuses to him and went to her bedroom. She closed the door, relieved to be on her own for a few minutes.

Through the open window she noted that the visitors' car park was empty and the windows of the ticket hut were closed. A crane-fly flew clumsily around the room, bumping against the window and the walls.

I hope you're not planning to sleep with my daddy.

A bead of perspiration slid down her forehead and Frannie put her hand in her pocket, but could not feel her handkerchief. She dug deeper, but the pocket was empty. She remembered wiping her forehead during the game, and went back up to the attic-playroom. The meagre daylight coming in from the small dormer windows, too high for a child to reach, gave a prison-like feel to the room.

A bird flew past one of the windows and its shadow skated along the wall. The total silence struck her. A floorboard creaked as she stepped on it and she moved forwards, treading more lightly so that Edward wouldn't hear her.

The handkerchief was lying on the floor beneath the ping-pong table and she picked it up and removed a bit of fluff from it. A sad room, she thought, staring around, and tried to imagine Edward playing up there on his own. There was an old rocking-horse, perhaps Victorian; it had probably been here for years, and generations of young Halkins had played on it. Oliver. Oliver's father.

She walked over to the bookshelves and looked at the titles. *William*. *Jennings*. *The Famous Five*. *Biggles*. Old books, some with their covers torn, others with no covers. There were some she used to read herself: *Grimm's Fairy Tales* and *Struwwelpeter* and the *Eagle Annual* and the *Beano Bumper Book*. Then she noticed a photo album and pulled it out.

It was heavy and she laid it down on the ping-pong table to open it. The first picture was a colour photograph of a naked baby lying on its back, gurgling, arms and legs raised in the air.

'Edward. 2 days,' was handwritten in black ink beneath.

She turned the thick page. There were various photographs of Edward's mother cuddling him in a hospital bed. She was fascinated to see this younger version of the Sarah Henrietta Louise she'd already seen in the kitchen collage. She noted the same poise, the same classic features, which made her feel rather plain in comparison. Her suspicions about Oliver's motives in inviting her down began to return. She turned on, through scenes of Edward growing up. She studied them closely, also trying to see his expression, searching for clues about his strange behaviour. Finding none.

As she turned the last page, she saw, folded in the back, a newspaper cutting. Curious, she opened it. It was from the *Mid-Sussex Times*, and dated 10th August 1991. An article in the centre of the page had been ringed with a red pen. Its headline read: SUSSEX MAN SHOT IN US STREET HORROR.

She began reading.

> A Sussex man has been shot dead by a mugger whilst on holiday in America.
>
> Jonathan Mountjoy, 25, a ceramics expert with Sotheby's, had left his home in High Street, Cuckfield, last Friday, for his dream holiday.
>
> Neighbours were shocked by the incident. 'He was a gentle young man who would not have harmed a fly,' said neighbour Ann Wilson.
>
> A spokesman for the Washington DC Police Department said, 'This was a particularly vicious crime perpetrated on an unarmed tourist. We are actively seeking the assailant.'

Frannie stopped and went to the start of the article again to make sure her eyes weren't deceiving her. *Jonathan Mountjoy*. But there was no mistaking his face in the photograph; it must have been taken around the time they were at university, or else he had not changed. The serious looks, almost gaunt with his high cheekbones and short black hair. A kind face. His colleagues were right; he was a brilliant young man, even if he had always seemed to be in a permanent dream.

She remembered Seb Holland in the restaurant last night, telling her about Jonathan's death. A curl of anxiety travelled through her as she remembered

Edward in the kitchen earlier, scanning through the newspapers as if looking for something. Had he cut it out? Or was it Oliver, thinking it would be of interest to her? The print blurred. Confused thoughts whirled through her mind. Oliver cutting it out did not make any sense. He would have shown it to her if he had seen it in the paper, surely, not hidden it in his son's photo album. And the article was a few weeks old.

She folded it up again and replaced the album on the bookshelf. Then she decided to have a bath, hoping Oliver might've returned when she'd finished.

CHAPTER NINE

She had a quick bath, then combed her hair, tugging the tangles free. Dark olive eyes stared back from the mirror. Frightened eyes. They watched the reflection of the closed door behind her. Maybe Jonathan Mountjoy was a relative of the Halkins? A cousin? But if that was the case, why had Oliver not mentioned it at the time?

Maybe it was just coincidence. Things happened that way sometimes. She remembered Oliver's words: *Coincidences make me uneasy ... I'm not sure there is such a thing as a meaningless coincidence.*

She dabbed the shine from her nose. Some people were scared of spiders; some of flying; of darkness; of the number 13; everyone had something they were scared of. Oliver Halkin happened to be scared of coincidences. That did not mean she had to be.

Oliver was waiting for her in the kitchen as she'd hoped. Captain Kirk was asleep on the floor in front of the Aga. 'Edward finally released you?' he asked, winking at her.

'Just.'

'I'm sorry you got lumbered.'

'He's been good company.' She hesitated, wanting to ask Oliver about Edward's strange silences but not able to think of a way of doing so tactfully.

'Would you like some tea – or something stronger?'

'I'd love some tea.' Her eyes fell on the stainless-steel draining-board and she swallowed at the memory of the fingers that had lain there a few hours earlier on the bloodstained tea towel.

'Ordinary or Earl Grey?'

'Earl Grey, please.' She watched his face. 'Does the name Jonathan Mountjoy mean anything to you?'

'Jonathan Mountjoy?' He pulled a tea-bag out of a tin, dropped it into a mug and then poured from the heavy kettle. 'Jonathan Mountjoy,' he said again with a slight frown. 'I think I recognize the name.'

'Last night,' she said.

'Ah! Was it the name of the chap – your friend – who was killed by a mugger?'

'Yes.' There was nothing that she could read in his expression at all.

'Why?'

She blushed. 'I – I got the impression that his name rang a bell with you, that's all.'

He shook his head. 'So where did you go this afternoon?'

'We went first to the chapel.'

'Oh?' Oliver pulled a tin out of a cupboard. 'Like a piece of cake?'

'No, thanks.' She eyed the spaniel. 'How old is Captain Kirk?'

Oliver thought for a moment. 'About three.'

'Is he OK with Edward?'

'Good as gold.' He hesitated. 'Why?'

'I thought he was going to attack him this afternoon.'

Oliver shook his head. 'He has got a bit of a sharp streak – he had a go at some gypsies last weekend, but he wouldn't touch Edward. He –'

'May I watch a video please, Daddy?'

Edward came in holding a Game Boy in his hand, and knelt beside Captain Kirk, who was stretched out on the floor, crooked his arm around the dog's neck and pressed his cheek against him. 'You'd like to watch a video, wouldn't you, Captain Kirk?'

'What do you want to see?' Oliver said.

'*Terminator 2.*'

Frannie watched the dog warily, but it licked Edward's face affectionately with no trace of its previous display. Oliver bent and tousled the boy's hair. 'All right. I'm going to show Frannie round the house. What do you want for supper tonight?'

As he removed his hand, Edward tidied his hair with a faint look of annoyance. 'Fish fingers,' he said. 'Captain Kirk likes them,' he said, looking at the dog fondly. 'Don't you?' He pressed his nose against the dog's.

Frannie looked at Edward curiously, wondering if the boy was being deliberately tasteless or not.

'I think we've had enough of fingers for one day.'

Edward looked crestfallen. 'Why?'

'I don't even know if we have any.'

Edward's face fell further. 'I *want* fish fingers; please, Daddy.'

He stomped his foot and Frannie felt uncomfortable, as if it was her fault he was overtired.

'OK. OK.'

Tears began to trickle down Edward's cheek. Frannie's heart went out to him. Perhaps the loss of his mother was still affecting him. Maybe that explained his behaviour. But not the news cutting. She caught Oliver's eye and he smiled wistfully back at her. A glint of sunshine slipped from an upstairs window across the courtyard, as if a light had been switched out. Edward cradled Captain Kirk tightly to him again, rocking backwards and forwards, tears flowing thickly. Oliver spooned the bag from Frannie's tea and raised the milk bottle as if it were a question mark. She nodded.

Oliver watched Edward for some moments, then

rested a hand on his shoulder and squeezed. Edward spoke without looking up at him.

'I'm scared, Daddy,' he said.

'It's OK,' his father replied. 'It's OK.' He handed Frannie her tea and gave her a weary smile, then he picked Edward up in his arms. 'Who's a tired boy? Sure you want to see a movie and don't want to go to bed?'

'See *Terminator 2.*'

Oliver winked at Frannie and carried the boy out of the room and down the corridor. Captain Kirk followed, excited.

Frannie sat at the table and blew on her tea, thinking of Edward's strange remark to his father. *Scared*. She wondered what of?

Oliver took Frannie round the downstairs first, starting in the basement, showing her the old, disused kitchens with their massive ovens and small high windows that reminded her of the ones in the nursery. She trailed along beside him, feeling slightly awkward, as if she were a sightseer; she was still very uncertain about her role. Upstairs, he showed her a bedroom with a roped-off four-poster where Oliver Cromwell had once spent the night. But it was the objects in the rooms that really captivated her. They seemed to be walking through an endless treasure trove. She recognized an Etruscan bronze mirror just for starters.

On the first floor they went into a long oak-panelled gallery. There were tapestried window-seats, elegant sofas, large tables on which open photograph albums of the family's history lay. The rich pinky-yellow glow of the sun filled the room with an ethereal light that the polished oak floor reflected like the surface of a lake. Massive chandeliers hung above it, each arm ornately wrought into the shape of a wyvern.

'Incredible,' she said, stopping in appreciation. She breathed in the rich warm smell of the wood and was aware of the complete silence.

'I think you're incredible,' Oliver said, putting his arm around her, surprising her.

'Me?'

He pulled her gently towards him. 'Yes.'

She turned to face him and smiled. 'I'm not. I'm very ordinary.' She watched his blue eyes that were staring straight into hers, and felt the strength of his arm around her.

'I say you're incredible,' he said again. 'And you're very lovely.' He squeezed her tighter.

Frannie flushed with elation, and experienced a sudden, intensely erotic pang of desire for him. He released her to walk over to a glass showcase and she followed him. 'Thank you,' she said. 'I think you're very lovely too.' Their shoulders were touching and there was a peacefulness between them; the same easiness again now as there had been when they had left the restaurant last night.

On the wall above them was a portrait of a man in seventeenth-century clothing. His head rose from the ermine collar of a purple velvet robe. The expression on his face was cold, preening arrogance. Thin lips were compressed into an inquisitor's smile. His shoulder-length hair was brushed immaculately in King Charles curls and tiny hands, the size of a child's, clasped a book to his chest. The same book, she realized, that now lay in the showcase on a velvet pad, its faded ink handwritten on what looked like badly preserved vellum. The writing was almost illegible, even without the failing light, and in a language she did not recognize.

Oliver moved and his shadow fell across the glass

and the book beneath. 'That's the one thing I really wish I did not own.'

'This book?'

'Yes.'

'Why? What is it?' There was a typed card in a mounting on the outside of the cabinet. It said: *Maleficarium*. c.1650 AD.

'An instruction manual of satanic rituals. It's supposed to be written on human skin.'

'Seriously?'

'That's what the family has always believed. I've no idea whether it's true.'

She leaned forward with morbid interest. It was as beautifully crafted as it was hideous. She stared at the grain of the pages, tiny criss-cross lines; the colour was a repugnant dark brown. She peered closer, revulsion spreading through her. Frannie had seen preserved human skin on mummies and on tribal artefacts. It always looked leathery, like this. 'Have you ever had anyone test it?'

'No.'

'I could get it done for you.'

There was an expression of wariness on his face. 'I'm not sure I really want to know. It's a bloody evil thing whatever it is. I've never even touched it and I don't think I want to.'

'What's the history behind it?'

'It was written by one of my ancestors – the second Marquess.' He nodded at the portrait.

'That's him?'

'Yes. Lord Francis Halkin.'

'Is he the only Marquess who's not buried in your family chapel?'

He frowned. 'How do you know that?'

'Edward told me when he was showing me the chapel.'

His expression darkened. 'He was a fairly evil man by all accounts.' He eyed the book uncomfortably. 'He was into witchcraft. Black magic. A whole raft of things. He was a sort of follower of Gilles de Rais.'

'I know the name. Who was he?'

'A rather unsavoury Frenchman who liked to have sex with small boys and cut their throats during the act.'

Oliver moved and as his shadow slipped away from the book, the effect made it appear for a moment as if the skin were breathing, and Frannie turned away also, unsettled, not wanting to stand near the cabinet any more. A floorboard creaked as her weight shifted.

He dug his hands in his pockets. The sunlight in the room seemed to be incongruous. She followed him as he walked slowly on. 'Gilles de Rais is reputed to have killed over nine hundred boys – the world's worst ever serial killer. I don't know how many the second Marquess killed. Nor where he got his writing-paper from.' He stopped and turned towards her. 'I can never take the notion of aristocracy too seriously. None of us are descended from terribly nice people.'

'There are plenty of ordinary people who are not very nice either,' Frannie said. 'Plenty of ordinary people commit evil acts and atrocities. You should see some of the weapons I've been sorting through at the Museum. Things like beautifully jewelled Indian knuckledusters with attachments for tearing ears off. Does tearing people's ears off advance mankind?'

'If it stops them being able to wear Walkmans it does.'

She chuckled, then looked back at the display case. 'Why do you keep the book? Why don't you sell it to a museum?'

He shrugged. 'It's part of the house's heritage,

whether I like it or not. There are a lot of other things here that I'm not wild about. I'd love to flog some of the dreary old portraits and buy some modern pieces, help encourage our young artists. But people want to see the family's history hanging on these walls.' He walked on again. 'The book pulls a few visitors – we get some of these odd occult characters travelling hundreds of miles to have a gawp – it's mentioned in quite a lot of reference works. I get two or three letters a year from the born-again brigade telling me to burn it.'

Leaving the gallery, they walked through a doorway at the end and into a dining-room. Places were laid for an elaborate dinner on the round mahogany table.

'This is where my ancestors would have intimate dinners.'

'Intimate dinners for sixteen?' She'd counted the places around the table.

'The table can be extended or contracted.'

A single picture hung on each of the four walls. The one that drew Frannie was a portrait of a man with a strong family likeness to the second Marquess. His face was slightly plumper, but there was the same hard arrogance and a look of fox-like cunning.

'That's the third Marquess,' Oliver said. 'Lord Thomas. He shopped his older brother, the second Marquess, to Cromwell, so he could inherit the title.'

Frannie could see the smugness in the man's face, and could well believe what Oliver had just said.

'It was during the Civil War. The family used to have a house in London – later destroyed in the Great Fire. There was a secret passage beneath it down to the Thames and the second Marquess allowed the Royalists to use it as a safe house in exchange for a supply of boys, the story goes.'

'What happened to him?'

Oliver's eyes roved around the room. 'He was hot-collared.'

'What's that?'

'The same thing that happened to Edward the Second. A red-hot poker pushed up his backside. It used to be a good way to murder someone – didn't leave any visible marks.'

Frannie squirmed. She was glad she could see no family resemblance to the portrait in Oliver's face. She looked at the round table again, cordoned by crimson rope to prevent visitors from helping themselves to the silverware or the cutlery. 'Do you ever use this room?'

'Very occasionally. There was a time when we did period banquets for American tourists.'

'Could we eat here tonight?' she said mischievously.

He looked surprised. 'You'd like to?'

'I think it would be amazing!'

He caught her mood. 'We could, I suppose!'

'Don't you think the house would like it – for it to be used again.'

He knelt down and crawled under the table. 'I'm not sure I can remember how to make it smaller.'

Frannie could see the family crest was embossed on the silver cruets, and on the handles of the cutlery. Much larger, in the centre of each plate, the Halkin motto was clearly legible in gold lettering inside the scroll. *Non omnis moriar.*

The words gave her the same feeling of apprehension she had felt earlier when she had read them above the front door. *I shall not altogether die.* From Horace. She had come across the quotation originally when she had studied Horace at school. But there was somewhere since. She read them again. It was there, on the edge of her mind, like a child taunting her then dodging behind a tree.

Like Edward. She shuddered as she suddenly thought of his strange question when he had been holding the fossil. *Do you think the dead always stay dead, Frannie?*

Non omnis moriar. She repeated the Latin silently to herself, then the translation, staring into the steely eyes of the third Marquess, as if he might help jog her memory. As if he might explain why the words made her feel so deeply and unaccountably afraid.

Spoons of flame hovered unsteadily above the twin silver candelabra; they fluttered in a draught and a hundred reflections shimmied in unison on the polished facets of the crystal goblets.

Frannie had her pullover on over her shirt, but still felt the dewy chill of the night air. Oliver sat opposite her across the mahogany table, which he had reduced right down in size. He was looking relaxed, wearing a denim shirt with the cuffs rolled back, and cradling his glass in his hands. His hair had slid forwards either side of his parting and rested across both temples, but he made no attempt to push it back. There was a mottling around the neck of the bottle on the table and the red of the wine in the glasses was dulled with a faint tinge of brown. The label said: Gevrey-Chambertin, 1971. Steam curled from the thick fillet steaks on their plates.

Frannie helped herself to mushrooms, a large tomato and tiny new potatoes from the foil pack in which they had brought the food. 'Are there any ghosts here?'

His mouth broadened into a warm grin and the blue of his eyes deepened in the candlelight. 'I don't think so.'

'I thought all old houses had ghosts.'

'All old families have skeletons in their closets, but

117

they don't all rattle and wail in the middle of the night.' He cut a piece of his steak. It was beautifully cooked, well done outside, pink inside, the way she liked them.

Frannie cut into hers, watching the band of juice trickle out in the wake of her knife. The sight made her feel queasy, reminding her of the blood from the boy's fingers. Her eyes went warily up to the third Marquess. She heard the sigh of a gust of wind outside, and the hiss of leaves. The window behind the drawn curtain was open slightly, and rattled in the draught.

She looked up at the unlit chandelier for the first time. The candlelight was reflected in its tear-drop crystals. The flames were burning upright again now; tiny ripples of heat warming the air above them. 'How did your wife die?' At last, she'd said it.

Oliver was silent for some moments before replying, then leaned forward as a sudden weariness seemed to sap him, and rested his elbows on the table. He interlinked his fingers beneath his chin. 'I – it was about three and a half years ago.' He gently tapped the base of his throat with his thumbs. 'I was taking Edward to meet Sarah for lunch – it was her birthday and we were having a day in London. She'd gone to have her hair done. We saw her on the other side of the road, and she started to cross towards us. A van being chased by the police jumped the lights and hit her.'

'God!'

'It carried her across the road and pushed her through the plate-glass window of a shop.'

Frannie looked at him in horror. 'You saw it happen? Both of you?'

He grimaced.

'Three and a half years ago?' she said, her voice trembling.

'Yes.'

'Whereabouts did it happen?' she felt her whole body clenching.

'In the City. I had to go to a meeting and took Edward with me into the office. We had a bit of time after it finished, before Sarah arrived, so I thought I'd show Edward the Guildhall. He was in a bit of a grumpy mood because I'd promised to take him to Hamleys and hadn't managed it. We had a drink in a café, then, as we came out into Poultry, we saw Sarah on the other side of the road. I remember not recognizing her at first because she'd had her hair cut short. She started to cross the road and a van being chased by the police jumped the lights and pushed her through a shop window. She was decapitated.'

'God, I'm sorry.'

He studied his wine and said nothing.

Frannie felt a strange and disorienting mixture of shock and surprise. 'Was it a bookshop?' she asked, quietly.

He looked at her oddly. 'Yes.'

'Edward had a chocolate milkshake and you had an espresso?'

'I can't remember exactly –' his face darkened into a deep frown. 'Yes, actually, I think –' He leaned back. 'How on earth do you know that?'

'I was the girl who served you. It was my parents' café.'

There was a long silence. Oliver shook his head in disbelief.

Then a sudden cold draught of air struck Frannie in the face. The flames on the candle heeled over sharply, almost tugging free of the wicks. A shadow moved behind Oliver. It was the door opening. Frannie pressed her nails into the palms of her hands. Oliver turned his head, following her stare.

Edward stood in the doorway in a woollen dressing-gown and corduroy slippers. 'Daddy, I heard a noise in the attic.'

Warm blood spread like central heating through her veins as her fear subsided. She slackened her clenched fingers, breathing out, almost exhilarated in her release, smiling at Edward as he came closer across the room. Oliver stood and put his arm protectively around the boy. 'Did you? Probably squirrels. I'll get someone to set some traps and put down some poison.'

Frannie continued to smile at Edward but there was barely any hint of recognition in his expression. He eyed their plates. 'Can I have some pudding?'

Oliver tousled his son's hair. 'You can have some tomorrow. Come on, I'll take you back to bed. Say goodnight to Frannie.'

The boy mumbled, 'Gnightfrannie,' then turned.

Oliver winked at her. 'Couple of minutes,' he said.

As they walked off, Edward grunted something she did not catch; their voices faded and their silhouettes became part of the darkness that stretched out into the corridor beyond the door. She looked back down at her steak which she had hardly touched and cut another piece, the silence amplifying the sound of her knife on the china. She was thinking back three and a half years, surprised she could remember so clearly what the man had ordered for the boy and himself. Thinking about the coincidence; or coincidences.

She drank some more wine and caught the arrogant gaze of the third Marquess on the wall. She became self-conscious, unable to dismiss the sensation she was being watched by the face in the portrait.

The horror of the death of Oliver's wife played on her mind. She could remember that scene clearly, also. And the stories that came back to her afterwards from other shopkeepers, from her parents. How the woman's head had been severed cleanly by the plate-glass and had rolled to the other end of the shop. How every single book in the shop had had to be thrown away because they had all been sprayed with blood.

She felt a strange mixture of elation and fear. As if there was some curious force of destiny at work and she was part of its master plan. But there was something that Oliver knew and was holding back. Had he known that they had met before? Did he have some reason for contacting her? For bringing her here?

The flames of the candles heeled again as another gust blew outside. There was a sharp crack behind her like a foot on a floorboard but she did not want the Marquess on the wall to see that she was nervous. Houses creaked and cracked all the time. The change of temperature from day to night. Contraction and expansion. The British Museum made the same sounds. She had been on her own many times down in its vaults, surrounded by mummies and unopened coffins; alone in crypts. It wasn't the dead who frightened her, it was the living. She was not afraid of ghosts.

She knew there was no one in the room; the door behind her was closed and she could see through into the darkness beyond the one in front. But when something touched the back of her head, she jumped, her larynx throttling the scream before it escaped. The same something flicked her cheek. Then her ear. A shadow flitted in front of her eyes. A moth, swooping in an uneven parabola in front of her. Its shadow strobed across the table.

Just as her breathing had calmed, the bang right behind her almost shook Frannie off her chair and on to the floor.

She turned in terror. The wall was blank; where there'd been a likeness of a white-faced girl from the past, there was now just a large dark rectangle and a crude hook in its midst. The picture of the girl lay face down on the floor, its frame split by the impact, like broken bones. She heard a deep hiss and the curtains were sucked into the window. Then both candles blew out, and the door slammed shut.

'Frannie?' Oliver's voice.

She opened her mouth and nothing came out. She heard a sharp click. Light filled the room and she blinked. Oliver looked anxiously at her, then beyond at the fallen picture. 'What's happened? You OK?' He walked over to the picture, knelt down and held up two strands of wire. 'Snapped,' he said. 'Bloody flimsy bit of wire whoever did this. Could have injured someone.'

'It nearly gave me a heart attack!'

His eyes moved to each of the remaining pictures in turn, giving each a stern appraisal. 'I apologize for Edward – he normally sleeps OK.'

'Probably still shaken by the accident on the speed-boat – or Dominic's fingers – I should think it would give any child nightmares.'

His face relaxed a little. 'You look as white as a sheet.'

'The painting gave me a fright!'

'I'm sorry.' His eyes focused intently on hers and he smiled. 'So. Not such strangers after all!'

Frannie shrugged. 'I had the feeling at King's Cross that I'd seen you before. It's been niggling me.'

'Do you often work in the café?'

'All the time when I was a kid, in the holidays, and when I was at university. My dad used to pay me, which was useful. But I haven't in the new café. The lease ran out and they were forced to move by developers a couple of years ago.' She looked at him quizzically.

He took a step towards her. 'I – I'm really happy that you're here.'

'In spite of our – coincidence?'

He slipped his hands around her waist and she felt the gentle grip of his strong fingers. He tilted his head back a few inches. His hair had slid further down over his temples and the crystals of light from the chandelier danced in his eyes. 'Maybe you're going to change my luck.'

'I hope so.'

They held each other's gaze and slowly their faces moved closer. Their lips dusted each other's lightly, tentatively, then parted. They stared, searchingly, into each other's eyes, then kissed again. She was surprised how soft and tender his lips were, how gently his mouth moved. His fingers pressed harder, held her more firmly, tracing the contours of her back, and she felt safe now, her fears melting, replaced by an intense yearning. She kissed him ferociously, pushing her fingers through his soft hair, breathing in the light fragrance of his skin, feeling the strength of his body.

Their mouths separated again and they eyed each other once more. Oliver cupped her face in his hands and kissed each of her eyelids lightly, then looked into her eyes, with hope and with fondness. 'Let's go to bed,' he said.

CHAPTER TEN

A sharp click woke Frannie with a start from a confusing dream. It sounded like a machine being switched off, or a drawer being shut. She sat up, confused, taking a moment to remember where she was. Then she breathed out and sank back against the pillow, held herself still, trying not to wake Oliver, who was sleeping deeply beside her. The stump of a candle burned unsteadily beyond him. Outside, the hoot of an owl probed the darkness.

She was wide awake, as if something was not right. The owl hooted again, a soft, lonely call, like an unanswered signal through space. The candle fluttered and shadows collided against the walls. Her eyes roamed the room, the dark canopy of the four-poster above them, the thick rugs on the floor, the walls ornately painted with cherubs and Rubenesque women.

Beneath the thin sheet Oliver's arm lay across her stomach. He stirred and his chin, hard with stubble, pressed against her shoulder. Then she smiled at remembered pleasures of the past few hours and her fear subsided. She felt drained, like a spent husk, and yet at the same time deliciously complete, as if the whole principle of equilibrium lay within her. They had made love almost the whole night through, catching brief snatches of exhausted sleep, then waking and starting again. The way they were starting now, the way she could feel Oliver nuzzling her cheek, slowly playing his fingers down her body.

She kissed him back, their lips tacky, their skin

damp with perspiration. He kissed her neck, then her chest, then each of her shoulders. He ran a finger lightly around the base of her neck and kissed that too, then he stared silently, approvingly at her face, and she was wanting him as if it were only the beginning of the night. She drew him to her, caressing him with her hands, kissing him lightly, then deeply, then lightly again; her body taut, resonating with increasing desire at each returned caress, each reciprocated kiss until she had to fight from crying out and clutch him tightly to her, cradling his head in her arms, whimpering with pleasure so intense it was barely distinguishable from pain, repeating his name over and over as if the world would cease to revolve if she stopped.

Afterwards they lay still, gulping air, her nostrils filled with the smells of sex, the salty taste of his skin on her lips. His face lay on the pillow beside her, nestled into her chest, and she stroked his hair, separating the strands, tidying them.

At the back of his parting was a tiny bald patch of white scalp. It made him seem vulnerable. As if she were looking at his skull. She shivered, but continued to stare in fascination. She knew that human beings shed skin constantly, a complete layer each week, shed enough particles of dead white skin to fill a soup bowl every day. She wondered, suddenly, how much skin it took to make a book.

Then she kissed his head, afraid of her thoughts, and buried her face for a moment in his hair.

He turned his face towards her, and looked serious for a moment, searching her eyes with a worried frown.

'What is it?' she said.

At first he said nothing. But then his hand squeezed her shoulder. 'How many languages do you speak?'

A little surprised, she answered him, 'English. A little French. Italian. And I understand Latin,' she added. 'Why?'

'You don't speak any Arabic? Or archaic languages – other than Latin?'

She smiled. 'No. Do you want something translated?'

He said nothing.

'I was quite surprised to hear Edward speaking Latin,' she said.

Oliver seemed to stiffen. 'He spoke in Latin to you?'

She was chilly, suddenly, under just the sheet and snuggled against him for warmth. 'His knowledge of plants is incredible. He seems to know the Latin names of all of them.'

'Plants?' he said quietly.

She lifted some hair from his forehead and pressed it back. 'Bright boy from a bright daddy.'

Oliver was silent again.

They slept.

The room was washed with light when she awoke to the sound of the clock chiming. Her eyes felt raw, the lids rubbing like sandpaper as she blinked. Oliver was sitting on the side of the bed in a paisley dressing-gown, smiling at her. His skin, white with tiredness, accentuated the darkness of his stubble, and with his hair dishevelled, hanging unevenly over his forehead, it gave him a rather savage appearance that she found appealing. His breath smelled minty as if he had just brushed his teeth. 'Morning,' he said.

'What's the time?'

'Six,' he said quietly. 'I don't want you to go, but Edward often comes in – and I –'

She nodded.

He squeezed her hand and looked thoughtfully at her for a moment. 'Have a lie-in in your room – get up when you feel like it and I'll make you some breakfast. Sleep in as long as you want – let's just have a lazy day.'

She heaved herself up and slid her feet out of bed, shaking her hair away from her face. Oliver peeled his dressing-gown off and draped it over her shoulders. 'Wear this.'

She pushed her hands in and they disappeared into the sleeves, then as she stood up she almost tripped over the bottom of it. She bundled up her clothes and shoes and carried them over to the door. Oliver came out into the corridor and they stood like clandestine lovers. He put his arms around her and she said farewell with her eyes. 'See you a bit later,' he whispered and kissed her lightly on the forehead.

She padded barefoot down the corridor, past the door of Edward's room, which was very slightly ajar, and she slowed, tiptoeing along to her own door which she opened, then shut behind her as quietly as she could.

She breathed in the bland smells of her own room, climbed in between the fresh, cold sheets, and fell asleep.

CHAPTER ELEVEN

Frannie had read the story on the front page of her father's newspaper when she was nine. A family on their yacht struck a mine that had been laid by the Germans during the Second World War. It had broken free from its anchorage and could have been drifting in the Channel for days. It was the first mine that had been encountered for a decade, a coastguard said. The whole family was killed.

She counted the chimes of seven o'clock, and wondered why she had suddenly thought of that story now. It had affected her deeply as a child and for years afterwards she had been scared of going anywhere by boat.

She heard seven-fifteen strike, then seven-thirty. She was wide awake, cocooned in a warm glow, too excited to sleep. Listening to the rising cacophony of the birds, she let the brightening light play on her closed eyelids. Finally, she slipped out of bed, pulled on her clothes and went quietly downstairs.

In the hall, she was surprised to hear the sound of a television. It was coming from the snug next to the kitchen, and she stuck her head around the door. Edward was lying on the floor in a Garfield dressing-gown, engrossed in a cartoon.

'Hello,' Frannie said. 'You're up early.'

He stayed glued to the television for some moments without acknowledging her. A large matchbox lay on the carpet beside him. The action reached its climax. Frannie watched the television with mild amusement. A cartoon dog skidded across a polished floor and through an open window. It hung upside down high above a Manhattan street, saved by a man's foot standing on its tail. A circle of darkness enclosed the image and shrank to a small dot. The credits rolled.

Then Edward turned his head. His face was pale and his eyes were red with tears.

Frannie was startled. 'What's the matter?' she said, kneeling down beside him.

'I've had the bad thing again,' he said.

'What do you mean?' she said with deepening disquiet.

He was silent for a moment. 'This is my last weekend before I go back to school.'

She smiled, relaxing, thinking she understood now, and feeling for him. 'We'll try and make the most of today, shall we?'

'Do you like insects, Frannie?' he said glumly.

'No. Why?'

He pressed the mute button on the sound, then picked up the matchbox. 'This is my new friend.'

She stared at the box warily as he slid open the lid. For a moment she could see nothing in it. He tilted it sideways, and tapped it. 'Come on, Mr Bean. I call him Mr Bean because I think he looks like Rowan Atkinson.' She saw twitching antennae. A small, dark brown beetle crawled into view. She felt a twinge of revulsion.

'Did you know Jonathan Mountjoy, Edward?' She lifted her eyes to his face, but all his attention was focused on the beetle.

'Turn round, Mr Bean,' he said and gave the matchbox a light shake. But the beetle plodded on to the end and then began trying to climb out. A new cartoon was beginning. He turned back to the screen. 'I have to see this. Would you like to watch it with me?'

'I'm just going out for a walk – I'll watch some with you when I come back.'

He grabbed the control and turned up the volume, his concentration already absorbed again by the television, and did not seem to hear her reply. The matchbox lay ignored beside him. Like her question.

Frannie had often heard of gifted children who behaved as if they were a little out of sync with everyone else. She wondered if this might be the case with Edward. She resolved to discuss it with Oliver.

She latched the front door, closed it behind her and headed for the lakeside. The morning was beautiful and she stopped to admire it from the graceful stone bridge that crossed the lake at its narrowest point.

As she rested her hands on the stone parapet, she noticed for the first time that they seemed to have aged; although the fingers were still slender the skin had dried and coarsened, probably from all the digs she had been on, she realized. She smelled Oliver rising from her unwashed skin and wished he was here with her now.

For all her recent happiness, a shadow moved through her mind. An undefined doubt chafing. Her feeling that there was something not right had returned. A rusting mine, broken from its anchorage, drifting unseen beneath the surface. Waiting to make contact.

She crossed herself, the habit of childhood.

The feeling deepened as she walked back up towards the house. She took a different path from yesterday and found herself lost for some minutes in the woods. Then she came to a track alongside an unfamiliar cornfield with a pylon in the centre, and worked out that she had gone too far over to the east.

She corrected herself and after a quarter of an hour the scenery looked more familiar again. She recognized the collapsed stone folly she had passed with Edward and some massive beech trees ahead.

As she entered their heavy shade she saw something strange in front of her. At first she wondered if it was a broken strip of foliage hanging down, but as she got nearer she realized it was an animal. It looked like a fox caught in a snare, she thought, her stomach churning. It was hanging by its neck, motionless, from a branch of a tree.

Then she clamped her hand over her mouth, cupping a scream, and stopped in her tracks, horror-struck. She could hear her own panting, and was aware of a dull ache in her stomach.

One dark brown eye watched her, shining like a marble in the ray of sunlight that played on it.

Frannie backed away, stumbled on a rut. The eye followed her every movement but recorded nothing. Unblinking. The open mouth revealed the gums that yesterday had been wet with saliva, but which were now as dry as old rubber tubing. Captain Kirk's limbs were splayed out as if he were asleep on the kitchen floor, instead of hanging from a noose of thin, bare wire.

Threads of fear pulled tight inside her, but she braced herself and walked slowly up to the dog, needing to make sure, just in case she could still do something for it. Just one brief touch was all she needed. Beneath the silky coat, the skin felt like porcelain.

She ran for the house, went straight upstairs and along to Oliver's room. His door was open and the room was empty. Across the landing she heard the sound of a bath draining and pounded on the door.

Oliver opened it, with a towel around his waist, and

gave her a warm smile which froze as he registered her expression.

'I don't know if Edward's seen it,' she said as he threw on some clothes. 'He was crying when I went down, but I'm not sure if that was because of going back to school.'

'Gypsies,' Oliver said grimly, as if he were not really listening, tugging the laces of his plimsoles. 'We had problems with gypsies a couple of weeks ago, camping on our land opposite. Captain Kirk bit one of them.'

They left the house quietly, hoping Edward would not hear them, carrying a bin liner and pliers. They cut the spaniel down. Frannie suggested Oliver should call the police but he seemed reluctant. Instead, he laid the dog in the bin liner in the back of the Range Rover and drove off to his gamekeeper, to have him bury it.

Frannie went back upstairs and ran herself a hot bath. She lay soaking in it for a long while, tired and distressed, trying to piece her thoughts together. Trying to dismiss, but unable to, the incident between Edward and Captain Kirk yesterday afternoon and the possibility that it was not the gypsies who had killed the dog.

Then she remembered the affection with which Edward had curled up on the kitchen floor with his arm around Captain Kirk last night, and she gave up trying to find an answer.

An hour later, the smell of fresh coffee and fried eggs greeted her as she came into the kitchen, and gave her an oddly reassuring feeling of normality. It reminded her, she realized, of one of the most familiar smells of her parents' café.

Oliver was wearing a butcher's apron over a faded denim shirt, and was pushing cloves of garlic under the skin of a chicken on a roasting tray. Edward was kneeling on the floor, his beetle inside a rectangular enclosure of Lego bricks. On the table, among the debris of Sunday papers, cereals and jams, there was an untouched place that she presumed had been set for her.

'Hi.' Oliver exchanged a conspiratorial grimace with her.

Edward did not look up. Inevitably the boy's presence made her feel subdued. Was it because she hadn't worked out whether he was friend or foe? But he was only a child, she reminded herself. And now his dog was dead. 'Feel up to some breakfast? French toast is the chef's speciality today.' Oliver was putting on a good act.

'Yes please,' Edward said, cheerily.

'Hey, you've already had some!'

'Can't I have some more? Please?'

'You really want another piece?'

Edward nodded. 'Daddy, would it be all right if I took Frannie riding this afternoon?'

Frannie looked at the boy in amazement then glanced at Oliver, uncertain whether the boy knew about Captain Kirk or not. He must, she thought, otherwise he'd be looking for him.

The telephone began to ring. 'You're going to a party this afternoon.'

Edward's face screwed up with disappointment. 'What party?'

'Jamie Middleton's ninth birthday.'

'God, Jamie Middleton.' He made a series of mock vomiting sounds. 'Do I have to go?'

'Yes, you've accepted.' Oliver picked up the receiver, covering the mouthpiece with his hand. 'I thought you liked him. You wanted him to come and stay a few weeks ago.'

'He's really silly, Daddy. He hasn't grown up at all.'

Oliver and Frannie exchanged a glance. Oliver removed his hand from the mouthpiece. 'Hello?' he said. 'Clive!' His voice became serious. 'I tried ringing you a couple of times yesterday evening. What's the news?'

Frannie watched him in silence. He said very little, listening mostly, then hung up glumly. Some of the morning brightness seemed to fade from the kitchen with his expression.

'Dominic,' he said. 'They stitched one finger back, but they're not very hopeful. They couldn't save the others – the bones were too badly crushed.'

Edward tapped the floor as the beetle moved towards a wall.

'Poor chap,' Frannie said.

'It would have been better if it was his left hand, wouldn't it, Daddy?' Edward said without looking up.

'You said that yesterday. It would have been better if it hadn't happened at all.' He turned to Frannie. 'Tea or coffee?'

'Coffee, please. Can I get it?'

'Sit and relax, read the papers. Have some cereal?'

Frannie poured herself some cornflakes, which she hadn't eaten for years, feeling hungry in spite of her distress, as if aware that she somehow had to stoke herself up for what was to come. Oliver dropped a knob of butter into a frying-pan.

'Daddy, are you making me another piece? I'm still hungry.'

'I'll make you another piece of French toast if you promise to go straight after breakfast and pick some plums for a crumble.'

'Can Frannie come and help me?'

'Frannie might just want to have a sit down.' He winked at her, rocked the butter around, then broke two eggs into a bowl, beat them, dunked two slices of bread in them, dropped them into the frying-pan.

'Frannie,' Edward said. 'Will you?'

'Yes, sure.'

She found herself smiling at his antics, being cheered by them, as he watched his father and mimed his hunger, hunching his shoulders up mischievously, then smacking his lips greedily.

Oliver served the toast up and poured maple syrup on top. 'Ready.'

'Daddy, look! Frannie!'

As the beetle approached one corner of the Lego enclosure Edward dropped a dried pea in its path. The insect pushed it forwards. 'He's going to score a goal!' Edward said, excitedly.

The beetle changed direction. 'No, stupid!' He blocked its path with his hand. 'That way!'

'Toast's getting cold!' Oliver said, putting the pan in the sink and turning on the tap.

Edward stood up. 'Bye-bye, Mr Bean,' he said and crushed the beetle flat with a single stamp of his foot. Then he sat on his chair and nonchalantly picked up his knife and fork.

Frannie looked at him in disbelief, then down at the beetle's remains. Oliver was rinsing out the frying-pan and had not noticed. Edward cut a piece of his toast, pushed it through the pool of syrup, then raised it to his mouth, a trickle of syrup running down his chin. He chewed enthusiastically, cutting his next piece before he had swallowed.

She looked back at the boy's open, freckled face; at his warm brown eyes and his springy ginger hair. 'Why did you do that?'

He continued eating without replying.

Whatever the reasons for it, his habit of not answering

tended to make her feel a fool. She cut her toast half-heartedly, her appetite gone, and forked a piece into her mouth. The sweet taste perked her a little. She tried not to look at the beetle but her eye was drawn back to it. 'Why did you do that, Edward?' she repeated.

Edward began to leaf busily through the pages of the *Mail on Sunday*, scanning the columns without reading them, as if he was searching for something.

Oliver frowned. Edward continued turning the pages in silence, shovelling his food into his mouth until he had finished, and put his knife and fork down, then he concentrated his full attention on the paper.

Oliver raised his eyebrows questioningly at Frannie and she pointed at the beetle's remains. When he realized what it was his face darkened. 'Edward, did you tread on the beetle?'

Edward ignored him and turned another page.

'Edward?' Oliver sounded angry. 'What did you do that for? Why kill it?'

'Beetles are vermin, Daddy.'

'They're not all vermin. And you shouldn't torture animals.'

Edward simply looked at Oliver as if it were he who was the child.

Frannie saw in the boy's face the same expression, the same power, that had made the dog tremble and back away yesterday, just as it now silenced his father. It chilled her. In Oliver's eyes she read both anger and bewilderment.

'For heaven's sake, Daddy, I wasn't torturing him; I was teaching him to play football. Frannie, have you finished? Shall we go and pick some plums now?'

Edward went to the scullery and brought out two wicker baskets with shoulder-straps. He held one for

Frannie. She swallowed the rest of her coffee, fetched her boots, then followed him outside.

They walked down a recently mown track beside the brick wall of the vegetable garden. The sun was hot, but the breeze was back, stronger, sucking and releasing the bushes and the leaves in the trees with a sound like distant waves. The grass had been left where it had fallen and had turned to hay in the dry weather; the air was tainted with its sharp, peppery smell and the more acrid reek of the cow-parsley that rose untamed either side.

'Captain Kirk's gone away,' Edward said suddenly, rather offhand.

'Gone?' she said, wondering what Oliver had told him.

'He's gone away,' he repeated, then lapsed into silence.

Frannie tried a different tack. 'Edward, in your photo album in the attic there's a newspaper cutting about someone called Jonathan Mountjoy, who was killed in America. Did you know it's there?'

'Yes.'

'Did you cut it out?'

He nodded.

'Why?'

'I don't know,' he said guilelessly.

'Do you cut out other things from newspapers?'

'Sometimes.'

'What sort of things?'

There was no reaction. She looked at him. 'Edward?' Still no reaction. He had sunk into silence, leaving her thrown as usual.

She walked on beside him into a large, hopelessly neglected orchard. There were rows of trees laden with fruit, their branches weighted down, some almost touching the ground. Plums and greengages lay all around in the long, weed-strewn grass – wasps, blue-bottles and flies crawling over them, burrowing into them. She trod on a plum, felt it squelch beneath her and looked at the mess of brown, overripe flesh. Through a gap ahead she could see rows of apple trees, similarly laden, the fruit looking less ripe.

Edward jumped up and grabbed a low branch and swung down on it, then released it. The tree shook and plums thudded down all around them. One struck Frannie's head and fell beside her. She picked it up, wiped it on her jeans and bit it. It was soggy and had a faintly rotten taste.

'The Victorias are the best, Frannie,' Edward said, and took her hand. 'Let's pick those!'

'What's the Latin for them?'

Edward did not reply as he walked on, suddenly taking her hand and holding it tightly, hurrying her as if afraid the fruit might disappear. He led her to a cluster of trees laden with large, egg-shaped plums, some green, some yellow with red streaks. 'These!' he said.

Frannie picked one and bit it. It was hard and sour.

'They ripen much later than the others,' Edward said. 'You have to look carefully to find the ripe ones. I'll get one for you!' He released her hand and scamp-ered ahead, his eyes scanning the branches of the next tree. He looked carefully at one large plum that was a deep yellow colour, curling his fingers around it gently as if worried it was fragile, and then pulled it very slowly, his face puckered in concentration. 'Here you are!' He held it out.

'Thanks!' She took it, raised it to her mouth and bit into it. As she did so, something tickled the inside of her lip. There was a strange fluttering sensation in her mouth, then a fierce pain on her inner lower lip. She opened her mouth, spitting frantically. There was a stab like a red-hot needle in the base of her tongue. She tossed her head, spitting again, then again something was flicking backwards and forwards in her mouth; it stabbed her ferociously a second time.

She spat again, then again, tiny fragments of plum flying out. A dark thing came out too, fell, dipping, then rose. A wasp; it flew away unsteadily.

She clamped her hand to her mouth, the pain almost unbearable, pinched her lip between her fingers, then her tongue, to try to ease the excruciating agony. She called out from her throat as another wasp buzzed around her, shaking her head in sudden panic. 'Edward! Help!' She pinched her tongue harder with her fingers, pressed her lips tightly together, stumbled forward, her vision blurred with tears. 'Edward!' A branch struck her face. 'Edward!' Another branch hit her in the eye.

Ammonia for bees, Vinegar for wasps. Her father had said that when she was stung as a child. AB. VW. The thought repeated itself. AB. VW. It became a chant in her head as she stumbled out of the orchard, and back along the path beside the walled kitchen garden, heading as fast as she could towards the house.

AB-VW-AB-VW

Sarson's vinegar. She visualized the bottle. AB. VW.

Sarson's vinegar. There was a bottle on each table at her parents' café. Vinegar and HP Sauce. The pain seared her mouth. She fought back more tears. It was worsening every second.

AB. VW. The words buzzed like a wasp in her brain. Willing herself on, she repeated them over and over in case she got to the house and did not know what to do. Edward was somewhere. She was still carrying the basket for the plums. A keening cry came from deep within her. She pulled her handkerchief out of her pocket and stuffed that into her mouth and stumbled on.

In the orchard, Edward shook another tree, and busily picked the best plums off the ground, checking each one carefully for insects, then laying them gently in the basket, careful not to bruise any, working methodically, remembering he must not fill the basket too much otherwise it would be too heavy to carry.

The house stood ahead beyond the beech grove. The pain would be better after she reached it. The house would stop the pain. Oliver would stop the pain. She ran in front of a young woman posing for her husband's camera as the shutter clicked. 'Sorry,' she said, but no voice came out and the word echoed, trapped inside her brain. Sorry. Sorry. Sorry.

She shook her head from side to side as if this might ease the burning in her mouth. She chewed on her handkerchief. Her lips felt like swollen bladders. Pain ate its way up behind her eyes, down into her gullet.

She opened the front door, charged into the hallway that was pitch dark after the brilliant sunlight, saw Oliver hunched over the kitchen table, phone pressed to his ear, in deep concentration. An egg whisk leaned out of a white china bowl on the table in front of him. The radio was on, the Archers weekly round-up.

'Eleven?' he was saying. 'The eleventh last night?' He gestured a greeting at Frannie with his left arm, barely acknowledging her, tapping the table thoughtfully with his right index finger. 'The same symptoms? Does the vet still reckon it's milk-drop syndrome?'

She turned to Edward for help and was surprised to

see that he was not behind her; she thought he had been following her. She opened a cupboard. It was full of china and glass bowls. She shut it and opened another, which was stacked with plates. Then another and stared through tears of frustration at a wok and an assortment of frying-pans. The pain in her tongue became unbearable. She squeezed it between her finger and thumb.

'Surely the vet must have some idea?' Oliver said calmly.

She yanked open another door, her eyes misting. The shelves contained a food mixer and various attachments. She clenched her mouth even tighter over the balled handkerchief, and managed an inarticulate sound.

'Charles, hang on,' Oliver said. 'Frannie – what was that?'

She was desperate, wondering why on earth he couldn't see her distress. 'Vrrngigr.' The handkerchief blotted up her words.

He looked at her properly and stood up, anxious suddenly.

'Vringar,' she repeated and lurched towards a cupboard. She turned back towards him, pleading with her eyes.

'Christ, Charles. I'll call you right back.'

She was trying all the cupboards, leaving the doors open. China . . . glass bowls . . . frying-pans . . . and then one full of bottles. Pickles, ketchup, Worcester Sauce, soy sauce, olive oil. Vinegar. She reached in. There were three different kinds: light vinegar, cider vinegar, dark brown vinegar. She took the dark one out, pulled the handkerchief from her mouth, unscrewed the top of the bottle and shook vinegar on to it, soaking it, then pushed it back into her mouth.

The acidity shot straight up her nose and her eyes snapped shut. She coughed the handkerchief out into her hand, staggered to the sink, hung over it and gagged. The taps and the stainless steel basin rolled past her as if they were on castors. She felt Oliver's hand on her shoulder.

'What is it, Frannie? What's happened?'

She looked up at him, trying to speak, but her tongue clogged her mouth and her lips wouldn't move properly. 'Wassp,' she hissed, and closed her eyes. When she opened them again he was holding her face in his hands, examining her mouth.

She tapped her lips then peeled the bottom one back. 'Wrsspp. Stnnng. In plum.'

'Wasp? You've been stung?'

She nodded feverishly, pointed to two spots on her lips, then her tongue.

'On your tongue? Oh, God! Did you stumble into a nest?' His face creased with anxiety and his cornflower-blue eyes seemed to lose their colour.

She breathed in sharply, clenching her eyes shut, then exhaling sharply. Oliver stood it for sixty seconds and then announced, 'I'm taking you to Casualty. I've got some sting-relief stuff upstairs but we can't put that in your mouth.' He gently pulled her lips, turning them over, looking inside. He checked the clock on the wall. 'Actually, no, it might be quicker if I try our doctor, see if he's in by any chance.' He picked the phone up.

Frannie opened her eyes. The taste of the vinegar made her gag again and she hung her head over the sink, stared down at potato peelings, the tops of carrots and a teaspoon covered in congealed coffee. The fire in her mouth was getting hotter. She rinsed it out with a glass of cold water and that made it worse.

She caught her reflection in the side of the kettle and tried to examine the marks, but it distorted her face too much to see clearly. She remembered there was a mirror in the hall and went out.

In the dim light, her skin looked pale and lifeless. Mascara ran in black streaks down her left cheek, but she barely registered it. As she leaned closer she was surprised that her lip was hardly swollen at all; just a little puffy. She peeled it back and there were just two tiny red marks that were barely noticeable. She curled up her tongue and could see just a tiny red spot, like an ulcer.

She pressed the handkerchief back in her mouth; the fire cooled just a fraction and the vinegar wrung more tears from her eyes. She wiped them with her sleeve and walked back towards the kitchen, bumping clumsily against the wall, and knocking a couple of pictures.

'Would you?' Oliver said into the phone as she came in. 'She's really in terrible pain.'

She sat down opposite him. A tear fell on to the front page of the *Mail on Sunday* and spread in a small grey stain. 'Bush Gets Tough', said the blurred headline. She wanted to be tough too, was trying to compose herself, to stop crying.

Oliver hung up. 'He'll be here in ten minutes – he only lives at Glynde. He says vinegar *is* the best thing.'

She closed her eyes, nodding gratefully.

He looked carefully inside her mouth again. 'You're not allergic to wasps?'

She shook her head.

'Your tongue doesn't look swollen. You can breathe OK?'

This time she nodded.

He put his arm around her shoulder and squeezed

her firmly; then he kissed the top of her head. 'I'm so sorry. Horrible. It's been a bad year with the wasps, we've been plagued by them.'

As she looked up at him, she caught him staring back at her, searching her face carefully with a troubled expression. Searching not for stings but for something else, trying to read her mind. Then he switched focus and she turned her head, startled.

Edward struggled in through the door, his wicker basket laden with plums, holding it with both hands, his face red from exertion as he carried it proudly to his father.

'See how many I got, Daddy!'

'Frannie's been stung by a wasp,' Oliver said starkly.

Edward looked shocked. He dropped the basket on to the floor, ignoring the plums that spilled from it and ran to her. 'Frannie, no! Wasps! Are you all right?' He looked at her face, his eyes wide open, so distraught she thought for a moment he was going to cry. 'Where?'

She stared back at him warily, and pointed at her mouth. Her expression was accusatory.

'In the plum? In the one I gave you?'

'Ysh.'

His face crumpled as if it had been deflated and his voice rose into a whine. 'There wasn't; there couldn't have been! Frannie, there couldn't, I was really careful – I nearly bit one with a wasp in once and I always look. Frannie, I'm sorry, does it hurt a lot?'

She nodded.

He turned to Oliver. 'I picked it, Daddy, specially for Frannie.' A tear ran down his cheek, and in spite of her pain Frannie suddenly felt a heel for her attitude. 'I did,' he said.

She reached her arm around him and hugged him. Then she buried her face in her free hand as the pain once more became unbearable.

The doctor examined each of the stings diligently and, with profuse sympathy, asked her if she had any allergies, then gave her an injection of hydrocortisone. He told her the pain might continue for a while and to take aspirin.

She spent the rest of the morning in a lounger beside the swimming-pool that was secluded from the prying eyes of visitors by a topiaried yew hedge. Edward stayed close to her as if he had personally taken charge of her recovery, lapsing into long periods of silent concentration on his Game Boy, to Frannie's relief, enabling her to read the papers.

A page of the *Sunday Times* on the ground beside her lifted in the breeze and rolled over with a crackle. She looked up and watched Edward, bent intently over his machine, biting his lower lip in concentration and pushing the buttons. She heard the faint tones of the synthetic music and the muffled explosions, and continued to watch him, as if she could somehow understand him by doing so. She needed to solve the enigma of how he could be so warm and alert at times, then suddenly switch off completely, seeming to be elsewhere. It was disturbing. Despite her earlier resolve, she hadn't liked to raise it with Oliver, because she sensed that she might be treading on forbidden territory.

Maybe there was nothing sinister about it. Maybe it was his mother's death that had caused it. The trauma of seeing his mother decapitated. She wondered how she would have reacted in the same circumstances. Perhaps Oliver was fortunate the child had kept his sanity at all.

She replayed in her mind the moment when Edward had picked and handed her the plum. Saw again the innocence in his face. Tried to compare it to the innocence of his expression on the boat yesterday.

He glanced at her suddenly, and she lowered her eyes to the pool. She watched the pipe that stretched beneath the surface, and the automatic cleaner working its way busily up and down. An unappetizing scum of froth and dead flies had gathered in one corner.

I hope you're not planning to sleep with my daddy.

Her unease was growing.

Edward was regarding her with his warm brown eyes. 'How are you feeling now, Frannie?'

'A little better,' she said.

'Would you like to have a go with my Game Boy?'

'Sure.'

'I'm going to kill every wasp I ever see,' he said.

She smiled. 'You don't have to do that.'

'I'm going to,' he said darkly. 'You're my friend. They're going to be sorry for what they did to you.'

The sun went behind a cloud, and she shivered as a sudden sense of fear swamped her. She remembered the beetle from a few hours ago. And the words Edward had used as he opened the matchbox. *This is my new friend.*

She remembered how he had parted company with it.

CHAPTER TWELVE

They had lunch in the courtyard. The sun shone intermittently between increasing spells of cloud. Oliver had cooked the chicken well, it was moist and lightly flavoured with tarragon, but eating was painful for Frannie and instead she drank too much of the ice-cold *rosé*. Edward waged a relentless war against the wasps, somewhat to Oliver's irritation, trapping them beneath upturned glasses, crushing them with his fork, and drowning one in his glass of Coke. Then he put down his knife and fork, leaving his food almost untouched.

'This chicken tastes funny, Daddy. What have you put in it?'

'A herb called tarragon.'

Edward screwed up his face. 'You always muck things up when you *gourmet* them.' He turned to Frannie.

Frannie smiled and saw that Oliver looked rather crestfallen. She wondered if his wife had been a good cook.

'There's gratitude!' he said. 'Back home for twenty-four hours and he's already criticizing my cooking.' He glared at his son with a mock-fierce expression. 'OK, Paul Bocuse junior, why don't you rustle us up something next time?'

Edward looked back at him seriously. 'Can't we just have things cooked normally? Like Mrs Beakbane does?' He turned to Frannie. 'He reads too many recipe books.'

Before she could speak in Oliver's defence, a man

and a boy of about Edward's age came into the court-yard. The man was tall and sturdy and looked a little younger than Oliver; he had a pleasant face with a healthy outdoors complexion, hair bleached by the sun, and was wearing grubby jeans and an old shirt. The boy had a round, rather watery face, with an impish grin, a high forehead and thin blond hair brushed vaguely flat – apart from one lock which stood defiantly upright. He was wearing a yellow Mickey Mouse T-shirt, clean but creased trousers, and train-ers.

'Charles, hi!' Oliver said, standing to introduce them. 'This is – ah – Frannie Monsanto – my brother Charles, and my nephew Tristram.'

'How do you do,' his brother said rather shyly, shaking Frannie's hand with a strong grip and looking down awkwardly at the ground. Frannie could see the family resemblance in their features.

'Tristram,' Edward said, 'would you like to see my new Game Boy cassette?'

The boy's eyes lit up. 'Yes!'

'Got time for a drink?' Oliver asked his brother.

'No – er – thanks, ought to get going; I've got to pick some stuff up from the vet on the way.'

'When's the homeopathic chap coming?'

'Tomorrow morning.'

Oliver suddenly shouted at the boys, who were scampering off. 'Hey, where are you going?'

'Tristram wants to play with my Game Boy.'

'Another time. Uncle Charles wants to get going.'

Charles scratched his head and looked at Frannie. 'Do you – er – know – er – this part of the world?'

'No, hardly at all.'

'Ah; right.' He looked down at the ground again as if trying to think of something to say.

'You've got problems with your cattle, I gather?' she said. The pain of the stings was being anaesthetized by the wine, but her lip still felt swollen and she wondered if she looked strange.

He dug his hands into the back pockets of his jeans and addressed the ground again. 'Yes, one or two, I'm afraid.' He looked at Oliver, at his watch, then back at her. 'Nice to meet you – excuse us dashing. The children are all being taken off somewhere for a mystery picnic and the mother was very insistent they should arrive on time.'

'Nice to meet you, too.'

'Don't forget the present,' Oliver said to Edward.

'Do I have to give Jamie Middleton a present, Daddy?'

'Yes, of course you do, it's his birthday.'

'I'd much rather give it to Tristram.'

His cousin's eyes lit up. 'Yes, please!'

Frannie felt a sense of freedom as Charles and his mud-caked Land Rover disappeared beyond the far end of the façade; the same way she used to feel as a teenager when her parents had gone out. It was exciting to have Oliver to herself for a few hours. She took his hand and squeezed it hard. Oliver took her other hand and kissed her lightly on the forehead. 'Feeling better?'

'Lots.' She looked into his eyes, seeking reassurance; reassurance that his son had not deliberately given her a plum with a wasp in it.

They lay on loungers by the pool, in the sun. Then, after a while, they went into the wooden changing-hut and made love on the hard, dusty floor. Rays of sunlight played above their heads like the beams of cinema projectors. And the stifling air contained the rubbery smell of some old swimsuits hung up and forgotten.

Afterwards they lay in silence. Frannie held his wrist, pulled his hand to her face and gently nibbled his forefinger. Then she caressed him lightly, feeling the warm, spent air of his breath on her face. Perspiration ran down her forehead and her cheeks, down her neck, and her hair was matted to her head. She watched a spider hover warily above them on its glinting thread. The pain was returning again now, so she sucked in cooling air through clenched teeth and after a few moments the burning subsided a little.

Oliver rolled on to his side, propped himself on his elbow and moved his face closer to hers. 'I'm sorry that you got stung,' he said.

'Do you think Edward could be a little jealous of me?'

Her words seemed to strike him like an electrical current. She detected the sudden change instantly; it was as if he were bristling. 'What do you mean?' He pulled away from her and the warmth left his eyes.

'Nothing,' she said, scared by his reaction.

'You think he did it deliberately?'

'No – not deliberately; not maliciously. I just wonder if there's a part of him that's – you know – that he's not even aware of – that resents me; or anyone you go out with.'

'You really think Edward would deliberately have given you a plum with a wasp in it?' His voice was cold; a stranger's. He sat up, morosely hunched over his knees.

Frannie watched the spider winding itself back up its thread, and was afraid to look at Oliver. 'No. No, I don't mean that.' Then immediately she was angry at herself, because she did mean it. It was exactly what she meant.

*

They swam in the pool separately, like two strangers, Oliver doing bursts of two lengths at a time in a powerful crawl, then lying back against the side, regaining his breath. Frannie meandered up and down in her steady breast-stroke. Each time she stopped, Oliver lunged off again.

They had tea by the pool in the last of the sun, their conversation awkward and banal. Frannie felt choked, trying to retrieve the situation and scared that she had blown it. Oliver did not attempt to touch her and failed to reciprocate with even the faintest squeeze when she took his hand. She cursed herself silently for what she'd said.

Then he left her by the pool, saying he was going to have another attempt at starting the plane, and did not ask if she would like to come with him. She heard the Range Rover roar off, being driven hard by someone in a temper. A few minutes later, the still of the air was broken by a muffled bang that sounded at first like a gunshot. There was another, then a distant but fierce roar that lasted about a second. The same procedure was repeated several times over the next quarter of an hour, until the roar grew into a steady, monotonous drone that went on for some minutes. It seemed to increase Frannie's loneliness.

They were going back to town tonight. Oliver was having a day's holiday to take Edward to London Zoo tomorrow. Frannie thought it strange that when she had first met them they were returning from another zoo; coincidence, she thought; barely worth noting.

In a few hours they would part on her doorstep and she would return to her world. To the flowers in the vase in her bedroom. To an angry phone conversation with her parents about why she had not told them she would not be coming to lunch today. And to an expectant phone call from Debbie Johnson wanting to hear all about the weekend.

All about how she blew it.

The clouds closed like curtains across the dying sun. She shivered as the warmth went out of the day.

The stable clock chimed five times. Each bong rang out, echoing in the still air like a warning. Bong, it pealed. Keep away! Bong. Danger! Bong. *I hope you're not planning to sleep with my daddy.* Bong. *Non omnis moriar.* Bong. *I shall not altogether die.*

The first spot of rain struck her cheek like a tear.

It was raining hard as they came off the end of the motorway into the haze of orange sodium that marked the beginning of the suburbs of London and the end of the weekend. The wipers squeaked and clunked, fresh spats of rain filling the arcs as soon as they were cleared. Tail-lights stretched ahead into the distance. They began brightening in sequence; brakes. A cube of ice-blue light hurtled towards them like a slingshot. It was followed by another. The Range Rover slowed.

'Why are we stopping?' Edward said tiredly from the rear seat.

Oliver changed gear. 'Looks like there's a pile-up,' he replied above the din of the engine and the tape of Michael Jackson's *Thriller* which Edward insisted on being played at an ear-splitting volume.

Edward pressed his face to the window. The traffic filed by a sign: POLICE. ACCIDENT. SLOW. A white car lay upside down across the central pavement, almost cut in half by a street light that was badly buckled. Another car with most of its front missing and its roof sticking in the air, as if someone had had a go at it with a tin-opener, faced the opposite direction. Two people sat inverted and motionless in the first car, their heads slumped forwards. The windscreen had frosted. Frannie looked away, feeling the dread accidents always gave her, but her eyes were drawn back involuntarily.

A siren screamed behind them. A policeman was stopping the traffic, moving everyone over to the side. A fire-engine pulled past them and, moments later, an ambulance. Blue lights slicked across the glossy tarmac.

'How do you think that crash happened, Daddy?'

Several people stood around a lump that lay in the road. Sickened, Frannie saw it was a girl, not moving. A dark pool was flowing from her head.

'Is that lady dead, Daddy?'

'I think she's just unconscious.'

A knot of people were standing around the cars and more were joining them. Two men were pulling hard on a door. As it opened, Frannie heard the shriek of protesting metal above the rumble of the Range Rover's engine and the music. It hit just the right frequency to grate on her nerve endings.

Edward tapped Frannie urgently on the shoulder and lowered his voice. 'I think she might be dead. She's not moving at all.'

A policeman was waving them on, agitatedly. Edward turned and peered at the scene through the rear window. 'Daddy, put the rear wiper on please. Quick. Quickly! I can't see!'

The traffic picked up speed and the accident receded behind them. The image of the girl in the road stayed with her.

Edward said: '*Elephas maximus.*'

She turned.

'*Loxodonta africanus. Giraffidae.*' He spoke clearly but quietly, and at first it was difficult for her to make out exactly what he was saying. '*Diceros bicornis. Diceros simus.*'

Frannie glanced at Oliver. He was looking in the rear-view mirror with a frown. She turned round again. Edward was unsmiling. The inside of the car was cold, suddenly, and she felt her body break out in a chill of goose-pimples. Shock from seeing the accident, she thought.

'*Hippopotamus amphibius. Hippopotamus libieriensis.*' Edward stared ahead, reciting expressionlessly.

'Are these the animals you are going to see tomorrow?' she said.

'*Lama huanacus glama. Panthera pardus. Panthera uncia. Neofelis nebulosa. Panthera leo. Erethizontidae. Hystricidae. Hyaena hyaena. Hyaena brunnea. Hyaena crocuta.*'

There was something compelling about the Latin words and Frannie felt the hairs on the back of her neck rising and something spiralling inside her. Fear. She looked at Oliver who continued looking at his son in the mirror, his face set like a mask. She was unable to read his expression.

'*Crocodylus. Osteolaemus. Crocodylus porosus.*'

'Edward, enough,' Oliver said suddenly.

The traffic had been moving steadily for a while, and familiar landmarks were looming ahead. The grimy, Odeon-style building that was a wine warehouse. The Gulf petrol station. Clapham South tube station. The weak red glow from the mosque-like windows of the Indian restaurant. The chemist. The wine bar and the pizzeria, their outside tables deserted in the rain.

'*Struthio. Gorilla gorilla. Gorilla berengei.*'

'OK, Edward, enough!' Oliver said more loudly and firmly. 'Next right, isn't it?'

She nodded gloomily. There had been no thaw in his frostiness.

'*Anthropopithecus troglodytes. Camelus dromedarius. Camelus bactrianus.*'

'Quiet!' he said, losing his temper. 'Tell us where you learned all that?' He looked in the mirror again.

'Turn right here,' Frannie said.

Edward fell silent.

Oliver turned down the street of terraced houses with cars parked on both sides, drove to the end and left into Frannie's street. He pulled up outside her flat.

Edward peered out. 'Is that your house?'

'I just have a flat there.'

'Can I come in and see it?'

'Not tonight,' Oliver said. 'It's late and you're tired.'

'I'm not, Daddy. Couldn't we just go in for a few minutes?'

'*No.*'

Frannie turned to him, and winced as one of the stings in her mouth suddenly pricked sharply. 'Bye, Edward. Back to school on Tuesday?'

He nodded, then his face crumpled. 'I don't want you to go, Frannie.' He put his arms around her neck and hugged her tightly. 'Am I going to see you again very soon?'

'I hope so,' she said flatly.

Oliver opened the tailgate and lifted out her overnight bag. She slid down on to the wet pavement. Edward looked totally doleful. 'Bye, Frannie.'

'Bye!' She blew him a kiss.

'Hey, Frannie!' Edward said, suddenly. 'Dead on!'

She frowned, then grinned. 'Dead on!' she said, and held out her hand. He slapped it. Then she closed the door, getting wet fast. Oliver carried her bag down into the basement, and held it whilst she fumbled for her key. Then he stepped into the hall with her and put the bag on the floor among a clutch of leaflets. She switched on the light. There was an awkward silence between them. Oliver lowered his head, opened his mouth as if to say something then patted his hands against his thighs. Frannie felt close to tears.

Suddenly he moved towards her and placed his hands on her shoulders and looked her squarely in the face. 'Thanks for coming. I'm sorry about the things that happened.'

She stared back for a while before replying. 'I'm still glad I came. Really.'

His expression thawed and he smiled for the first time since his anger in the changing-hut. 'I – I have an invite to a private view of a painter I rather like, Andrew Kiewzka, on Wednesday. Would you like to come?'

'I'd love to.' She dismissed all thoughts of her aerobics class.

'It starts at seven. I could pick you up from here or the Museum.'

'The Museum might be best as it's early. What time?'

'About ten to seven?'

'The Great Russell Street entrance?'

They put their arms around each other and hugged tightly. 'I enjoyed being with you,' she murmured. 'I'm sorry about what I said. I didn't mean it.' Her eyes were wet; as she clung tightly to him she could smell faint traces of chlorine from the pool on him.

'I'd better go, before Edward decides to come down,' he said. They kissed lightly, then she stood in the front door as he ran back up the steps, his head ducked against the rain, and she waited, listening to the bellow of the Range Rover's engine as it drove off, and the slosh of its tyres.

She closed the front door and scooped the leaflets off the floor. A pizza delivery service, a DIY removals service and a builder called STACKMAN – CHEAPEST IN TOWN! She dropped them on to the hall table. A baby cried upstairs and she heard a man's voice raised in anger. Then silence; just the drumming of the rain.

The gloom of the hall closed around her and she shivered once in reaction. The passage down to her bedroom was dark and a hundred miles long. She walked down it slowly, listening for any sound. As she stood outside the bedroom and gripped the handle, her eyes checked the living-room door; the kitchen door; the bathroom door. She turned the handle and went in and was met immediately by the smell of Oliver's flowers. She switched on the light.

And breathed out.

The flowers were where she had put them, in the white vase with the green ceramic bow, on the mantelpiece. Lilies and carnations. She walked across and smelled them; they were still fresh and their scents were sweet. The phone rang. Probably her parents or Debbie. She let it ring twice, three times, breathed the scents again. Another ring. Then she went over to the bed and lifted the receiver.

It was a man's voice that she knew and yet she could not immediately place it.

'Hello, Frannie?'

Serious; she did know it, but it was different; not the way he usually spoke, whoever he was. It sounded wrong, like a recording played at the wrong speed.

'Hi!' she said, trying not to reveal that she could not place the caller.

'I've been trying to get you all weekend.'

'I've been away.'

Silence.

Paul Bryce. Meredith's husband. That was who it was.

'Oh,' he said. 'Right. You haven't heard?'

The words came out heavily, charged with leaden portent. Her reply was weak, her vocal cords constricted, 'Heard?'

'About Meredith?'

She felt the sudden pull of gravity tugging her jaw, the base of her neck, her stomach, her thighs. The floor pushed up through the balls of her feet and her legs buckled to meet it. She sat down on the bed, her dread rising like water in a lock. 'No? About Meredith?' Whispering now.

'She was killed on Friday morning in a car crash.'

CHAPTER THIRTEEN

The landscape slipped by the window of the train, the colours flat and lifeless as if the sombre grey of the sky had leaked over everything. Chimney-stacks, housing estates, reservoirs, factories, canals, coalfields, lines of traffic at level crossings. Frannie watched a woman unpegging her washing in her back yard. A man stood near a bridge, his dog cocking a leg on a lamppost. A lorry crawled up a hill. Life was going on; the daily business; relentless, remorseless routines, patterns. For all except Meredith and her family.

She used to love this journey so much. Now she was making it probably for the last time. It was a month ago that she had brought the double bass up here and met Oliver and Edward on the platform. Meredith had been alive and Frannie had never imagined she would see Oliver again. She had not even known his name then.

The train shook and some coffee spilled over the rim of the polystyrene cup and scalded her fingers. She took a bite of the soggy breakfast bun; the hot meat and the slimy tomato burned the roof of her mouth. She chewed disconsolately; the food was tinged with the cardboard flavour of its carton. It was half past nine and the train was due in York shortly before eleven. The cremation was at twelve.

On Sunday night she had lain in bed wondering about coincidence and remembering Oliver's comment that there was no such thing as a meaningless coincidence. She thought about the accident involving Oliver's wife and the one they had seen on their way up to London and then getting the news about Meredith. Too many accidents. So many coincidences. Meeting Oliver and Edward at the station after they had come into the café three years before; bumping into Seb Holland in the restaurant and hearing of Jonathan Mountjoy's death; Edward's news cutting; Meredith and Jonathan: two people from the same year at university dead within weeks of each other.

She tried to work out whether there was any significance, any meaning. Oliver had talked at dinner on Friday night about Jung and meaningful coincidence; she had read a little about Jung herself at a time when she had been interested in dreams. Synchronicity. The collective unconscious. Causal connections. The only link she could establish was that they had all happened since she had met Oliver; but there seemed no reason.

She had had a miserable day at work yesterday, in which her mouth had still hurt and she had been too upset about Meredith to concentrate. She had only cheered up in the evening when she'd finally called Debbie Johnson to update her on the Oliver situation and then Oliver himself had rung to say hello. He'd been very sympathetic about Meredith. Edward had come on the line as well and told her about his day at the zoo, his voice sweet and gentle and excited. She had wished him luck at school, wondering again as she hung up about his silences; about his strange Latin vocabulary of plant and animal names. And about the wasp.

She recalled how Oliver's temper had flared when she had hinted that Edward might have deliberately given her a plum with a wasp in it, aware of the very deep nerve she must have touched. Oliver's reaction still bothered her, the way it bothered her that he had been quick to dismiss calling the police when Captain Kirk had been killed. Was he protecting Edward?

Even so it did not diminish the intensity of her feelings for Oliver; if anything, bizarrely, it made them deeper still. She thought back to past relationships and wondered if she had always felt disquieted by the people she had loved the most. But the comparison was hard; she had never before felt as deeply in love with anyone.

The taxi drove in through the gates of the crematorium, and along the smooth drive through the tended lawns to the squat, red brick chapel.

Frannie paid the driver, then stood for a moment rather awkwardly. There were two hearses outside the chapel, a row of black limousines and a large number of people split into small clusters, each a short distance from the next. It was like a cocktail party at which there were no drinks.

She scanned the faces, uncertain which people were gathered for Meredith's funeral and which for an earlier one. She felt chilly in her black cotton two-piece and wished she had on something warmer; she always forgot how much colder Yorkshire was than London.

The men were in dark suits and several of the women wore hats and veils. A smell of mothballs and perfume mingled with the scent of freshly mown grass. She recognized a face from university, but it was not someone she had ever met. Then she saw Meredith's husband, Paul, working his way through the clusters, shaking hands, his normally ruddy face clenched and drained of colour, and she found herself fighting to keep control of her own grief.

The same gutted feeling in response to the news over the phone, which had remained with her since, was now intensifying. The coffin was visible through the rear window of the hearse, rising out of the sprays and wreaths that surrounded it. Two undertakers in black suits were busily unloading and taking the flowers around the side of the crematorium, where they were laying them out. Beyond, Frannie could see an ornamental fountain and a long wall with inscribed stone tablets, and rows of single rose bushes, each bearing a large perspex tag.

The other hearse was empty, its contents currently behind the closed oak doors of the chapel from which she could hear strains of organ music and the muffled singing of 'Jerusalem'. Already, another hearse was nosing its way in through the gates. It hove to at a respectful distance, like a ship waiting for the tide.

Frannie walked into the garden of remembrance and joined several other mourners in looking at the flowers. She found the spray she had sent and read the tag: *Meredith. Love you and miss you always. Fondest love. Spags.*

Spags had been her nickname at university; Meredith had still called her that, and sometimes Paul. A tear rolled down her cheek, and as she pulled her handkerchief out of her bag she saw someone making their way towards her. Her heart sank a little as she recognized Phoebe Hawkins, one of her fellow Archaeology students from university.

Phoebe Hawkins was a strange, rather lonely girl, who kept her own affairs strictly to herself but at the same time was a source of gossip about everyone else, as if she desperately wanted to belong with the crowd, and believed gossip was the currency with which she could buy her way in. She had an angular, somewhat masculine, face that was neither attractive nor ugly, and which was made more severe by her close-cropped hair and wire-framed granny glasses. She was wearing a matt-black smock and leather sandals, and stood badly, her head stooped forwards, the way Frannie remembered. She looked like a tortoise peering from its shell.

Frannie had always felt a little sorry for Phoebe and had tried to include her in things at university, even though she had never really liked her very much. She had never heard Meredith speak of her since leaving and was surprised to see her here. Yet she remembered how Phoebe had always hated to miss out on bad news. The thought had often struck her when they were students that Phoebe appeared to get pleasure from the misfortunes of others.

She shook Frannie's hand with a deadly seriousness that seemed genuine. 'This is terrible, Frannie,' she said.

'Yes, it is.'

'So how are you?'

'OK, thanks,' Frannie said, looking around to see who else she recognized. 'How about you?' she asked, mechanically.

'I'm fine, really well.'

'Spags! You made it.' Paul stood in front of her suddenly and kissed her on both cheeks, mustering a welcome. 'Really good of you to come all this way. I thought you were going to phone and let me know what train you were on – I'd have picked you up.'

'You had enough to worry about.' She smiled. 'I don't know what to say about Meredith. I'm sorry, I'm just – wiped. How are the kids?'

'I don't think they're old enough to really understand.' He glanced inquisitively at Phoebe, but without recognition. 'How do you do?' he said.

'I'm Phoebe Hawkins – I was at UCL with Meredith.'

'Ah, right,' he said politely, but rather formally. 'Very kind of you to come.' He looked back at Frannie. 'Will you come back to the house afterwards?' He glanced at Phoebe. 'You'd be most welcome also. The undertakers have laid on a couple of limousines – just get straight into one when you come out.' He moved on to a man and a woman who were hovering close by. 'Aileen. Richard. Thanks for coming.'

'Heard you are at the British Museum?' Phoebe said to Frannie.

'Yes.'

'Do you know someone there called Penrose Spode?'

'We share an office,' she said, surprised.

'For heaven's sake!' Phoebe's smile showed a warmth and a vulnerability Frannie had never before noticed, and she was beginning to wonder if perhaps she had misjudged her.

'How – how do you know him?'

'We were on a four-month dig together in Iran the summer I graduated. Bit of a strange fellow.'

'A little. He's all right.' Frannie studied her face for any information it might yield about Spode, hoping for something that she could tease him about, and she wondered suddenly whether anything had happened between them. She glanced at Phoebe's hands, but she wasn't wearing a ring. 'How about you – what are you up to?'

'I was working in Bath – at the Roman Baths Museum. But I've just moved up to London about a month ago to the Natural History Museum.'

'How's it going?'

'It's really good, I'm enjoying it.' She hesitated. 'Dreadful way to die for poor Meredith.'

Above the subdued chatter of the crowd, Frannie

heard the clank of a handle, and the chapel doors opened. Mourners filed past a clergyman who stood in the entrance shaking their hands. She looked back at Phoebe. 'Do you know what happened?'

Phoebe Hawkins hesitated, as if reluctant to part with a good secret, then she looked around as if to ensure she was not being overheard and leaned a little closer to Frannie. Frannie could smell her soap, it had a carbolic, institutional smell about it that was unattractive. Phoebe imparted the details proprietorially, as if she alone had been entrusted with them:

'It was on Friday morning, apparently; she had dropped the boy, Charles, at nursery school, and she was driving to some bric-à-brac auction near Harrogate. She was at a traffic-light; when the lights changed, she pulled out and a car crossing on red hit her broadside.' Phoebe stopped, but signalled with a widening of her eyes that there was more she could tell.

'God, poor Meredith!' Frannie said.

'There'll obviously be quite a lawsuit. And the police are going to prosecute him.'

Won't do Meredith much good, Frannie thought but did not say. She noticed another friend she had not seen for a couple of years, but Phoebe did not want to release her.

'At least she didn't suffer for very long,' Phoebe said, 'but it was a pretty horrific scene, I gather.'

'Suffer for long?'

'The car went up in flames. She was conscious but they couldn't get her out.'

Frannie closed her eyes, feeling sick. 'Oh my God!'

'A total fireball; she was burned beyond recognition.'

When Frannie opened her eyes again she saw the

pallbearers were unloading the coffin from the hearse. Meredith was in that. She stared up at the bland, red brick wall. The vapour trail of a jet lay across the sky.

Burned beyond recognition.

She tried to push the image from her mind but she could not. She saw Meredith driving: her hair a tangle, cigarette between her messily painted lips, leaning forward to turn up the volume on the radio, pop music blaring, then looking up and seeing the light go green, pushing the gear lever forward, accelerating. One moment of horror. Stabbing her foot on the brakes. Squeal of tyres. The bang. Then the flames. Trying to open the door that was stoved in, buckled. Other people pulling at the door, the way they had pulled at the door of the Volvo outside Meston, with the boy's trapped fingers. The flames increasing. Burning alive. Meredith screaming, pulling the door handle, pounding on the window. Just like the driver in the motorway inferno she'd witnessed four years ago.

She prayed not.

She swayed on her legs and swallowed the bile that rose in her throat, shivers raking her skin. 'That's awful,' she said, weakly. 'My God.' She closed her eyes again for a moment, immediately opening them, frightened by the image that came into her mind.

'Terrible.' Phoebe nodded at the cluster of Meredith's family filing in through the door behind the pallbearers. 'Imagine having to go and identify her.'

'Do you keep in touch with any of our lot?' Frannie said, trying to change the subject.

'Sarah Hobday's down in Bath doing a six-month project at the museum. And I bumped into Keith Stanley at a seminar at the Middlesex Poly last year. And of course I've been down to see Susie Verbeeten a couple of times.' She hesitated, then added the rider: 'Poor thing.'

Frannie saw a faint trace of the spiked smile of the old Phoebe; it was like the probe of a mosquito drawing something out of everyone she met, exchanging blood for poison. 'Why do you say that?'

'Oh, you didn't hear?'

Shadows rose inside Frannie. 'Hear what?' She remembered Susie Verbeeten clearly: The organizer, always the organizer, but fun too at times, although she tended to know everything.

'She went blind.'

'Went blind?' Frannie echoed in horror. 'Susie?'

'Yes, I thought you knew?'

'I haven't seen her since I left.' Frannie's brain fogged as a new and undefined fear seeped through her. 'How – do – you – I mean tell me – what happened? Permanently blind?'

'Oh yes, there's no chance, her retinas have been destroyed.'

The clusters were thinning around them as the mourners filed into the chapel. 'But how?' Frannie was aware of the desperation in her voice.

'From a virus she picked up in Malaysia. The pollution in the South China Sea – there's some bacteria the locals are immune to but Westerners aren't. It attacks the retinas.'

'But that's – why isn't – I mean – there's nothing they can do?'

'Nothing at all.' Phoebe glanced around. 'We ought to go in.'

Something stirred deep in Frannie's mind. Faint, only faint; like a hibernating monster not quite roused from its slumber. She followed Phoebe lamely into the chapel and sat beside her on the hard, shiny pew, staring silently at the oak veneer coffin on the catafalque. At the single wreath of white lilies.

Death was a lonely place; and a silent place. In a short while Meredith would be wheeled alone into the furnace. Was that necessary when she was already charred beyond recognition? Frannie pondered. And the door would be shut on her for ever.

And maybe God would take her spirit. Maybe she was already with God. Frannie was not sure. Her faith was at a low ebb. She closed her eyes, unhooked her kneeler and slipped down on to her knees, cupping her face in her hands.

She cried softly throughout the service, whilst Phoebe sat stonily beside her. She barely heard the words of the chaplain; Meredith had never been much of a believer and it did not sound, from the way he spoke, as if the chaplain had ever met her.

Odd thoughts came in and out of her mind. Appearance and reality, suddenly remembered from a school essay. Shakespeare wrote about that. About nothing being what it seemed. Susie Verbeeten had seemed strong, indestructible. Leader of the pack.

Blind.

Meredith had been full of life. Charmed. Always cheery, always lucky. Frannie knelt and prayed again, but as she did so she felt a stiffening sensation spreading through her body and a cold sweat broke out on her skin. She was very frightened now. She had to work it out.

Back outside in the drizzle Paul directed them to one of the undertaker's Daimler limousines. Frannie turned to Phoebe. 'Remember Jonathan Mountjoy?'

'Yes. Have you seen him lately?'

'He was murdered in Washington by a mugger, a few weeks ago.'

Phoebe paled slightly. She seemed reluctant to look at Frannie. The driver held the door and they stepped into the rich leathery smell of the interior and sat down. 'Seriously, Frannie?'

'Yes.'

'A few weeks ago?'

'Early August.' Frannie clasped her hands together for warmth and comfort. 'There seem to be a lot of things happening to our year, don't there, Phoebe? Meredith dead. Jonathan dead. Susie blind. Three things. It's a rather horrible coincidence, isn't it?'

Phoebe shook her head. 'No, I don't think it is coincidence.'

'What do you mean?'

She was quiet for a moment, then she asked the driver if he could drop her at the station as she had to get back to London. 'I'll call you, Frannie.'

'What is it?'

'I can get you at the British Museum?'

'Yes.'

Phoebe changed the subject, chatting as they drove through York with false jollity about old acquaintances, watching the passing scenery with bird-like wariness rather than meeting Frannie's eyes.

She climbed out of the limousine at the station. 'I'll call you tomorrow,' she said. Then she went inside without looking back.

CHAPTER FOURTEEN

'Not unless you wish to buy a chariot, madam,' Penrose Spode said into the telephone receiver.

He had a sticking-plaster on his forehead and the tip of his chin was grazed from having fallen off his bicycle on his way into work. His black hair, as usual, was as flat and smooth as sealskin. He sat stiffly at his desk, opposite Frannie, in a shirt that had the same pasty whiteness as his complexion, a green corduroy jacket and a carefully knotted tie the colour of gravy, holding the telephone a short distance from his ear as if it were a bag of dirty laundry belonging to someone else. 'No,' he articulated frostily. 'No,' he repeated.

Frannie was transcribing her notes of tagged but uncatalogued objects stored down in the basements on to the Museum's computers, and she was having difficulty deciphering her own handwriting. She felt cold and tired and her head ached. The morning rain seemed to have followed her into the Museum and was wrapped around her now like a sodden coat. Chilling her body the way Phoebe Hawkins' strange reaction to the news of Jonathan Mountjoy's death was chilling her thoughts.

The rain had fallen all night and the wind had risen. She had lain alone in bed in her flat and shivered, lapsing from time to time into short periods of troubled sleep

'No, most certainly not,' Spode said.

Frannie clenched her throbbing forehead and typed:

Ram-Dao buffalo sword. Jewel-encrusted hide handle.

Gupta Dynasty bone-handled thruster.
Nepalese iron-bladed kukri with copper-banded
    handle.

'Madam,' Spode said. 'As I have told you, I'm afraid you've been put through to the wrong department. This is Oriental Antiquities. You need to speak to someone in the Roman department.' He covered up the mouthpiece. 'Bonkers, complete nutter.'

Frannie was uncertain whether Spode was addressing her or the room in general. He had been carrying on this way all morning, and she had tried to ignore him, the way she usually did when he was in a tetch. But she was finding it hard to concentrate on her work. She had taken some more aspirin an hour ago, but they seemed to have had little effect. She took another long pull on the can of Coca-Cola that sat on her desk; Coke sometimes worked for her as a hangover cure or when she just felt lousy.

It was ten-thirty. Two and a half hours to lunch. Her will-power broke and she pulled out of her handbag the Twix chocolate biscuit she had bought for her dessert. Spode stared disdainfully as she tore open the wrapping and bit a piece off one bar.

'Yes, madam,' Spode said, 'I *am* well aware of that.'

The cursor on Frannie's VDU blinked patiently, a small orange square on the black screen. There was a moment of quiet, as Spode listened without commenting. Some people walked down the corridor outside. She heard the jovial Irish accent of Declan O'Hare, the Deputy Keeper of Oriental Antiquities, and a guffaw of laughter from whomever he was with. The door opened and she turned round as O'Hare stuck his head into the room.

'Ah, Frannie. Looking so smart today. Must have an important date, could it be?'

She smiled faintly, not in the mood for his jocularity. A man in a goatee beard and anorak hovered behind him.

O'Hare went on. 'Frannie is about to be rescued from the eternal drudgery of the basements. The dawn of a new world is nigh. Might even include Penrose if he's very good. Could you come to my office tomorrow at half nine? We're planning a new exhibition and I'd like you to be involved from the ground up. How far have you got with the cataloguing?'

'Nearly finished.'

'Could you get it done today?'

'I could try.'

'Perhaps you could work late?'

'I have to leave at quarter to seven. I'll work through lunch.'

'That's my girl!' He went out and shut the door, and she felt a beat of interest, pleased to have the possibility of a change from the monotony of her current work.

'Madam,' Spode said again into the receiver, 'I think if you check your history books you'll find that the Iceni were not Romans. And that Boadicea was in fact a woman, not a lost Indian princeling.'

Frannie adjusted the brightness of her screen, turning the glare down a little, and stared at her pad. Then her phone rang and she felt irrational panic that it was Oliver calling to cancel. She had an intense yearning to see him again. To hold him. To be reassured by him. She lifted the receiver. 'Hello?'

'Frannie?'

It was another research assistant, Julian Egon. 'Declan O'Hare said I was going to have to take over the cataloguing in the basements. Can you let me have a note of the ones you've covered – save me some time.'

'Sure. When do you need it?'

'No rush. Next couple of days.'

'I'll do it later today.' She replaced the receiver and stared at her unfinished Twix; the chocolate was making her feel queasy.

Penrose Spode hung up. 'Really!' he said.

Frannie raised her eyebrows.

'Bloody female.' He frowned as Frannie drained her Coke. 'You know how much sugar's in that stuff?'

'Probably why it works,' she said, and began to type in the next entry.

The phone rang again. But it was Carol Bolton, asking her if she would like to join a small crowd who were going to be taken around the excavations beneath a construction site after work, and then go on for a Chinese. She thanked her for the invite but said she was already going out. Carol said she could guess who with, giggled and rang off.

Frannie found her fingers and her brain were hopelessly unco-ordinated and she made constant mistakes. Penrose Spode was in a phoning mood and his icy sarcasm to the operators, librarians and archivists made her cringe. She took a break at eleven, asked Spode if he wanted anything, went along to the machine outside the canteen and bought them each a coffee. When she came back he was off the phone and twitching with indignation at some fresh injustice.

'I gather you know someone I was at university with,' she said as she set the plastic cup down on the barren neatness of his desk, and he warily eyed a drop that was trickling down the side.

'Who's that?'

'Phoebe Hawkins.'

He looked at her suspiciously, as if she had made an unwelcome intrusion into his private life, his expression reminding her of a crow guarding its nest. 'Yes,' he said evasively, 'I vaguely remember her. We were on a dig in Iran.'

'Steamy Arabian nights?'

He bristled in silence as if a reply was beyond dignity and made a pretence of returning to his work for some moments. 'As a matter of fact, no,' he said, suddenly, and Frannie realized that Spode's view of the friendship or relationship had been less happy than Phoebe's. She wondered out of pure curiosity what the relationship really had been. From a comment he had once made, she got the impression he lived with his mother, but he always gave ambiguous answers to her questions. None of her other colleagues knew any more, either. In a year of sharing the office, she had found no chink in the armour around his private life.

'Bit of a coincidence!' she said.

He did not reply.

She ate an egg-and-tomato sandwich in the canteen, swallowed it down with an apple juice, bought another Twix, which she dropped into her handbag, and went straight down to the basement. She had two final cupboards to catalogue and she would have finished this storage room. If she worked fast she might just get it done today, as Declan O'Hare had requested. Although the cataloguing on Indian weaponry would not be complete, Julian Egon would have a clear starting-point when he took over from her.

She hurried down the long, gloomy corridor, deep underground, with its overhead fluorescents, rows of fire extinguishers and numbered storage doors packed with treasures. Some were antiquities that had been brought down for safety during the Blitz and never taken up again. Some were objects for which there was simply no room and which awaited a relevant exhibition. Others were items for which the records had been lost.

She opened the door marked 2(f), switched on the light and went into the windowless, airless room. A three-foot-high red marble gargoyle grinned at her, inches from her face. It squatted on top of a stone coffin, guarding it. Its face was hideous and gave her the creeps. Declan O'Hare had told Frannie with an evil gleam that the coffin had never been opened and carried a curse worse than Tutankhamun's.

Artefacts were piled up to the high, vaulted ceiling all around: shelves of statuettes, death-masks, totems, vizors, helmets. A torture chair with upright nails sat in the gloom of the far corner and she eased her way past it to unlock the door of one of the two cedar-wood cupboards she had not yet touched. To her amazement, the cupboard was empty, except for one damaged and jagged brass sculpture of a tiger surrounded by curiously shaped symbols, right at the back. To make sure there was nothing else, she pulled out the steps, and climbed up. Each of the ten slatted shelves was bare.

She climbed down and put her hand around the figure. As she tightened her grip on it she felt a stab of pain in her finger. For a moment she thought she had been stung by another wasp, then she saw dark red blood welling out of the tiny puncture. She sucked it clean, and bound her handkerchief tightly around her finger.

When she turned the figure round, she saw what had cut her: it was the broken-off point of what looked like a sword. Frannie eased the figure to the front of the shelf, surprised how heavy it was, and looked at the old buff tag tied to it. She opened her notepad, and removed the top of her pen, settling down to the usual routine.

The writing on the tag had been done a long time ago, in ink that had discoloured to a watery brown, but it was still clearly legible: *Damaged brass figure of a tiger found at the siege of Seringapatam, Mysore, 1799. Date: early 18th Cent. AD. Donated to British Museum 1865 by William Halkin, 14th Marquess of Sherfield.*

A smile pushed its way falteringly across her lips, like a crack through ice. She tried to convince herself that there was nothing sinister, that it did not mean anything, tried to push away the creeping doubts that had been stalking her since Meredith's funeral. But she had the sudden eerie sensation that someone was in the room with her, watching her. She turned around. Nothing. She looked back at the tiger, read the label again. Then she heard the unmistakable scrape of a footstep. It came from the far side of the cupboard, near the door.

'Hello?' she called.

There was no reply.

'Hello?' she called louder.

Silence. But the ceiling was watching her. The walls seemed to move in a little towards her; her skin felt unseen fingers drawing it in, pleating it. She fought her panic. There was no one down here to hear her if she shouted. She stepped lightly between the shelves, looking for an object to hold, something heavy; the cupboards were full of weapons, hundreds of them. She moved round towards the door, then stopped, astounded. The red marble gargoyle that guarded the unopened coffin was no longer on the lid. It was standing on the floor beside it. Blocking her path.

A low croaking voice beyond the door said: 'I'm just going out for a stroll. You can come out of the coffin whilst I'm gone if you promise to be good.'

Then her boss appeared in the doorway, grinning imbecilically.

'Declan O'Hare! You bastard!' Frannie said.

He rocked his head from side to side and slid his hands into his blazer pockets. 'I always said this room was spooky, didn't I?'

She pressed her hand over her heart. 'God, you frightened me!' Her relief was tinged with anger. 'That really freaked me!'

He grinned again. 'Fear is one of the spices of life, Frannie. How can you respect the past if you don't fear it? You can't love anything in life without being afraid of it. Did you not know that?'

She wondered if he was becoming unhinged. 'No, I didn't know that; there are a lot of things I love without fearing them.'

He stroked the gargoyle's head as if it were a cat. 'Oh yes? Tell me one?'

'My parents.'

He shook his head. 'No, you only love them because the first thing you learned was to fear them. It's the difference between like and love, Frannie. You can *like* all sorts of things – a pretty view, a nice vase – but you can only love something you respect. And if you respect it, you're afraid of it in some way.' He bent down and with some difficulty lifted the gargoyle back on to the coffin. 'Cesare Lombroso said that the ignorant man always adores what he cannot understand. Do you?'

'What is this? Twenty questions?'

'Tell me, do you?'

'Adore what I can't understand? I don't know. What

are you getting at?' She wondered suddenly if there was some connection between Declan O'Hare and Oliver Halkin of which she was unaware. The wording on the tag she'd just read was giving her ideas. Maybe the Halkins were patrons of the Museum or something. Was Declan trying to warn her off? Put her off Oliver? Ridiculous.

He was wandering through the room with his normal, slightly swaggering walk. In his early forties, passionately in love with his work, he had the smooth good looks of a television presenter. He paused to tap a ferocious mask. 'Know why warriors used to wear these in battle?'

'To frighten their enemies.'

He smiled his television presenter's smile. 'No, Frannie. To hide their fear from their enemies.'

'This isn't a very good day to talk to me about fear, Declan.'

'Oh?' he looked at her quizzically. 'Are you OK? What have you done to your finger?'

'Nothing. Just a prick.'

'You look a little peaky. Ah, of course. I'd forgotten. The funeral. Bad?'

'Yes.'

'The Western way of death always is. But that's another story. So, freedom from fear you want today?'

She nodded.

He stared at a death-mask. 'You're a good girl, Frannie. A good researcher – you have a great future ahead of you. Just don't get blasé about the past, that's all.'

'I didn't think I was.'

He gave a brief shake of his head. 'No, no, I don't think you are.' He ran his hand over a crocodile shield. 'Don't you think it would be wonderful if you could access the past? If you could run a machine over something like this and pick up the energy field of the man who once carried it into battle, find out all about him, his thoughts, his emotions, how he lived?'

'Yes, it would be.'

'That's what antiquities do for me, Frannie. Do they do it for you?'

'You mean you can really read the past in them?'

His expressive blue eyes widened. 'Unfortunately not. I wish I was psychic, then maybe I could. There are people who can. Or so they claim. You should talk to Penrose, he knows about these things.'

'Penrose?' she said, surprised.

He rolled his eyes in a rather sceptical affirmation. 'But I'll tell you what I think: we humans can remember everything that's ever happened to us, everything we've ever seen and done. A lot of it we can't access unless we go under hypnosis. It's there, but it's buried. I believe objects and places remember things too; their atoms, their subatomic particles, whatever, are affected by everything that happens close to them. It must be possible to access them somehow.'

'Is that what you want to do? Find a way how? Invent a machine that can read them?'

'No,' he said with a smile, and walked back to the door. 'No, not at all. I'm just a simple archaeologist who digs around in dust for old bones and pots and garden gnomes.' He departed silently on his rubber-soled shoes and she shook her head, bemused by his typical eccentricity.

'Declan!' she called after him.

He stopped by the door at the end. 'Yes?'

'There's a small bronze in one of the cupboards – eighteenth-century Indian, donated in 1865 by William Halkin, fourteenth Marquess of Sherfield. Is there any family connection with the Museum and that family?'

He looked at the ground, clasped his hands behind his back and frowned. 'I seem to think there's some connection between them and the East India Company. And they were quite big patrons of the arts at one time.'

As she reached him he started walking again, through the door and up the staircase. She kept pace with him.

'Strange lot, the Halkins, mad as hatters, half of them. But so are most of the aristocracy,' he said.

'Why are the Halkins strange?'

'Oh – I can't remember which one of them it was – in the eighteenth century, I think – the eleventh or twelfth Marquess's wife died, but he totally ignored it, carried on as usual, had the servants continue to dress her for dinner and bring her down every night. He dined with her for years after her death. Half the servants left because they couldn't bear the charade.' He held the door at the top of the stairs for her. 'And of course there was the old second Marquess in the seventeenth century up to all sorts of occult tricks. Very involved in numerology.'

'You seem to know a lot about them.'

'No, not really. I'm interested in English history, that's all. They were a significant family, in a minor way. A few MPs and soldiers, that sort of thing. I'm not even sure if the line isn't extinct now.'

'It isn't,' Frannie said.

'Ah,' he said without much interest. 'If you want to know more you could try looking them up in the library.'

'Yes, I was planning to.'

'There's a whole section on genealogy. They're bound to be in it. *Debrett's* would be the place to start.'

When she went back into her office, just before five, Penrose Spode was not there; she glanced up at the back of the door and saw that his crash-helmet and fluorescent strap had gone, indicating he had left for the day. Then she saw the note in his neat handwriting as she sat down: '2.35p.m. Phoebe Hawkins telephoned. Very urgent that you call her back ASAP. She is in a meeting but they will put you through.'

She wondered, as she dialled, whether speaking to Phoebe had prompted Spode's unusually early departure. Whatever the reason, she was quite glad that he wasn't there to listen in.

'Frannie?' Phoebe sounded edgy.

'Sorry, I only just got your message.'

'Look, I can't talk at the moment. Can we meet up this evening?'

'I can't,' Frannie said. 'Impossible. What about lunchtime tomorrow?'

'No good, I have a meeting – could we meet tomorrow evening? Come round to my flat and have supper?'

'Yes – I – I suppose so,' Frannie said, reluctant to commit herself to an evening in case she and Oliver wanted to meet up. 'Where do you live?'

'In Clapham. Thetford Avenue.'

'I know it. You're only a few streets away from me.'

Phoebe did not react to that. 'It's really important, Frannie, I mean it.'

'Don't worry. I'll come. What time?'

'About seven?'

'Sure.'

'It's number thirty-eight. Flat Three.'

Frannie jotted it down.

'Does the number *twenty-six* mean anything to you, Frannie?'

As Frannie thought for a moment, she said, 'Why?' She could hear someone calling Phoebe impatiently.

'Look, I've got to go. Just be careful of that number.'

'Careful? What do you mean?' She heard the impatient shout again.

'See you tomorrow. Seven o'clock.' Then Phoebe hung up.

CHAPTER FIFTEEN

The rain had stopped some time during the afternoon, and the streets were slicked and shiny beneath the dusk sky. It was five to seven. Frannie waited outside the Museum in her mackintosh. The rush-hour traffic had thinned down now, but the fumes still hung heavily over Great Russell Street. There was a sharp toot, and Oliver roared up in his Renault.

As she climbed in the car he apologized for being late, saying he had been stuck in a meeting, then greeted her with a long kiss that left her breathless and flushed. 'You look gorgeous,' he said.

'You don't look too bad yourself.' She liked his soft blue shirt and striped tie that was predominantly orange. She kissed his knuckles, then they stared into each other's eyes as the engine ran busily on. He was looking relaxed and some of the anxiety wrinkles that had stressed his face over the weekend had gone, making his features even clearer and stronger.

'I missed you,' he said.

'Missed you too.' She was aware they were in full view of anyone coming out of the Museum but she did not care.

'Edward go off to school OK?'

'Yes, he seemed very happy.' He raised a finger. 'I had to make one solemn promise. That'd you'd be at Meston on Saturday afternoon when he comes home for the weekend.' He angled his head and smiled. 'Would that be a possibility?'

Her sadness about Meredith and her concern about Phoebe's words were forgotten for a moment. She slid

183

her arms around him, intoxicated by the sheer warmth he was exuding towards her and by her own response to it. 'I think it could be arranged,' she said softly.

'How are the stings?'

'Hurting a little but they're a lot better today.'

Oliver eased out into the traffic. Frannie leaned back in her seat and asked, 'Edward's allowed home every weekend?'

'From lunchtime Saturdays.'

'Did you miss him today?'

'As I took Monday and Tuesday off work, I had to knuckle down today; didn't have too much time to think about him.'

'What did you do at work today?'

'I've been analysing and discussing motor-accident statistics.'

From the speed and aggression of his driving, Frannie concluded that the statistics must have left him unmoved. 'What was that for?'

'The bank's involved in reinsurance for some of the motor-car insurers. We have to make decisions based on statistics.' He was quiet for a moment as he changed lanes, aware of the direction of her thoughts. 'So, how was the funeral?'

'Grim. Her husband's being very brave. I think he's going to feel the shock later.'

'You got back last night?'

'Yes. I had some good news at work today. I'm going to work on a new exhibition, which I'm really pleased about.'

'Great! Well done!'

'Just a bit of luck, I think. And I had a rather interesting coincidence involving your family,' she said hesitantly.

'Oh yes?'

She told him about the brass tiger, but did not mention the cut she had got from it.

'The fourteenth Marquess. William Halkin,' he said thoughtfully. 'He was involved with the East India Company, I think. And with Indian politics. He gave quite a lot of works of art to museums.'

'Actually, when I first saw it I found it a bit eerie. I think your own fear of coincidences is starting to get to me.' She was jerked forward against her seat-belt as he braked hard for a red light.

'How do you mean?'

'You know on the drive back to London we saw that accident?'

He nodded, his expression turning more serious.

'Well, as soon as I got home the phone rang with the terrible news about Meredith. And after what you'd said about coincidences always seeming to mean something, I thought that was quite weird.'

The lights changed and Oliver accelerated more slowly. 'I didn't have very good news either on Sunday night. I didn't mention it on the phone. Charles rang to tell me another six cows have gone down with the virus, and the vet has said we have to stop selling our milk until the herd's clear of it.'

'Are you going to lose a lot of money?'

The traffic was snarled up ahead of them in the Charing Cross Road. Oliver halted behind a taxi that was disgorging some passengers. 'Yes; and our insurance doesn't cover it.'

'Maybe the homeopathy you're going to try will help.'

'Maybe,' he said without conviction.

They drove around Trafalgar Square into Pall Mall, then Oliver slowed, found a parking space, and backed into it. Frannie enjoyed walking along the front of the white Georgian terrace on the Mall, her hand linked with Oliver's, watching the last spangles of daylight through the trees.

At the entrance to the gallery Oliver showed his invitation, and beyond was the refined hubbub of the party in progress. A waitress stood at the top of a short staircase with a tray of drinks. Frannie could smell smoke and perfume, and a tinge of alcohol. She went across to the cloakroom, slipped off her mackintosh and laid it on the counter. An elderly, silver-haired attendant pushed a hanger inside and gave her a plastic disc.

Frannie opened her handbag and dropped the disc in. As she did so, something jolted her. Something about the disc. She dug her hand into her bag, rummaged with her fingers and retrieved the disc. It was number twenty-six.

Sudden goose-pimples prickled her neck as she remembered Phoebe's words; and her scared voice, quite out of character. *Just be careful of that number.*

She saw, to her surprise, Oliver reading the number also and frowning, with a distinct look of unease on his face; or perhaps he was frowning at something else, she wondered, dropping it back into her bag and trying to brush the moment off with a smile. She was going to enjoy herself tonight. She very definitely was not about to get spooked by a cloakroom tag.

The party was a crush of wall-to-wall glamorous women, and tall men in City suits with loud ties or unstructured jackets with T-shirts. In her black cotton jacket, tailored shorts and white T-shirt, Frannie felt fine, although she knew she should perhaps have been dressier. But Oliver seemed to approve, introducing her proudly to friends and acquaintances.

She met an art dealer called James Shenstone who

had been at Trinity College, Dublin with Declan O'Hare, and who regaled her with stories of the mischief O'Hare had got up to. He then introduced her to the artist, whose name she had already forgotten and which she failed to grasp when she heard it again. The artist was small and rather embarrassed-looking, and repeated several times to Frannie that it had not been his idea at all to hold an exhibition. When he learned that she was an archaeologist, he launched into a deep conversation about the relationship between archaeology and anthropology, before being wheeled away, shyly and rather reluctantly, for a photograph.

Frannie was then collared by an immensely boring man with a voice like gears meshing, who proceeded to lecture her for ten minutes about a lawsuit in which he was engaged, and which he assumed she had read of in the newspapers, whilst asking her not a single question about herself.

She was finally rescued by Oliver who put his arm protectively around her. 'Shall we slope off?'

She nodded gratefully, gave the bore a sweet smile and followed Oliver to the entrance. He helped her on with her mac and they stepped outside; it was almost dark. 'Sorry you got stuck with him. Did you enjoy yourself otherwise?'

'It was great. I've got some good ammunition on my boss.'

'Oh yes?'

'That art historian I was introduced to?'

'Jimmy Shenstone.'

'Yes. He was at university with my boss at the Museum. Another coincid –' She stopped in mid-sentence and gave him a guilty smile.

He gave her a hug. 'You are allowed to mention the word; I'm not totally paranoid about it. Only slightly.'

Frannie laughed. 'Race you up!'

She broke free and ran up the steps to Pall Mall, leaping them two at a time, Oliver shadowing her. They stopped at the top, breathless. 'You're crazy!' Oliver said, exhilarated.

But when they got back to the car, his face fell. 'Bugger!'

In the glare of the street light the wording of the paper square on the windscreen was clear:

WARNING. THIS VEHICLE HAS BEEN CLAMPED. DO NOT ATTEMPT TO MOVE IT. Beneath was the large star emblem of the Metropolitan Police.

Oliver insisted they leave the Renault and said he would sort it out in the morning; they took a taxi to his flat in Cadogan Square.

In contrast to the grand elegance of the exterior of the building, the flat was small and furnished almost entirely in modern furniture. There were a few ancestral oil paintings, but most of the decor and pictures were modern also. The place felt snug.

Frannie smiled, but was feeling subdued. Phoebe Hawkins' warning, *Just be careful of that number*, was lodged in her mind like an old tune. She followed Oliver into the tiny, high-tech kitchen, and waited as he removed a bottle of wine from the fridge and a couple of glasses from a cupboard.

'Are you hungry? Would you like an omelette or something?' he asked.

'I'll make it if you like.'

'Don't worry; I'll do it in a minute – let's have a drink first.' He pulled a corkscrew out of a drawer and began opening the bottle.

'Do you think there are different types of coincidence?' she said.

'How do you mean?'

'Can you make a distinction between what's just pure chance, and – I don't know – something supernatural, I suppose?'

He carried a tray through into the drawing-room, and put on a jazz cassette she did not recognize, then sat down beside her on a comfortable sofa. Behind her, through the window, she could hear the muffled sound of the traffic.

'Man has an innate need to try to make sense of things he cannot understand. One of the perverse paradoxes of physics is that there is order in chaos. As I said, I was working with road-accident statistics today. In England in 1986, 5,618 people died in road accidents. In 1987, 5,339. In 1988, 5,230. In 1989, 5,554. In 1990, 5,402. You have the same constancy in the United States only the figures are much higher.' He raised his hands in a despairing gesture. 'How the hell can they be so consistent, year after year?'

She looked at him in amazement. 'You can remember those in your head?'

'Uh huh.' He poured some wine into the glasses and handed her one. 'Cheers. Don't you think it's strange? If you think of all the combinations of bad luck and chance that make up a car crash, you would expect to get peaks and troughs – some years more, some less. But it's almost exactly the same number every year. It's constant for road deaths, for dog bites, for air-travel deaths, for cancer, heart attacks. Everything.'

'So why is that?' Frannie asked.

Oliver drank some wine then looked serious. 'There is a mathematical law of large numbers, but I don't believe that's the answer. I think there has to be something behind how the world works that we don't yet begin to understand.'

'Something supernatural?'

'I think coincidences *are* signals that a greater intelligence or consciousness is at work. But I don't have a firm conviction as to whether it is some supernatural force or entity, some God figure, or something that is simply inside us all – part of our programming.'

The music was soothing her, now. 'So was our meeting part of the chaos or part of the cosmic order?'

'Not necessarily either.' He said the words sharply, almost chidingly.

'Isn't there a theory that we read too much into coincidence? That given infinity everything is possible? That if you sat a monkey at a typewriter it would eventually recreate the entire works of Shakespeare?'

'I don't believe in infinity. Life is finite; neither humans nor monkeys live for ever. It would be far more interesting if playwrights in three different parts of the world, who had never met, all sat down and wrote exactly the same play.'

'I've heard of things like that happening.'

'Yes. They do happen. All sorts of strange things happen that are dismissed as chance. People meet on railway stations and dismiss that as chance.'

Frannie smiled.

Oliver took a small sip of his wine and pondered it for some moments. 'When we met at King's Cross, Edward and I should have been on an earlier train; we only missed it because I remembered I had to make a phone call.'

'Hey! I should have caught an earlier train also. I missed it because I had a phone call just as I was leaving the office.' She watched his face, but could read no reaction.

'We meet three years ago in your parents' café. We meet three years later at a railway station. I place an advertisement in a magazine you don't read, and you see it.' He dipped his head and raised his eyes at her.

'Didn't Jung believe in meaningful coincidence? What did he call it – Synchronicity?'

'He never explained it to his satisfaction. I think he accepted that telepathy had something to do with it.' Oliver traced a finger around the rim of his glass. 'Who was it who said that man doubts everything that can be doubted and hopes what is left over is the truth?'

'I don't know,' she said. 'That's rather beautiful.'

'I think it's a sad indictment.'

'Don't mathematicians tend to be sceptical about coincidences because the odds on things such as meeting someone you know – like at a station or an airport, or someone phoning just as you're thinking about them – are much smaller than we realize?'

'I used to think that once.' His eyes widened and he looked sad, suddenly. 'I used to really hope that was the case.' He cupped his glass in both hands beneath his chin and mustered a weak smile.

'I'm sorry, I'm talking about a sensitive subject.'

'It's OK. It's good to talk about it.'

She reached across and squeezed one of his hands. His skin was like ice. She lifted her hand away with a start and studied him. In his eyes was the same look of fear that she had seen in his car the first time he had taken her out. Then it had been fleeting, so fast she might have imagined it. This time she gripped his hand and squeezed again, alarmed. 'What is it?'

He smiled. 'I'm fine.' He squeezed her hand back. 'I'm fine,' he repeated, then stood up abruptly and walked towards the kitchen.

Chapter Sixteen

Frannie walked down Phoebe Hawkins' street shortly after seven, tired and in a bad mood. Oliver had been given tickets to a royal movie première and had asked her to go with him.

It was a damp night and a light drizzle was falling. She walked with her head bowed, clutching a bottle of Valpolicella in its tissue wrapping from the off-licence.

She itched to see Oliver again, had been missing him all day. He had rung and left a message at the office in the late morning, but she had been tied up almost the whole day with Declan O'Hare and a group of colleagues and had not seen the message until half past six.

Now, instead of being with him, she was plodding through the rain to spend an uncertain evening with someone she did not like, and her doubts were increasing. Phoebe Hawkins was sly; a manipulator who had become unpopular for that reason. At university you'd had to be careful what you told her because it would come back at you weeks later, distorted. An innocent comment about a friend would be turned into an insult and recycled to the person concerned in a quiet, underhand way, as a chance remark. Or a message would be subtly altered. For Phoebe the truth was no more than a raw material waiting to be fashioned. Frannie wondered if that was all Phoebe was up to now. Her old tricks. Making something out of nothing.

If Meredith's death and Jonathan Mountjoy's death and Susie Verbeeten's blindness were nothing.

With every step she took closer to Phoebe's street,

she felt a growing feeling of gloom. A taxi drove past, and she was tempted to hail it, to get it to take her to Leicester Square, to join the crowds outside the cinema and watch for Oliver, see who he was with. The more time she spent with him, the more she enjoyed being with him. After he'd relaxed again last night, they had made love all night through, as tenderly and as forcefully as they had on Saturday.

It had not escaped Penrose Spode's notice that she had arrived for work in the same clothes as the previous day. The shorts were not her usual office togs. He had not commented, of course, not in words; he had conveyed it all with one brief and complex manoeuvre of his facial muscles. Declan O'Hare had also noticed, because he missed nothing, and made a subtle joke connecting the brevity of her attention span to her sartorial consistency, but she had been able to keep him at bay by casually dropping that she had met an old friend of his, James Shenstone, and that he had been reminiscing about their days at Trinity College, Dublin.

She walked slowly past the parked cars that lined both sides of the street. She smelled cooking as she passed an open window, something garlicky, but she was not hungry, did not want to spend the evening drinking Valpolicella and eating nut rissoles, or whatever else Phoebe might cook, in a grotty kitchen.

A strobe flash of blue light skidded down the pavement and she heard the wailing of a siren. Frannie felt something walk over her grave. A gust of wind shook the trees in the street and a solitary leaf shuffled along the pavement.

Two coincidences yesterday: finding the bronze tiger; the number twenty-six. Then Oliver's car getting clamped. Was that a connection? Any more than

Meredith's death had been a connection after the up-turned car? Getting paranoid. She shivered. It seemed bitterly cold suddenly. Winter, not late summer. An old Buddy Holly song blasted from a window across the street. As she turned the corner, she saw ahead of her a jumble of vehicles and the stark white glare of an arc light.

For a second she wondered if there was someone filming, then a solitary blue cube of strobed light hurtled towards her and was gone. A policeman in a luminous yellow waistcoat was standing in the middle of the road, stopping a car. The next cube of blue light turned green on his chest.

In the brilliant white light behind him the first thing she saw was a bicycle wheel. Then the huge shadow of a lorry halted at an angle across the pavement. Its cab had demolished the brick wall of someone's front garden. A small crowd of people stood on the street corner, watching.

'Sorry, sir,' the policeman was saying to the driver of the car. 'Could you use another route?'

The bicycle wheel glinted in the glare of the light mounted on a tripod near it. A gear whined. A man shouted. She saw an ambulance. A fire-engine. A tender. A vast truck with a crane on the back from which a large metal hook was being lowered. Two men were trying to find a purchase beneath the front bumper of the lorry. On the panelled sides of the lorry were emblazoned in large letters: HUNSTONS WHOLE-SALE FRUITERERS. GARDEN-FRESH PRODUCE!

Frannie looked at the bicycle wheel again. It was buckled like the rest of the bike, twisted and broken like some weird modern sculpture in the Tate. *Bicycle on Paving Slab*, she thought, her brain trying to occupy itself, to distract her, to draw her away from the body under the front wheel of the lorry.

Is that lady dead, Daddy?

Edward's words as they had driven up to London on Sunday night came into her mind. Shards of blue light skidded across the wet pavement, across the woman lying in the road. Sparks of orange light followed intermittently from the roof light of the truck with the crane. Puffs of dark diesel smoke drifted across. The woman was in her twenties; Phoebe's build, she thought. About Phoebe's height. She was dressed in a kaftan and Roman sandals.

Frannie's knees collided together. Her stomach was pitching. She did not want to look any more. The woman wasn't moving but she might not be dead, she was not underneath the lorry herself; just had one arm pinned beneath its massive front wheel, as though she were stretching underneath it to reach something.

A shopping bag lay in the gutter beside her. A carton of yoghurt was on its side a short distance from it, its contents spilled on the tarmac; apples, a bunch of bananas; a polythene pack of fresh tagliatelle; a tube of tomato purée. A large shoulder-bag lay in the gutter also, a comb and a notebook beside it.

An ambulanceman walked towards the woman, shining a powerful lamp and taking slow, wary steps on the slick black tarmac as if he were walking on ice. The wheel of the lorry was turned at an angle and in the beam of the light she could see the woman's hand splayed out on the far side, flat, like a dead starfish.

Blood oozed from under the tyre. Her eye caught the word 'Pirelli' embossed close to the rim, and she read it and reread it until it became meaningless. It gave her something to concentrate on, saved her from having to look back at the woman.

Then the beam of the ambulanceman's lamp struck the woman's face. It was turned forwards, eyes closed, trails of blood already congealing.

Frannie's scream got caught in her throat and came out at first as a yammering wail of disbelief as she mouthed Phoebe's name, then ran towards her.

'Stand back, please! Stand well back, please!' a policeman shouted.

Frannie ignored him, knelt and took Phoebe's free hand, her good hand, squeezed it. 'It's OK, Phoebe, it's me,' she said, but the words came out silently, high-pitched, inaudible, like a dog whistle. Something metallic clanged above her. Someone was easing her away. A doom-laden bell clanged deep inside her. She had heard its warning knell before.

'Have to move, please,' a voice said. 'We're lifting now.'

The shadow of the lorry's bumper quivered. Frannie shook helplessly with shock. A voice called out; an engine roared; she heard the rattle of a chain. The wheel lifted a fraction of an inch and then some more, lifted clear, and a shadow swung beneath it.

Frannie could see underneath now; could see that what had once been an arm was now a flattened pulp of flesh indistinguishable from crushed bone, obscenely printed with the zigzag tread pattern of the tyre.

CHAPTER SEVENTEEN

The plastic cup dropped into place: hot black coffee jetted from the nozzle; then frothing milk; there was a sharp clunk and the machine fell silent.

Frannie removed the cup carefully, trying not to slop any over the side, and carried it back to the waiting-room, which had a depressing, lifeless feel, enhanced by the dreary green paint of the walls and the smell of vinyl from the slashed and torn leatherette seat covers.

A trolley clattered past the door. Then silence. After about five minutes a flurry of footsteps came down the corridor and Frannie looked round as the door opened. A nurse whom she recognized from earlier walked in, followed by a tall bear of a man with a tired and rather belligerent expression beneath shaggy eyebrows. He was wearing a grey suit which fitted him sloppily, the top button of his shirt was undone and his tie was loose.

'This is Miss Monsanto,' the nurse said. 'Mr Gower has been operating on your friend.'

When Frannie stood up, the surgeon gestured for her to sit and perched himself on the edge of a chair. 'We haven't been able to contact Phoebe's parents,' he said tersely. 'They'll keep on trying.' He fixed a lengthy stare on Frannie, sizing her up. 'We couldn't save her arm, I'm afraid; the bones were too badly crushed.'

Frannie heard the words one at a time, in slow motion. She felt as if something had been injected into her stomach, numbing it, and the numbness was spreading through her, up her chest, her neck, into her brain. She shook her head in dismay as the words kept on coming, each resonating, made noisier by the buzz of the faulty fluorescent above her.

'We had to amputate above the elbow. But at least she's alive.'

'Yes,' Frannie said, blankly.

'Did you see the accident happen?'

'No – I was –' She suddenly noticed the bottle of Valpolicella on the chair beside her, still wrapped in the off-licence's green tissue. 'Just going round to have supper with her.' She touched the bottle; it felt hard and cold. 'When can I visit her?'

'She'll be conscious enough to talk a bit tomorrow afternoon, but she'll be rather woozy for a day or two from the painkillers.'

Frannie walked out of the front gates of the hospital shortly after half past ten, turning her collar up and bowing her head against the worsening weather.

She was shivering, wanted someone to hold her, to put their arms around her, to tell her that she was going to be all right, that she was silly to be worried, that it was just a series of appalling coincidences, that was all.

She entered the tube station and bought a ticket. Just saying the name of the station seemed oddly comforting.

'Bethnal Green,' the man behind the glass screen repeated, an Indian with a soft voice; he smiled at her, as if the destination was special to him too, a shared secret, the place for everyone in the world who needed help. He pushed her change into the metal dish beneath his glass window and a ticket fluttered from a chute.

A long, empty escalator carried her down to the

platform. Phoebe Hawkins was not ill. But she was never going to get better. Something about that did not make sense; that was the hard part. The arm was never going to grow back. The same way that Meredith was never going to come back. Nor Jonathan Mountjoy. Susie Verbeeten was never going to see again. And young Dominic's right hand would never be the same.

Rain as hard as grit stung Frannie's face as she came out of Bethnal Green Station and hurried along the road. She enjoyed a brief respite under the twin railway bridges, running her hand along the metal railing like she used to as a child, lifting it at each join, her nostrils filled with the familiar unpleasant reek of urine.

She came out into the rain again, passed a used-car lot, a filling-station forecourt, and a grubby parade of take-away cafés and shops. There were few people around. Across the road was the playground of her school. Once, it had seemed so big you could get lost in it, now it was just a small tarmac yard with painted lines and a practice basketball net fixed to a wall; a place where a little girl she could now barely remember had once gone every day except holidays, for twelve years.

A few blocks away, set back from the main road in a backwater of quiet darkness, was the church and priory of Our Lady of Assumption. It was an old, solid church, red brick Gothic, traditional.

Frannie had gone with her parents to mass every Sunday of her childhood. Her faith had begun to dwindle during her mid-teens, but it wasn't until she had left school for university that she had given up going altogether. There was no one thing that had changed her heart, only a gradual build-up of doubts over the years, and a need to search for answers her own way.

An old woman at a bus-stop struggled with a small umbrella. The cinema had 'Kevin Costner' in lights above the porch. The fish-and-chip shop was closed; the Quikburger two doors along was open, with a solitary punter slouched against the counter, reading the menu. The smell of frying onions made Frannie feel queasy. Her thoughts swung around inside her head.

One by one. Chance. Coincidence. Nothing more. Please God, nothing more.

Fear was inside her bones. A bus thundered past; a truck. Her feet were sodden and her right leg ached badly. She removed her right hand from her pocket, slid it inside her mackintosh and up to her neck. Lapsed Catholic Francesca Monsanto pulled on the thin chain around her neck until she could feel the small silver crucifix, and squeezed it lightly. She had put it on this morning for the first time in ages.

It was half past eleven when she rang the bell of the door that was bounded on one side by the dark premises of Sandwich Paradiso and on the other by the dingily lit and smoky office of King Minicabs.

After a few moments a light appeared in the window above the door. She heard the stairs creak and the door juddered, once. A motor cycle caterwauled up the street behind her and a cloud of oily two-stroke fumes drifted over her; her father's voice shouted: 'Yes-sawhoseit?'

'It's me, Papa. Frannie.'

She heard the rattle of a chain; bolts sliding; then the door opened. Her father stared at her in surprise, his face heavy with stubble as it always was in the evenings. He was wearing a ragged towelling dressing-gown over striped pyjamas; his hair was tousled and she suddenly saw how grey it had become, surprised she had not noticed before.

'Francesca! Hey! Why you here so late?' He put his arms around her and they hugged each other, kissing both cheeks in turn, and she held him tightly, the slight, bony man who was no taller than herself. She smelled the wine and tobacco on his breath, the hair oil he still used and the laundered freshness of his pyjamas. She felt the hard bristles of his stubble against her cheek. She wished he could envelop her in his arms the way he had when she was small, wished he still felt like her father and not a stranger.

He released her gently, standing back a little, shaking his head. 'Where you was on Sunday? Why you no phone? We was worried abou' you.' The bones of his face pressed through the sallow skin and his eyes were sunken, as if he had a wasting disease, but it was just the years of working long hours, the lack of exercise and fresh air that had left him with a weary air of defeat; as if he was aware that life was too big for him and he had abandoned trying to match up to it. Instead he lived vicariously through movies, to which he was addicted, spending almost all his free time in front of the television. He looked down at her leg and his face became tender with concern. 'Was happen? You had an accident?'

She glanced down and was surprised to see a rip in the right leg of her jeans. She touched it with her finger and it hurt. 'I – I hadn't noticed.'

'Where you fell?' He touched her cheek lightly with his finger. 'You look terrible.' There was a sudden flash of suspicion in his eyes. 'You had a fight? Boy kick you? Come in.' He pressed against the wall to let her past and closed the door.

She climbed the steep stairs, still clutching the Valpolicella. She heard the television; there were loud voices, shots, an engine roared and tyres squealed. Her mother's voice called out: '*Chi è, Papa?*'

'Francesca. *Ha avuto un incidente!*' he replied urgently.

Tyres squealed again; there were more shots; the sound of a siren. At the top of the stairs her father opened the door to the sitting-room and switched on the light. 'Get you some stuff; bandage; antiseptic. You like coffee? Glass of wine?' There was a faint aroma of fried garlic.

The walls were bare, but the small room with a dining alcove was cluttered by a huge three-piece suite, too many chairs, and by the china ornaments her mother collected.

'Coffee would be nice.' Frannie held out the wine. 'A present,' she said. 'To say sorry for Sunday.' She sat in an armchair and looked at the artificial brick fireplace. On the mantelpiece there were photographs of herself, her sister and her two brothers, as well as a vase of silk orchids, a Capo di Monte tramp on a park bench and a white plastic Virgin Mary statuette. The window faced the busy street; through the net curtains she saw the lights of a lorry that was grinding up the street, then she saw the top deck of a bus slide past, empty apart from one glum-looking man. The car chase continued on the television in her parents' bedroom, down the landing.

'So who kick you, who wasa it? You gotta boyfriend?'

'No one kicked me, Papa. A friend of mine has just had a horrible accident on her bicycle. I must have got cut when I knelt down.'

'*Mamma mia! Povera Francesca!*' Frannie turned,

alarmed by the hysterical high-pitched yell of her mother who ran towards her in her dressing-gown, her hair inside a bath cap and cream on her face. She knelt beside Frannie, gave her a kiss on each cheek. 'Accident? You have accident?' She ran a finger through Frannie's hair, shaking her head in distress, and talking quickly in Italian, barely giving Frannie a chance to reply or explain. She left the room and came back moments later with a towel, a wet flannel, iodine and sticking-plaster, firing questions in Italian at Frannie as she helped her out of her jeans.

Her father came in with coffee on a tray and sweet biscuits, and she suddenly felt weepy at the simple kindness of her parents, feeling as if she did not deserve their pampering. She had no appetite but remembered she had skipped lunch, had had no supper and needed something to give her energy, so she managed a sandwich forced on her by her father.

'You know what?' her father said. 'Saturday I went into the City to see the new building where the café was. And you know something? They don't built it yet.' There was astonishment in his voice; and despair. 'They don't start it! Poulterers' Alley, the café, not demolished yet!'

'Nothing at all, Papa?'

'They is working on the demolishing – but that should have been two years ago. Is another two years we could have stayed there.' He lit a cigarette and she saw her mother's frown of disapproval. 'Is probably archaeologists digging.'

'I have a new boyfriend,' she said, changing the subject, not wanting to rise to his bait.

Her father's eyes widened with interest and he leaned forward further.

'Boyfrenna?' her mother said, her expression also changing. '*Come si chiama?*'

'Oliver,' Frannie said.

'Oliv*i*er!' her mother pronounced, boldly. '*Un bel nome!*'

'Oliver,' her father echoed.

Frannie smiled, feeling faintly embarrassed, wishing she hadn't mentioned it now, afraid that it might be bad luck; they had only been going out for just over a week.

'So what he do, this Oliver?' her father said. 'Archaeologist or he got a real job?'

She shook her head lamely. 'No, he's not an archaeologist; he's a mathematician.'

Her father stared at her sadly. 'Archaeologist; mathematician; what the difference? *Ecco.* You come here in the middle of the night in this state . . .' He drew on his cigarette, pinching it between his finger and thumb, and shook his head despairingly. 'When you gonna grow up, Francesca?' He stroked her hair down over the back of her head. 'When you gonna understand the real world?'

She looked back at him, the distance between them as great as ever.

Her father sighed. There was a long silence, which he finally broke. 'You stay here tonight, OK? I clean your clothes, make them nice and dry for the morning, give you a good breakfast.'

She closed her eyes and nodded, too tired to argue, even to think. A wave of exhaustion overcame her, sapping her. She wanted to sleep.

In the morning, when Frannie woke, her clothes were laid out on the chair in the tiny spare room. It was seven o'clock and the flat was empty. She showered and dressed, then went down to the café beneath. The radio was on, playing schmaltz. Her father was cutting and buttering bread, and her mother was silently mixing tuna and onion.

'Can I do anything?' she said.

Her mother wiped her hands down the front of her apron and kissed her on both cheeks; her mother's skin felt soft and cold.

'You sit, I going to make you nice breakfast,' her father said. 'Get soma food inside you.'

'Thanks,' she smiled and it felt like old times, suddenly. It was a fine morning outside, and the sun shone straight in through the window. A street cleaner drove past and the rush-hour traffic was already building up, heading into London.

She sat on one of the familiar hard chairs at a narrow table, moving the ketchup and bottle of brown sauce out of the way.

'How you sleep?' her father asked, cracking eggs into a bowl. Butter sizzled.

She told him she had slept soundly. Not adding that it was for the first time in several days; deep, dreamless sleep. She felt more refreshed this morning; and hungry.

Her father held up an egg, then looked at her uncertainly. 'But you was a having bad dreams, huh?'

She shook her head. 'No.' She smiled.

'You give your mother and I a big fright.' He tapped the egg gently without breaking it, then looked at her again. 'You talking in your sleep.'

She frowned and a little of the light seemed to fade from the room. 'What did I say?'

He shrugged, broke the egg with one hand and released the contents into the bowl. Then he beat them hard with a fork, before grinding in some black pepper. 'Is mumbo-jumbo. No make sense. Is a foreign language.' Her father looked worried. 'You scared us, your mama and I.'

'What do you mean?'

'Not like you talking. Like someone else is a talking through you.'

She saw the seriousness on both their faces, and felt her skin go clammy.

'Something is no good, Francesca,' he said solemnly. 'Something no good at all.'

CHAPTER EIGHTEEN

'You look very white,' Penrose Spode said across the barren gloss of his desk. 'Are you all right?'

Frannie nodded.

'Late night?' The perfect circle of his mouth stretched into a knowing smile.

'Wasn't like that, Penrose. I'm afraid I didn't get lucky last night.' She still didn't know how well he'd got to know Phoebe, but she wasn't ready to face telling him about the accident.

Her reply caused a rather stranded expression to appear on his face, as if he did not know quite how to take it. He opened his mouth, then closed it again, cancelling whatever further observation he had been contemplating.

As soon as he left his desk to go down the corridor, she looked up the phone number of a florist and ordered some flowers to be sent to Phoebe in hospital, and a note with them, charged to her Access card. Whilst part of her brain did that on autopilot, her active waking consciousness contemplated the coincidence of four people from the same year at university dead or maimed within a short space of time.

She confronted it with clear logic; with rational thought; with the probability theory that had rubbed off from a few conversations with Oliver Halkin. She could also hear her father's worried words echoing through her, but everyone sleep-talked when they were worried; and mostly in gibberish.

Later in the morning Oliver rang to ask how she was, and about her evening. She told him about

Phoebe's accident and he was both horrified and sympathetic. Just as he had been about Meredith's. She asked him how the première had gone. Even when he said it had not been any fun without her, it only lifted her spirits a little.

'Pick you up at half nine tomorrow?'

'Right.' She kept it simple, aware of Spode's ears.

She held the receiver to her ear for several seconds after he had hung up, scared suddenly that it might be the last link between them; that she might never see him again.

Scared of the rest of her life.

Frannie stared at the name of the ward written in grey lettering on a green strip above the double doors: LYTTLETON. She steeled herself.

Hospitals scared her; they always had done: their smells, their sounds. You walked into a hospital and you took a step too close to death for comfort.

She pushed open the door and went over to the nursing station. The ward sister told her that Phoebe was down at the end, around the corner; she said her parents had just left, and asked her not to stay too long as Phoebe was sedated and tired, and should go back to sleep soon.

There was a reek of polish and disinfectant and the bland, lingering smell of mashed potato. A commotion was going on behind the curtains screening one bed. She passed an elderly, almost bald woman whose cheeks were indented, making her mouth look like a belly-button, and a woman in her fifties, knitting busily and holding court to her family.

The ward opened into an L-shape at the end. Phoebe was in the far corner, lying prostrate with a cage over her midriff. There was a window beyond her with blue curtains that had not yet been drawn against the darkness. Frannie felt a lump in her throat. Phoebe was staring at the ceiling, eyes half closed, her face the colour of chewing gum. Headphones hung from a hook above her; the anglepoise lamp was switched off; a bowl of fruit, a vase of flowers and several cards sat on the table.

There was a drip stand beside the bed that was not connected. Phoebe's right hand lay outside the bedclothes; a cannula was taped to the back of it and a yellow plastic bracelet was strapped around her wrist.

Frannie saw flesh coming out of the other sleeve of the hospital gown and for a brief moment thought that Phoebe was all right, that the surgeon, Mr Gower, had been wrong, had been able to save her arm after all.

Then she saw where it ended, a thin little stump with the bandage over the end like an outsize thumbstall. A dwarf, handless arm, like a Thalidomide child's. Slender and pathetic.

Her head suddenly felt hot and a swell of giddiness disorientated her. She looked at Phoebe's face, then at her stump again. For a moment the two became disconnected, belonged to separate people. The stump belonged to someone else. The Phoebe she knew had two arms.

She stepped closer, then stood still again, struggling to keep her composure. She looked harder, just to make sure Phoebe wasn't playing a joke on her the way Declan O'Hare had played a joke on her yesterday, and that the arm wasn't bent back, the way her father used to bend back his pinkie, hold up his hand, show the rest of his fingers and pretend he had bitten the pinkie off.

On Phoebe's forehead there was a small Band-aid and a larger strip on her cheek. Her eyes registered

Frannie's presence impassively. Frannie tried to keep a bright face, knowing that she must be strong, must not let Phoebe think losing an arm was a disaster, mustn't let her think it was any worse than having her tonsils out; needed her to understand that people lost arms and stuff all the time and it was no big deal. No bigger deal than having a cold or missing a bus. Or leaving the fridge door open.

Who the hell needed two arms?

She breathed in hard, stood by the bed and numbly took Phoebe's right hand. There was a faint hint of a squeeze back.

'Hello, Phoebe,' she said.

There was a delay of several seconds before Phoebe responded, in a weak and slurred voice. 'Frnne.'

Frannie sat down on the chair beside the bed and looked at a large humorous card with nurses whizzing across a ward on skateboards. She squeezed Phoebe's hand again. 'You poor thing.'

Phoebe's eyes moved slowly to Frannie's face. The lids closed, then opened again as she struggled against sleep. Frannie again felt a light pressure reciprocated on her hand. She felt she had better not waste time.

'You were going to tell me something last night, Phoebe, that was very important. Can you remember?'

After a few seconds, the girl in the bed gave a single nod. Then there was confusion in her eyes. 'Made me ride out in front of she lorry. Made me shink I could beat she lorry.'

'*Who* made you?'

There was a long silence. Phoebe's eyes closed and Frannie waited, praying they would open again, that she wasn't going to drift into sleep. She looked around, saw that there were no nurses looking, and shook

Phoebe's good arm gently. 'Who made you ride in front of the lorry, Phoebe?'

Phoebe's eyes opened and she looked at Frannie in confusion and surprise. 'Ouija,' she said.

'Ouija?' Frannie repeated.

Phoebe reached out suddenly, tugging feebly, pulling Frannie towards her, pleading with her eyes. Her lips parted. Her eyes were trying to communicate something; she spoke but it was too faint. Frannie leaned further forward, laying her cheek close to Phoebe's own.

'The Ouija. Warn them, Frannie.'

Frannie was confused. 'Ouija? Can you explain? Please.'

Then suddenly she realized what Phoebe was talking about; and a small bomb of fear exploded inside her.

Chapter Nineteen

March 1988

As the dilapidated Volkswagen, crammed with eight other third-year students from London University, pulled into the kerb, Frannie Monsanto slipped her fingers inside her T-shirt and felt comforted by the touch of her crucifix. She knew that what they were doing was wrong. An hour ago it had seemed a great idea, but now the booze was wearing off, and the courage it had given her was replaced with a deepening disquiet, and the knowledge of what had happened the last time she had been down there.

'Just over on the left, past the garbage bags,' she said.

The camper halted with a lurch and the thump of music died with the engine. They piled out and stood on the pavement, an incongruous gaggle with wild hair and beat-up clothes, blinking in the fine rain and the orange sodium twilight of the street lamps as if they had been deposited in an alien land by a spacecraft. Above them on either side rose the dark, silent windows of banks and insurance companies. In the square mile of the City of London, the streets that teemed with people in the daytime were quiet every night; on Saturday they were dead.

A solitary car drove past, its tyres cutting crisply through the puddles, the reflections of its tail-lights following like a ghost across the varnished tarmac. Seb Holland locked the camper's doors. Flecks of drizzle tickled Frannie's cheeks as she led the way around the corner, past the John Templar Employment Bureau

with its cards in the window: SECRETARY FOR MD. SALES
– COMMISSION ONLY. PART-TIME 2-DAY BOOK KPR. SHIP-
PING CLERK. And into a narrow alley that was much
darker. She walked past a barber, a newsagent, a heel
bar and a tailor, then stopped and rummaged in her
bag for her keys. Water seeped through the cork soles
of her canvas shoes.

'Hey, wow!' Seb said. 'This your dad's place?'

Frannie nodded.

'Great!' said someone else.

Above the small shop-window was a row of twelve-
inch-high dayglo letters, two of which were missing:
SANDW CH S LUIGI CAFE.

Four small suction cups held a white plastic menu
against the inside of the window. EAT IN OR TAKE AWAY
was printed along the bottom. A cracked plastic sign
suspended across the window on a thin chain proclaimed: BREAKFAST SPECIAL! Salamis and sausages
hung from butcher's hooks; an ultraviolet fly-trap
above the counter filled the dark interior of the café
with a purple sheen.

Frannie unlocked the front door and went inside,
into the familiar smells of the spiced meats and olive
oil, coffee beans and cleaning fluid. She pressed one of
the light switches; a fluorescent threw a stark pool of
light over the rear of the sandwich bar, emitting a
steady buzz that joined the hum of the fridges.

The shelves inside the glass counter were bare. A
solitary wicker basket containing packets of crisps sat
on top. There was an electronic cash register, a row of
bar stools in front of a formica-topped shelf along the
far wall, and a cluster of tiny tables with banquette
seats and plastic chairs. A creased poster of Naples
and one of Amalfi adorned the back wall. Both posters
were old, their colours faded, their corners uneven,

with bits missing where they had many times in the past torn away from the crude strips of Sellotape that held them up.

The posters were as much a part of the place as her father's cheery greeting to each customer, whether he knew them or not: 'Hi, how y'doin? What y'gonna 'ave today?' Together with her mother's silent concentration, preparing sandwiches, making hot drinks, pushing earthenware bowls of pasta into the microwave. People mistook this silence for sullenness, but it was only that in the twenty-eight years since they had left the backstreets of Naples to come to England in search of prosperity, her mother had never succeeded in mastering enough of the language even to hold the most basic conversation.

A moth fizzed and crackled on the mesh of the fly-trap. The place was old, unchanged since her parents had taken the lease in 1957, and spotlessly clean, the way they left it every evening, Mondays to Fridays, at around six, when they closed. Frannie had spent more time in here as a child than she had at their flat in Bethnal Green. Almost every day of her school holidays she had worked in here, and she still came in and helped during vacations now she was at university, although less than before.

'I'll have a pastrami and dill on rye,' Max Gabriel said, staring across the blank counter, shaking his tousled blond hair away from his eyes.

'Hey, Luigi, one alligator sandwich – and make it snappy!' Seb Holland boomed, towering over the counter, then looking round and grinning. 'Hey, Luigi! Service, hey!'

There was a sharp crackle as the moth's wing burnt and the creature fell to the floor of the trap where it lay twitching among the carcasses of the flies and wasps. Frannie locked the front door. The sign SORRY CLOSED swung gently against the glass, and she made sure it was still facing outwards; she felt a lump in her throat and was not sure whether it was fear or guilt, or the realization that she had made a mistake in having brought all her friends in, in having suggested the place, in having gone along with the idea at all.

The trapdoor to the cellar was in the tiny passage that separated the front of the café from the kitchenette and toilets. As a child Frannie had been fascinated by the cellar and at the same time terrified by it. Paolo, her eldest brother, said the bogeyman lived down there, and Frannie had believed him; it was big enough, and dark enough. The bogeyman could have lived there for ever, scraping water off the damp walls, nibbling at the stores her father kept. The bogeyman stayed out of sight, lurking somewhere in the shadows (watching her, Paolo said) whenever she went down with her father to open one of the crates of cheeses, meats and olives that were regularly delivered from Palermo when she was a child; the bogeyman was afraid of her father. But not of her.

She had seen the bogeyman once: the last time she had been down there.

At least, she had seen his shadow. It was five years ago, maybe longer. They didn't use the cellar any more, hadn't really used it for a good ten years; a wholesaler started stocking all the items her father needed and he found it easier and more profitable to pick up his requirements on a weekly basis than to have goods shipped in bulk from Italy.

'We need some paper,' Susie Verbeeten was saying bossily. Her black hair was cropped short around the sides then spread vertically above her scalp as if it had sprung from a jack-in-the-box. Her mother was supposed to be a white witch, which was how Susie Verbeeten knew about the occult. 'And a thick marker pen.'

Jonathan Mountjoy stood as he usually did with his hands in his pockets, staring vacantly upwards, his brain focused on a different spectrum. Lynn Frickers, small and bird-like, looked nervously at Frannie. 'I'm just wondering whether I ought to get back. I have a lot of reading to get done by Monday.'

Bob Castle, whose face muscles rose and sagged between the fronds of his flimsy ginger beard, nodded. 'Yes, I –' His eyes darted around the room. 'I have to be up early – I think I – ought . . .'

Frannie went into the tiny alcove behind the fridges, to the cabinet where the stationery was kept. 'How much paper?' she called out, and was startled by how edgy her voice sounded.

'We need to make twenty-eight squares about three inches by three inches,' Susie Verbeeten replied.

Frannie took out several sheets, some scissors and a black marker pen. Lynn Frickers, with Bob Castle standing like a faithful dog behind her, was trying to open the front door. Frannie unlocked it and let them both out, then locked it again behind them, secretly wishing she could follow. The back of her scalp felt tight and her throat was dry.

'Dunno why they bothered coming in the first place,' Meredith Minns said. 'They're no bloody use to anybody!'

Frannie tossed her long brown hair away from her face and grinned, the cheery normality of Meredith's voice allaying her fears for a moment. She handed the paper to Susie, then went into the back of the shop, knelt on the old linoleum beside the trapdoor, slid her fingers under the metal hoops and lifted hard. The heavy door came free with a crackling sound, and a cobweb rose up with it. An angry spider scuttled out of sight. Cold, musty air that smelled of damp stone and rotting wood poured out, enveloping her, seeped through her wet clothes into her skin, and she stared at the wooden steps that descended almost vertically, their bottom rungs swallowed by the blackness, with a sudden sickening feeling of dread.

Five years ago she had scrambled, whimpering, up those steps. Chased by the bogeyman. She had been looking for the entrance to a secret passage that was supposed to lead down to the Thames and that had been bricked in centuries ago. Then a shadow had moved behind her, and with it had come a sharp scrape. As she had turned her torch towards it, the bulb had failed.

It might have been her imagination, she knew. Or a tramp or a wino. The cellars interconnected. You could crawl under the arches, working your way beneath half the City of London. This part of London was riddled with secret passages dating back to the Middle Ages and which were used by prisoners escaping from the Tower, by Royalists during the Civil War, by smugglers.

For five years she had wanted to go back down to that cellar and prove to herself that the shadow had been nothing, just a trick of light. Each time she had plucked up courage she had chickened out because there had been no one else to accompany her. But tonight in the downstairs room of the pizzeria they had been fooling around, joking, a little drunk, telling ghost stories and trying to scare each other. So when Seb Holland had suggested a Ouija board session, or maybe it had been Meredith Minns, and Susie Verbeeten had said it needed total darkness, Frannie told them she knew the ideal place.

'Seb, do you have a torch in your van?' she said, remembering now that there was no light in the cellar.

'Yes, I'll get it.'

Meredith Minns wandered over and stood beside her, staring down. 'Yeeech! God, what's down there?'

'Nothing,' Frannie said. 'Empty boxes and stuff.'

'Perfect,' Susie said, peering over her shoulder.

'Looks horrible,' Max said. 'Why don't we do it up here?'

'Because you need somewhere where there isn't anyone else around, and total darkness,' Susie said.

'Why total darkness?' Meredith asked.

'Because, daaahlink,' Seb said, his voice turning Slavic, and running his fingers up her back, 've are going to summon up ze Prince of Darkness. Yee ha hahhh!'

Meredith shivered and grinned. 'Stopppit!'

Seb unlocked the front door and went to get his torch. Susie cut twenty-eight squares of paper, wrote in capitals a single letter of the alphabet on each one in turn and on the final two the single word *Yes* and the single word *No*.

'We need a glass,' Susie said, 'and a flat surface, and a candle.'

'There's probably a crate down there that's suitable, otherwise we can bring down a table,' Frannie said, resting the trapdoor back against its hinges.

Max stared around the café. 'Should think this place is a gold-mine – right in the middle of the City – perfect.'

'The rent's very high,' Frannie said, and thought for a moment about her parents: up at five every morning making the sandwiches; always struggling to pay the bills, struggling to gain a few more years on the lease the landlords wanted to terminate for redevelopment; always dreaming of returning to Naples laden with riches. But the reality was that they would never return, not now. Their family and friends had died, or moved or changed; the past they had left behind them in Italy was as threadbare as the future that lay before them in England. In a couple of years the lease ran out, this time for good, and the whole building would be coming down. Her parents would have to move on, start again elsewhere; tired, ageing people, their hope beaten flat like old metal.

Frannie found a box of candles in the cupboard beside the kitchen sink, took one out, picked up the matches off the gas ring and waited for Seb. He came back in the front door, locked it behind him and gave her a large rubber torch.

She switched it on, flashed the powerful beam down into the darkness and saw the blob of white light slide across the floor. Then, tucking the candle and matches into the back pockets of her jeans, she climbed slowly down the wooden steps, holding the torch with one hand and each step, in turn, tightly with the other.

As she reached the bottom she felt an uncomfortable sense of isolation. Susie Verbeeten's face seemed a long way above her. The cold air bit through her clothes, blew on her skin. She shone the torch out into the bitumen blackness that surrounded her, tried to dispel her unease. Shadows jumped. A steady, echoing ping . . . ping . . . ping rang out as rainwater leaked through from somewhere above.

Columns stretched out into the distance either side of her and behind her: squat stone columns and ribbed arches that had been built to shore up the cellars after the spreading waters of the Thames had eaten away some of the foundations centuries ago. Far thicker than they probably needed to be, they dated from a time long before engineering stresses and tolerances had been understood. The walls were brick, damp and crumbling, and it was rumoured that victims of the Plague were cemented in behind them.

She played the beam around, but could see nothing she didn't recognize. Several empty cardboard boxes listed badly, their bases eaten by the damp that came up through the floor. Then she swung the beam away with a shudder as she realized it was shining on a decomposing rat.

'OK?' Susie called down, and her voice echoed. *Ok-ayyy?*

'Yup, fine!' she called back. *Yup-ine-ine-ine*, her voice echoed; then she guided each of them down the steps with the torch.

'Spoooooky!' Seb said, shoving his hands into his pockets and looking around.

'Perfect,' Susie said; then looked dubiously upwards. 'I think we ought to shut the trapdoor. We don't want any light at all.'

Seb climbed up and reached for the handle. The trapdoor fell with a heavy thud that gave Frannie a sudden claustrophobic feeling.

She guided him back down, then swept the torch over each of her friends' faces in turn for reassurance. They nearly all looked uncomfortable. Even Seb seemed to have lost some of his bravado. Only Susie seemed unconcerned as she selected a wide plywood packing-case with a flat base, placed the glass upturned in the middle, then laid the letters randomly in a surrounding circle, with the words *Yes* and *No* among them. 'Make a circle round the packing-case with things to sit on,' she said.

'Yeek!' Meredith screamed, clutching Jonathan Mountjoy. 'I saw something move.'

Frannie swung the torch and saw a rat or a large mouse disappear behind the arches at the far end.

'Have you got the candle, Frannie?' Susie asked.

Frannie pulled the candle out of her pocket and struck a match. The acrid smell of the sulphur was comforting against the dank mustiness. Susie took the candle, let a few drops of molten wax fall on the packing-case and stood the candle firmly in it, cursing as a drop of hot wax fell on her finger. A barrel scraped across the floor as Jonathan Mountjoy moved it. Frannie turned her head, startled by the sound, the memory of the shadow and the scrape returning. Then everyone sat down.

'Torch off, please, Frannie,' Susie said.

Frannie switched it off. The darkness seemed to jump in towards them, the weak, oval, yellow glow of candlelight barely keeping it at bay. A small pool of shadow rocked around the base of the candle as the flame guttered. A cold draught blew like a breath across Frannie's neck. She could smell the hot wax and the fainter smell of the spent match. The drip of rainwater out in the darkness still pinged steadily. The flame guttered again, more so, and Frannie felt the downy, invisible hairs on her arms stiffen. Her cotton 'Free Nelson Mandela' T-shirt clung to her like a wet towel.

Three sharp raps rang out, startling her. Then a ghostly voice boomed: 'Is anyone there?'

Meredith giggled.

Three raps again.

'Seb,' Susie said sharply.

'Yeeh-hahh-hahhh!' he replied, his voice low and resonating.

Fingers crawled up Frannie's neck and she jumped. 'Seb – for God's sake!' Then she grinned, momentarily relieved of the oppressive tension she felt. Maybe this was the best thing, just joke, fool around, don't get too serious.

'I can feel the spirits,' Seb said. 'I can feel them all over me.' He wriggled.

'Seb,' Max said quietly, 'I think we should all calm down now and be serious.'

Meredith Minns was smiling uncertainly. In the weak light, the pasty whiteness of her skin against her brilliant red lipstick and her gelled black hair presented a ghostly appearance. Susie Verbeeten stared imperiously around.

'Hey, darlings, I'm just wondering whether I should really stay,' Meredith said, tossing her head theatrically. 'I have to get some reading done – I have another exam on Monday.'

'You can't possibly leave now!' Susie said. 'We need at least six to create enough energy to summon the spirit. And someone to control it.'

Meredith chewed the inside of her cheek.

'Right,' Susie said, 'everyone put one finger on the glass. Very lightly, don't push. It's really important you don't push.'

Frannie could read the name 'Helix' stamped in the base of the glass as she reached out tentatively, touching other hands that were jostling for space, then rested her index finger on the glass. It was vibrating, jerking in different directions.

'Stop pushing it,' Susie said. 'You're all pushing it!'

The glass became still.

'Now close your eyes, everyone.'

Frannie stared out into the darkness beyond the glow of the candle, then down at the fingers on the glass. She closed her eyes.

They sat in silence for some moments. Frannie could feel the pressure on the glass.

'Is there a spirit here?' Susie said, quietly. 'If there is a spirit who has joined us will you answer us by moving the glass.'

There was a low rumbling in the distance. It grew louder. Louder still. Frannie could feel the glass twitching. The rumbling increased, echoing around the cellar, rising to a crescendo din.

'Jesus!' Jonathan said.

'Tube,' Frannie said, her eyes shut. 'Just a tube train – Central Line.'

'Bloody good, Susie,' Seb said. 'You've managed to call up the spirit of a tube train.'

Meredith giggled. The rumble faded.

'Could you get us a cross-Channel ferry next?' Seb said.

Meredith giggled again.

'How about a Boeing 747,' Max said.

'Quiet,' Susie hissed angrily. 'Concentrate!'

The glass jigged.

'There *is* something here. Something is in here with us. I can feel it.' Susie raised her voice. 'Is there a spirit with us? Is there a spirit here who wants to talk to us?'

Frannie swallowed; the silence of the cellar magnified every sound. She could hear the boomf-boomf-boomf of her heart, the blood coursing through her veins like the roar of distant traffic, the gurgling as she swallowed again. The cellar became sharply colder, as if the door to a freezer had been opened. She stiffened. She could sense the change, as if there was something or someone else in here with them now. It was standing behind her, passing a magnet or a sheet of cellophane a few inches over her skin, drawing up the hairs, its icy breath blowing through her bones as if she were transparent. She kept her eyes tightly shut, clenched the lids together, too frightened to see.

'A spirit has joined us,' Susie Verbeeten announced.

Icy claws raked Frannie's skin. She wanted to stop now, she was too afraid to go on any more.

'We have a spirit with us,' Susie said, louder. 'Do you want to talk to us?'

The glass jerked sharply with a loud scrape, several inches to the right, and then stopped.

'*Yes,*' Susie said, her voice rising in pitch with excitement. 'It says *yes*!' Her voice regained its imperiousness. 'Who are you? Please tell us your name.'

Frannie felt the glass move again. It skidded across the surface of the packing-case and stopped abruptly.

'The letter N,' Susie said.

The glass moved again. 'Don't push it, just let it move, let the spirit move it. O,' she said, her voice tight with concentration.

It moved again.

'N.'

'*Non,*' Jonathan Mountjoy said. 'French for *no.*'

The glass moved again. 'O – M – N – I – S,' Susie spelled out.

'*Omnis,*' Max Gabriel said.

'It's Latin,' Seb said. 'You've got hold of a Roman centurion. Hi there, Polonius!'

Meredith giggled.

The glass moved again, startling them all. 'M – O – R – I – A – R,' Susie spelt. '*Non omnis moriar.*'

'*Non omnis moriar,*' Max Gabriel echoed.

'Who can remember their Latin?' Susie said.

'Me – I can,' Frannie croaked. Her throat was now so dry that she was barely able to speak.

'What does it mean?'

'It's a quote from Horace,' she said, her voice barely louder than a whisper.

'*Doris* did you say?' said Seb.

Meredith giggled again, a forced, nervous sound this time.

'Horace,' Frannie repeated quietly. Her arm was trembling. '*Non omnis moriar*. It means: I shall not altogether die.'

CHAPTER TWENTY

September 1991

The tube doors opened and Frannie looked up with a start, snapping out of her thoughts. Clapham South. She scrambled to her feet and just made it out of the doors before they closed again, then stood on the platform, remembering.

Oliver's family motto. *Non omnis moriar.*

Tension coiled through her. Another coincidence. Unless her memory was wrong. The train slid out of the station behind her, accelerating with a fierce whine. A gust of grimy underground wind curled around her, then followed the tail of the train into the tunnel.

Altering the past to make it fit. The mind did that; the mind played tricks constantly. She thought back hard as the escalator carried her upwards. Three years ago – longer – three and a half years ago; it had been near the end of the spring term in her last year at university and they had been out celebrating someone's birthday in the basement of the cheap pizzeria they used to frequent.

It was Susie Verbeeten who had suggested the Ouija session. Susie Verbeeten who had run it. Bossy Susie, far bossier than Phoebe. Susie had claimed her mother was a white witch, and that was how she knew about doing the Ouija properly.

But Susie was now blind.

As Frannie hurried back to her flat she wondered how she could get hold of her. She knew that her mother lived in Sussex, remembered Susie telling her it was the village where Virginia Woolf had once lived. Rodmell! She remembered that, although she wasn't sure why. The number should be easy to get, Verbeeten wasn't a common name.

She picked two days' worth of post from the hall floor: bills, mostly, and a birthday card with Italian stamps and a Naples postmark, from her aunt, who every year sent her a card that unfailingly defeated the Italian postal system and arrived early. Then she went into the living-room and dialled Directory Enquiries, doodling on the back of a telephone bill envelope as she waited.

NON OMNIS MORIAR, she wrote in capitals, then scrawled down the number and dialled it immediately.

The phone was answered by a woman with a small, high-pitched voice that had a hint of a smoker's gravelliness about it: 'I'll just get her for you. Who's calling, please?'

'Frannie Monsanto. We were at university together.'

She heard the sound of the receiver being lifted. Then Susie greeted her with a warm and cheery 'Spags! How are you?!'

Frannie was taken aback. It was as if they hadn't spoken for a couple of days; not for over three years. 'Fine, I'm fine.'

'What are you up to?'

Frannie told her. Susie seemed genuinely interested to know about her work, to know exactly what she had been doing since university, with whom she had kept in touch.

'I wondered if you are going to be down in Sussex over the weekend?' Frannie said.

'Yes, I'm here all the time.'

'Are you anywhere near a village called Meston, outside Lewes?'

'Yes, why?'

'That's where I'll be this weekend.'

'For heaven's sake, Frannie! That's about four miles away! Come over and see us – have a drink or a meal.'

'Love to. When would be best?'

'Any time at all – I've got no plans.'

Frannie hesitated. 'Susie – do you remember that Ouija session we once had underneath my parents' café?'

'Funny you should mention that.'

'Why?'

'Phoebe Hawkins asked me the same thing.'

'Recently?'

'Yes. She rang me on Tuesday evening and told me she had just been to Meredith's funeral. That's when she asked about the Ouija. She asked if I could remember who had been there.'

Frannie was silent. It did not sound as if she had heard about Phoebe's accident. 'Can you?'

'I always used to keep a diary; I would probably have written the names down in it. It's rather difficult looking through things like that in my –' her voice tailed.

'Perhaps I could give you a hand? I think I can remember but I need to make sure.'

'What is it, Frannie? What's up?'

Frannie didn't want to talk about it on the telephone. 'Can you think about it overnight? I know it was some time ago. See what you could find, or remember?'

'Yes,' Susie said uneasily, 'I'll do my best. Do you think there's something –?'

'I don't know. I think it's just coincidence.'

'I've always thought that.'

'Oh?'

'I've always remembered the message the Ouija gave me.'

'What was it?'

'It was just one word, that was all. *Dark.*'

The traffic heading south out of London crawled forwards then stopped again. Oliver braked and put the Range Rover's gear into neutral. It was a blustery day: fat, overripe clouds wallowed in the blue sky; trees bent in the wind; leaves and empty cartons scudded down the pavements.

Oliver was wearing a thin blue jumper over a rugger shirt, and blue jeans; his hair was untidy and he looked tired. Frannie wondered if he was all right, as they sat in silence, each preoccupied with their own worries.

Phoebe Hawkins. Phoebe had gone straight back from the funeral and phoned Susie Verbeeten to ask her who had been at the Ouija session. Then she had rung to warn Frannie of the number twenty-six. Why? She thought about the cloakroom tag at the art gallery on Wednesday night, then Oliver getting clamped. Ridiculous. Then she thought about her birthday next week and felt a prickle of unease. Her twenty-sixth. What did Phoebe know?

Non omnis moriar. The harder she thought back, the more uncertain she became. She could remember being scared, blocking her ears at some point, not wanting to hear the message that came through for her. More than scared; she could remember being terrified.

The Ouija had given each of them a message, but she could not remember what they were. She had never known what her own was, had asked them not to tell her. She knew that sometimes, if you were told something bad, you could end up turning it into a self-fulfilling prophecy.

Dark. Could Susie Verbeeten have willed herself to go blind?

Oliver took her hand suddenly, and kissed it. 'I never apologized to you for getting angry at you on Sunday. I'm sorry.'

She shook her head. 'It was my fault. I was in such pain I wasn't thinking straight. I didn't mean to accuse Edward. I just –'

They joined the motorway; the traffic was lighter and moving more freely now. Oliver accelerated hard, moving over into the fast lane. 'I should have explained to you about him earlier.' He ran his right hand through his hair, then lowered his window a fraction. There was a sharp hiss of air. 'He has a behavioural problem; what the shrinks call a disturbed child. I don't know whether it's his mother's death or whether it's me.'

'You?'

He talked quietly, keeping his eyes on the road ahead and she had to listen hard to hear him.

'I never had much of a relationship with my parents. I was sent to boarding-school from the time I was seven and I was brought up by staff in the holidays. My brother and I had nannies until we were quite old; and Mrs Beakbane. I was never able to relate to my mother or father. So I don't find it easy to be close to Edward. After what happened to his mother, I knew that he was going to need me to be there for him, but I'm not sure I've ever succeeded.'

'You seem to have a really good relationship with each other,' she said, feeling sad for him. Sad for his son. 'I haven't seen that much of you together –' She stopped, as she remembered when she had met them at King's Cross: Edward's tantrum and Oliver's helplessness. And then her mind went back further to the morning the woman was decapitated in Poultry. The father and son coming into the café: the son's tantrum.

'Only since I've met you,' Oliver said. He slowed down, his mind wandering from his driving, and moved back into the nearside lane. The traffic they had just passed began to overtake them. 'You seem to work wonders with him. That time I met you at King's Cross, he had been vile the whole journey; he was good as gold the rest of the day. Last Saturday he was great; and Sunday, except –'

'Except when I accused him of giving me the plum deliberately. God, I'm sorry!'

He took his left hand from the wheel and patted her thigh. 'Listen, he might have done it.'

'No,' she said. 'It was an accident.' She looked at him. 'There's no reason on earth why he should have wanted to hurt me, is there?'

I hope you're not planning to sleep with my daddy.

'No,' he said with a weary smile that contained no conviction, and placed his left hand back on the wheel.

She experienced the familiar feeling that he was holding something back. 'When you say he's "disturbed", what do you mean? The strange silences he lapses into, and the Latin he starts speaking?'

'It's a whole raft of things. He's very disruptive at school – some of the other boys are quite wary of him. I've had a couple of warnings from the headmaster that they might not be able to keep him there.'

'Disruptive?'

'Things like refusing to attend the chapel, which they're meant to do every morning. How do you convince him God loves him when he knows that God took away his mother?' He looked at Frannie and she had no reply. 'Gets into a lot of fights with other children. And the worst thing was last term when he set fire to a wastebin.'

Frannie stifled a grin, guiltily, her heart going out to

Edward. 'Bloody nearly burned the school down,' Oliver said.

'Has he seen anyone?'

'Shrinks?'

'Yes.'

'I've done the rounds. Behavioural psychologists; psychiatrists. Been to the best people. He's sweet as pie with them. Angelic; they end up getting nowhere with him. I've tried a homeopath; dietary changes; drugs.' He shrugged. 'So far you're the only thing that's worked.'

'I'm very flattered.'

He took her hand and squeezed it, then drove on in silence for a while. She saw a police car sitting on a motorway bridge ahead, but Oliver was driving below the limit. A jumbo jet came alarmingly close and flew low across the motorway in front of them, landing at Gatwick, filling the air with the screams of its engines.

She stroked his hand. 'With your fear of coincidence, what do you make of my finding the tiger in the cupboard at the Museum?' She detected a faint tremor in his hand.

'I don't know,' he said.

'It's odd, isn't it? It's almost as if there's something that's drawing us together, bit by bit. One connection after another.'

'Yes,' he said tersely.

The road slid beneath them. The Range Rover's grimy bonnet vibrated a little; a large fly exploded on the windscreen in a smear of blood; its wings continued flapping as if they were trying desperately to fly off without the body.

Oliver drove on for a couple of miles in silence, then indicated left and they turned off the motorway at an earlier junction than last weekend. 'Edward's school,' he said by way of explanation.

A short distance on, he braked and turned into a driveway between brick pillars and over a cattle-grid, past a large sign saying STOWELL PARK PREPARATORY SCHOOL. As they drove up a long avenue of poplars and beech, Oliver's face came slowly back to life, like a creature awakening from hibernation; as if he was filled with yearning at the prospect of seeing Edward again, and Frannie was touched; it was the first time she had really felt the intensity of Oliver's love for his son.

'If there's anything I can do to help with Edward in any way, do tell me. I'll gladly do it.'

'You are helping,' he said. 'Just by being around. It'll be a real surprise for him that you've come with me to collect him.'

There was farmland beyond the trees on both sides; sheep were grazing and the soft hills of the Downs lay beyond. Frannie compared the idyllic setting with her own old school yard in Bethnal Green, and wondered how she would have viewed life if she had been here instead. Yet she felt no resentment; that was life's lottery. She also wondered how she would have viewed life if she had seen her mother decapitated when she was five.

It was warm in the car and she wound her window down a little. 'Rodmell's quite close to you, isn't it?'

'Yes, just down the road.'

'There's an old student friend of mine who lives there. I'd like to pop over and see her some time today or tomorrow. The poor girl's gone blind.'

'Christ. What happened?'

'I'm not exactly sure. I gather it was some virus she picked up in the Far East.'

'You're not having much luck with your friends,' he said grimly.

She did not reply.

'Why don't you go over this morning? I have to go and look at some machinery with Charles in the afternoon and I was hoping you might keep an eye on the boys for a couple of hours. I can run you over and pick you up, or you can take the car, if you like.'

'Sure, if you don't need it; thanks.'

'Mrs Beakbane would normally look after them but she's going to a wedding or something. You don't mind?'

'No, not at all.' And she didn't. She had got over her feeling of being a surrogate nanny and looked forward to spending some time with Edward and gaining his confidence.

'Tristram can be a bit of a monkey sometimes; and Edward rather encourages him.'

A squat Victorian baroque pile came into view. Oliver slowed for a sleeping policeman and the Range Rover bumped over it. Two boys pedalled down on bicycles towards them.

'A lot of children can be pretty mischievous,' she said. 'Maybe Edward gets blamed for more than his fair share.'

Oliver said nothing.

Her eyes rested on the signet ring on his wedding finger. She could just make out the wyverns on the crest.

Non omnis moriar. She swallowed.

Chapter Twenty-one

Frannie steered the Range Rover through the narrow wooden posts of the gates, craning her neck as she tried to gauge the width of the vehicle. She pressed the accelerator and the engine bellowed; the tyres munched the balding gravel drive and her wing mirror slid past the post with a centimetre to spare.

There was a ramshackle farmhouse fifty yards ahead, looking as if it had recently weathered a trip around the world lashed to the deck of a ship. A tired Volvo station-wagon sat in the yard, sagging on its suspension, its sills shot with rust, a faded yellow *Nuclear Power – No Thanks!* sticker visible through the grime on the rear window.

She pulled the handbrake on with difficulty, and switched off the engine. Then she unbuckled her seat-belt slowly, in no hurry to get out now that she had found the house. She felt anxious about meeting Susie, worried about how blindness might have changed her.

As she climbed down, she heard hens clucking and smelled the stench of pigs. A strong gust scattered her hair and she pushed several strands away from her eyes. A combine harvester droned through a large cornfield behind the house. Harvest. Autumn was coming. If she lived that long.

High above her the mid-morning sun glinted like a mirror but gave her no warmth. She walked up to the house, glancing through the double doors of a barn across the yard. Inside she could see a canvas on an easel; a window had been cut into the far wall, opening a view out on to the fields.

Bits of gravel stuck in the tread of her trainers and clicked as she stepped on the porch tiles. She pressed the doorbell but heard nothing ring and wondered if it worked. She waited a moment, then lifted the rusty iron knocker and rapped loudly.

The door was opened by a woman in her late forties wearing a grubby artist's smock and plastic flip-flops. Her hair was a bush of brown and grey wire. She wore no make-up and although ravaged by pock-marks from childhood acne she had a doll-like prettiness about her, spoiled by yellow and black nicotine-stained teeth as she smiled. A lump of rock crystal hung from a leather thong around her neck and there was a heavy charm-bracelet on her wrist. She held a cigarette in one hand and knelt, brushing two cats away from the door with the other. 'Hello, Frannie?' Frannie recognized the voice immediately from the phone last night, like a little girl's, with the faintest hint of a smoker's rasp.

'Yes! Mrs Verbeeten?'

'So sweet of you to come. Susie's thrilled.' She stepped back and waved the cats away again with paint-covered hands. 'Tonga, Biba, my little honeys, shoo, out of the way for Frannie, go on, dears!'

Frannie stepped into a shabby hallway that smelled of cats and joss-sticks. A moth-eaten Aztec rug hung on the wall in front of her, and dusty-looking ethnic rugs were scattered on the floor. A huge tapestry filled the wall on her right and it took a moment for her to notice the five-pointed star motif that was its main design. A pentagram, she thought. Pentacle. A floorboard creaked above them and they both turned. Susie was coming down the stairs, confidently, as if she could see perfectly well.

She was wearing a blouse, cotton skirt and leather

slippers, and clutching a small blue book in her hand. She looked exactly the same as when Frannie had last seen her three years ago. The upright, angular figure, the slender, handsome face harshened by her hairstyle, which was also the same: shorn at the sides and sticking up like a topiaried hedge on top. Only the way she stared past Frannie with a rather vacant expression gave her blindness away. And Frannie noticed that she had made a mistake buttoning her blouse; it was one out in the sequence.

'Spags!' Her greeting was cheery but carried a hint of uncertainty.

'Hi, Susie!' Frannie tried to sound natural, as if nothing was different, but it came out all wrong, sounded as if she was greeting an imbecile. She reached out and took Susie's right hand, then put her free arm around her and hugged her, clumsily. Susie hugged her back warmly and they kissed on each cheek. Frannie smelled the raw, astringent smell of underarm perspiration. Susie was nervous of this meeting also.

She released her hand, and was surprised when Susie suddenly touched her on the arms, patted her ribs, then lifted her hands up and felt her hair.

'Slim as ever,' Susie said. 'And your hair's still long.'

Frannie relaxed for an instant from the tension. 'You're looking great, you know? Really pretty.'

In the silence that followed she wondered if she had said the wrong thing. She watched Susie's eyes uncomfortably; for a brief moment they seemed almost to focus on her, then they moved away.

'Would you like a drink? Some tea, or coffee?' Susie asked.

'Love some coffee.'

'I'm going back to the studio, darling. Call me if you want anything.' Mrs Verbeeten looked at Frannie, giving her a stare she could not read. 'So nice to meet you. Susie's talked so much about you over the years.'

'And you too,' Frannie said, thrown by the stare.

'You're very welcome to stay for lunch, if you like. It'll just be a salad.'

'Thank you, but I have to get back.'

Susie led the way through into the kitchen which was old-fashioned and grimy. A cat slunk out. 'God, I don't know what happens to time, Frannie. I've been meaning to call you. I did try a couple of times but you were away on digs.'

'I would have called you too, but I thought you were out in the Far East.'

'So tell me about you,' Susie said. She put the book down on the wooden table in the middle of the room, and Frannie saw that it was an old diary. She watched Susie open cupboards, remove coffee, mugs, and open the fridge. She did everything slowly, methodically, setting things down carefully. She shook the kettle, switched it on, unscrewed the jar of coffee, then felt below the worktop for the drawer with the spoons.

'Do you have a boyfriend?' Susie asked.

Frannie hesitated. 'Yes.'

'Great!' Susie said with a warmth that surprised her. 'What does he do? You're at the British Museum, you said? Is he an archaeologist?'

'No – he's a –' Frannie wasn't quite sure how to describe Oliver. 'Mathematician. A statistician.'

The kettle started to boil. Susie pulled a gadget from behind it that looked like a radio pager, with one short and one long wire. She clipped it to the side of the mug, the wires dangling in, and poured from the kettle. As the water reached the top of the first mug, a sharp electronic beep rang out. She clipped the gadget to the second mug and filled that.

'That's clever,' Frannie said.

'There's tons of tricks,' Susie said with a trace of bitterness. 'I've got a machine I'm learning on that can read printed books – scans the words and converts them into Braille. In six months' time I'm getting a guide-dog – I have to go on a training course.'

'Is there any chance of getting your sight back?'

'Milk?'

'Just black, thanks.'

'No chance at all,' Susie said with finality, as if she did not even want to discuss it. She poured some milk into her mug, then set the bottle dangerously close to the edge of the worktop, turned away, picked a tray off a shelf behind and put the two mugs on it, her arm passing inches from the bottle. Alarmed, Frannie reached across and moved the bottle.

'Sugar?'

'No, I don't take it, thanks.'

To her horror, she saw Susie reaching towards the back of the worktop, her hand sweeping towards the sugar bowl. She had put the milk bottle right in her path.

She lunged forward, but it was too late. Susie's hand struck the bottle, sending it flying like a skittle. It spun across the surface, spewing out milk, striking one mug, sending it smashing to the floor. Scalding coffee exploded in all directions, lashing Frannie's jeans and burning her legs, splashing over Susie's legs and over her cotton skirt, spraying the units.

Frannie grabbed a tea towel, ran it under the cold tap, and pressed it against Susie's legs, apologizing frantically, explaining that it was her fault.

'Afraid I'm not much good at clearing things up,' Susie said.

Frannie steered her away to the other side of the

kitchen, and Susie told her where to find the squeegee and mop and bucket.

'I'm so sorry,' Frannie said, feeling very small, making herself another cup of coffee after she'd mopped up.

'It's OK. I have to get used to people helping me,' she said ironically.

They went through into the drawing-room. It was dark, with a battered sofa and two armchairs with their backs draped in antimacassars. There were several pictures on the wall, strange, rather disturbing abstracts, which she wondered if Susie's mother had painted. An assortment of stones and crystals were arranged on the mantelpiece, along with some small, rather ugly figurines. A creased pack of tarot cards sat on a lace cloth on a round table.

She waited until Susie had set the tray down and had removed her mug before taking the other, wary of any more mishaps.

'Did you have any thoughts about that Ouija session, Susie?' she asked.

'Mummy found my old diary – damn – I left it in the kitchen.' She jumped up and went out, neatly sidestepping a cat; Frannie watched her agility in amazement. She came back and handed the diary to Frannie. 'Seven of us,' she said. 'You, me, Meredith, Phoebe, Jonathan Mountjoy, Seb Holland and Max Gabriel.'

'That's what I thought,' Frannie said, a band of tension tightening in her. 'And you were given the message *Dark*?'

Susie gave a hollow laugh. 'Yes. We were all given stupid messages.' She hesitated. 'Except Meredith. I'd forgotten until Phoebe rang me.'

'Do you hear much from Phoebe?'

'Not a lot, because I've been out of the country most of the time since university. When her contract ended in Bath she was going to come with me out to China, a few months ago, to join a dig in Szechwan, but then she got the job offer in London. She was lucky. Might have got the same thing as me.'

'It was a *virus*?' Frannie said.

'Yes. I got it on the way, in Malaya. It's from the pollution in the South China Sea. The locals are immune to it, and they like to keep it a secret from tourists. Most people who get it come back with a bad eye infection and are fine after a few days – but if you get it really badly, like I did, it destroys your retinas.'

'I'm sorry I didn't know about it sooner,' Frannie said awkwardly. 'I'd have come to see you.'

'I didn't want to see anybody until recently. I'm not very good company, I'm afraid. I just keep thinking about all the things I'll never be able to do.'

'Medicine and technology are improving all the time.' Frannie said the only thing she could say. 'There might be some real breakthroughs in a year or two's time.'

Susie was silent for a moment. 'Our year from university has done pretty well in the disaster stakes, hasn't it?'

'Is it *us*? Or is it something else?'

'The Ouija?'

'Yes.'

'Is that what you think?'

'It was Phoebe who – I guess – made the connection.'

'Actually, I'm surprised Phoebe hasn't rung me back – she said she might come down this weekend.'

Frannie looked at her. 'You haven't heard?'

Susie stiffened and her voice turned to alarm. 'No?

What?' When Frannie told her about the accident, she seemed dazed by the news. 'I – I ought to go and see her. I'll get Mummy to drive me up. How's she taking it?'

'She was pretty doped up when I saw her last night.'

'She'll go through a lot of emotions. Same as I did. God!' She put her mug down and gripped the edge of the sofa, as if for reassurance.

'Four of the seven who were there have had something happen,' Frannie said. 'That's quite a coincidence.'

Susie thought for some moments before speaking. 'Four?' she echoed, dubiously. 'Have a look in the diary, Frannie. It's around about 24th March.'

Frannie picked up the diary and opened it. The cover was battered and the pages were creased, filled with large, untidy handwriting. There was a page to a day and almost every inch of space was crammed with lists, telephone numbers, reminders heavily underlined. Several pages were missing or partially torn out. She turned to the page with 24th March on it and noticed that the bottom two inches of that, also, were missing. Through the morass of writing she could see, heavily underlined, the word: 'Seance!!!' Packed in beneath it were the names of everyone who had been there. Beneath them, in list form, was written:

> Me – DARK
>
> Phoebe – FRUIT MACHINE
>
> Jonathan – CASH AND CARRY
>
> Max – LOSE WEIGHT
>
> Meredith – DEAD BY 25. CAR CRASH

Frannie looked up with a start. '*Dead by twenty-five.
Car crash*. Meredith?' she said.

'Yes.'

'You wrote this down at the time?'

'Yes. Well – probably a few days later. How old was
Meredith when she died?'

'She'd have been twenty-five in October.'

'Shit,' uttered Susie and then repeated it. 'Shit.'

'That's really freaky,' Frannie said.

She shivered, turned the page, compelled to look for
her own message.

Susie was silent. 'Fruit machine,' she said suddenly.
'That was Phoebe's message.'

Frannie could find nothing relevant on the reverse
page. It looked as if her own and Seb Holland's messages had been on the strip that was torn off the
bottom. She looked back at the list. 'Yes, *fruit
machine*.'

'One-armed bandit,' Susie said.

Frannie didn't react at first; she was hunting again
in case her own entry was written somewhere else.
Then she stopped and stared at Susie, understanding
the gruesome connection. 'You were told *dark*, and
this has happened to you. Jonathan *cash and carry* and
he's shot by a mugger. Phoebe *fruit machine* and she's
lost an arm. It's easy to make them fit. But that
doesn't make them predictions or prophecies, does it?'
She could hear the anxiety in her own voice.

'What does it say for you?' Susie asked.

'Mine and Seb Holland's are missing. Someone's
torn off the bottom of the page. Can you remember
what they were?'

Susie thought for a moment then shook her head.
'No. Too long ago. It was just a lark, I didn't take it seriously.'

'Some lark,' Frannie said.

Susie grimaced.

'You don't remember if I had a number in mine, Susie? The number twenty-six?'

'No, I really can't remember. Is that what you think it was?'

'Phoebe told me to be careful of that number the day before she had her accident.' She shrugged and looked back down at the diary. 'Max Gabriel – *lose weight*,' she read out.

Susie seemed not to react for a few moments, then she said, 'Well, he's doing that all right.'

'What do you mean?'

'I was going out with him – before – what happened. He was working with some loony environmentalists; tried to sabotage a French nuclear power station and ended up getting heavily irradiated. He's in a hospice dying of leukaemia. It's not four out of the seven who were there, Frannie. It's five.'

Frannie looked down at the knuckles of charred wood and the grey ash in the cold grate, and wondered distractedly if they had been there since last winter. The ceiling was low, a grubby cream that was unevenly stained with nicotine. The room felt so gloomy and dark she had to look through the window at the blue sky to convince herself that it was not raining outside.

Her hands opened and shut. Her body felt leaden, as if she had buoyancy tanks inside her that had been ruptured and she was going to sink. The sofa sagged beneath her weight; there was a stone floor beneath the sofa, and earth beneath that. She felt the vastness of the planet and the smallness of the room, and the strength of the pull of gravity drawing her downwards.

'Why's all this happening to us?' she whispered.

Susie began to pull each finger in turn, cracking her

knuckles. Frannie remembered she used to do that at university and it had got on her nerves. 'I'm scared, Susie,' she said. 'I'm really scared.'

She heard birds singing and the distant drone of the combine harvester. She closed her eyes, trying to staunch a flood of tears. 'I'm sorry. You're the one who's had the awful thing happen and I'm sitting here crying.'

'I've done plenty of crying,' Susie said quietly.

'It needn't have happened,' Frannie said. 'Maybe if we'd thought about the things the Ouija said, we could have stopped all these –'

Susie leaned towards her. 'I don't think there's anything anyone could have done that would have made any difference. They're all so vague, so joky, you could interpret them in dozens of ways.'

Frannie hunched her shoulders, closing them in protectively, cocooning herself. 'Not Meredith's.'

'Do you really think if any of us had worked out what they meant we'd have done anything different? If I'd known I was going to go blind, do you think it would have occurred to me not to go swimming in the South China Sea? That Phoebe would have never gone bicycling? It's easy to understand things after they've happened, isn't it?'

Through the window Frannie watched a blackbird on the lawn and envied the creature's innocence, and freedom. She watched it dip its head then look up, and saw a worm writhing from its beak. She had never in her life felt so completely helpless.

She looked at the books crammed round the fireplace: *Astral Projection*; *Paranormal or Normal?*; *The Presence of the Past*. She had never taken much interest in the occult before; now she read the titles hungrily, wondering if there was one amongst them that might have an answer.

'I ought to warn Seb,' she said. 'If he's still all right.'

'Do you know how to get hold of him?'

'Yes. But what do I tell him?'

Susie did not answer.

'How do I stop this, Susie?'

The blind woman lifted her arms helplessly, and the gesture swung Frannie's mood suddenly, to anger.

'Susie,' she said, her voice rising. 'If it is the Ouija that's brought all this on us, and not some other freak explanation, there must be a way of stopping it. You were the one who knew the rules about it, told us all what to do. You said your mother was a white witch.'

'Mummy a witch?' Susie sounded astonished. 'She's not a witch, she's just a bit – I don't know – fey.'

'Why's she got a pentagram on the wall?'

'She's got hundreds of occulty things all over the place. She dabbles in everything that's going, but she's not a witch. God, she can't even do the tarot without looking it all up!'

Frannie retorted in disbelief. 'But you're the one who knew all about the Ouija. You insisted we had to have darkness, which is why we went down into the cellar.'

'Mummy used to do the Ouija here sometimes, that's how I knew.'

'Great,' Frannie said bitterly. 'Just great!'

Susie's voice stayed calm. 'Frannie, it never occurred to me that it was anything other than a game. Do you think I want to be like this? I wake up in the morning sometimes and wish I were dead.' She lowered her head and sank her face into her hands. Then she stood up unsteadily, and walked towards her friend, putting her arms around her. Frannie felt the wetness of her tears.

'I'm sorry, Frannie.'

Frannie squeezed her back, she was crying too.

'Jonathan Mountjoy,' Susie sobbed. 'Seb. Meredith. Max. Phoebe. All such good people.'

'I'm going to beat it,' Frannie said. 'I'm going to put a stop to it, whatever it is. And get your sight back.'

'Nothing's going to get my sight back, but I want you to be OK. I'll help you and Seb any way I can. But I don't know how. Perhaps you should go to a priest?'

'Your mother's done the Ouija before. Has she ever had any problems?'

'She never told me. You could have a word with her, but I don't think she'll be much help.'

They went across the yard into the studio in the barn. The reek of linseed oil and turps reminded Frannie of the picture-restoration room at the Museum. It was surprisingly tidy and airy; there were modern skylights in the roof as well as the window looking on to the fields, and the walls had recently been whitewashed. Canvases hung on display and dozens more were stacked on the floor.

Mrs Verbeeten was working at her easel with her back to them, and did not appear to notice their arrival. Her palette was gripped firmly in one hand and with a fine camel brush in the other she was adding colour to a detail. A cigarette burned in a tin lid crammed with butts on a milking stool. The picture was of a group of hooded people crowded on a rocky promontory below a castle wall.

Frannie looked closely at the couple of portraits on the wall. One was of Susie in her teens; the other of a bearded man behind an untidy desk. Then she looked at one of the landscapes. It was a disturbing work, with a foreboding sky, eerie buildings and a tormented quality which she did not care for, but she was impressed by the technique.

'Do you paint, Frannie?' Mrs Verbeeten spoke loudly without looking round and her voice startled Frannie.

'No.'

'Susie's blindness has taught me to see things in a different way. She can tell people apart by their footsteps. I've learned to do that. I'm learning to paint what the mind sees, not the eyes.'

Frannie fingered through a stack of canvases leaning against the wall, glancing at each one: all expressing the same troubled theme as the landscape she had just looked at on the wall.

'Images,' Mrs Verbeeten said. 'They come to me all the time. From every thought I get an image.'

'They're very good.'

Mrs Verbeeten turned and tilted her head in a childlike way. 'How very sweet of you, Frannie.' She laid her brush down at the edge of the easel, picked up her cigarette and dragged on it.

'Frannie wants some advice about the Ouija, Mummy.'

Mrs Verbeeten studied the end of her cigarette for a moment, then stared right through Frannie. 'The best advice I can give is not to touch it,' she said.

'It's a bit late for that, Mummy!'

'I haven't touched it for years,' the woman said. She inhaled deeply and jetted the smoke out through her nostrils.

'Why's that?' Frannie said, still flicking compulsively through the pictures.

Mrs Verbeeten glanced at her picture as if she was anxious to get back to it. 'There were too many occasions when –' she hesitated. 'When it was just too accurate, and unpleasant. Tarot cards give you a bit of guidance. The beastly Ouija just gives you a *fait accompli*. *You will die in three days' time*, you know? That sort of stuff. And people do.' She crushed out her cigarette in the metal tin, picked up her brush and stroked a vermilion splodge on her palette, signalling the interruption was over.

Chapter Twenty-two

The needle of the speedometer bounced wildly between 60 and 80 m.p.h., and the Range Rover swayed and lurched along the uneven two-lane road as Frannie wrestled with the steering-wheel. She knew she was going too fast, but she kept the accelerator pressed to the floor up a gentle gradient, the engine bellowing gruffly, the needle bouncing higher on the dial, touching the 90 mark. She felt strangely light-headed, enjoying the recklessness, the sense of freedom; pleased to be away from the claustrophobic gloom of Susie Verbeeten's house, pleased to be away from Susie's strange mother. High on adrenaline, she was experiencing a forgotten feeling of confidence.

The tailgate of a truck she was gaining on vanished over the brow ahead. The clock which was sited to the left of the dash in front of the passenger seat, and was hard to read, said 1.10. She had promised Oliver she would be back by one.

The road curved left more sharply than she expected, and the row of trees on the far side of the bend hurtled towards her. She jabbed her foot off the accelerator as the Range Rover heeled over and her shoulder slammed against the door, the tyres yowling beneath her as if they were shedding their treads. They slewed over on to the wrong side. She jerked the wheel hard, too much; the heavy vehicle yawed, snaked, veered left then right, crossed the white line again. A car was coming in the opposite direction, flashing its lights and blaring its horn angrily. She tramped on the brake pedal, her mouth dry. Going to hit it! Going to hit it!

Her throat expelled a gasp of choked air. The car screamed towards her; she could see the horror on the driver's face, could see him wrenching his wheel. Their wings missed by inches. She heard the shriek of his horn like a train passing through a station. She thought her wing mirror was going to go, but that missed too.

Relief pumped through her. She felt clammy with shock. The truck in front was two hundred yards ahead now and there was a long, straight stretch of road. A fresh shot of adrenaline pumped through her. She could get past. She pressed the accelerator back to the floor, indicated, looked in her rear-view mirror. And froze.

Edward was sitting behind her.

A shockwave kicked through her whole body as if the wheel she was holding were electrified, and she swerved wildly. 'Edward,' she mouthed, turning her head round.

The seat was empty. She blinked. A chill blast of air blew down her neck. Something flashed in the corner of her eye. Red. Danger. Amber. Her mouth opened. Her eyes widened, levered by terror.

The lorry had stopped and was indicating right.

Her foot dived for the brake pedal, and she threw her weight forward on to it. The wheels locked, the tyres howled across the dry tarmac; the bonnet snaked right, left. Now the tailgate of the lorry hurtled towards her as if someone had pulled the lever on a zoom lens. She saw its brake lights go off. Its right indicator still flashed. It was starting to turn, moving slowly, crawling.

Faster. Please move. For God's sake faster.

She was locked too, just like the wheels. A passenger. The Range Rover lurched left, jolted hard, and the howl stopped abruptly as the tyres tobogganed across the grass verge. For a moment the vehicle slid in almost complete silence; not even the sound of the engine. It missed a bus shelter, but was hauled in by the hedgerow. Brambles clattered like hail against the windscreen, ripped and tore. The car then dipped forward, tobogganing still, its shocks creaking as it bounced on to the soft earth of a ploughed field. Several rooks took off and a panicked pheasant lumbered into the air. The car bounced again, then slewed round in an arc to the right, as if caught in a giant rut.

When Frannie opened her eyes a red light was shining on the dash in front of her. She hugged herself. And she looked in the mirror again, then turned. Nothing. No Edward in the car. Just the empty rear seat.

Something ticked busily. The engine had stalled, she realized. She opened the door and leaned out, peering behind her. There was a wide, messy hole in the hedge, and she could see the black tarmac of the road beyond. She heard the distant roar of a lorry changing gear, moving away, fading. Then just the ticking of the fuel pump again.

She looked around, feeling slightly foolish now, and pulled the door shut. Water trickled down her wrist. The palms of her hands were wringing wet. She wiped them on her jeans, then turned the ignition key. The car jumped forward and stopped. She pressed the clutch and put the gear into neutral, then tried again. The engine revolved several times without firing. Come on, please! She twisted the key hard over, then pressed the accelerator slowly forwards as the starter motor clattered. Oily blue smoke rafted past the windows. She put the car into first gear, then slowly let out the clutch.

The wheels spun and mud and stones rattled against

the underside. Then the car slid sideways. She stopped. Think. She knew she ought to be able to get out. On a dig she had once been in a Land Rover that had got bogged to its axles in sand. The driver had pulled something on the transmission tunnel and it had got them going. She scanned the carpeted hump and saw a small plastic knob. Faded white lettering on the top said: 'Diff Lock', and there was a plate screwed to the bulkhead in front with instructions. She pulled the lever up then pushed the gear forwards and let out the clutch again.

The Range Rover slewed sideways; she accelerated harder and suddenly they began to crab forward. Turning in a wide arc towards the gap in the hedge, she drove through it and stopped. There were deep brown furrows where the locked wheels had gouged out the grass. The wing mirror had been knocked flat against the door, but that was the least of her worries.

She looked guiltily at the hole in the hedge, then scanned the road once more. No sign of anyone. Oliver might know the farmer who owned it; she'd phone him and pay for the damage. Then she turned her head once more and stared at the empty rear seat. She unbuckled her belt, climbed on her knees on to the seat and peered over into the tailgate area, just to be sure: some jump leads lay on the carpeted floor; a chewed plimsole from the days of Captain Kirk; a can of de-icing spray and part of a chocolate wrapper. No Edward. She sat back down. She had imagined it.

Cracking up.

She edged forwards and pulled out on to the road. Then she began to shake.

CHAPTER TWENTY-THREE

Frannie turned in beneath the wyverns on the gate pillars, past the sign that said MESTON HALL. OPEN TODAY 10 A.M. – 5 P.M. and down through the arch beneath the stable block. The hands of the clock said 1.25.

She slowed as she emerged into the milling visitors, acknowledged a prim smile from a woman member of staff, and parked on the gravel drive along the front of the house.

Then she climbed out and inspected the front of the Range Rover. The tyres and the wheel arches were coated in mud and there were brambles tangled in the bull bar, which she hurriedly removed and dumped on the bonfire tip beyond the formal garden.

As she walked up to the front door of Oliver's wing, a muffled bang rang out in the distance, followed by a roar, then a steady drone. She had heard the same sound last week, she realized: Oliver's aeroplane. Good. She hoped that meant he wasn't back yet.

She closed the oak door behind her with a heavy clunk, still shaken, wondering whether she should tell Oliver about her accident, and fretting about the damage to the hedge.

She called out 'Hello!' but there was no response. Motes of dust drifted silently, and the eye of a dead pheasant glinted from an oil painting on the far wall. She walked through into the kitchen; there was ham salad on the kitchen table and five places laid, together with a note from Mrs Beakbane saying that baked potatoes were in the bottom oven.

She collapsed on to the decrepit sofa, but the rubber bone that rolled on to the floor only reminded her of what Edward had called 'the bad thing'. Her mind went upstairs to the cutting of Jonathan Mountjoy's death in the nursery. Then to the glass showcase with the book written on human skin. The *Maleficarium*, or whatever it was called. She wondered if there was a curse on the family, and whether the violent death of Oliver's wife could be explained by it. And if so, was she next in line for presuming to love him?

Declan O'Hare had told her there were mentions of the Halkins in quite a few books; she had been planning to go to the British Library all week but had not had the time. She now walked back down the corridor and across the hall, through the grand panelled door into Oliver's library-cum-study.

There was a damp chill, as if the room had never been heated, and a strong smell of stale leather and decaying paper. The sky was darkening; through the window she could see heavy grey clouds. She glanced at the sheets of mathematical calculations on the desk and the charts with their hieroglyphics on the wall, then up at the bookshelves, scanning the titles, uncertain where to begin.

Winston Churchill's *History of the Second World War. The Canterbury Tales.* Walter Pater's *History of the Renaissance Studies.* Tomes and tomes of military history, political history, biographies. A whole section on mathematics, and several books on numerology. She hesitated, then went across to the charts on the wall. Numbers; algebraic equations; she noticed the number twenty-six at the core of a ring of concentric circles. But as she leaned forward to look closer, Frannie heard an electronic ting-tack-tang sound, and a shadow fell across the desk. She spun round in alarm and nearly knocked Edward over. He was standing right behind her.

'God, you gave me a fright!'

'I just got four thousand, Frannie.' He showed her the Game Boy's screen. 'Score. On Level Four. Level Four's the hardest. It's my new record,' he said.

'That's very good,' she said, slightly lost.

'What are you doing?'

She blushed. 'I was seeing if I could find any books on your family history.'

He looked at her solemnly. There were dark bags beneath his eyes as if he had not been sleeping well, which she had not noticed before. Or was it just the lighting? 'Can I talk to you for a moment, Frannie?' he said. As he did so, he glanced around, as if checking there was no one else there.

'Of course,' she said, his expression making her feel nervous.

'Can you help me, Frannie?'

'Help you do what?' She smiled at him, because he looked as if he was close to tears. When he said nothing for a while, she wondered if he was lapsing back into one of his silences. Then he spoke again.

'Do you ever have funny thoughts about people, Frannie?'

'How do you mean?'

'Like there's some bad thing inside you that makes you do things you don't want to do?'

She knew this was an important moment and she tried to handle it without fluffing. 'I sometimes think of things I'd like to do which I know I can't.'

'No, I don't mean that. I mean do you have something inside you that makes you want to harm people?' He fixed his warm brown eyes on her, looking scared and vulnerable. 'I have this bad thing, Frannie. I don't want it.'

'What does it do?'

'It makes things happen when I just think about them.'

'What sort of things?'

'Do you remember last Saturday when Dom got his fingers caught in the car door?'

'Yes.'

'I made that happen.'

'But you were with me.'

'I know; but I saw it in my mind first; I wanted it to happen. Except I didn't after it happened.'

Impossible, she thought. It was impossible. Then she remembered the strange, almost suicidal feeling she had had in the Range Rover, as if she were high on a drug, indestructible, could do anything; and how vividly Edward had appeared to her. She squeezed her hands together, then picked at her nails. 'How often has this happened?'

'Sometimes it happens at school. And I got really scared just now, while Daddy was working on his aeroplane engine, because I had this bad thought about you.'

'What was it?' she said, conscious of the chill rippling through her.

Tears began rolling down his cheeks. 'I wanted you to crash the Range Rover,' he said.

She stared at him numbly. 'Why, Edward?'

'I don't know. Sometimes there's a bad part of me that I can't stop.' His eyes widened. 'You can help me, can't you, Frannie?'

'How? Tell me more about it, about this bad thing.'

He said nothing, lapsing into a long silence.

She took a deep breath. 'Did you have it when your mummy was killed?'

His eyes flashed at her, startling her; they had

changed completely, seemed to be burning with venom.

He ran out of the library and the next thing she heard was the slam of a door upstairs.

She was left wondering if she should go up and apologize, calm him; but she felt drained. She sat down and tried to work out what on earth he'd meant. To make some sense. She lowered her face into her hands. All she knew was that Edward had been in the back of the Range Rover; she had seen him clearly.

Willing things to happen? Dom's fingers? The wasps? Captain Kirk? Was it possible? With voodoo it might be, but not with an eight-year-old boy? His mother was decapitated. Why would he will that? Was it the bad thing inside him?

I hope you're not planning to sleep with my daddy.

Was he possessed?

She tried to laugh the idea off but it stuck in her mind. *Possessed*. She barely noticed the sky darkening further as she sat engulfed in her thoughts, looking round unfocusing at the shelves of books and then looking up at the strange mathematical hieroglyphics on the wall, her mind churning, searching for logic.

She tried to tag everything the way she would on a dig, every fragment that might eventually help make an identifiable object, that in turn would build up an image of the site in which it was found, and the people who had put it there. In archaeology tiny fragments were all you needed. They were all she had now. Jonathan Mountjoy. Meredith Minns. Max Gabriel. Phoebe Hawkins. Susie Verbeeten. Edward. Oliver's wife. The boy's fingers. The wasps. Where was the connection? Was Edward possessed? Mad? Or psychic? Telepathic? Reading her mind? That might explain the Range Rover where something had definitely influenced her own behaviour, but not Dom's fingers; or the wasps.

As she had done so many times recently, Frannie thought back to when she had first seen Oliver and Edward. In the café; the boy's tantrum. Then at King's Cross, and the tantrum again. *Can you help me, Frannie?* Something about her that he seemed to trust, to respond to. And at the same time hate?

There were stories about disturbed people having strange powers. Particularly children being psychic; disturbed children caused poltergeists, that was well known. Oliver had said Edward was disturbed. You could hardly see your mother being decapitated and not be.

Especially if you'd made it happen.

Her thoughts were broken by the sound of the front door opening and closing, then Oliver came into the library in grubby overalls, his hands covered in grease and streaks of it on his face. He kissed her lightly on the lips.

'Hi, sorry to be so late.' Then he gave a triumphant smile. 'Got the plane's engine running properly at last!'

She reciprocated the smile. 'Good. I'm looking forward to my first flight.'

'Won't be long.' He looked at his hands. 'Better go and clean myself up. Charles is on his way; he and I are going to skip lunch and shoot straight off – do you mind terribly having lunch with the boys?'

'No, that's fine,' she said, hoping it would be.

'How was your friend in Rodmell?'

'She was OK. Up and down, I guess.'

There was a sharp rap on the front door.

'That's them,' he said and went out. She heard the door open, then Tristram's voice.

'Uncle Oliver!'

'Hello, little brute!' Oliver said.

'Hello, big brute!' the boy replied.

Frannie went out into the hall. Oliver's brother was a little taller than she remembered and more gangly. He was looking very much a farmer in an old shirt, worn-out grey flannel trousers and wellingtons.

'You met Frannie last week,' Oliver said to him.

'Yes,' Charles said. He pushed his fingers shyly through his straw hair, taking a step towards her. 'Hi, nice to see you again.' He gave her hand a rather clumsy shake.

Tristram stared at her silently, his small frame engulfed by a yellow Snoopy T-shirt that was a couple of sizes too big, and pink Bermudas that hung below his knees. She remembered last week his blond hair had been plastered down in an attempt to make him look neat for a party, but no such effort had been made this time; it flopped, unruly, over his forehead and it suited him better. She smiled at him warmly. 'How are you, Tristram?'

He raised his eyebrows quizzically. 'OK.' He shrugged.

She heard the musical ting-tack-tang of the Game Boy again, and saw Edward standing in front of the suit of armour on the half-landing, looking down at them with a distant expression in his eyes, as if he was not registering them. He turned his attention back to his toy and slowly walked down into the hall without taking his eyes off the screen.

'Uncle Charles and I are going in a sec, Edward,' Oliver said. 'You and Tristram are going to have lunch with Frannie.'

Edward continued concentrating on his game and did not acknowledge his father.

'Did you hear, Edward?' Oliver said, irritated.

Edward flapped a hand, equally irritated. 'I'm busy.'

'Aren't you going to say hello to your uncle, or to Tristram?' Edward looked up. 'Hello, Uncle Charles.' Then he looked at his father. 'Can I show Tristram the aeroplane?'

'No, I don't think that's a very good idea.'

His face fell. 'Why not?'

'The engine's been running and it'll still be very hot. We'll go down there when I come back.'

'Promise?'

'As long as we're not too late.'

The ting-tack-tang beat of the Game Boy resumed, and Frannie saw Edward pressing the buttons again, biting his tongue in concentration.

While Oliver went to have a quick wash, Frannie asked his brother how the cattle were. He told her there seemed to be some improvement but it was too early to tell, and explained the homeopathic treatment the vet was giving them.

Oliver came back out, wiping his still grimy hands on his overalls. 'Right,' he said breezily. 'We're off! Think you can handle these monsters, Frannie?'

'OK, you guys, what would you like for pudding?' Frannie said, clearing away the plates.

'Ice-cream and hot choccy sauce!' Edward said. 'Can you make hot choccy sauce, Frannie?'

'If there's some chocolate.'

Tristram whispered in Edward's ear and the two boys burst into giggles.

Frannie found some chocolate and made the sauce. When Edward had finished, leaving a brown-and-white trail around his mouth, he looked up at her and asked if he and Tristram could go out and play.

Frannie tried to engage his eyes, to read behind them, but could see nothing. 'Wait until I've cleared up, and I'll come with you.' She was in charge of him and she felt he needed watching.

He dug his hands into the patch-pockets of his cotton trousers and his forehead furrowed in thought, making him look for an instant like an elder statesman. 'I think we might go and see the horses. If you come with us we could give you a riding lesson.'

'No, not today.'

'It won't be dangerous, Frannie, honestly. We'll just go out in the field. If you ride Sheba she's very gentle.'

'I think your father should be with us if I'm going to have a riding lesson.'

'Daddy's useless with horses; he only knows about aeroplanes. It won't hurt, Frannie. I'll hold her by the reins.'

Tristram was absorbed in scraping his bowl clean. 'I'll hold him too, Frannie,' he said without looking up.

She smiled, not wanting to seem a coward, but equally determined she was not getting on a horse. 'I'll just get ready then we'll go down and have a look at them.'

'Promise?'

'I promise I'll come with you, but I don't promise I'm going to ride.'

'OK.' The boys scrambled off, chattering excitedly.

'Hey! Where are you going?' she called, following them into the hall.

'I want to show Tristram my Game Boy score,' Edward said. 'In my room.'

She returned to the kitchen, glad of a few moments' quiet to try to collect her thoughts. The shakes were coming back in another wave of shock from the accident, and she was deeply disturbed by her visit to Susie Verbeeten. She switched on the kettle to make herself a cup of coffee, stacked the dishwasher and washed the remains of the chocolate from the saucepan.

She blew on her coffee, sipped it, and went out into the hall. The house sounded quiet; the boys were probably engrossed with Edward's game. She went back into the kitchen, wiped the table clean, sat down and glanced through the 'Weekend' section of *The Times*. But she was unable to read more than a short way through any of the articles before her attention wandered.

She finished her coffee, then went up to Edward's room, hoping they might have changed their minds about going down to the horses. As she opened the door she felt the first prick of concern. They were not there. And when she went up to the nursery they were not there either.

Her concern deepening, Frannie ran back downstairs, and out of the front door into the bright sunlight, but there was still no sign of the boys. She glanced at her watch. It was about twenty minutes since they had left the kitchen. There was a muffled bang in the distance. A few moments later she heard another, and she felt a sharp jolt inside her.

Couldn't be.

Then another bang, followed by a blattering roar that died almost instantly.

No.

She was already racing down the gravel path before the noise had faded in her ears.

Faces blurred as she tore along the front of the house. She weaved through a group of visitors moving away from the ticket office and collided with a large man taking a photograph, who was as solid as a sandbag. Her mouth would not work; she apologized with her eyes, holding him at arm's length as if to get her bearings, slipping past him, and sprinted up the road past the chapel, towards the noise. Again, there was an ear-blistering roar, much louder, an angry sound that rasped through the grounds, shattering the peace of the still afternoon.

She cut across the grass, then on to the asphalt path, the route Edward had taken her last Saturday, just a week ago. A week ago when she was unaware that Meredith was dead and that Max Gabriel was dying. When Phoebe Hawkins still had two arms. She prayed silently as she ran.

Please don't let anything bad happen. Please let them be all right.

Past a huge cornfield that was all cut and baled up, she saw the tall, rusting corrugated iron barn ahead of her. There was a bang, a short, fiendish roar that drummed the walls of the barn, then silence. Rafts of oily smoke drifted towards her. Her speed quickened in panic. Then as she hurtled round to the front she saw Edward and Tristram standing on two oil drums in front of the aeroplane, turning the propeller, that was much higher than either of them, with difficulty, having to stretch up and strain hard. Having a great game. Frannie stopped, horrified.

'OK!' Edward yelled, bracing himself.

'OK!' Tristram yelled back, bracing himself also, holding the propeller steady for a moment.

'Edward!' Frannie screamed. 'Edward! Tristram!'

There was a clattering sound as they swung the propeller sharply downwards. Then it began revolving, slowly, on its own, and with a deafening noise the engine burst into life, picking up speed, the blades of the propeller vanishing into a transparent blur. Thick exhaust fumes billowed out. The biplane shook and the barn drummed with the din.

The boys were swaying, fighting to keep their balance in the vortex of suction from the propeller. Edward windmilled his arms desperately, the drum rocking crazily beneath him, pitching him forward; he was beginning to fall towards the propeller.

Frannie was half demented with horror. 'Edward!' she screamed but she could not even hear if her voice had come out. 'Edwa –'

He struggled to get his balance back, grabbed Tristram by the shoulders and they both fell forwards, then rocked back, swayed forwards again. Then, suddenly, the drums pitched over, throwing them both backwards on to the ground. Tristram lay motionless. Edward covered his head with his hands and rolled clear.

Frannie never forgot what happened next. Tristram climbed to his knees, and remained there, dazed, looking directly at her. The plane began to creep forwards towards him. 'Tristr –' she choked on her own terror. Launched herself towards him. Her foot caught in a crack and the hard concrete slammed into her chest.

Winded, she saw movement to her left, someone running, it was just a blob. The blob became a man in his late fifties, wearing a soiled lumberjack shirt. But Tristram stayed on his knees, looking at her and at the approaching man.

The concrete tearing skin from her hands, Frannie powered herself forward to the little boy who was kneeling less than two yards in front of the propeller. She stumbled back to her feet, felt the air sucking at her, 'TRISTRAAAAMMMM!'

By now her T-shirt was ripped from inside her jeans and icy air flailed her bare back; her hair beat her face like knotted string.

A look of guilty panic sheeted over Tristram's face and he stood up, then backed away. Backed towards the propeller that was looming up on him.

'Tristram! It's OK, Tristram!' Frannie called, but her voice was choked and raw, and it came out as a squeak rather than a shout. She stretched forward with her hands, only a few feet away from grabbing him. The propeller closed on the boy like a shadow.

Out of the corner of her eye she could see the man closing also. Then everything slowed as if suddenly there was all the time in the world. She was aware of strange details: the rubber soles of her trainers compacting on the concrete then expanding, springing her into the air, absorbing her weight as she landed again, compacting, expanding, the wind from the propeller lifting the strands of grey hair from the man's head, exposing the bald area beneath; the wind billowing his shirt like a sail.

There was a strange sound that echoed in her head. A *chinnggg* like a lawnmower blade striking a stone. At first she thought Tristram had been hit by a pillow. Thousands of tiny little shreds hung in the air, like feathers. Then they were gone.

He'd disappeared.

The propeller was inches from her own face now, its draught tearing her mouth open, freezing her eyes. She flung herself sideways and the blade scythed over her; the din of the engine drilling out her eardrums, fumes filling her lungs like cotton wool. A wheel struck her in the back and the shadow of the wing passed across her as she lay flattened. Dust, pebbles and grit peppered her face, stinging it like hail.

Slowly, she climbed to her feet. Through blurred eyes she saw Tristram standing near her. He was fine. He was OK! Relief surged through her. Then she realized it wasn't Tristram, it was Edward, with fluff in his hair and spots of blood all over him. He was staring at a pair of Bermudas that had legs sticking out of them at one end, the feet in tiny trainers. Out of the other end protruded ragged flesh, unwinding coils of intestine and a few inches of sharp, white backbone like the shaft of a broken spear. A small lake of blood was slowly spreading out across the concrete and draining into the weed-filled cracks.

Someone was clambering into the cockpit of the plane: the man in the lumberjack shirt, she dimly registered. The roar of the engine ceased suddenly and there was just the shuttering sound of the propeller. Then silence. The plane was no longer moving. The tiny shreds of hair and bone and flesh that hung from the fuselage and wings also lay scattered across the concrete. Later, when she looked in the mirror, she saw that she was covered in them, too.

CHAPTER TWENTY-FOUR

Fragments of the afternoon played themselves back to Frannie at random. Moments; segments of moments; details. She could not focus on any one part of what had happened for more than a few seconds without her brain switching channels.

She stared blankly around the drawing-room, trying to orientate herself. The drawing-room was real time. She was in the drawing-room. Then she was outside on the concrete hard, hurtling herself towards Tristram. Brambles tore at the windscreen of the Range Rover, rattling and shrieking. The roar of the aero-engine drummed through the barn. The Tiger Moth rolled forwards. The propeller came up behind Tristram like a shadow. The Range Rover was returning with Charles and Oliver inside it: the lusty bellow of its engine; the crunch of its tyres on the gravel; the two men emerging, cheery voiced, innocent of what lay ahead, glancing with only mild curiosity at the police car drawn up behind Charles's battered Toyota Landcruiser and the sign that said PRIVATE. NO VISITORS BEYOND THIS POINT. The policeman approaching Charles and Oliver, Frannie beside him. Edward at that moment coming around the side of the building with his Game Boy, and the ting-tack-tang ... ting-tack-tang ... that seemed for a brief instant to be the only sound in the world.

Then the hideous sound Charles had made, a howl of anguish that sounded as if it were drawn from the bowels of the earth.

Now she sat on a sofa, holding a glass in her hand,

in front of an unlit fire. Wind rattled the window-panes. 'My fault, all my fault.' She heard herself speaking as if she were somewhere else, in another room, detached.

There was whisky in the glass: hard, neat Scotch that singed her mouth, burned her stomach. It did not relieve the shock or the pain, but it battened them in another compartment and as long as it did, she would be all right.

The pills helped too, helped to dull everything a little, delay reality by a few more hours. Oliver had given them to her. The doctor had given them to Oliver. The doctor who had made her stings better last weekend, who had come and taken Charles away. Oliver's face seemed to get bigger and smaller. It stretched out sideways then shrank. The doctor had told Oliver she should not drink with the pills.

The channel changed. Tiny scraps clung to the silver fuselage and to the engine cowling. The propeller still spun but the sound had gone mute. Then she was back in the drawing-room again. Bands of tension etched like scratches across her scalp.

'My fault,' she repeated.

Oliver sat beside her. 'No,' he said.

'It is.'

'Kids have to be watched all the time. No one understands that until they have kids of their own. It's not your fault.'

His voice sounded strange as if she were hearing it through glass. She wondered if she had died. Oliver was looking at her oddly. Maybe I was killed by the plane and no one told me. She reached out to touch his hand but closed on air. She tried again, took his wrist, felt the hairs and the firm muscle, pressed her face into his neck, smelled his ears, his shampoo, his skin, held him tightly.

There was a picture of the aeroplane on the mantel-piece, and in the kitchen; there seemed to be pictures of it in every room. Oliver, Edward and Edward's mother standing in front of it, laughing at the camera.

'I should have stayed with them, followed them.'

'I should have padlocked the barn,' he said.

'Where was the ignition key for the plane?'

'It doesn't have a key; just a couple of magneto switches on the dash. It never occurred to me that he – they –' his voice shuttered off, like the propeller, into silence.

Frannie drank some more, held the glass close to her face, inhaling the fumes. Everything was out of kilter, as if new laws of the universe had been written and nobody had told her. The world was now a place where a group of kids could get killed and maimed just by sitting around a table with an upturned glass; where a small boy could kill and maim just by thinking about it. Maybe it was Oliver who had written the new laws? The stuff on the wall in the library. The hieroglyphics. She closed her eyes. Madness was not very far away; just a glass of whisky or a small blue pill separated her from it.

Her own turn was not very far away either. And she did not know what separated her from that.

A crash of breaking glass upstairs startled them both. Oliver jumped up and ran out into the corridor. She followed him into the hall, and up the stairs to the landing where all they could hear was a low moaning sound that Frannie thought at first was the wind.

It was coming from Edward's room. She realized it was not moaning but chanting. Oliver gripped the round brass handle; his knuckles were white. For a moment he remained motionless then he slowly opened the door, pushing hard against the draught of cold air that blasted out at them.

The room was in darkness, the windows were broken. The curtains thrashed, tearing at their rods, the rings sliding and clacking, the fabric hissing. In the midst of it all Edward lay in his bed, asleep on his back, the steady chant coming from his mouth.

'... *murotaccep menoissimer ni rutednuffe sitlum orp te sibov orp iuq iedif muiretsym itnematset inretea te ivon iem siniugnas xilac mine tse cih* ...'

Frannie felt panicked. A toy car rolled along a shelf and fell at her feet. Oliver ushered her back out of the room and closed the door softly.

'What on earth is it?' she whispered. 'What's going on.

He raised a hand, motioning her to stay, strode down to his own room and came back moments later with a small ghetto-blaster. He opened Edward's door a few inches and switched on the red recording light, and the tape revolved with a shuffle. Edward's flat monotone sounded along the passageway: '... *muem suproc mine tse coh. Senmo coh xe etacudnam te, etipicca: snecid, sius silupicsid euqtided, tigerf, tixid eneb, snega saitarg metnetopinmo muus mertap mued et da muleac ni siluco sitavele te saus sunam selibarenev ca satcnas ni menap tipecca ruteretap mauq eidirp iuq* ...'

Oliver closed the door and stopped the tape, then walked back along the corridor to his room, switched on the light, waited for her to come in and closed the door. The room looked neat and orderly, but it felt very cold. The candles in the two iron holders either side of the bed had been replaced. In the bright light the room felt strange. Oliver's face was white and lined, had aged twenty years since the morning. He sat on the edge of the four-poster bed and put the recorder down beside him, then looked at her gravely. 'You didn't recognize that?'

She stayed close to the door, feeling unwelcome.

'What is it? One of the Arabic languages?' She observed the cherubs and nudes painted on the walls; the thick rugs, the shirts on their metal hangers hooked on to the wardrobe door. The row of polished shoes with their wooden trees on the floor. Alien. It was all alien.

'I'll play it backwards,' he said. 'You might find that helps.' He opened the wardrobe, rummaged in the back and pulled out an old reel-to-reel tape recorder. He played back the tape, recording it on to the reel-to-reel, then pressed the machine's reverse play button. Edward's voice immediately sounded clearer.

'. . . *Hic est enim Calix Sanguinis mei, novi et aeterni testamenti: mysterium fidei: qui pro vobis et pro multis effundetur in remissionem peccatorum.*'

She prowled near the door like a caged animal. He watched her with haunted eyes. His worn plimsoles were sunk into the shag rug beside the bed and his head was sunk into his shoulders. She translated, her voice trembling, the words that she knew so well, had memorized since earliest childhood. It had been a long time since she had heard them in Latin.

'For this is the Chalice of my Blood of the new and eternal testament,' she said falteringly, unable to take her eyes from Oliver. 'The mystery of the faith; which shall be shed for you and for the multitude of mankind so that sins may be forgiven.'

He stopped the tape.

'Mass,' she said. 'He's reciting the canon of the mass backwards.' She walked across the room and put her hand on the cold ribbed radiator beneath the window. The ghost of her face stared back from the glass. She turned and faced Oliver. 'Mass isn't – isn't held in Latin – in this country –' She faltered. 'Backwards. I –' She stopped and suddenly thought of the plants he had reeled off in Latin. And the animals.

He spoke in Latin to you? Oliver had said when they were in bed in this room last Saturday, sounding surprised, but not commenting further. The way he had not probed deeply when Edward had started reeling off Latin names in the car on Sunday night going back to London.

'Isn't saying mass backwards something to do with black magic?' she said.

'Yes,' he said stiffly. 'I looked it up after the first time he did it.'

'He's done it before?'

'He's been doing it at school for years. Three and a half years, to be precise,' he said, giving her a strange look.

'And the windows? Did that happen?'

'No.' He was silent for a moment. 'That hasn't happened before. He'll calm down. And in the morning he won't remember anything.'

'Where's it coming from?'

Oliver said nothing.

'The doctors and shrinks you've taken him to – did you tell them about this?'

'I've played them tapes.'

'And what did they say?'

'That it's not uncommon. Apparently, disturbed children often speak strange languages or gibberish in their sleep.'

Frannie felt trapped between the light of the room and the darkness outside, the darkness that pressed against the glass, trying to push through it and to crush her up against the light. She shuddered, her skin absorbing the coldness like blotting-paper.

Oliver stopped the machine, then pulled another tape out of the drawer of his bedside table and slotted it into place. 'Last Saturday when we slept together,

273

Frannie, you began talking in your sleep. It woke me up. I thought you'd stop, but you kept going on, talking complete mumbo-jumbo. I couldn't work out what the hell you were saying. I recorded a bit of it because I thought it might amuse you; then I realized it might embarrass you so I didn't say anything about it.' He stared at the floor, then back at her.

She remembered now, being woken by a click in the middle of the night and wondering what it was.

'Then I suddenly realized on Sunday night when Edward started his chanting that it was the same sound. I knew there had to be a connection – it couldn't be coincidence.' He started the tape.

'*Muem suproc mine tse coh senmo coh xe etacudman te etipicca snecid sius silupicsid euqtided tigerf tixid eneb snega saitarg ibit metnetopinmo muus mertap mued et da mulaec ni siluco sitavele te . . .*'

Frannie listened, transfixed, to the chanting sound of her own voice.

Oliver pressed the stop button. 'I don't know what gave me the idea to play it backwards.' She watched Oliver's finger hover, hunting for the reverse play button, then push down on it, and she listened to her words again, mechanically translating the Latin into English as she did:

'. . . and looking up to Heaven to thee, God, his almighty Father, giving thanks to thee, he blessed the bread, broke it, and gave it to his disciples, saying: Take and eat of this, all of you. For this is my Body –'

Oliver stopped the tape abruptly, leaving the house in silence. She was numb.

'You asked me where it's coming from.' Oliver's face was tight. 'The first time it happened was that night after we had seen you at your parents' café – although we didn't know you then.'

The cold air in the room was now burrowing deep into her veins, into her bones. She felt as cold as dead flesh.

'It's you, Frannie,' he said quietly. 'That's where it's coming from.'

CHAPTER TWENTY-FIVE

Frannie sat in silence whilst Oliver's words sank through her, dissolving like chemicals, paralysing her. As long as she did not believe it, she would be all right. She could cope with what he had said as long as she knew he was making it up.

She stared at the chromium-plated grilles of the speakers at each end of the ghetto-blaster, and the shiny red plastic casing. She wondered, irrelevantly, why he owned such an ugly thing. Perhaps it belonged to Edward. Or to Oliver's late wife. Perhaps Sarah Henrietta Louise Halkin had liked music blaring wherever she went. Perhaps she had played it loudly to keep out the silence of the house that was now closing around Frannie herself and entering into her.

She wondered how long she had been talking in her sleep. A few months? A year? Six years? All her life? A memory released itself, rose, like a bubble detaching itself from the floor of the ocean, to the surface of her mind. Her father yesterday morning.

You scared us, your mama and I . . . Not like you talking . . . Like someone else is a talking through you.

Who else had heard her? The bubble of memory expanded. Tom Dufferin, her last boyfriend, had said she mumbled in her sleep. So had Elliot Dumas before him. And on the dig in Iraq after leaving university, when she had shared a tent with three others, they had commented then that she woke them sometimes with her mumbling. The end of her last year at university. She thought back harder; no one had commented before then; no one at home, where she had shared a

276

bedroom with her kid sister. Maria-Angela would have said something. The many previous occasions when she had shared tents on digs; others would have commented. She had shared a room in her second year at university with Meredith; she had not said anything. The end of her third year was when it had started. From worry about her exams?

Or –? She tried to dismiss the thought, but it persisted. The Ouija. They had done the Ouija at the end of that last year. Only days before the end of term. They had all been so happy that night; most of the term's coursework was over and they were winding down for the breather of the Easter holiday before the onslaught of finals. So innocent then. Unaware of what lay ahead; of the spirit they had attracted, angered, the thing that had come after them, pursued them.

Possessed her.

She looked down at her hands, unable to meet Oliver's gaze. She studied her nails; the tips of the fingers went blue after death; she remembered seeing her grandmother's fingernails in an open coffin in Naples; almost black.

Edward in the library came back to her.

I have this bad thing, Frannie. I don't want it . . . It makes things happen when I just think about them.

Edward influencing people. Surely it was coming from him. She spoke to Oliver. 'Edward said –' she stopped.

He raised his eyebrows, waiting for her to continue. But confusion swirled in her brain, because it might begin with herself, not Edward, in which case it was she who was making Edward will bad things on other people. It couldn't be.

'Why do you say it's coming from me?' she said.

'How do you know that Edward's picking it up from me, and not the other way round?'

'It's inconceivable from pure chance that you would both say mass backwards in your sleep, isn't it?'

She said nothing.

'You told me you'd heard about what Jung called Synchronicity; well, that's what I believe. That one of the explanations for what people call chance is unconscious telepathy between them. Channelling of thoughts.'

She watched him blankly.

'I think that one of you is instigating it, the other picking it up.' He uncrossed his legs, folded his arms and leaned forwards. 'Edward had never done this before he met you.'

You're wrong, she wanted to say. *You're wrong!* But she did not have the conviction.

'It's not you, Frannie, not your conscious self, any more than Edward knows what he's doing when he suddenly drifts off into those silences of his in the daytime. There's something else causing it. You're just the channel for it.'

'For what?'

He stood up and walked across to rest his hands on her shoulders. He squeezed them gently. She felt his warm, whisky-laced breath, saw the shadow of stubble that had begun to form, emphasizing his harrowed expression, his drained complexion. She became aware of the tears that were trickling down her own cheeks, and pressed her face into his chest, nestling against the skin of his neck and the soft wool of his pullover.

'Have you ever done the Ouija?' she asked.

'No.'

'I did, once.'

'What happened?'

Frannie told him everything and he listened carefully, leaning on the window-sill. When she had finished, his first reaction was, 'Have you checked on any of your other fellow students? Ones who weren't at the Ouija session?'

'Why?'

'To make sure you have the right causal connection. You're assuming it's the Ouija session, but it could be something else.' He flexed his toes inside his ancient plimsoles, studied them for a moment then went on. 'If odd things have been happening to other students who weren't at that Ouija session, that would put a different light on things.'

'You mean contact every student who was at London University during the three years I was there?'

'Yes. It wouldn't be impossible.'

'It would in the time,' she said quietly. 'And what would I say?' *Hello, just wondering if you're still alive?*

Oliver was silent for a while, deep in thought again. 'Do you have a tame priest?' he said finally.

'No. Not any more.'

He looked at her with heavy eyes. 'I think we need to find one.'

They made love because they each needed solace, but afterwards Frannie lay in Oliver's bed unable to sleep. The booze had worn off and she was troubled by her thoughts. She started to picture her own funeral, wondered which of her old boyfriends would turn up. Perhaps they'd feel guilty for not having loved her enough. Then she wondered whether she should phone Directory Enquiries to see if there was a Ouija helpline. Like Alcoholics Anonymous.

Beside her, Oliver's breathing deepened: strong, deep intakes of air. Physical strength, all the privileges of his birth and yet he still had his fears. Scared of coincidence.

Twenty-six.

She opened her eyes in a cold sweat. The hieroglyphics on the wall. And the number twenty-six inside the concentric circles! The tragedy with Tristram had knocked her out and because of that she still hadn't asked Oliver about what she'd seen in his own library. Now, suddenly, she couldn't wait.

Oliver moved; the bed clanked as he slipped out, and she heard him pulling something on, then treading carefully across the floor. The click of the door then another click as he closed it quietly behind him. She switched on her bedside light and sat up a little. A lavatory flushed, then Oliver returned.

'Hi,' he said.

She gave him a tired, strained smile, then the words poured out. 'In the library you've got charts on the walls with calculations all over them. What are they?'

He sat on the edge of the bed hunched in his paisley dressing-gown. 'Numerology,' he said simply.

'What is that?'

He yawned. 'Part of it is a theory that numbers provide the clues to understanding – I suppose – the underlying mysteries of the universe.'

'What sort of numbers?' She had to understand.

'All numbers have significance.'

'How are they worked out?'

He remained on the edge of the bed. 'It's a combination of metaphysics and religion. There are numbers in the Bible. Aristotle was very into them. Pythagoras. It all stems from a very logical base. Numbers provide a principle of order in a seemingly chaotic universe.'

'And how do you get the numbers?'

'Do you know what a palimpsest is?'

Frannie reached for her glass of water beside the bed. 'Yes – you get them a lot on parchment used by the old monks. When a text is erased and a new one written over it, you can still read the imprint of the old writing if you look hard enough, or in the right light.'

Oliver nodded. 'Numbers are in everything if you look hard enough. In the atomic molecules of everything we see and touch. In the Bible, there are hundreds of codes, messages. In our names and dates of birth.'

'How did you get interested in this?'

He leaned back against the headboard. 'Part of what mathematics is all about is order; patterns; trying to make sense out of chaos.' He reflected for a moment. 'The universe is chaotic, but our solar system is ordered – we have life on this planet because we happen to be exactly the right distance from the sun, the moon. Just a bit further away from the sun and it would be too cold to exist; a bit closer and it would be too hot. Is that chance? Or design?' He gave her a half smile. 'Human life is chaotic, yet we create ordered society, of a sort. We divide our planet into countries, establish governments, laws, education, codes of behaviour. All from random evolution? Natural selection? Or some greater design?'

She watched him, wondering where it was all leading. The despair in his eyes gave him the look of a man who has stared into the pit of Hell and cannot get the image from his mind. He seemed to be talking to himself, rambling almost, as if in doing so he might stumble across the answer. His bewilderment frightened her; she needed him to be strong. In the darkness beyond the undrawn curtains the stable clock was striking two.

'When Sarah died, for a long time I just couldn't

accept it; and when I finally did, I wanted to die too. I loved her so much, and I couldn't believe that I could ever –' He fell silent and Frannie drank some water. 'It was only Edward who kept me going. I had to be there for him; so I buried myself in work during the week, and I made myself a project down here for the weekends, to give me a focus on something. I was handling the theme of connected coincidence in my work at the bank and I thought it would be interesting to look back through my family to see whether coincidence ran through our history in any way.'

'Do you mean genetically?'

'No, not specifically.'

'Did you find anything?'

'Just one very odd coincidence. About a number.'

'What number?'

'Twenty-six,' he said.

Some water slopped over the rim of Frannie's glass and trickled down between her fingers and thumb.

He studied her, registering her lost composure. 'It's a rather interesting number in numerology. *Two* is a number that has a lot of evil significance. And so does *six*. The combination of the two digits, making twenty-six, is twice thirteen. Thirteen is a two-six number. Two times one is two. Two times three is six.'

'I think you're losing me,' she said.

He pushed some hair from his forehead then traced the contours of his face with his fingers, as if to reassure himself that he was still intact. 'I'm lost half the time as well; there are layers and layers. A sort of multiple palimpsest.'

'Why the number twenty-six though?' she persisted. 'Is there a reason for that particular number?'

'That's what I'm trying to find out. I came up with

one connection that's quite curious, although it doesn't mean anything. I mentioned to you that the second Marquess was into numerology?'

'He was the evil one?'

'Yes. I've discovered he was very keen on this number for some reason – it was sort of his signature, his mark. Except it didn't do him much good in the end. He was executed – murdered, whatever – on 26th March, 1652.'

Frannie smiled weakly.

'Does twenty-six mean anything to you?' he said.

'Yes it – might. Phoebe Hawkins warned me off it just before her accident, but I couldn't get much sense out of her when I saw her later in hospital. She was too shattered. I need to see her again.'

He frowned, returning to his previous line of thought. 'My wife, Sarah, also died on 26th March. And it was her twenty-sixth birthday.'

Frannie absorbed the words in silence. Her mouth felt dry. She looked at Oliver for an explanation, for an assurance which he couldn't give. Fear rose up her spine then spread like cold water across the base of her scalp. She bit her lip before she spoke again, tried to affect a normal tone of voice and failed.

'It's my twenty-sixth birthday next week,' she said. 'On the twenty-sixth.'

CHAPTER TWENTY-SIX

In the morning, Frannie left Oliver's room for her own shortly before six. At breakfast, they were all subdued.

The police came back whilst they were clearing up, took a lengthy statement from Frannie and increased her feeling of guilt, and were then closeted in the library with Oliver and Edward for over an hour.

When they finally left, Oliver said that he had to go to the farm and give Charles a hand as his brother was in no fit state to do anything. Frannie and Edward spent the remains of the morning mooching around the estate hunting fossils, and by lunchtime had collected a dozen good samples, which Edward proudly washed and told her he would be taking back to school with him.

She tried more than once to steer him back to the conversation they had had yesterday in the library but, each time, instead of answering her, he plied her with questions about fossils, about archaeology in general. And she had to promise, with a heavy heart, that if she was down next weekend they would do a mini dig in the grounds, just the two of them, somewhere around the site of the old Roman villa.

Then she turned and confronted him directly. 'Edward, in the library yesterday you told me how you could make things happen to people just by thinking about them. Did you have bad thoughts about Tristram before he got hit by the propeller?'

His response startled her. His eyes became hard and fierce, and his face tightened into a similar expression of fury. '*No!*' he said in a voice that was almost a shout. Then he burst into tears and ran upstairs.

Frannie waited some minutes then followed him. She found him in his bedroom, sitting in a chair, sobbing. She put her arm around him and talked quietly. 'Tell me more about this bad thing, Edward.'

He reached out a hand and picked a small white sports car off a shelf beside him; he pressed a switch underneath it and the rear wheels began to spin.

'Want to dry your eyes?' she said.

He shook his head.

'Do you have any bad thoughts about anyone else? Do you have any about me?'

He switched his car off then on again without replying, back in one of his silences again.

Frannie tested him. 'What would you like for lunch? Shall I make you something nice?'

He stayed silent. Eventually she left him and went back downstairs. She hesitated in the hall, listening hard for any sign of Oliver, then walked through to the kitchen, and listened carefully again. Then, as quickly as she could, she removed one small shot of Edward from the photographic collage, and slipped it into the pocket inside her handbag.

At six o'clock they dropped Edward back at school and he went off glumly, his fossils carefully wrapped in paper in his small bag, having reminded Frannie of her promise of the dig. Then they drove to London.

'I've been thinking hard all day about a priest I could contact,' Oliver said. 'I have met the Archbishop of Canterbury; we're both in the House of Lords. I could have a word – but –' he shrugged. 'I don't really know if that's such a good idea. If he believed the story he'd probably delegate and it would take time.'

A lorry thundered past, its slipstream rocking them. 'But I could go and see the Bishop of Lewes tomorrow. He's quite a reasonable chap.' He squeezed Frannie's hand. 'It'll be OK.'

'And I ought to go and see your brother,' she said.

'Not for a bit; I don't think he can cope with seeing anyone.' He put his hand on her shoulder and stroked it lightly. 'Come with me tomorrow; we'll go and see the Bishop of Lewes. I'll ask him if he can see us tomorrow evening?'

She nodded bleakly.

'Stay with me tonight?'

She tilted her head and pressed her cheek against his hand. 'Could we make a detour?'

'Where to?'

'I'd like to pop in just for a few minutes to see Phoebe.'

The linoleum floor of the ward was spongy beneath Frannie's shoes. A trolley laden with surgical instruments rattled and she stepped aside to let it pass, the discomfort of being in a hospital adding to the leaden fear inside her.

There was a young woman sleeping deeply in the bed next to Phoebe, her face a sickly grey. Phoebe's table and the tray across her bed were stacked with flowers and cards, and more cards surrounded a massive basket of fruit. She was sitting up in bed, looking a better colour than Thursday, and even greeted Frannie with a smile.

'Thank you for the flowers you sent, Frannie – they're really beautiful.' She pointed to one of the vases on the table.

'You've got some life back in your face.'

'Drugs,' Phoebe said.

Frannie saw her dilated pupils and realized she was right, doped up; reality was at bay. She looked away so Phoebe could not see her grimace. Declan O'Hare had talked about the warriors who wore masks into battle so as to hide their fear. Frannie hoped she was not going into battle but knew that she had looked away to hide her fear from Phoebe just now.

'You went to see Susie,' Phoebe said.

'Yes.'

'I'm glad. I spoke to her today.'

Frannie sat down heavily on the chair beside the bed. 'When you rang me on Tuesday, Phoebe, you asked me if the number twenty-six meant anything to me, and you told me to be careful of it. Why exactly?'

'I always remembered it from the Ouija session. It stuck in my mind.'

'What was my message?'

'I seem to think that was it.'

'What do you mean?'

'*Twenty-six.* Or maybe it was *the twenty-sixth.*'

'Just the number?'

Phoebe nodded. 'I think so.'

'That was the whole message?'

'I don't know if it was a message, Frannie, or a prophecy.'

Frannie closed her eyes, then opened them again, afraid of the thoughts that waited behind her lids. 'Seb Holland,' she said, weakly. 'Do you remember what he was told?'

'No, Susie asked me that. I can only remember mine, yours, Jonathan and Meredith's.'

'Do you think all this is just chance? Coincidence?'

'No.'

'What is it?'

'I don't know.'

Frannie pushed some strands of hair from her face and glanced down evasively, waiting for some moments before speaking. 'How did your accident happen, Phoebe?'

'I'm not sure. I don't understand.'

'Understand?'

'Why I didn't stop.'

The expression in Phoebe's eyes changed as Frannie watched them; her blinking became faster and the lids quivered.

'Was it your brakes? Did they fail?'

'I didn't try to brake. I didn't put my brakes on at all.'

Frannie studied the dilated pupils. 'Why not?'

'That's what I don't understand.'

'Are you sure you're not still a little confused – the anaesthetics can – you know –?'

Phoebe shook her head. 'It's not the happy pills either. They think I don't know they're giving me happy pills.' Her voice was slurring as she raised it in anger. 'But I do know.' Her face contracted and the anger scared Frannie. 'I know. Right? I know.'

Frannie smiled gently, trying to defuse her anger. 'Yes, I'm sure.'

'They won't pull fast ones on me. I know which way's up in here.'

Frannie heard the sharp clack of a curtain being pulled around the bed next door. 'You saw the lorry, but you didn't brake; is that right?'

Phoebe shrugged and the stump rose and fell. 'Maybe I thought that if I stopped I would be late.'

'Late for what?'

'I don't know. I don't remember. Late for the game.'

'Game?'

'Playing fruit machines.' Phoebe's voice was slurring and her mind was drifting. She smiled.

Frannie summoned up a smile in return, but as she did, Phoebe's face changed, began to rumple and crinkle as if she were an inflatable doll from which the air was leaking. Changed from adult to child; to a pink-faced baby bawling in its cot.

Frannie pulled out her handkerchief, dabbed Phoebe's eyes, trying to staunch the flow of tears. She squeezed her hand, cradled her face, trying to stop the sobs.

A nurse came over. 'I think I'd better give her something.'

Phoebe shook her head fiercely. 'Go away. I don't want your fucking pills. I want my fucking arm back.'

She sobbed some more and then the tears subsided and she lay back, spent, against the pillow, her mouth open, gulping air as if she had emerged from swimming several lengths underwater. 'Sorry. Sorry, Frannie,' she whispered hoarsely.

'It's OK,' she whispered back and stroked her hand.

In the distance a floor polisher whined. 'Fruit machine,' Phoebe said. 'One-armed bandit. Obvious, wasn't it?'

Frannie hesitated. 'Phoebe, I want to ask you something. This might sound silly – but – did you see a small boy before the accident?'

Phoebe looked at her, puzzled. 'A small ginger-haired boy?'

Frannie stiffened.

Phoebe's mind seemed to clarify; her eyes brightened. 'Yes, Frannie, I did. He's been on my mind quite a lot.'

'What do you mean?'

'There was a boy standing on the kerb. I passed him

289

just before the accident. I remember thinking it was strange that he was out there on his own – and the way he was standing there – as if he wasn't wanting to cross the road, but was waiting for something.'

'Strange?' Frannie echoed, but her thoughts were elsewhere. Oliver's words last night. *It's you . . . That's where it's coming from.* She was remembering the Latin she learned at school. Remembering the Latin teacher who was a crabby, elderly man with a voice like a saw. Remembering when she was thirteen and asking him why it was necessary to learn a dead language. He had exploded in rage. Then, when he had calmed down, he had made her learn by heart, first the names of dozens of plants, then dozens of animals. Made her recite them out loud to the class. She was remembering Edward giving the plants their Latin names as they had both walked through the grounds of Meston. Edward reciting the names of the animals in the Range Rover driving back to London last Sunday night.

Frannie removed the photograph from her handbag and handed it to Phoebe. 'Is this him?'

Phoebe studied it carefully, then stared back at her suspiciously. 'Is he a witness? Has he said anything?'

Frannie was trembling. 'Is it him? Is it the boy you saw?'

Phoebe looked again. 'Yes,' she said. 'Definitely. Because I can remember him so clearly. When I saw him, it was like one of those freeze-frames on a video – as if time had stopped. He didn't look real. It was almost as if I was imagining him.' She smiled distantly. 'Or as if he was a ghost.'

CHAPTER TWENTY-SEVEN

The boy was curled in a foetal position, face downwards in a scooped-out hollow of rock inside the glass case. Urns and vases lay in there with him, as well as some metal bangles and an earthenware drinking-vessel. His face had long gone and his desiccated skin had hardened so that he looked more like a grotesque wooden sculpture than someone who had once been flesh and blood.

Declan O'Hare patted the top of the case with a paternal air. 'Egyptian Predynastic, this fellow,' he said. 'Gebelein. We date him around 3250 BC. The baubles and jugs are typical of the grave goods that would have been buried with him at the time.'

Frannie stared through the glass; she had done so several times before and she was never comfortable with the sight. There was something she found both morbidly fascinating and at the same time deeply disturbing about a dead human being in a display cabinet.

She watched the reactions of the other two research assistants who had been assigned to the preparation of the exhibition: Hermione Wallis, a friendly but slightly dozy girl with a beaky nose, hair swept back by an elastic band, hands rammed into her dungaree pockets, was glancing uncomfortably round the mummy room; Roger Wencelas, in Doc Marten boots, starched blue jeans and a pristine white T-shirt, was peering fiercely through his wire-framed spectacles at the corpse's tiny buttocks.

Mummies lined the walls of the room: several in

upright showcases, and one in a rotting wooden box. Frannie was tired. The monochromatic overhead lighting in the exhibit rooms became oppressive after a while. You forgot whether you were above ground or below it.

It was half past ten and the room was already teeming with tourists. The living posed in front of the dead, smiling to hide their unease; and smiling because they were on the right side of the glass, Frannie thought, suddenly.

'Attitudes to death,' O'Hare said. 'The way a civilization views its own mortality tells you a great deal.' He looked at each of them in turn, then nodded at Frannie. 'You're a good Catholic girl, perhaps you can enlarge on that for us?'

'Our civilization's afraid of death,' she said.

'Very good. Indeed we are. Afraid of that Great Unknown. Afraid of what we can't take with us.' His gaze scanned all three of them again, his bright blue eyes sparkling with the near-manic passion with which he addressed his work. 'Look at this chap.' He tapped the glass cabinet again. 'What kind of a world did he leave behind? What did he think of in those last moments before death?'

Frannie stared at the cabinet. The remains of Tristram were lying in there. The pink Bermudas with his thin legs and the tiny trainers. The coil of intestines like a dead snake; the splintered shaft of his backbone.

She pressed her hand over her mouth and turned. Jonathan Mountjoy stared out from another cabinet. His mouth was open and there was a bullet hole in his forehead. She spun her head, saw a blackened, shrivelled mummy; but it wasn't a mummy, it was Meredith, her socketless eyes staring back through the glass.

292

Frannie backed away, perspiration running down her neck, bumped into a cabinet, put a hand out to steady herself. Declan O'Hare was looking at her, so were her two colleagues. 'Sorry,' she whispered. 'I'm sorry.'

The meeting finally ended at twelve. Frannie hurried back to her office, wanting desperately to phone Seb Holland.

Penrose Spode was seated primly behind his desk, looking unusually fashionable in a yellow Lacoste shirt buttoned to the neck beneath a white jacket; he gave her a rather self-conscious smile as she came into the office, as if he were seeking reassurance.

He was normally in before Frannie, but this morning he had been late and it was the first time she had seen him today.

'Hi, nice weekend?' she said.

'Yes, thank you.' He watched her expectantly, like a puppy awaiting praise. 'Did you?'

'I've had better.' She gave a smile that felt like a twitch. 'I like the gear – is it new?'

'It's – ah – a birthday present to myself.' He blushed.

'When's your birthday?'

He blushed even harder. 'Today.'

'Oh, Penrose! I wish I'd known.' She switched on her word processor and sat down, then began rummaging in her bag for Seb Holland's business card. 'Are you celebrating tonight? Having a party?'

Spode wetted the point of his pencil with his tongue and tested it on his pad. 'Having a quiet dinner,' he said.

She thought he sounded rather sad. 'I think small celebrations are the nicest,' she said as cheerily as she could.

Spode opened his mouth as if to say something more then seemed to change his mind and returned to his work.

She found the card. It was embossed with the address of a skyscraper office block in the City which she had always liked immensely. She dialled, praying silently that Seb Holland was going to be all right. She was put on hold by a faintly hostile secretary, then Seb's cheery voice came on the line. 'Great seeing you last week – no – the week before,' he said. 'Real surprise!'

'Congratulations on your engagement.' Her relief that he was all right was tempered by anxiety.

'Have to give me your latest address – you must come to the wedding. Anyhow – we have to get together before that, have a drink or a bite or something.'

'Actually I'd like to – there's something I need to talk to you about.'

'Oh? Business?'

'No –' She saw Spode's ears were busy. 'It's not something I can talk about that easily over the phone.'

'Sounds mysterious!'

'I need to see you as soon as poss.'

'You've just caught me – I'm off to New York on Wednesday, and I won't be back until . . .' he paused and she heard the flick of a page, '5th October. How about that following week sometime? Are you free for lunch?'

'I need to see you before then, Seb. It's really urgent.'

'It can't wait?'

'No.'

There was a pause. 'Christ – I just haven't got any time – how long do we need?'

'Not long. Half an hour?'

'Could you come here at lunchtime tomorrow – we'll shoot off round the corner somewhere?'

'Yes, that would be fine.'

'Know where we are?'

'Yes, I do.'

'Come up to the fortieth floor and ask for me in reception. About one?'

'One. Fine.'

'You'd better give me your number in case something comes up.'

She gave him her home and office numbers, then hesitated. 'Seb, listen – this may sound a bit daft, but will you be really careful until I see you?'

'Careful? Of what?'

She wished Spode would mind his own business and stop listening; he was making her feel even more foolish. 'I – I'll explain tomorrow.'

'Right. OK.' He sounded uneasy; not about her warning, but about her. She tried to think of something to salvage the situation, but Seb terminated the conversation before she had a chance. 'Listen, I have to dash. I didn't want to be rude and not take your call. See you tomorrow, here, OK?'

She turned back to her screen and tried to apply her mind for the next hour, compiling the list Declan O'Hare had asked her to do from the central memory bank of every item of Egyptology in the Museum. She thought, glumly, that only a few days ago she had been relieved to be taken off a monotonous cataloguing job. This one was going to be even worse. If she lived long enough to complete it.

She stared at the screen; the cursor blinked, waiting for her next tap on the keyboard, for her next command, for the next piece of stored information she wanted to access.

Information. She thought about Oliver's research into numerology. When he had dropped her at the Museum this morning he had made a big effort to be bright, positive, to reassure her. But she could see it in his eyes: he was as scared as she was.

She thought hard, her brain tired, blunted by the pills she was taking to help her sleep and damp the shock. They were doing neither. There had to be more she could unravel. She had met Oliver at King's Cross. Before that their paths had crossed in the café. Maybe she had even met him before then, somewhere else. A connection. Something between her and the Halkins. Or her family and the Halkins. All this horror wasn't limited just to the group who were at the Ouija. Tristram hadn't been there. Nor had Dom. Nor had Edward's mother. Oliver was blaming her. But maybe there was something in his past, which he was hiding from her.

Or wasn't aware of.

At one o'clock Frannie hurried outside, weaving through the tourists and the pigeons. She crossed Great Russell Street, went into a newsagent and found a selection of birthday cards that were all either dull, or lewd and suggestive. She opted for one with a picture of the Horse Guards Parade, bought a packet of tiny candles then went into the café next door where she bought a pastrami sandwich, a lemon cupcake and a can of lime-flavoured Perrier. She perched on one of the stools, ate quickly, signed the card and put the cupcake into her handbag. Then she went back into the Museum, glancing at her watch. It was twenty past one.

She showed her pass and went into the hallowed domed silence of the British Library. There was a sharp contrast between the Library and the Museum even though they shared, for a short while longer, the same building. Whilst the interior of the Museum had a modern, progressive feel, the Reading Room of the Library felt as if it had been unchanged for centuries. Ancient volumes lined the grand circular shelves. The room smelt of old bindings, old paper, buffed leather and wood polish. The silence was disturbed only by the squeak of shoes, the rustle of turned pages, the putter of word-processor keys.

Frannie noticed Archie Weir, a genealogist she had met a couple of times. A kindly, worried-looking man, he sat behind piles of tomes that were stacked like a barricade, engrossed in some research. He was wearing an ancient tweed jacket with leather patches on the elbows, and an even more ancient shirt and tie. The tufts of grey hair on either side of his bald dome looked as if they had been glued on as an afterthought, and his wire half-framed glasses were perched halfway down his nose. His lips chattered wordlessly as he scanned a document, reminding Frannie of the rabbit in *Alice in Wonderland*.

Frannie quietly stood in front of him. After some moments, he looked up with a start, a frown of recognition spreading across his forehead as if a name and a face were speeding somewhere through his memory banks but had not yet collided.

'Frannie – Francesca Monsanto,' she said. 'Oriental Antiquities.'

'Ah, yes, yes, yes!' He put down the document. 'With Mr O'Hare.'

'That's right.'

'Ah, yes, yes, yes.' He was blushing and she wondered why. Then through a chink in the barricade she saw a flattened paper bag and a half-eaten sandwich.

Eating was strictly forbidden in here. 'I'm sorry,' she said. 'I don't want to disturb you.'

'Not at all, no, no, not at all.' To emphasize this he placed his hands firmly to either side of him on the desk and sat more upright.

'I was wondering if you could tell me the best books in here on the English aristocracy?'

'English aristocracy, yes,' he said. 'Yes. General history or a specific family?'

'A specific family. The Halkins – Marquess of Sherfield.' She thought as she whispered the name that she detected the faintest hint of distaste in his expression.

'Ah, Sherfield, the Halkins, yes.' A slight brake seemed to have been applied to his enthusiasm. 'Ah, yes, let me see, we're bound to have their family archive here if it's been printed up; most of them have been at some time, fortunately. Might be under the family name or in the name of their principal residence. There'd be something in *Debrett's* of course, and *Burke's Peerage*. Let me see.' His fingers, soft and wrinkled like old carrots, drummed the table. '*Arkwright's History of the British Aristocracy*, might be something in that. How much detail do you need?'

'As much as I can find.'

'You might also find a few mentions in one or two books on witchcraft.'

Before she'd digested this last remark, he'd picked up a stub of a pencil, a piece of notepaper and was writing down some titles in fat, slanting writing. When he'd finished, he gave her a list of a dozen books.

She thanked him and walked across into the vast Reading Room, awed as she always was in here by the sheer quantity of the volumes stacked floor to ceiling. Her watch said it was half past one. In her haste she walked straight past the Genealogy section the first time, and did a complete circuit of the room before finding it and scanning the titles.

She searched first for the name Halkin, then Sherfield. Then she went along the Ms. Marlborough, she read. Montagu. Melbourne Castle. Melksham. Mentmore. Then she saw it. A blue volume an inch and a half thick, with the wording *The Meston Hall Archives* embossed in gold on the spine. Next to it was *Meston and the Halkins – A History* by Keenan Towse.

Frannie pulled it out. Although the book was slim, it felt heavy. There was a ring on the cover where someone had once stood a glass or a mug. She opened it where she stood and smelled the dry, faintly woody smell that rose up from the pages. The frontispiece was an oval vignette of Meston Hall, in much better condition than now, with a horse and carriage outside. On the facing page was the family crest.

She glanced at a few pages further on. There were references to the Halkin family pedigree, the family archives, manorial records, title deeds and leases . . . She turned forwards a few more pages and came to the family tree which was on a triple page, folded over. She read some of the names: Sir Godfrey Halkin; Marie, dau. of Henry Le Sabanne; Agnes de Bournelle; Francis Edward Alwynne, second Marquess; Thomas; Lady Prudence.

There were several pages detailing the contents, followed by a dozen introductory pages in minute type that gave the French origins of the family, the first recorded instance of a Halkynne arriving in England in 1066, and where he'd settled.

She turned back to the contents: The First English Halkins 1066–1300, Halkin Rôles in the Crusades – Home and Abroad, Elizabethan Halkins, Halkins and the English Civil War.

She turned to that chapter and scanned through it. Six pages along, the second Marquess of Sherfield's name jumped out at her. She went back several paragraphs until she found the start of the section, then read through it slowly.

Francis Halkin. Second Marquess of Sherfield. 1600–1652. Unscrupulous and tenacious in asserting the right of the Halkin family, he inherited the title and the family's estates on the death of the first Marquess in 1625, and immediately came into conflict with his overlord, the Archbishop of Canterbury, and even with a group of tenants of his manor of Meston who complained of his 'daryke and bullynge behaviour and hideousness to defie ymaginacion amonges them'.

It is fair to say that Lord Francis Halkin was unique among nine centuries of Halkins for his sheer evil and depravity, a one-off in a family that in general contributed in many ways to the growth of the country and British Empire.

Francis Halkin, a true Jekyll-and-Hyde nature, outwardly a fickle political animal, inwardly a greedy and brutal sadist, deeply involved in the dark arts of Satanism and Numerology which he manipulated both for political and financial gain and for sexual gratification of the most perverse nature. In the Civil War he sided first for his own protection with the Parliamentarians, providing finance and men to Cromwell but subsequently provided help to the Royalists in the City of London, in particular the use of the underground passageway from the Halkin residence to the Thames, in exchange for a supply of children for sexual favours and ritual sacrifice.

In 1652 his younger brother, Thomas Halkin, informed on him to the Parliamentarians (whether from disgust at his perversions or in order to inherit the title is not established). His arrest warrant was signed personally by Oliver Cromwell, but soldiers, sickened by what they found in the premises, carried out their own fitting execution.

She turned forward, flipping through several pages of detailed information on the Halkin family properties – covering, in the thirteenth and fourteenth centuries, several counties. Then several plates of photographs. As she flipped through them, she stopped with a start, turning back to a scene of London that looked familiar.

Frannie felt her skin tightening around her body. The book shook in her hands as she was confronted by a print of Victorian London. The City. Hansom cabs and horse-drawn carts travelled down the street, and the shops were different. But she knew exactly where it was. She had spent most of her childhood there. The junction of Poultry with Cheapside. The front few buildings of Poulterers' Alley were clearly visible in the centre of the print.

Her eyes dived down to the caption at the bottom. Her focus blurred and she had to concentrate her vision: 'Site of original London residence of Halkin family. (Destroyed in Great Fire of 1666.) Now occupied by offices and shops of Poulterers' Alley.'

Where their sandwich bar had been.

CHAPTER TWENTY-EIGHT

Frannie ran out of the gallery and down the stairs, raced down the corridor to the phone booths, wanting to be more private than back in her office. She spilled a handful of coins on to the surface of the box and dialled Oliver's office number.

His secretary informed her, in a very formal voice, that Lord Sherfield had left at midday to go to the country, owing to a family bereavement and was not expected back today.

She rang Meston and Mrs Beakbane answered. She had not seen Oliver and gave Frannie Charles's number. Hesitantly, she tried that, but there was no reply.

She headed back to her office, her heart thumping. Declan O'Hare appeared out of a doorway and walked down towards her, moving in slow motion like a character in a dream.

'Are you all right, Frannie? With us? You don't look as if you've quite made it to Planet Earth today.'

'I'm OK,' she said.

OK OK OK. The word reverberated down the corridor.

'Well that's good. Not happy about working on the exhibition?'

'Very happy.'

'Good.'

GOOD OOD OOD. The echo followed her boss's footsteps. The corridor stretched and shrank, then a double door swallowed him and closed with a bang like a muffled shot.

She opened the clasp of her handbag with fingers

that were not working properly, fumblingly removed the lemon cupcake, pressed in one of the tiny candles she had bought, then tried to strike a book match. It fell from her fingers. She tore another out, lit it and carried the cake into her office. 'Happy birthday!' she said, trying to sound cheerful.

Spode looked up, startled, from a phone conversation. She put the tiny cake on his desk, pulled the card from her handbag, put that beside the cake and went to her own desk.

Spode terminated his conversation hastily. His eyes went from the card to the cake to Frannie and back. He read the card then set it carefully on his desk.

'Thank you,' he said. 'Thank you, Frannie. Thank you very much.' His voice was choked with emotion.

Her phone rang, startling her. It was Oliver.

'How are you, Frannie?' he said.

'I was trying to get hold of you,' she told him. Her throat felt as if it were full of rocks. 'I've found it!'

'Found what?'

'The connection. I've found the connection!' Her voice wasn't working properly, wouldn't let her speak at the speed at which she was thinking. 'You're not going to believe it. It's the café. Poulterers' Alley. Does that address mean anything to you?'

'Not a thing,' he said blankly.

'Your family home in London that got burned down in the Great Fire, in 1666?'

'What about it? I'm not with you.'

'It was on the site that is now Poulterers' Alley. That's where my parents had their café!'

He was silent for some moments. 'Godfathers,' he said. 'That's where you had the Ouija session?'

'Yes. That's the link, isn't it? It must be!'

'You're certain about the site?'

303

'It's in the library here.'

'*Non omnis moriar,*' he said.

Fear crawled across her skin like a living thing. '*Non omnis moriar*,' she repeated. She no longer cared whether Spode was listening or not. 'I think I'm beginning to understand,' she said.

'I haven't been able to speak to the Bishop yet – he's away until late tonight. His secretary's trying to get hold of him to ask him to call me. Charles is in a terrible state, I had to come down and try and get him a bit organized, make some arrangements. Got to sort out the funeral, got to get the body released by the coroner after the post-mortem. There's more cattle gone sick and I've got the vet coming this evening but he doesn't think he'll be able to get here until nine.'

'Can I do anything to help?'

'No. I just want you to be careful. Best thing is I'll call you later, as soon as I hear from the Bishop – I hope we can see him some time tomorrow.'

After he had hung up, Frannie stared bleakly at the kinked and twisted cord attached to the receiver. At the grubby dial; at the grain of the wood of her desk, noticing holes, scratches, the dull shine from the light bulb above.

The cursor on her word-processor screen blinked at her. She untwisted the plastic cord with her fingers. Spode's fountain pen scratched busily across the lined paper of a notebook. She smelled a faint trace of molten wax from the candle he had extinguished on his cupcake, and it reminded her of the candles in Oliver's bedroom.

She tapped in a fresh file access code on her keyboard, her brain on autopilot, her thoughts on Oliver, on Tristram, on Poulterers' Alley, on a night three and a half years ago.

She shivered. Tentacles stretched back into the past. She closed her eyes. If she could turn the clock back. Could have told Seb Holland that night to keep on driving, not to stop, could have told him she had changed her mind, that the cellar wasn't really a good idea after all . . .

Twenty-five years they had had that café. Her parents had taken it before she was born. All her childhood she had played in there, worked in there. On the site of Oliver's ancestral London home. The site where the second Marquess had murdered small boys. Where he himself had been murdered; by a red-hot poker.

What the hell had they contacted and picked up down there in that cellar? What had been there all along? All the time she had been scared as a child to go down? The bogeyman? The shadow, the scrape that was like a dragging foot – was that who it was?

The wrong file came up on the screen. She read the words, too scared by her thoughts to be irritated. '*Homo habilis*. Skhul. Vindja. Upper Palaeolithic. Java Man. Peking Man.' Bones. Dead, long dead, whatever had happened mattered no more, unless you lived in some kind of parallel universe or whatever it was Declan O'Hare had gone on about not long ago.

There were no such things as ghosts.

Penrose Spode was looking at her. 'Are you all right, Frannie?'

'Yes, I'm fine.'

'You're crying.'

She put her hands to her cheeks, startled. They were wet. She sniffed, pulled out her handkerchief and dabbed them. 'Sorry,' she said, sniffed again and forced a smile.

His lips closed in a silent apology for his intrusion, but he continued to stare at her. She thought he was never going to return to his work. Then he laid his elbows on his desk, pressed the fingertips of both hands together and inclined his head, shyly. 'I don't know – if you have any other plans – but – er – if you don't – er – would you have dinner with me?'

'Come to your birthday party?'

'I'm not having a birthday party,' he said quietly. 'I wasn't doing anything tonight.'

She looked back at him, surprised, and feeling sorry for him. Considered the prospect of going back to her empty flat, waiting for Oliver to ring, sitting alone with her thoughts. Did not want to be alone.

'Sure,' she said. 'I'd love to.'

Penrose Spode was getting drunk. Frannie could see it in his co-ordination, in the way he was articulating with his hands; in the way his expression was becoming soppier and his voice slurring. She was getting drunk too; the booze cheered her, made her feel safe, made everything seem all right, just a bad dream, that was all.

Spode tried to pick a peanut out of the goo of dark sauce with his chopsticks. The points of the sticks clacked together a full inch short of the nut. He persevered, focusing with difficulty, and finally held the nut up triumphantly. As he moved it towards his mouth, it slipped free and tumbled down his chest leaving a sticky brown trail through the grains of rice that already adorned his yellow T-shirt.

'Ooopsh!' he said.

Frannie wanted to stay drunk, to get drunker still. She signalled to the waiter for another bottle of Pinot Grigio. Spode registered mock alarm with his eyes and went for a mushroom in another of the array of Thai dishes on the table. He hoisted it up, trapped between the points of his sticks, then it shot out and skidded across the white tablecloth like an ice-hockey puck.

'Have you always been interested in archaeology?' Frannie asked him.

He hovered his chopsticks over the errant mushroom as if he was hoping to catch it unawares. 'Yes.'

'What in particular interests you?'

He inclined his head, leaning forwards a fraction, and drawing her in towards him as if he was letting her into a great secret. 'The past speaks to me.'

'Speaks?'

'Yes.'

She plucked out a hot, spicy prawn, and Spode's eyes followed her chopsticks as if he was watching a conjuring trick. 'You mean you have conversations with the past? What do you say to each other?'

Spode grinned, then hastily covered his mouth with his hand and resumed his inert expression of seriousness.

'Psychometry,' Spode said, keeping his voice low.

'Huh?'

'I have this gift.'

'Psychometry?'

The waitress presented the bottle for inspection, hovered between Frannie and Spode and was rescued by Frannie. Her mouth burned from a hot prawn and she could barely detect any flavour as she tasted it. 'Fine,' she said, then looked back at Spode. 'What's psychometry?'

'I can tell things about the past by touching objects.'

'You mean you're psychic?'

Spode blushed. 'Sort of.'

She ate a mouthful of cod in ginger. 'You're a dark horse, aren't you!'

He cradled his freshly filled glass, and drank by

lowering his mouth to it. Wine trickled down his chin. 'People think you're a bit –' he tapped the side of his head. 'You know – if you talk about these things.'

'So what sort of things can you tell by touching objects?'

'Depends.'

'On what?'

'On the strength of the imprints.' He eyed a prawn, then stared dubiously at his chopsticks. 'On the condition of the object. Where it's been stored.'

'Why does that affect it?'

'Objects pick up everything emotional that happens close to them.'

'How?'

He leaned forwards and she thought for a moment he was going to try to kiss her. 'They absorb things, the same as walls do, in their subatomic particles, or somewhere. I can read them. Usually works best if it's a personal object – or something that's been buried and undisturbed for years.'

'What sort of personal objects?'

'Rings. Watches. Bracelets.'

'Could you read my watch?'

He looked at her scratched and battered Citizen quartz. 'How long have you had it?'

'My father gave it to me for my sixteenth birthday.'

He put down his chopsticks. She unclipped it and gave it to him. He closed his hand around it and stared up at the ceiling with such intensity that his pupils almost disappeared and all she could see were the whites of his eyes. His expression alarmed her, short-circuiting her feelings of pleasant oblivion.

'I'm getting a young man with a red sports car, and a link with fish. I think you had a boyfriend who was a fishmonger. Not really a boyfriend, a boy you went out with but did not like. People wanted you to marry him but you were not interested; almost like an arranged marriage, I am sensing. A source of anger between you and your father. Your father was keen for you to marry him, there was plenty of money in the boy's family. And now I'm getting more anguish between you and your father. Always you and your father, your mother is meek; it's your father you fight and you feel guilty about it but you never give in because you are a very determined girl.'

She stared at him in amazement. He was talking louder, his voice sounding increasingly excited. 'Yes, yes, archaeology; a source of contention! Your father was angry that you wanted to do archaeology because there is no money in it. You have fought with him often over this. You have a younger sister who always wears a black hat. You are deeply in love at this moment with a man you met at a railway station.' He fell silent.

People were turning round and looking at them. Frannie was aware that conversation at other tables in the restaurant had subsided; she was trembling with a strange current that was flowing through her, disturbing the rhythm of her body, and she was blushing hard. It took her some moments before she had collected her thoughts enough to speak.

'That's extraordinary, Penrose.' Her face was in a tight frown, trying to think back, to remember if she had ever told him any of this. They had exchanged pleasantries and talked about work, but never conversed about anything personal before. 'Can you tell me any more about this man I met at a railway station?'

He closed his eyes. 'He has a boy. No wife. She is dead.'

'And the boy? Can you tell me about him?'

She watched him sit in silent concentration. Again the pupils almost completely disappeared; his fist was clenched tightly around the watch, shaking with the tension. He looked as if he was about to say something. Then suddenly, quite unexpectedly, he shot his hand out towards her and uncurled his fingers, presenting the watch to her with an intensely reproachful expression. 'You'd better take it back.'

She felt herself sobering and her nerves shimmying. 'What's the matter?'

'Take it,' he said. 'Please take it.'

'Can't you tell me some more? Please, Penrose.'

'It's just a blur – too many conflicting emotions. Too much to drink. I can only pick up the past not the present.'

'I thought mediums could divine the future through psychometry?' She clipped her watch back on, reluctantly.

Spode ran his eye suspiciously across the dishes, as if he was surveying enemy territory. 'That's a rather presumptuous thing to do,' he said, hovering the chopsticks over a mange-tout that stuck like a green fin out of a dish that she did not remember ordering. 'Objects are not crystal balls; they are like video-recorders; the past is imprinted in them, not the future. And I'm not a medium.' He looked uncomfortable; evasive.

The mange-tout fell on to the tablecloth and he picked it up with his chopsticks with a sudden deftness that surprised Frannie, and clearly surprised him also. She heard the crunch as his teeth bit the crisp vegetable, then saw him lick his lips with the satisfaction of someone who has achieved a small but significant personal landmark of progress. He studied his chopsticks through new, triumphant eyes, as if they had changed from being his enemies into his friends.

'That wasn't just telepathy, what you did? You didn't subconsciously pick those thoughts out of my head?'

'I might have done.' He suddenly looked sullen and she saw a trace of the old Penrose Spode she knew in the office, the supercilious, petulant introvert. 'But when I hold the teabowl that belonged to an Ashokan warrior two thousand years ago and learn about things that happened to him, I don't imagine his decomposed remains are in much of a condition to communicate to me telepathically.'

'I didn't mean to be rude – it's just – I mean – what you told me is incredible – so accurate.'

He looked appeased and drank some more wine. Then he lowered his voice right down and leaned close again, glancing warily around him before he spoke. 'I've helped my brother a couple of times.' He nodded, knowingly.

'I didn't know you had a brother.'

'He's a priest.' He raised his glass to his mouth and noticed to his surprise that it was empty. He lifted the bottle out of the ice bucket and a rivulet of water trickled on to his plate as he filled both Frannie's glass and his own to the brim.

'Are you religious, also?'

He shook his head. 'We don't get on very well.'

'How've you helped him?'

'Hauntings. Place memories. He's a diocesan exorcist. He knows what I can do isn't telepathy.'

'Exorcist?'

'Not his title – but that's what he is.'

'Who does he work for?'

'Church of England.'

'They have an exorcist?'

'Several. He has to investigate – when people in his

parish think they have a ghost in their house or their pub or something. He has to go and see what it is. I've gone along and done my bit.'

'By reading objects?'

'Objects. Or walls.'

'I don't see the connection with exorcism.'

'Some ghosts are place memories that people trigger off. I can read what they are for him.'

'Off the walls?'

'Mostly.'

'Does that scare you?'

He carefully raised his full glass. 'There's nothing scary about the past; it can't harm you.' He looked down as if he did not want to meet her eye.

'Do you know anything about Ouija boards?'

He inspected the top of his glass, lowered it unsteadily and picked up his chopsticks again. 'My brother doesn't like them.' He ran his gaze across each of the dishes and fished out another mushroom. 'He gets a lot of people with problems after the Ouija.'

'What sort of problems?'

The mushroom fell from the chopsticks inches from his mouth but he did not notice; he suddenly stood up, the colour drained from his face, and without saying anything, walked hurriedly and erratically to the back of the restaurant. Ten minutes later he had not reappeared. Frannie went down the narrow stairs at the back of the restaurant to look for him. At the bottom were two doors, one with the silhouette of a man, the other a woman. She knocked on the one with the man but there was no response. Timidly she opened it and there was a strong reek of vomit. Spode was curled up on the floor beneath the wash-basin, asleep.

Frannie cleaned her colleague's face with a damp paper towel and the manager called a taxi. She paid the bill for the two of them and Spode recovered enough to stagger to the taxi, supported by herself and a waiter, and tried to give his address to the driver. 'Spenrose Pode, Number Sheventy-sheven.'

The taxi stopped outside the Victorian mansion block in Wandsworth where Frannie knew he lived, and she helped him along the corridor to his flat and made sure he was safely in. His flat was as neat and bland as his desk. He looked at her with barely focusing eyes, and made a supreme effort to be coherent, 'My brother could help you,' he said, then she had to catch him as he stumbled.

'Yes, please.'

'Call him in morning.'

She climbed back into the waiting taxi, her own head swimming from the wine and the exertion, and fell asleep herself. She woke with a start to find she was outside her flat, paid the driver a sum which would normally have grieved her and heaved herself out, walking unsteadily down the steps, clinging to the rail as she went, and bashed noisily into the dustbins at the bottom.

She let herself in, staring at the post scattered on the floor. As she closed the front door, silence enclosed her.

Too silent.

Suddenly as sober as a judge, she stared down the empty hallway with a feeling of apprehension, backed towards the door, put her hand on the Yale latch, listening. Something was not right. Silence except for the hum of the fridge. Took a step forward. Then another. Her bedroom door was open. So was the kitchen door. Darkness spilled out of them into the hall. The sitting-room door was open also. The faint haze of orange from the street lighting shone through.

Through the silence.

She took another step forward. Waited. Heard the voices above her. A man shouting. Then a woman. The couple rowing as they often did. The baby crying. The sounds of other life in the building gave Frannie courage and she stepped forward again. Then pushed the sitting-room door open, reached in her hand and snapped on the light.

Nothing moved. Nothing there. Empty. The curtains hung open, undisturbed. Her Roman vase sat on the coffee table. She walked in slowly, looking around. Something caught her eye in the hallway; a shadow moving; or maybe it was her imagination. She stared at the doorway, watching the emptiness. Her ears popped as if she were going up in an aeroplane and she swallowed to relieve them. Then the phone rang and the stillness was shattered like exploding glass.

She snatched at the receiver, brought it to her ear. 'Yeshallo?' she said, talking quietly, as if afraid someone in the flat would overhear her.

'Frannie?' It was Oliver's voice.

'Frannie? You all right?'

'Yes.' Just a whisper again.

'I've been calling you all evening. I've been worried out of my wits.'

She watched the hall. The shadow moved again. Stopped. Moved again. 'Where are you?'

'Down at Meston.'

Shadows suddenly jumped all around her. She looked up. The light that hung from the ceiling was swaying wildly in the breeze.

Except there was no breeze.

Alarm coursed through her nerves. The light began to swing faster. The cheap fringed shade the colour of parchment; the brown flex. Faster. The wire frame creaked against the bakelite collar. Faster. The shade hit the ceiling and the flex went slack for a moment; then it swung and hit the ceiling on the opposite side; the shade cracked and a piece of dry, papery material fell to the floor.

'Frannie? Frannie? Are you there?'

The light swung the other way, hit the ceiling even harder, hurled in anger; a huge chunk of the shade fell away. It swung back the opposite way. Hit the ceiling again. Hit it in fury.

She shrieked, putting her hands up as a chunk of the shade and its wire frame fell away, missing her by inches. She jumped to her feet, pulling the phone with her behind the sofa, staring at the lamp in blind terror.

'Frannie?'

This time the lamp swung even harder. The rest of the shade fell away, leaving the bare bulb and a few spikes of wire.

'I'm leaving right now, Frannie. I'll be with you in an hour.'

There was a flash above her head. Then the entire flat was plunged into darkness.

She threw down the phone and ran out into the hall, down to the front door, jerked it open and stumbled up the steps to the pavement, then stood gulping down air, leaning against the railings in a cold sweat.

Without moving and without looking back at the flat, she stayed there for over an hour until the lights of Oliver's Range Rover shone in her face, and he was cradling her in his arms.

'I didn't imagine it, Oliver.'

He had mended the fuses and they were sitting on the sofa in her living-room.

'I didn't.' She noticed for the first time how

exhausted he looked. His face was white, with a patina of grease, and his hair was limp. His dark grey pin-striped suit was crumpled, his top shirt-button was undone and his tie hanging loose. His hands were grimy. He stared at the Roman vase. 'The Bishop rang. He was very helpful. I told him you're a Catholic – or used to be, but he said it made no difference – he's referred me to a rector in London who's the diocesan exorcist for the area. Protocol, I suppose.' He shoved his hands into his trouser pockets. 'I tried ringing him, but he must have been out. I left a message on his answering machine. Are you free any time tomorrow?'

'I'm having lunch with Seb Holland.'

'Perhaps he ought to come too if we go to this clergy-man?'

'If I can persuade him.'

'Are you going to work in the morning?'

'Yes.'

'The message I left the rector – I asked him to call you if he couldn't get hold of me – I gave him both your numbers.'

'What's his name?'

'It's – ah –' He clicked his finger and thumb a couple of times. 'Rather odd name.' He pulled out his diary, opened it and turned several pages; then he seemed to have difficulty deciphering his writing. 'Canon Benedict Spode,' he read out finally.

'Spode?'

He nodded. 'I think so.'

'S-P-O-D-E?' she spelled out.

'Yes.' He looked at her with surprise. 'Why? Do you know him?'

She stared back at him. 'Where do they stop, these coincidences?'

He frowned. 'I'm not with you.'

She shook her head in disbelief. 'I share an office with his brother. We had dinner together tonight.'

The page of Frannie's diary said 'Tue 25th Sept'.

She sat at her desk trying to work, waiting for the phone to ring, running through in her mind what she was going to say to Seb Holland. She was trying hard to hold her sanity together, trying to think of everything that had happened and not think about it at the same time. Not thinking about Tristram. Phoebe's stump. Max Gabriel being eaten away.

Her head ached fiercely. It was a damp, overcast morning and a strong wind was blowing outside; a chill fear soaked through the whole of her body, mildewing her insides and making her feel sick. She wished she had dressed in warmer clothes than her navy linen two-piece and the cerise blouse which she had put on to look smart for Seb, as well as for seeing the priest.

Penrose Spode did not appear until after eleven o'clock, and when he did he slipped in wordlessly, hung his cycling kit on the hook and walked across the office in a curious, upright manner as if he had just come from a lesson in deportment.

He eased himself into his chair and carefully placed his hands on his desk. His face was a similar shade of white to when Frannie had found him on the washroom floor. He smiled apologetically then winced, as if the act of stretching his lips had hurt his face.

'Morning,' she said.

Spode mouthed a silent reply.

'How are you feeling?'

'Rather fragile.' He stared around the office as if trying to remember where he was. 'I think the food

must have been a little rich for me. Thank you for –'
He raised his hands and dropped them, blushing. He
sat down, closed his eyes and pinched his forehead
tightly between his hands. 'I'm not very good at
drinking.'

'We had quite a lot.'

He looked as if he was about to stand up again.
'I think I might get a coffee – would you like
one?'

'You were talking about your brother last night.'

He cradled his forehead in his hand for some moments, then he nodded slowly. 'I spoke to him already.'

'You have?'

'That's why I'm late in. I went round to him.'

'Oh?'

'I wanted to make sure he understood.'

'Thank you,' she said, surprised.

'I've arranged for you to see him at half past six this
evening. All right?'

'Yes – yes, thank you.'

'Good. I –' He fell silent and his mind seemed to
wander. Then he stood up. 'Black, no sugar?'

'Yes, thanks. Want me to get them?'

'No, it's OK.' He shuffled across the room like an
old man. As he reached the door, he stopped and
looked at her for some moments. 'You will go, won't
you?'

'Of course.'

'It's very important.'

'Yes, I know.'

'It's just sometimes I'm never quite sure when you
are being serious.'

'I am serious. Penrose. Really serious. There's someone else I'd like to take with me if it would be all

right.' She looked at him, but was unable to read his reaction. 'His name's Seb Holland.'

He said nothing else, and shuffled out of the door down the corridor.

CHAPTER TWENTY-NINE

Frannie came out of Bank tube station at a quarter to one, blinking in the sunlight which had broken through the cloud. The autumnal wind was freshening, blowing right through her thin clothes. Her hair thrashed irritatingly around her face, her jacket and skirt flapped and billowed.

She waited for the lights to change before she crossed over. A sightseeing coach chuntered past. A taxi followed, then a BMW, its driver talking on his telephone. A motor-cycle courier weaved by, its engine blasting. A road drill pounded and her own nerves pounded with it.

On the far side, a pretty girl came tripping out of an office and greeted a young man in a suit with a hug and a long kiss. Frannie enviously watched the carefree way they linked arms and walked away. Normal life was going on and she felt excluded from it.

The pavements were crammed with people moving quickly, urgently. Men jostled past her in funereal suits and peacock ties, women in two-pieces, their necks trussed importantly in Hermès and Cornelia James scarves. The traffic stopped and she crossed over.

People were queueing in the sandwich bars, and she heard the usual lunchtime hubbub as she passed a pub, then silence as she walked through the shadow laid across the pavement by the Gothic façade of a church. She glanced up at the windowless wall. Fear pressed to her skin like brass against tracing-paper, rubbing dark lines across her face. A siren wailed. She slowed her pace, her feet weighted with uncertainty. An ambulance flashed across, ahead, its siren a swirling banshee that beat her stomach like an egg whisk.

She passed sights so familiar from childhood that she scarcely noticed them. In the City, things rarely changed; when they did it was brutal: radical surgery; a familiar comfortable sight cut away like a mastectomy; cranes, skeletal girders rising like prosthetic limbs. She passed the Record Album shop, Boots the Chemist, Austin Reed, reassuringly unchanged, then orange lights winked ahead of her. Temporary bollards in the middle of the road. A triangle of barriers; the reflectors of unlit red lanterns. She felt the first prickle of apprehension as she saw the hoarding sticking out into the road, encasing an entire block of empty buildings; as she saw the huge sign on it: MACFAZEDEAN BROTHERS PLC. CITY FIELDS DEVELOPMENT.

MacFazedean Brothers. The name lodged in her gullet. Bastards. The slick young men in their grey striped suits who served the eviction notices, took her father's ranting with barely a twitch of their facial muscles and had the gall to tell him it was the best thing for everyone.

It was a large development. Seven acres. Two giant cranes rose from its midst, one with a demolition ball suspended from its jib and swinging menacingly in the wind. There was a cacophony to jar the ears and a pall of dust hung in the air above the entire site.

On some of the buildings visible above the tall hoarding the façades had been torn off, leaving rooms that were open to the elements, like a scene from a war movie of the Blitz, and Frannie felt for an instant as if something had been torn from herself, leaving her raw and exposed. Number 14 Poulterers' Alley was behind that hoarding; somewhere. She crossed over and ran along a boarded walkway where the pavement had once been, past the words GARBUTT MCMILLAN ARCHITECTS on a smart red sign.

Taking her bearings from the shops opposite, she reached what should have been the start of Poulterers' Alley, but the hoarding went across it, sealing it off. There were small viewing slits cut into the hoarding and she pressed her face to one and found herself looking straight down the alley. It was gloomy and forlorn; the windows were boarded up and all that remained were the names of the shops and offices, and closed doors. She could see the café, and the sadness she felt was tempered by a rising fear.

The whole central core of the site had been disembowelled. She could see right into the cellars. One was filled with water; another was now bare mud, shored up with iron pilings. A hook was sinking down from the jib of the massive crane and she saw the demolition ball swing out of sight. There followed a crash of rubble, the gears of a bulldozer meshing, metal clanging, and then a steady hiss of compressed air.

Dust dried the back of her throat as Frannie walked on and reached the site entrance. She went in through the wide-open gates, on to rubble-strewn mud that was rutted with tyre treads, and was confronted by a hive of activity: bulldozers; dumper trucks; tippers unloading; men in hard hats measuring, digging, drilling. Two men were attaching an iron piling to the hook of the crane. Three others on a rooftop were hauling up tools on a rope. Someone was shouting instructions. Over to her right the demolition ball swung against an unsupported wall belonging to one of the buildings immediately behind Poulterers' Alley. The wall buckled. The ball swung again. In its wake a bulldozer was clawing at the rubble like a crab scavenging a carcass on the seabed. In one of the deep rectangular pits a yellow JCB digger was pounding a stone floor, tearing great chunks of it out, lifting them up and dumping them in a skip. It looked as though it were ripping out the entrails of the earth itself. She stepped over some cables, then had to move out of the way of another truck. She checked her watch. Five to one.

She turned and left the site, then crossed the road, quickening her pace. As she reached the end of the next street, she could see Seb Holland's office building ahead. The Winston Churchill Tower, its bronze walls rising sixty storeys high out of the open square in which it sat. Her favourite modern building, which she had watched go up as a child, but which she had never been inside.

She remembered how it had always seemed to absorb the different moods of the weather and now it darkened suddenly as a cloud slid across the narrow corridor of sky like a roof hatch closing. A ferocious gust ripped across the open square, whistling eerily like a mountain wind, bending the conifers in their marble tubs and blowing the spray of the fountains sideways; the spots of water striking Frannie's cheek gave the illusion for a moment that it was raining. Her jacket thrashed like a loose sail and she had to hold it tight around her chest. One of the local criticisms was that the building created a wind tunnel around it.

Frannie pushed through the revolving door into a vast marble lobby that was strangely quiet. She heard the ping of an elevator, then another. The names of the companies housed in the building were engraved on a tall brass plate like a roll of honour on a cathedral wall. She scanned down it.

The fortieth floor, she remembered Seb Holland had told her.

The centre of the lobby was dominated by a Henry Moore sculpture, and presided over by an elderly commissionaire in black serge, his jacket breast covered in rows of decorations and his shoulders looped with bright white rope. Beyond him the lobby narrowed to an alcove containing two banks of four elevators each. One of them disgorged a group of men who walked across the lobby in silence. Two office girls came out of another and walked past Frannie, snippets of their chatter trailing behind them.

A man and a woman emerged from another, the woman talking emphatically. Frannie stepped into the elevator. It had a deep bronze carpet, black lacquered walls with bronze-tinted mirrors and reeked of a perfume she did not recognize.

She touched the button marked *40* on the panel and it lit up, but for a moment nothing happened. She tidied her hair in the mirror, then pulled a tissue out of her handbag and quickly wiped the mud from the building site off her dark blue shoes. The doors closed, decisively and smoothly. For an instant, again, nothing happened. Then an unseen hand lifted her by the insides of her stomach. The carpet pressed up hard against her feet. She felt a great weight on her knees. There was a rush of air and a faint drumming. Numbers spun on the digital dial above the doors. Her stomach rose up through her body. 15 20 25 30 35.

The pressure eased. The floor shrank away from her

feet. Her stomach was lowered gently. The display slowed, 38, 39, then halted. 40. Ping. The doors opened. She walked out, slightly dazed, into a hallway. The four elevator doors opposite faced her, and there were double oak doors to her right and left. The one to her left had a large brass plate which said: HOLLAND DELARUE PLC. RECEPTION.

Frannie went through into a sumptuous oak-panelled room, with deep leather armchairs and sofas on either side of the reception console. Large gold letters on the wall behind her proclaimed the dozen countries around the world in which Holland Delarue plc had offices, and the centre-piece was a large blue and gold 'Queen's Award for Export' emblem.

The receptionist was a woman in her late forties with silver highlights in her coiffed black hair, chatting busily on the telephone in a nasal voice and filing her nails at the same time. 'Melanie didn't come in today, another of her migraines, so I'm stuck over lunch hour. I thought I might try the new Asda superstore this evening. I'll just put you on hold a moment, don't go away.' She pressed a switch then looked inquisit-ively at Frannie.

'Could you tell Sebastian Holland that Frannie Monsanto is here, please.'

'He's expecting you, is he?'

'Yes.'

She pressed two buttons on her telephone, lifting the receiver to her ear. 'Oh, would you tell Mr Sebas-tian that Frannie Monsanto is in reception. Yes, no, I'm still here. Melanie didn't come in today, so I'm covering lunch hour.' She held the receiver to her ear in silence for a moment. 'Righty-ho. Thank you very much.' She looked at Frannie again. 'He'll be out in a couple of minutes. Take a seat.' She flicked a switch and resumed her conversation.

Frannie sat in a deep leather armchair and glanced at the magazines and papers on the table beside it. The *Financial Times. Fortune. Business Week. Lloyd's Log.* The walls were hung with framed colour photographs of modern office blocks. The telephone warbled again. It was a different world in here; a long way from the one in which Seb Holland, the archaeology student, had gone down into a cellar beneath a sandwich bar for a lark.

The doors behind her opened. 'Frannie! Hi! Sorry to keep you!'

She stood up and turned round. Seb was looking tired but cheery, the same slightly larger-than-life Seb: tall and hefty with his generous grinning face, big white teeth, black hair fashionably long and with a hint of gel, and his rich green eyes. His well-cut clothes and the executive trappings suited him. He looked good on them.

He gripped her shoulders and kissed her on each cheek, smelling heavily of aftershave as she remembered he always did. 'God, you look great! Hope you're still available in case Lucy dumps me at the last minute!'

She smiled. 'You look good too. Being engaged suits you.'

'Yah. It's great! Right, let's dash. I've booked at a little place around the corner. We'll have to be quick if you don't mind – bit of a crisis has come up and I've got to be back here by two o'clock.'

'You're off to New York tomorrow?'

'A hassle. We've got some real problems over there at the moment. So where are you working? British Museum, did you tell me?' He held the door for her, then stepped across and pressed the elevator button. 'Are you doing something with archaeology? You don't look like an archaeologist.'

'How are we supposed to look?' she said with mock indignation.

'Thought you'd be in an anorak and wellies.'

'Like I was wearing at dinner?'

He grinned. 'So, smart dates, eh? You're going out with Ollie Halkin?'

'Yes.' It sounded strange hearing Oliver's name abbreviated.

'Good stuff. How long?'

There was a ping behind her and they turned. A strip of green lights was flashing on an art deco display above an elevator. The same one she had come up in, she noticed.

The door slid open and Seb stepped forward quickly, holding his arm out to catch the door. 'Hello, young fellow!' he called out. Frannie felt a blast of cold air. 'Have to get in these things quickly,' he said; 'the doors are really vicious bru –'

His voice stopped in mid sentence. She saw his eyes widen in wonder. Another blast of wind curled around her, sucked her, as if it was trying to draw her in towards him. There was blackness all around him. The wrong blackness. Not the black lacquer of the elevator walls and the bronze tint of the mirror.

No bronze-carpeted floor.

A dark, matt blackness. Air poured out. Cold air that smelled dank like a cellar. The blackness of the bare shaft. Cables ran down the back wall. Grooves were cut into it; ridges and guides.

There was no fear in his eyes; just a look of surprise; like a child opening a parcel and finding nothing inside it. His hand grabbed once at the steel door-frame; his fingers slid for a few inches down its shiny surface, without any hope of purchase.

Then he dropped from her sight in complete silence.

CHAPTER THIRTY

For a moment, for just a fleeting instant, Frannie thought it was one of his pranks. She stepped two inches forwards, moving slowly as if she were wading through water. Her hand touched the cold steel frame of the door and she stared into the darkness, breathed in its dank, oily smell.

A bunch of bright yellow wires, held together by thick black tape, ran down the far wall into a junction box with a warning bolt-of-lightning label on the outside. Ducting pipes ran down beside them; she dropped to her knees and inched forward on her hands, still protected by a layer of disbelief.

'Seb?' she called out in a feeble croak, her throat clamped shut like a sprung trap.

Her hands touched the metal rim and her eyes strained into the square black tunnel that dropped sheer away for forty storeys. The dust in the draught made them smart. 'Seb?' it was a whimper now. She looked up. The ribbed black ceiling was only ten feet above her; wires looped down from it. It was a moment before she realized it wasn't the ceiling, but the floor of the elevator that had stopped inches above the top of the door. 'Seb?' the darkness sucked up her voice. She looked up at the elevator and down into the shaft again.

Then the reality hit her and tore the scream from her throat.

She backed away from the edge, scrambled to her feet and burst, stammering, through the double doors into the reception area, her eyes transmitting her terror like semaphore flags to the woman she'd seen earlier and who was still chatting merrily.

'Get help! Oh God, get help!' Frannie screamed. 'He's fallen. He's fallen down the lift. Call an ambulance. For God's sake call an ambulance! Keep people away from the lift. Don't use the lift, the door's open.'

She ran back out through the doors, stared at the open elevator shaft, then looked around wildly. There was a fire extinguisher against the wall and a flat hose on a reel. She grabbed the extinguisher and stood it in front of the open door, then hefted the hose reel down and laid that beside it, blocking the way.

The double doors opened behind her. It was the receptionist. She looked at Frannie then at the open shaft. Horror shrivelled her face as if it had been punctured. 'Mr Sebastian? Did you say Mr Sebastian?'

'Where are the stairs down?' Frannie yelled at her, too afraid to risk another elevator.

'Just inside the other doors, on the right,' the woman's voice had become a whisper. 'Mr Sebastian?'

Frannie nodded.

The woman covered her mouth with her hand.

'Call an ambulance! Please call an ambulance!' Frannie said. She ran through the double doors and came into a large open-plan office, most of the desks abandoned for lunch. She saw immediately on her right a door marked FIRE EXIT, pushed it open and found herself on a stone staircase. She ran down, clutching the metal guide rail, turned, turned, turned again, saw the number 39 crudely painted in black on the raw concrete wall.

She raced on down, the echo of her tapping feet chasing her. 36 . . . 35 . . . 34. She was getting giddy, her hand was burning from the rail. 33 . . . 32 . . . 31 . . .

She passed fire buckets, a discarded cigarette pack, a grubby J-cloth. The light was weak and for a couple of floors the bulbs had gone and she ran in almost total darkness. 25 ... 24 ... She was conscious of the sound of her own breathing, her own sobbing. 20 ... 19 ... The walls swirled past her. 14 ... 13 ... 12 ... She could feel the ground getting nearer. 7 ... 6 ... 5 ... She stumbled, lost her balance, grabbed the rail tightly and swung against the wall. One of her shoes came off and tumbled down several steps, rolling to a rest on the landing.

She hobbled down, gasping, tears streaming down her face, pulled the shoe back on and began to run again. 3 ... 2 ... 1 ... Then she reached the bottom, a poorly lit basement corridor with thickly cladded pipes along the ceiling. There was a steady roar of a machine and a hiss of air, the whine of pumps. She saw a bucket and a mop just beyond the banks of the elevator doors; a squeegee was propped against the wall beside them and a plastic drum of cleaning fluid. Further along was an open doorway and she heard a tapping sound, like a hammer on metal, and called out.

Her voice was swallowed by the roaring. She ran down the corridor, saw an open door and went in. She heard the rumble of a furnace. There were racks of stores on metal shelving: lavatory paper and towelling paper, plastic containers of soaps and detergents. The ceiling was low and gridded with pipes. It was as hot as an airing cupboard and the air was thick with flecks of lint. At the far end a light shone through an open doorway. 'Help!' she called out.

A shadow moved across the light. She heard the tapping again and ran across. A black man in a blue boiler suit was hammering a bracket in a vice inside a small workshop, his face glazed in concentration.

She dashed up to him. 'Please, are you in charge of the elevators?' She was so short of breath she could barely speak.

He looked up at her in surprise. 'I'm the caretaker, yes, ma'am.'

'Please come! Someone's fallen down the lift shaft . . .'

His face was streaked with grease and his hair was a grizzled grey. He wiped his hands on his overalls, studying her for a moment, absorbing her expression with tired brown eyes, one of which had a burst blood vessel. 'That can't happen, that's impossible.'

'Please, I was with him on the fortieth floor. The doors opened. The elevator wasn't there. Please come.' She shook her head in desperation. 'Please!'

He looked at her as if about to argue, then his expression softened. 'They've only just been checked. It can't happen,' he said, slightly defensively.

'It has. Oh God, it has.'

The tone of her voice seemed to get through to him.

'On the fortieth floor?'

'Yes. The door opened – he said he had to grab it quickly and stepped in and there was nothing there. Please,' she said. 'Please.'

He ran his hand along a row of shelves, hitched a long ribbed instrument and a bunch of keys off a hook, picked up a rubber torch, then walked with a limping gait out into the corridor and down to the elevators. 'Which one?'

Frannie had to think for a moment, trying to regain her bearings. She turned around and pointed to the third one along on the right.

He gave her a chance to reconsider. 'You sure?'

'Yes.'

He hesitated. 'Fortieth floor?'

'Yes.'

'A man, you say?'

'Yes.'

'I don't think anyone could have fallen, ma'am.'

'Please,' she whispered, the salty taste of her tears in her mouth. Perspiration torrented down her chest and back. 'Please check.'

She noticed the framed maintenance certificate that was fixed beside the elevator door.

> MAINTENANCE RECORD.
>
> DATE OF LAST SAFETY CHECK.
>
> DATE OF ANNUAL INSPECTION.
>
> SAFETY OFFICER. D. PAPWORTH.

The records were neatly typed. She could see the last date clearly. 27th August. Less than a month ago.

The caretaker tapped it with his forefinger; his nail was dark blue as if it had recently been hit by a hammer. 'Been checked, you see.'

She nodded.

'It's impossible. The doors can't open. Not without the elevator car there.' He pushed a key into a box on the wall, turned it and pulled open a small metal door. There was a battery of switches and winking lights inside. One orange light was static and he stared at it for a moment, pressed a switch a couple of times and looked dubious. He then pressed two more switches and a bell sounded. He pressed another and the bell stopped ringing. 'Have to stop the whole system,' he said. 'Won't be too popular.' He pulled a lever and there was a loud clunk. All the lights stopped winking and remained on.

He knelt down and inserted the long ribbed tool into a tiny hole in the bottom of one of the elevator's doors and turned it sharply. He repeated the procedure in a hole at the top, and then again in the other door. Then he slowly levered his fingers into the gap and began to prise the doors open. They slid back until there was enough gap for him to get his head through.

He gave Frannie a cautioning signal with his hand for her to stay back, picked up his torch, leaned in and pointed the torch downwards.

'Oh God . . .' he stepped back, gagging. His eyes looked at Frannie without focusing, then swung away unco-ordinated. His mouth quivered. The torch fell from his fingers. He lurched towards the bucket, knelt and threw up.

Frannie picked up the lighted torch and stepped, terrified of what she would see, towards the gap in the door. She slowly lowered the white blob of torch beam down the back wall of the shaft.

Where it met the bottom she saw dust spun into a fine moss, cigarette butts, keys, a milk carton, a child's rattle. There was a vile stench of excrement. Her chest tightened as the beam slid across a crumpled shape in pinstriped cloth. A shiny loafer shoe with a green and red band across it, and a gold buckle. Her heart jigged. Something pale white gleamed out at her. It was Seb's face, his eyes wide open as if something was trying to push them out of their sockets, and for a brief moment she thought he was all right, thought he was fine, just in shock.

Until she realized his body was chest and stomach down, and his head had been wrenched round 180 degrees, saw a gleam of white bone sticking out of the side of his neck. And then she saw, also, the mess of red and orange pulp that was spreading through his hair and which lay like a cushion behind his ears. She whimpered. Something was sticking several inches out of his back like a bent spar impaling him; sharp and pointed, it had pierced cleanly through the centre of his jacket, between his shoulder-blades. A bone, she realized; one of his ribs.

She gulped, and her insides rattled as she staggered back, the image of his face imprinted like a developing photograph in her brain. She backed into the wall. Bells were ringing one after the other: desperate, panicky drilling sounds. She breathed in hard rasps, horror guttering through her, staring at the dark slit between the doors as if expecting Seb to climb out of it at any moment.

She turned her head. The caretaker was dialling a phone on the wall. The smell of his vomit churned her own stomach; she turned and ran, up the stairs, out into the lobby. Bells were ringing there, also, and she saw the commissionaire in his smart braided outfit walking anxiously past her towards the basement door.

She ran across the marble floor on legs that would barely hold her weight, pushed through a revolving door into the howling wind and slumped down on a teak bench, still holding the rubber torch in her hands. She switched it off, then on. Off then on again, the rubber button bending then clicking under the pressure of her finger.

She watched the spray from the fountains being bent by the relentless wind. Where a pigeon landed with a crack of its wings and eyed her expectantly, she saw only a grey blur on the ground. People were still at lunch. She could hear the distant clatter of their knives and forks, of laughter and chatter. She and Sebastian should have been in the restaurant now, talking about how to stay alive. She buried her face in her arms, plugged her ears with her fingers against the whoosh of the approaching siren and shook silently in grief. And in terror.

★

The tea was sweet and she sipped it gratefully, then placed her mug back down on the cork coaster on the mahogany boardroom table that shone like an ice-rink. A man who bore a family resemblance to Seb looked down from a portrait on the wall opposite her, a hard-looking man with Seb's large features, but not his warmth, wearing ermine and with a shrieval chain around his neck.

She turned to the policeman, Constable Boyle, who sat opposite her, his notebook in front of him on the table. He held himself well, sat upright with broad shoulders. In his mid thirties, his face had babyish, underdeveloped features, with half-moon eyes and thick, rubbery lips, but his manner was firm, adult, toughened with street wisdom. He exuded a faint aura of sadness as if there were things about human life that were beyond his comprehension, beyond his ability to change.

He smiled at her periodically, and each time the small act of kindness made her feel weepy again, and she sniffed, blinked away some tears and continued with her story, inching it forward, then being taken back, retracing each step a dozen times, adding fresh detail.

'You're sure it was ten past one, Francesca?' His voice was flat and pedantic and she had to fight the urge to snap at him with irritation.

'Yes.'

Then she managed, 'I can remember looking at my watch as we went out to the lifts.' But she was thinking, *He's dead. Nothing's going to bring him back. What the hell does it matter what time it was?*

'I was meeting him for lunch at one, and I was late. I didn't get here until ten past and when he came out he told me we'd have to be quick because he had to be back by two. He had some problems in the office he had to deal with.'

'What made you late?'

She drew her breath in sharply, fighting irritation again. The clock on the wall said 2.45. Her stomach ached. She sipped more tea. Someone on the construction site would remember her she thought, knowing it was irrational. 'I didn't leave enough time, I suppose. And whilst I was in the area I wanted to take a look at my family's old sandwich bar – it's on the City Fields development – so I took a detour over there.' She shrugged.

'And no one else came out to the lifts with you?'

'No one.'

Hello, young fellow!

'Did you have lunch with – er – Mr Holland regularly?'

Hello, young fellow! Seb's voice like an echo.

'No. We were at university together.'

'What was the reason for your lunch today?'

I wanted to warn him about the Ouija.

'We – hadn't seen each other since we were students – and we bumped into each other in a restaurant a couple of weeks ago. He told me he was engaged and said we ought to have lunch some time.'

His eyebrows rose. 'Excuse me being personal, Francesca, but was there anything – you know – between you and Mr Holland?'

'No.'

'Not at university?'

She hesitated. Almost. Once. They had snogged on a sofa at a party. But she had been dating someone else at the time and it had gone no further. It was one of those things that might have been. 'No.' She looked at him. 'You think I pushed him or something? In a fit of

337

jealousy? Or so that I could get to marry him?' Her face flushed with anger and she saw he had at least the grace to blush a little.

'I'm afraid it is my job to look at all the angles.'

Hello, young fellow! The expression on Seb's face as he had stepped into the lift. As if he was greeting someone in there. A small boy.

Edward.

He had seen Edward.

'So I'm a murder suspect, is that it?'

He raised his hands. 'Please! Nothing like that. But I do have to make a full report.' He smiled. 'You have to understand that I've come into this cold. A man is dead; the circumstances are very odd. At the inquest we will have to show we have looked at every possibility, for everyone's sake – and particularly for the deceased and his relatives.'

Wet, heavy sand heaved in her guts. The image of Seb's face brightened in her brain. She saw him again, lying there, amongst the dirt. The policeman's face dissolved into Seb's and drifted up away from the table. The table slid sideways; she gripped it, tried to prevent it from crashing to the ground. Her cheek pressed against it and she saw her blurred reflection in its mirrored shine, and tears flooded from her eyes.

A hand touched her arm, gently. 'I'll get someone to run you home. Do you have the number of your doctor? We'll ask him to pop in and see you.'

She lifted her head slowly, feeling giddy. The table was fine, solid, had not moved and she looked at it in confusion. 'I have to go to the office. I have a meeting this afternoon at three. My boss is going to be really angry.'

'Would you like to phone him?'

'How much longer do I have to stay here?'

'We're almost finished.' He smiled. 'Don't worry; no one's accusing you of anything.'

I'm guilty, she wanted to say. *I'm guilty. You're quite right to accuse me. It was my idea to have the Ouija session in the cellar. I made it happen. Seb would be alive now if –*

She sipped some more of her tea, as tears welled in her eyes again. 'I'm sorry,' she said to the policeman.

'I think you should go home and go to bed, have your doctor give you something that'll make you have a good night's sleep.'

She shook her head. 'I can't. There isn't time.'

He smiled again, but did not ask her what she meant.

CHAPTER THIRTY-ONE

Frannie got back to the Museum shortly after half past three. She stopped in the middle of the hall, feeling giddy and sick, and looked numbly at the crowds, at the queues for the bookshop tills, the souvenir shop, the information desk. Feet clacked all around her on the hard floor. Voices. She fumbled in her bag for a handkerchief and dabbed her eyes, tried to still the image of Seb's last look of amazement, which spun like a fairground centrifuge in her brain, pressing her back against the walls of her skull. If she had been quicker she could have dived forward and –

Hello, young fellow!

Constable Boyle had told her she could not have done anything, that she'd never have held his weight, that she would have been dragged down also. She felt the floor swaying beneath her. She could have seen the elevator was not there, could have screamed out.

Could have realized when he had said *Hello, young fellow!*

She collected her key, nodded at the security guard without noticing him, walking in a trance, then stopped outside her office, forgetting where she was for a moment, shock and fear clogging her mind. Eventually she opened the door and went in. Penrose Spode was not there, and had left a note on her desk: 'Not feeling well. Have gone home. Benedict is expecting you at 6.30, address and directions on reverse. If I can help, call me at home.'

There was another note also in his handwriting: 'Kate Hemingway phoned, *Evening Standard*. 2.50. Will call back.'

She looked with a feeling of hopelessness at the message from the newspaper. Calling about Seb, no doubt. She sat down, closed her eyes and began to pray. The phone rang and she answered it warily, afraid it might be the *Evening Standard* reporter. But it was Oliver, and he sounded distraught.

'Edward's disappeared,' he said.

'From school?'

'He had breakfast, then he didn't turn up for any classes. No one's seen him.'

Spode's neat handwriting blurred. 'What does the – the headmaster – say?'

'He doesn't know what to do.'

'Are the police –?'

'They're looking for him.'

'God, I'm sorry.' She bit her lip. 'What's happening?' she said quietly. 'What are we caught up in, Oliver?'

'I don't know.'

Her knees were knocking together; she felt the pressure of her knuckles against her cheek as she held the phone to her ear. She had to tell him. 'It's even worse than you think. Seb's dead.'

'Seb? Holland?'

She started telling him what had happened, but her voice became too choked with tears to go on.

'Christ, you poor thing,' he said, and was quiet for a moment. Then he grasped at the only shred of hope they had left. 'Did the priest – rector – get in touch?'

She stared into the tiny holes in the mouthpiece. 'I'm seeing him this evening.'

'If Edward turns up, I'll come straight to London.'

'I'm sure he's all right. He's very resourceful.'

'Yes,' Oliver said grimly. 'What time are you seeing the priest?'

'Half past six.'

'Will you call me afterwards?'

She promised she would in a choked whisper.

The Reverend Benedict Spode's address turned out to be a grimy, detached Georgian house on a busy main road south of the Thames, behind London Bridge Station.

Dark clouds with pink underbellies from the setting sun slid like burning boats across the sky. The wind was freshening, and occasional fat splodges of rain burst on the pavement around her as Frannie approached the front door and rang the bell.

She was surprised by the appearance of the man who answered it, quite different from the image she had in her mind. He was ten years older than his brother, short and bald, with a small round head as solid as a cannon ball and thyroid eyes. The only feature he shared in common with Penrose was the same bung-shaped mouth. His body was parcelled inside a billowing black cassock and what neck he had was squashed, fleshily, inside a tight dog-collar.

'Frannie Monsanto?' he said fiercely.

'Yes.' She held out an uncertain hand. The clergyman discarded it almost before he had shaken it, as if it were a package he had been handed for an Oxfam sale and should have been passed on to someone else. 'I was expecting you at six o'clock.'

'I'm sorry. Penrose told me half past.'

He looked at his watch. 'I really don't have any time

342

left – perhaps you could come and see me at the beginning of next week? Say Monday evening?'

She looked at him aghast. 'But I need help now. It can't wait that long. Please could we have a talk tonight? I can wait if it's not convenient; I must see you tonight.'

He looked exasperated. 'Bloody brother of mine. I told him six quite clearly.'

'*Please*,' she said again.

He hesitated, assessing her, then stepped back and gestured for her to come in.

The hallway had a shabbiness that reminded Frannie of a student rooming-house, and stank of wet dog. The hall carpet was worn down in places to the underlay, and strewn with moulted hairs; the paint was yellowed and chipped, and the walls virtually bare. The clergyman took her mackintosh and hung it on a Victorian coat stand, which stood out rather proudly, and then led her into a small, austere study.

There was a marble fireplace with an unlit gas fire in the grate, and a crucifix dutifully resting on the mantelpiece – a postcard of a pyramid beside it. A plain oak desk cluttered with papers, amid which sat a weary-looking manual typewriter and a small fax machine, fronted a typist's chair that looked as if it had been salvaged from a skip. The room also boasted a beat-up armchair and a sofa with shot springs that appeared as lumps in its blue covering. The window beyond the desk looked out on to the street, and rattled from the passing traffic.

Frannie heard a pattering sound, and an elderly Old English sheepdog limped inquisitively into the room.

'Basket, Shula!' Benedict Spode said in an equally

dictatorial but kinder tone than the one in which he had greeted her. 'Back to your basket!'

The dog turned and padded slowly back out. Benedict Spode gestured Frannie to the sofa, then perched on the swivel typing chair and gave her a more thorough inspection. With his air of disdain and conceit, he reminded her of a portrait she had seen of one of the Borgias.

He raised his head a fraction when he spoke, as if in order to throw his voice to an entire congregation, and his aggressive tone was belittling. 'Penrose tells me you've been mucking around with the Ouija?'

'Once. When I was a student,' Frannie said.

'Once!' He tapped his foot on the carpet; he was wearing polished black loafers that seemed too small and dainty for him. 'What is it about this word *once* that seems to make everything all right? There are circumstances where once is more than enough, young woman. Went bankrupt *once*. Mugged an old lady *once*.'

He shook his head in frustration, as if there were some inner demon trapped within him. 'I'm fed up with intelligent young people who should know better, who dabble with the Ouija then come running to me for help, expecting me to wave some magic wand and make everything all right.'

Frannie's spirits dropped to an even lower ebb. This was all wrong. She should not have trusted Penrose, not listened to him. She balled her fists in anger and despair. And yet, last night: Penrose at the table. The things he had said were not lucky guesses. And she tried to remind herself that the Bishop of Lewes had recommended this clergyman. The diocesan exorcist. He must know what he was doing. *Must.*

'I don't imagine you even go to church, do you?

Except for Christmas carols?' he added with a faint sneer.

'I used to.'

'How long ago is *used to*?'

'Seven or eight years.'

He squeezed his hands together. 'I'm fed up with non-attenders! They either come to me because they want a church wedding – so they can have pretty pictures to stick on the mantelpiece, or else because they've been dabbling with the occult.' Then his tone mellowed, just a fraction. 'OK. Lecture over; time is short.' There was even a hint of sympathy in his face. 'Would you like to tell me the full story?'

'How much has Penrose filled you in?'

'Let's make no assumptions, then we won't make any mistakes.' He leaned back, waiting.

Frannie began. The clergyman nodded impatiently several times as she told him all about the Ouija session and the messages that had turned into predictions. He sat motionless as she related Edward's plea to her in the library, the Latin he had been reciting in his sleep, and which she had too. And he listened without comment as she told him about Oliver's research into his family background, his studies in numerology, and her discovery of the common ground shared by her parents' sandwich bar and the Halkin residence.

'Twenty-six,' Benedict Spode said when she had finished, sucking in his cheeks as though he had a boiled sweet in his mouth. '*Twenty-six*. This man who died today, this friend, Seb Holland, you don't know what he was told by the Ouija?'

'No.'

'Do you really think it would have made any difference if you had known?'

She stared back bleakly. 'I don't know.'

He gathered a fold of his cassock, lifting the hem a few inches and inspecting his shoes. Then he looked at Frannie with a new intensity. 'Birds never sing at Auschwitz. Did you know that?'

'No,' she said, surprised by the apparent *non sequitur*.

'There's a reason. All the suffering that went on there is imprinted in the land. Animals sense it and they avoid it; those that do pass over it are silent.' He lapsed into silence himself for a moment. 'People leave imprints behind them when they die. Imprints of their energy, emotions. Some, like my brother, can read these imprints. There are other people who simply act, without knowing it, as channels, like radio receivers and transmitters, passing those imprints on to others who can either visualize them in the form of ghosts, or be subconsciously influenced by them.'

Channel. The word Oliver had used.

'It sounds,' Benedict Spode continued, 'as if you might be channelling the spirit of this second Marquess to Lord Sherfield's son, Edward.'

Her voice faltered. 'Do you really think that's possible?'

'What do you think?' he retorted sharply.

She regressed, pushed herself back through her mind, back into the darkness of the cellar. Something in there imprinted in the walls? The spirit of a man dead for 350 years who was still thinking, scheming, planning; still able to make others do his bidding? Able to make her do it? Edward do it? To kill Meredith, Jonathan Mountjoy, Seb Holland. And to strike Max Gabriel, maim Phoebe, blind Susie Verbeeten? To kill Oliver's wife? Tristram?

'I don't understand what it is – exactly – that lives on – how it works.'

The clergyman spoke more civilly. 'I believe there are forces of evil that exist in their own right and which we all have the choice to accept or reject. Every time we accept evil, allow it to enter, we feed it and it becomes stronger; and sometimes when we die it remains behind. The second Marquess accepted and embraced evil. It perhaps did not die with him but remained dormant; a strong enough force to survive for 350 years.'

'To survive in bricks and mortar? In stone?'

'Bricks and stone are inert, but they contain many elements – including electricity and carbon – that are capable of storing energy. When people play with the Ouija they are inviting intense energy into one focal point. Creating a fusion of energies. The energies of six or seven people all focused into one glass. That concentrated mass can disturb whatever is in the room around them, and sometimes reactivate the place memories – or a dormant evil force. I would think that cellar, with all the evil that has taken place around it, was a highly dangerous place to play the Ouija. I can't imagine anywhere that could be worse: sexual perversion; mass murder; a hideous end.' He shook his head. 'What do you expect?'

Frannie was silent.

'Evil is immensely cunning, but it can only work through adult humans who will accept it, or through young children who are not yet aware of the distinction.' He smiled ironically. 'The second Marquess was murdered on the premises, more than likely down in the cellar, by *seven* soldiers. Numerology was his big thing.' He looked hard at Frannie. '*Seven* students held the Ouija session.' He shrugged. 'Maybe significant, maybe not. What *is* significant is that Lord Sherfield, with his five-year-old son, came into the café after you had re-energized the force. You were the natural link.'

'Why?'

'A young child's consciousness is not fully formed until at least the age of seven. Here the evil force or the spirit, or whatever you care to call it, saw a child not only young, but also with direct ancestral and therefore genetic lineage back to the second Marquess. By using you as a channel, it could slowly become part of that child's consciousness; test the boy out without him realizing, until he became used to it, accepted it as part of himself. And then –' he looked away for a moment.

'And then what?'

'Then it – or he – doesn't need either of you any more.' His ironic smile returned.

'Why?' said Frannie. 'Why would it want to carry on? Surely there – there's no reason –' her train of thought stumbled.

'Evil is the corruption of good. That is its sole purpose: to corrupt, destroy, nullify. It requires no reason, only energy. The energy of a seance; the energy of a host body.'

'Why would it harm everyone who was at the Ouija session?'

'You know the expression "Let sleeping dogs lie"?'

'Of course.'

'A sleeping dog has no gratitude for being woken.' He rested his hands on his lap and surveyed the room imperiously. 'If the second Marquess was into numerology, the spirit probably finds it amusing to continue. Seven soldiers put him to death. Seven people bring him back into existence. Repeat the pattern.' He parted his hands. 'Evil does not have to account to anyone for its actions.'

'But how does that explain the friend of mine who went blind? She picked up a virus swimming – how could a spirit have made her do that?'

He flicked some tiny fleck off his cassock. 'We understand very little about the body's abilities to look after itself. The immune system is still largely a mystery. I should think most people don't go blind from the virus your friend caught. Probably only a tiny percentage do. Was she unlucky? Or did something get channelled into her subconscious, blocking her immune system for her? To make her prophecy come true?'

Frannie felt as though a nerve had snapped inside her. 'Is there nothing I can do?'

'There's only one thing we can do. We go to that cellar and we hold a requiem mass. And we go now.'

'Who?'

'Just you and me.'

She bit the back of her hand. 'I don't know if we can get in.'

'We'll worry about that when we get there.'

'What – what happens in a requiem mass?'

'We hold a simple communion service to lay the spirit to rest.'

'And if that doesn't work?'

He looked at her as if she was mad. The skin around his mouth tightened in determination, 'We are going armed with the authority of the Church. The authority of God. That is stronger than anything belonging to Satan. You do understand that, don't you?'

She could feel the hairs rising on her body and the goose-pimples creeping across her flesh. She had hoped that in coming to the clergyman she would somehow find comfort. Instead she had found even greater fear.

CHAPTER THIRTY-TWO

Frannie walked with Benedict Spode across London Bridge, her mackintosh pocket weighted with the torch he had lent her. The clergyman carried a small vinyl holdall which he swung at his side in a deliberately carefree manner that did not reflect the anxiety in his face.

They waited for a stream of traffic to pass, then crossed into King William Street and walked down towards Bank. Over to their right, brightly lit against the night sky when Frannie looked down one of the side streets, was the Winston Churchill Tower. But she had to look away again.

'Do you think,' she said, 'this could be the reason why Oliver and I met? That it was all manipulated, contrived – by – the – this –?' She stopped, uncertain of the word she was searching for. *Spirit? Force?*

'I believe that there is order in disorder,' Benedict Spode said tersely.

She remembered Oliver had said the same thing. 'How do you mean?'

He did not reply until they had stopped to wait for the traffic lights at the end of the street. 'I mean that there are patterns even in apparent chaos. Sometimes one is too close to them to see them.'

'I'm not sure I understand; I –'

The lights changed and they crossed into Poultry. The air in her lungs felt heavier by the second. Ahead, up to the left, she could see the lights of the hoarding. She slowed her pace and the clergyman slowed his also.

'I just want to say something before we –' she said, and she saw the soft, baby-like skin of the clergyman's cheek in the glare of a street light as he half turned towards her. 'I'm sorry for everything. For all the grief I've brought to everyone. For being so bloody stupid.'

Benedict Spode turned further to face her full on. The anxiety had not left his face but his voice was calm. 'Seven of you made the decision to play the Ouija, Frannie,' he said quietly. 'It's not for you to take the blame alone. God will be the judge of that.'

A sharp blast of wind seized her hair and her clothes. The clergyman's cassock billowed beneath his raincoat and his holdall swayed in his hand. The hoarding rocked; even from a hundred yards away Frannie could hear the loose boards banging and tarpaulins cracking like sails, metal chinking.

She looked back at Benedict Spode. 'Can I ask you something really naïve? If people can do this – attract evil spirits – on their own, why does it need a priest to stop it? Couldn't anyone stop it with prayers?'

'Priests have no magic,' he said. 'Good is stronger than evil; but when evil becomes out of control, those who have the authority of the Church are stronger in dealing with it than anyone else. The Church acts on God's behalf, with His authority. And God is stronger than Satan. God defeated Satan.'

A bus rumbled past. The door of a pub across the road opened and two men came out. Behind them the interior looked cheery, and Frannie felt a pang of envy.

'I still find it hard to believe – with all that's gone on – that just saying a few prayers will end it.'

Her companion stopped, 'Why?'

'It seems too simple.'

He rounded on her with logic. 'Is it any less simple than the way it started? Just a bunch of drunken friends with an upturned wine glass and some scraps of paper?'

She smiled weakly, but Benedict Spode did not smile back. She looked at her watch. A quarter past eight. It was much brighter lit here than she had expected. The pavement, the hoarding, the site; they were all bathed in a milky-orange haze. Conspicuous. But towards the tops of the buildings that towered around them, the artificial light faded. And far above, only hard white stars pricked the oily blackness of the sky.

The landscape was as Frannie had seen it earlier that day: the jib of a crane towering over the alley; the silhouette of a massive lead demolition ball suspended beneath it like something hanging from the beak of a giant bird of prey. But the building that had been there at lunchtime was no longer standing. Shock ripped through her guts. She raced across the road towards the hoarding and peered through a viewing slit but could see nothing. She ran on to the next slit, which looked straight on to the remains of the corner building at the start of Poulterers' Alley. It had been almost completely demolished, its façade torn off, its innards opened to the elements. But, on either side of the alley behind it, the rest of the buildings were still standing.

Part of her wished they weren't; wanted to pretend that it was too late. The clergyman wouldn't know. Then Seb Holland's face came into her mind. Then Tristram's. Meredith's coffin on the catafalque. Frannie shuddered. She imagined never seeing Oliver again. Nor her family. Being crippled, or dead or disfigured. She nodded at Benedict Spode and pointed.

He looked up at the hoarding. 'Let's see if we can find a gap,' he said decisively.

They stopped outside the main gates, which were chained shut. She tested them, but there was no play in them. A taxi drove by, the knocking rattle of its engine echoing in the quietness, the fumes of its exhaust staying in their nostrils after it had gone. She walked on, leading the way down to the end of the block, then turned left and the pavement became a covered boardwalk as they followed the hoarding along a street that was quiet and less well lit. Benedict Spode pressed a section of hoarding on the join with the scaffolding and it gave, reluctantly, then sprung sharply back. He glanced around, rather shiftily, pushed hard and held it for Frannie, then followed her through, releasing it behind him with a fierce bang.

They stood on an unstable mound of rubble; the sounds of flapping and loose metal were much louder now. Frannie switched the torch on, and the beam jumped hungrily into the shadows beyond the haze of light from the street lamps. It struck the caterpillar tracks of a bulldozer. Then the cabin of a crane. She played it along the partially demolished terrace that housed the site office. The air was full of the oddly sweet smell of rotten wood and damp, and the harder, drier smell of old plaster. The beam slid over a stepladder, a skip, then flared off the windows of a Portakabin. She stepped forward nervously, picking her way past a broken supermarket trolley, then walked across rotten plasterboard which broke beneath her feet and on to a track of churned mud.

Benedict Spode walked on tiptoe, his cassock hitched up like a skirt. As they passed a Portakabin with 'Supplies' stencilled on the door, a van drove fast down the road and halted outside the gates, its engine still running. Frannie snapped off the torch as footsteps and the crackle of a two-way radio were heard. Then a man's voice.

'City Fields. One nine five five. Site secure. Moving on to Docklands. Roger and out.'

A chain rattled and the vehicle sped away. Frannie switched on the torch, revealing the clergyman's raised eyebrows. 'Could have been a bit embarrassing,' he said.

Frannie couldn't raise a smile, and walked on until Poulterers' Alley stretched out in front of them like a ghost town on a movie studio lot.

Fear had returned to the clergyman's face and she felt it infecting her, flowing into her. Had to keep going now; to somehow be brave. Had to keep going. Had to. She imagined two eyes watching them from behind the boarded windows. A small boy's eyes. She felt her heart bang like a shuttle inside her chest, weaving a tapestry from the raw yarn of her nerves.

She almost walked right past it. What had once seemed such a very big place now looked so small. She swung the torch up above the door as if she needed to make sure: SANDW CH S LUIGI CAFE.

The windows were boarded like all the others, but the door still had its glass panels. She took her key-ring from her bag, separated the old Banham and pushed it into the lock. It slid in almost too easily, and allowed herself and Canon Spode to gain entry to the premises she'd known for most of her life.

Inside, the floor was a mess. Part of the ceiling had come down, leaving exposed beams. Frannie trod slowly, waited for Benedict Spode, and played the torchlight around, scooping the darkness out. A flesh-white rectangle indicated where the counter had stood. The old poster of Naples had fallen and lay on the floor. The other, of Amalfi, was still on the back wall. And it was this one on which the clergyman had fixed his gaze, eyes widening. Frannie followed his stare.

The poster was moving, the top left-hand corner tearing as if an invisible hand were pulling it. The other corner was already free. She felt her own flesh tearing in sympathy, parting. The whole place felt as if it was charged with electricity as the poster carried on moving from the top downwards until it dropped to the floor, curled over on itself and lay still.

The effect was petrifying. Just the draught from opening the door, Frannie tried to convince herself, pushing her way through the darkness to the hoop of the trapdoor which she could see glinting dully. She laid the torch down, knelt and signalled to Spode to do the same.

The cold metal bit into her fingers like ice as she pulled. The bogeyman was down there beneath the hatch, waiting for her in his dark, silent lair. He lived in the cellar. The bogeyman who pricked every bone in her body now with sharp needles of terror. The second Marquess – Francis Edward Alwynne Halkin.

The hatch lifted a few inches and dropped back down. She had forgotten how heavy it was. She resisted the clergyman's attempts to help and, bracing herself, lifted harder; it came away, pulling a stringy cobweb with it. A draught of air poured out, as cold as if she had opened the door of a freezer.

She pulled the hatch right back until it was resting against its hinges then shone the torch down the wooden steps into the darkness. Dark as a lift shaft. Frannie was shaking uncontrollably by now, as if she had convulsions. She rocked on her knees, staring down as darkness coiled like smoke around her.

The clergyman offered, 'Shall I go first?'

'I'll go,' she heard herself say, 'and you can pass your bag down.'

Slowly she eased herself over, and grabbed the torch with one hand. She felt as if she were descending into a bottomless pit. But eventually her feet touched the hard flagstones. They felt unsteady, then she realized that it was herself, swaying in her fear.

'OK,' she called out, shining the torch back up. The word echoed back at her. *OK . . . OK . . . OK.*

Benedict Spode's foot clumsily struck the top step. 'Careful!' she shouted out into the blackness. *CARE-FUL . . . FUUULLLL.*

The cold of the flagstones seeped through her shoes. Her skin prickled and she felt the downy hairs on her arms, her legs, on the small of her back rising and her skin erupting into goose-pimples. She could hear the steady metallic drip . . . ping . . . ping . . . ping and remembered it from the last time she had been down here.

She raked the steps with the torch, too afraid to look around her, stretching for the bag which Spode was holding down to her.

The clergyman reached the bottom but stayed holding on to the rails with both hands, collecting his breath. 'My bag,' he said anxiously, as if he was frightened to be separated from it.

She handed it back to him to the accompaniment of a low, rumbling echo that came out of the darkness, growing deeper and louder, like a hundred boulders rolling towards them. She had heard the sound thousands of times but it always scared her. It began to fade as rapidly as it had started, becoming a distant hum, and then died completely. 'Tube train,' she said. 'Central Line.'

Spode released his grip on the rail and walked a few

steps away from her as if drawn across the room. She watched him open his bag; he removed a small torch of his own then went over to one of several upright barrels, and using it as a table began to unpack. In the extra light of the second torch, she saw a packing-case with a candle stuck on the top, a pool of wax around the base. Scraps of paper lay on it. It was the packing-crate they had used as a table for the Ouija.

Memories washed over her. She walked over, afraid to go too close. The letters of the alphabet lay in random order, the words *Yes* and *No* in their midst, mottled now with black spots of mildew.

The clergyman had pulled a phial of holy water and a silver salt cellar from his bag and set them on the barrel. Then two silver candlesticks, into which he pushed candles, which he lit. A chalice, a silver tray and a silver stoup were also produced. Mouthing a silent prayer, he poured some water into the stoup and added some salt. Working in the flickering candlelight, he was slow, tidy, methodical, as if he had all the time in the world.

He raised the stoup, 'Protect us, O Lord, we beseech you.' He said the words firmly, but without raising his voice. Then he pulled what looked like a silver ball and chain from his bag. The ball had tiny holes, like a sugar shaker. An aspergillum, Frannie realized.

He carefully immersed the head in holy water, before raising the aspergillum by its chain so that it swung gently. Then he raised it higher as if making sure that whoever or whatever was present could see it. He began to swing it on its chain, slowly at first, then faster, until flecks of water sprinkled the wall. At the same time the clergyman began to move around the cellar, repeating the words and procedure over and over.

'Protect us, O Lord, we beseech you.'

Outside the lead demolition ball that hung from the jib of the crane, twenty feet above the rod, moved a fraction in a gust of wind. As the gust died away it continued to move, in a faint, barely discernible, rocking motion; the ball gradually began to swing faster, making wide, sweeping arcs until it was swinging too hard for the jib to contain it and the whole crane began to sway with it. The lead ball swung like the aspergillum in the clergyman's hand. Like the lampshade in Frannie's sitting-room. Harder and harder. Until it rose too high and the chain went slack. Then it fell with a dead-weight of five tons. Plummeted unchecked through the air as the slack of the chain paid out. Then tightened. Sharply. Too sharply.

The top of the jib's superstructure sheared away and was yanked sharply downwards by the demolition ball as it plunged straight down through roof tiles and rotting timbers.

Below in the cellar, Benedict Spode made another swing with the aspergillum. Holy water spattered on the brickwork.

'Protect us, O Lord, we beseech you.'

He took a step to the left and began the same performance. As he did so, Frannie heard a faint splitting sound like sticks of firewood being snapped. Then a deep rumble. A train, she thought at first, but it was different: deeper, more threatening. She saw jagged spidery cracks rip across the walls and ceiling. Dust and small stones showered down on them, striking her head, her hands.

'Get out!' she shouted. 'Get out!'

The whole cellar was shaking and dust was avalanching down through the open hatch. Frannie shouted again, then something slammed into her shoulder, sending her crashing to the floor. The noise had become deafening. She heard someone scream, but dust and plaster filled her own mouth and she choked, blinded by dust.

Then there was silence.

She felt wind on her face and tried to move. But she was pinioned, trapped. She spat out a mouthful of dust. 'Mr Spode?'

A faint haze of light made its way through the mist that was stinging her eyes. Then the mist itself started to clear. Dust, settling. Above her was a strange orange glow and familiar pinpricks of white in an oily blackness beyond. Shadowy walls rising up. Then Frannie realized, confused, that she was looking straight up at the night outside.

There was a face. Someone staring down at her. A small man standing looking down through the crater in the floor above. He was smiling and she thought that was incongruous. Smiling, and there was a gleam in his eye. Then she saw with blind terror that it was not a man at all.

It was Edward.

CHAPTER THIRTY-THREE

As Frannie watched, Edward disappeared.

She struggled to free herself from the dead-weight crushing her legs and her left shoulder, but panic snaked up and down inside her.

'Mr Spode?' she called out.

Silence. She felt like an insect trapped in a match-box. *Beetles are vermin, Daddy*.

'Mr Spode?'

She choked on dust and coughed again. She strained her eyes but could see nothing. Something sharp was digging into her wrist; she pulled, twisted, but it dug in further. She looked up again but could see nothing except the faint orange haze.

A shadow moved. She heard a scrape, like a dragging foot, and her muscles went into spasm. But still she couldn't shift her legs; they felt set in cement.

She heard another scrape. Louder. Then again. Behind her. She could still move her head and now she spun it round frantically.

A silhouette standing; someone small. A torch came on and the beam blinded her. It moved away from her eyes and in the spill of light she could see that it was Edward.

He was motionless, concentrating on her.

'Edward!' she called out. Try to talk to him, get through to him, she thought desperately.

His lips moved but she could not hear what they said. The beam of his torch raked the cellar. It had caved in and she was in an enclosed pocket. Then the beam struck a face to her left.

It was Benedict Spode; his back and his legs crushed flat by the demolition ball. His tongue was sticking out and a trail of yellow bile dribbled from it, down into the pool of blood that was spreading slowly out across the floor and towards Frannie.

Bursts of a throttled scream gouted from her throat. Edward took a step towards her. Then another, his lips moving, talking, saying something she could not hear.

Her right arm was the only limb she could move and she slid it across the rubble without taking her eyes off him, then closed her fingers around a chunk of masonry, gripped it tightly and swung it back, demented enough to use it.

Edward walked solemnly towards her, eyes glazed, lips still chanting inaudibly; he was wearing his school uniform of grey jacket and shorts, and striped tie. She lifted the stone chunk higher, bracing herself. He continued chanting, and as he came closer she realized with rising terror that it was not his own voice coming from his mouth, but that of someone much older.

He walked on past her, knelt and picked up the aspergillum that lay just beyond the outstretched fingers of the dead clergyman, stood and swung it from the chain. Droplets of holy water struck Frannie in the face.

'Protect us, O Lord, we beseech you. Protect us, O Lord, we beseech you,' he repeated much louder and clearer in a no-nonsense voice that she recognized.

He knelt again and began pulling away the rubble beside Canon Spode, chanting to himself. Now he was saying the Lord's Prayer. Frannie watched as he unearthed the silver tray and the chalice, as if he knew exactly what he was looking for, and what to do next. From the buried holdall he removed a bottle of communion wine and some wafers.

'Listen to our prayers, Lord,' he said. 'As we humbly beg Your mercy.'

Frannie could not comprehend it, but the voice coming from Edward was that of the clergyman who was lying dead on the floor. The clergyman was speaking through the boy.

Edward continued with calm assurance. With authority. 'Listen to our prayers, Lord, as we humbly beg Your mercy, that the soul of Your servant Francis Edward Alwynne Halkin, whom You have called from this life, may be brought by You to a place of peace and light, and so be enabled to share the life of all Your saints. Through Christ our Lord, Amen.'

'Amen,' Frannie echoed involuntarily, releasing her grip on the masonry.

'We pray You, Lord our God, to receive the soul of this Your servant Francis, for whom Your blood was shed. Remember, Lord, that we are but dust and that man is like grass and the flower of the field. Lord grant him everlasting rest, and let perpetual light shine upon him. O God it is Your nature to have mercy and to spare. Grant to Your servant Francis, Lord, a place of rest and pardon.'

The boy with the presence of an adult was quiet for a moment. A siren faded into the distance, and Frannie had the strange impression that someone else was standing beside them. But she did not dare look away from the miracle taking place in front of her. Edward had begun saying the Lord's Prayer again, and she joined him.

When they had finished, he picked up the Host and broke a piece into the chalice. 'Lamb of God,' he said, 'You take away the sins of the world; have mercy on us. May this mingling of the Body and Blood of our Lord Jesus Christ bring eternal life to us who receive it.' He carried the host to Frannie and placed it in her hand.

'Take, eat,' he said.

She raised it to her mouth and put it on her tongue. The sweet, papery wafer dissolved.

Then he brought her the chalice, and placed the rim to her lips. She tasted silver polish; then heavy, sweet wine, swallowing gratefully.

'This is the Blood of Christ.' Edward's words were spoken confidently and he put the chalice down. 'Lord God, Your Son gave us the sacrament of His Body to support us in our last journey. Grant that our brother Francis may take his seat with Christ at His eternal banquet: Who lives and reigns for ever and ever.'

'Amen,' whispered Frannie.

The air felt warmer and she was no longer afraid. Edward knelt beside her. The darkness had lifted and she could see that his eyes looked bright, and he was smiling. His voice was normal again.

'Are you OK, Frannie?'

She nodded.

'It's all right now, isn't it, Frannie?' He knelt and began to pull the rubble off her. As he worked, she stared at the small boy's face and remembered his question: *Do the dead stay dead?*

Benedict Spode had been armed with the authority of the Church and he had died. But not quite. By killing Spode, the second Marquess had not diminished the clergyman's authority, but had given him a new weapon: Edward.

Non omnis moriar.

In his death Canon Spode had channelled his spirit through Edward.

Frannie put her arm up and gently took Edward's hand, the clergyman's words echoing in her head.

When evil becomes out of control, those who have the authority of the Church are stronger in dealing with it than anyone else.

Something else that he had said echoed also. *I believe that there is order in disorder.*

Frannie pulled Edward tightly to her; he did not seem to mind that tears were streaming down her face. It was as if they both knew that here in the rubble of the past, and in the presence of death, somehow they were now free.

EPILOGUE

When Charles Richard William Halkin was seven he discovered his half-brother's secret place, where Edward would go and smoke. He discovered it by following him through the attics beyond the nursery. He had watched Edward crawl out of a window, and had crawled after him, along the parapet and into a hollow beside one of the massive chimneys.

Edward had been annoyed the first time, but now he let Charles join him whenever he wanted. On a fine day you could see across the hills and far out into the English Channel. Edward said that the line on the horizon was France, although Charles didn't really believe him. There were a lot of things Edward told him that he didn't really believe and he preferred to try to find the truth out for himself. Discovering things gave him a great thrill. He liked to work everything out and had inherited a logical, analytical mind from his mother; he was always piecing things together from little fragments.

Once when he was bored and rummaging through some old suitcases in one of the attics, he found a battered case with a faded Alitalia luggage label. Inside it was full of photographs of his mother and some of his uncles and aunts, as well as old magazines and bundles of letters. As he was closing the case, he noticed an envelope that looked more recent than the rest and he glanced at it. It was addressed: 'Francesca, Lady Sherfield, Meston Hall, Meston, East Sussex.'

Inside was a brief letter with a strip of paper attached. The letter was in rather scrawly handwriting.

Dear Frannie,
Mama found this the other day when she was helping
me clear out some old stuff when I was down for the
weekend. I thought you might like to see it in case
you've always wondered. Horribly appropriate for
poor old Seb, but I don't know about yours. It seems
Phoebe was wrong in her recollection, it wasn't just
the number 26, after all. Not that any of it matters
now.
I will try and call you next time I'm down. Second
baby's due in August. Lots of love.
    Susie.

Charles unclipped the strip of paper. It was about two inches wide, and lined, and looked as if it had been torn from a diary. On one side there was an address. On the other were two names, in list form:

Seb Holland – HUMPTY DUMPTY
Frannie – YOU'LL BEAR THE 26th

When he was younger, Edward had told Charles that he wasn't like a proper brother because they did not have the same mummy. Charles understood that; he knew Edward's mummy had died a long time ago.

He understood also that it was Edward who would inherit his father's title one day. His father was the twenty-fourth Marquess of Sherfield, and Edward would become the twenty-fifth Marquess. When Edward died, his eldest son would become the twenty-sixth Marquess. Unless Edward died without having a son, in which case the title would pass to Charles.

On the whole, Charles liked Edward, and in spite of their age difference they got on well, although sometimes he had a weird thought about him. He would imagine that he was watching Edward falling to his death from the parapet.

available from

THE ORION PUBLISHING GROUP

All Orion/Phoenix titles are available at your local bookshop or from the following address:

> Mail Order Department
> Littlehampton Book Services
> FREEPOST BR535
> Worthing, West Sussex, BN13 3BR
> *telephone* 01903 828503, *facsimile* 01903 828802
> *e-mail* MailOrders@lbsltd.co.uk
> (Please ensure that you include full postal address details)

Payment can be made either by credit/debit card (Visa, Mastercard, Access and Switch accepted) or by sending a £ Sterling cheque or postal order made payable to *Littlehampton Book Services*.
DO NOT SEND CASH OR CURRENCY

Please add the following to cover postage and packing:

UK and BFPO:
£1.50 for the first book, and 50p for each additional book to a maximum of £3.50

Overseas and Eire:
£2.50 for the first book, plus £1.00 for the second book, and 50p for each additional book ordered

---

BLOCK CAPITALS PLEASE

name of cardholder ....

address of cardholder ....

....

....

postcode ....

delivery address
(if different from cardholder)

....

....

....

postcode ....

☐ I enclose my remittance for £.............................

☐ please debit my Mastercard/Visa/Access/Switch (delete as appropriate)

card number ☐☐☐☐☐☐☐☐☐☐☐☐☐☐☐☐☐

expiry date ☐☐☐☐   Switch issue no. ☐☐

signature ....

prices and availability are subject to change without notice